LOVE & DARK SERIES

HINA MCCORD & BECCA C. SMITH

Published by Red Frog Publishing, a division of Red Frog Media

First published in 2014, 2015, 2020

ISBN 9781949877526

Printed in the United States of America

VESSEL

PROLOGUE
LUCIAN

The alcohol in her perfume was strong enough to burn my eyes. I sank my teeth in deeper as she moaned with pleasure. I was already full, but what was the point in leaving her alive? So that she could continue to wait tables at The Bargain's Inn, married to Floyd the town's drunk?

Not that he was of any use to her now.

I wasn't Lucian the Merciful . . . not anymore. But it was more convenient to kill someone who was already dead inside. Her eyes rolled back and I languished on the last few drops as her body trembled then orgasmed.

Would her dismal life have given her this sweet of a death?

I let her body thud to the floor. I wiped my mouth and straightened my back, kicking an empty beer can at Floyd's carcass. His severed head sat on top of the TV he'd been yelling at before he'd hit her.

My body surged, their blood filling my hollow cavities with

warmth. I wasn't supposed to stop in for a snack, but when I'd passed and saw what he was doing to her, I just couldn't resist cutting him open.

Things like that weren't men.

They were monsters . . . like I was.

I walked steadily out the door, their rocking chair creaking in the warm desert breeze as I gazed up at the quarter moon. Where was the Vessel hiding? It had been five hundred years since the last one, and he should be of age by now. I shifted restlessly. Waiting was an agony I'd become all too familiar with.

Adnachiel was probably keeping the Vessel from activating his powers so that I couldn't track him. As if that had stopped me before. Any mistake, any misstep, and I'd be at that dog's doorstep ready to rip him apart.

This game of ours had gone on for too long. My eyes were dull with boredom. If only I could bring Adnachiel enough pain to satisfy my rage. I couldn't fill this growing emptiness, even after a hefty feeding like tonight.

Maybe this time I'd end it and drag that Vessel, boy or man, to the depths of hell with me . . . to meet my maker.

CHAPTER 1
SHEA

"Shea Harper?"

Even the way the woman said my name made me want to punch her. I'd been sitting in the housing registration room for about three hours now. All this lady had done so far was tell me to sit down and shut up until my name was called. Of course, this was after I had asked her five times if she could help me. The room was empty for God's sake, and I could tell she was just futzing around on the Internet. She was making me wait on purpose, and now that she was bored, she was finally going to talk to me.

Seriously? Would anyone *really* mind if I punched her? Maybe a little slap? Kick in the shins? Anything to inflict some kind of pain?

All I wanted were the keys to my new abode. Was that too much to ask? Apparently for this woman, it was.

It wasn't like Arizona State University was my dream school, but I grew up in Phoenix, and my parents didn't want to pay out-of-state fees. It had taken every ounce of manipulation I could muster just to get them to agree to let me stay in a dorm!

So here I was.

Sitting in a room.

Waiting for condescending-annoying-lady to grace me with her time.

I should have taken care of my housing situation months ago, so I only had myself to blame. But that didn't justify the attitude from Ms. Dorm-pants over there.

I stood up and walked to the front desk. She sat behind it, ruffling through papers with an irritated grunt here or there.

Finally, she made eye contact and handed me a sheet of paper. "Fill that out, please," she ordered tersely.

"I already filled out an application. They said all I had to do was come here and pick up my keys." I told her what I'd been trying to tell her the entire three hours I'd been there.

She sighed and her nostrils flared a bit, but she didn't raise her voice. It was more of a gritted-teeth-I-freaking-hate-you tone. "This is not an application, Ms. Harper. It's a release form for your keys. I do know what I'm doing, after all."

Normally, I'd blush and apologize profusely, but this lady brought out the worst in me. "Got it, thanks," I said with a roll of my eyes. Pretty stupid since she was the guardian of my coveted keys, but I couldn't control myself.

"If you want to come back tomorrow, the office opens at noon," she threatened.

That did it.

Attitude gone.

I needed my room tonight or I was going to have to sleep at home, and since my car was already full of everything I owned, there was no way that was going to happen.

"Nope. I'm good. I'll just fill this out. Anything else you want me to fill out? Can I get you some coffee? Snack? Anything?" I went into full-on *sweet*-mode.

"Just the form will do," the woman said.

I thought for just a second I could see a hint of a smile. I was glad my pathetic-ness could entertain her.

After that, I was surprised at how quickly everything came together. I handed her the fully filled out form and she handed me the keys. I tried not to think about the fact that she could easily have done this hours ago. I just took a deep breath, smiled, and left before she could find some excuse to take away my new home.

The intense Phoenix September sun hit my body like I had stepped into an oven. It was 107 degrees today and that was nothing compared to the 120-degree summer days the city experienced all of July and August. 107 was actually a cooldown! I despised Phoenix. I couldn't really hate on Arizona completely since it did have pretty spectacular places like the Grand Canyon and Bell Rock in Sedona. But Phoenix? Phoenix I could loathe with all of my soul.

I'd wanted to go to UCLA for my undergrad degree, but every time I was about to get a loan, scholarship, or grant, it would fall through. It wasn't long after that I'd become convinced that there was such a thing as "the Phoenix gods." They never let anyone leave once they had them in their grasp. That was what it felt like anyway. When an opportunity came my way to get out of this city, something random and, frankly, absurd would keep me here. Why else would so many people live here? It couldn't be by choice! It had to be something supernatural. There was no other explanation, in my opinion. I was beginning to think Phoenix was stalking me, it wanted to keep me so badly.

I could barely breathe because of the intense heat, but I'd been dealing with this crappy weather my whole life. I just had to grin and bear it. First things first, I needed to cool down. I grabbed an elastic band from my jeans pocket and tied my pale blond hair back into a sloppy ponytail. I had been growing my hair out since last year, so it was just past my shoulders, making it a furnace on my neck anytime I went outside.

I took my sunglasses out of my purse and put them on. My eyes were extremely sensitive to the sun. They were technically hazel: gold some days, green others, and every once in a while they managed to be a boring brown.

I peeled off my small black cardigan. It was essential when I was in overly air-conditioned ASU offices, but outside it might as well have been a fur coat. Jeans and a tank for me. It was the only way I could survive.

I never had to worry about eating crappy food, at least when it came to weight. Digestion was a whole other story. My roll of Tums was a permanent addition to my list of essentials.

"Shea! Where's your car?" A voice sounded behind me.

I whirled around to see my very best friend in the whole wide world, Aidan O'Connell. You couldn't get a more Irish name than that! Aidan's roots may have been in Ireland, but he was born and raised in Phoenix as well. He'd been my next-door neighbor since . . . well . . . birth.

Our moms would always laugh about the fact that Aidan and I were born on the exact same day, minute, and second. I used to question the minutes and seconds part, until our parents showed us our birth certificates. Sure enough, it was one of those weird anomalies in life. We called ourselves the "spirit twins." Totally cheesy, I know, but we were four! Give me a break!

I suppose any other girl with a pulse would go all aflutter for someone like Aidan. He was pretty gorgeous. I wasn't blind, it was just that I always thought of him as a brother, so it was difficult to see him in a "hot" kind of way. But the boy was a stunner, that I couldn't deny, whether I liked him that way or not.

His hair was dark brown and short, with a swoopy kind of messy look that guys seemed to be into nowadays. It suited his sculpted face, giant blue eyes, and those crazy long eyelashes I was secretly jealous of. Though on the surface he could easily fit the title "pretty boy," Aidan was actually the toughest guy I knew. He wasn't "body-builder" huge, but he was a little over six feet and in incredible shape. That boy had a ten pack at least, if that was possible.

Yup, my best friend the hottie.

Sometimes I almost wished I liked him in a romantic way. It would be so much easier. I knew Aidan would die for me. He'd been my protector since preschool when the resident bully, Greg Chanto, had decided he wanted my Pokémon card collection and grabbed it at playtime.

When Aidan had found out, he'd had Greg in a headlock until he cried and gave me back my cards. Aidan had even made Greg apologize and promise never to do it again. This had been the first of about a million events where Aidan kicked someone's butt because he thought he was protecting me in some way. It was very "big brotherly" behavior, which was probably why I saw him like family instead of boyfriend material.

And to be fair, it wasn't like Aidan had confessed some undying love for me and I was choosing not to be with him. Aidan was just Aidan. We were best buds. That was that. As far as I knew, neither one of us wanted anything more.

Right now, he had this adorable, silly grin on his face, like seeing me had made his day. His sparkly, warm eyes looking at me like that always gave me a surge of fierce loyalty toward him. I was just happy we were both going to ASU so we wouldn't be separated. I wasn't ready to live life without my BFF yet.

"What do you mean where's my car? You parked it." I rolled my eyes as I reached his side. He was holding a large box that looked heavy for me, but was probably as light as a feather for him.

"I know, but I got all turned around. There are too many courtyards. They all look the same." Aidan shifted the box uncomfortably. "I just want to drop this off in my dorm."

"Is that seriously all you're bringing?" I asked incredulously. My car was filled to the brim with all my stuff. We'd barely had room for Aidan's one box. "And don't you want to know where the dorm is and not the car?" I was a little confused at his logic.

"I mapped out where the building was from where I parked the car, but when I forgot where the car was, I couldn't find the dorm. I've been wandering around campus since you went into housing registration," he admitted lamely.

"You've been walking aimlessly for three hours holding a

fifty-pound box in hundred degree weather? Didn't you think to ask anyone for directions?" I would have been appalled, but it was so Aidan to do something like that.

Aidan gave me a sly smile. "I don't ask for directions, you know that."

I sighed heavily, shaking my head in amusement. "Come on. I know where the building is."

Aidan was instantly by my side as we walked through the maze that was the ASU campus.

"You got into McClintock Hall, right?" Aidan asked with a slight worried tone.

"Barely. The housing lady was being such a jerk." ASU had what was called "residential living," which basically meant on-campus housing for students with the same major. Aidan and I still weren't sure what we wanted to do with our lives, so we opted for majoring in Liberal Arts and Sciences. It sounded good and we figured we could always change it later.

That left us a few options for housing, but since Aidan was way more prepared than me, he'd gotten into McClintock Hall ages ago. It seemed like the best place to be since it was near the library and central to campus. I was just happy Crazy-Lady had given me my first choice. It wouldn't have been horrible to be in another building, but Aidan was my security blanket at this point, and I was glad we'd be living in the same place.

It took us about ten minutes to arrive at our new home. It was an L-shaped building. One side was three stories and the attached side was two stories. It looked like it was built in the '70s from the blocky architecture and the brown-and-white paint job. But at least there were lots of windows. I hated dark houses.

I needed my space as bright as possible. Natural sunlight was the best and I was thrilled that I'd have that, but I had come prepared just in case. One of my suitcases was completely filled with every table lamp I could stuff in it.

"What room are you in?" Aidan asked as we approached the bottom level.

"What room am *I* in? What room are *you* in? You have to put that box down before you pass out." Just like Aidan to be more concerned with me than himself.

He half laughed and nodded toward his back. "I forgot already. It's on a slip in my back pocket. Could you grab it?"

I was about to grab the white piece of paper sticking out of his jeans but stopped myself. It suddenly occurred to me how intimate it was to reach into someone's pants pocket, even if it was just a piece of paper. And for the first time in our entire lives together, I felt embarrassed. Or at least self-conscious. "Um, why don't I take the box and you get the paper?"

Aidan's face turned a little pink, and it wasn't from the heat. "Oh, right, sorry." He didn't hand me the box, but simply placed it on the ground in front of him. He grabbed the paper and read his room number aloud. "222."

I felt horrible making a "thing" out of something that should have been so normal for us. I'd known Aidan since forever. We'd had sleepovers and campouts. We'd slept in the same sleeping bag, for crying out loud! We'd been eight, but still.

Officially, we were adults now. Standing in front of our dorm. In college! And suddenly, touching Aidan's butt, even if it was just to grab a piece of paper, was just weird. I couldn't explain my crazy logic. I didn't want to cross any lines. Not with Aidan. He was too important to me to screw it up.

He brushed the whole thing off as if it'd never happened. Picking up his box, he gave me a goofy grin that told me everything was fine between us. "Shall we?"

I smiled back, relieved at how he handled my insanity. "Maybe your roommate will be there already."

"Ha! I'm a single occupant, sucker!" Aidan teased as he walked up the small flight of stairs to the second level.

"What?" I punched him in the arm playfully. "How did you pull that off?"

"It's called filling out the request early. As in before the due date. You wouldn't know anything about that," he laughed.

"You suck," I grumbled, but I wasn't mad. I was extremely jealous! I was going to have to share my room with someone called Gerta Jones. Who would name their child Gerta? I had an image in my head: a cross between Godzilla and Jabba the Hutt. I just hoped I was wrong.

"Yeah, I know." Aidan had his triumphant-face on.

"You're still going to have to share the bathroom." I had to knock his victory down just a little bit. The way the floor plans worked, there were two people to a room and two rooms shared one bathroom. So basically, four people to every bathroom.

"True, but still. I win," he laughed.

We reached his room and he put his box down on the two-seater couch on the left. The rooms were all the same from the research I'd done. They were set up like a small one-bedroom apartment. The front room consisted of the love seat and two desks with chairs. The back room had two twin beds side by side, a sink, a closet, and a door to the shared bathroom. Pretty simple.

I took out my dorm slip and looked it over. "I'm a couple rooms down from you, 225. I'm going to unpack my car. I'll meet you back here when I'm done?"

Aidan looked at me as if I was insane. He placed his hands on my shoulders and his eyes met mine. "Do you honestly think I'm going to let you unpack your car alone? You practically brought your whole house!"

"Which is why you shouldn't be forced to help. I got this. No worries." Though I knew it was a useless argument, I had to try. I hated moving with every fiber of my soul, so to have my best friend help lug all my crap seemed like a horrible abuse of friendship.

"Um, you're crazy. Now, where's your car?" Aidan wasn't budging. He was going to help no matter what I said.

"You keep forgetting that you parked it." I grinned.

"Oh, yeah." He grinned back. "Follow me."

Two hours later I was finally done. It was early evening, so at least it was in the nineties now instead of the 107-degree madness. And after going up those stairs five hundred times, I was drenched to the bone in sweat. Okay, maybe it wasn't five hundred, but it certainly felt like it! And at least I was able to leave the heavy box of extra lamps in my car since the dorm was perfectly lit to my satisfaction.

Gerta had arrived and she was actually quite pleasant. She was a short, pretty girl with brown hair and brown eyes, and as far as I could tell, she appeared very sweet.

The only difference between Aidan's and my apartment was the fact that the furniture setup was reversed.

Aidan was currently plopped on our couch. Gerta didn't

seem to mind. She was eyeing him like a piece of prime rib.

I felt a pang of . . . something. I wouldn't call it jealousy, but it was definitely territorial. I suddenly had the need to sit right next to Aidan. He was so exhausted he leaned his head on my shoulder and I fought the urge to be smug to poor little Gerta, who looked like I'd taken away her favorite toy.

"Are you two a couple?" Gerta asked with a forced smile, but really she was hiding her disappointment that Aidan might not be available.

He took his head off my shoulder and immediately shook his head. "Nah, just best buds. We've known each other since we were kids."

I wasn't expecting the knot that abruptly lurched in my stomach. It actually hurt. Not because it wasn't true, but because I wanted Gerta to think we were a couple. What made it more confusing was the fact that I didn't actually want to be a couple.

What was wrong with me? I didn't want Aidan romantically, but I didn't want him to be romantic with anyone else. It made no sense, but I felt it as strongly as anything I'd ever felt. I was being so selfish! How much of a jerk could I be? What if Aidan was so quick to say we were friends because he liked Gerta? I couldn't be the a-hole friend who cockblocked him from every potential girlfriend.

I swallowed my feelings of . . . whatever the heck I was feeling and simply said, "Nope. Just friends." When Gerta's eyes lit up, I added, "Good friends. Best friends. As in, if anyone even came close to hurting him, they'd have some serious hospital bills."

Aidan laughed and nudged me with his shoulder playfully. "We look out for each other." He gave me a smile that made my chest swell with affection. I really would tear anyone apart who dared to mess with him.

Gerta leaned back against one of the desks across from us. "There's a party at Delta Delta Phi. You guys want to come?"

I wasn't normally a party person and neither was Aidan . . .

"We'd love to!" Aidan's face lit up with so much enthusiasm I didn't have the heart to disappoint him.

"Yeah," I said with as much gusto as I could muster, "that sounds awesome. Let's do it."

Aidan went to go clean up and I did the same. A quick shower to wash off all the moving-slime felt amazing, although I was super paranoid that our next-door neighbors would walk into the bathroom at any time. The shower was closed off, but people could still come in and use the "other" facilities. I wasn't used to sharing anything, being an only child, so splitting a bathroom was making me jumpy.

I dried off and got dressed at super speed. I decided on jeans and a tank top. Yes, pretty much the same outfit I wore earlier, but this was a different tank; it had black and white stripes. I called it my "Paris" tank.

Gerta was wearing a killer short dress that made her look like a movie star. I suddenly felt very frumpy.

"You're going to dry your hair, right? You're seriously not going to let it air-dry at a party?" Gerta looked downright appalled.

I was going to do exactly that, but from the look of horror on Gerta's face, I said instead, "Of course not. I just can't find my hair dryer."

"Here. Use mine. And I have a ceramic straightener so it won't fry your hair." Gerta loaded me up with an expensive-looking hair dryer and flat iron. They were the kind that super swanky salons used. I realized then that Gerta was definitely a girly-girl and I'd have to adjust my personality accordingly.

"Thanks," I said with a grateful smile, though I felt more frustrated than grateful. I really didn't want to go to this party. I really didn't want to dry my hair. I just wanted to curl up on my new uncomfortable twin bed and read my Kindle until I fell asleep. Was that so wrong?

Despite my desire to be a hermit, I went into the bathroom to get ready. After all was said and done, I was impressed with myself. I looked pretty darn good. My hair had never been this straight in my life. Not that my hair was curly, but it had a natural wave to it that the iron completely flattened. The style really ended up suiting my oval face.

It was all worth it when Aidan arrived and his jaw dropped to the floor. All he could say was, "Shea."

I took that as a compliment, especially when he hardly noticed Gerta. And, trust me, he was going to be the only boy who didn't. That girl looked good!

Once the three of us started walking over to the frat house though, Aidan was back to his non-gawking self, talking about how excited he was to start school. We all gossiped about our classes and how lame it was that we had to take math and science as a requirement. Although, my heart was half into that argument. I actually liked science and math, but I didn't feel like being the lone sheep in the conversation, so I complained heartily with Aidan and Gerta.

When we arrived at the Delta Delta Phi house, it was already spilling over with people. Apparently, this was "the" party to go to, and from the looks of it, most of the campus had crammed inside. Even the lawn and porch were stuffed with students.

"I guess we came to the right place," Aidan observed. I looked over at him and could tell he was fighting the urge to leave.

I was about to suggest we do just that when Gerta wrapped her arm around his and pulled him toward the front door. "Let's get some alcohol in you."

I followed close behind them, not wanting to be stranded in a sea of people I didn't know. Aidan kept giving me smiles of encouragement while Gerta led him through the throng of drunk coeds. It was getting harder and harder to keep up with them until finally I realized I needed to grow a pair and let Aidan have fun.

I stopped in the middle of the room and watched Aidan and Gerta get swallowed up by the ocean of people.

Okay.

Here I was.

Getting more and more claustrophobic by the second.

I was about to become a human bulldozer and shove my way out of this hot, sweaty, crowded place when an ice-cold red cup was gently placed in my hand. "You look like you could use a drink."

I peered up at the guy who had handed it to me. I had to say, he was pretty beautiful. He had smoldering brown eyes, pale blond hair, and cheekbones for days. He was way too good-looking to talk to me. It must have been dark in here.

"I don't take drinks from strangers. Leave me alone." Why did I just say that? It was like I couldn't control what came out of my mouth. I mean, I'd uttered some pretty stupid things before, but I was fully aware that I was saying them. This was different. It was as if someone else was pulling my vocal strings and wanted to tell this guy to go away.

That was it.

My instincts told me Blond-Boy was bad news.

He looked at me as if he was butt hurt. Like it had taken all his courage to come up and talk to me and I had blown him off. The people pleaser in me felt like a complete jerk.

Maybe I was being crazy-paranoid-girl. It might not be instinct; it could be fear-of-hot-boys. I'd definitely been known to choke up when talking to a cute guy. They intimidated the crap out of me.

"I'm sorry. It's all these people. It's freaking me out a little." I lifted the cup to him. "Thanks." I didn't actually drink it. I still had unreasonable fears of poisoning and roofies, but I pretended to so he wouldn't feel bad.

"I'm Frank," he said with a shy smile. "We can go outside and get some air if it'll make you feel better?"

Okay. He was being sweet.

"Sure," I responded with what I hoped was a pleasant smile. "I'm Shea."

"Hi, Shea." From the relief on his face, I'd say I did my job recovering from my earlier nastiness.

We walked through the packed partiers and finally emerged into the night air. It was warm outside, but not nearly as suffocating as the frat house. There were almost as many people outside as inside, but somehow being in the open air made it psychologically better.

"Over here." Frank placed his hand on the small of my back

and led me to an outcropping of sycamore trees. They were in full foliage, making it hard to see anyone through the low branches. "See? Private, but still close to the party for an easy getaway if you decide you don't like me," Frank whispered charmingly.

The hairs on the back of my neck rose. Something was off.

"You know what? I completely abandoned my friend in there. I should go get him." I wanted to run from Frank. He was nice and I was probably acting like a scaredy-cat, but all I could think about was finding Aidan and being as far away from this guy as possible.

"How's your drink?" Frank ignored my statement completely.

I dumped it on the ground. "Excuse me," I said and tried to push past him.

He grabbed my arm. "That was rude." His face went from sweet and charismatic to angry in about a second.

I tried to shrug him off, but his grip was like a vise. And by vise, I mean I couldn't move at all.

Frank leaned down so his eyes met mine, and even though it was dark out, they constricted right in front of me as if someone had shone a flashlight in them. "You won't scream. You won't even remember this. Just relax."

I screamed.

I would never forget the creepy look in his eyes.

And relaxing was entirely out of the question.

But Frank's reaction was the opposite of what I expected. He was shocked. As if simply telling me not to scream would have actually worked. Did he think he was some kind of hypnotist or something?

The shock wasn't enough for him to release his hold on me

though. He pulled me closer, and I was pretty sure the guy was about to bite the back of my neck! Who did this guy think he was: Dracula? Freaking psycho!

I tried to move, but he was strong. He didn't look like he'd be that powerful, but the more I grabbed at him and tried to wriggle away, the more he just stood there like stone. I wasn't that weak, was I?

And you'd think with a party right next to us someone would have responded to my scream, but no such luck.

That's when I felt his teeth on my neck. On my neck! He was seriously going to bite me like a raging lunatic! I'd read about nutzoids like Frank in a magazine once. They really thought they were vampires. All I could think about was the part in the article that said it was a lot harder to bite into flesh than the crazies thought. For Frank's teeth to actually break my skin, he would have to bite down really hard and possibly take out a chunk of me.

Oh, God. This was going to be bad.

I tried again to move Statue-Boy, but he might as well have been rooted in cement.

I felt his teeth puncture my skin. The sensation of blood trickling down my back was surreal and terrifying. Not to mention the fact that Frank was moaning like he was having an orgasm.

Terror raced through me.

I was trapped.

No one was coming.

Something deep inside me snapped.

I screamed once more, but this time it sounded like a battle cry.

My eyes burned and I saw a flash of white.

Frank pulled back instantly, horrified.

The white was gone.

I felt like myself again.

I was about to run when I saw a blur of muscle beside me. Frank's body suddenly flew in the air and smashed against a nearby tree.

Aidan stood next to me. I could feel the rage flowing off him like waves of power. It was much more terrifying than Frank's attack. The fact that Aidan's fist had made a six-foot college student fly ten feet in the air and smash into a tree was a little mind-blowing. I knew Aidan was strong, but seriously!

Frank recovered more quickly than I expected. He pleaded to Aidan, "I didn't know she was yours."

Aidan snarled. He sounded more like an animal than a man. He leapt at Frank and grabbed him by the throat. "If there weren't so many witnesses . . . "

Aidan was right; we had gained quite an audience. He must have caused a scene by racing to save me. The only thing I could think of was that he had heard me scream. Out of all the noise and people at that party, Aidan had heard me above everything else. If I hadn't know it before, I knew it now: he and I were connected. He'd always be there for me, no matter what.

Frank was a blubbering mess and barely choked out the words, "I didn't know she was claimed!"

Aidan made sure Frank was looking him in the eye. "I'm not one of you," he growled.

I had no idea what they were talking about, but Frank's eyes went round. He choked. "What are you?"

Aidan didn't answer. He must have been amped up on adrenaline because he threw Frank by the neck like he was a rag doll.

Frank scrambled to his feet as if it had been a gentle shove. He knew better than to stay at this point and ran into the darkness.

People were asking me if I was okay and trying to high-five Aidan. I just wanted out of there. I needed to be in the quiet. I needed to be away from people. I needed a freaking Band-Aid.

Aidan ignored everyone's praise and lifted me into his arms, cradling me like a baby. I leaned my head on his shoulder and let him carry me. Normally my feminist side would tell him to put me down so I could walk on my own, but feeling his arms holding my body made me feel safe.

And I really needed to feel safe at the moment.

Aidan took me to his dorm room so that we could have some privacy. He laid me on one of the twin beds and gently examined my neck. "Not too bad. You won't need stitches. I've got a bandage here."

I touched his arm. "Thank you," I said. Talking made all my emotions flood to the surface. Tears streamed down my cheeks and I couldn't stop them. Everything that had happened hit me full force. I hated crying. I wasn't a crier. But being attacked on my first day was too much for me to process. I was completely overwhelmed.

Aidan's arms were instantly wrapped around me. He held me close. I clung to him like he was air. He had saved my life. My best friend. My Aidan. I couldn't love him any more than I did in that moment.

He pulled out of the embrace and smiled. "You're going to sleep here tonight." He left no room for argument.

I simply nodded and let him clean the bite marks and bandage them properly. I was exhausted. My head barely hit the pillow and I was asleep.

***

I awoke to the sound of someone knocking on the door.

Aidan was out cold on the twin bed next to me. I didn't want to wake him. From the light coming in through the window, I knew it was morning. Or, I hoped it was morning. I had been known to sleep in pretty late from time to time.

I tiptoed past Aidan and walked through the bedroom to the main living space where the desks and couch were. Cracking open his front door, I was not prepared for the hot guy standing there.

After last night, I didn't think I'd be interested in another boy . . . ever.

But . . . this guy?

He had a kind of half smirk, which made him ridiculously sexy, but he held himself in a way that pretty much told me he knew that already. I hated it when really good-looking people knew that they were really good looking. He had piercing . . . was it teal? Holy crap, this guy had almost turquoise eyes! But a deep, deep teal like they could be dark green or dark blue depending on his wardrobe.

His face angled in all the right places and his dark hair was short and perfectly in place.

He wore a simple black T-shirt and jeans, but he managed to make that look like he had stepped out of a modeling shoot. And from the look in his eyes, I could tell he thought I should be falling all over him.

Not going to happen.

No way was I going to let this guy know I was attracted to him. Not after last night.

"Yes?" I said as snarkily as I could.

It took him aback.

Good.

I liked bringing down egomaniacs a notch or two.

He took a moment before he spoke, but when he did, his voice was calm and commanding. "I'm Lucian, the dorm monitor. I wanted to introduce myself to all the new students."

A part of me felt bad for being rude, but after what I'd gone through with that crazy jerk, I wasn't in the mood to be nice. Especially to gorgeous boys who had the nerve to stand there and be . . . gorgeous.

"Nice to meet you," I replied flatly. "I'm Shea, but this isn't my room. I'm in 225. This is Aidan O'Connell's room." Being the dorm monitor, he should already know that, but I thought I'd make his job easier. "Did you want to meet him, too?" I asked, and was surprised at how much attitude I had.

He had done exactly nothing to deserve my wrath. It must have been residual feelings from my experience with Bite-Boy.

No matter how hard I tried to put on a nice smile, a scowl would instantly replace it.

Lucian appeared to sense this as well because he suddenly leaned down close to me. "Nice to meet you, Shea."

Then his eyes constricted.

Like Frank's.

I stepped back in fear.

"Are you on drugs?" Was this some kind of new campus drug that messed with people's eyes? Maybe this guy would think he was Dracula, too. "Get the hell away from me. I'm going to report you to . . . to someone . . . I don't know who yet, but you shouldn't be in charge of anything if you're doing drugs!" That even sounded lame to me.

Lucian was more surprised than before. He looked like Frank had when I'd refused to obey his "no screaming" order.

"I'm not on drugs," he stated simply.

"Yeah, right." I crossed my arms defiantly. "Well, you did your job. You introduced yourself, now go introduce yourself to everyone else." I slammed the door in his face.

I knew I had completely overreacted, but I didn't care. Cute or not, there was something about him I didn't trust.

I turned around and jumped slightly when I saw Aidan standing in the bedroom doorway with a huge grin on his face.

"What are you smiling about?" I found his amusement contagious.

"You certainly told him," he beamed.

The boy looked positively proud of me. I suddenly needed a hug. I ran up to him and felt relieved when his arms wrapped around me. "Can we just have a first-day do-over please?" I mumbled into his chest.

"How's breakfast sound?" He pulled away with a grin.

"Perfect." I sighed in relief. "I'll meet you in the lobby in a half hour. I'm going to complain to somebody, damn it." I wasn't sure if I was actually going to make a formal complaint, but I hated making empty threats.

I hurried to my room, successfully avoiding the "Lucian welcoming wagon." After showering quickly and slopping my hair into a wet ponytail, I hurried down to the lobby to wait for Aidan.

It was a small lobby with one main desk and four couches. Of course, no one was there, so I couldn't report anyone at the moment. That somehow made me feel better, and I was starting to rethink my whole complaint rant anyway. Maybe I had just been upset about what had happened to me with Frank, so I'd taken it out on Lucian. I felt the bandages on my neck. The injury barely hurt, but the whole experience had been pretty terrifying.

Whoa.

My stomach dropped.

I whirled around, expecting to see Frank, but there was no one there, just a door to the supply closet.

For no reason that I could explain, I knew something horrible was behind that door.

And like every idiot in a horror movie, I walked over to it. Before I could chicken out, I grabbed the knob and turned.

Locked.

Of course it was.

My feeling didn't go away though. Something felt wrong.

"Shea? You ready?" Aidan's voice interrupted my crazy obsession with the closet. I really was going nuts.

"Yeah." I turned around and walked over to Aidan. "But I think I'm going for a nice chamomile tea instead of coffee this morning."

"Good plan." Aidan nudged me affectionately.

CHAPTER 2
LUCIAN

I stared into his brown eyes. So many humans in America had brown eyes now. Maybe it was being in Arizona again, but I hated this place. I hated the dry, dusty air of the desert, the artificial plants and plastic breasts, the bleached-blond hair and the smell of slathered cocoa butter.

It was a den for lizards. The sun made their skin leathery, and the more insane among them fried and cooked it in tanning beds. I'd never been one for beef jerky. Human flesh should be kept tender, juicy.

I knew he couldn't pick where he'd been born, but it was a good move for Adnachiel to stay here. Keep Shea in the desert . . . the middle of the desert, where the sun was high and night was short. After all these years of losing, maybe that little beasty wanted to win. It didn't matter. He could even hide her in the arctic land of the midnight sun, and I would burn in the gray light of her shadow and still take her.

The putrid heat rolled a long line of sweat down my back, and I smiled at the distasteful sensation. It wasn't pleasant like the heat of Egypt. There were no turning sands, and the people didn't smell of frankincense and myrrh, like the Babylonians and Assyrians. Now those were a people. They used to bring boatloads of resins from the Phoenicians. Queen Hatshepsut had reeked of the stuff.

These paper dolls had no depth and no weight. They couldn't fathom such a rich fragrance. The women in this generation smelled of rotten flowers and alcohol. Nothing of the earth, the soil. No, it was nothing like Egypt . . . nothing like Nefertiti.

Shea Harper wouldn't be any different. She'd be cheap and easily controlled. This round would be easier than the last; she'd make number seven. Poor Adnachiel. With Shea being a woman, she didn't stand a chance against me. The men were harder, but my skill and age won over every time. They were just playthings for this immortal game. Still, a female. That was new.

Women in this generation didn't have willpower like they used to centuries ago. My pupils barely had to constrict and I was inside their minds. Puppets; that was all the human race had amounted to. They were even controlled by their own devices and creations. Larger puppets sat in big buildings, making advertisements to brainwash the smaller masses. It was a joke. The whole "class system," I'd seen it before.

I touched my shoulder, feeling the deep scars underneath. I wondered if any of them would fight back. I laughed to myself condescendingly. Of course they wouldn't. They'd have to acknowledge that they were modern slaves. Working, fighting, just for food on the table and a roof over their heads, all the while their small fragile lives consumed in work and believing the lies of the invention of "retirement."

In a way, I pitied them. It made humans easier to feed on. I was putting the poor bunnies down before the factories and offices slowly squeezed the life out of them. I laughed again at the thought of my own mercy.

Lucian the Merciful. Now that brought a smile to my face as I stared at the mangled body shoved into the supply closet, his brown eyes still open wide in frozen horror.

I wondered about his life, if I had taken something too carelessly, but one glance at him and I knew what he'd become. He'd been a young man, enthralled with the power of being Dorm Monitor. A small power for a slave. I shook my head. He would have lorded himself over the "lessers" the rest of his life. Even his blood had a sour tint to it . . . but that hadn't stopped me from drinking him dry.

Have not, waste not.

I yawned, throwing his body over my shoulder. It was a shame Shea had been so curious about this closet, and a good thing I'd locked it behind me. She'd almost pried it open, strong for a small-framed woman. I needed to take her before she understood what she really was.

Although, knowing hadn't helped the others.

I wondered what the next one would be like. Was this female thing a trend, or a different tactic? I would have to wait another five hundred years to find out. At least this was a change, unlike Adnachiel trying this old middle-of-the-desert move. Honestly, I'd already looked up their files. They'd both been born and raised in Phoenix. By now, Adnachiel should have convinced them to move to some secluded valley where they could live out their days in hiding.

Did he really think I wouldn't find her? It didn't matter. Even with the sun and heat, I'd still beaten him last time. I'd played this chess game before. He thought he could castle and move his king safely behind these plastic Arizona pawns, using the daylight to his advantage.

To me, unfiltered light was a curse. What good was the sun, that raging orb fueling all life, surrounded by the blackness of space? It's only saving grace was the reflected light it cast on the moon, that soft controller of all the oceans.

I swallowed, thinking about the correlation throughout history between women and the moon I so adored.

I resolved that it didn't matter that Shea was a woman. She may have slammed the door in my face, but that was just a fluke. She would succumb to me like all the rest. Still, she had noticed my eyes. Most humans weren't quick enough to see the millisecond they constricted before they were under my control.

Her powers protected her from my mind. I laughed, unable to fight the surge pulsing through my dead veins. This might be a fun challenge.

It had been centuries since I'd felt . . . anything, watching time pass and ages shift from glory to decay. If she were a man, I'd just take her, force her. I was so much more powerful than their greatest of strengths. Adnachiel, he always stopped me, if you could call what he did to them *stopping* me.

It was losing, any way you looked at it. His face sickened me, even after all these years. That would-be loyal dog. Shea didn't know that he'd slit her throat just as readily as I would. She'd die oblivious in his arms after he'd lanced her. That last look of betrayal on their faces . . . like Moses . . . how could he stand it? Every time.

I breathed in the air and coughed it out, so much dirt in every inhalation. Seducing her the old-fashioned way wouldn't be a problem. I'd kissed my fair share of desert rats with sand in their teeth while waiting for the Vessel to reveal its location. I'd known it would be in the desert, I could feel it. I just hadn't known which one.

Now that I had found her, this might be entertaining. I always enjoyed the hunt, but adding seduction to the fire could be enough to satiate my growing distemper with eternity.

At least for a while.

A small drop of the dorm monitor's blood dripped down my back. My nostrils flared at the scent. I should top up before talking to Shea again. I walked candidly through shadows until I was outside. I had to wait until nightfall to ditch the body.

I moved quickly past a few meat-bags. I nodded graciously, explaining that the boy was a friend of mine who'd passed out from drinking. They didn't notice the dried blood down his mangled arms. They laughed, agreed, and went inside; no mind control needed.

Oh Adnachiel, was this really the safest place for her, to stay where she'd been born, never leaving the desert? It didn't make sense. Unless he thought she'd never use her powers.

If that was the case, then he was a fool. No matter how careful he was, every Vessel eventually did.

***

I sighed. Normally, the fresh night air was a relief, but it was still ninety degrees. The only benefit to my brief stay in this sweltering hell was the cactuses. Desert plants bloomed at night. Their biggest pollinators weren't butterflies or hummingbirds; they were bats. I breathed in deep. The scent was made to attract them. The fragrance was too pungent for most mortals, but for me it was the smell of bliss. If vampires were cursed, why did nature itself procure a gift for us, to bloom in the hours when we roam?

A yearning grew in my stomach. How long had it been since I had a garden and tilled the soil? I growled, hating the idea. That'd been over three thousand years ago. It was strange, how just being in the desert was stirring up old memories, feelings I had long since buried with my mortal flesh. The sooner I took her and left the desert, the more I'd feel like I always felt.

Calloused and powerful.

I jumped into the air, flying over the city lights. If I soared high enough, all of that noise, all of that movement below slowed. Above the cloud cover, it was silent. Except for planes. I wouldn't make that mistake again. However, when a passenger had screamed upon seeing me hovering outside his window, the noise had been worth the reaction. The stewardess restrained him as he continued to call out hysterically.

What a sight.

Now it was still. I glided slowly in the atmosphere, watching the small lights fade in the distance. I could be lazy and drop the dorm monitor's remains in some canyon, but I needed a break from the desert. I thought about taking him to the Pacific Ocean. It wasn't a far fly from here. Maybe I'd pick up a few snacks to refuel on the way.

No. No sense being careless now. She had awakened, and I needed to use every moment to my advantage. Why this nostalgia? It wasn't like me to delay a battle, even a pathetic one. I had waited five hundred years to stick it to Adnachiel again. Besides, Caelius grew restless in his cage. If he knew about my little ocean excursion, or any sort of misstep from the goal, he'd be furious. Furious, but helpless to do anything about it. Unless he sent my Second-Borns, in which case I was his, caged or not.

I sighed, letting the body slip from my hands and splat thousands of feet below in a deep, desolate canyon. The desert would bake his bones and rid me of the mess in a matter of days. I straightened my shoulders, brushing off the now dried blood from my black T-shirt.

Time to go do some dorm monitoring.

Even though her classes were now over, I landed close enough to the school to walk to where I'd last seen her in history class, a useless subject. A human had said it best: history was written by the victors. Then it was taught and force-fed to the masses. Besides, her history wasn't something she was going to find or learn about in books; it was in her blood. Her sweet, nourishing blood.

I felt my irises expand, covering my pupils. A little hint from my body. I definitely needed to eat something again before we met.

I scanned the treats walking by in their short-shorts, the strong smell of bleach still lingering in their platinum hair. One caught my eye as she bounced over.

"Hi! You must be new here, or I know I would have totally seen you by now. I'm Melissa." She giggled as the words spilled out of her mouth like warm honey. I smiled, pointing down to my dorm monitor badge as her cheeks burned red.

"Oh, I didn't know we had a new monitor. I was *very* close with the old one." Again, every word was pinned on seduction. Her breasts heaved in her paint-by-number shirt. One foot fidgeted with the other as she raked her manicured nails through her hair.

I let her continue. It was a child's game. A real woman could seduce any man, but not a vampire. Although, I'm sure Nefertiti could have. Living or dead, she could have moved the oceans. Her eyes had burned like the center of the sea in a storm. I missed those magnificent purple eyes.

I coughed, looking away and feigning embarrassment. I shouldn't toy with my food. Again, why was I so wrapped up in nostalgia and comparison? Meaningless comparisons about beauty and a life long dead. I should just eat her and find Shea.

Now, I'd done it. The whole swarm followed Melissa over: five more large-breasted, tan, flirtatious women. Another one stepped forward, her shorts just an inch above the curve of her cheeks, leaving little to the imagination. "Don't let Melissa embarrass you. I'm Audrey. If you didn't guess already, we're the main bitches in the cheerleading squad. You don't seem like the kind of nerd who would be a dorm monitor. You're too hot." She winked, unashamed of her brash nature.

My eyes constricted, and like the mindless bunnies they were, all their mouths dropped open. "Now Audrey, that's not a nice thing to say. I like being a dorm monitor." They all leaned in as I spoke. My mind was blank. I couldn't decide what to fill their fragile brains with.

I peered at all of them at once: father issues, competitive mothers, self-worth fed by false gods in Victoria's Secret catalogs, boob jobs at young ages before their bodies had fully grown.

The saddest case was Melissa. I looked deeper into her eyes. She was a copy of all the other girls. She'd end up just like her mother before her, and then she'd have two more daughters just like her. Over and over through her bloodline, the mindlessness would continue. Lucian the Merciful. I took her hand and spoke gently, compelling the other girls.

"You don't know where Melissa went. The last you saw her, she was getting drunk with some boy named Adnachiel . . . no . . . you'd know him by his mortal name: Aidan. You saw her with *Aidan* at a party. If anyone knows where she is, it's him. And you feel like he's a liar. At least, that's what you'll tell the police when they come looking. He's hiding something. You want to make his life hell while he's here in college. I'm the new dorm monitor and you want to help me, anytime I need it. You trust me without fear."

They nodded, and one of them drooled slightly. I jumped into the sky with Melissa. It was too quick for their human eyes to register the strong breeze that shook the trees beside them. And night could play tricks with the senses after all.

Melissa struggled for breath in the thinning atmosphere, but her eyes remained fixed on mine, full of lust and servitude. "Melissa, such a sad life. Do you want me to end it for you and give you bliss?" I let her regain control of her mind for a moment.

She saw the earth below and screamed, squirming from my grip. I watched her fall a thousand feet. When I caught her, I wrapped her in my arms. She cried into my chest and I felt a pang of guilt. Lucian the Merciful indeed. *It's not nice to play with your food. Just finish it.*

I clenched my jaw over her soft neck. She flinched for a moment, but I took the time to fill her body with a deep, aching sort of orgasmic pleasure. Her limbs trembled as she peed herself. Something turned my stomach. Was it boredom? The taste of silicone from a leaking bag in her breast? Whatever it was, I just couldn't finish. All I could think about was Shea. Why was the Vessel a woman this time?

In this generation, they were nothing more than household pets. If men were modern slaves, women were the slaves of slaves. There was a time when they'd fought for something. Not too long ago they'd burned bras and demanded to be astronauts and physicists . . . now they wanted to be mommies.

The anti–birth control propaganda had created another generation of slaves. It was a simple tactic I'd seen the ruling class use throughout centuries: keep the numbers at the bottom of the pyramid large. It was called a *working* class. And that's what they did, until they died. Such servitude and breeding was all done in the pursuit of wealth. It was the carrot held by those in power, driving the masses to their graves.

Wealth: a sickening disease that turned humans against themselves.

Melissa was just a plastic toy caught in the system. Marketing worked. Imperfections were now damnations that had to be paid for with blood and credit cards, anything to fill the void of real self-worth.

I laughed as she moaned in bliss, still alive.

Suddenly, I shook her hard. An unknown fury began to radiate from my bones, my inner thoughts boiling to the surface.

"Don't you see what they've done to you? To all of you? Are you that mindless? Imperfections are the beauty of life! And all life was made from a mutation in genes! Do you really want to remain an amoeba? Is that what women are now: replications, empty dolls? If your only desire is to be slaves to a ruling class, if that's what mankind has become, you deserve to be harvested and fed on like the cattle you are by Caelius himself!"

I let her body drop. This time she didn't scream, still wrapped in the pleasure of my mouth. When it thudded, dust encircled her like an iris. I shook my head. What had come over me? "Disappointing Lucian . . . and wasteful." I quickly landed in the mush that was Melissa and blood splattered everywhere.

It was too close to the campus. They would find this wreckage. I smiled, biting my own lip. "It's unwise to top up and use my powers. I'll just need to eat again." I kicked a piece of her pelvis bone. "But you have to do what you have to do. You made this mess . . . now clean it up." I gritted my teeth. I'd have sand coming out of every hole for days. I spat her lingering blood out as I felt my eyes burn.

My body rose, a sandstorm mounting behind me. "Remember this little move, Moses? Lock your windows, kiddies, and pray to your gods. It's going to be a dark night." There was nothing like a small plague of locusts to cover up a miss-feed.

Their buzzing was heard miles off. The ground shook as swarms of insects covered the night sky with the blackness of their large bodies. They hurtled mercilessly toward the campus, along with dust and anything else the tornado-like wind drew in by the flapping of their wings.

An inch. An inch of dirt and locusts would dissolve Melissa.

My little friends could carry the bones away and feast in the canyons.

It wasn't a smart move. Taking a pawn with a rook. I might be revealing my power too soon to Adnachiel. He didn't know how much I'd grown over the last five hundred years, but he'd seen this move before. I smiled, unable to filter the rage as the swarms crawled onto my body, taking over the school. He'd asked me to use this power once, and I had, out of sheer loyalty.

I heard all of their rushed footsteps as the meat-bags ran. I heard the screams. Now, I felt like I was in Egypt again. To think, in the end they'd blamed all those plagues on God and not Moses. The bible was not the most accurate form of history. They talked about Moses's power, but they missed the part about being helped by a vampire and a beast. And they missed the very greatness of the man himself. At that time, there'd been nothing Aidan, Moses and I couldn't accomplish for the betterment of all mankind.

His real name was Adnachiel, but during Moses's time, we'd called him Aidan. It had been brotherly-like affection. We'd been so bonded then. And now, after all these centuries, the family he'd been born into had actually given him that name. I hoped it pained him every time his mother stroked his hair and called him the same name Moses had gasped in his last breaths. I hoped it reminded him of his betrayal. I'd hate that name and that beast forever for what he'd done.

I refocused on the present as power surged through me, the pain in my chest stirring old wounds savagely patched by the passing of centuries. Things that went bump in the night had been more readily accepted and seen back then. Today's locust infestation would have to be scientifically explained. Global warming maybe?

Caelius wouldn't be pleased. This kind of exposure wasn't done anymore. I was tired of sitting on my hands, only using my gifts once or twice every five hundred years, all so that Caelius could have his numbers quietly increased from the shadows, preparing for his final release from the cage. Caelius only wanted the world to burn if he was the one ruling it.

I had only turned seven men into vampires. Still, those had been particular circumstances and unique humans I'd selected. But that had been a long time ago. I hadn't turned anyone in close to five hundred years. I hadn't been tempted. Only after I took the Vessel and battled with Aidan did I feel so compelled, hollowed out, and desperate for camaraderie. It was a pattern that repeated, despite my arrogant protests of needing no one.

Only one human could have broken the routine. It was a shame women didn't survive the transformation. There'd been a brilliant botanist a hundred years ago: Helena Madison. She'd deserved to have more time. The things she could have done for this planet—that might have been exciting to see, to stay alive for. Still, she would have seen the world become this.

Why a woman? This Shea Harper. I'd assumed the Vessels were only male, like us. But to come in this form, this fragile form . . . something was different. I could sense it. Let Caelius rage. If the game was different this round, I might as well dust off some of my old favorite tricks, show this Shea what she was in for.

I heard their voices, all of their mindless, fear-driven voices coddled inside buildings and cars, even over the beautiful storm of locust wings. I continued to let them crawl over my body like old friends, touching my skin. A girl nearby didn't make it inside in time. She was suffocating as the winged creatures crawled into her mouth.

I sighed. My arms dropped as I calmed the storm. The insects scattered, flying back into the night they'd been called from. I looked at the thick layer of dirt and bug carcasses covering the mess that was once Melissa.

Lucian the Merciful indeed.

I stepped on a large, juicy one and it crunched under my black eel-skin shoes. I breathed in the dirt and the fear. It had been so long since mass terror rippled in the air at my presence. It was like Pompeii. The panic alone was thick enough to feed from. The power sharpened my senses. I could smell her. I hadn't noticed before, but her sweat . . . it was almost sugared, like a foreign nectar I had never tasted.

Perhaps I would taste it now. When I was charged like this, humans melted at my very presence. I leapt quickly into the air, landing in an alley behind a small coffee shop. She was drinking water. I smelled him too: Adnachiel.

His scent changed every time. Now he reeked like all the other boys at college, no doubt covered in expensive cologne. He did his best to blend in. But I knew the beast that was underneath.

I walked casually to the front and stepped in. The noise was the first thing that hit me. All of the voices were frenzied about the storm and dead locusts outside. My presence calmed the atmosphere. I heightened my sexual energy. It was like a magnet in the room. Men and women stared at my form as I walked by.

I ordered a tall coffee, black. A perky boy with curly hair left the register and insisted on giving it to me himself, bypassing the other employees. A line formed behind me, but they didn't seem to mind the wait. I looked back, casting a small side smile. That was enough for them. They laughed uncomfortably, nodding, trying to mutter something about how good the coffee was here.

The curly-haired barista returned. His hand shook as he gave me an extra-large cup, on the house. The hot liquid sloshed and burned my hand, to his horror. I reached up and grabbed one of his curls, pulling his soft, newborn-like face to mine. The room quieted further. They were all holding their breath, hoping to see something more.

I patted his cheek, whispering in his ear. "Relax. You didn't hurt me. But later tonight, you'll wait for me in the alley. I'll need something else to drink then. You'll tell no one."

He nodded, smiling from ear to ear. I casually looked toward Shea and Adnachiel. Nothing. She didn't even turn. She'd missed the whole display. I laughed, letting my hold of the room go. The bustle begun again, everyone asking about the bugs. I sneered, walking past the line. Turning the empty chair next to her backward, I plopped down, my legs spread casually open as I leaned forward.

Her eyes caught mine, but her mouth didn't unlock with desire. She was genuinely angry that I'd joined them. I straightened my back, coughing as I took a sip of the scalding liquid. I let my smile peel back farther, but it seemed to aggravate her even more. "I just popped in for a break. I've been running around campus, trying to make sure everyone's okay. Freak storm, right? How are you guys holding up?"

"We're fine," she spat, turning her body toward Adnachiel.

I took a moment, trying to figure out my next move. A tall woman with long legs invited herself to the table, sitting obnoxiously close to me. She laughed, using the same line I'd just used on Shea.

"Hey guys, whatcha talking about? I'm Kristy, number 150 in your dorm, and we are all super freaked about the bugs! Gross, right?" She shook her head, setting her hand on my thigh. Shea and I both eyed that hand.

I picked it up as if it were diseased and returned it to her. I could easily have compelled Kristy away from us, but Shea had noticed my eyes constrict before. It wasn't worth the risk.

I gritted my teeth. At least this paper doll had helped me realize how rusty my pickup line was. If I wanted to charm Shea and not have this be another smash-and-grab like in the past, I'd need another angle.

Kristy was undaunted by the rejected flirtation. "So, the word that's spread around campus is you're the new hot dorm monitor. All us cheerleaders are talking about it. There's this party tonight, I'd love you to come with me." There was that hand again. This time it reached deeper and squeezed, her long nails leaving marks in my thigh.

I eyed Adnachiel, who seemed bemused. I wondered how he tolerated this sort of mortal and if his tastes had changed along with mine over the centuries. To my knowledge, he hadn't loved anyone after I'd killed Mailid decades ago.

Kristy looked briefly at the other two. "Oh, you can totally invite your friends . . . just as long as you're there." She laced her other small talon through my dark brown hair, now more wildly tossed than usual.

She grabbed a handful tight. "Look at this shaggy scruff. Did you get caught in the storm?" She inched her way closer for a kiss. That was enough.

I stuck up my hand and her face landed in it. I slowly pushed her back. "Listen . . . Kristy, was it? I don't know you, or your little friends. If I liked you, you'd know. These bold advances of yours reek of how many men you've let take you. You have nothing for me that I want. You can take your plastic eyelashes and bat them somewhere else."

It was hard to stop myself. I was furious that she had interrupted my conversation with Shea. I used to not mind cheap women throwing themselves at me. But when it was all the time, when everyone could be so easily drawn in, it became shallow and empty. It added to the loneliness aching in my hollow bones.

I looked down, closing my eyes. I didn't open them again until I heard her retreat out the door, the small bell jingling as she passed. I couldn't let my eyes show their rage. I took a few deep breaths. When they opened, my gaze fell on Shea's soft face.

I sighed despite myself, my brow furrowed. She still looked angry. She leaned back in her chair and crossed her arms, looking at me squarely. "That was a bit harsh, don't you think? It takes a lot for a girl to approach a guy."

Before I could rationalize, the words came rolling out like hot lava. "Do you *think* it takes a lot for a girl like that to approach a guy? Really, Shea? I don't think it does." I leaned closer to her, my anger boiling over. She winced slightly, but I couldn't stop myself, just to breathe her in a little deeper.

"I've been stalked, chased, and had trash like that throw itself at me for as long as I can remember. They don't want *me,*

Shea. Not what I really am. They're just addicts, addicted to the pleasure they think I can give them. They want this body, and their fake beliefs in what I am, and that's fine.

"Sometimes I want to play, but it's nothing. It means nothing. Girls like Kristy will breed, and with each generation, there'll be more of them. Soon they'll swarm just like the locusts outside. Then, the last beautiful, unique spark of humanity will die out along with the inventors, freethinkers, and radicals. Perfection is a diseased idea that has infected mankind." I wanted to spit out my own disgust for what humanity had become . . . for what I had become.

She leaned so far back in her chair, I was sure there were groove marks on her spine. I sat, truly embarrassed for the first time in ages. What was I saying? I was always in control. It couldn't be the desert alone that was making me act this way.

Something was off.

"I'm sorry. I don't know what came over me. Just . . . people like that, that's all I've encountered for so long. I mean, since I started working here. It got to me, but that was no reason to . . . I . . . I apologize," I stuttered.

This had gone horribly wrong. Was I that out of practice with having a real conversation with someone? It had been a while, at least a hundred years since I'd found anyone worth talking to. Still, this was humiliating. I didn't know if her face was more shocked by my venomous words about humans, or my apology after. What was worse was the smirk that hadn't left Adnachiel's face since I'd sat down. I should address that and put the pup in his place.

"So, Adnachiel, what did you think about that storm of

locusts? Remind you of anything . . . or anyone?" Now my smile returned as his faded.

He literally growled, scraping the table with his nails as he spoke. "My name is . . . Aidan. Just as familiar and easy to say as the word *locust*."

I scoffed. "Is it *easy* to say? After what you did to him?"

If it had been a cold day, I'd have seen a stream of hot air blowing out of his flaring nostrils as his eyes bulged. "Listen, this table is for two *friends*. Not for some freak with obvious daddy issues. Why don't you draw some black eyeliner under your eyes and go tell your sad story somewhere else?"

Good move.

Should I play the wounded guest, or should I just grab her now and forget my plan and see what strength Adnachiel had in this new form? I paused, letting the anticipation build. "Just trying to make conversation. You and Shea don't seem as mindless as the other kids on campus. I thought we might have something in common . . . *Aidan*." He almost winced, hearing me spit his endearing nickname out like a curse. I had to admit, I winced as well. I hadn't called him by that name since Moses.

I swallowed hard and continued my ruse. "And Shea, about my eyes this morning, I'd like to apologize for that as well. When you asked if I'd been drugged, I was shocked. I actually went to Rapid Care. It turns out there's been a new drug around campus. One of the cheerleaders gave me a drink when I first arrived. I think she slipped it in, like a roofie. I'm new to the school and wasn't expecting that kind of welcome. That's also why I came off a little harsh to Kristy. Although, I do stick by everything I said."

I casually stood, surveying the air outside, taking a long sip of coffee. "I hope we don't have any more strange weather. There's blood in the water after all." I eyed Adnachiel one last time, whose hands were still frozen in claws on the table. He'd love to rip my skin off . . . just as much as I'd love to see him try.

"Shea, be careful. There are enough male Kristys out there, too. Don't take any drinks from anyone you don't know." My cold stare stayed on Adnachiel. "Or from anyone *you think you know* for that matter." I coughed, wiping dust from my black shirt. "Better get cleaned up and continue checking on everyone."

Without giving her another glance, I walked to the door, tossing my coffee in the trash on the way out.

I casually made my way to the back of the shop, my thirst burning. I remembered how food used to taste. Now it tasted like water. Everything did. It all had no flavor. Candies, drinks, meats . . . all of it was nothing. The only thing my taste buds picked up was blood. Again, why was I reminiscing about things dead, like my old senses? I was so much more than all of that now.

I leaned heavily against the brick wall before turning the corner. I could smell the shampoo the young curly-haired boy had used this morning. I could feel his perspiration covering his milky skin as if it was my own. Would I really trade these sensations, the power, all for one sip of coffee? No.

But what about sugars, salts, and spices? My only variation was the different blood types. But at most, that ranged from sixteen groups. With food, you could make a thousand dishes, and they'd all taste intrinsically different.

I licked my lips and my body surged with anticipation as my fangs grew. I knew his blood would be sweet enough for me: B-positive if I wasn't mistaken. The air was still, the perfect moment to strike. But I didn't move. I froze.

I should take him. Now that I'd pushed, who knew what Adnachiel would do? I doubted he'd pull out his queen or his bishop yet . . . but he might. In the next few days, I should feed as often as possible.

The curly boy was wringing his hands. His body language was wide-open and easy to read. He looked about seventeen. His accent gave away that he wasn't from the city but the South. The sweetness in his voice was undercut by the small traces of pain, a fractured life that he couldn't hide. I could imagine. It must have been hard, being homosexual in what was no doubt a small town. The scars on his hand and upper arms were old. He had received the blows in childhood, no doubt.

Still, he had freed himself and moved away. His earlier experiences hadn't broken him. Even a cold monster like me could feel the warmth of his radiating open heart.

My stomach turned. I knew better than to use my heightened perception before I fed. It was easier to let myself assume that he was like everyone else here. Now I had soured the meal. My palms sweated, but I controlled the sensation. I had gone hungry before. I was not like these new vampires who had to scratch every time that itch made their skin crawl.

It was painful resisting a feed, more painful than anything I'd experienced in human form . . . but not impossible. At this point, I was more controlled by my own desires than the blood that churned in my ancient veins.

My lips moved slowly as I spoke to the boy's mind. "Leave. Go to your dorm. Never again listen to any voice that says to meet you in a dark, secluded location. You're smarter than that. You will live in the light. You'll move as soon as possible out of this hick-area to a more progressive city where you'll meet a good-hearted man like you . . . and you'll find happiness. You'll have a good life. You'll stay away from shadows and anything or anyone that smells, feels, or looks like the man who came in earlier and told you to meet him here."

Quickly, the boy shook his head. As if coming out of a fog, he turned the corner, passing me without a second look, and headed toward the dorm. Another embarrassment. What was this, Lucian the Merciful again? I knew what I really was. No sense changing. That ship had sailed thousands of years ago . . . with Moses, and before that, with Nefertiti.

I should have just taken him. I bit my own tongue, letting my body slouch to the ground as I rested my palms on my eyes. Why couldn't I get my head in the game? I was acting like it was another century passing, waiting for Adnachiel. What was it about Shea that threw me?

A college kid with a large letterman jacket walked by and tossed some quarters at my face. "Buy yourself a new life, you homeless trash," he muttered, laughing to himself.

I lunged and buried my hands through his chest, cracking his rib cage open. I ripped out his heart and swallowed it whole. He fell to the ground, lifeless. I leaned toward his face, wiping the blood from my mouth. "Who's trash now?" With one hand, I pulled his body over my head and threw it into the open dumpster as I lumbered toward the football field behind the café.

I compelled a handful of maimed, grounded locusts, forcing them to crawl their way toward his body. It would no doubt be their last meal.

CHAPTER 3
SHEA

The ego on that guy! What did he say? *They're just addicts . . . They want this body . . .* Dude! What a narcissist! Lucian was hot, but not that hot! I wanted to high-five Aidan when he told him to draw on some black eyeliner. Lucian was definitely a bit on the emo side. His apology had seemed sincere though. I still felt a burning hatred for Frank biting me on my first day. So, if he was telling the truth and he really had been drugged, maybe I should cut him some slack.

Ugh!

No. He was a dick and I needed to stick to that! This was how *bad boys* did it. They were total a-holes to everyone except their prey. Then once they had their prize, they'd treat them just as crappy as they did everyone else. What on earth would make me think he wouldn't treat me exactly the way he'd treated Kristy? Granted, the girl was coming on strong, but holy cow! Lucian was so cruel. And he had made a point to say he stood by *everything* he had said. *Everything.* That included his mean-boy remarks to Kristy.

Nope. Still on my shit-list.

Aidan and I were walking to our dorm. We didn't take our usual way back because he insisted that we stick to the lighted path. He said it was safer and made some comment about people lurking in the shadows or something. I guessed my encounter with Frank had freaked him out, too. I didn't argue. I just wrapped my arm around his and let him lead the way. It took a bit longer than it should have, but we arrived at our dorm unscathed.

Walking me to my door, Aidan leaned down and lifted my chin with his hand. "You okay? That Lucian guy didn't scare you, did he?"

"Scare me? No. Annoy me? Yes," I said with a roll of my eyes.

This appeared to worry him because his forehead got all crinkly. "Annoy? That sounds like a girl fighting the urge to like someone."

Did it? I guessed if I used every romantic comedy ever written as a reference, the word *annoy* was usually followed twenty minutes later by true love. This was definitely not the case with Lucian. "You've been watching too many John Hughes movies." I reached up and hugged Aidan. "Good night."

His hug was a little tighter than normal, but I didn't mind. It was actually quite comforting after the last two days. He whispered in my ear, "Good night, Shea. If you need anything, I'm two doors down."

"Really? I had no idea." I pulled away with a smile and hit his chest playfully, but when I saw that his worry crinkles hadn't gone away, I looked at him seriously. "You're the first person I'd call for anything, dufus."

Aidan smiled at that. He walked down the hall and entered his abode with a small wave. I waved back and went inside my room.

Apparently, Gerta was still partying because she wasn't there. I took my second shower of the day. For some reason, my run-in with Lucian made me feel dirty. Like I had let him manipulate me, and now he thought he had gotten away with it. Things like that always bugged me.

I remembered when I was in high school and Paul Butters had talked me into drinking a beer. I had made it clear to everyone in our small class that I planned on never drinking. I'd felt pretty strongly about it. I didn't like losing control and alcohol epitomized *losing control.* But I'd wanted Paul to like me, so I drank it anyway. For weeks, Paul had bragged about the fact that he'd talked *the pure Shea Harper* into drinking. I'd felt so crappy. Like I had let myself down. Like I had let a boy manipulate me into doing something I genuinely didn't want to do.

Of course, it helped when Aidan threatened bodily harm to Paul unless he stopped talking about the incident. Don't get me wrong, everyone loved Aidan. How could you not? But when it came to messing with me, everyone was scared stiff. Needless to say, Paul never teased me again.

I was feeling like I had back then. Like Lucian had convinced me to do something I didn't want to do. He'd made me have an iota of sympathy for him. But he was an egomaniac liar who probably saw me as a challenge. The girl who wouldn't fall all over his every word. I had to keep reminding myself that I was no more than a conquest to him.

It depressed me for some reason.

I put on my most comfortable jammies and snuggled deep into my down comforter. Maybe a good night's rest would cheer me up.

***

Okay. I was definitely in dreamland. The forest was really green. It was too bright and colorful to be real. Even the bark of the trees was a light copper-red and the trunks were at least the size of my car.

"We're in the redwoods," a voice said behind me.

I turned around to see Lucian standing in the shadow of one of the giant trees.

Great. I was dreaming about a-hole-boy now. I tried to control the dream by making Aidan appear to kick this guy's butt, but dream-Aidan was a no-show.

"You can make him leave now," I said to my subconscious. "I love the place, just not him in it."

"Why? Can you sense what I am?" Lucian was in front of me in the blink of an eye.

"A jerk? Yes. And wake-up call: a rock could tell that." Maybe this was my brain's way of telling him off and relieving all that stress from earlier this evening.

Lucian tilted his head. From the look in his eyes, my words stung. "It's deeper than that." He brushed his hand against my cheek.

Even in a dream, I felt every cell in my body tingle. Stop it! I wouldn't let this guy win!

I smacked his hand away. "Keep your hands to yourself. And stay out of my dreams!"

***

I awoke drenched in sweat. What was that? I hated the fact that I'd dreamt about Lucian. It was Aidan's fault. If he hadn't planted the *romance* bomb in my head, I never would have given Lucian a second thought, except to avoid him like the plague. He seemed to bring those with him anyway: locusts heralding his entrance. I knew that was unfair, but it somehow felt fitting in the moment.

I looked over at my clock and hoped it was morning. There was nothing worse than thinking you'd slept the whole night through only to find you were asleep for an hour. I was both relieved and slightly annoyed to see it was five in the morning. Technically, I had been asleep for seven hours, which was just enough time to make me feel rested but too early to make me want to get up at five in the freaking morning!

I sat there staring at the ceiling for another twenty minutes until I finally decided to get up. Gerta was sleeping soundly on the bed next to mine. I tried to be as quiet as she must have been when she'd come in last night since she hadn't woken me. Grabbing my running clothes, I quickly dressed in sweat shorts and a tank, then laced up my tennies. I put my dorm key on a chain and placed it around my neck. I winced slightly when the metal hit my bandage, just a reminder of the crazies who roamed the planet.

Carefully, I exited my dorm room and walked out into the morning breeze. It was still dark. Sunrise wasn't for another half hour or so, but it felt good to breathe in the semi-cool air. I stuck to the lighted pathways since I could hear Aidan's lecture-voice scolding me: "*Stay where people can see you.*"

As I ran, I had a sudden burst of energy, as if I could take on the world. I knew it was just the endorphins from running, but either way, it was amazing.

Every muscle cried out in joy as I ran faster and faster through the campus. It was exhilarating. I felt alive.

"Shea?" I heard my name being called behind me.

I stopped, breathless from running, and turned to see Lucian standing near a tree. It was so close to my dream I almost thought I was dreaming all over again. But when he walked toward me, I knew I was completely awake.

And completely defensive.

"Still up from a night of partying, are we?" I was surprised to hear how much judgment was in my tone.

Lucian simply stared at me, as if he couldn't decide if it was worth pursuing any type of conversation. "I'm afraid we've gotten off on the wrong foot. It's my fault really."

"We can at least agree on something," I said. Wow. I was rivaling him in meanness at this point. But my instincts told me there was more to this guy. After the Frank debacle, I planned on listening to my instincts from now on.

"So much hostility. I'm not sure I deserve it," Lucian continued. "Can we start over?" He was a few feet away from me now. His eyes were filled with so many different emotions—insecurity, anger, confusion—I couldn't tell which one was real. The boy apparently didn't know what to think of me.

"Just stay where you are, thank you very much." I put my

hand up for emphasis. "I don't know what your obsession is with trying to be my friend, but reality check, there's something about you I don't trust." I crossed my arms. "Or like." Harsh, but true.

"And I want to know why. I admit, it fascinates me." Lucian looked at me with a quizzical expression. I could tell it really *did* puzzle him.

"Well, you're going to have to ponder that one on your own time. I'm in the middle of a run."

And I was off.

I couldn't believe how rude I had been. I was never like that, even to people I couldn't stand. The weird part was the fact that I really didn't hate Lucian. Sure, he was obnoxious. Sure, he'd been a jerk to Kristy. But he had been nice to me. I guessed I felt like I had to be the defender of everyone he had wronged, as if somehow treating him the way he treated others would be a good wake-up call.

I decided to head back to my dorm and cut my jog short. The Lucian confrontation had thrown off my whole Chi. The more I thought about it, the more it irritated me. What were the odds that I kept running into him? Was he following me? Maybe the guy who claimed *he'd been stalked his whole life* was actually a stalker himself. For some reason the thought didn't scare me as much as I thought it would, or *should*. It wasn't that he seemed harmless, it was that he seemed genuinely befuddled at the fact that I wasn't fawning all over him.

I shook Lucian from my head as I saw Aidan jogging straight toward me from our dorm.

"Out for a run?" he asked with a smile as he stopped in front of me. I could tell he was trying very hard to sound relaxed, but those darn worry crinkles on his forehead gave him away every time.

"Yes, *Dad*. I brought my mace and rape whistle with me." Now that I'd joked about it, that wasn't such a bad idea. The thought of spraying Lucian with mace gave me a perverse satisfaction.

"Did I say anything? I just asked if you went for a run," Aidan responded defensively.

"But I could see your worried-face."

"Can you blame me? You were *bitten* on the neck by some vampire wannabe. I can't help it. It's my job to protect you." The way he said that made me pause. He didn't sound like the boy I'd grown up with. He sounded like he was a guard on duty and I was the princess who needed protecting.

"Your *job*? I thought I was your friend." I was kidding, but something in my tone must have made him feel bad because he looked upset.

"Shea. You know I didn't mean it like that. You're my best friend—" Aidan began.

"I was joking. Geez, lighten up. And as much as I love having you as my personal guard dog, I *am* capable of taking care of myself. I know it didn't look like it, but that Frank guy was about to book before you got there."

I thought back to that moment: Frank was biting me and my eyes burned, then I saw a flash of light. The guy had been freaked. How could I have forgotten that? With Aidan coming in and throwing Frank into a tree, I had pushed it from my brain. What *had* happened? I was about to spill everything to Aidan when something held me back. I didn't know why, but some inner voice was telling me to keep quiet. It went against every instinct, since he had been a part of my life since birth. But it was so powerful I listened. I kept my mouth shut.

"I don't know, Shea. That guy was strong." Aidan didn't sound convinced.

He was right, the guy had been like a steel wall, but I knew what I'd seen. After my eyes had burned, Frank had been afraid. As in terrified. What could he have seen in me that would scare a guy like that? A thought to consider on my own. In the meantime, I had to play it cool. "I'm telling you, Frank was about to leave. Now, can we drop it?"

Aidan took a moment to respond. I was surprised when he pulled me in for a tight hug. "Of course. I'm sorry," he mumbled in my ear.

"You know, for a bronzed Adonis like yourself, you certainly are a sap." I smiled as I pulled away.

He grinned back and shook his head. "Sun's up. Breakfast?"

I nodded. "This time I'm going for the good stuff: chai tea with a shot of espresso."

He raised an eyebrow. "I might have to try me one of those."

***

The next two weeks were a lot more mundane than I thought they would be. The only excitement was when the campus police came to question Aidan about some missing girl named Melissa. But when Gerta and I gave Aidan a solid alibi, they backed off.

My classes weren't as great as I had hoped. I was rudely awakened to the fact that everything felt just like high school. I guess I hadn't really known what to expect, but almost nodding off in Precalculus hadn't been it.

I met a couple of new people, but no one special. I pretty much hung out with Aidan most of my free time. We would take walks around campus when the sun was about to go down since the temperature was slightly cooler. He'd always want to get back to the dorm before nightfall though. I seriously thought the boy was getting a phobia of the dark.

Gerta was okay. She tried to rope me into a mani-pedi day, but I managed to squirm my way out of that one. Not that I didn't appreciate a good mani-pedi, I just didn't want to spend the day with Gerta gossiping about all the campus drama. Too many people sleeping around, breaking hearts, and at least one full-out girl-catfight every few days.

Nope. Not for me. I was as drama-free as you could get.

Aidan and I pretty much hung out in his dorm room every night watching movies. Gerta was convinced that we were an item no matter how many times I told her otherwise. I realized most people thought the same thing, looking at us like we were adorable puppies. I didn't mind. Even though I knew I didn't have those kinds of feelings for him, we were still pretty possessive as far as friendships went.

The one thing I couldn't confess to anyone was the fact that I was kind of upset I hadn't seen or heard from Lucian the entire two weeks. He must have finally gotten the hint. But now that I hadn't seen him, I felt a little guilty about my offensive behavior. I knew I shouldn't feel that way, but the people-pleaser-nice-girl part of me wanted to find him and apologize.

There was no way in hell I would tell Aidan that I even

remotely thought of Lucian in any way, shape, or form. He had made it quite clear how he felt about him. So I kept my crazy-guilt-obsession to myself.

I was walking back from art class where I'd had to sketch a naked dude. Not exactly a comfortable moment. I hated admitting how much of a prude I was, but I had never seen a boy naked before.

Pictures, yes, as in biology class, but never in person. The teacher had made him pose lying on the floor with his arms outstretched. From where I'd been sitting, I was staring at a full frontal. I didn't think my face would stop being red for at least two more days. I just hoped no one had noticed.

I was about to walk into my domicile when I decided to see if Aidan was home yet. Knocking on his door, I waited a few minutes before giving up. I went into my room and plopped my backpack on the desk.

Gerta walked out of the bathroom in a robe with a towel wrapped around her head. "You're not hanging with your boyfriend?"

"Aidan is not my boyfriend," I said for the millionth time.

Gerta gave me a knowing look. "Of course he isn't. You keep telling yourself that." She smiled.

There was a knock on the door.

"Speak of the devil . . . " Gerta laughed.

"You don't know that's Aidan," I replied more defensively than I'd intended.

"Who is it?" Gerta called at the door with a grin.

"Aidan," came the muffled sound of bad timing.

I didn't make eye contact with Gerta as I opened the door.

"Let's get out of here." I took his hand and left the room.

But I could hear Gerta's words as we walked down the hall. "Have fun, you two!"

He stopped me. "What was that all about?"

I kept pulling him outside toward the walkway. "Nothing. She's just giving me a hard time." I paused and then blurted, "Everyone thinks we're a couple."

Instead of shock or repulsion or any other reaction I had imagined, he simply shrugged. "Yeah, I've been getting that too."

I self-consciously let go of his hand and looked up at him. "Does it bother you?"

"Not really. We know how we feel about each other. I don't really care what other people think." He smiled down at me. "Does it bother you?"

Did it? It was too complicated for me to say. But I didn't want to leave him hanging or hurt his feelings, so I playfully slugged him in the arm. "Nah. I just didn't want other people to mess up what we have." Saying it out loud made me realize that was exactly why it bugged me. If anything (and that was a big if) were to happen between Aidan and me, I wanted it to be a natural progression, not shoved down our throats because everyone was pressuring us to date.

"Good," he said, then placed his hands on my arms, looking me in the eye. "Don't freak out, but I think we should be social tonight."

Social? That sounded horrible! "You mean hanging out with other people?"

Aidan laughed, and it made his whole face light up. He really was a cutie. "Yes, I know. What could I possibly be thinking? But

Shea, it'd be good for you. There's a party at the Pillar House."

"I'm still healing from the last party." I touched the small scabs from Frank's bite two weeks ago. It was almost completely healed, but the psychological wound had grown exponentially. The thought of a party made me feel physically ill.

"Come here." He brought me in for a hug. Even though his chest was as hard as a rock, it was still my soft spot to land. Aidan hugs were the best hugs.

"You really want me to go to this party, don't you?" I mumbled into his chest.

He pulled away slightly so we still had our arms around each other but he could see my face. "Don't let some jerk ruin your whole college experience. We're supposed to have fun, get drunk, and party at least . . . three times before we graduate."

I laughed. "Three times, huh? You just come up with that number randomly or is there scientific research involved?"

"Definitely scientific research." He grinned. "So, you coming?"

I pushed him away with a playful grunt. "Yes, you big doof. But I swear, if that Frank guy is there—"

"If Frank is there, I'll kill him."

He was smiling as if he were joking, but the way he said it made the hairs on my arms rise. I didn't think he was capable of killing anyone, but in that moment, I was actually scared for Frank.

"Or maybe just call the cops," I responded.

"Or that." He nudged me affectionately. "I'll be knocking at your door at nine."

I mock-saluted him and we walked back to the dorm.

Nine o'clock came a lot faster than I'd expected. Probably because I desperately didn't want to go to this party. Gerta had already gone to some other shindig she'd been invited to, so I only had Aidan as my security blanket for the evening's festivities.

He and I walked to the Pillar House, which was about a mile off campus, so it was quite a trek at this time of night. I felt completely safe with him, but I couldn't help looking over my shoulder every few minutes or so. I hated that the whole experience with Frank had sent me into paranoia-zone, but it had only been two weeks and I hadn't bounced back yet.

The party was certainly hopping by the time we arrived. It looked like a giant hand had taken a heaping scoop of people and stuffed them in the house.

Aidan carefully led me inside. He was being overly protective tonight, sweetly so. Once we were in the mayhem, I found that I wasn't as claustrophobic as I'd been at the other party. People stood around in tight groups as opposed to the shoulder-to-shoulder action like before.

"You want something to drink?" Aidan asked over the noise of the music and crowd.

"Maybe some water," I replied.

He rolled his eyes but didn't argue with me. We walked by a set of stairs going up to the second floor and he gently placed me on the fifth step. "Stay here where you can see everything. I'm getting those drinks."

Before he left, Aidan smiled at me. "You going to be okay?"

"I'm fine, geez. It's not like I'm socially inept."

"Inept? Isn't that an SAT word?" he joked.

"Just get me my water," I said as I moved all the way to the railing so that people could still use the stairs if they needed to.

He walked into the maw of the party and disappeared from view.

I loved that Aidan had scanned the whole house and picked the most strategic spot for me to sit. I really could see if anyone was coming toward me. He was doing his best to make me feel as safe as possible.

"Hey." A familiar voice came from behind.

My heart jumped into my throat.

Lucian.

My magic spy-spot didn't work as well as I thought it would because he seemed to come out of nowhere. He walked down the few steps that separated us and sat down next to me.

"Mind if I sit with you?" he asked.

I felt so horrible about the way I had treated him before, I instantly nodded my head. "You kind of disappeared," I admitted.

"I didn't think my company was welcome," Lucian confessed carefully. He looked neither arrogant nor mad, just confused.

"Yeah, sorry about that. I took out all my issues on you. You just rubbed me the wrong way, I guess." Was that mean too? I couldn't control my words with this guy, and for some reason my words *wanted* to bite.

"I'm not used to that." He looked like he was trying to look vulnerable but failing miserably.

"See? It's not what you're saying, it's the way you say it. Admitting that you're not used to rubbing people the wrong way is fine, but you say it like you're the Queen of Sheba or something. Like everyone has always worshiped the ground you've walked on, and now you can't handle the fact that some lowly plebe doesn't like you." Wow. This apology was going fantastic. And I couldn't seem to stop. "You said at the café that you've been stalked your whole life? What are you, like twenty? Did little Rosy in kindergarten follow you home after school?" I suppressed a laugh by covering my mouth with my hand. The visual image of a five-year-old Lucian all broody and egotistical thinking he was being stalked by a kindergartner was somehow amusing.

And what was that?

Lucian actually cracked a smile. Albeit a very small one, but it was there, I was sure of it.

It made me instantly feel better about him. Like he wasn't such an arrogant jerk. I stopped my tirade and smiled. "Have you ever been in love?" Where had that come from? All I could think of was Aidan shaking his head at me. But for some reason, I really wanted to know if a guy like Lucian was capable of love. Usually, condescending, self-important boys thought they were God's gift to women, but never really opened up to anyone.

"Once," he said, and his eyes suddenly looked ancient. I never knew what people meant when they said they could see an old soul, but if they saw what I just saw: I got it. It was strange. He looked at me as if he had lived a thousand lifetimes.

"What's that on your neck?" he suddenly asked.

I unconsciously touched the small scabs, the last remnants of my ordeal with Frank.

"This weirdo-guy Frank thought he was a vampire. He bit me." I didn't want to talk about it, but Lucian asked with such concern I didn't want to be rude either.

His face revealed a whole lot of anger. "He *bit* you?"

"Yeah, I got away before too much damage was done. It's

all right." I felt weirdly pleased at the way Lucian stared at me. He looked like he would smash Frank like a pea if he had been standing in front of us.

It made me want to know more about him. "What was the name of the girl you fell in love with?"

I didn't think he was going to answer me. He paused, as if wrestling with pursuing the Frank conversation or opening up to me about his ex. Then he said, "Nefertiti."

"Nefertiti? Wow, her parents went old-school. But that's kind of cool. From what I've read of the chick, she was pretty badass." Being a history nut, I gushed, "I guess she was so loyal and in love with her husband they ruled Egypt side by side. And that was over three thousand years ago when women weren't exactly on the top of the food chain." I could feel my face burn red. I didn't normally puke out history lessons to strangers, but Nefertiti was kind of a hero of mine.

In the awkward silence that followed, I muttered, "Romantic, huh?"

Lucian didn't speak.

His expression went dark in less than a second.

I was terrified.

Before I could think to move, Aidan had lifted Lucian off the stairs and thrown him clear across the room.

"Aidan!" I yelled in shock.

He whirled to me. "Lucian looked like he was going to hurt you, Shea."

I just nodded. I'd seen it, too. And now Aidan confirmed it.

Lucian was off his rocker. My instincts had been right the first time. The guy was dangerous.

Lucian practically flew at Aidan as he body-slammed into the railing of the staircase.

Everyone watched the show at this point. I went for my phone to call the cops.

No signal.

I'd never seen a fight like this, and I was scared Aidan would be crushed.

But to my surprise, he was holding his own. I couldn't say the same about the Pillar House though. Their body slams were smashing holes in the walls left and right.

I ran out of the house to get a signal. Others were following me, not wanting to accidentally get hurt from testosterone-boys in there.

One bar. I dialed 911.

My phone was snatched out of my hand before I could hit "Call." My eyes went round in terror when I looked up to see Frank.

"Looks like your bodyguard is busy," he sneered.

I tried to run, but he grabbed my arm.

"You're all I've been thinking about, the taste of you . . ." Frank looked at me like I was a Big Mac.

I tried screaming at the people passing by, but they ignored me completely.

Frank recognized the danger of being out in the open, so he pulled me toward the side of the house. I tried to get away, but the guy was like Superman. I couldn't even loosen his grip on my arm.

This was happening.

He was going to finish what he'd started.

Frank was going to kill me.

Seriously? Death by a guy who thought he was a vampire? It couldn't get any lamer than that!

When he had me pinned to the side of the house, he put his finger to my lips. His eyes constricted like before. "No more tricks. Keep quiet and this will be over before you know it."

"You know that eye thing doesn't do what you think it does, right?" I was amazed at how condescending I sounded considering I was about to pee my pants.

Frank was more than shocked. He was downright baffled. "Impossible," he muttered in astonishment.

I kicked him in the groin, but he didn't flinch. What the heck?

Frank gained his bearings and looking as if he knew he didn't have much time. He pried my neck to the side and bent down to take another bite.

I screamed. A guttural scream.

I didn't know who was more surprised, me or Frank.

Long, sinewy strands of wood grew out of the planks on the side of the house. They slithered their way past my body and wrapped around Frank's neck like wooden vines going in for the kill.

It was safe to say both of us were seriously freaked out. Houses coming to life to save me? Had I done that? I didn't want to admit it, but I knew somehow I had.

Frank was choking. He lost his hold on me.

And I ran.

Straight into the safety of Aidan's arms.

Aidan and Lucian were no longer fighting. Apparently, my

scream had stopped them and they had come running.

Aidan gave Lucian a nod, almost like they had come to some sort of understanding. And the way Lucian looked at Frank . . . I was actually scared for the boy. I was about to suggest we call the police when Aidan made me look him in the eyes.

"We're going back to the dorm," he said, leaving no room for argument.

I nodded.

We left without looking back to see what Lucian was about to do to Frank.

CHAPTER 4
LUCIAN

To those hungry eyes still looking for party drama, there was nothing left of Frank. Nothing but a small fleck of dust picked up by the scuff of his dress shoes as I snatched him from the grip of wood around his neck and flew into the air. He coughed when we landed, desperately grabbing his throat.

I watched, turning over a small metal trash can and sitting on it as he gathered himself. First appreciation filled his eyes, then confusion. "Where are we? I mean, thanks, man. I think that bitch almost staked me!" He walked over to a window. "Are we in Boston? Did you *fly* here? No vampire can fly . . . I mean, we can move really fast, but . . . and we're inside, that's—"

I was now inches from Frank's face as his words recoiled into his sick, small-minded mouth. His pupils constricted as his meager powers tried to sense what I was.

Quickly, he bowed. "I'm sorry. You must be a Second-Born. I've heard . . . there are only a few alive. I thought your kind was a myth, but . . . I can *feel* your power." Frank's eyes widened in amazement as a small bit of drool left his still-exposed incisors.

I laughed, keeping the volcanic rage just under the surface of my skin, all the while planning what to do with him. "I'm not a Second-Born, boy. I *made* the Second-Borns. I'm the *First*!"

It was too much. The vampire cowered, kneeling on the ground in full servitude. "To think you saved a lowly vampire like me, I can't thank you enough."

My eyes burned like hot coals inside my skull. "Save you? Is that what you think I've done? You are nothing but a smear, a stain on the tip of my heel. Which fool turned you? Who's your father?"

His lips trembled, his mind moved beyond fear. "Please, I'm nothing. I've only been alive two hundred years. I don't know anything. My father's a good man. His name is Raphael, from the Louisiana District."

I leaned down and grabbed the scruff of his neck, letting my menacing voice sharpen his terror. "I do not know this Raphael, or his line. Who is *his* maker?"

Tears streamed down Frank's cheeks. "Please, master, I-I don't know his maker. I'm very young—"

My fangs enlarged so drastically they split the gums. Blood filled my mouth and the taste of it enraged me further. It had been ages since I'd felt this much fury. The idea of him "drinking" the Vessel. He didn't even know his lineage.

He was no better than the mindless, classless slaves of humans who roamed this earth. His blood was diluted. He was no vampire. He wasn't worth the title. *I should show him what a real vampire is.*

"It matters not the name of your line. I will smite them. I will hunt Raphael, your blessed father, and I will drink him like the mule-rat he is. He will curse the name Frank as he writhes in an agony unknown to our kind.

"All those he's turned will tremble in fear at their own demise. I will devour *every* drop of lineage that brought you here, save the original elder I myself turned. I will wipe the earth clean of their stench simply because you, you worthless, spineless worm, even dared to touch . . . to think that you could taste Shea Harper. I should thank you. You'll be an example of what happens to anyone who tries to touch what's *mine*!"

I started slowly. I exposed him to filtered sunlight at a gentle, intimate pace, enough to drive him mad. He experienced all the things that could cause agony to my kind, but not death. I couldn't stop. Every time I thought about his teeth being where mine had not, his lips on her neck . . . I wanted him to live another day, if only just to watch him plead over and over for me to kill him. Eventually his end did come, when I repainted my entire Boston flat with his entrails.

I'd been foolish thinking I should seduce Shea. I needed to take her. If bottom-feeders like this could get close, then Adnachiel was failing more than usual. She was not safe with him. I had to be there before he turned on her.

Aidan. My blood boiled and I wished I hadn't ended Frank, just so I could kill him again in this moment. When that dog had nodded to me, we'd agreed Frank needed to die. It was almost like it had been with Moses, as if all the thousands of years hadn't changed what we were, what we had been to each other.

I watched the blood slide over the darkened window like

sludge covering a smooth surface. That was what killing Moses had done to our friendship. In one moment, I'd lost them both. I should have listened to Caelius. I hadn't known what Adnachiel was capable of then. But for years we'd been like brothers. The three of us had freed slaves and changed the world. He'd made us better, both of us. Yet *Aidan* had killed him, and the way he'd done it . . .

My thoughts turned black with the memory. Shea was not Moses. I wouldn't be fooled again. I'd had a judgment lapse, but I would never side with that beast. I was going to take her straight out of his weak, pathetic grasp. Forget seduction. With other Vessels, I'd force Adnachiel to choose and he'd always end them. He'd prove where his loyalty was, and where it wasn't. He'd never choose me, or the Vessel. Not now, not ever. Maybe it really was time to fulfill my promise to Caelius and free him.

That thought produced a strange feeling. The idea of anyone's hands on her sickened me. Shea was *mine*.

I licked the blood from my palm and made a fist.

First things first.

Retribution.

***

Weeks passed. They rose and fell like waves over the ocean. It had been a month since Frank. My ears rang from the desperate cries pried from the flesh of thousands of devoured vampires. Some I ate, some I just ripped apart with my hands, watching the marrow spill out of their bones.

It was like the Viking era all over again, but this time I didn't have Gunnhild by my side to relish in the torment. We'd ended the Vikings. They'd been a challenge, but we'd wiped them from the earth. All to add salt to Aidan's eyes. His people, *that round.*

A warrior class, but still he couldn't protect the Vessel. Even in front of his brother, in front of Gunnhild, he'd shown his true beast. Always a servant to the Light, his master.

Poor Gunnhild. I'd turned him just to increase Adnachiel's agony, but he'd grown on me over the centuries. Admittedly, he'd been one of my favorites.

Remembering the tenderness and fondness I'd had for my children in my youth faded as I ripped open a young vamp's chest and pulled his spine through. They were so few, my original seven, and the trash they'd made was unacceptable, even if Caelius wanted the numbers increased incrementally. With every thought of Frank touching Shea, barbarity seeped into my mind, and I relished having an outlet for my confusing emotions.

I hunted.

I stalked.

And I alone reaped vengeance on the lineage of my son, Gracuri. But before I could finish devouring his New Orleans branch, he came to me.

It was a hot summer night in Louisiana. He placed his hand on my shoulder as if greeting an old friend. In my bloodlust, I popped it from its socket.

Shocked, he reeled back and reset it. "Lucian, Father . . . I've heard that someone in my family has displeased you. I've come to make it right." He reached to hug me as he always had. Something inside shifted. He held me tight, resting his head on my shoulder like he had in Thebes when I'd been displeased with him then.

When he pulled back, his eyes were warm and his golden hair picked up the light of the moon. I'd taken him in Athens. He'd always looked like the sun, as if he belonged to daylight. I remembered likening him to the Roman god Helios, who drove a fiery chariot across the sky. Romans and their gods; it was nonsense, but at least it was inventive.

He pulled me in again, tenderly lengthening the embrace, bowing his large gladiator frame to mine. "It's been so long, Father. Please, tell me what I can do to appease you."

I smiled, pushing him back. "You've always had the tongue for philosophy. And flattery isn't lost on you, my son."

He touched my cheek with the back of his hand. "Why have you been killing my children?"

Only now, after nearly a month of slaughtering, did I feel the pang of guilt. "They didn't deserve your name. Some didn't even know it. They were unworthy."

He laced his arm through mine boyishly as he pulled me forward. He was quick, unlike his sluggish descendants. I hadn't noticed the sound of a lake nearby, but sure enough, within a few steps we were there.

Water. He loved to walk along the water. That was where I'd met him for the first time. That was where I'd befriended him. I'd been younger then, and so had he.

He laughed, looking at my bloodied face as he pulled me into the lake. He took his time, tenderly washing my crimson frame. The cold and his soft touch changed my temperament.

I again looked at him like he was the boy I'd known then, before the wasted city and his slaughtered family had colored my view of him forever. Was it my blood that had corrupted such a sweet soul? Did I ruin everything I touched?

He smiled. "Why Lucian, you're looking at me as if you've ripped the wings off a butterfly. Do you still regard me with such sentiment?"

My jaw hardened. He knew that I did. He was using that sentiment now.

He pouted at my callousness. "I didn't mean to provoke you. It's just . . . I've missed you. It's been so long. Will you ever see me like you did before Thebes? That was the last we spoke, and now this. I fear I'll never be in your favor."

I hated it, the way my heart melted toward him. I knew it was the curse. You were bonded to those you turned. A strange sort of familial, loving bond. That was why I'd turned so few. It was not like with Aidan, where I felt bonded despite our differences. This was instinctual.

I paused, taking in the night as my wet hair dripped in his warm hands. He should let the back of my head go and stop holding me as if I were his world. My chest swelled. This must have been why Caelius had only turned me. He had one child to break his heart. I had seven to break mine.

His smile widened, his large white teeth sharp as a lion's. "Caelius really broke the mold with you. There will never be a need to turn others. You're too perfect, Lucian."

I growled as I smacked his hand away and lunged at his throat. Gracuri knew me too well. He could read my body language, my scent, my words like he was reading an open book. As hard as it was to hide my true self from Caelius out of fear, it was harder to hide that vulnerability from someone I had trusted. Someone I had come to love.

His smile didn't fade. "What are you doing, Father? Honestly, I'm worried about you. I know the hunt is on. It's that five hundred year time where you go after the Vessel and do your dance . . . but I've heard things."

I tightened my grip on his neck, trying to push all that I felt for him deep inside. "What things?"

Now he scowled. He looked more like the thing I should have killed in Thebes and less like the boy by the river. I left my mind open so I could direct my thoughts to him loud and clear: *Gracuri, I'll never see you without looking twice—once at the boy, and once at the monster. Those innocent people you killed, the blood from your eyes . . . the madness of it.*

He coughed, shaking his head, feigning like he wasn't still hearing my telepathy. "The rumor is that . . . well, you're sending a message not to touch what's yours. And what's yours is Shea Harper." His eyes fell flat as he pushed the pressure point in my wrist, loosening my grip.

I sneered, taking in a deep breath. The tips of my fangs opened as they sucked in air like they would blood. His concern shifted to amazement, as it always did when I accomplished something he could not, simply because of the dilution from my blood to his.

"You can breathe through your fangs?" he asked in wonder.

I let my hand fall from his throat and ignored his childlike curiosity. "I'm glad, Gracuri. Your words please me. The message has reached the Second-Borns, and no doubt Caelius himself by now. This should stop any of them from *accidentally* interfering in my affairs. The rumors don't misspeak. Shea is mine." I looked at him with a strange feeling clawing underneath my skin, a feeling

I couldn't yet describe. Was it territorial passion? Something lit within when I mentioned her name. All I could think of was one word: *mine*. Over and over, and nothing else.

Tears welled in his eyes and rolled like rain as my mouth fell open in shock. What was this?

He grabbed me with all the fervor of an estranged child. "Father, I was misguided once. I was lost in Thebes. I know Caelius asked you to end me there. I overexposed our kind. I was supposed to build slowly, quietly like the others. You know why I did what I did. You alone came for me then. You pulled me out. You showed mercy and saved me from the madness that had infected my mind.

"Please, let me do the same for you now. Your hands are soaked in blood, *our* blood, vampire blood. It's lunacy. There's territory, but this has stretched far beyond that. Caelius will be furious if he finds out how emotionally involved you're becoming with this Vessel. It's dangerous for you. Please, stop now, Father. Kill this Shea Harper and play your games with the *next* Vessel. It's only five hundred years. This Vessel has gotten to you, or maybe the hunt has. Whatever it is, you need to end it and walk away."

Fury rose inside of me as I directed my thoughts to all the living creatures in the water at our feet. Then the whole lake. One thought emanated from my mind: *Cut yourself open.*

Within moments our legs were no longer soaking in water, but blood. Gracuri gasped and slowly stepped out of the wet. He shook his head as his eyes darkened, his favorite white suit dipped in red.

Snakes with fresh gashes bleeding down their sides lifted me out of the blood and set me by his side. He didn't move or flinch in fear as they slithered by his white shoes. "How dare you doubt my intentions. I don't need you to look after me. I am your father, not the other way around. So listen well because I will only tell you this once more: Shea Harper is *mine*!"

He closed his eyes and took a deep breath, his curls still bouncing in the soft summer breeze. "I'm sorry, Father. Then I can't save you as you did me. You always were stronger. Is it done then? Have you killed enough of my babies to satisfy your rage?"

I stared into the forest beyond him. Maybe he was right. I wasn't acting like myself. Did I look like he had then? What would he think now that he too could see the savage, unkempt madman before him?

I wanted to embrace Gracuri one last time. I didn't know why I was feeling all of this nostalgia. What was wrong with this Vessel, or with me?

Why was the entirety of my years only desiring to be reflected upon now? I grabbed the back of his neck, pulling his forehead to mine until they touched. We stood there in the silence of our long years and hardened hearts.

"Remember when we first met, Gracuri? Do you remember what you said to me?"

He nodded. Another tear followed the dried traces of the ones before. He was the only one I'd turned who could still cry. It endeared him to me further.

Gracuri half smiled. "I will always feel that way about you. Even if you soak your hands in the blood of my line, even if you were to gut me and soak your hands in the juice from my still-pumping heart, I will never stop believing in you, Lucian. Who you really are. Time may erode all that's in me, all that we are and were to each other, but what I said to you that night will never change. And I will hold dear the deal we made the night you turned me and wear it like a code of honor until my death."

If I could cry, I would have done it then. His words shook me further. I imagined the tears that should be flowing down my cheeks with his.

The last time I'd cried had been when Aidan had died—for the first time—with Moses, and taken my tears and heart with him in the desert. That had been so long ago. And now, a son I had all but forsaken because of his brutality had brought me back to what I'd been before: a young heart that still hoped it could be more than Caelius's servant.

But was it Gracuri alone? Why did I feel more alive now than I had before Caelius found me near death in a ditch under the light of Nefertiti's window?

For the first time in a thousand years, my voice trembled as I spoke, revealing a moment's vulnerability. "I will leave the children you have left in your line. I know they are the oldest and dearest to you." Without a word, he grabbed me tight, holding me, his head instantly on my shoulder.

When he pulled back, his eyes were fiery, no doubt ready to start a new line. I pitied the town he showed up in next. "Then I will do this for you, Father. I will spread the word that Shea Harper is your *mission*. That you will kill anyone who intercepts that mission out of fierce loyalty to Caelius."

I nodded, a curious sort of coldness sweeping over me. "You will not be spreading a lie. It *is* for Caelius that I cleared your line."

His face softened, as if he saw something that I did not. "I am always on your side, Lucian, no matter what you do as the centuries pass. I will defend your honor with my dying breath, even if I cannot protect you from yourself." He took one last look as he stroked my cheek with the back of his palm. Then, like a lightning bolt striking the surface of the water, he was gone.

I fell to my knees. My nails grew into the dry dirt as I clenched fistfuls of it and forced it into my mouth. *Swallow it, Lucian. That dirt, that dry dirt is all you are. You're nothing but ash. Smother this heart. Your heart is dead, remember. It died once in Egypt, then again with Moses. Bury what you're feeling now. The dirt is what you are.*

I choked on the grit as it filled my stomach. Vampires got nourishment from being underground because that was where Caelius was buried, but this was toxic. I'd done this after Nefertiti died. Every night for months, just to kill the pain, I'd swallowed the sands of Egypt.

I had forgotten the sensation, the agony of it. Damn Gracuri. Damn Shea, Adnachiel, all of them. They didn't know what it was like, what I was. They thought they could make me feel something. But I was dead.

"I'm *dead!*" I screamed to the stars, bellows of dust escaping my lungs into the shadows of clouds.

I gasped, choking on the pain.

Only one thought remained . . .

This ended tonight.

***

I pounded on the door of her dorm room before catching the idiocy of it. I didn't need to knock. Ripping off the handle, I peeled the wooden door back like a flimsy piece of paper. My eyes first met Aidan's. Of course he'd be inches from her. I scanned his body. At least he wasn't holding anything sharp to fillet her with.

I stretched my hand out to the Vessel, her face still reeling in horror from the damage to her room. "Shea, step away from Aidan and come with me. I'll keep you safe." What was I saying? Safe? I wasn't going to keep her safe. I had to stop these feelings from taking over. Dragging her to Caelius would kill what was left of my human weakness. Maybe it really was time to give up this game.

I firmed my gaze, resolute.

Instantly, Adnachiel was at my throat. I doubted Shea could hear the thunder of his giant wings furiously flapping just out of mortal sight. But there it was in all his glory: the dog revealed. "You're uglier than your four brothers, *Aidan*. All those eyes, a mangled mess between lion, ox, man, and eagle. Tell me, if Shea saw your *real* form, do you think she'd still call you friend? Or would she tremble in fear like all mortals?"

Without a word, he flung me through the large window just past her. Had I been a lesser vampire, his well-angled toss would have cut open my throat.

He'd revealed his hand.

Even after our mutual agreement about Frank, he wouldn't hold back. Good. I was in no mood to fight the pain that mounds of dirt couldn't vanquish. His blood would make it easier.

I laughed, stepping casually on the broken glass of the window frame. My mouth barely moved as I spoke. "I know you used Shea at the party last month to lure me out. I only killed Frank so you wouldn't hurt her. Is that all you know now, Beast? Betrayal? Once we were like brothers, now I will use *against* you what was once *for* you.

"The wrath of fire still burns in my veins. Let the earth tremble. Let the ground quake and swallow you whole like it swallowed me for a hundred years in Pompeii!"

I didn't care about overexposing our kind. If Caelius was finally freed, I was sure he would forgive the infraction. Even if he didn't, I couldn't control myself. The agonies of betrayal swallowed me whole.

I connected to every drop of insect and animal blood crawling and squirming inside and around the building. All their blood was now the same pulse, beating to my rhythm. Then it was beating too fast. It beat faster and faster, like the ache in my chest, until they exploded. The whole building trembled from the impact. Cracks formed along the walls, their gruesome deaths shaking its foundation.

Lucian the Merciful indeed.

In Aidan's confusion, I grabbed Shea. I wrapped her safely in my arms, covering her mouth as the building started to collapse around us. The other meat-bags were running from rooms like fleas on a drowning rat. Still, I had to bury him. First the ceiling caved in, then the floor. He was quick, but not quick enough. The rubble would be his tomb, even though it couldn't kill him. Only one thing could end that beast. Still, I could crush his bones to dust and leave his skin for worm food, alive and in agony, like he'd left me in Pompeii.

I had Shea. The rest of the earth, and him with it, could burn for what they had done to me . . . for what they had done to themselves.

Blinding white light filled every pore. I couldn't see, or feel my body. Shea was my only thought. Aidan's brothers . . . no, maybe I was too late. I couldn't feel her in my arms anymore.

They'd killed her.

I'd won the game.

My heart wrenched. All these years, I'd thought it was Adnachiel losing, but with the loss of Shea I realized that his failing and mine were the same. The Vessels always perished. They lost, every time.

This couldn't keep happening.

Not again.

Not to *her*.

In that moment, I felt my heart break. I'd rather die than feel what came next. Fresh tears rolled down my cheeks like they had with Moses. My voice cracked. "I couldn't save them." My mother, my people, Nefertiti, Moses, Aidan, and now Shea. Grief, held back by an eternity of denial, hit me all at once. No matter how powerful I was, they'd all slipped through my hands.

Slowly, my vision returned. All I could see at first was a palm, then the person behind it took shape. It wasn't Adnachiel. It was *her*. Shea had used her powers against me.

Her face looked as shocked as mine. I was flooded with emotions I hadn't felt since before I'd been turned. Deep feelings, just seeing her alive: hope.

I followed her gaze to the giant burned chunk of flesh that was melted off my rib cage, exposing bone. That would take some time to recover from.

Her eyes moved from the blood up to the tip of my chin. Her lips trembled as she stared at the fresh teardrops hanging there. When her gaze met mine, she was vulnerable for a moment, then she closed off, unsure.

I struggled to stand, but my legs were like water. How could she be this strong already? She had no practice or knowledge of her powers. I looked toward her other hand. It was outstretched to the rubble that was supposed to bury Aidan. She'd blasted it off. In one motion, she'd nearly ended me and saved him.

I coughed as blood rained out of my mouth. "Wait, Shea, you don't understand. He's not who you think he is. He'll kill you . . . I won't let anyone touch you. Just come with me. I know I'm a monster. I know what I've done . . ." I closed my eyes. Enough. I let the wet of my tears fall off my chin as I tilted my head upward. What was this? I pleaded to *no one.* She was not Nefertiti, and I was not some love-torn adolescent slave. She was just another Vessel. She was nothing.

When my eyes opened, I met her gaze. *Maybe I should provoke her, let her end me now.* Adnachiel would finally win and I'd be free of this weight I'd carried for so long. A powerful wind dried the blood on my lips as he ran next to her. His face was as angry as mine.

I laughed, gurgling on my singed tongue, my voice filled with sarcasm. "Do you miss it, Adnachiel? Being so close to the Light, hearing the biblical cries of 'holy, holy, holy, is the Lord Almighty; the whole earth is full of His glory?' Tell me, after all you've seen, is it? Is it full of His *glory*?"

He didn't answer. A sadness overtook his features. It was a look I hadn't seen since the first time we'd been reunited after

Moses. "Don't look at me like that, Dog. You haven't won. This isn't Pompeii. This isn't goodbye either. Our fight doesn't end like this. We will have our day. I'll tell you what I told Frank and two thousand slaughtered vampires in my wake, Shea Harper is *mine*!" I flew into the air before either of them had a chance to move.

CHAPTER 5
Shea

"**S**hea, come on, we have to go!" Aidan screamed over the sound of the collapsing building that used to be my dorm. It looked like an earthquake had decided to target McClintock Hall and nothing else. Had Lucian done that? Had Aidan? Had I?

I remembered looking at the rubble and being terrified that Aidan was buried alive. With one thought, all the broken pieces that used to be my dorm room, had flown into the air, revealing Aidan crouched on the ground. When he saw me, he'd jumped to his feet and was by my side.

Now that he was safe, my mind was reeling. I couldn't think straight. I had no idea what was happening, and frankly, I just wanted to wake up from this nightmare.

Aidan touched my arm and I jumped back a few feet. Lucian's words had somehow stuck with me even though they were lies. *He's not who you think he is. He'll kill you.* Lucian, the dorm monitor, had a hole inside his chest where I could see his ribs. I'd made that hole! I had been so scared for Aidan I'd felt my eyes burn and suddenly I'd been seeing a close-up of Lucian's guts. Then he'd vanished. In a puff of smoke, fog, ash? What the hell was that? The absurdity of the moment made everything spin.

I was going to faint.

Aidan's arms were welcome this time. How could I have even considered a word that monster Lucian had said? Aidan had been my protector since we'd been kids. But he *knew* Lucian, they had a past.

And they hated each other.

Lucian had tried to kill him.

Kill him and take me all in one swoop.

Aidan's voice was calm now as he whispered in my ear, "Shea, we have to leave. It's not safe here."

My terror and shock turned to anger. I pulled away. "Safe from what? From whom? From . . ." It was too much. I was pretty sure I was short-circuiting.

I was about to collapse.

He lifted me up and cradled me in his arms. "I'm sorry, Shea, but Lucian heals fast. He'll be hunting us soon."

I didn't struggle. I let him carry me. The word "hunting" rang in my ears. It was paralyzing. "What happened? What just happened?"

"I'll explain everything to you." I felt his soft reassuring kiss on my cheek. "We have to get somewhere safe."

That was enough for me. My brain didn't want to process anymore. It was seizing from shock.

I laid my head on Aidan's shoulder and closed my eyes.

***

"Shea?" Lucian's voice called out to me.

I opened my eyes. I was in the middle of the desert. There were hills and hills of golden sand for miles in every direction. It wasn't hot, even though the sun was beaming down on my face.

A dream.

Another dream . . . with Lucian.

Ugh.

Maybe everything that had happened was all a horrible nightmare, and now I was finishing off the night with some kind of sexy desert dream. I tried to picture myself waking up in my dorm with Gerta snoring softly in the bed next to me. I would laugh and tell her all about how I'd dreamed that I demolished our room and seared a hole in the new dorm monitor's chest. Funny, huh?

I almost believed it.

Until Lucian was up against me. I could feel the heat from his body radiating off of him. We weren't touching, but standing this close made me ache to be held. Even just a small touch would be enough. I imagined his soft lips on mine, then I remembered his forceful hands grabbing me, the fury in his eyes as he tried to bury Aidan in the debris, his ribs staring back at me like a grotesque statue.

I pulled away. "What are you doing here?"

"I've never been able to Dream-Walk before. *You* pulled me in," Lucian said quietly. He was different somehow. Not the arrogant boy I thought I knew, but not the raging hunter I had seen before either.

"Well . . ." I was at a loss for words. Why *had* I brought him here? And how the heck could I bring anyone anywhere while I was asleep? Dream-Walking? That sounded like some kind of horror novel where the heroine gets trapped forever in Nightmare Land. Maybe that was what this was? I decided just to be honest.

"I don't know why I brought you here."

"I see." Lucian reached up and lightly touched my cheek, sending shivers through my whole body. "I meant what I said before. Aidan will kill you. You're not safe with him."

"Aidan would die for me," I uttered defensively.

That made Lucian pause. It was a few moments before he responded. He pulled his hand away, both to my relief and disappointment. "True enough."

Before I could think better of it, curiosity overtook me. I reached out and pulled up his T-shirt to examine his stomach. It was deep red, like a third-degree burn, but his flesh was no longer open and broken. "Was I the one who blew that hole in your chest?" I asked, not really wanting to hear the answer.

Lucian nodded slowly. He stared at me so intensely I wanted to look away, but couldn't. There was something intoxicating about keeping his gaze. I didn't know what was wrong with me. I'd pretty much hated this guy up until the Pillar House, where we'd had a decent conversation. But then Aidan had attacked him and I'd gone back to hating him.

Then Lucian had disappeared for a month and I'd found myself thinking about our conversation. The way he spoke of Nefertiti.

The way he spoke. The way he looked at me. The way he looked at Frank for hurting me. It had been intense, to say the least.

That was the problem with time. The more of it that passed, you either softened your feelings or turned them into raging hatred. I had done both.

But in this dream . . .

This Lucian standing before me felt different somehow.

I tried to shake myself out of it, to remember how I truly felt, how my hatred for him had made me burn a hole through his chest.

Instead, I traced his red, inflamed skin with my finger. He shuddered from my touch. His eyes closed in contentment. I didn't know what had come over me. Every part of me wanted Lucian to take me right there in the warm sand.

I yanked myself away from him. "How did I do that to you?"

I didn't expect him to know, but having the power to rip holes in people with my mind terrified me.

"Honestly? I don't know. You shouldn't be this powerful yet," Lucian admitted. His fingers brushed against my hand as if he had to be touching me. I cringed as it sent a thrill through my spine.

There was a connection between us.

I had denied it before when I thought he was a pompous dorm monitor. But now it was as if a veil had been lifted. Even though he acted like a vicious monster in life, in my dream I could see deep inside him. His soul was pure. And the way he looked at me . . .

"What are you?" I asked.

"I think you know what I am." Lucian parted his lips and suddenly he had fangs. *Real* fangs.

Um.

"A vampire? Seriously?" Then a thought occurred to me. "So Frank was . . . a real . . ." Even though I knew it was a dream, I touched my neck for the remnants of Frank's bite. He wasn't a crazy guy. He was actually a freaking vampire.

My head started to spin.

Lucian's hand steadied me as his fingers intertwined with mine. It only made my head spin more. "You'll never have to worry about him, or those like him, again. I'll keep you safe."

I had to pull away. "Don't. I shouldn't admit this, but when you touch me, it drives me a little nutty. So just keep your distance. I'm hoping this is just a weird dream thing."

Lucian ignored my "no touching" request and took a step closer, holding my face in his hands. Oh man. *I think my brain just froze.*

He leaned close so our foreheads were touching. I almost lost my breath from the power of it. He spoke gently, "You are mine, Shea Harper."

Danger.

The word hit me like a gale force wind. I practically fell on my rump from pushing Lucian away so fast. "No, I'm not. That sounds stalker-y. And no biting! And no hurting Aidan! And just *no!*"

***

"You awake?" Aidan's voice welcomed me from my weird-ass dream.

My heart sank as I realized I was in a hotel room and not my dorm. All of it had really happened. My life had just gone from normal to insane-o in fewer than sixty seconds.

I tried to shake myself out of the coma I wanted to retreat into.

I could still feel Lucian's touch. I didn't want to admit it, but I knew with certainty the dream had been real. Whatever Dream-Walking was, I could do it, and I had been with Lucian.

It excited and terrified me at the same time. I knew he was the enemy, but a part of me saw something in him—something kind, something yearning to come out, but his monster wouldn't let him.

I rubbed my face, trying to think of something else besides Lucian. I needed answers, and not from vampire-boy.

From Aidan.

The person I trusted most in this world had been lying to me, or at least hiding some kind of truth, which equated to the same thing in my book.

I pulled my hands away from my face and looked him in the eye. "What in the *hell* is going on?" I could hear the anger in my voice.

My heart faltered when I saw the genuine hurt and shame in his expression. No matter what had happened, he still loved me. I knew that because I loved him just as much. It may not be romantic, but sometimes familial love like ours was stronger, fiercer. As if it was a living thing coursing through my veins, knowing that we'd die for each other.

I took a deep, calming breath. "Just tell me."

Aidan ran his hand through his hair nervously and started to pace. The room was small, so he didn't have much space to work with. "Trust me, Shea. This wasn't supposed to happen. None of it was."

I could tell Aidan was seriously stressing. I'd never seen him so panicked. He had always been my rock. *I* was the panicky one in our relationship, never him. I glanced out the window and saw trees. Pine trees. "Where are we?"

"Colorado Springs." Aidan continued to pace.

"What?" I was shocked. "What about my parents? Did you call them? How long was I asleep? Why are we here?" I was babbling, but having my best friend kidnap me and bring me to Colorado was way out of my comfort zone.

"One thing at a time, Shea." Aidan stopped pacing and sat down next to me on the bed. He reached over and held my hand in his. I didn't pull away. Holding his hand kept me grounded, as if mere contact could prevent me from going cuckoo.

"You've been out cold for about twelve hours, and no, I didn't call your parents. You can call them later, but in order to keep them safe I had to get you out of town. Lucian might try and use them as leverage."

"He wouldn't do that," I said, not knowing why. I wished I hadn't.

Aidan's expression turned dark. "Did you forget he tried to kill me?"

"Don't get mad. I just know he wouldn't use my parents as leverage. And of course I didn't forget he tried to kill you. I blew a hole in his chest, didn't I?" The look on Aidan's face confirmed it was true.

He nodded slowly. "Yes, you did."

I was overwhelmed again. "And I lifted that rubble with my mind?" I couldn't believe I was asking that. What was my life turning into?

He read me like he always had and let go of my hand, wrapping his arms around me. I leaned into his chest.

The lump in my throat made it impossible to swallow, but I was too numb to cry. "Oh, Aidan. What am I?" Was I a monster like Lucian? *I must be if I can rip a hole in someone.*

He kissed the top of my head and I felt a moment of relief. It was surprising how much Aidan's presence comforted me. I knew that no matter how crazy my world was about to get, he would protect me from it all.

"I never wanted any of this for you. I've tried to keep you away from danger your whole life. If you had never activated your powers, Lucian would never have been able to find you."

Aidan's words made sense to him, but not to me.

"So it was my fault?" I asked. "When did I *activate* my powers? Because Lucian has been around for over a month now." Then it hit me. "Frank." The first time Frank had attacked me, I'd felt my eyes burn. The guy had looked terrified. The next day Lucian was knocking on the door, introducing himself as the dorm monitor. "Lucian wasn't the new monitor, was he? I wonder what happened to that guy."

"Dead," he answered definitively.

I pulled out of Aidan's embrace. "How do you know?"

"Because I know him. He's a killer, Shea." He left no room for argument. "This is going to sound ridiculous, but Lucian is a vampire."

I knew he wanted to see a more shocked expression on my face, but Lucian had showed me what he was in my dream. It only solidified my belief that the dream had been real. "I sensed that," I lied. Why was I lying to Aidan? I just couldn't tell him that I was dreaming about Vamp-Boy. I knew he'd freak out.

"That doesn't surprise me. You're the first Vessel who's gained control of their powers so quickly . . . and the first female." Aidan was talking gibberish again.

I stood up. I couldn't be next to him anymore. He knew too much about me that I didn't know myself, and it scared me. I leaned against the dresser and stretched out my hand toward him. "Just stay there. I need to process. What's a Vessel? That sounds really *Lord of the Rings.*"

Aidan smiled, though there wasn't much humor in it. "This is serious, Shea."

"You don't think I know that?" I shouted. "I'm in Colorado for God's sake! I've never even left Arizona before! And my best friend in the whole world has been lying to me and cohorting with a vampire!"

"Cohorting?" Aidan smiled for real this time. He stood up and faced me, gently pulling me in for a hug.

It was so easy with Aidan. Despite all the chaos I had just experienced, falling into him felt right. Like home. His chin rested on top of my head. Sometimes I forgot how tall he was. His chest vibrated as he spoke. "Lucian is very old, Shea. Like, over three thousand years old."

I lifted my head off his chest to make eye contact. I'd somehow known that Lucian was ancient. It didn't surprise me like I knew it should have. I was more concerned about Aidan. "What about you? You two acted like you knew each other, like you had a past, but I grew up with you. I know you're my age because I've been in your life every second of every day. Spirit twins, remember?" There was no way Lucian could know Aidan, unless they'd become enemies when Aidan was in diapers. The whole thing didn't sit right.

Aidan sighed deeply. He leaned down and kissed my forehead. It felt so natural. So comfy. "You should sit."

I didn't argue. I sat back down on the bed and he joined me.

"I'm going to tell you everything and it's going to sound insane, okay?" Aidan didn't continue until I nodded in agreement. "You're called a Vessel, Shea. The first Vessel was born over three thousand years ago, and it took almost eight hundred years before another was born. But after the second Vessel's death, a Vessel was born every five hundred years like clockwork, and your sole purpose is to break a seal. But that curse can never be broken, Shea. Ever."

"Okay," I interrupted, "so I promise not to break this curse or whatever. Done. Couldn't you have just told me, so none of this crap with Lucian would have happened?"

He gave me a look that said I should be quiet and listen.

"Lucian wants to *break* the seal. He'll do anything to get his hands on you and *make* you do it. The seal is a prison created by my brothers and me to trap a very evil being. His name is Caelius. He's Darkness trapped in human form, and he's Lucian's father."

The words coming out of Aidan's mouth made sense logically, but I felt separated from their meaning, as if I was in someone else's body looking in. Even the word "evil" was foreign to me. I had never met anyone evil. What did that really mean?

I was starting to become dizzy again. I would have sat down, but I was already sitting.

"So I won't do it, no matter what Lucian says or does to try and convince me. If his dad is truly that evil, then I would never let a guy like that loose. That would be like springing Jeffrey Dahmer from jail, right?" I was trying to put what I was hearing in real-life terms. It kept me from hyperventilating and passing out on the hotel room floor.

Then something else Aidan had said hit me. "You and your brothers? Three thousand years ago? No, Aidan, you're my age," I insisted, "the *exact* same age. We were born on the same day, the same second . . ." I stopped myself, understanding creeping into me like an unwanted flu virus. "That's the way it works, doesn't it? You're born with these *Vessels*. You protect all of us." I'd always known Aidan was my personal bodyguard, I just hadn't known how literal that actually was.

Aidan nodded and tucked a piece of hair behind my ear. "My brothers and I were given a job eons ago: to protect the Light, with our lives if need be. Caelius is Darkness itself, and he decided he wanted to take human form and live among you. But once he became human, he realized he wanted to feed off life. He was the first vampire, Shea, and he turned Lucian. My brothers and I wouldn't stand for it. We had to seal Caelius before he destroyed what the Light held most dear: humans. So we trapped him deep within the earth, protected by wards that no one can break. No one but you, Shea."

"If you're supposed to be protecting this *Light*, why aren't you?" I asked.

"I am," he said simply.

It took me a few seconds to understand what he was saying.

"Wait. *I'm* the Light? Um," was all that came out of my mouth.

"A piece of it, yes. My brothers protect the true Light. We disturbed the balance of good and evil, and you are nature's way of preserving it. No action comes without a cost. The prison we forged for Caelius was unnatural. It may have been made for the greater good, but it was made against the will of the natural order. That's why a Vessel is born. It's nature's way of trying to fix what we did. Darkness was not meant to be bound.

"The Vessel is the key to breaking Caelius's prison. When my brothers and I realized this, I volunteered to be the human guardian of each Vessel. There have been six Vessels before you and we've managed to keep Caelius in his prison every time. I'd just hoped you'd live your life without using your powers and Lucian would never find you." Aidan's eyes were full of pain and regret.

I could see that he was holding back emotion. It pained him to talk about his past . . . his past what? Lives? Six Vessels. That meant he had lived six other times in the last three thousand years.

"Do you have all the memories of your past experiences?"

"Shea, I'm born aware every time. I remember everything."

There it was. The pain. If he had been successful every time, then why so much pain?

"So what? Normally the Vessels live long, happy lives and then they just die? That's how you've succeeded every time? And I ruined it by using my powers?" If I hadn't alerted Lucian by scaring the crap out of Frank, Aidan and I could have had a normal life?

But then I never would have met Lucian . . .

Good! What was I thinking? My life would have been a whole

lot better if evil-vampire Lucian hadn't eaten the dorm monitor and pretended to be a college student. Killer. He was a killer. I needed to remember that.

But Aidan's expression made me pause. There was the sadness again, and something more: shame. I had a sinking feeling in the pit of my stomach. "What happened to the other Vessels?" I stood up, needing to be separate from him. He averted his eyes. That was never a good sign. "Aidan?" My shouting forced eye contact.

"Yes, they died," he admitted softly, then stood up and held my arms to steady me. "But they didn't die from old age. Lucian killed them all."

I shoved Aidan away. For some reason, his words felt wrong. Why was I surprised that Lucian had killed all the other Vessels? He was a vampire. He had tried to kill Aidan . . .

But he had never hurt me.

"If Lucian wanted me dead, why did he tell me he was protecting me? Why didn't he try and kill me at the dorm, or earlier? He had plenty of opportunities, and I wouldn't have known what hit me." I had no idea why I was defending Lucian. Aidan's accusation just felt off somehow. Maybe Aidan misunderstood.

He rolled his eyes, angry now. "You totally like him! I knew it!" His eyes met mine with a fury I had never seen before. "He's a predator, Shea. He likes playing with his food before he eats it."

That rang true.

I couldn't explain why, but it hurt.

"But you said I could break Caelius's prison open. Why would he kill the only thing that could free his father?"

"I can't explain what goes on in a monster's head! Lucian destroyed the Vessels for the sheer joy of it." Aidan turned away as he said it.

There it was again.

More proof that Lucian was evil.

Why did I want to defend him?

I'd known from the beginning he was bad news, from the first second I saw him. So why was I so conflicted? It made me feel like an idiot. And why was I attacking Aidan, the one true friend I had? He had brought me all the way to Colorado to protect me, to save me from a vampire who wanted me to break his daddy out of some kind of hell-prison.

I practically leapt into Aidan's arms. I needed to feel close to him. He was more than a willing participant. "I'm so sorry, Shea," he whispered in my ear.

"What now?" I mumbled into his chest. The tears were coming, but I held them back.

"We keep running. I teach you how to use your powers. And we live." Aidan's voice was soft and reassuring.

I pulled my head back to look up at him. "Forever?"

Aidan's eyes were sad, but determined. He nodded.

I nodded back. My heart ached. My body was numb.

Before I could say another word, he leaned down and kissed me gently on my lips. It was so unexpected I didn't respond at first. But then all the chaos and mayhem of the last twenty-four hours poured out into that one kiss. The moment grew in intensity as we lost ourselves. I had only a passing thought of Aidan in a romantic way, but feeling him pull me in and the power of his lips on mine made my head spin.

I forgot about everything: the last few days, Frank, the blood, the rubble. There was only Aidan in front of me. His strong hands lifted me off my feet and onto the bed.

He softly pressed up against me, then pulled his lips away from mine. He lightly touched my cheek with his hand, his eyes staring at me with . . . love.

When Aidan leaned in to kiss me once more, I pushed him away. "We can't," I said suddenly. I loved Aidan, but I didn't know if I *loved* Aidan. I cared about him too much to lead him on if I didn't really feel that way. I needed time to think.

He was immediately gentle and backed off. "I'm so sorry, Shea. I didn't mean—"

"Don't be sorry. I was a full participant. I just . . . I'm not sure how I feel. I need time."

Aidan genuinely didn't look hurt at all. He looked hopeful. "You have all the time in the world."

I nodded slowly, letting that sentiment sink in. I suddenly felt tired, even though I had just slept for hours. "I need to rest."

"Of course. We have to keep moving though, so don't freak if you wake up in another state." He smiled.

I smiled back. "I won't." I leaned on the pillow.

"Sweet dreams, Shea," I heard him whisper as I closed my eyes and fell asleep.

***

I was in the desert again. Uh oh. I didn't want to see Lucian right now, not after everything Aidan had confessed. A part of me wanted to know his side of the story, but the other part was afraid he'd fill my head with lies.

And why a desert? I'd never liked the desert. I lived in Arizona, it was desert enough. Sand dunes were pretty on TV, but in person, they were messy and . . . sandy. If I was controlling this whole thing, why didn't I create some kind of cool environment like a beautiful waterfall or hot springs?

Nope. Just hills and hills of sand. "Seriously?" I said aloud to my subconscious. "At least give me a pyramid or something."

Three pyramids grew out of the dunes in front of me like giant triangular fingers grabbing for the sky. I gawked at the spectacle. It was breathtaking.

"I was a slave here once."

I turned around to see Lucian standing in the sunlight.

"I thought you burned up in the sun," I said with as much attitude as I could muster. I didn't want to fall for his act. I had to stay strong.

Lucian looked hurt at the anger he sensed from me.

I really wished he wouldn't look at me like a wounded puppy.

I was a sucker for a guy with a butt-hurt face. Especially if I was the cause of it.

He responded, "In your dreams I can walk in the sun. Even though it's not warm and doesn't feel the same, it's the closest I've come for centuries. I forgot what it felt like. Thank you."

"Don't thank me for anything. I don't like it when you thank me. I don't like it when you're nice to me. I just don't like any of it!" I sounded like a four-year-old and I knew it, but I couldn't seem to control myself around Lucian. Even in dreamland.

He stepped closer. Our faces were within inches of each other.

He stood staring. I stared back, thinking I'd win this contest, but Lucian took the prize when he brushed his hand through my hair.

My knees almost buckled.

"Your hair is luminescent in the sun. I didn't know that. It's like the surface of the Nile under the moon." His hand gently rested on the nape of my neck.

I shivered from his soft touch. I should have pulled away from him, kicked him, punched him. Anything! But his agonizingly gentle caress made me want to reach up and kiss him. What was wrong with me?

I changed the subject instead. "You were a slave?"

"When I was human, yes." Lucian's other hand traced the edge of my jawbone as if I were some kind of porcelain doll he was admiring. My stomach did flip-flops in response. "I hate these deserts. It reminds me of a time when I was weak and vulnerable."

"I can't imagine you weak," I admitted.

Lucian gently reached down and took my hand in his. I could feel every nerve in my fingers tingle at his touch. "You make me weak." He leaned down, his lips almost touching mine.

I'd never wanted anything more, but . . .

Aidan.

I pushed away.

Instead of angry and annoyed like I thought he would be, he looked genuinely wounded.

I shook my head to gain my senses back. "Just stay away from me. I'm not your food!" I warned threateningly.

Lucian stared with an expression of confusion. "I would

never feed on you."

"Yeah right!" I was starting to get angry now. "Aidan told me everything!"

Lucian snarled, anger growing in his eyes. "And just what did Adnachiel tell you?"

"He told me how you killed all the other Vessels, how you want to kill me! And that you're just toying with me until I fall for your little act and then you'll take me to Caelius or eat me!" I started to back away from him.

I had never seen anyone look that mad.

"He said *I* killed the Vessels? *Me?*" Lucian was fuming.

"Don't bother trying to deny it!" I exclaimed.

Lucian was on me in less than a second. I was so startled I didn't know how to react. His face was millimeters from mine. His eyes were balls of rage. "Why don't you ask him about the first Vessel, Moses?"

I snapped out of my stupor.

Before Lucian could do anything to hurt me, I made myself wake up.

***

I jumped slightly when my eyes opened. I was in the passenger seat of my own car with Aidan in the driver's seat. We were heading down an empty highway with no other cars or lights anywhere in sight.

"You okay?" he asked.

"Yeah, fine," I said, though I didn't mean it.

I turned away and stared out the window. I wished I could

erase Lucian from my mind forever. I never wanted to see that guy again.

And even as I thought it, I knew it was a lie.

Chapter 6
Lucian

"Lucian, Lucian, Lucian . . . am I not your father? Do you have no love for your maker? No loyalty?"

I half knelt, refusing eye contact.

"Ur-Nammu found you in some cavern, surviving on bats, near death, chunks of your flesh burned to ash. You were muttering in a lucid dream: Shea, you are my weakness . . ."

Now my eyes raised, but they weren't full of gratitude as they should have been. It was hatred, raw and unkempt. "I'm sorry, Caelius."

He instantly coughed, grabbing his chest as if I'd struck a mortal blow. He paused, breathing in deep. "Caelius? Not even the least among my grandchildren call me this. Babies that you created, that have created hundreds of children, don't dare to speak my name, though close to none have seen my face. And you, you say it as if I weren't your *father*!"

Even caged, his power was magnificent. He tossed my large

frame through a stalagmite without so much as a twitch from his brow.

I lifted myself slowly from the rubble. This wasn't the first time I'd been covered in the dust of his cavern, half-alive, and I doubted it would be the last. He'd beaten me worse than any pompous master in Egypt.

I gritted my teeth and kept silent, readying myself for another lash.

He smiled, and for the first time in over three thousand years, he sat down. My mouth fell open at the sight of it. He leaned back casually, his auburn eyes fixed on my slumped frame. His white teeth gleamed as he used his mind to take off my shirt. Once off, he tore it to shreds with a quick snap of his fingers. "Come closer, my son. I want to look at that wound."

The cavern was vast. I looked around for a moment, a ridiculous gesture, but I had to think quickly. In this weakened state, he could do what he wanted with me and I'd have no defense. He'd done it before.

I let my feet drag on the loose dirt. With every step toward him I did what I could to harden, to gut anything that felt alive inside.

My eyes fell to a large bestial skeleton behind him. It was the size of a building, its skull alone the mass of a house. Its wingspan spread out for yards. Ashliel, one of Aidan's brothers.

His life was said to have been offered freely like Aidan's other brother, Herostel, the earthbound angel like Aidan was now. They were the final ingredients to seal Caelius, or so Aidan claimed.

But I'd been there.

Herostel may have resolved to give his life over for the cause, but I'd *seen* Caelius drag Ashliel unwillingly to the pit with him, alive and terrified.

Caelius had taken his time slowly devouring him, inch by inch. Now he was just bones perched like a mantle behind Caelius, adorning his enormous cage like a prize. But some nights when I was forced to visit, I swore I could still hear the ghost of Ashliel's agonizing screams echoing throughout the chamber.

I stepped closer and swallowed hard. In all of the archeological digs in Egypt, they'd never find Caelius. No mortal would be able to follow the caves down this deep—it was too much of a labyrinth. Besides, the angelic seal in the hollowed-out catacomb would prevent that from happening, making Caelius and his angel bones invisible.

He motioned his hand in an appealing manner. "Sit with me, my son. We have much to discuss."

I was hesitant.

I knew my head wasn't right from my encounters with Shea, and if anyone could tell, it would be Caelius.

Of course he would send Ur-Nammu to retrieve me. We hadn't spoken since he'd tried to take Moses to Caelius. Only he would have the power to track me, break my protective seals, and lug my unconscious body back to Egypt.

I watched as Caelius's eyebrow raised and he motioned one last time. A final warning.

I closed my eyes, and for a moment I was back in the dream with Shea, feeling the soft texture of her pale blond hair. It had no place in Egypt, and yet it was as if she'd always been there, standing with me in the misery of that life I'd left behind with

Nefertiti.

I swallowed hard. Enough. If I wasn't with Caelius, I'd shove more sand down my throat. Who was I to feel like this? I was a creature now. A monster. I shouldn't have still been alive. I shouldn't have existed.

There it was, I'd found it: that familiar numbness and pain. Now I could speak to him.

I casually walked inches from his cell, if one could call it a cell. It was simple enough in design: a vast empty space, except for Ashliel's corpse. But outside of his cage, the Enochian beauty took form. The entire cavern was covered in the seal keeping Caelius in place. The writing looked even stranger than Egyptian hieroglyphs.

They were immovable. No amount of water, destruction, or torrent could break their script. It was written in the very air, burned into the core of the earth.

I sat as close as I could to him. It was the way he liked it, so he could almost touch me with his long fingertips. "I've never seen you sit down in here before. All these thousands of years. Have I upset you this much?"

He reached his hand toward my face and motioned as if stroking my hair. "I'm worried about you, my son."

I instinctively flinched, not thinking about my words before they spilled out. "You have nothing to worry about. I will bring you the Vessel."

He squinted, tracing his tongue over his enlarged incisors. They reminded me of the saber-tooth tiger before it'd been hunted to extinction. They were small now, but they could grow thicker and fiercer than any nightmare. When he'd fought the beasts of Heaven, I'd seen them grow along with his body. He'd had spiderlike black limbs and had been the size of a mammoth then, unstoppable, with blood eyes and teeth that had made Aidan's body quake in terror. He'd always been the weakest of his brothers.

That last thought made me grin despite myself. This seemed to change Caelius's temperament slightly. "You've always had a beautiful smile."

My lips recoiled. I averted my eyes, biting the inside of my mouth, reminding myself to think of nothing but pain.

He laughed openly, again pretending to touch my face. "You think you can hide from me now! You may be the strongest because you are my only child, but you are *mine*! I will always see you, Lucian."

His invisible touch moved along the surface of my skin, curving around my muscles, slithering up my legs. He was making his point. Even like this, he could touch, he could *own* every part of me. He opened my mouth and I felt his invisible lips on mine. He smiled, sitting there candidly like a god watching some puppet.

I couldn't stand to look at him. I stopped myself from explaining, protesting, or playing his game. If he wanted to pry information from my lips, let him taste the dirt still lingering in my belly or the ash of Shea's burn. Let him feel my agony and not my pleasure.

Shea . . . I cursed myself for even thinking her name.

His pressure shifted from my mouth and weighed heavily on my hips. "Do you want to know how much I know about Shea?"

There was no escape. He had me. I had to shut it down, to

kill my heart. I squeezed my hands into fists until my knuckles were white, filling my mind with death and blood.

He dragged a hand carefully through his short, pitch-black hair, biting his bottom lip while unzipping my pants. "When Ur-Nammu brought you, you were half-asleep, as if in some dream. I remember you as a boy. I wanted you then. It's because of that heart of yours that I saw fit to turn you in the first place. Then there was your undying love and devotion to Nefertiti, even as you lay dying by her window, beaten to death because of your passion. You know, the sculptures you made of her are everywhere. Most museums use it as her likeness."

It was good that he'd mentioned her. I snapped, letting my fury mount. "And what would you know of the outside world, or of passion? You've been sitting in rot for—"

Long nail marks moved down my chest. I watched his hand as he grabbed the air and tore down; peels of my flesh curled in thick slabs under his invisible touch. I clenched my jaw and said nothing. I hated the desert. It was the place where I'd been a slave. And now . . . had anything really changed? In the world amongst mortals and cattle, I was like a god, but in here I was just the whipping post.

His eyes swelled. He stopped just before the seam of my pants, blood seeping into the fabric. "You always ruin such tender moments between us. You know I have ears all over the world that tell me what you find too taxing to explain. I've even seen a sunset on an iPhone."

The auburn in his eyes turned bloodred. His skin paled further as he tilted his perfectly sculpted face toward me. He crushed it against the barrier. It singed his cheek as he whispered in a dark fury, "You were supposed to be my hands in the world, Lucian. Why do you always push me this way? You have sired children of your own; you know how you *love* them. Even when you don't want to think of them, they drift into your mind and you long to touch what is yours. That's only a fifth of the way I feel about you. You are my *only* son . . ."

His voice trailed off. I felt it. I could lie to myself for a thousand years, and still it would be there: the sickening connection I couldn't escape from. It was an unholy, unfathomable devotion to him, and to those cursed souls I had foolishly turned in my youth. The closest words in mortal tongue were father and son. But that wasn't right either. It was deeper, sometimes purer, sometimes intimate, but mostly it was like an inexplicable possession. To love as a vampire was to *own*.

I'd had a real father when I was human. Onack the Great had been an honorable man who'd died fighting in the wars with Egypt. He'd been a Gutian, like Nefertiti, before those left of our kind had been enslaved or slaughtered.

Onack had given his life fighting by our code. I had no such honor; he'd robbed me of it when he'd begged me to hide amongst the Elamites and become a tradesman. It had saved me the fate of becoming a slave like Ur-Nammu and the others, or worse: a concubine to the Pharaoh like *her*.

And how had I repaid him, my real father? With loving the one woman who would guarantee my slavery for all eternity. His name, I barely noticed as it passed, was a murmur between my lips.

"Do you think of him often? Your *mortal* father?" Caelius's eyes burned like molten lava, but his voice was soft, almost tender.

"Not often." I spoke, again trying to freeze my mind. In this proximity, even an inaudible whisper could be heard by Caelius. He was watching me intently, listening to every ragged breath, looking for an opening: a way inside.

The numbness I'd relied on all these years always helped me in these encounters. It kept him from seeing, from really knowing me. Still, in the end he'd always win, breaking me down one way or another until I obeyed and acknowledged that I was *his*.

Even though the blood inside me longed for Caelius, I would *never* come to him willingly. But now, these past few months I'd been cracked open by strange feelings. I was *raw*. It was a dangerous time for me to be this close. If Caelius could twist me in his grasp when I was strong . . .

He sighed heavily. "I know you serve me. My blood inside you will guarantee that. But me? I've always wanted you. I *chose* you for a reason. Do you think there's anyone else I'd rather spend eternity with?

"My love, the love of our kind, is so much greater than what any other life-form can offer; you know that. You're my *only* son. If you were to free me tomorrow, I would not turn another. And yet, that same heart that I cherish within you has caused me nothing but misery.

"I'd hoped you'd placed childish notions of romantic love behind you in Egypt. Now I hear that you've been killing our own kind because this Shea Harper *belongs* to you?"

My stomach churned and my esophagus was flooded with a burning sensation. If I were mortal there would be acid eating away at my insides. "You misunderstand," I began. "These young vampires know nothing. One almost killed the Vessel. I made an example of him in order to send a message to the lesser amongst our kind not to interfere. I did this for *you*, so I can bring her here."

He cocked his head, pleasure overtaking his immaculate features. "I heard you smote the entire line of Gracuri. Did you finish him as well?"

I moved to speak, but he snatched the words from my lips.

"Don't lie to me, boy. I know you left him alive! I ordered you to kill him in Thebes! If you'd wanted my blessing to do it now, you didn't need it."

I rose. I knew it was because he'd mentioned Gracuri. The thought of him dead with his head skewered on a post and presented to Caelius, like he'd requested all those years ago, sickened me.

He was my son, but more than that, he was a friend.

Caelius closed his hand into a fist and my body crinkled like a crushed tin can. I was forced to kneel before him in a heap.

"You'll spend the rest of our conversation this way until you learn some manners. Since you are such a fan of eating dirt, you can speak to me from it. Oh, Lucian, when will you stop tormenting yourself like a worthless slave?"

I spat on the ground, my saliva mixing with the sweat rolling off my body as I tried to resist his brute force. *When you stop treating me like one.*

I directed the thought toward him, but he ignored it like a fly buzzing around his ears. "I'm pleased the Vessel is a woman. This means change, and change means opportunity. The Light is wanting to right the wrong of my imprisonment. Shea was destined to be the key that frees me.

"I want to give you aid. You have been unsuccessful all of these years. Whether Adnachiel was involved or not, it is still *your* failing. This time you will not fail because you will not touch Shea Harper.

"I will send *all* of our kind with instructions to bring her to me. You are the eldest, the most feared, but this task is not fit for you. You will stand down and our armies will drag her to my depths."

"And what will happen to the girl once you're done with her? Will she survive this *dragging to the depths*?" The words rushed out. It was unwise, but I could think of nothing else.

He leered in silence. With my face pressed against the rocks, I could still feel the heat of his glare as a large shadow stood over me. Even if he'd released my body so that I could look in horror at his true form, I wouldn't have. I'd seen it once, and that was enough for all eternity. His shadow form extended past the seal, holding me down. His breath grated on my skin like sandpaper and shook the cavern like a trapped tornado.

I felt the tips of teeth hold my neck. They punctured either side. I winced momentarily but relaxed my muscles. Why did I always speak? It had been the same in Egypt. If I'd kept silent, I could have lived a long life. But I'd had to reach for the moon just to touch Nefertiti, and now I'd spoken on Shea's behalf. Maybe Caelius was right to break me every time I came to him. Maybe eventually that fire inside me would die. It would save me from this at least.

"You could beg me to stop and I would," he laughed, knowing my response.

"I have agreed to serve masters, but I have *never* begged. Not since my mother died. You know that. And you know I never will. Not even to you."

"Fair enough." He grinned.

His phantom teeth pushed in deeper as he held me in place, having his way with my small immortal form in every bestial way possible. He dragged out his pleasure to the brink of my sanity, bringing me to the edges of both ecstasy and pain until I moaned in madness what he longed to hear. "I will do as you say, Caelius. I will obey."

When he was done with my body, if you could call what was left a body, I was in a pile and his shadow was back inside his mortal form, looking satisfied and bored. It was always that mixture of looks, of conquest and new desire. That was what Caelius called love.

What sickened me was that I believed him. The way he worked over my body confused all of my senses, until I'd believe that his version of love was all there was in the universe and that I was powerless to stand against it . . . but I'd had real love before. I'd *felt* it. It had been long ago, but it still lived, even if I had died. It was out there in the world somewhere, for those who were lucky enough to find it, and it was not this. It was not an immortal kiss of servitude, a compassionless void of ownership. This wasn't love: it was breaking a wild horse.

He moved his mouth as close as he could to the lump of my frame. "In answer to your question, now that you've agreed to obey, I am not a murderer like the children you have chosen and their children. I don't need constant blood to survive. I fed once, on you! Once in Egypt before I was imprisoned! I've gone three millennia without food. That's not what I want.

"I'm not looking to end this Shea or humankind. I merely wish to be free. I may sometimes seem cruel to you, Lucian, but understand that I've been trapped and restless for over three thousand years. Sometimes my temper boils. But I'm kind underneath, don't you think?"

My lips moved without provocation. "Of course you are."

He laced his hands through his hair, somewhat pleased with my obedient response. Still, it only caused the look of boredom to grow further. I knew it every time, and there it was again: he wanted to break me, but only as long as I kept getting up. His pleasure was in the conquest.

"When I turned you, it was to save your life, Lucian. You, having been a slave, should understand what it's like to be imprisoned. My power leashed like this is tormenting. I'm in agony."

His hold on my body loosened. I trembled as our gazes met. His face looked like it had on the night he'd turned me. I saw now that the only agony he was in was his own. "I had no idea that you were in pain."

His expression saddened. "And why tell you of my torment? For guilt? You carry enough of that around on your own. That's why I don't want you handling this Vessel." Now his invisible touch was soft, cupping my face.

After what he had done to me, I could think of nothing but obedience. That yes, I belonged to him. Yes to whatever he said, whatever he wanted.

He bit his full bottom lip, eyeing me with more obvious displeasure, knowing that he had full control. "I will send all the others, but you . . . you she's already come close to killing. No Vessel has touched you before. And with my blood surging through you as my first and only born, I'm not surprised. But this Vessel is different. I'll send every vampire your sons have created, but not you. She might kill you, and for that I would not live, free or caged, to see the sunrise."

I nodded in acceptance. There was nothing else to do. Every thought was his. My own blood longed to please him. But it wasn't my blood. It was his blood in me. His blood keeping me trapped by a similar invisible cage.

Still, he could own this body, he could confuse my mind, but I knew deep inside why I was his favorite pet: because even now, completely subservient, my soul was starting to burn. Burn against every word in his mouth.

I couldn't kill that growing fire, even with a body beaten and trembling from his pleasures. "Ur-Nammu brought me here, but he said nothing. Is he still close? May I speak with him?"

Caelius shook his head tentatively. "You know he will not. It's because of you that his daughter is dead. He may be the first son you turned, but you will always be the vampire who killed his Nefertiti."

The words themselves ripped a larger hole in my soul than Shea ever could. "So . . . he still hasn't forgiven me then."

Caelius took a deep breath, his eyes full of fake empathy. "Will you forgive yourself?"

"No." The words were flat and moved out of my lips before I had a chance to stop them.

"Then you have your answer." I felt his phantom hand around my waist. It still sent chills up my spine. "Go now, Son.

Egypt is not good for you: too many memories here. When Shea is captured, and I am free, I will find you. If your children fail, come to me when you are rested and this Vessel is dead. Together we'll plan our strategy for the next Vessel, like we did once… before the first Vessel, Moses, came between us."

His last words stung, but I shook my head in acceptance and left. I didn't need to give him a reason to break me again. If it pleased him, he could make leaving grueling.

And it was.

When he wanted, his power snatched me from the entrance to the cave and dragged me back at such a fierce speed that my mind couldn't even register the movements. Then I would have to start climbing all over again.

It took an entire month to claw my way out of the catacombs. I cursed him with every breath for making it slow and forcing me to wander large periods of time lost.

I couldn't think about the Vessel . . . I couldn't think about anything but obedience and my loyalty to Caelius. Every broken bone in my body begged me to do as he said. Every sore muscle, every chunk of missing flesh. He was my creator, my savior. I had to obey.

I had to.

****

When I emerged, it was day. I hid under the surface of the sand for hours waiting for nightfall as the shadows moved inch by inch, ticking away the minutes with their slow stretching.

When the moon finally appeared, I tore through the sand,

leaving tunnels like a giant anaconda in my wake.

I headed toward Shea, sensing her location from the dream we'd shared before my encounter with Caelius.

I waited until I was in Colorado to think again, to feel anything that was mine.

I began what I called the "separating." It was the process of determining what was Caelius and what was real. It was always hard to distinguish at first, but I'd mastered it by now.

He could break me for a moment, a day, a year, but I would always come back to myself. Maybe that was the problem. If I could just stay broken, keep my head bowed and serve, if I could just be weak . . .

My thoughts found their way back to Shea. With her, I *wanted* to be weak.

I held the blanket that she must have been lying in at the Morning Star Hotel close to my face. Just breathing in her scent brought me a strange sort of peace. I recalled the way her fingertips had glided over my healing flesh when we'd Dream-Walked. I covered my eyes and felt her, the exposure cleansing me of Caelius's painful touch.

If Ur-Nammu hadn't come, I'd have sought her out that night in person, just to protect her from Aidan's lies. But Ur-Nammu's arrival had heralded bad news. Caelius wanted me to forfeit her to scum, to lesser immortals. All for whom? *Him?*

I laughed openly. I knew that trash wouldn't bring her in alive. Even if Ur-Nammu told every last vampire that only a *living* Vessel could break the curse, they wouldn't be able to succeed where I had failed.

And their idiocy could cost her life.

Caelius. It felt good to be free from his gaze. He should have listened more carefully to the message engraved in Frank's skin and the clan of Gracuri.

Shea was *mine*.

CHAPTER 7
SHEA

"What? No, seriously, say that again." I asked Aidan to repeat himself for the hundredth time.

"Just remember, you are a part of creation itself. Your blood has pure Light inside of it, and it allows you to connect to the earth, whereas Caelius is your opposite: Darkness. He can only consume and destroy.

"As a result, you can control any element: earth, wind, fire, water. You're an elemental, of sorts." Aidan sighed deeply. He may have been frowning in frustration, but his eyes were smiling.

"Of sorts? Elemental? So you're saying *I control the elements?*" I said that last part in a deep Gandalf-type voice because saying something like that was *crazy*. I couldn't decide if I had jumped into delusional-land or not.

We had been on the run for over a month now, and I was starting to wonder if any of the insane-o things that had happened to me had *really* happened to me. Maybe I had imagined everything and now I was giving myself superpowers.

Although, powers were easy compared to the conversation I'd had with Aidan a few weeks ago. I'd finally figured out how I felt about him. I loved him with all my soul, but I just didn't see him *that* way. He had taken it well and told me he'd always be there for me. I felt horrible, but he was like my brother. I had seen him in Spiderman Underoos for goodness sake! It wasn't that I didn't find him attractive—he was gorgeous—it was just . . . I didn't know how to explain it. I loved him and that was enough for me.

I could tell it hurt, but his mood had brightened considerably over the last couple of weeks. He seemed happy just to be with me, whether it was romantic or not. It made me love him all the more.

"Try again," Aidan instructed.

I had been trying for the last three hours to make a tree branch move. Aidan figured since I had connected with the wood in the Pillar House to fight Frank-the-vampire that it was a good place to start.

But so far?

Nothing.

Not even a twitch.

About an hour ago, I'd had a small surge of hope when the branch had moved slightly, until I'd realized it was the breeze.

Apparently, summoning strangling tendrils, ripping holes into vampires' chests, and lifting rubble with my mind were abilities only available when I was in extreme stress.

"Maybe you should attack me or something. Get me to activate my powers," I suggested, desperate for something to happen.

Aidan didn't like the sound of that because he reached out and touched my cheek, his eyes filled with determination. "I will never hurt you."

It was weird. It was almost as if he was convincing himself more than he was trying to convince me. I couldn't tell if I was just being paranoid or not.

Lucian's words always seemed to ring in my ears: *Aidan will kill you. You're not safe with him.*

Not that I should've given a crap what Lucian had to say. Aidan had given me the skinny on that particular monster. Caelius was his father for crying out loud! Aidan had told me about the many lifetimes he'd spent with Lucian, and that Pompeii had actually happened because of the fight between him and Aidan's brothers. Apparently, it had been the second Vessel, and when Lucian had decided to torture him by drinking his blood (ew), Lucian had gone too far and had started to drain the Vessel's soul. It had been enough for Aidan's brothers (though his name had been Atticus back then, weird!) to come down from wherever it was they came down from, and it had turned into a serious volcano-worthy smackdown.

But the worst was Moses. Freaking *Moses!* I was still reeling from that one. It sounded like Aidan and Lucian had actually been friends. Like brothers, really. And Moses had been their third musketeer. After years of living together as a family, Lucian had betrayed them both and taken Moses to free his father, Caelius. When confronted by Aidan, Lucian had chosen to kill the Vessel rather than let Aidan save him.

I'd managed to keep him out of my dreams. Well, that was a lie. I'd tried to connect with him, just to hear what he had to say for himself, but it was like he was gone, as if he wasn't on Earth anymore. I knew that couldn't be true. When Aidan had told me Lucian could fly, I'd imagined him floating in space or something ridiculous like that, but deep down I knew he was somewhere dark. Somewhere deep.

I only saw a flash of him once, like a tiny piece of a nightmare. He'd been in some kind of cavern, standing in front of a hideous monster, and behind him were the bones of another hideous monster. Then suddenly Lucian was thinking of my hair?

I'd woken up after that. It had been so strange, I hadn't known what to make of it. I still couldn't tell if it had been just an ordinary odd-bird dream, or an actual Dream-Walking experience. Either way, I hadn't been able to connect with him after that.

Telling Aidan definitely wasn't an option. The guy would kill me if he knew I was actively seeking out Lucian in my dreams. And besides, after the dreaded "talk," Aidan and I had grown much closer. I didn't want to do or say anything that would ruin it. I felt safe with Aidan, and safe felt pretty darn good at the moment.

"I'm not asking you to *hurt* me. I'm asking you to provoke me so I can get this juju going." I was getting pumped up. "Let's do this."

Aidan grinned. "All right, calm down. You need to control your power *without* provocation."

I sighed heavily, repeating the "rules" Aidan had drilled in my head. "Don't use your power out of the circle, and don't use too much of it. It will act as a beacon to any vampire, but especially the old ones."

I looked at the circle Aidan had created. Seared into the grass were strange symbols that apparently kept my powers hidden from all vampires as long as I stayed inside their border.

We were somewhere in the middle of the country, Missouri, off Highway D. It was all grass fields for miles with a smattering of trees here and there, and quite stunning in a peaceful kind of way. The tree in front of me broke up the monotonous rolls of green. My car was the unnatural sore thumb parked at the side of the highway.

I couldn't imagine Lucian or any other vampire finding us here in the middle of nowhere. They would've had to be randomly driving past or flying by. Of course, according to Aidan, Lucian was the only vampire he knew of who could fly. That didn't exactly calm my mind though. Vampires on Harleys could be just as scary. It was daylight anyway, so we didn't have to worry about any of them finding us at this particular moment, but I still didn't want to alert them to our general vicinity either.

Only one month and these thoughts were already becoming natural to me. I wished it were otherwise, but I had to accept that this was my life now. Unless Aidan planned on killing every vampire on Earth, we would always be on the run.

Aidan brought me back to our current task—getting that branch to move. "Good, you remember the rules. I can't shield your powers unless I prepare the ground with the Enochian symbols. Now concentrate on this little branch here." Aidan wiggled the branch.

"Oh, that branch? I'd been trying to move *that* one," I joked. Sometimes Aidan could be so teachery it drove me bonkers. But it was cute.

"Ha, ha," he said sarcastically. "We've been at this for hours. My feet hurt and I'm hungry. Make this branch move so I can eat a burger."

"You were eyeing that diner twenty miles back, weren't you?" I smiled. "You love the greasy-spoon diet. If I have one more patty melt I'm going to puke."

"Then stop ordering the patty melt," Aidan teased.

"I can't. It's a thing now. I have to find the best patty melt in the country. Hey, a girl has to have goals."

"Speaking of goals . . ." Aidan eyed the branch purposefully.

"Right," I groaned.

Here went nothing.

I focused on the branch with every iota of concentration I could conjure up.

Nothing.

Really?

So. Frustrated.

I decided to use that frustration, feed on it, make it breathe. I stared at that branch and thought only of connecting to it, to its core, to its essence.

Then I saw it—the inside of the tree.

Sap. Veins. Pulp.

Alive. Growing. Life.

It was as if I was inside it, a part of it. Its limbs were my limbs.

I opened my arms wide.

The two front branches opened with me, mimicking my every move. I made a branch wave at Aidan in a friendly hello.

"Holy crap, Shea! That's amazing!" Aidan's eyes were wide

with wonder.

"Watch this," I said.

I made all the branches twist and turn into beautiful braids of leaves and limbs.

As I did this, I started to feel light-headed. The power surged through me. I panicked and wanted to disconnect, but I couldn't. My own heartbeat pumped with sap. I felt my feet plant into the ground. I was becoming . . .

"Aidan," I cried out.

Then everything went black.

***

How had I gotten here?

Dreaming. I must have passed out.

At least I was standing in my own backyard in Phoenix. It was one of the few places I actually enjoyed when it wasn't a hundred thousand degrees out. It was magic hour, my favorite time of day. The sun was just getting ready to set and the clouds in the sky were a million different shades of purple and pink.

My backyard wasn't huge, but it wasn't tiny either. It didn't have any grass, only small lava rock like most Arizona homes. I walked over to the swinging bench my dad had built when I was four. It was made of wrought iron and wood. I thought it looked like it belonged in an East Coast brochure; it was out of place in Phoenix. But that was why my father had built it that way. He'd wanted to give us something different than what everybody else had. Thinking of my dad made me miss him terribly.

My heart almost leapt out of my chest when Lucian appeared

on the bench.

"Lucian," I exclaimed. Stating the obvious was a gift of mine.

He looked at me as if hearing me say his name was somehow painful. "It's been a while," he whispered.

I sat down next to him on the bench and my leg casually rocked the swing until we moved in a steady rhythm. "I thought I saw you once, but I think it was just a nightmare. The guy you were with looked like some kind of demon-monster-beast." I didn't mention the memory of him noticing my hair. It was too embarrassing.

Lucian stared at me. His eyes were full of so much emotion, I didn't know how to respond. "It wasn't a dream," he answered quietly. "I was visiting Caelius."

"Aidan said Caelius is your father." For some reason I needed Lucian to confirm it.

"He made me into a vampire, but I refuse to call him 'Father.' He wants me to stay away from you. He's commanded every vampire in existence to hunt you down. There are too many; I can't stop them all. If you stay with me, I'll keep you safe. The weaker children won't even try to stand against me. I sent a message to the lower class about what happens to any vamp who touches you through Frank's lineage."

I sat back, creating some distance between us. "Aidan will protect me, and I can protect myself. I controlled a tree today." I knew I shouldn't be sharing, but for some reason I wanted to. I needed Lucian not to be the monster Aidan painted him to be.

Lucian appeared disturbed by the news. "But you're so young."

"The younger the stronger?" I shrugged.

"That's never been the case. Moses didn't have full use of his powers until he was a grown man." Lucian leaned forward to be closer to me.

I leaned back until I felt the armrest dig into my back. "Well, I'm different, I guess. Probably because I'm a girl. Girls are better, you know." I cracked a smile.

Lucian paused, then the shadow of a smile ghosted his face. "*You* are better. Stronger."

"Thanks?" I wasn't sure how I was supposed to respond to that. The way he looked at me made me blush. "I shouldn't be here with you."

"Because of Aidan?" Lucian gracefully slid toward me until our knees were touching. I could barely focus on what he'd asked. My mind went numb from sensory overload.

"Aidan doesn't know about this." I closed my eyes. It helped keep me grounded.

When I opened them again, Lucian's face was an inch away, his lips almost touching mine. If I wasn't already unconscious, I would have lost consciousness right there. He was so close. I wanted to pull him in, kiss him, feel his chest pressed against mine, his hand caressing my thigh.

Whoa.

I stood up, leaving Lucian on the bench swing.

"Are you working some kind of vampire seduction magic on me? Stop it!" I reproached him breathlessly.

"Believe me, I tried. It didn't work, remember? You accused me of being on drugs." He stood up as well. I could feel the heat of his chest like a giant raging fireball of making-me-crazy.

"The eye thing. Right. Well, it seems to be working now." I

didn't want to believe I was having these feelings all on my own. I wanted something to blame. *Someone* to blame.

"Shea." When he said my name, it gave me shivers. "I *can't* compel you." Lucian reached down and cupped my cheek with his hand. I closed my eyes again, leaning into his palm. I was starting to enjoy this a little too much.

Then he asked, "Where are you?"

***

My eyes snapped open.

I was in the passenger seat of my car, parked in front of Lucy's Diner. It was dark outside, so I had no idea how long I'd been out. Aidan was next to me, stroking my hair worriedly. "You okay?" he asked.

"What happened?" I sat up, rubbing my eyes.

I could still feel Lucian's hand.

I shook my head to rid myself of my own foolishness. All Lucian wanted to know was where I was so he could take me and then feed me to his father. How could I have been so stupid? On TV shows or movies, I always hated when girls acted the way I had acted. I used to think no one would feel *anything* for a jerk. Just because a guy was hot wasn't reason enough to lose all reason! I hated that I was becoming a stereotype. It made me feel weak somehow, like I was an idiot.

Aidan nodded toward the diner. "I'll tell you over a patty melt."

I groaned, but didn't argue. Even though I'd devoured a patty melt every day for the last month, it somehow still managed to sound delicious.

In fewer than twenty minutes, I was sitting in a red vinyl booth with a patty melt placed before me on a Formica tabletop. Why did every diner look like it'd been built and decorated in the '50s? It was comforting somehow, an American staple that no one wanted to change. I took a large bite of my sloppy-cheesed, grilled-onion-filled burger.

And. Yum.

Once the protein entered my bloodstream, I started to feel more myself. "So, spill," I prodded Aidan.

Aidan finished a bite of a huge stacked burger. "I don't know how to explain it. You connected to the tree and your mind tried to make you . . . merge somehow. It was too much for your consciousness, so your body protected you by knocking you on your arse. You're lucky I was there to catch you." He smiled teasingly, then continued, "Only Moses was as strong as you. Remember the old parting of the red sea? That was him tapping into the water and separating it with his arms like you did with the branches."

Hearing Aidan talk about Moses only reminded me that my dream with Lucian had been real. Moses had been the only person the two of them had cared about mutually. It was strange to hear two enemies talk about a man who they'd both obviously loved. It made me wonder if Aidan and Lucian would ever *not* hate each other.

"Maybe I should take it easy for a while then." I felt weak, and the thought of connecting to another living thing like that scared me, almost as if I didn't have the right to feel that kind of power.

"Agreed." Aidan looked relieved. Even though he'd been keeping the conversation light, I could tell that my abilities scared him. Or at least how apparently fast I was learning them.

We sat in silence and quietly ate our cholesterol-filled delicious food. When the last fry was consumed, Aidan's eyes met mine. "Shall we?"

Before I could respond, a man slid into the booth next to me. With a quick flash of fangs, the vampire motioned to the crowded restaurant. "Hear me out before you decide to wreak havoc on me and possibly hurt some of these innocent people."

I glanced at the vampire to have a better view. He wasn't that attractive, which surprised me. I thought it was a prerequisite that all vampires be stunning. He had shaggy brown hair and a long, crooked nose. He wasn't exactly fit either. Kind of a general pudge all around.

"Speak," Aidan growled.

I was getting used to this growl of his. I knew he wanted to rip the guy's throat out, but the patrons of the diner were holding him back. The vampire was smart. He knew neither one of us would be willing to put anyone in harm's way.

"I'm the only one who knows you're here, so don't worry. I'm not calling in the big dogs," the man began. "I'm Chris, by the way."

"Chris, you'd better get to the point before I tear those fangs out of your mouth," Aidan snarled.

Damn, that boy was scary. But considering it was all about protecting me, it made me all warm and fuzzy inside. Was it weird that I wanted to give Aidan a big hug in the midst of Chris-the-vampire's spiel of why Aidan shouldn't kill him?

Chris put his hands up in a placating manner. "I was only turned thirty years ago, so I'm still young. I have no doubts you'd demolish me in two seconds. I used to be a detective in my human life, so I was able to track you two down the old-fashioned way: through witnesses. I admit, being a vampire makes it much easier to get people to tell you the truth, but that's not the point."

"What *is* the point?" Aidan was losing his patience.

"*This* is my point."

Before Aidan or I could react, Chris ripped the bolted-down table out from the floor and shoved it as hard as he could into Aidan's chest. The force was so great that Aidan, and his booth, were pulled up from the ground and flung back, destroying three booths behind him in his wake. The poor couple sitting in the next booth were pinned between their table and the other two booths.

Chris's iron grip grabbed me by the waist and the world whooshed past me at lightning speed. Faster than any car, Chris was running as if he were made of wind. It was nighttime, so it would have been difficult to see my surroundings anyway, but going as fast as we were going, all the lights looked like streaks of fluorescent markers written in the sky.

I tried to struggle out of his grasp, but these vampires were made of steel.

Louder than any lion, I heard a roar fill the air.

Aidan.

Even though I was helpless in Chris's grasp, my heart surged with hope and pride.

I almost felt sorry for the guy.

Almost.

Boom!

Aidan materialized in front of Chris as if he had teleported there.

Chris stopped and tried to run back the other way.

Not going to happen.

"Shea! Crash position!" Aidan called out, and I almost laughed from the absurdity of his statement, but I knew Chris was about to be bitch-slapped into next week, so I did as he said.

I curled into a ball in Chris's arms.

Bam!

I was free.

I was free because Aidan's fist hit Chris's jaw with such strength that it flew off his face—off his face! The guy had no bottom jaw!

He choked and coughed, shocked at the blood pouring from the open gape where the lower half of his mouth should've been.

It was pretty gross.

Chris's eyes were filled with panic.

And panicked people did stupid things.

Unfortunately, that included tackling me to the ground.

I couldn't fight him. He was too strong.

Aidan grabbed Chris's neck from behind and yanked him off.

Chris used the only weapon he had left on Aidan.

His fangs.

He bit down into Aidan's neck. It would have been comical if it weren't so terrifying. Without his lower jaw, his teeth sank easily into skin. Aidan grunted in pain, but couldn't get enough of a grip to pull Chris off of him.

I freaked.

I didn't know what biting meant. Did it mean he was turning Aidan into a vampire? Would it kill him?

I screamed.

I felt the wind around me, like nature was breathing. Breathing into me. Spinning. Building. Growing.

Until it was *mine*.

The tornado hit Chris full force.

He was off Aidan in the blink of an eye.

His body was torn into thousands of pieces as the tornado ripped him to shreds.

My mind spun. Rotating. Spinning into oblivion. The power flowed through me. I was made of air.

"*Shea!*"

Aidan's voice broke my connection with the wind.

The tornado evaporated instantly.

Then it rained.

I looked at my skin. The water was red.

It was raining Chris-the-vampire.

Ew.

"We have to leave. You shouldn't have used your powers. I could have taken care of him." Aidan helped me get to my feet.

"I couldn't let him bite you. He could have turned you or something." I was still dizzy.

"I can't be turned, Shea. We have to go." Aidan's voice was urgent. "You used your Light outside of my protective seals. Lucian knows where we are."

I tried to walk, but my knees wobbled. "I can't walk."

"I'll carry you back to the car." He lifted me in his arms. This was becoming our new thing. I couldn't really complain. Being carried by Aidan felt nice.

Initially Aidan had showed off his super speed, but after I'd almost vomited, he decided to walk like a *normal* person. In such a short time, Chris had taken me pretty far from the car. It made me realize the urgency of Aidan's warnings. If a newbie could move that fast, how fast could an ancient vampire move?

I really wished I hadn't thought that.

Two vampires suddenly appeared, one in front of us and one behind. If I hadn't known that they'd ran, I would have thought they'd materialized out of thin air.

Aidan set me down on my feet.

I wobbled, still light-headed.

The Nordic-looking vamp in front of us stepped forward. He had long, blond hair pulled back into a low ponytail. His skin was ivory and sculpted, his eyes bright blue even in the darkness.

"Hand her over, Beast." The blond man's voice was smooth yet powerful.

"Never going to happen, Gunnhild." Aidan kept me behind him, though it was futile since we were surrounded.

I tried to tap into my powers, but I could barely stay conscious. Aidan would have to get us out of this one.

"You're standing against two Second-Borns, Dog. You can't win. Even you know that." Gunnhild seemed so sure of himself as the other vamp moved closer from behind.

"We were brothers once, Gunnhild. Lucian turned you to hurt me. He never loved you. But *I* did." Aidan was genuinely hurt.

Brother? Lucian must have made this Gunnhild dude *because* he was Aidan's brother. It made my stomach wrench.

Gunnhild paused a moment. I could see Aidan's words affected him, but it turned to hatred in a flash. "Lucian is my father. You are the beast that betrayed me. You weren't even human, just a monster brought to Earth to kill *my* brother!"

"He was my brother too," Aidan said softly.

Why would Aidan kill his own brother? This conversation was confusing, but maybe it would buy me some time to re-juice.

Gunnhild spat. "My human life with you was fleeting. With Lucian it is eternal, and what he's done for me, he turned Ashgar—" He paused, catching himself.

I looked up at Aidan as he glanced behind him to who I could only guess was Ashgar. Unlike Gunnhild, the vamp had almost-black eyes. He was huge, and his black shaggy hair shadowed his face in an ominous way.

Aidan's eyes darted back and forth between them and I was horrified to see fear, doubt, and uncertainty. He didn't know if he could take them. Why couldn't I use my powers?

I had to try.

I concentrated on the wind around me. If I could create a hurricane, I could scatter these "Second-Borns" and we could run.

The more I concentrated, the more I stumbled.

My knees buckled.

Aidan caught me by the arm before I fell.

Everything wouldn't stop spinning.

I almost thought I had passed out completely because it took a few seconds to realize that Lucian had landed right in front of us.

"Give her up, Aidan," Lucian commanded.

"You know I can't." I could hear Aidan's voice crack.

Was he crying?

We must've really been about to lose.

"I'll go with them," I whispered to Aidan. "I promise I won't break the curse. I don't want you to die for me." The thought was unbearable. If Aidan died trying to protect me, as he had died protecting all the other Vessels, I could never live with myself. I loved him too much.

Lucian stepped forward carefully. "Aidan, I'm asking you just this once . . . to spare the Vessel."

"I can't." Aidan spoke so quietly I could barely hear him.

Then a chill went through my spine.

My blurred eyes peered up into Aidan's.

What I saw there scared me to the core.

I knew with every fiber of my soul that Aidan was going to kill me.

"Aidan, no," I said lamely.

Tears streamed down his cheeks. "I made an oath, Shea. Thousands of years ago. It's the world or you. You're the Light that frees the Dark."

"Aidan," I choked.

I felt the blade of Aidan's knife enter my stomach.

The pain was so intense I couldn't breathe.

The scream was so loud it was deafening, and then I realized it wasn't my own.

It was Lucian's.

I stumbled into Aidan's arms, this time because of the blood pouring out of my wound.

Aidan had stabbed me.

I dropped to my knees.

I looked into his eyes. They were full of anguish, but his pain was a slap in the face.

"I trusted you," I sputtered, blood trickling out of my mouth.

"I had to, Shea. I had to," Aidan kept repeating.

"I loved you," I choked, unable to hide my devastation.

Aidan grabbed his own stomach and his whole body twisted like it was in agony, like he'd been stabbed too.

I pushed away from him and crawled toward Lucian.

Lucian was on his knees, but when he saw me coming toward him, still alive, he rushed to hold me.

Everything Aidan had said was a lie.

He had killed them all.

Aidan had killed all the Vessels.

Aidan had killed me.

Suddenly a boulder came crashing down on Aidan's face. I screamed. As much betrayal as I felt, it was horrendous to see him crushed in front of me.

I looked up to see a smiling Gunnhild, proud that he had smashed Aidan to a pulp. "That's for Halfdan, Beast!"

Halfdan. Their brother. A Vessel. Aidan had killed his own brother.

Gunnhild turned to Lucian, his voice full of hate and contempt. "Take her, Father. Take her to Caelius. Or *we* will."

I didn't want to die like this.

Stabbed by my best friend.

My dead best friend.

I wanted to cry, but I was too terrified.

As I looked into Lucian's eyes, I could see the truth.

He'd never let anything happen to me.

"Lucian," I cried. "Help me."

CHAPTER 8
LUCIAN

"Help me."

Shea's words moved through my mind like jagged nails against the back of my skull. Everything inside my brain scrambled, leaving only one compelling thought: *mine.*

I had to think fast.

I had to save her.

"The Vessel must be alive to break the seal. If I take her now, she will die and be useless to Caelius. She's too weak. I need to help her heal, then I'll take her myself." My mind was moving the chess pieces. It was only a matter of time before Aidan lifted that boulder and tried to finish her off.

I squeezed her tighter in my arms.

"*Father*, she already has enough Light in her to break the seal, half-alive like this. We just need to drag her there." Gunnhild looked to Ashgar, confused.

I paused, then looked at them both. "If I take her now, she

won't *survive* Caelius."

"Why does that matter?" Ashgar squinted, his dark eyes assessing the situation. I had always enjoyed the fact that he was one of my brightest children, even though I hadn't turned him for my sake, but for Gunnhild's. Now, however, that same ruthless determination was working against me.

"It matters to *me*." That should've been enough for his tactical brain to figure out.

I moved my hand possessively to the small of her back, resting her head on my chest. The action sent both men reeling. I myself was at a loss for how it might look.

I'd only turned seven men total. Five weren't here, including Gracuri. I didn't believe in his gods, but I thanked someone for that. As much as Gracuri loved the theater, I couldn't face him or the others, not like this. Especially because this was beginning to look like a Greek tragedy.

Two of my own children waited for me to do what I knew I should: to honor Caelius and drag her to his cage. But these sons had been turned during dark times, and they were the most savage and cunning of my children. Gunnhild and I had ended the Viking era together before he'd met Ashgar. He had been crazed from the loss of his brother Halfdan then, and I'd ridden that madness with him.

He'd owned a century of my life, a time when I'd been something other than what I was now. They were both my living memories in that way, pieces of me that had scattered, but remained alive through their image.

It was unsettling to see them now, with my arms frozen, wrapped protectively around a Vessel. I let Shea go, propping her up on the ground before I stood in front of her like a shield.

"We will not relent, Father. This Vessel has poisoned you somehow. She's dangerous; let us take her," Ashgar growled.

I scanned their faces. I'd shared so much with each of my sons, and they were hard like I was, savage and wild. It was part of what I loved about them, and what I hated in myself.

I felt their footsteps move, inching closer. They would dare to cross me if it meant pleasing the larger master: Caelius. They were hungry for power. They were so much like I'd been when I'd turned them.

These were my shadow children.

The side that was unseen, but living, breathing and demanding that I take her to Caelius.

Or *they* would.

That statement alone filled me with an unimaginable rage.

Again, one thought pulsed through my veins stronger than any bloodline: Shea Harper was mine.

"Lucian, *please*," she cried out again.

With the sweetness of her mouth, the word "mine" melted away. When Caelius had turned me and I'd died, my life hadn't flashed before my eyes. There hadn't been a holy experience, only a deep ache. Now, Shea's words were slow and all around me time shifted.

I saw Nefertiti, how the light had left her eyes when I'd tried to make her immortal. I saw Caelius explaining that we couldn't turn females, how there was nothing he could do to save her. Then there was Ur-Nammu's rage as he took her body to be buried, followed by endless wandering in the desert where that emptiness inside me grew larger than a black hole.

Then there was Aidan. When I'd met Moses, it had been the first time I'd felt alive again in centuries. That aliveness had ended when I'd held him, the knife in his heart still warm from Adnachiel's betrayal. That night I'd lost them both: Aidan, and what had been left of my soul.

Only the clenching of my fists returned me to normal time. I wouldn't lose Shea like I had lost everything and everyone before. I couldn't explain what she meant to me; I only felt it, deep and raw like the failures of my past. "Don't say another word. If you touch her, I'll rip out your throats and your bodies will be as lifeless as you were before *my* blood entered your mouth."

The two recoiled but did not flee.

Gunnhild ran quickly to Ashgar and stepped coyly behind him as Ashgar puffed his chest and widened his stance protectively.

It was a shame that Ashgar was even here. He was loyal and would never betray me, but I had seen them fall in love, and I knew that my words would never again reach him. If Gunnhild asked him to stay and fight to the death, Ashgar wouldn't hesitate if it meant protecting his beloved—vampire blood be damned.

Gunnhild addressed me from behind Ashgar's broad shoulders. "Father, just finish her and we'll leave this place *together*. We only hunted the Vessel because it was commanded by Caelius. All of these years you've failed him, but I know you. You never fail. I understand. I'm more than happy to hunt and kill every Vessel from here to eternity if it means you being in charge.

"You would have saved Halfdan. You would have let him live through the ages *with* us. After he was killed by that dog Adnachiel, you gave me vengeance, this new life, and a chance to love again." His hand wrapped tenderly around Ashgar's bicep. "I owe you everything." His voice was flat, but underneath his tone was a genuine plea.

I sighed, looking at his stony blue eyes. "I wish you hadn't come."

I had already crossed a line by killing Frank, but killing my own children, no matter what they had become, was a crime. I could feel the pangs of connection twisting in my body, screaming in agony at the fear of loss. Still, as much as we were bound together, I couldn't lose Shea.

I tried again, knowing that Ashgar was already calculating his next move to support Gunnhild. If he didn't accept this final offer of peace, I would have no choice.

"If you are both truly loyal to me, I *command* you to leave. Back down from this battle. You are connected to me with more than just blood. Gunnhild, you are one of my favorite beings. This world would be less for me without you in it. When you asked me about Ashgar, I was the one who turned him so that he could be strong for you. I made him a Second-Born for *you*. Ashgar is loyal, a warrior, and a *good* man. I've enjoyed watching from afar as your affections bloomed through the ages. Leave now, and it can continue to grow. Your lives don't have to end here.

"If you have any regard for me as your father, get as far away from me as possible. It's true what I wrote in blood through all of those worthless children of Gracuri's. Shea is *mine*."

Gunnhild stepped forward, incensed, but Ashgar pulled him back. "I care not what you've done to his line," Gunnhild spat. "Gracuri was never a warrior like us. We've fought side by side.

I know you, Father. And this, this isn't you. Gracuri is soft. He came to all the Second-Borns asking them to stay out of this for your sake. The *weaker* among us agreed. His way of helping you may be to withdraw those you care about so that you don't have to fight them. But I never thought you'd raise a hand to your own children. And I believe that if you've crossed that line, then forcing you to face us *is* helping you.

"We have our ways, Father. You know mine. So I'm asking *you* one last time: give up this woman, this worthless Vessel. She makes you weak. We can all see it. Kill her or take her to Caelius and end the madness that's taken hold of you. Come with *us*. It's been so long since we've all traveled together. We can claim a town or two on the way to Caelius if you'd like. We can bathe in blood, relishing death in the moonlight. Please, Lucian, choose *us*, like you chose us once before."

I didn't move. I could hear every gasp as Shea fought for breath as if they were my own. Even if I saved her, would she survive? Was this madness, or was it the thing I feared most?

What was this all-consuming emotion?

Fear and shame filled my gaze as it met Gunnhild's. This feeling . . .

Nefertiti.

Moses.

Aidan.

After all this time, I felt it again . . .

Love.

I closed my eyes for a moment.

I would mourn them, but if I walked away from Shea now, no amount of mourning would stop the anguish of Aidan's twisted blade.

When my eyes opened, they were hard, resolute. Gunnhild only nodded, reconciling his own thoughts to my actions. He drew out a long broadsword from behind Ashgar, the one I had given him when we'd taken the Walled City.

The sight of it only increased my pain, but I knew them. They would try and take her to Caelius, and if it meant going through me to do it, as much as it pained them, they wouldn't hesitate. They were warriors, and that was our creed and armor: to kill anything that made us weak. It was what they were asking me to do to Shea. It was what they were willing to do to me, because just as she was my weakness, I was theirs.

They'd decided and sealed their fate before they'd gotten here. Nothing I had said or could say would convince them otherwise.

But they were wrong. Inside my dead, cold, hollowed-out carcass, I knew that it was stronger to fight for that tender spot. Fight to keep it alive, to keep the weakness breathing. But it was more than that. My heart, my soul . . . *needed* her.

I had to mend Shea quickly. I didn't have time to draw this out, even if I should, to honor them. It was not in me to elongate their pain. Even the pain of trying to kill me.

Lucian the Merciful. I laughed at the mockery of my own thoughts. What I was about to do to them would be no mercy.

I stepped forward, letting the tip of Gunnhild's blade press against my neck. "Last chance. Betray me now, and I will kill you both. You will lose him, Gunnhild. Are you willing to pay that price?"

Gunnhild hesitated, but Ashgar cleared his throat. "Do not

fear for my life. I am yours, Gun. Whatever you decide, we do it together."

I winced as Gunnhild thrust the sword forward and lunged, his voice whispering under the ferocity of his movements, "I'm sorry, Father. This is for your own good." Ashgar leapt forward as well, trying to pin me down as the blade grazed the side of my neck.

It didn't matter.

As the only First-Born, I was faster than the both of them combined.

I twisted Gunnhild's wrist behind him just as Ashgar leapt full force. The turned blade plummeted deep inside his throat. I pulled it through and across as quickly as possible, but I saw it: the millisecond of horror and grief on Gunnhild's face as he realized that I had used his own hand to behead his world.

The sight made his arms instantly go limp. I took the blade easily from his hand, like taking a plastic sword from the grip of a small child, as Ashgar's head rolled away from his body.

"I warned you." The words weren't enough to conceal my exposed guilt.

His eyes were wide as he stared at Ashgar's dead, headless body. His voice became hoarse, squeezed, like the air escaping the lungs of someone punched in the gut. "No. I played this through in my mind a thousand times. We convince you, if not with words, with actions. We don't back down if you want to fight, and in fighting you remember . . . remember how much we mean to you. You're grateful. We save you, like you saved us once. You come with us. We live . . . forever together, Ashgar and I, we live . . ." His voice trailed off as he knelt by Ashgar's head, pulling it into his lap.

I reached a hand toward him. To soothe him? To apologize? I wasn't sure. His reasons seemed genuine, mistaken as they were.

His eyes finally met mine as he clutched Ashgar's head to his chest. I couldn't stand it. He looked just as lost and betrayed as he had when Aidan had gutted his brother.

But this time, it'd been me.

I had made promises then, to comfort him. Promises I had just broken.

"Gunnhild, I . . . if you would have just listened," I stuttered.

"Do it." He spoke his words into Ashgar's hair like whispering a prayer. "I won't forgive you for this. I'll hunt you to the ends of the earth," he choked. "Do it."

I lifted the blade from the ground, aiming it at his throat. My hands were shaking as I stared at them both.

It had to be done.

"I had to kill Ashgar. You wouldn't stop."

He shook his head, drawing deeper into his shell. "We would have followed you forever."

I raised the blade. "You were loyal to Caelius."

"We were only loyal to you, *Father.*" His voice was mournful, and the tone cut me deeper still.

I dropped the blade.

I was weak. He was right.

"I'm sorry." I spoke the words, but they felt as pathetic as they sounded.

"Coward." He lifted the blade against his own throat. "You dishonor me, even in death."

"Wait—"

He plunged the blade through his own neck, yanking it across bone and flesh, falling limp, his own head rolling down to meet Ashgar's.

I looked in horror at what falling for the Vessel had cost.

"Lucian," Shea called, this time her voice a whisper.

I choked down my grief.

I had no time to mourn.

If I didn't save her, their deaths would be for nothing.

I wrapped my arms around Shea, cradling her face in my hands. "It's going to be all right." She barely nodded, her skin paler than before.

I pulled the knife out of her stomach, covering her wound quickly with my hand. "Stay with me, Shea. Don't pass out. I need you, I love . . ."

My lips parted hers. I wanted to breathe life back into her. I had given the kiss of death to all I'd cared for, and now I longed, just this once, to give life.

Her lips warmed beneath mine. My eyes closed as I fell into the feeling of her: her essence, her Light. I wanted to lose myself in that moment, to forget that I had just killed two of my most precious children.

Then something moved.

My eyes flashed open as I pulled her against my chest. I looked toward the headless bodies of my children, then to the boulder; Aidan was stirring. That stone wouldn't stop him for long. Even unconscious, there was only one way to kill that beast.

I leapt into the night air and flew.

I tore through city after city, ransacking jewelers for supplies while clutching her small body. As long as I felt her heart beating,

I was able to push on.

Finally, I took her home.

It was the place I went to when I had nowhere else to go. As far as amenities, it had the bare essentials: a bed and a shower, no need for a kitchen. Mainly, it was the place where I kept my keepsakes.

They were all around, like trophies of the life I'd lived, proof that I'd seen decades pass. It was my secret treasure trove. Even Caelius didn't know of its location. I couldn't think of anywhere else to bring someone so valuable.

I laid her gently on my large four-poster bed, the blood from her stomach inking the white fur blankets bright red. Her eyes were closed, but she was conscious.

I had to be quick.

In all my years home, I'd never seen out the windows. I savagely peeled off the black tint. Dawn was coming and every moment could be the difference between life or death for Shea.

I placed all the crystals and diamonds I'd collected along the window. When the last jewel was in place, I kissed her forehead and whispered into her golden hair. "Rest. You're safe now. Let the Light in. Feel its life. I'll bury myself in the dirt under this bed. I'll be right under you, still able to hear your heartbeat. Know that I'm with you. I won't leave you, Shea. But you need what I can't give. You *need* the sun."

I saw the first few rays as they hit the window and reflected in the crystals I'd placed there. It burned my eyes and a piece of my neck instantly turned to ash. Good. None of my kind could touch her here.

I quickly dug a shallow hole under the bed as the light hit the jewels and reflected in every direction. I didn't want it too deep; if anything happened, even if my whole body turned to ash, I would leap out and save her with my last breath.

As I covered my face with the wet earth, I imagined what the room must look like. I had learned something like this with the sunshields in Egypt, but more so with the botanist, Helena, and her obsession with refraction.

I hoped it would be enough.

It had to be.

I needed her. I needed . . .

My thoughts paused as the black soil over me warmed slightly. My chest ached.

My longing for the sun was nothing compared to what I felt waiting in darkness . . . waiting for her heartbeat to gain strength.

And it did.

With every hour that passed, as she bathed in the heat and awe of thousands of reflected lights and colors, the sound of her beautiful heart solidified.

She would survive.

My children hadn't died for nothing.

"Aidan," she cried.

She repeated his name for hours. "Aidan, Aidan . . ."

It was torture, hearing both his name and her lamenting it. I hated feeling so helpless. I had to lie there and listen as she processed the betrayal of her best friend. I'd seen the betrayal of every Vessel by that dog. But they'd always *died*. They'd only felt the sting and surge of pain for a moment. They'd never lived to feel the full extent of heartbreak.

Only I had.

When he'd taken Moses and I alone had been left to grieve his death.

The bitterness of decades washed over me as I eventually heard her rise. I nearly jerked out of the dirt when she said my name.

I shifted in the soil as she walked around the room slowly. Then she knelt down and her hand gently traced the soft dirt covering my form. It sent a chill through my bones as all logic and reason left my mind. I wanted to embrace her, to pull her close to me.

"I need you." Her voice was cracked and raw from crying.

My mind connected with hers. I could use telepathy with any human, but Vessels were different. This connection was only possible, consciously or not, because Shea was letting me in. *Don't leave.* I spoke to her mind. *None of my kind know about this place, and the walls are engraved with Egyptian symbols that will ensure Adnachiel and his brothers can't find your Light. I am sorry, Shea. I will hold you. I'll give you whatever you need. Just wait for nightfall . . . and I am yours.*

"He's still alive?" Her voice was full of anguish and hope. Shea lay back down on the bed. "You were right about Aidan." She started crying again.

The very words made my blood boil. Of course I was right. That beast had killed them all. Caelius could wait to be freed, because after Moses, the Vessels hadn't mattered to me anymore. I just wanted to see Adnachiel in pain, to see if he really could do it every time. So I hunted, and sure enough, his blade would always find them.

This time had been different.

I didn't know why, but I'd actually thought he wouldn't do it.

When I'd killed Frank, I'd thought I'd seen the old Aidan. But when his knife had lanced her gut everything went white, and the pain of a thousand betrayals came rolling out of my tongue as I screamed with every broken thread of sanity. He'd gone through with it. He'd stabbed her like all the others.

He'd never be my brother again.

He'd always choose the Light.

I breathed slightly as dirt fell into my mouth. I was gutted and my mind was a jumbled mess, flipping back and forth from decades ago, to hours. Vampires didn't sleep, but being covered in earth like this gave rise to living dreams, like a film reel was playing across my irises, and I couldn't stop it.

I thought of Ashgar's severed head. I hadn't honored Gunnhild's last request, even though, in that moment, I'd understood perfectly how he'd felt. If Shea had died, I would have gladly lanced my own throat and lay clutching her in my arms. You could only lose love like that so many times in one lifetime before living itself became worthless.

In truth, I should have died with the other Vessels, or at least with Moses. Either way, I knew I couldn't go through it again in another five hundred years. Not with the loss of Shea. She was different. I *needed* her: my skin touching hers for her last breaths, for every breath.

If I wasn't buried, I'd scratch my nails down my face.

Gracuri was right.

Something was *wrong* with me.

I was thankful that he'd saved the rest of my Second-Borns, my most faithful, beloved children who would never face me like that in battle. But my Gunnhild, his Ashgar . . .

My warriors . . . were dead now.

By my hand.

How could I have done this?

It was only now, as Shea grieved her loss, her sobs cutting open my soul, that I felt the full severity of my own. I'd spent hundreds of years with each of them. Their faces and names were tattooed in my blood. They didn't make men like that anymore. Each had been unique. I was completely gutted by their loss.

Still, I hadn't been surprised to see them there. They'd wanted me to take her to Caelius, had needed me to. It was as if they'd known before I had, that I loved—

I choked down the word, trying to harden myself.

Was I a fool?

How could I have let something like that blind me?

I had told them that she needed to be strong when Caelius used her to break the seal. I knew what he did to things that were weak. He'd said he wouldn't kill her, but if she was vulnerable, he might, despite himself. That didn't matter anyway, because in truth, from the moment I'd held her in my arms, I'd had no intention of letting her go.

My stomach rolled in agony at the idea of Caelius's hands on her. How exactly would he "use" the Vessel to break the seal anyway? He had never spoken of the action, only the need for a *living* Vessel. But what did he *need* her for? I swallowed hard, still feeling his large jowls around the nape of my neck. Would he have bent Shea to his will in the same manner?

I growled in fury at the idea as my mind flashed again, moving to three thousand years in the past, to a time when I'd been as innocent and heartbroken as she was now. And like a maddened fever, I heard my own cries anew, remembering how Caelius had turned me under the light of Nefertiti's window.

It had been painful.

Savage.

He'd taken me and made me his, body and soul.

I'd all but forgotten that night, how I'd longed for death. His words, "But then you'll never see her again," had convinced me, and I'd let him continue on until the light of morning. We'd been able to walk in the daylight then. It was the seal that kept his blood and ours bound to shadow.

I cringed with the memory.

I'd *never* let him touch Shea.

I had never turned a son in that way. It had been by accident that I'd killed Ur-Nammu. It was only when I'd brought his bleeding carcass to Caelius's cell, asking him to tell me what to do, that he'd instructed me on the simple art of turning. It was easy enough, and it didn't have to be painful.

Even then, he hadn't told me that I couldn't turn females. He should have known that Ur-Nammu and I would go back for his daughter, that I would have wanted Nefertiti to be mine forever.

My lips around her neck had been soft. I'd taken great lengths to make it pleasurable . . . but as the light left her eyes and she slipped into death, I'd been struck with a sense of horror, which only increased as my blood didn't revive her.

Nothing ever would.

I'd brought her to Caelius.

It was *then* that he'd told me I could only turn males.

I'd killed her.

The woman I had sold my soul for.

I thought of Shea's warm lips, the way they curved when she said my name. Would knowing me turn those same lips cold? Would I fail her like I had failed Nefertiti? My insides twisted further.

After that night, Caelius had sent me away. Ur-Nammu hadn't spoken, but the hate I'd seen reflected in his eyes when he took his daughter's ashen body away from me still haunted my vision when the moon was high and full like it had been that night.

Only when Caelius discovered there was a Vessel had he summoned me back. He'd called me son again and said that I could make it up to him, that my foolishness with Nefertiti was shameful, but time had passed and she was gone. He'd hoped I'd buried all notion of being anything but his with the bones of her memory.

And in a way, I had.

I'd sworn without hesitation that I'd find the Vessel and bring it to him, that indeed I belonged to him alone. But I hadn't been expecting Moses.

My mind shifted back and forth, from Nefertiti to Shea to Moses. In their own way, they were all alike.

Moses had been charismatic and brave, an irresistible force of life, and I'd been wandering the desert for so long, eating death and sand, mourning Nefertiti.

At first he'd reminded me enough of the Pharaoh to hate him, but then he'd changed. He'd given up his title, worked as a slave, and been hell-bent on knocking down the golden scepter of Egypt. He'd wanted every man, woman, and child to be free.

He'd reminded me of the Gutians, of my father before the

wars with Egypt, before I'd been a slave to the Pharaoh myself.

And then there'd been his devoted: Aidan. The last time I had seen him was when he and his brothers had sealed Caelius. This time, he'd been by Moses's side and earthbound.

He'd still had wings, but only immortals could see them. Back then he couldn't hide what he was as easily. He hadn't been the practiced, polished dog I knew now. Back then we'd had long conversations about the Light and how he missed home and his brothers.

Living bound to the Vessel in human form for a divine creature like himself . . . how had he described it then? Ah, yes, like a shadow was always over his heart. Just breathing was painful. Death and hopelessness saturated everything he saw. He marveled at how humans could live in such a state. I'd marveled at his ignorance.

It was Moses who had stopped us from initially ripping each other apart. He united us. He united everyone he talked to.

There was just something about the way he'd explained things . . . like hope moved in his every thought, and he passed it on to those who'd stay and listen.

Even now I could hear his words, "Light and Darkness are not so different from one another. If we unite, here and now, we have a chance to do something, to really change this world. Join me, *brothers*. Together, let the three of us show Egypt that nothing can break the spirit of man or beast. Let us show them what it means to be free."

I should've opened my eyes and let the dirt fall in. I should've let every small rock cut my irises. Anything to stop the memories. I hated being in soil; it always had this effect. I didn't want to remember what I'd done for Moses, what I'd done for *us*: the plagues, the bloody water, the glory of freeing an entire people.

The betrayal.

Nefertiti, Moses, Aidan . . . everyone I loved suffered.

"Lucian, it's night." Shea's voice was shaky.

Quickly, I ripped my hands out from under the dirt and lunged forward. She fell backward, startled by my sudden eruption. I caught her just before her soft, pale hair hit the corner of my desk.

"Careful." I stared at her open mouth as her swollen eyes gazed over my dirt-covered form.

Her arms wrapped around my chest, then she pulled away. "Do you sleep in the ground all the time?"

I shook my head, the dirt from my hair falling on her legs. "Not often. It's restorative to our kind, but I hate the soil—the feel, the taste of it, the memories it evokes. I'd rather not be tethered to the earth with Caelius. This . . . place really isn't meant for sleeping. Having a bed was more for nostalgia than function. It's just another trophy for my room." I motioned my head to the keepsakes littering the floor and walls.

She nodded as I released her slowly. I stood up, making my way to the shower. "Wait a moment longer and we'll talk."

I needed to clear my head from the effects of being buried.

"Okay," she mumbled as I entered the shower.

I wanted to stay in the hot water, to let it wash away all of my past, but I couldn't just leave her out there, suffering as she was. I rinsed off the dirt quickly, then walked out to join her.

Before she could stand, I rushed to help her up, a towel tucked around my waist. My hair dripped down her hand as she raised it to my chest. I was ripped apart inside. Looking at her just increased the racket that had started the moment I'd seen her in the dorm all those months ago. More than the warm water, I needed her to wash away the grime of my life.

"Shea . . . I couldn't protect them. I want to protect you—if I'm strong enough, if you'll let me." I slowly pushed her down onto the bed, feeling the quickening of her heartbeat. "I want to check on your wound." Her heart continued to pound as loud as a Viking war cry.

Her skin was smooth to the touch and completely healed, save a small scar next to her belly button. I rested my hand there longer than I should have, brushing it over the soft hills of her hip bones.

"I would have died . . . if Adnachiel had killed you." I leaned my face close to hers, surprised by the gentleness in my own voice. Her lips trembled underneath my breath. "The whole world can burn, but not you, Shea. I would give anything . . ." I didn't have to lean in closer. She grabbed the back of my neck and kissed me hard. Without thinking, my arms pulled her up to the top of the bed and my heavy frame fell over hers.

I wanted her. I needed to taste her. Every inch. I pulled my hands over her leg and raised it to my hip. Her kisses were deep, rich, and I felt with them all the longing of a young man deprived of fruit in the desert. She was my Eden, an oasis in a forgotten land.

Stop.

Even as my hips sank into hers, I needed to stop. She was still healing and confused. I knew I couldn't take advantage of her exposed emotions like this. She moaned and I lost all clarity.

Pushing harder, I ripped her shirt off, pressing the purple of her bra against my heaving chest.

Stop.

I slipped my hands down her thigh, cutting open her jeans with an elongated nail.

Stop.

Her hands moved for my towel, and I moved my mouth over her ear. My hot breath spoke to her in my native language, things I'd never said to anyone before, as I kissed the exposed pink just behind her small earlobe.

Her neck arched as my hand pushed from under the small of her back. I pressed my lips against a throbbing vein and kissed her soft flesh. I had to taste her.

Stop. Stop!

I shoved myself mercilessly from her voluptuous frame and walked to the center of the room. "I'm sorry, Shea. Forgive me. I'm not myself. You need rest, not this. There are clothes in the cabinet by the shower. Clean up and dress yourself. I'll dress as well. Then we can . . . figure out what to do next. We'll plan and prepare. I'll keep you safe."

I didn't meet her gaze as she ran to the shower, slamming the door behind her. I heard the quick panting of her breath and sighed, ashamed. Why did I always ruin everything I touched?

No. It wouldn't be the same with her. I wasn't going to rush this just to fill that ache inside. That hole. The need for every ounce of her. It was better if she hated me. She needed to keep her distance.

The door slowly clicked open. Her face was downcast as she stared at my frame. "Lucian . . . your back . . ."

With a small motion of my hand, I pulled a shirt out of an antique cabinet and laced my arms through. I coughed as I buttoned the front.

"I told you, I was a slave in Egypt before I was turned. The scars you have in life follow you in death. But rest assured, nothing can scar me now. Nothing's permanent." Even as I said the words, I felt their falsehood. Internal scars, those could be new, and those would last until my dying breath.

CHAPTER 9
SHEA

I had been seething, ready to give *the vampire* the cold shoulder. How dare he tease me like that? I had wanted to do anything to forget about Aidan and how he'd *stabbed* me . . .

I still couldn't wrap my head around it.

Aidan.

It hurt so bad I could barely breathe.

I didn't think I would ever stop crying. I had never felt pain like that before. And it wasn't the knife wound. Healing had been easy compared to what he had done.

Aidan had crushed me.

He was my best friend. The man I loved and trusted. The man I had joked with, laughed with, shared my whole life with . . .

My whole life!

Our whole lives.

My brain squeezed with pain.

It was excruciating.

It hurt too much to think.

To feel.

To exist.

And Lucian had given me the perfect distraction. Even thinking about how he'd touched me, kissed me, held me . . . it gave me shivers. I had never felt that way about anyone before.

But then he'd stopped. He freaking stopped! I was so humiliated. Did he know how hard it was for me to give myself to *anyone* physically? How vulnerable I was? And I had pulled *him* in. *I* was the aggressor. And he'd given me everything I had ever dreamed. Then he'd ripped it away from me like I was an annoying *fan*. Like I was one of those girls he used to talk about when I thought he was ego-boy: one of his *stalkers*.

So, I did what any completely mature girl would do; I got up, ran to the bathroom, and slammed the door. Yeah, real classy.

After stewing in my own humiliated juices for a while, I decided I was going to go out to Lucian and refuse to let him touch me. Okay, I was still being a shining star of maturity, but I didn't care. I wanted him to be tortured like I was tortured.

When I stormed back out of the bathroom, I saw his scars. Long, thick striations all across his back as if he'd been whipped continuously for years.

My heart melted.

As in a big gooey puddle on the floor.

All I wanted to do was run up to Lucian's back and kiss every scar.

And the way he looked at me. It froze me where I stood. His turquoise eyes stared with such intensity, I couldn't speak. Even if I tried, I wouldn't have been able to play it cool. I wasn't a game player and I never would be. Some girls could make guys like Lucian eat out of their hands by playing hard to get. Whenever I tried that, I just ended up not saying anything and making the guy feel uncomfortable until he excused himself and flirted with someone else.

I decided honesty was the only way I could handle the situation. "Look . . ." I stopped, not sure of what I wanted to say. He stayed silent, as if anything I said was important. I was used to Aidan interrupting me with a quip or a joke.

Breathe. Tears threatened to overwhelm me. I had to block Aidan from my mind. Even thinking his name caused me anguish. I ran my fingers through my hair and refocused my attention on Lucian. "I realize that I'm probably just another one of your conquests, and I apologize for being so forward. I'm not normally like that."

Suddenly all the emotional craziness of the last ten hours made me angry. "So, congratulations, I'm just like every other girl on the planet. I fell all over you. You were right the first time. I guess you're just too irresistible for any human." I was so ashamed and embarrassed I couldn't continue. I hated being the girl who *gave in*.

Before I could run back into the bathroom and slam the door again, Lucian was in front of me. He brushed his hand against my cheek and stared into my eyes. "You are not a conquest." His voice was almost a whisper.

I wasn't going to let him *lure* me into his charming-sexy-gorgeous stare. "When I was Dream-Walking or whatever, you said I was *yours*. That sounds pretty 'conquest-ey' to me." I knew that wasn't a word, but he knew what I meant.

Aidan would have made fun of me for it.

I screamed inside and pushed Lucian away from me.

I didn't want to think of Aidan!

But I couldn't stop.

He was so much a part of who I was and where I came from, it was impossible not to. It was almost like if I concentrated hard enough, everything that had happened would just be a nightmare. I'd wake up, he would be a couple doors down, and we would grab breakfast together.

I made it as far as the bed, where I not so gracefully collapsed and started to cry *again*. I didn't want to look that weak in front of Lucian, but I had no control over myself anymore. He was over three thousand years old; I was sure he'd seen a crying girl or two in his lifetime. I just didn't care. Everything hurt too much.

Before I could react, I felt his arms lift me up and place me in his lap, my head on his chest. I didn't struggle. I didn't have the strength. And I didn't want to. His strong arms wrapping around me was the only thing that made me feel sane.

A thought hit me.

I didn't want to care about the answer, but I did. "He's really alive?" My voice was choked with tears. I knew logically he'd tried to kill me, but I still loved him.

I still love him.

I could feel Lucian tense up, but his voice was calm as he said, "Yes. There's only one way to kill him . . ." He paused. "Even if I wanted to, I couldn't. And I've wanted to, believe me."

"So when Gunnhild smashed him with a boulder?" I asked.

Watching Aidan get crunched like that had been terrifying! And now that I'd had time to process, I found myself worried about him. I knew I shouldn't be. But it was second nature. My brain didn't function any other way.

"He's still alive, and he'll be fine. He's no more human than I am. He's a beast. Other than harming himself, his kind can't be killed by anyone but Caelius. They can only be slowed down." There was anger and admiration in Lucian's voice.

I pushed away from him. "I heard the crunch! No one could survive that!"

Aidan was dead; I was sure of it.

I stood up and started to pace frantically. "I just wanted you to save me. I just wanted to escape. I didn't want him dead. What have I done?" I was rambling, but my mind wouldn't let go of any of my fears. I should've hated Aidan. I should've been glad he was dead.

I started to cry again. I was such a mess.

Lucian was off the bed and wrapping his arms around me in seconds. "Shea, he is very much alive. He's tracking us even as we speak. The only way he can die is if he *kills* you. Once the Vessel is dead, he dies . . . then is reborn with the next."

His words cut me to my core.

Aidan didn't just kill the Vessels; he killed himself . . . every time. My heart suddenly hurt for him, even though I knew it shouldn't.

Every time he was faced with an impossible situation: let Caelius out into the world or kill the one he loved and save it.

He chose the world.

A part of me understood, but the other part of me was devastated.

Lucian's hand reached down and softly touched my stomach.

It was electric. "After what he did to you, I'm surprised you care." Then anger flared in his eyes. "Maybe I killed my children for nothing."

It felt as if he had punched me in the gut. "I get it." I turned away from him, trying to hide the catch in my voice. "I wasn't worth saving."

Lucian pulled me back around and held my face in his hands. "You are worth *everything*, Shea Harper."

I shook my head in his hands, trying to hold back my tears. "You didn't have to kill them! We could have flown away or something! I would never expect . . . I would never ask you to do something like that! I'm sorry. I'm so sorry." Hearing Lucian admit that he had killed his children for me made me feel like dying. "Oh God, Lucian, I'm not worth it. I'm not worth any of this. How can you look at me?" I stared at him through blurred vision. "I didn't want you to . . . I'm so sorry." It was all I could say.

Lucian leaned down and kissed my lips softly. When he pulled away, he said, "It wasn't your choice, it was mine. If I hadn't killed them, they would have taken you to Caelius, or worse . . . killed you. And that's something I could not allow."

"Because you want to be the one to take me to your father." Everything was coming out before I could stop it.

I wasn't blind. I could see that Lucian cared for me on some vampire-possession level. But one truth I knew for certain: Lucian needed me alive to rescue his dad. I wished it was because he cared about me, but I knew I was fooling myself.

How could someone like Lucian love someone like me anyway?

He was Dark; I was Light.

Literally.

But it didn't stop the way I felt. It didn't matter if Lucian was using me to release his father from his prison. I knew with certainty that we were connected. I was crazy to feel this way, but I'd known from the moment I opened Aidan's dorm room door and saw Lucian's face that we belonged to each other. I'd never believed in destiny before. It was always some fantasy or something people made up to justify how strongly they felt about each other.

But in this moment, standing in front of him, regardless of his intentions or faults . . .

I love him.

As soon as I thought the words, a flood of warmth surged through me. It was as if admitting the truth set my soul free. With all the anguish I had experienced over the last few days, this very second I was filled with a joy I couldn't explain. It surprised me so much I almost stumbled.

All of this happened in seconds.

Lucian's face still looked broken from what I had said about him keeping me alive for his father. "Shea, Caelius will never have you. I swear on my life."

He was intense. My knees finally gave out and buckled.

He caught me in his arms.

"Lucian." My voice was small. I could barely even hear myself.

He brought me in tighter. "I'll prove it to you. Now that my two disobedient sons are gone, I can take you back to Aidan. He won't try to kill you if he's not cornered. And I swear, I will kill any of my kind who even try to put you in that situation again. I'll spend all of my days protecting you from afar, until your final breath. You'll never see Caelius. Will you trust me then?" His eyes were desperate. He'd be willing to give me up just to show his intentions were pure.

I reached up and touched his beautiful face. "Lucian." The warmth still spread through me like wildfire. Being with him felt right. No. It didn't *feel* right—it *was* right. Like everything in the universe was in perfect alignment.

He saw it then. The spark in my eyes. The love that I had forced down and denied existed . . . It was real. It was as if he couldn't believe what he was seeing. As if I were some kind of illusion.

"Lucian," I repeated. "I love you."

Gone was the monster, the killing machine, the vampire.

Before me stood Lucian, the boy, the once slave, the human.

His bright turquoise eyes looked at me with the same fire that flowed inside my body.

I could tell that he could feel it too.

Something bigger than us.

The Vessel and the one sworn to take it.

We were meant to be.

Our fates the same.

Lucian lifted me in his arms and placed me on the bed. I could feel the heat of his body against mine as we came together in a kiss. His lips were soft yet forceful, making my head spin. At the small of my back, I felt Lucian's hand grip tightly and pull me close so our stomachs were touching.

Clothes felt like barriers between us. I couldn't pull my bra off fast enough, and in one fluid rip, Lucian's shirt lay on the floor next to mine. This time our skin touched and it felt like fire. My hands held on to his back. It was the only thing that kept my mind grounded. Every touch, every sensation was charged with electricity. I honestly didn't know if I'd survive this. My heart pounded in my chest, loud and fast. This seemed to draw Lucian even more.

His kisses grew in intensity as he moved over every inch of my body. I almost lost my breath. But being near him became my breath. No matter how close we were pressed together, it wasn't close enough.

His back muscles tightened as his hands explored my curves with fevered passion. I wasn't sure how much more I could survive. I desperately wanted to devour him.

I couldn't see straight, the power was so overwhelming.

The more I kissed, the more I wanted.

Nothing had ever felt so amazing. I didn't want this moment to end.

Lucian moved his way up my neck with toe-curling, mind-blowing kisses until he reached my ear and whispered, "I love you, Shea Harper."

After that, my body and mind were his.

I'd never wanted anything more.

"I love you," I answered back.

Lucian and I became one.

***

I awoke later. I could tell it was still nighttime from the moonlight pouring in through the windows. It was Lucian's absence that woke me up. I'd felt his arms wrapped around me, but a few minutes ago he had left my side. I wondered if it was almost daybreak. Maybe he had to go underground again.

"Lucian?" I called out.

But there was no answer.

I didn't panic like I thought I would. My *normal* neurotic self would have jumped to horrible conclusions like "Lucian left me" or "Lucian got what he wanted, now he's over it." Granted, those thoughts obviously flitted through my brain, but they held no truth. I knew with complete confidence how Lucian felt. And I felt the exact same way.

I lay back in bed and smiled in contentment.

It had been my first time. It wasn't as if I had been holding out for anyone in particular. I'd just never met anyone who I wanted to do it with. And let's face it, Aidan made dating a little difficult. He'd be so pissed if he knew about Lucian and me.

My heart squeezed.

I tried to ignore the gaping hole of pain that crept up every time I thought of Aidan. Thinking of him used to conjure up warm fuzzies, but now it just conjured up tears and bile.

Still, it would take a lot more than Aidan to ruin my mood.

I had no idea how a Vessel and a vampire could make a relationship work, but I felt completely safe with Lucian.

We had talked for hours after making love, and he'd told me all about his travels and life. He was the oldest vampire out there besides his dad, and I guessed that made him the most powerful. I was pretty sure he'd left out a bunch of killing and mayhem, and I was grateful for it.

I loved him for who he was now, not for who he'd been then. I knew the Lucian today wouldn't hurt anyone who didn't deserve it. He had changed. I'd physically seen it with my own eyes. Our connection had brought him back to his humanity. I had no doubt he would still do whatever was necessary to protect me, but he wouldn't kill innocents. He'd made me a promise and I believed him. Lucian admitted that he didn't have the stomach for it anymore. He had already let some barista-boy go that he had planned to eat. (Gross!) He knew he had been changing then, but he hadn't wanted to accept it yet.

I grabbed a shirt and jeans that looked like they would fit from the cabinet and put them on. Maybe Lucian went to get food. I was starving. I could've used a patty melt right now. Of course, that reminded me of Aidan again, and I suddenly lost my appetite.

When my feet hit the hardwood floor, I surveyed my surroundings. The place was like a museum. There were shelves on every wall filled with trinkets, artifacts, and objects I couldn't even recognize. Knowing Lucian's age, it made me wonder how old some of the relics were.

I walked over to the wall next to the front door and examined his stuff up close. One item stood out more than any of the others. It was a necklace enclosed in a glass box. It looked ancient. It was made of gold and had what looked like hieroglyphs carved around its round border. In the center of the medallion was a perfect green stone. I assumed it was an emerald. It was stunning. Probably worth millions. I wondered if Lucian even used money. He didn't really need to with his "compelling" thing, but still.

I heard something.

It sounded like voices coming from outside.

I pressed my ear against the front door and I definitely recognized Lucian's voice, but I couldn't tell what he was saying or who he was talking to.

Normally, I wasn't a snoop, but my situation made me suspicious.

I tiptoed over to the window and as slowly and as quietly as possible, I cracked it about a half inch.

It was enough.

I could hear Lucian perfectly.

He was talking to another man, and from the way they were arguing, I could tell they knew each other. Maybe another one of his children? I hoped not. I didn't want Lucian killing anyone else he cared about for me. My heart couldn't take it, and I didn't think his could either.

"You should go back to Caelius, Ur-Nammu." Lucian's voice was angry.

"Caelius has been trying to contact you, and you've been ignoring him." The man named Ur-Nammu sounded disgusted.

"I don't wish to speak with him at the present moment." Lucian's anger was rising.

"I didn't believe what he told me. I had to see for myself." Ur-Nammu didn't seemed pleased.

"How did you find me?" I could tell Lucian was annoyed. He had told me this was a secret to all other vampires. As far as he knew, no vampire had set foot anywhere near this place.

Ur-Nammu laughed. "You think you can hide anything from Caelius? You underestimate his power."

"I never underestimate his power," Lucian growled.

"Is that why you killed your sons? You want to stay top dog forever?" Ur-Nammu accused.

Ouch. I didn't like this Ur-Nammu guy. He was acting like a real dick. But apparently, Lucian wasn't as shaken by his comment as I was.

"They were going to kill Shea. I did what I had to," Lucian responded flatly.

"Don't lie, boy. You may have turned me, but I fought alongside your father and helped raise you as a child in Gutium. They weren't going to kill her, they were following *my* orders. They would have taken her straight to Caelius. And Shea? You haven't called a Vessel by name since Moses. You've grown too close to her," Ur-Nammu implicated.

"And if I have?" Lucian's voice was quiet.

"I worry about you. You must take her to Caelius's prison, Lucian." Ur-Nammu's tone was pleading.

Screw him. I waited to hear Lucian's answer.

"Know this, Ur-Nammu: as sure as the sun swept over the eastern mountain in Gutium every morning, and as sure as you and I will never see that sunrise again, I will *never* bring Shea Harper to Caelius." Lucian's voice was like ice.

I had a surge of love for Lucian. He'd never let me go. My heart felt like it was going to burst with affection.

"Lucian . . . reconsider. The last time I saw you like this, you were in love with my daughter. And remember how that ended." Ur-Nammu's voice was just as cold as Lucian's.

"You of all people should understand, Ur-Nammu!" Lucian snapped back. "I had to watch Nefertiti die in my arms! I won't let that happen with Shea."

Ur-Nammu was quiet for a long while. When he spoke, his tone was different, almost vulnerable. "After all this time, have you finally left Nefertiti buried in the sands of Egypt?"

Now Lucian was quiet.

I held my breath, waiting for him to respond.

When he did speak, his voice cracked in agony. "I would have moved heaven and earth for her. Ever since we were children, she held my heart. I was enslaved because I tried to free you both, whipped to death and killed by the Pharaoh because of my devotion to her. I was enslaved again by Caelius because he tempted me to take his *bargain of life*, if only so that I could see her again.

"I've been dead for thousands of years, and inside I've had nothing but the pain of her loss. I know I don't deserve forgiveness, but I feel the way I used to feel when I'd see Nefertiti. Even more so. And I know that makes me a fool like it did before. But my soul *needs* Shea in a way I can't explain. I think she could help me heal. Ur-Nammu . . . I love her."

The man sighed. "Then it's as I feared."

Again they were both silent.

Ur-Nammu spoke brashly, this time tempering his voice with passion. "So be it, Lucian. If this is what you want, I will not require you to bring this Vessel to Caelius. I won't tell him that I saw you here and in this state. This never happened. Enjoy tonight . . . and all the days after."

Lucian sighed and his voice turned lighter. "I have your word then?"

"Of course, Lucian. I will do as I've said."

"Thank you, Ur-Nammu. I know Caelius is my father, but

you were close to my *real* father. You were like brothers, and your home was a second one to mine all growing up. I've missed talking with you—"

"We have nothing more to speak of," Ur-Nammu interrupted.

Lucian's words came out gritty, crushed. "Then all I have left to say is thank you. I won't forget this."

"I'll handle Caelius," Ur-Nammu replied thoughtfully.

"Goodbye, Lucian."

"Goodbye, Ur-Nammu."

A gust of wind shook the whole house, and just like that, Ur-Nammu was gone.

***

In less than a second, the door opened and Lucian stepped inside. I didn't have time to move from my obvious spying spot. I tried to stand up as gracefully and innocently as possible.

"Hey," I said lamely. I smiled. "Sorry."

Lucian was next to me in a flash. He leaned down and kissed me.

I put my arms around his neck and stared up at his big beautiful eyes. "Another bullet dodged?" I asked.

"Looks like it. He was the last bullet I was worried about." Lucian was visibly relieved. "I hadn't spoken to Ur-Nammu for thousands of years." A far-off look crossed his face.

"You okay?" I could tell he was in pain.

Lucian's attention focused back on me. "I am now."

He lifted me off the ground and brought me back to the bed, his body instantly on top of mine. The force of his lips parted my mouth and I was pretty sure I went cross-eyed. Dang, that boy could kiss!

He traced his fingers over my body. "Now why would you put clothes on? It just makes my job more difficult," Lucian teased.

"Nothing good is easy," I teased back.

"Oh really?" He kissed the hollow of my neck.

Oh man.

I was in serious trouble.

I could no longer speak as he performed his magic and my head entered the clouds.

***

"Come to me." I heard Lucian's voice calling me.

I was asleep.

I knew I was asleep, but I couldn't seem to wake up. I was in that weird state where you're half-awake but still dreaming.

I couldn't tell if I was imagining Lucian's voice. I was aware of his body resting next to mine. Why would he be asking me to come to him if he was next to me?

I tried to wake up. I wasn't thinking clearly.

"*Please*, Shea. I need you. Come outside," Lucian's voice pleaded.

You're right next to me, I rationalized. But it didn't come out of my mouth. I started to feel trapped in my own body. I tried shaking my hand, arm, leg, anything to wake up. It was so frustrating!

"Shea! I'm in trouble! I need you! Please!" Lucian's voice was urgent enough to make me move.

I was walking.

But I was still sleeping.

Was I really walking then?

It felt real.

It felt like I was opening the door.

It felt like the cold night air was on my face.

But I was still asleep.

Something was wrong.

I was losing control.

"There you are, child." Now that wasn't Lucian's voice.

It was Ur-Nammu's.

I woke up.

It was too late.

I felt Ur-Nammu's hand clamp over my mouth before I could scream.

The world spun around me as his lightning speed took me away from the safety of Lucian's arms.

The door was open. *Open.* She was gone. It didn't make sense. The glyphs I'd inscribed on the walls prevented any vampire or beast from entering this safe haven. Even Ur-Nammu, with all his powers, couldn't step inside.

There was only one person she would have opened that door for. Only one beast that could have convinced her to "talk to him."

Adnachiel.

My blood boiled like the fires of Pompeii. I'd track him and take Shea if he hadn't . . . if he hadn't already killed—

I flipped the bed and threw it into a wall, shattering artifacts from Beijing to Iceland. It didn't matter. It was all junk. Every memory, every artifact was empty. This room was nothing more than a relic to house my lonely passage through death. But Shea had been here, filled with Light. We'd made love, and for once in my very long existence, I'd felt alive.

I was going to pluck every feather covering Aidan's wings one by one. I couldn't kill him; the only thing that could was killing the Vessel he was sworn to protect. If he had killed Shea, then he was already dead.

When backed into a corner, that dog would do it to save what? The world? He may not have cared about his own life because he'd just be reincarnated with some new Vessel, but Shea was worth letting a million worlds die for.

It always came down to the fact that Aidan loved the Light and its creations more than the "drippings," the Vessels. Even if the dripping was in human form, a form that could love, live. A form that had become his *best friend.*

If he were dead, if he had killed Shea, I'd wait patiently for five hundred years.

I'd wait.

I'd never hunt the Vessel again.

I'd hunt *him.*

If he was reborn, I'd go to great lengths to make sure the Vessel lived as long as possible, so that I could torture Aidan in every way that hurt a beast. He'd curse his immortality as I had mine. He'd beg for me to kill the Vessel, just to end his torment.

I hoped that she was still alive . . . for his sake and for mine.

I walked to the end of the room and shoved my hand through the glass case around a golden necklace with a green emerald. This was my first time touching it since they'd excavated it out of the ruins of Pompeii.

I'd looked everywhere for it, digging around in the ash and waste to no avail. The museum had encased it for display, and after taking it back I'd left it like that. To gaze at and never touch—like *her*. I latched it around my neck and tucked it under my shirt.

I kicked into a floorboard. It flew up and I dug the earth beneath until my nails raked over the top of a fresh pine box.

I placed it under my arm and walked out into the night air. I took a few steps then looked back at my home.

My sanctuary.

I turned away from it. Stretching out, I reached my fingers into the cool breeze. I summoned all of the nearby insects and beasts, as I had done with the dorm building. This time they would not explode—I would spare the creatures' lives. I had promised Shea that no more innocent blood would be spilled on my behalf.

The command was simple: eat, dig, tear until there is nothing left.

I closed my eyes, hearing the walls cave in behind me. I heard every treasure breaking as I squeezed my outstretched hand into a fist. My home collapsed into itself like a supernova. Nothing was left but a writhing pile of beasts and insects. If this place couldn't protect Shea, then it and all it housed was *worthless*.

Now that Shea's power had been exposed, Aidan's beast form was easy for me to see. Unfortunately, he was clever enough to hide Shea and himself under Enochian seals. That had never stopped me from tracking him before. It just took patience and time. I didn't have that luxury now. Caelius would send everything after Adnachiel, and that dog would try and kill her again.

He may have taken my queen in this chess match, but I wasn't without options, and I was better at this game than he was.

I opened the box and stared at it: the blade Aidan had stabbed

Shea with. It couldn't be done with simple metals, she was already too powerful for that, so he'd lanced her gut with a blade forged from heaven. Normally, it would've disappeared after he'd killed the Vessel, but because Shea had survived, it remained.

I stared as it gleamed with a strange sort of light that the box and mud had concealed. Her blood was still lingering on the serrated edge, and because of the contact, it glowed brighter than the knife. It was radiant like the sun and colored like the film of soap on top of water.

This was going to be painful.

I held its ivory handle and let the box drop. The sooner I found him, the better chance I had of keeping Shea alive. If she wasn't already—

I couldn't think of that now.

I sank the knife between the bones of my forearm and dragged it to my elbow.

This was a trick I'd learned from the Book of the Dead while trying to rescue Nefertiti's children from the Pharaoh Akhenaten. I'd never done it with an angel blade, but the idea was the same.

"*Ingrata dosu betan. Eakta norat shenu.* I call upon the Light to seek what is its own. Light to Light, follow the blood and show me Shea Harper!"

I screamed with an intensity that Caelius had never been able to derive from my bones as the Light poured into my veins and devoured my flesh. My whole arm turned to mush then ash in a matter of moments.

Nothing.

The Light did not respond.

The way was blocked.

As it moved up my chest, melting my right leg, I gathered what was left of my sanity beyond the pain. I had one shot left before it exploded and shattered my body. "Then show me the dog! Show me Adnachiel! The Light must go back to its keeper! If not the Vessel, then the earthbound angel!"

It ripped out of my skin, shredding my veins as it torched through the black sky like a banshee in search of a virgin sacrifice. My body collapsed. There was no time. I knew that the heat trail of that small speck of Light wouldn't last long. I needed help.

I closed my eyes and whispered. Within moments, he was by my side, forcing something into my mouth. I couldn't think. I just kept drinking, my eyes fixed on that distant stream of Light.

When I finally stopped, I was mid-gulp, staring into the frightened eyes of a woman in her forties, still clutching her BMW car keys.

Her look of shock matched my own.

I shoved her away and tried to stand. My newly formed leg and arm were weak. The rips over my limbs and the pinprick holes out of every pore in my skin freckled my whole body with pink. I fell as Gracuri grabbed my frame and leaned it over his own.

He stroked the back of my hair. I felt his tears land on my neck, wetting my muddied white shirt. Every inch of my body burned. The fresh blood was combatting the liquid fire I'd poured down my veins by injecting her blood into mine through a holy blade.

The curse of Caelius being bound in darkness, forbidden from the sun, from all light, was raging through my body with every breath, reminding me of what I really was, and who I belonged to.

It had been a suicidal move.

But it was worth it if it meant finding her.

Gracuri pulled my sloppy frame back, his eyes swelling. "*Father*, who did this to you?"

I laughed, which only seemed to frighten him further. "I did."

Confusion filled his features as he motioned the half-alive woman to walk toward us. He feigned a half smile. "You're delirious. You've been mortally injured. You need more blood."

I turned to her. She hesitated and I noticed the dried mascara frozen on her lower jaw from tears.

I turned away. I couldn't look at her, at myself. My horror only mounted as my eyes rested on a pile. No. A small mountain of dead bodies lay heaped where I'd stood.

I staggered from Gracuri, pushing him back. "What have you done?"

He reached for my arm to steady my balance, but I bared my fangs and he stood back.

Looking even more confused than before, Gracuri shook his head. "But, you called me, and when I came, you were near *true* death! There was a town nearby. My only thought was of you, the thought of losing you . . ." Gracuri began crying again. "I'm sorry. I know you don't feed en masse like this. I know it's like when you found me in Thebes—the entire city dead at my feet—but please don't abandon me again. What I did then was for love, and that's what I did now! Father, I don't care if this exposes our kind! I don't care if you're morally against it! You were dying and I was so afraid of losing you forever, I—"

I grabbed his head and cradled it in my arms. He wrapped his gladiator frame around mine and trembled as he wept, "I can't lose you," over and over again.

I knew in that moment I could never blame or judge him. He wasn't thinking clearly because of me. Just like I wasn't thinking clearly because of Shea. I would do anything for her, even *this* if it meant saving her life.

I buried my head deeper into his back.

All this death.

I truly was a monster.

After we'd made love, I'd changed. I'd felt as if the killer in me had died. But now, with Shea gone and my only hope drifting into darkness, the monster had re-emerged without my consent.

I sighed, pulling him back. Gracuri was my responsibility. "Forgive me for blaming you. I called you here. This was my fault, not yours.

"Thank you, Gracuri. You saved my other children from slaughter, you saved my life, and because you exposed us again, Caelius will no doubt demand your head as he has before. But I promise, I will defend you with my last breath. He will never have you."

He smiled, pushing my hair away from my face, his eyes full of concern. I touched a curl in his hair and pulled it straight. "I have to go and find her, Son. I need you to clean this up and never speak of it, even to the others. And I need . . . I need to feed."

He nodded, quickly pulling back. "There was another town close by. I can have you a dozen more—"

"No." I gently placed my hand around the side of his neck. "It will take too long, and even though, in hunger, I broke my promise, I still intend on keeping it. I won't kill anyone else, but I need to be powerful when I face Aidan. Do you understand?"

He rested his palm over mine. "Then I will go with you. I'll call the other Second-Borns. We'll save her together if that's what you desire, Father."

I shook my head. "If Adnachiel's outnumbered, he'll kill her. I won't be forced to stand against them, or you. I can't do it. I'm not strong enough, not after Gunnhild and Ashgar. Just clean this up and keep the others safe, hidden from the eyes of Aidan and Caelius . . . and me. Without Shea's Light, no one should find you. I taught you the symbols once, when we were younger. Do you remember?"

He nodded slowly, his eyes filling with horror. "But I have to be there . . . if you need me. And the others, you know not one of us would stand against you, even the sons you've abandoned."

I pulled him closer, my lips resting on the small of his neck just before the muscle of his shoulder blade. "You can be here for me *now*, Gracuri."

His eyes widened, his fear and confusion melting away to sheer pleasure. "But you've never—you don't feed on your children like we all do. Even when asked . . . when *begged*."

I sighed heavily. There was a reason for that. It was bad enough turning them, linking their hearts to mine for eternity. But sharing blood, feeding on them, it was the part of possession that gave Caelius such pleasure when he consumed me in shadow form.

It was owning.

To feed on your children ensured their loyalty and love for you. They would think of nothing else for hundreds of years, depending on the power of their own free will and the power of their maker. It would be complete. An obsession. Caelius's version of love.

"I've never asked because I don't want to harm my children. I don't want to hurt you, Gracuri. I have cared for each and every one of you, and my heart is pleased that you have all been free and without my influence, or as free as you could be with my infected blood pumping through you, not to mention the drop of Caelius's foul blood that gives all vampires eternal life. But to do this—"

He grabbed the back of my head and pushed my lips onto his neck.

He sighed, relaxing his muscles. "I have longed for nothing else, Father. Please, if this will help you, to feed on a Second-Born, then take me. I'll clean this mess up after and hide your children. Take what you need. It's an honor to serve you in this way."

It was sweet, like it had been the night I'd turned him in Athens. I made it painless and pleasurable. His body sank into mine as I felt my limbs growing in strength. And there it was. The link. With every drop, more of me was inside him, our blood and hearts fusing.

Instantly, I jerked away, thinking only of Shea. I wiped my mouth as my muscles surged with the borrowed power of a Second-Born.

I stared at his soft features. He looked weak, pale. I grabbed him as he staggered forward. "Gracuri, are you all right? I've taken too much."

He only smiled. "You really do love her, don't you?" He

grabbed me fiercely and kissed my lips. Before I could respond, he was gone and the pile of human bodies set aflame. I shook my head, already feeling the pangs of guilt and regret.

Gracuri was loyal and wild of heart. I'd taken more than blood—my final acceptance of his body, my final rejection of his feelings toward me . . . I'd hurt him this time.

I took in a deep breath. If I survived this, I'd apologize, I'd make up for it somehow.

I looked at the already weakened trail of Light and hissed, "I'm coming for you, Beast." I leapt into the air and followed the path.

I tracked it all over the world.

Aidan had been everywhere I'd traveled in the last millennium. Places we had battled before. That winged dog hadn't been able to fly since killing Moses, but he was still fast.

As useless as those wings were to him now, they were still made of spirit, and a dark creature like me could grab hold. And I would. I'd break every bone, flightless as they were.

The thought of his suffering didn't calm my growing unease. His behavior didn't make sense. Why was he visiting every place he had chosen to kill a Vessel? Was he also nostalgic, or was this a part of his deception?

It had to be his leftover trail from following me while looking for Shea. It wasn't fresh; the Light was dim. I kept following the heat until it got brighter and I finally discovered a fresh track. It wouldn't be long now before I ripped him open.

And there he was. In a forest near Amsterdam. He was just waiting there by a cave. Thinking? Plotting?

Seeing him filled me with relief and rage.

If he was alive, then so was Shea.

But why here? Had he stopped in town to buy drugs? Was he keeping her comatose so she wouldn't escape and come looking for me?

I ripped through the night air like a comet hurtling toward the earth. The sound barrier snapped in my wake as I crashed into him. The force of our bodies created a crater that demolished the surrounding trees and sent them flying like toothpicks spilled on a dinner table.

Before he could recover, I held his bloodied face to mine. "Where is she?" I screamed. "Where is she, you worthless, blind, senseless, Light-suckling dog?" I threw his body into a mountain. His bones crushed as he propelled through the other side, landing somewhere in a small town.

I didn't have much time. I scavenged the area. She was nowhere. I couldn't feel, see, or smell her. What had he done?

I flew to the town square, where his body had fallen chest-first on the spike of a metal fence. I bared my fangs as he growled.

He pulled the skewer out of his chest and took a step forward; the ground quaked beneath his feet. His power was alive in the very air we were breathing.

My eyes burned as I gained control of the animals in the forest behind me. Two could play at this game.

Instantly, he stopped. "Let's end this, but not here. There's no reason for this town and the ones around it to go down like Pompeii."

I spat, and it landed on his cheek as I laughed. "That was your doing, not mine."

He growled again, a sound so deep and ravenous it shook all

the houses and broke the windows. "That may be, but there's no reason for *these* people to die."

I paused.

For a moment, I felt something. Something strange. Why did he care? Who were these meaningless people he would postpone our battle for? I thought about the pile of bodies next to Gracuri, and of my own guilt and promise.

I was not the same vampire I'd been in Pompeii, and he was right: there was no reason for innocent humans to die just because he was a treacherous dog. I could torture him and find Shea without their lives being lost.

"Fine. We'll fight over the water just to remind you of Halfdan, the seaman. You remember Halfdan, don't you? Gunnhild and your *brother*?"

He clenched his jaw and nodded bitterly. In a flash, he was racing toward the North Sea. He arrived moments before me, running on top of the water. His kind could stand on it without penetrating the barrier. It was something about the essence of the ocean being likened to the spirit.

He turned, a fraction of a second before I could stop, and pounded his clenched fists into my chest. I smacked the surface of the water. The waves rose up around my body like concrete skyscrapers.

I sank.

Every bone in my spine was broken, blood pouring out of every orifice. It drew the sharks.

Let them come.

I extended my power and attracted anything alive in the vicinity. With quick movements, I shredded them like a ravenous tornado of death. Blood rose up from the depths and I with it. If blood was in the water, I controlled that water.

Aidan looked shocked. He shouldn't have been. It was I who had frightened the Pharaoh for Moses, turning all the water into blood and using it to attack the city.

I wrapped the tides around his invisible wings, pinning him in midair. I plummeted my fists into every inch of his muscled frame. His bones broke under my knuckles.

Eventually, my knuckles broke too, but I still pounded them into his body until they were mush.

Our strength diminished until we were both barely hovering inches above the water, my hold on his wings as light as a child's, yet he still couldn't resist it.

I spat blood onto his face in disgust. "Just tell me where she is, Adnachiel. I'm not taking her to Caelius, but *you* can't have her. She chose *me!*"

That did it.

We both had a surge of strength, our eyes alight in joint fury. He broke my hold over him. I quickly called the locusts, which he easily drove away, his wings sending small tornadoes across the ocean. I was surprised. They were useless for flying, but they still had power. Maybe it was something internal that had stopped him from flying after Moses's death, not the physicality of it.

I stood firm and sneered, unmoved. Gust of wind or not, he'd have to do better than that.

And he would.

I had to think quickly. I had to find anything alive in the water that I could control.

I had an idea.

I'd done this once before on a pious man as a joke. Later it'd been put in the bible as God's will, but it would do.

A large whale leapt into the air and swallowed us both. It swam fast and hard through the deepest, darkest cave toward the center of the earth. Aidan didn't react fast enough. Odds were, even as a beast, he'd never been swallowed whole before, and rolling around in an acidic giant whale stomach threw his game.

I had been swallowed by Caelius's shadow enough times to know the routine. It would burn, in an unimaginable way. But it would pass.

I grabbed his invisible wings and snapped them backward. I broke every bone. I pushed a handful of stomach acid into his chest as he screamed in agony.

"Just give her to me, Adnachiel, and I'll keep her safe while you live a long, boorish dog life! Why are you so incessant on keeping her only to kill her later?" As the acid peeled back layers of muscle, I pushed my fist through his rib cage and ripped out his heart. It would grow back eventually, but it was still pleasing, feeling it warm and pumping in my hand.

I let the pleasure get the better of me. He rammed his palm through my sternum and ripped out my heart, then stood back.

There we were.

Once like brothers.

Now and forever enemies.

Holding each other's hearts.

I couldn't help but smile at the irony. For some reason, he did too. He looked at me. For the first time in centuries, he really looked at me. "Lucian, what would Moses think, seeing us now?"

I dropped his heart and crushed it with my heel. "I don't know, because he's dead. Because you cared more about this precious world than him, than our friendship. You're just mindless and obedient that way."

He lowered his hand, still holding my blackened organ. "I do. I do care about this world. All the people in it. And it kills me, literally, every time I end a Vessel. And whether you believe me or not, I *am* sorry, Lucian."

I gritted my teeth as my incisors ripped my gums. I'd tear him apart. "You're *sorry?*"

His eyes grew downcast as he took a deep breath. He tossed the heart and I caught it, confused. What tactic was this?

He spoke without wavering. "I think we've been played here. When you had this thing swallow us, it hit me: you don't know where she is either. You kept asking, but it didn't register. I thought you were toying with me. But you're not, are you? You genuinely don't know where she is."

My mouth opened. No. This couldn't be right. The heat trail, all the places Aidan had gone looking for me . . . it never doubled back. It should have at least passed by the rubble that'd been my home if he'd grabbed her then.

"Impossible . . ." I staggered as I shoved the heart back in its hole. It would heal faster that way.

I needed to think.

I needed to start building my strength again.

I needed to get the hell out of this whale.

Within moments, I had it vomiting us up on the closest shoreline. Aidan gasped and brushed his arms and legs, as if that would remove the smell from his memory. I grabbed him and shoved him into the sand. "If you and I don't have her, then where is she?"

He shrugged me off, still gasping. "I don't know, Lucian! I was tracking her scent when you found me."

I clenched my jaw and spoke through my teeth. "We hate each other. That's fine. I'll *never* forgive you for Moses, but that's not going to help either of us find Shea. We can find her faster together. United . . . Light and Dark." I stopped. I knew this speech.

Although Moses had been more elegant, Aidan still smiled at hearing it. It was an awkward thing. It always was. I doubted his kind used their mouths in that way. Still, I couldn't help but feel strange seeing it again.

He reached out and grabbed my forearm in a pact like we'd made all those centuries ago.

"This time, *Aidan*, save her. Promise me. If we do this together, no matter how bad the situation looks, promise you won't kill Shea."

He winced, withdrawing his hand. "I love her, Lucian," he admitted. He shook his head, averting his gaze. "I know she loves you. I saw it even before she did, so I won't get in your way."

When his eyes met mine, they were wet with tears. "When I sank the knife in, it was like with Moses, but *worse*. I wanted to die. I needed to, just so I wouldn't have to see the look on her face." Aidan took a deep breath, then stared at me with conviction. "I will never hurt her again. I promise on my soul, on my brothers, on the end of the world . . ." His eyes were heavy and full of a deep, unrelenting sorrow.

I didn't move. The wind was calm around us. My chest tightened. Despite the feverish pumping of my regrowing heart, it was hard to breathe.

Never in all these centuries had he agreed to not kill a Vessel if the time came. He had his duty, his obligation to the Light, to his beastly brothers. His *real* brothers.

I didn't know what to say. My eyes were fixed on his, and I nodded. We looked so much the same in that moment. Younger than our ancient souls, young and in love with Shea Harper. That was what it was. We had both loved Moses, but this was different. This was more.

His mouth barely moved as he spoke. "And I will *always* regret what I did to Moses . . . and to you."

He didn't meet my gaze then.

"What you did to me," I growled, "changed me. You made me into the monster you feared I was."

His mouth opened, but nothing came out.

Words couldn't repair the distance his actions, and lifetimes of misunderstandings, had created.

"Lucian, I want us to be—"

"Enough sentiment." I brushed the sand off my chest as if brushing off his words.

He coughed, unlocking the broken bones in his wings and straightening out.

We didn't have time for this. We needed to buck up and hunt whatever had Shea.

I turned from him back toward the vast body of water. I called and feasted on the bloodied delicacies of the sea while he bathed in the bright light of the moon.

When we were ready, we were both eager, refreshed from blood and light. "What have you found so far, Adnachiel?" I began.

He shook his head. "It's all masked, her scent thrown in every direction. Her blood, drops of it splashed here and there. I thought it was from you feeding. Whoever did this, they were good. Maybe even better than you. And if it's not *you*, that tells me we're dealing with one of your initial children. Someone ancient."

I shook my head. "No. I killed the two that would have betrayed me. The other five are loyal. They'd die before dishonoring their father in that way."

He grimaced. "I've always found the father thing a little creepy."

I shrugged and half smiled. "Yeah, me too. But it's—"

"And what do you mean you *killed* two?" he interjected.

Now my smile faded. I did my best to quell the anger ready to mount and break his wings all over again. "When you *knifed* Shea, they wanted me to end her. I refused and chose instead to end their lives. Like I told you before you gutted her, there was no need."

He looked over the sea and sighed. "I couldn't have guessed that, Lucian."

My fangs grew impulsively. "I thought after I *tortured* Frank and killed his entire lineage, we had an understanding."

His eyes widened. "I didn't know any of this. I was obsessed with keeping her safe. I didn't want . . . I didn't think I could trust you. It doesn't matter. The important thing now is finding her. It had to be one of your children who took her. Did anyone know where you were?"

I shook my head. "No." Then the reality set in. "Wait . . . Ur-

Nammu, but he wouldn't—"

"Ur-Nammu?" He lunged, pinning me to a towering palm. "You idiot! He was the one who made me think you were going to take Moses! He's Caelius's right hand when you fall through!"

I shoved him violently into the sand. "Moses would have lived if you'd given me time to explain it to Ur-Nammu! Had he known our relationship, he wouldn't have come. When you saw me take Moses, you just assumed the worst! I was trying to protect him, not take him to Caelius!"

There was a long pause as we stared at each other with unkempt fury.

Then Aidan cooled, looking away, not meeting my gaze. "I know."

I ground my teeth, tilting my head. "What was that, Dog?"

His voice was low and soft. "I *know*, Lucian. It was my mistake. I thought . . . I thought maybe you'd turned on us. It was only after I stabbed him, when we were dying as we fell from the sky . . . the look on your face, the betrayal. I realized then that I'd been wrong."

I took a deep breath. It had been thousands of years, and now he'd admitted his error. "You and Moses died that day, and all the goodness and hope I had left died with you. At that time, I didn't even know that killing the Vessel was the only way to end your life. I would have never betrayed Moses, Aidan. I would have never betrayed *you*. And it's the same for Shea now."

He looked up, his sky-blue eyes wet with shame. "I'm sorry, Lucian. After Moses, when the next Vessel was born, I tried to find you. When you found us, you were so full of rage. You took the Vessel without question and attacked me. You'd changed. I wanted to explain, but you wouldn't listen. Then after Pompeii, all of that death . . . I just thought you were dead to me as well."

I stepped toward him. "Not dead. You buried me under that rubble. It took a hundred years to claw myself out. I had plenty of time to hate you as I ate ash and molten lava."

He took a step back, furrowing his brow. "And what was I supposed to do? You tapped into the Vessel's soul! My brothers thought you were freeing Caelius in Egypt, so when they realized you were in Pompeii and cracking open the Light of a Vessel, they showed up to stop you. The fight cost countless of innocent people their lives. I couldn't let you do that again. All those people died because of us. And burying you was foolish. I know that. But my brothers . . . they would have *killed* you."

I grabbed his wrist and jerked his face to mine. "Don't play innocent. You didn't bury me to save my life."

"Of course I did!" Aidan shouted. "You may have hated me then, but I hated myself more. I didn't blame you for it. I accepted your hate as my penance. All these years . . ."

I squeezed his wrist, my incisors cutting my tight lower lip. As the blood ran down my chin, I could hear the sincerity in his voice.

"Yes, we've done things to each other, fueled by hate and regret, but I know the first blow was mine. I've carried the blame for what you've become. I'll never be able to apologize enough. But after Moses, you kept taking the Vessel, forcing me to kill my friends, brothers, the Light. I knew you were doing it to punish me. And I deserved it. I deserved every moment of anguish it caused me.

"But as much as I deserved your torment, the Vessels didn't.

And I prayed you would never find Shea because she's different, like he was. A part of me thought . . . if anyone could unite us like Moses, it would be her. Granted, she's not an eloquent speaker, but her spirit is like his was. I know you see it too.

"I've wanted to ask for centuries, but I couldn't risk the fate of the world on a theory. So here it is: you're still my brother, you don't like Caelius any more than we do, and you're not interested in destroying the Light. And this time, despite my feelings about her, you've fallen for Shea. When you talk about her, it's like how you used to talk about Nefertiti when we first met."

I let his wrist fall from my hand. The shallow hole in my ripped-out heart was mending. I could feel the fibers as they welded themselves back together. A dead black thing, but now I felt it as if it were whole again.

Care, concern, hope—they were strange things to feel for a beast I'd sworn to torment for all eternity. "If you thought I wouldn't kill Shea, why did you try to take her life?"

Again, his face filled with shame. "It was a risk. I could have been wrong. I could have been seeing things that I wanted to see in you, that I *needed* to see, to believe. I've been away from home, from the Light for so long, I worried that . . . I just wasn't sure. And I couldn't risk the death of this world for a theory. No matter how I felt about you, or her."

"I understand." It was a short response, but I couldn't hear any more. It was easier to despise him, to be callous, than to face the truth that all of this time, all of this wasted pain and misery, had been for nothing.

I looked at my empty hands. He was right. In all of our battles, no matter how much we tore into each other, he had never actually *killed* me. This whole time he'd been waiting for me, hoping I'd change.

"I don't want to believe that Ur-Nammu would turn on me. After Moses, he never interfered with another Vessel. He's Nefertiti's *father*, Aidan. I trust him as much as I trust my own left hand." I clenched my hollow palms into fists. "But you're right. He's the only one who knew where she was, and he's the only one who can Dream-Walk like Shea. He could have convinced her to come outside." I nodded to Aidan and he crossed his arms, resolute.

I scanned my memories, the look on Ur-Nammu's face as I'd held Nefertiti's cold body in my arms. "I just don't know why he would do this. He was my father's . . . my *real* father's best friend. They fought side by side in the Gutian wars with Egypt. My father knew I wasn't a fighter and sent me off to be a tradesman, but he kept Nefertiti by his side to fight. I asked her to come with me then, but she wouldn't. She was a warrior, as was he. That's why they were captured.

"When I saw them again, we were older. She'd already been forced to birth children for the Pharaoh as his concubine. I risked everything to free her, but I was a boy, not a vampire.

"I ended up enslaved alongside her father. He took care of me and found ways for me to see her. They were *family*. And she was . . . could I have been blind? I know he can't forgive me, the fact that my kiss took her life. But neither of us knew then that we couldn't turn women. After I turned him, *he* asked me to turn her. How could he take Shea, just to punish me for Nefertiti?"

Aidan took a long breath as he watched what must have been obvious pain pour over my features. "Can you track him,

Lucian? I've been trying since you left with Shea, following trails I thought were yours all over the world. He's better than I am at hiding her."

My eyes cleared as I shifted my focus from Nefertiti to Shea. "I'll need to feed. Don't worry, I'll feed on animals . . . and I have Gracuri who I can feed on, one last time. It won't take long. Stay here, and when I get back, we'll go *together*." I looked into his eyes. Yes, it was a test. If we were about to do what I'd planned, we had to trust each other without question.

He nodded slowly. "I'll wait here for you. No matter how long it takes—"

I was halfway across the world before he could finish his sentence. I fed on anything and everything that moved, except humans. My pile of dead bodies before I'd encountered Adnachiel still troubled me.

I'd become a killer, a monster, but I hadn't always been that way. Shea had brought me back to the boy who wasn't a warrior. I was a craftsman. I loved to build things with my hands. I knew all of that was outdated now but just the memory that I wasn't *this* was enough for me to despise all of the life I'd drank to kill my own pain and guilt.

Gracuri was more than willing to let me drink from him. His passion had doubled since our last encounter. I hated it. I hated seeing him so maddened with loyalty and desire. It would fade and normalize, and eventually he'd go back to his own nature and remember himself.

I cherished his nature. It was so unique and childish, despite his gladiator frame. It pained me seeing him like this. This wasn't the secret love Gracuri had always believed I couldn't see. This was complete and utter possession without refrain.

***

It didn't take long before I was on the beach next to Aidan again. I would have made him wait a hundred years to test his loyalty if not for Shea. For her, I couldn't stand to have him wait longer than what was needed for me to be at full strength.

Aidan eyed my mouth and I slowly wiped the warm blood from my lips. He spoke clearly. "Are you ready then? Let's track Ur-Nammu and get our Shea back."

I laughed candidly and grabbed his shoulder. "Now that we know Ur-Nammu has her, I know exactly where she is. He's taken her to Caelius, and if you want to get her back, you'll have to face my father with me. I'll die, but if you're willing to do this, you should know, you'll probably die too."

His mouth fell open as he stared at my resolute face.

I spoke slowly, needing him to digest my words. "You think that nothing can kill you, unless they kill Shea. Caelius *can* kill you. He's killed your kind before."

He swallowed hard. His eyes widened like a child's at Sunday school upon hearing that the devil was *real*.

I sighed. "But if he kills you, you're dead forever—no more being born again with the next Vessel. Your spirit doesn't go to the Light. I'm sure you remember your brother who was dragged to the pit with him: Ashliel?"

He coughed as if all the air had been sucked out of his lungs, his tan features turning as pale as my own skin. He nodded. "He sacrificed himself to make sure Herostel could complete the seal."

My brow raised. "You don't really believe that. You just don't want to look Darkness in its twisted face. Caelius *ate* your brother out of spite. He devoured him and keeps his bones framed on the cut stone behind him like a mantel—"

Before I could finish, Aidan was on his knees vomiting in the sand. He lurched, grabbing his gut and shaking his head violently. It was only then that I realized how much these beasts must mean to each other. Aidan and I had called ourselves brothers with Moses, and it'd always felt that way. Brothers not by birth, but by choice. But his *real* brothers, they'd probably circled the throne of heaven for—how long is eternity? A loss like that . . . no wonder he was loyal to them.

"I didn't say that to hurt you, Adnachiel. I just want you to be prepared. He will use any angle against you. He should be easier to face because he's still sealed, but if you're thrown off by seeing your brother's bones, he'll use that advantage in battle." I stared at his back as he rose, firm and resolute.

"Thank you for telling me, Lucian. I know it must be hard for you to stand against Caelius, to give up what has become your new family. I'm aware that if you do this and live, you'll be hunted by your own kind. I'm also aware that you're right: we both won't make it out of this alive. But one of us can save Shea."

His eyes were strong and fierce, the warrior inside hardening like stone. He nodded, and I did the same, wrapping up my own raw feelings and emotions. I filled myself with ash and flame. Fighting side by side, we would use every ounce of our powers, every trick, every ruthless and cunning tool we'd sharpened on

each other over the years on Caelius.
Together, we could save her.

CHAPTER 11
SHEA

Where was I?

My eyes opened to darkness and I couldn't make out any familiar shapes. For a second I thought I had woken up in my dorm and that everything had been one long dream.

But then Ur-Nammu's face came into sharp focus when he lit a small oil lamp.

We were in a cave. I could tell we were farther back from the entrance because there was only a small pinprick of light in the distance. I was about to make a run for it, knowing Ur-Nammu couldn't chase me in the sun, but his iron grip held me down.

"You'd be dead before you went five feet," he warned casually.

"You won't kill me. You need me alive," I answered back a little more brazenly than I had intended.

Ur-Nammu's eyebrow rose slightly. "I'll rephrase: you'd be unconscious before you went five feet."

That I believed.

Maybe I could use my powers. I tried to concentrate on the cave itself, the earth—make it move, make it crumble.

Nothing.

Maybe I was too scared.

I took deep, calming breaths.

Then I tried to connect to anything. Air. Water. Rock.

Anything!

Still nothing.

"Are you quite done?" Ur-Nammu asked.

How did he know what I was trying to do? But like a lame-ass, I nodded.

Why wasn't my power working? Sure, I was still a noob, but at this point I should have been able to shake a rock or something.

Then it hit me.

"I'm already unconscious, aren't I? You can't control me awake, so you're keeping me asleep." I knew I was right. It was the only thing that would explain my complete lack of power.

Ur-Nammu actually smiled. I'd impressed him. Good to know.

"Very good," Ur-Nammu responded. "I guess I can lighten up the scenery now that I don't have to deceive you."

With little more than a wave, the cave turned into a house with a wraparound porch surrounded by acres and acres of wheat fields. I was now sitting on a wooden bench swing with a glass of lemonade in my hand while Ur-Nammu sat across from me on an old-fashioned rocking chair. The house was quaint and right out of a Norman Rockwell painting. The breeze was soft and the sun was shining. If Ur-Nammu wasn't sitting across from me, I'd actually be relaxed and wishing I was there.

"This is what you Americans like, right?" Ur-Nammu's voice was flat, as if he didn't really care but wanted to placate me.

I suddenly didn't want to admit how nice it was. I didn't want to be "cliché girl." But I guess I was to a certain degree because sitting there on that porch with a cool glass of lemonade felt pretty darn good. Screw old vampire a-holes.

"I think most *humans* would appreciate this scenery, thank you very much. Not that you'd know, since you're stuck in the dark all the time." I sounded like a spoiled brat.

I could only imagine how I came across to an ancient vampire.

"Just drink your lemonade," Ur-Nammu replied dismissively.

I threw the lemonade in his face. "Why don't *you* drink it?"

To my surprise, Ur-Nammu laughed. Being a dream, the lemonade was gone in an instant, leaving him completely dry.

But he looked over at me and his eyes kept a bit of the amusement he'd felt at my outburst. "Would you like another?"

I couldn't help it. I reluctantly smiled back. "Yes, please."

Another lemonade was suddenly in my hand. I drank its cool deliciousness. Taking a deep breath, I realized fighting with Ur-Nammu would get me nowhere. The fact that I entertained him with my temper was something I could use to my advantage. He liked 'em feisty, I guessed.

I glanced down at the glass full of liquid. "Is this how you're keeping me asleep? Drugs or something?" For some reason it didn't freak me out as much as I thought it would, and the more information I had, the better off I'd be. Maybe I could find a way to wake up and get the heck back to Lucian.

Even thinking his name sent butterflies through my stomach.

He had been my first. And to be honest, the experience had

been mind-blowing. It was all that was keeping me sane at the moment. Feeling him against me, his mouth ravaging every inch of my body—I shuddered.

I didn't have much of a princess complex, but seeing as I was unconscious, I kind of hoped Lucian would swoop in and save me. It went against my feminist nature, but I'd always been a sucker for a good romantic rescue, so my two sides were fighting with each other.

And frankly, I could use all the help I could get.

Normally, Aidan was the first person I'd think of to protect me. Maybe he had come to his senses. I didn't want to hate him. I didn't want to lose him. I rubbed my belly where he had stabbed me. It wasn't really there, so I didn't feel much, but the wound was deeper than physical injury. Aidan might as well have stabbed my soul. It certainly felt the same.

Ur-Nammu broke me out of my reverie by answering my question. "No. I'm draining you to the point of unconsciousness."

"As in, my blood?" I asked in horror.

Ur-Nammu gave me a look that I could only describe as curious. "You're with Lucian. I'm sure he's fed from you before."

I stood up from the porch swing, smashing the lemonade on the ground. "No, he's never *fed* off me. Gross."

Ur-Nammu was taken aback. "Gross? What's *gross* about drinking life? It's more intimate than anything you can imagine."

The guy looked like he was going to orgasm in front of me.

I tried to hide my disgust, but I was pretty sure my expression was in a permanent grimace. "Do you even remember what it was like to be human?"

Ur-Nammu's face went still. "That time in my life is burned

into my memory forever."

"You know what? I don't think it's *burned* enough. If you really remembered being human, then feeding off people would revolt you. Infuriate you. Make you sick! Anything but *intimacy!*" I had a feeling I was projecting my own issues onto the vampire, but I couldn't fathom that he wouldn't remember that humans pretty much thought drinking blood was repulsive.

Ur-Nammu was silent for a moment. He was watching me closely. I couldn't tell what he was thinking. I felt stupid standing in front of him while he sat quietly in his rocking chair staring at me. It was like when a stand-up comedian told a joke that no one understood.

Awkward silence.

When he didn't respond, my anger faded. I plopped back down on the porch swing and made it rock with my foot. "Sorry," I apologized. "You've been a vampire a lot longer than you were human." I examined his face. "Although you are kind of old looking."

Ur-Nammu laughed again.

It was such a startling contrast to his silent stares I actually jumped back in my seat.

"You remind me of my daughter," Ur-Nammu suddenly admitted.

I sighed. At least he was talking. "What was she like?"

"She was the most beautiful creature in existence." Ur-Nammu's expression was far-off like he was reliving his past. "So much so, the Pharaoh stole her from me and made her his slave, though he called her his wife," he practically spat.

I suddenly remembered his conversation with Lucian.

"Nefertiti?"

Ur-Nammu's eyes went wide with surprise. "Did Lucian speak of her?"

"He said she was his first love." I couldn't tell if knowing that Ur-Nammu was Nefertiti's dad was good or bad for me. And another thing that was bugging me was the fact that Ur-Nammu said I reminded him of Nefertiti. Was that why Lucian liked me? Because I reminded him of Nefertiti? Kind of cool in a seriously geeky way, but also awful in a heart-crushingly insecure way.

"Never were there two people who belonged to each other more. Soul mates of the truest form. Lucian tried to turn her, but men can't turn females, and she died in his arms." Ur-Nammu was watching my every reaction. It must have been bad, because he smiled, savoring my pain. "Did you think *you* were Lucian's soul mate?" He laughed, but this time there was no humor in it. "You're just the Vessel. He's attracted to your Light, nothing more. Look how easily he let me take you. Lucian got what he wanted and let you go."

Ouch.

I thought I was going to puke.

Ur-Nammu was tapping into my worst fears: That Lucian had never really cared about me. That he only wanted me to save his evil father.

But I knew in my heart it wasn't true.

Lucian loved me.

The thought filled me with a surge of light.

It was true.

It was pure.

And no jealous father-in-law-turd-face was going to take it

away from me.

I gave Ur-Nammu the snarkiest expression I could when I said, "Is that supposed to upset me?" His face gave me what I needed: shock and anger. "The thing about love is, when you're in it, there are *no* doubts. None. So nothing you can say will convince me otherwise. Lucian is coming for me. That's a certainty. The question is: what do you think he's going to do to you when he finds us?"

Ur-Nammu showed a flash of fear, then he went back to his stoic demeanor. "We'll see."

"So are you taking me to Daddy, or what?" I crossed my arms, annoyed at the old-looking vampire.

"It's not just to free Caelius that I'm taking you to him." Ur-Nammu eyed me with his annoying observation-mode.

I tried to keep my lame poker face up, but I was curious. "So what else happens when the curse is broken?"

"All vampires will be able to walk in the light."

Whoa.

Lucian and I could be together in the daylight without fear of him turning into ash.

"Do I have to die?" I figured I'd ask.

Ur-Nammu's eyes met mine and there was almost affection there. "I don't know."

"It probably doesn't matter anyway." I stopped rocking the swing. "Aidan will try and kill me first. Either way, it looks like I'm dying. Maybe if I died for Caelius, at least Lucian could live a normal life." Ugh. I hated to be a Debbie Downer, but my chances weren't looking all that great. There was no way Aidan would let Caelius free, which meant he was probably tracking me . . . to kill me. And even if he didn't find me in time, Caelius would kill me anyway. My future wasn't looking too bright.

When I peered up at Ur-Nammu, he was staring again. I wasn't that tough of a nut to crack, seriously. The way he examined me was like I was an anomaly he'd never seen before.

His voice was soft when he asked, "You'd willingly die so Lucian could be what? Happy?"

"Yeah, so? What do you care anyway?" I had no patience for Ur-Nammu anymore. The fact that he was drinking my blood to keep me asleep made me want to strangle him. And if I was going to die, it might as well be for love.

But I wasn't ready to die yet. I fully planned on using whatever power I could muster to kick Caelius's butt.

"I'm bringing you to Caelius to make things right and restore the balance. It doesn't reflect my feelings," Ur-Nammu admitted cryptically.

"What's that supposed to mean?" I wanted to know any chinks in his armor.

"It means spending over three thousand years in the dark is a torture I can't explain. I find myself escaping by Dream-Walking for years at a time, just to feel the sunlight. When I saw that Lucian would never bring you to Caelius, the thought of waiting five hundred more years was unbearable. I'm sorry it has to be this way, but you were born for a purpose, and I'm allowing you to complete what you were destined for. I have others to think about as well. We all need the sun, and as long as Caelius is trapped in his cage, we will never be free." Ur-Nammu definitely believed what he was dishing.

"Gee, thanks." My voice was laced with sarcasm.

A thought hit me.

I was always in control when I Dream-Walked with Lucian.

Obviously, Ur-Nammu had about three thousand years of experience on me, but I was also the *Vessel*, so that had to come with some kind of power perks, didn't it? I was about to find out.

I closed my eyes and concentrated as hard as I could.

"What are you doing?" I heard Ur-Nammu's voice, but I didn't open my eyes.

It must've been working.

I focused on Lucian.

If I could just get him here in this space, he'd know where we were and then he could come for me.

"You can't break my protection spells. Stop trying." Ur-Nammu's voice was commanding, but there was a note of worry in there too.

I could hang on to that. If he was even slightly worried, it made me more confident that I might get a message out. I kept my concentration up, remembering our night together. The way Lucian had touched me. The way he'd kissed me. The way he'd looked at me.

"*Stop!*"

My eyes jolted open when Ur-Nammu shook me.

I was awake!

He was scared enough that I'd get a message through that he'd actually woken me up.

It wasn't what I'd intended to happen, but maybe this was even better.

Of course, that's when I realized I could barely move. I felt so weak that it was difficult to keep my eyes open. Blood loss.

Serious blood loss. I'd always wondered what that would feel like.

I was so sleepy I just wanted to drift back into dreamworld, but I had to stay alert.

What do you know? We *were* in a cave. That first vision he'd given me had actually been accurate. The sun was shining outside in the distant exit like before, but it was setting.

I needed to get to that light.

"You've created quite a conundrum. I can't let you sleep because you may get word to Lucian or the beast, but I can't let you be fully awake or you could use your powers against me. You leave me no choice," Ur-Nammu said as he leaned down, with his fangs out toward my neck.

No.

I couldn't let him drink any more of my blood. He needed me alive, so I knew I wouldn't die, but my instincts were to make him stop. His teeth sank into my neck, but it wasn't the sharp pain of breaking skin as it had been with Frank. I realized this was because Ur-Nammu had been drinking from the same spot the entire time he'd had me. He didn't need to puncture new wounds, there were premade straw holes.

Ew.

I thought about his fangs. His teeth. The violation I felt. I was exhausted, but my fury kept me awake.

There was pure wrath in my veins.

Ur-Nammu screamed and flew back against the rough cave wall. He was spitting up my blood like it was made of fire.

My fire.

I felt a surge of satisfaction. So much so, I wanted to rub it in his face. "My blood will be poison to you, and you will rot and die if you drink it."

Ur-Nammu's eyes were full of terror. He believed me.

That was the first successful bluff of my life. I was pretty proud of myself. Maybe it was true. I really didn't know the extent of my power, so it was possible I could make my blood kill him. I was the Vessel, after all, and made out of Light, whatever that meant. The plus side was Light killed vamps, so intensify the heat, and blood equals liquid sunlight.

Of course, I didn't know if I could repeat the trick. My anger had triggered it. But I needed to continue the bluff in order to get outside.

I stood up with every ounce of strength I had. I wanted to make it look like I wasn't weak, like I had full capacity of my body. It worked because Ur-Nammu stayed where he was.

Although his expression turned back to that of a hunter, which I didn't like, I kept my voice strong as I said, "You're going to let me leave right now." I tried not to show any fear.

Ur-Nammu stood up. He wasn't a tall man, but he was intimidating. "I don't have to drink from you to keep you weak. I can break your legs and Caelius would still have his sacrifice."

"I ripped a hole through Lucian's chest, so I'd be careful with threats if I were you." I was terrified, but I needed to convince him I was at full power. I really didn't want him to break my legs. Once I had broken my pinkie and cried for a week. I wasn't good with pain, especially my own.

Ur-Nammu smiled wickedly. "My daughter used to lie to me as well. She was better at it."

Okay.

Run.

I whirled around as fast as I could and ran for the pinpoint of light in the distance.

Snap!

Excruciating pain ripped through my body. He'd broken my right leg! I could see the jagged edge of bone piercing through my upper thigh. It was so surreal I froze in place. I didn't even scream, though my body was on fire. I was in such total shock that I was still standing.

Ur-Nammu's arms cradled me to keep me upright.

I snapped out of my stupor and felt the roaring pain as if a stick of dynamite had ripped open my leg.

I screamed.

Ur-Nammu whispered in my ear, "Give into the blackness. Let yourself pass out from the pain. I'll fix it when you sleep."

Rage.

Rage.

Rage.

I wanted to break every bone in Ur-Nammu's lame vampire body.

I wanted the pain to stop.

Stop! I screamed in my head.

Crunch!

The pain was gone.

I shrugged myself away from Ur-Nammu with ease. His face was full of astonishment and fear.

I looked down at my leg. No wound. No broken leg. Not even a scar. Just smooth skin and the remnants of blood from where the bone had shot through.

I'd fixed it.

I'd fixed my own freaking leg!

I wanted to celebrate, except I was still with the ancient vampire madman who'd broken it in the first place.

"What else you got?" I taunted.

I felt like a true badass.

My nature wasn't to hurt anyone, not even Crazy-Pants in front of me, but I would if I had to. Or I'd try to anyway. I backed away from him, heading steadily toward the cave entrance.

Ur-Nammu didn't move. He watched.

I could see he wasn't exactly scared, but he wasn't sure how to proceed either.

Just a few more feet and I could run into the safe sunlight.

When I was positive I should be at the exit, I turned around to make sure I had gone the right way.

I had gone the right way, all right.

It was simply that the sun had gone down.

I was screwed.

Before I could think, Ur-Nammu's teeth dug into my neck.

Damn it.

Everything went black.

***

The next thing I knew, I was waking up again. I hadn't had any dreams. It felt instantaneous. One moment I was being bitten by Ur-Nammu, the next I was in some kind of chamber. I was definitely underground. The walls, ceiling, and floor were all stalagmites and stalactites, rough stone and dirt. I couldn't see any exits.

I could barely see anything it was so dark.

"Is this better?" a voice sounded in the blackness.

The cavern began to glow a dull blue.

It was huge.

Five football fields huge.

I skittered back when I saw the bones of a giant winged beast sitting in front of me. It filled the whole back of the cave, its wingspan too big to see. It looked like a dragon. A dragon! My mind couldn't seem to accept that as reality. It had barely accepted my current life as reality, but dragon bones? Serious overload.

The remains had been so distracting I hadn't noticed the man standing in front of me.

Caelius.

I knew it instantly.

I had expected to see pure evil incarnate, something like a black piece of coal with hands and legs like in the vision I'd had when Lucian had visited him. But Caelius was stunning. He had an ageless quality to him. If I saw him on the street, I'd think he was in his late twenties, but his eyes were prehistoric.

It was like when I first met Lucian, but about a million times more powerful. And speaking of those eyes. I thought Lucian's turquoise eyes were unique, but Caelius's were auburn. Was having crazy-colored eyes a prerequisite for turning?

I stood up and tried to appear more confident than I felt.

"Where's Ur-Nammu?" I wondered aloud. Had he just left me with the father of all vampires?

"He's standing right there." Caelius smiled with his pearly white fangs showing.

I turned my head to see him about ten feet behind me. His

face was stoic.

"Hey." I nodded in what I could only describe as a friendly manner. I had no idea why, but for some reason Ur-Nammu felt like dealing with a puppy compared to Caelius. I almost wanted to run up to him and beg him to protect me, but since he was the one who'd brought me here, I was pretty sure he'd veto that.

"You are an interesting girl." Caelius brought my attention back to him.

"Thanks?" I wasn't sure how to respond to that.

It was kind of annoying how all these ancient beings were somehow *fascinated* by me, like I was some kind of revolutionary science experiment.

I suddenly noticed that I was outside of Caelius's prison cell. The wall was invisible straight on, but I could see it out of the corner of my eye like a hologram. There were all kinds of symbols around it as well, which I could only assume were the seals that kept him in.

I was grateful that I wasn't inside with the monster, but it also made me wonder why Ur-Nammu hadn't delivered me straight to Caelius's feet. Why carry me thousands of miles only to drop me off five feet short of the intended target? I decided not to bring it up. I didn't want to give Ur-Nammu any ideas. Maybe I could escape as long as I stayed outside the angel barrier.

Caelius's face was amused, as if talking to me was like talking to a chimpanzee. He definitely thought I was beneath him. "You're the first female Vessel. Did you know that?"

"Um, cool?" I felt extremely weird having a conversation with the evilest of evil. It was so . . . *normal.*

"Females carry life, and you carry mine, Shea Harper. When

I feed off your soul, I will be made whole, and I will finally be free of this prison. You should consider yourself honored to be such a sacrifice." He had an air of arrogance that made me want to kick him. I didn't like the word "sacrifice" either. I really didn't want to die so this freak could wreak havoc on the planet. I had to come up with some sort of plan.

"Yeah, not so much honored as repulsed. You're kind of an a-hole," I said before I could think better of it.

I hated smugness more than anything, and Caelius had it in spades.

He was silent for a moment. When he spoke, his words were icy. "How could *my* Lucian love a vile thing like you?"

Thanks for confirming that Lucian loves me.

It was as if a huge weight had been lifted from my chest. If Caelius was upset that Lucian loved me, then I knew it was true. Not that I hadn't known it before, but hearing it from the father of all evil made it more real.

Caelius apparently didn't like the expression on my face, which was something akin to dreamy. "Your insecurities make you weak and pathetic. You are a flawed, unworthy Vessel."

"Sticks and stones, dude." Okay, "dude" was a little Valley girl, but the more casual and non-caring I was, the angrier Caelius became. Not that I should've been trying to provoke the most powerful vampire on Earth, but I really hated him.

Caelius threw his hand out and an invisible vise clasped around my neck. I choked instantly, clawing at my throat, trying to breathe.

He laughed at my terror. "Lucian loved only one woman in his lifetime. *One!* And for over three thousand years he pined over his loss. It made it *pure*. *True*. Then *you* come along and he falls in love with another! You ruined the perfect love story. You defiled it. I will enjoy killing you. I'll savor every drop of life from your body!"

"You'll have to kill *me* first."

Through sputtering coughs, I turned my head to see Lucian snarling at his father like an enraged lion. My eyes smiled at him even though my face couldn't. I told him through my thoughts, *I love you, Lucian.*

With a loud thud, Aidan dropped down next to him.

His expression said it all.

He was my Aidan.

He was sorry.

They were there to save me.

I blacked out.

CHAPTER 12
LUCIAN

Caelius dropped Shea to the ground like used newspaper. Her body thudded, and my heart with it. Even after my thoughtless trust of Ur-Nammu had dragged her here, she still loved me.

Everything inside ached and burned for her. Caelius smiled, reading my body language. "So it's true. You love this Shea Harper—*disgusting*. I had such plans for you, for us. I had my Adam and Eve. We would have ruled the world together . . . you were my chosen."

His jaw clenched as he took a casual step to the edge of his cage. "You are *still* my chosen. Once I release us into the daylight, I'll reveal everything to you—the plan, your place by my side. You'll have *real* love. And everything you've wanted. The only thing in our way is the Vessel. I had Ur-Nammu bring her just to the outside of my prison so you, my son, could deliver her to my arms. That's how much I trust you.

"She's the Vessel, so she'll slide right through the barrier.

Watch as I break the seal, and this world will be ours, my Lucian."

His hand stretched out as his shadow caressed my frame.

Aidan growled.

I was glad to have him by my side. "You know I can't let you have her, Caelius."

I lunged while he was still wrapped up in the pleasure of his fondness for a future I couldn't allow. I threw her body to Aidan. He instantly raced toward the opening.

A black and beastly shadow, one that had ravaged me for years, burst out of Caelius's chest as he screamed in fury.

It moved toward Aidan. Everything slowed. I couldn't let this happen. If I could keep Caelius back, Aidan could escape with Shea. He could hide her and keep her safe.

They could live.

The only thing it would take was my life, which meant nothing without her.

I sank my hands into the earth. A spark ignited inside me as Gutian words filled my lips, chants my father and Ur-Nammu had prayed to the gods before battle. It enlivened my blood with the heritage of a powerful people. I pushed my palms in deeper and called upon every ounce of ability I had. And then I called on the Darkness. The black itself.

I couldn't breathe. I felt a hole ripping in my mind, like a tear in space. My body shrunk and I fell inside. I watched as a puppet master—a shadow boiling red, filled with ash and smoke—rose from my body. My actual limbs remained still and frozen, but my soul was attached to the monster. My thoughts were its thoughts.

I grew its shape then surged toward Caelius's shadow just before he ripped out one of Aidan's wings.

Aidan shrieked in agony as the bone tore the skin down his back, but kept moving.

Caelius stood there, the true beast that lived inside him, staring at my own creation in *pleasure*.

He laughed.

The sound moved through the shadow in bursts and waves. He looked back at our frozen bodies, so small and insignificant now on the vast cave floor beneath us.

His words were thoughts and they penetrated mine. "So, my child, you've finally given in to the Darkness. Now it has your soul . . . now you are truly mine. Even if I release you, your shadow form will *always* belong to me."

I hissed, reedifying my words, keeping his control and the Darkness from overpowering me. "I am merely using the emptiness. I am not one with it. But I would give myself over to oblivion and worse for her. As my real father would say to me on the eve before battle: ours is a proud people."

I shoved my shadow talons through his chest and ripped as his form shifted around mine. "We are many, but united we beat with one heart."

No matter how I tore, he kept shifting. I couldn't fix my shadows around him, but our dance was blocking Shea well enough. He'd stretch and grab Adnachiel, dragging him back here and there, but Aidan was quick and making ground with Shea in his arms.

I shifted my form, absorbing rock and dirt, anything that his shadow couldn't seep through.

Now Caelius's anger boiled. His form grew ten times the size of mine. I'd never seen it so large. I felt myself being pulled into it.

I added more stalagmites and anything else I could consume. I kept my mind focused on my true father's words: "Though we may fall, we will never fail because we have given ourselves over to glory. To fight for those we love."

That was it. I knew what to do. It was simple, but the worst thing I could have imagined. I had to let go, to get sucked into him. This wasn't going to be like when he'd taken my body before. There was no coming back from this. I pushed the shadow of my spirit *into* his.

At first he howled as I burned his insides right through to the edges, then he squealed with delight as he began breaking apart my soul. Thoughts, memories, they all became fragmented. Feelings, cares, anything that I thought was mine was gone.

I couldn't remember the last words of my father's code. They were *important*. What I was doing was important. It was for someone, but for whom? What was I?

Nothing.

Everything slipped, and I began dissolving into him like paper into water.

Then something whispered. It was a hook, pulling me out.

"Ours is a proud people. We are many, but united we beat with one heart. Though we fall, we will never fail because we have given ourselves over to glory. To fight for those we love. Though our bones may brittle with time. Life may wear and kill the tenderness of affection, but the burning heart, the flame that is our people and what we stand for, cannot be stamped out of time. We are etched into the very existence of all things. We are, and forever will be, a people who fight for what we love. And love is the soul of all that's worth fighting for."

It was spoken in my own tongue, in Gutian. The words burst me through Caelius' shadow, forcing us both back into our small vampire frames. I stared into the wet eyes of Ur-Nammu as he held my flimsy limbs. He'd been whispering into my ear, bringing me back.

Tears welled in my own eyes upon seeing his face. "Why did you betray me? Why did you bring Shea here?"

He shook his head, replacing his vulnerable stare with a hardened mask as he stood me back on my feet. "I have my reasons. Believe it or not, I'm still fighting for the ones I love. Your father's words will never be forgotten by our people. We created that chant together as boys, and when we ruled side by side, we wore it like a code of honor."

Caelius coughed and our eyes found his, burning red like phosphorescent blood. "Am I interrupting this moment by wanting to get the *Vessel*?"

I was flung to the other side of the cavern wall, the impact crushing every bone in my body. I'd never actually walked that far in all my thousands of years. As I clawed my chest, trying to quickly shove my rib cage back into place, I saw the tip of the beast's outstretched wing. I hadn't realized how long it was. Aidan's brothers were a thousand times his mortal size.

I coughed blood. With all the speed I could force out of my soggy flesh, I propelled myself forward, only to find the worst. In that small moment, one fraction of a second out of Caelius's sight, he had dragged Aidan all the way back. He was pinned next to Shea's unconscious body on the dirt just outside the glyphs of Caelius's cage.

Before I could move, Caelius shoved me down next to Aidan.

Adnachiel's lips trembled as he spoke. "I was halfway across Egypt! I didn't think—I'm sorry. I wasn't fast enough." Blood spilled out of his mouth, matching mine. He was ravaged. I had no doubt that he'd fought harder and fiercer than he had when I'd faced him, but still, he was torn open, with only one wing left that hadn't been ripped from its socket.

Caelius laughed.

He slowly raised my body and Aidan's so that we could see him. He tilted Aidan's chin up toward the mounted skeleton of his beast brother, and mine toward Ur-Nammu, who was held up next to it, unconscious.

Caelius eyed Aidan's horrified face. "Do these bones look familiar to you, boy? I must say, I've eaten life for a long time, but nothing was as delicious, as *supple* as the heavenly skin of your brother, Ashliel."

Aidan tried not to respond as his eyes took in the full view of every meat-stripped bone. He gave into grief and unwillingly released a bestial howl that shook the cavern's foundations.

This pleased Caelius to no end. "You know," he continued, "I've taken Lucian in every way I've been able to imagine over the past centuries. It helps kill the time. But most of those methods I developed and refined by working on *your brother's* soft flesh.

"Oh, how he screamed and begged, pleaded for death. 'Mercy, Caelius,' he would cry. And he would call out for you, by name. For all of you, actually, hoping that you'd hear him, that you'd come and save him . . . his loyal brothers. But you didn't! You abandoned him to the Darkness! All too afraid to come down here and see for yourself what was becoming of his limbs.

He was still alive as I devoured each one.

"I guess there's no loyalty among dogs. You left him here, knowing full well what I'd do, didn't you, Adnachiel?"

Horror.

Sheer horror filled Aidan's eyes as he stared, fully taking in Caelius's words and the skeleton of his beloved brother.

He stared at the holes where his eyes must have been and gasped the words, "I'm sorry," before he began weeping in sobs, his broad chest shrinking in convulsions as he cried, speaking in an inaudible tongue that only his kind could understand.

I finally shouted, hoping to draw his attention away from Aidan. "Caelius, stop!"

He bared his fangs and spoke through clenched teeth, his grip re-collapsing my rib cage as I coughed blood in agony. "That's *Father* to you! Is it so hard to say? Watch . . ."

Caelius used his shadow form to pick up Shea's motionless body. He moved her lips like a puppet, forcing them to say "father."

Aidan's eyes shifted to mine, full of fear. I shook my head, then whispered, "He can't pull her in himself. Someone has to toss her in there. We still have time."

Aidan tried to rein himself in.

Caelius's grip tightened as he dropped her and pulled me inches from his face. "Time? What is this time that you have? I *am* time. I am the void. I am *everything*. When will you acknowledge that truth?"

His lips twitched as he spoke. He pulled Ur-Nammu's unconscious body next to mine and snapped his fingers. Ur-Nammu gasped, his eyes flying open. Caelius smiled. "Did you enjoy that little rest? Remember what I told you before. That nightmare is just a fraction of what I'll do to everything you love if you disobey me again."

Ur-Nammu didn't respond. He hardened, wearing the mask of a warrior. Caelius took a deep breath and sat down. "Now that you've been punished, I will allow you to speak. Just what do you think you were accomplishing, stopping me from devouring my Lucian?"

Caelius freed him from his hold. Ur-Nammu stuttered, gathering his strength as he forced his frame to stand tall and upright. "He would have died. I was saving him, Grandfather. He was like a son to me before we were turned, so . . . I . . ."

I could see the gears in his mind shifting, always the strategist. "I could only imagine, if that's how I felt, a lowly worm, how you would feel if, in your rage, you had accidentally killed him. I know how you adore him. You would have regretted it for all of time. He is, after all, the Adam to your Eve, isn't he? You have a plan that you've been waiting to exact for thousands of years. I merely wanted to honor that plan. I am, and forever will be, your loyal servant." He bowed.

I bit my tongue. I didn't want to believe it. When he'd pulled me out, I'd seen in him the same look my Gutian father had worn when he'd said his last goodbye. There was the code . . . there was love there. Loyalty. Trust.

Caelius sighed, his eyes shining with a mischievous look. "Ah. And after all, I do have claim to something very important to you. I suppose that's factoring into your whimpering now. But all in all, you're right. There is no replacing Lucian. I want my story, and I want it perfect. This world will begin again with me as ruler. I have my Adam and Eve. I can break him. I've done it before. He'll be who I need him to be . . . and when he's not, I'll enjoy the process of convincing him.

"You are right, Ur-Nammu, there's nothing for me in daylight without my boy. Oh, and if you cross me like that again, that nightmare I spoke of will be nothing in comparison to the real thing."

Caelius motioned his head. "If Lucian won't throw the Vessel in, then you must do it." Ur-Nammu stepped toward Shea.

I rallied, and so did Aidan, but to no avail. Our bodies, inside and out, were hemorrhaging. He was too powerful for us.

I did the only thing left that I could do, which broke the last part of my dignity, something I'd managed to keep alive all these years. "Please."

The room fell silent. I'd never uttered the words after my mother, Anna-Steen, had died. Even when I was being beaten to death in Egypt, I'd never begged. I'd never said please.

Caelius leaned toward me, enthralled. "What was that?"

I didn't meet his gaze. I focused on Ur-Nammu alone. "I'm sorry, Ur-Nammu. I'm sorry for turning you and bringing you into this horrible existence where you've been enslaved by a creature more powerful than we can stand. I'm sorry that, in my ignorance and youth, I killed Nefertiti . . . my morning star. I'm sorry that I am who I am. I'm sorry that, on the eve of battle, my father sent me to be a tradesman with the Elamites because I was no warrior, but a sculptor and a poet. I should have trained. I should have been the warrior that you, he, and Nefertiti deserved, maybe if I had—"

Ur-Nammu turned, his eyes again soft. "Stop, Lucian. Your

father knew what you were and loved you for it. In our chant, you're the heart he died to keep alive. It was my failing. He kept you safe. And when I saw you trading in Egypt, I was a slave. I had failed to protect Nefertiti. I should have sent her away with you . . ."

I gurgled as blood moved through my punctured organs. "No, Ur-Nammu. She refused. And if you could turn back time, there are no words you could say to make her listen. She was always more of a warrior than any of us. She was strong, beautiful . . ."

He stepped toward me as Caelius's eyes and smile widened, as if we were performing some Greek tragedy for him. "I should have given her the medicine you'd created to make her sleep, Lucian. You'd wanted to escape with her then. I should have listened."

I sighed. He was wrong. "I've always hated myself for surviving, and she would have hated us both, Ur-Nammu. Had she awoken next to me, her people slaughtered and the remnants enslaved . . . she would have fought to get you back and been *killed*."

The air around him was silent, cold, as if he'd seen something I had not. "That might have been better. Instead she fought by my side, and we were all enslaved, but hers was the worst. The Pharaoh took her as a wife. She bore *him* children. He allowed her to see me in the slums. She brought me water as I worked in the mud on the statues of his likeness.

"I should have never reached out to you. You were a slave in Egypt because of me—because of what you felt for her. I betrayed your father's memory and risked your safety for hers. And now she . . ."

Tears ran down my eyes as I pleaded, "She's *gone*. But Shea is *alive*. I can't take back our past. I can't forgive myself for Nefertiti, but this isn't going to bring her back. Serving Caelius will only cause more pain and chaos.

"Whether I love Shea or not, she doesn't deserve to die at the hands of this monster! This planet isn't perfect, but it shouldn't have to suffer for *our* mistakes. Please, Ur-Nammu. If you've ever cared for me or my father, the code of our people, please protect her."

Ur-Nammu stepped back, then took a deep breath. Quickly he picked up Shea's body and threw it into Caelius' cage.

My jaw dropped in shock.

Ur-Nammu's eyes didn't meet mine as he said, "I *am* protecting our code by doing this. I am and will forever fight for the ones I love."

Caelius laughed as he held Shea's slumped body. He laughed and laughed, tears finally rolling from his eyes as he gasped for breath. "Lucian, you really thought *Ur-Nammu* would save her? You're so blind. And you begged! I never thought I'd see it!" He paused, the cavern falling silent. "Why not try your luck again?" His eyes were more terrifying than when he'd been a bestial shadow made of Darkness. "Go ahead, Lucian. Beg for her life."

I clenched my teeth, my insides shaking. It was too late. He had her. Aidan managed to get his arm free, Caelius's attention being solely focused on my agony.

He grabbed my wrist so tight his fingertips were clenching together. "*Don't*, Lucian. He's going to take her right now, no matter what you say. Don't give him the satisfaction."

Caelius scowled. "Oh, look at this. The two buddies back

together. I'm guessing you've resolved the whole Moses issue. Well, good for you. Lucian may have distracted me from explaining the heights of your brother's torture, but I haven't forgotten about you, Adnachiel.

"In fact, after I drink this whore dry, I'll show you firsthand what he experienced. I'll show you both, at the same time. You can bond in that as well. Although, you I'll kill and frame next to your brother. Lucian, however, is mine to keep and play with for *all of time*. He's like no other."

His eyes warmed as they traced over my haggard frame. Aidan growled and I bared my fangs. Caelius just shrugged as he moved the hair from Shea's neck. "I really would like to hear you beg, Lucian. How about this: if you beg, I'll start sucking her blood and breaking the seal."

Aidan scoffed. "That's what you're going to do anyway!"

Caelius shook his head. "Oh, you haven't been here long. But Lucian knows better. Drinking from her can be the *last* thing I do. My real flesh and bones haven't felt something alive and warm like this for a very long time. I've had to take pleasure in my shadow form, but with her body, there's so much I can do like this. I think I might just start—"

"Please, Caelius, just drink her."

The words came out, but not from my mouth. Ur-Nammu stood by my side, pleading so I wouldn't have to.

Caelius scoffed as he tossed Ur-Nammu's body carelessly into the black depths of the cave. "He'll wake up somewhere in Egypt. He's served his purpose and doesn't need to be here for the rest of this, not when there's so much fun to be had. A girl, a vampire, and a dog . . . all here for my pleasure."

He slid his hand along Shea's body, cutting a small gash down her side as he tore her shirt off.

Seeing him on top of her—

"Please." My voice cracked. My love for her meant more to me than all the pride I'd saved over three thousand years. Now, I finally understood my Gutian code of honor.

I continued, unashamed. "Whatever you want from me, I'll give it to you, just don't hurt her!"

He stopped, his face unamused. "You need to do better than that, *Son*. I've done things to you, unimaginable things, and never once did you do me the honor of begging me to stop. I've never heard the word 'please' uttered from your lips until tonight. Not once.

"Even when you were a mere mortal, hanging on to your last gasps of life as I pleasured myself, you didn't beg. This dog creature from heaven mounted behind me begged daily! Hourly! And I have done no worse to you! And *for her*! For her you beg to the likes of *Ur-Nammu*!"

I stuttered, my mind blank, flatlining in fear. This couldn't happen.

He took off his shirt and pressed his naked chest against hers, eyeing me with satisfaction as he rested his hips onto her frame. He ground his pelvis on top of her jeans as he grabbed her breast.

"Please, just drink her!" Aidan begged. "You miss your freedom, don't you? Why wait? Just end it!"

I stared at Aidan as his lips trembled with every breath. His face was ghost pale. He was as afraid as I was. Our love for her was that strong.

Caelius released his force over our bodies. We fell like puddles to the floor, both coughing and trying to unsnap the bones that were protruding out of our skin in every direction.

He licked the side of her face and feigned unzipping his pants.

Aidan and I shouted in unison, "No!"

He stopped for a moment, boyishly resting his body halfway on hers. "I want something that you two just aren't giving me. Let's make it sweet." He licked the space between her breasts as he peered back up into our desperate eyes. "Both of you are free from my hold. You can leave *now*. You won't get another opportunity like this.

"Adnachiel benefits because I don't kill and torture him in unfathomable, pleasurable, decadent ways. Lucian, you benefit because you don't get to sit and watch me suck the life from something you love more than yourself. Of course, I'll still have to break you once I'm out."

He looked at our hardened jaws and goaded, "However, if you both stay, bow and plead over and over into the dirt, calling yourself worthless worms, speaking my glory, and begging for me to drink her, then I will do just that. I'll start drinking until her body is lifeless. She won't experience any pain at the cost of my pleasure.

"Again, Adnachiel, you have much to gain by leaving, and more to lose by staying. If you stay, you'll be forsaking the Light by *praising* the Darkness. But you will save the Vessel from horrible things. And then I will *ravage* you.

"Lucian, it will be agony watching her die, and in all the years I've stripped you bare, you've never begged. I will require you to beg in the most *demeaning* way now. I'll want to hear it, loud and true from the both of you, or . . ." He again began grinding on Shea's motionless body. Though she was clothed from the waist down, it was still gruesome to watch. The pressure of his hips caused her to involuntarily gasp for breath as he moaned with delight.

Instantly there were two thuds: Aidan's body and mine kneeling to the ground. Caelius stopped as we both began pleading, loud and shamelessly in every tongue we could speak. He smiled, breathing in deep the torture his request had caused, ripping proud men apart from the inside by using what they loved the most. He smelled the soft spot between her jawbone and then sank his teeth deep into her neck.

Chapter 13
Shea

Um. Ew.

I woke up *half-naked* with Caelius crunching into my neck.

I knew I should be terrified, but I was seriously repulsed.

He hadn't . . . ?

I did a quick mental check of my girl parts and thank God, the douche bag hadn't sank that low.

It pissed me off.

I concentrated as hard as I possibly could, focusing on my blood, turning it to liquefied sunshine like I had done with Ur-Nammu.

Caelius coughed and stumbled back a few feet, clawing at his neck.

"Choke on that, asshat." I couldn't resist.

I grabbed what was left of my clothes and put them on. It covered what needed to be covered, but I still felt vulnerable.

I turned at the sound of pounding on a window. In front of

me were Lucian and Aidan trying to claw their way through the invisible barrier that kept Caelius inside his prison.

I ran to them, but I couldn't touch them.

I was stuck inside the mystical jail.

The two of them looked like broken puppies, their eyes full of terror and concern.

Aidan spoke first. "Shea, you have to use your powers to get out of there! He can't use you if you're outside the barrier!"

I nodded worriedly. "Okay, let me concentrate."

Lucian's voice cracked as he placed his hand flat on the invisible wall. "Shea, I tried to save you, but he was too strong. I love you."

I placed my hand over his, though they didn't touch. "I love you too." Then I smiled. "And I can save myself." I nodded toward the sputtering Caelius. "See?"

Aidan cracked a very small smile, but it was Lucian who spoke. "It won't last. Get out of there."

"Right," I said and closed my eyes.

I thought about the wall and turning it to water. It was the only thing I could think of in that moment of insane distress.

That's when I felt it.

Like black ice seeping into my back.

I could barely hear Lucian and Aidan screaming at me as Caelius's shadow entered my body.

Caelius spoke to them, his voice full of what I could only describe as merriment. "You both begged me to drink, so I drank." He laughed. "Blood doesn't break this curse—it's just tasty. You humiliated yourselves for nothing." He was quite amused.

I tried to push out the Darkness growing inside of me. I

thought only of the Light and how it could defeat Caelius. His shadow was cold and instantly made my body shake, but still the Light grew bigger. I could do this.

Then I felt Caelius's mouth against my ear. "That's it. The more Light you generate, the sooner I can free myself."

"Caelius!" Lucian screamed. "What are you doing?" His face was wracked with panic.

Caelius turned to Lucian, furious. "Her blood is ecstasy, I'll give you that, when she's not tainting it with Heaven. But my prison was created by the beasts of the Light, and only the Light can break it." He licked the side of my cheek. "I need her *soul* to restore me. You should remember this, boy. You unknowingly tapped into the Vessel's soul in Pompeii."

Caelius's shadow pierced my heart. I could feel it wrap around my very being, like a boa constricting the life out of its prey.

I reached my hand out for Lucian and Aidan, but they were stuck on the other side of the prison.

Caelius had me.

He was killing me.

By devouring my soul.

Thump!

Thump!

Thump!

The ground shook as three giant men landed on the ground next to me. They were well over ten feet tall and all muscle. But as my consciousness started to drift off from Caelius's attack, I saw a flash of their true forms, beasts with wings the size of the bones in front of me. They weren't dragons; they were a mishmash of every animal imaginable all rolled up into one terrifying foe.

With the blink of an eye, they were in human form again. My mortal mind apparently couldn't comprehend what they really looked like. But even as giant human beings, they were horrifying.

Aidan's brothers were here.

The protectors of the Light.

I just hoped they didn't try and kill me first, as Aidan's original plan had been.

I had to be on my toes as much as Caelius at this point.

Caelius pulled back from me with a grin.

I wasn't happy in this situation, but Aidan's brothers evidently amused him.

"So the beasts have arrived. Sabrael, Harahel, and Gavreel, oh how I've missed you. Have you come to visit dear old Ashliel? You only had a few thousand years to save him," he laughed. "Or are you here for your baby brother, Adnachiel? He's doing a bang-up job keeping the Vessel from me."

"Adnachiel may have failed at his duty, but we will not," the one called Gavreel said.

"I'll devour you three quickly, unlike Ashliel," Caelius boasted.

Was he *that* powerful?

Everyone in the room was about to find out.

Gavreel seemed to be their leader, as he was the first to strike.

Whack!

Caelius smashed into the invisible barrier like a rag doll.

That was my cue to get the heck out of the way.

If they meant Aidan had *failed* by not killing me, then they were *definitely* going to kill me.

Probably now-ish.

I need to get the ef out of there.

The angel named Sabrael whirled on me before I could move. His hand was the size of half my body as he wrapped his fingers around my waist. "Go to Adnachiel. He will protect you." His voice sounded like music as he lightly pushed me through the barrier and into Aidan.

Oh how I missed those arms.

I felt him kissing the top of my head and all my anger and worry and horror at what he had done to me vanished. I hugged him back fiercely, trying to drown out the epic battle now commencing behind us.

"Shea," Lucian's voice called out to me.

Aidan gently pulled away and let me fall into Lucian. Being with the two of them made me feel like we were going to survive this. I was with my love and my best friend. Nothing could stop us.

Except maybe the full-on supernatural battle exploding in front of our faces.

Aidan's eyes met Lucian's. "Get her out of here. I have to help my brothers fight."

Lucian nodded and took my hand, but I stopped him. "We can't leave Aidan to fight that *thing*."

Aidan looked at me pleadingly. "Please, Shea. Go with Lucian. I need to know that you're safe."

"Safe? Are you high? If you and your brothers lose, then Caelius is going to send every one of his minions to come after me again and again until the end of my days!" I said furiously.

"End of your days?" Aidan grinned.

I grinned back. Even in the mayhem of the epic battle taking place around us, Aidan still had to tease me. We'd grown up together. We had spent almost every moment of our lives together. He knew me better than anyone on the planet, and he still knew how to make me smile.

"Yes, the end of my days. Dork."

"Adnachiel!" Harahel called out.

Aidan was a warrior through and through. He turned to his brother. "I can't get past the barrier!"

Harahel reached his giant hand out and pulled Aidan through with ease. Aidan was a big guy, but he looked like a boy compared to his brothers.

Caelius was using the bones of Ashliel as a weapon against Sabrael and Gavreel, who had him pinned against the invisible barrier. Caelius stabbed Sabrael in the chest with a shard of bone. Sabrael yanked it out and stabbed it into Caelius's throat.

Caelius sputtered up blood and pulled the bone out just as easily as Sabrael had.

Trying to kill immortal beings was going to be harder than it looked.

Maybe Caelius couldn't be killed.

Maybe that was why they'd trapped him here in the first place.

Aidan, being roughly the same size as Caelius, ran at him full force. He looked like a linebacker taking down his opponent. It caught Caelius by surprise, so he wasn't able to protect himself. The two tumbled onto the ground, slashing and clawing at each other.

"I have to do something," I announced.

My heart jumped into my throat when Caelius pinned Aidan down. He was smaller and weaker than his brothers.

He was going to die.

"Shea, we have to go. Aidan wants you safe. Don't make his sacrifice for nothing," Lucian pleaded.

I looked into Lucian's turquoise eyes and saw nothing but worry there. "I'm not *sacrificing* him. That's not who I am."

Lucian held me back before I could pass through the invisible wall. "No, Shea. We have to go now."

Aidan cried out in pain as Caelius smashed his ribs with his hands.

I pulled free from Lucian, ran for the barrier, and passed through.

Lucian pounded his fists on the prison wall in fury. "I have to protect you! Let me in!"

"I don't know how."

"Just concentrate on my body! You passed through on instinct! You should be powerful enough to bring me in too!"

His unwavering confidence gave me the boost I needed. I thought of the barrier being made of liquid again. With a slight tug, Lucian was stuck half-in, half-out. I focused all my energy on getting him through to the other side. Within seconds, he stumbled inside the prison unscathed.

I had to get to Aidan.

His brothers couldn't pry him loose from Caelius's grasp.

Lucian's face was fierce. "Stay here and use what power you can." He leaned down and kissed me briefly. When he pulled away, I nodded.

Aidan's face was beet red from Caelius's grasp.

I shot out my hand and Caelius screamed in pain as I used wind to make his arm snap. He released his hold on Aidan.

Lucian bared his fangs and joined the beatdown of Caelius.

Not knowing which side Lucian was on, Gavreel shoved him aside like he was a blade of grass.

Aidan screamed at Gavreel, "He's on our side, Brother!"

Lucian held his hand out as if he was going to summon some kind of power.

Caelius laughed. "Your powers don't work inside this prison. Mine are limited and you are a dilution of me!"

Lucian recovered quickly. With lightning speed he wrapped his arm around Caelius's neck from behind and squeezed.

Caelius choked in pain and what looked like a little bit of pleasure. It was enough of a distraction for Harahel to rip off Caelius's legs and throw them clear across the prison.

It was gruesome.

But like a bad Frankenstein movie, Caelius's legs flew back to him and attached themselves instantly.

Caelius threw Lucian off with ease.

How on earth were they going to kill him? It seemed like a hopeless cause, and Caelius appeared to be enjoying the whole ordeal even though he was grossly outnumbered. I knew then that Caelius had been raring for a fight for quite some time. His visits with Lucian must have been few and far between.

Caelius was just bored.

I didn't blame him. I'd be batshit-crazy if I had to stay in a prison for thousands of years. And being that he was a creature of violence, this fight was like throwing him into the briar patch.

Home.

I was about to make his life suck.

I could feel my powers flow through me like a living being. The one thing Caelius had done when he'd tried to chow down on my soul was tune me into what made me tick. I knew I was something more than human, which was hard to wrap my head around. A few months ago, I'd been excited to get my dorm room. Now I was standing in an underground cavern watching angels fight with Darkness itself. To say my life had changed was a serious understatement.

But it had.

And I had power.

I closed my eyes and thought of daylight hitting Caelius's skin. I pictured the strength of the sun heating his skin, boiling his flesh like fire.

Caelius screamed in anguish.

I opened my eyes. His body was covered in boils and he no longer looked amused. His eyes met mine and there was burning hatred oozing out of them.

I kept up my concentration, though the sight terrified me, especially since I knew I was the one responsible for it. The blisters on his arms and legs were starting to burst and pop large amounts of puss.

I wanted to throw up.

I stopped my attack.

Sabrael turned to Aidan. "Remove the Vessel from here! Caelius cannot break the seal!"

Aidan's response was a resounding kick to Caelius's face. "She's done more damage than any of us. She can tip the balance!"

Gavreel chimed in, "Sabrael, listen to Adnachiel. Maybe we

can destroy Caelius, if it's possible."

"I'm right here!" Caelius mocked the angels, laughing. "And you know I cannot be killed, even in this humanlike form. We've known each other since the dawn of time. Three thousand years isn't even a blip for us. And you've forgotten one important detail."

The fight had stopped momentarily.

I wanted to roll my eyes. Angel-beast-thingies were such suckers. Caelius not only made them stop attacking him, but they were actually waiting to hear what he had to say.

Caelius's blisters continued to burst as he spoke. He looked like some kind of leprosy reject. "My dear beasts, if you're down here, who's protecting the Light?"

The fear that ran through that room was palpable.

Even Lucian had stopped to listen, as if the power of his father's voice kept him at bay.

"Don't listen to him!" I called out, feeling the need to step in. "He wants to even the playing field by forcing some of you to return to your Light or whatever. Caelius is imprisoned here; there is no way he can hurt the Light." I wasn't 100 percent positive, but my gut told me I was right.

And so did Caelius's face when he looked at me. I was ruining his plan and he loathed me for it.

"If I use the Vessel to break the seal, then return to my unbound form as Darkness, I will devour the Light without you protecting it. Do you really want to risk the Light on the word of a *girl*?" He was trying to gain back momentum.

I could see that Aidan's brothers were trying to figure out what to do. If they left, Caelius would win for sure. I had to do something.

"I'm the Vessel, moron. I'm the dripping of what they're sworn to protect. Don't you think I'd know if the Light was in danger? I can feel it in my bones, my blood, my *soul*. The Light isn't in danger, but *you*? It ends here," I said with as much confidence as I could.

Aidan and his brothers nodded and they repeated in unison, "It ends here."

It was frightening hearing them speak as one voice. I could feel the power race through my veins.

Caelius was scared.

Lucian looked over at me, pride beaming.

Caelius's voice practically squawked as he frantically turned to Lucian. "*Son*, help your father."

Lucian snarled. "Not even if you *begged*."

Caelius's eyes flashed betrayal and hurt. "You are my son, my only *true* son. How can you turn against me?"

"I was never a monster until you made me. I should have died in Egypt under the light of Nefertiti's window. Shea's finally brought me back from the edge of your madness—back to myself. Seeing you die will only bring me closure." Lucian leapt first, baring his fangs.

Aidan and his brothers quickly followed suit and ripped Caelius limb from limb, pieces of his flesh flying everywhere. His parts couldn't reattach themselves fast enough. The whole scene looked like a pack of dogs digging into Caelius's broken body.

It was horrifying.

I stood watching, not knowing what to do or how to react.

They clearly didn't need me.

I jumped suddenly.

It felt as if something had brushed up against my leg, but nothing was there. I was about to chalk it up to the wind from the slaughter I was witnessing when—

Boom!

The ground shook so violently everyone fell to the ground, including me.

It was instantly calm.

Everyone slowly rose to their feet.

My blood turned to ice as Harahel's voice broke the silence. "Where's Caelius?"

I searched the cavern with the others, but he was gone. Not even the tiny bits of torn flesh remained.

He'd disappeared.

Gavreel was by my side before I could think to move, but he wasn't focused on me. "The barrier is gone. With the power he absorbed from the Vessel, Caelius destroyed the seal."

"But the Vessel is still alive and her soul is intact." Sabrael tried to hide the confusion in his voice.

Gavreel shook his head. "Caelius used enough of the Vessel's Light to break out of his prison, but he is still weak. As soon as he feeds, he *will* try to finish draining the Vessel to regain his full strength."

Aidan walked over to me protectively. "I will never let that happen."

Harahel breathed in deep. "Caelius is vulnerable." He eyed Aidan knowingly. "Huntable."

Aidan nodded. "Killable?"

"We don't know," Sabrael admitted. "But you must try."

Sabrael placed his giant hand on Aidan's shoulder. "You are no longer tied to the Vessel. Your bond is broken, which means Caelius may not be able to be killed, but you can. Be careful and find him, Adnachiel. If he can't be killed, force him back to his true form."

"I will." I had never seen Aidan more determined.

Then Gavreel looked down at me. It was quite intimidating staring up at a giant angel beast. His voice was kind as he said, "Caelius no longer needs you to break free of his prison, but he still needs your soul to be at full strength in his mortal form." He nodded to Lucian. "This one will keep you safe while Aidan hunts Caelius down." Gavreel turned to Lucian. "All vampires can walk in the sunlight now, which makes the Vessel even more vulnerable. You have been an extension of Caelius's evil for over three thousand years, but the Light has made you whole again. We see inside your heart and know you will die for this Vessel. We are entrusting you with her safety. Are you willing?"

Lucian nodded. "I will protect her with my life."

This seemed to be good enough for Aidan's brothers. They all placed a hand on Aidan. They had a moment of silence and I was pretty sure they were communicating with each other. I was glad these guys were on my side because they were really scary.

"We must go back to protect the Light. It is our most sacred duty. If Caelius goes back to his true form and destroys the Light, the Universe will collapse. It's up to you to stop Caelius on Earth. Don't fail us again, Adnachiel."

"I won't fail you," Aidan vowed.

Before I could process what had just happened, Sabrael, Harahel, and Gavreel were gone.

Caelius free or not, I felt an overwhelming sense of relief. I knew the panic and mayhem would begin soon enough, but in an instant of zen, I just appreciated the moment.

It was over.

I was alive.

And I had my two boys.

CHAPTER 14
LUCIAN

I looked at her face. It was hopeful and somewhat elated. I guessed Caelius being gone and the fact that she was out of danger momentarily must have come as some sort of relief.

My only relief was that she was alive. For now. But Caelius being free meant the whole world was at risk. And the world could die for all I cared, but she was a part of it. If it burned to the ground, she'd be nothing but ash and smoke.

I pulled her close to my chest. She leaned in for a kiss, but I moved my head back. I just wanted to look at her, to feel the thudding of her heartbeat: alive. I stroked her hair. My Shea Harper.

A thought chilled my bones.

How long could I really protect her from all of this?

She leaned in again, and this time I didn't resist. I let my mouth melt into hers. The soft curve of her lower lip rested gently between my teeth as I moved deeper into the embrace.

I pulled the air from her lungs and it filled my own. I was hers, and she was mine.

Aidan placed his hand on my shoulder and coughed awkwardly. Shea instantly jerked back, blushing. His eyes didn't meet hers as he spoke. "I will definitely give you guys some alone time. I just need to be clear. My brothers are back protecting the Light. They can't track him, even if they stayed, but I can. I had enough practice through the centuries by tracking the scent of Caelius's blood in Lucian as we battled over the Vessels."

Shea shook her head and touched his arm. Now he looked at her. And for a moment, they were silent. I could see relief move through his body as his one remaining wing trembled with the loss of the other. In any other battle it would regrow, but it'd been severed by Caelius's shadow form, his touch of Darkness marring Aidan for the rest of his life. However long that was, for any of us.

She smiled. "Why can't your brothers track him? We're not leaving you alone. We'll hunt him together."

He shook his head no. "I can track him because he's Darkness willingly keeping itself in human form. I'm an angel in human form linked to the dripping of the Vessel, aka you. It's a similar energy exchange and should make it easier for me to find his influence.

"Lucian will keep you safe in the meantime, and he can train you . . . he trained Moses. You'll get stronger. You can Dream-Walk with me *every* night. He's weak right now. When I find him, you can meet me then, and we'll ground and pound him together and destroy his human form. All of us." Now he smiled. He and Shea had this "I get you" moment. I didn't interrupt as I could see the warmth of familiarity and kinship move between them as natural as breathing.

I sighed despite myself. It wouldn't be as easy as that. Caelius was clever and cruel. I could only guess as to what his next move would be. "You should start here in Egypt. It's obvious that he wouldn't be here, but that may be his game. He's sentimental, and injured or not, he'll want to lash back at me in any way he can for my disobedience."

Aidan growled. "He's weak from breaking the seal. I'll track him, and you and I will both have our revenge. He can't hurt you anymore."

I wanted to smile. I wanted to join this A-team mentality of happy endings. But I *knew* Caelius.

He shook my shoulders, seeing that I wasn't readily convinced. "I've tracked you and hidden from the likes of slime for centuries. I can do this, Brother."

I gave him a sly look. "Are you referring to the slime of my children?"

He grinned unabashedly.

I nodded. He'd roped me in with his use of the word "brother." He hadn't called me that since we'd been like brothers, before he'd killed Moses.

Aidan did have a way about him. With that small gesture, I was pulled into their illusion. The Darkness had its persuasions, but it was nothing to the small touch of the Light tugging on what you really were and what you needed.

"All right, *Brother.*" It didn't feel right to say it back. But I had to try. "Keep your updates frequent, and I'll have Shea pull me into some of the dreams for counsel. I'm also pretty good at tracking myself, if you haven't forgotten. Found you every time—"

"Caelius is different. You know if you tried to track him he'd just mess with your head. You have his blood in you; he might use that. And it's easier for Light to find Darkness and vice versa. Your job is to keep Shea safe and *train* her. I'm sure you'll be better at it than I was. She . . . she lights up when she's around you."

We both looked at her and she stuttered. Aidan lunged in and wrapped his arms around her. She probably couldn't see it, but I saw his wing encase her entire body. That was the way his kind embraced. Rare as it was, it was beautiful, beast and all.

A tear rolled down his cheek as he whispered, "I'm so glad you're alive."

She nodded, a tear matching his falling from her face. "I missed you." He held her for a moment longer. Then with a gust of wind, he left the cavern. She stumbled forward, thrown off by the thrust and power of his movement.

She started shaking.

With Aidan gone, the reality of all that had happened was starting to sink in. She rushed toward me and threw herself into my arms. I smelled her hair, cupping the nape of her neck with the palm of my hand, pressing her torso to mine. "I'll keep you safe, Shea. Caelius will never take you from my grasp again. I'll train you. You'll get stronger—"

She pulled back. "There's time for that later. Now I just *need* you."

I looked around at the devastation. All I could smell was everyone's blood. The stalactites were dripping, but the darkness had lifted. All that had made this cave a prison, all that had made it torture for over three thousand years, had gone with Caelius. Now it was just a slash house in some horror film.

I brushed the back of my hand against her cheek. "I can take you anywhere. Just name a place, and it will be ours."

She leaned close to me, her chest resting on mine. I could feel the warmth of her blood pumping erratically through her veins. "I need you *now*."

For a moment I stared, confused. This wasn't like her. She grabbed a handful of my hair and pulled me in. She whispered in front of my lips before tasting them, "You could have died, I could have died, we still might die, but I know now more than I know anything else . . . you, Lucian, are *mine*."

A surge of passion rolled over me like a vacuum of air exploding a sealed burning building. Her breath. Her lips. Saying what I'd always said. *Mine*. It was a powerful word to a vampire. But it meant more than Caelius could understand. It was body, soul, and *heart*.

All of me.

I placed her onto the cold stone and kissed her neck. I didn't drink, I just held her there with my teeth while my hands peeled off the thrashed layers of her clothes. She moaned in ecstasy as I hissed, instinctually moving my hot mouth to hers. I kissed her like a man deprived of water in the desert.

And I had been.

All the years of feeling nothing, of being empty. She made me whole. But it was more than that. With her, I was more alive than I had been as a young man before I'd been turned.

She grabbed the necklace I was wearing and eyed it as she

kissed my ear. "This was from your safe place?"

I pushed the small of her back into my hips. "I've had it since I was boy."

Her breath was hot as it whispered into my ear. "I like it."

My fingers laced over the soft pressure points on her abdomen and into her thighs as I pressed her body deeper into mine.

Here, in the place Caelius had taken me in every way but one—love. Here, at the root of my torment, she was offering healing with the Light of her body. Amongst the blood and waste, she was planting a seed, a different memory to cling to.

I lunged deeper and she gasped as I licked a small trace of blood from her neck that had survived the battle. It was sweet like nectar. I wanted it. All of it.

My desperation, no, my *need* for her to fill my very being caused me to pull back. "Wait, Shea, I'm losing myself. I can't control—"

She grabbed my face and pulled me back in.

I hovered my growing fangs over the soft curve of her neck. It pulsed and I could feel my eyes lose their color, the pupils dilating, filling the irises to black.

Then she said my name. It was a whisper, but enough to make me blind. My teeth retracted. As much as instinct mixed with desire, my love for her was powerful, all-consuming. I'd never drink her. She was *mine*. I'd give up life and all its essence to never hurt her.

With every kiss, she penetrated the Darkness inside of me. She was in me as much as I was inside of her. My soul came alive, and it beat with hers.

I kissed her mouth, her hair, the small of her back. Everything stopped, like all of time was nothing but an illusion and we could speed it up or slow it down given our pleasures. I could move quicker than any human, but I hadn't moved this slowly before. Every breath, every motion was drawn out.

Before this cave had echoed the sounds of horror and pain, and now it was filled with the pleasured cries of two lovers.

It was terrifying.

More than any anguish Darkness could cause, losing myself completely like this . . .

A day passed until we both collapsed from exhaustion. The last thing she said to me was "France."

***

Shea was still sleeping in the apartment I'd bought for us in Paris. She looked beautiful, wrapped in white down blankets. Everything felt clean, new somehow, despite the relict architecture.

I sat on the terrace and braced myself as I looked at the Eiffel Tower. It was coming. There was no stopping it. It would come as it always had, except now, I wasn't going to hide. I would face it and myself.

Just beyond visible sight, I could hear it. The subtle shift in sound. All animals could. It was part of their internal clocks, knowing when night or day was approaching. Everything inside me shivered. Maybe the seal being broken had no effect on the sun. Maybe Aidan's brothers were wrong.

Either way, I had to know. I had to see it. As new as I felt on the inside, I wanted to drench my skin in the light, whether it would burn me alive or not.

I ripped the necklace off my neck. I'd kept it for so long, like an anchor keeping me where I was, keeping me who I'd been before. It had reminded me of all I'd lost. I'd sculpted it as a child, pressing the symbolic words of our tribe into the gold. I rubbed my thumb over the glyph of my name—my *real* name. Branded as it was, the necklace was never meant to be mine. It was *hers*.

And now that I was with Shea, I wanted to let it go with the coming of my first sunrise in centuries.

Light poured over the horizon. I winced instantly in pain. My skin felt warm, all of the hair on my body standing on end. Before I could back up, Shea grabbed my hand.

"It's okay, Lucian. You're okay."

She pulled the necklace from my fist and placed it back around my neck, smiling as only she could.

I stared at her face as the sun rose, casting oranges and pinks across her warm cheeks. Tears welled in our eyes. It was the first time in over three thousand years that I'd seen anyone look so warm. "You, Shea Harper . . . you are my sunrise."

EPILOGUE
CAELIUS

That worm. That insolent maggot. After all these years of fathering him, he'd turned against me. I laughed, unable to stop the feeling of pride welling in my chest. My son should've been wild and rebellious like I was. After all, he was *mine*.

I was still being dragged. I knew it wasn't Lucian because it didn't smell like him. I could hear the confusion of the beasts and their Light as they vanished back to the heavens above, back where they could protect their blessed maker. I spit and scowled. Only the Light would be happy with such obedient dogs. They didn't need any breaking or training. They came molded, sculpted, and created to serve.

I breathed in deep. They were nothing like my boy. He was over three thousand years old. Just a baby. And that Ur-Nammu . . . he thought I would have killed my Lucian. I laughed again, letting it ring through the sand as my body left a trail like a sidewinder in the dunes.

I would have kept Lucian inside me, totally consumed in Darkness, in all that I was. And when I spat him out, he would have been riddled with confusion. It would have taken him ages to put himself back together, and he'd be better for it. Stronger. And more mine than before.

That didn't matter now. One way or another, I'd have him.

As the sun rose above the pyramids, I scowled. I hated the light. I wanted to break free, but to break the seal meant that vampires could once again walk in the sunlight.

I only wanted free in order to spit at the Light itself. To walk under its brilliance, then kill and devour all that it loved. See—I was a good son, just like Lucian.

Those beasts, didn't they know I was allowed to live, that my very existence gave the Light pleasure? Or maybe the Light just didn't have the balls to finish what it'd started: to end Darkness completely.

I stopped. Or, rather, the person dragging me got tired. I casually looked up, eager to feed on the helping hand that had pulled me away from the fight.

I smiled, and she smiled back.

"Good girl," I said, moving my hand through her jet-black hair.

She heaved me up into her lap. "They thought you were torn to shreds, but I dragged you through the opening the Vessel left when she convinced Lucian to fight you. You came through easily because you drained some of her Light, but you are weakened. What can I do? You need your strength, Father."

I grabbed her wrist and took a long drink. She moaned in pleasure like she always did. My Eve to Lucian. I moved my thumb over her elongated black eye shadow. It was strange that even after all this time, she wore the paintings of Egypt. Strange, but fitting. She still matched those sculptures he'd made of her all those centuries ago.

"Now that I'm free, he belongs to us. We'll have our family like I promised. He'll just need some . . . convincing." We both smiled, baring our fangs at the sunlight. The desire in her heart matched mine. "Don't worry, Nefertiti. Lucian and this world are *ours*."

FIRST BORN

PROLOGUE
CAELIUS

The sound of his sobbing filled my heart with more warmth than my first day under Egypt's sun. No amount of light could penetrate me the way his cries did now. And I'd waited. So many years ago I'd longed to see his flesh torn apart.

It was bittersweet. I smiled, licking blood from my arm as I dropped another one of his lifeless children. I could make this so much sweeter. My patience had worn thin over the centuries, but what were a few more days to relish in his agony? This kind of theatrics needed an audience, and the spectator I had in mind would be moved beyond reason with this display.

I laced my hand through the curls of his golden hair. His blue eyes were wet as his lips trembled. "Oh come, Gracuri," I said. "You can do better. These are the children you first turned that I'm feasting on; surely you can beg louder than this. Just call Lucian's name, and I'll spare them."

He was weak. In the last few days he'd submitted himself

to my every whim, every bodily pleasure and destruction, all to save his children, but I was just carrying out a sentence I'd given Lucian. I was finishing the cleansing of his line.

I decapitated Gracuri's *favorite* child. His body sagged. I leaned my head close to his slumped frame. If he wasn't dead, if my Lucian hadn't given him the blessing of an immortal kiss, this would have killed him.

I listened as his heart seized in his chest. His body twitched and convulsed: a heart attack. The fresh human blood I'd force-fed through his veins kept him alive. I wanted him awake and fully charged for today's tortures.

"I'm so sorry. Did you *love* him? You know, the *first* one we turn is always our most dear. The pain of love lost, well, it's driven immortals and gods greater than yourself to madness."

I smiled, leaning on his back. It was like resting on a bed of stones. Lucian was more comfortable. I glanced up at the night sky, thinking of my son. It was beautiful, all that black emptiness. I growled and, for a moment, Gracuri's agony left me hollow. All those stars were ruining the darkness with their light; all that noise was polluting the silence.

I missed it, the power. The feeling of twisting into a black hole and devouring galaxies was thrilling. But when the Light became obsessed with these small worlds, with mammals and in particular humans, well, I was curious enough to make a bargain.

This small form was nothing compared to my true essence. It wasn't even a fraction, yet I clung to it desperately. That was the agreement: I could take *this* form *once*. And it was worth it. All of that power as Darkness seemed meaningless once I was solid. Before my essence was scattered, but now I could think clearly. I was free from the burden of balance.

His convulsing stopped, and I sighed. "You know what the most irritating thing about you is, Gracuri?" I rolled to face him, cupping his chin in my hands as his pupils constricted and his fangs bared.

I looked at the poor thing with unexpected gratitude, whispering into his ear, "You're so pathetic. I've killed you in hundreds of unique ways this week, but my Lucian would take all of this without dying and reviving. Lucian would take it until he was mangled, near death. He wouldn't let himself go. But you, Gracuri, you're not worthy of such a father. Your very existence shames him and, in that way, shames me. Your love makes him *weak*. But *my* love will make him strong."

CHAPTER 1
SHEA

It was impossible to concentrate when Lucian looked at me like that. He was supposed to be teaching me how to use my powers, but his eyes would go all intense, and it made me want to jump the guy.

"Shea, don't look at me like that," Lucian said.

"Me? You're the one with smolder-face. I just really want to make this water move." I'd been trying to connect to a small pond just outside the villa near Paris where we were staying. Lucian had shown me a few tricks for focusing my energy, but my mind tended to veer back to him rather than the dirty pool of water.

He stepped closer, and my heart raced. Talk about having it bad for someone. One gesture, move, look, kiss . . .

I put my hand out before he could touch me, almost touching the necklace he always wore around his neck. "Hold it right there, bud-o. You start with the kissing, and my brain is mush for the rest of the day."

He didn't listen.

As usual.

His arms pulled me close, and my knees almost gave. How could one guy be so freaking hot? It wasn't fair to the rest of us mere mortals when someone like Lucian existed. With his teal eyes and sculpted face, not to mention his perfectly coifed dark hair, he was too perfect.

I wasn't *ugly*. I was cute by most standards—long blond hair, decent body, hazel eyes—but standing next to *him*? It was the difference between a Michelangelo and a hotel painting.

Of course, I was probably biased because I loved Lucian with every fiber of my soul. I hated being insecure, but I still couldn't totally believe he felt the same way for me.

Then I felt his lips against mine.

Yup. Pure mush.

I felt his hunger as he pressed his body against me, his mouth passionately devouring my lips. It was how we spent most of our days. We weren't even married, but our honeymoon phase showed no signs of abating.

Which I had zero problems with.

Before this inevitably led us back to our bedroom, I managed to muster up enough self-restraint to pull away, uttering breathlessly, "We can't. Caelius is still out there. I need to be strong."

At the mention of his father, Lucian nodded and took a step back. "You're right. Your power may be the weapon we need to stop him. His blood pumping through my veins makes me vulnerable to his influence."

That must have been hard for him to admit.

Lucian had tried to explain it, though it was still difficult for me to fully grasp. Apparently, Lucian was the first and only vampire made by Caelius, who in turn was Darkness in human form.

From what Lucian knew, it was Caelius's blood that turned a human into a vampire, which was why Lucian was the strongest. But Caelius's blood diluted from there with each person turned, so the weakest vampire would probably only have a single drop of Caelius's blood in him. It would make him strong, but nowhere near "Lucian strong." Plus, Lucian had said when a vampire *made* another vampire they shared some kind of blood bond with each other as well.

In the simplest terms, the maker's blood was also running through their veins. And, with that kind of connection, makers could control their offspring—to a certain degree. Lucian had explained that resistance against makers depended on how strong the vampire was. The more inner strength a vampire had, the less control the maker had over them.

I knew Lucian was strong even if he didn't. When the time came for the two of us to face Caelius, I trusted Lucian to fight against the blood of his maker like he'd done before when he'd fought Caelius in his prison. If I saw Caelius again, it would be too soon, but fighting him was our destiny.

We had to kill him before he wreaked havoc on the planet. After all, the odds were on our side already: Caelius was still weak from escaping.

I still couldn't believe he'd broken free. I knew it was my fault, but Lucian and Aidan wouldn't let me take the blame, so I kept the self-loathing to myself.

"You'll be able to face him again and be even stronger this time." I tried to sound as encouraging as I could.

Lucian didn't respond, he only nodded, which translated to "I don't want to argue the point." I understood. He wasn't looking forward to a daddy-son reunion outside the cage any more than I was.

Avoiding the issue, Lucian reverted back to instructor mode. "Take a deep breath and focus on the water. I want you to create a whirlpool."

The fact that we were doing this during the day was pretty amazing. When the prison had broken, so had the curse that'd kept vampires from the sun. Lucian couldn't seem to get enough of the stuff. After three thousand years in darkness, I could hardly blame him.

"A whirlpool . . ." Lucian's voice nudged me back to the task at hand.

"Okay." I shook out my hands and jogged in place as if I were a boxer about to enter the ring. "Pond, right. Swirly motion, okay." I clapped my hands together and took in a gulp of fresh air and . . . nothing.

"You're getting frustrated. I can see it in every tense muscle on your beautiful body." Lucian had meant to be encouraging, but hearing him say the word "beautiful" in regard to me made my head spin. Then he added, "You can connect to the earth and trees easily now, but if you could master *all* the elements, you would be a real threat to Caelius."

"Rub it in," I grumbled under my breath. I knew he was trying to give me props for my earth mastery, if I could call it mastery. After Caelius's escape three months ago, Lucian had decided earth was a good place to start, since I'd had some luck with it in the past. Within a few days I'd turned the foliage outside our villa into serious bodyguards. From swiping, to strangling, to punching, I felt like I'd created my own Ents from *Lord of the Rings*. It was kind of awesome.

But mastery over earth was as far as I seemed to be able to go; every other element was like a brick wall to me. Okay, I'd had a little luck with air once when I'd created a tornado to save Aidan from a vamp, but I'd been under extreme stress then. For some reason I couldn't recreate what I'd done.

It had been my idea to try water today. I'd been reading Greek mythology books about Poseidon and had felt inspired. Not that we'd be running into Caelius on a sea voyage, but at this point I wanted to add another element under my belt. Besides, manipulating water, creating tidal waves, and controlling whirlpools just sounded cool.

But right now all I was doing was staring at a mossy, stagnant body of water that I could barely cause a ripple on. And I was pretty sure that ripple had been from the wind, not me.

"I'm trying to get you to relax." Lucian gave me a half smile that never failed to make my face flush.

"Well, relaxing isn't really an option around you." I shook my head. "It's easier when I'm being attacked or I need to protect someone."

"I'm not going to attack you, if that's what you're asking. At least not in a way you wouldn't enjoy."

There was that smile again.

The boy was going to give me a heart attack. He was so damn sexy. And *mine*.

Lucian cocked his head to the side. "Did you just pinch yourself?"

Busted. But I couldn't help it. The good parts of my life felt like an amazing dream I never wanted to wake up from, and the bad parts felt like nightmares I *couldn't* wake up from. "I'm going to concentrate," I announced.

If it wasn't for distraction-boy, I might've had a shot at making this water do *something*. At this point I debated jumping in just to cool off.

I closed my eyes and thought only of the pond in front of me. I imagined touching it, letting the soft liquid trace through my fingers, energizing every molecule with my intentions.

I felt it.

There was a tiny ounce of connection.

I held on to it as if the water itself was a part of me: my limbs, my fingers, my toes, my mind.

"Shea. Open your eyes." I heard Lucian's voice as if he were miles away.

I did as he asked and couldn't believe what I was seeing.

Before me was a giant cyclone of water over ten feet tall. Small splashes of dirty pond hit my face as the raging vortex spun faster and faster.

I couldn't stop it.

Panic seemed like a good call.

Lucian's arms wrapped around me from behind. His breath was soft on my ear as he whispered, "Just relax and disconnect."

The water swirled wider, out of control. I wanted to run, but feeling the strength of his arms gave me power from within.

I stared at the inverted whirlpool. *I'd* created that.

With sudden clarity, I knew I could bend it to my will. Whatever I wanted to do with it, I could, like it was a part of me.

It *was* a part of me.

With a large sigh, the water collapsed back into the pond. It was still. Not even a ripple.

I turned in his arms, my adrenaline pumping. "I did it!" I cried excitedly.

Apparently, my enthusiasm made me irresistible because before I could utter another word he was kissing me. After what I'd just accomplished, the energy that surged through me only fueled the fire, and before I knew it, Lucian was carrying me back inside.

Even though this had happened every day for the last three months, I still had butterflies. Being with Lucian was like nothing I could put into words. Every touch made me blind with desire. Every kiss felt like the first time.

We were made for each other.

He carefully set me down on our bed, his hands never leaving my body. Wrapping my arms around him, I drew him in closer, wanting to feel the heat of his chest against mine. Being with him was so powerful I found myself gasping for air.

My head floated in the clouds as we made love.

***

"What is it, your nap time? It's only two thirty in the afternoon, or is it later?" Aidan stood before me in a forest.

I was Dream-Walking.

I must have dozed off after being with Lucian. The boy

zonked me out.

Lucky me.

Aidan always brought me a rush of happiness. Seeing him there with his big blue eyes, messy brown hair, and abs for days, I reached up to his six-foot frame and gave him the biggest hug I could muster.

I pulled away with a huge grin, which he returned in kind. His eyes sparkled with an inner kindness that always took my breath away.

"Yes, smart-ass," I answered. "It's two thirty in the afternoon, and maybe I just wanted to see you. Is that so wrong?" I nudged him affectionately. Looking around at all the trees, I had to ask, "Where is this place?"

"In the Angeles Forest, just outside Los Angeles." Then, in a quick change of mood, Aidan's face turned serious. "I think I'm close."

He didn't have to say what he was close to.

Aidan had been hunting Caelius since he'd escaped three months ago. I'd been Dream-Walking with him to stay up-to-date on the situation, and to visit because Aidan was more than just my best friend. We'd been born on the same day, minute, and second for a reason. I was called a Vessel. And Aidan was one of four remaining brothers who protected the Light, which I was apparently made out of. Yeah, it didn't sound crazy at all!

He'd been sent down in human form to protect me from, well, Lucian. Before we'd known we were made for each other, Lucian's job had been to hunt down Vessels to help free his father, Caelius, from where he'd been imprisoned. "Help" may have been the wrong word; draining my soul until the prison cracked open was more like it.

Once Lucian had realized his feelings for me, he'd flat-out refused to take me, but Lucian's first son, Ur-Nammu, had kidnapped me and taken me there anyway, hence Caelius's "get out of jail free card." Luckily, he hadn't finished the ritual, which would've ended up sucking out my soul and restoring him to full power. But Caelius had still managed to drain enough of my Light to escape.

It was all a big mess, but I trusted Aidan with my life.

Even though he'd stabbed me in the gut.

One would think my trust might have wavered at that point, and, I'll admit, it had for a little while. But I understood his decision. His brothers believed that if Caelius was freed it would mean the end of the world as we knew it. Since I was the key to opening his prison, it was better to destroy the key than risk the chance of Caelius obliterating the planet.

It made sense, so I understood the "why" of his actions. Still, the emotional betrayal of my best friend had been far worse than the knife he'd twisted in my gut. But when Aidan had showed up with Lucian to save me from Caelius, I'd seen in his eyes that he would never hurt me again.

It was hard to explain, but my loyalty to Aidan was even fiercer than before. There was something about finding out I was an elemental created from Light—a Light the beast-brothers had protected since the dawn of time—that put the matter into perspective.

"Caelius in Los Angeles?" I rolled my eyes. I was actually surprised he hadn't gone to Las Vegas. The irony would've been that much sweeter.

Aidan gave a chuckle. "Right?" His face turned contemplative. "I'm just not sure what he's doing here. The whole time I've been tracking Caelius, I keep getting the feeling he's tracking someone as well, but it's not you or Lucian."

"Or you," I added.

"Or me," he conceded. "Lucian is Caelius's *only* son. Why wouldn't he want to find him and convince him to come back to the fold?"

"Maybe he's pissed. I mean, Lucian did align himself with you and your brothers and try to kill him." That last battle in Caelius's cell had been brutal: five against one with me in the mix. I hadn't thought the monster had a chance in hell of surviving. But one moment the boys had been tearing the vampire to shreds, and the next he was gone and the curse was broken.

I'd felt something brush up against me. In hindsight I now knew it'd been Caelius. If I'd figured it out, I could have stopped him. But I'd let him slip right past me . . .

I shook my head from the memory. I needed to focus on the here and now.

"Caelius didn't know anybody before Lucian, right?" I asked aloud. "I mean, wasn't he 'Darkness incarnate' before he decided to take human form? Lucian is the only one he met who's still alive."

Aidan shrugged. "I thought it might be Ur-Nammu Caelius is hunting, but that vamp is in Miami."

"Miami?" The image of Ur-Nammu sunbathing on Miami Beach popped into my head, and I couldn't stop from laughing. "That's the last place I'd imagine him going."

Aidan smiled, but it was a hollow smile; he didn't find it that funny, which made the hairs on my neck rise.

"Miami is no joke, Shea. It used to be a nighttime feast for vampires down there, what with the party scene, but now that they're active during the day, the missing person reports are piling up. Ur-Nammu is probably there on Caelius's orders to punish a few of the overzealous vampires. Caelius wants to be the main show; he doesn't want his 'diluted grandchildren' stealing the spotlight. Until he gets his power back, he wants his kind to live in secret. If there are to be mass killings, Caelius will want all the credit . . ." Aidan's expression took on a far-off look.

"You have thinky-face. What is it?" I asked.

"Nothing. I just thought of something. I might know who Caelius is after." Aidan didn't look pleased.

"Who?" For some reason I didn't want to know. Aidan's expression said it all. Whoever papa-vampire was after, it wasn't good.

Aidan grimaced. "I don't want to say. Just hope that I'm wrong."

"I'll definitely do that. Your face is freaking me out." I cringed.

Apparently, not wanting to worry me further, he smiled, trying to ease the tension. "So, how's your training going?"

I had to brag. "I made a whirlpool."

Aidan nodded his head, impressed. "That's really good. You're getting stronger."

Then I added with a bang, "I made it in the air, sucker!"

His eyes widened. "Holy crap, are you serious?"

"It was ginormous! It looked like a water tornado!" Okay, yeah, I was proud of myself.

"That's amazing!" His eyes were still wide. "No Vessel has

been this powerful this quick. Even Moses took years to learn his strengths. Maybe it's because you're the last one."

"Or, like I've told you over and over, it's because I'm a girl, which on principal makes me better," I teased. All the Vessels before me had been men. I was the first female.

Aidan's eyes did all the smiling for me.

"I can't argue with your logic," he said with a laugh. "Still, you'd better wake up, lazy butt. Tell Lucian where I am, and be careful." He was suddenly full of concern.

"I will, but you be more careful. Contact me as soon as you find Caelius. Don't be a hero. We need to confront him together." I sounded like a mom.

Aidan didn't seem to mind. He reached down and gave me another hug. "Love you."

"Love you too," I said into his chest.

***

I woke up to see the sun slowly setting through the window. It was almost as stunning as Lucian lying beside me. He watched me with his usual mixture of love, desire, and concern.

"I just talked to Aidan," I said at last, breaking the silence.

Concern won out. "Did he find Caelius?" Then, as if he didn't want to ask, he added, "Is Aidan okay?"

The bromance between Lucian and Aidan was pretty adorable to me, but I'd only witnessed the tail end of their long history. The first Vessel had been Moses. Yes, *Moses*, and he'd bonded the two of them like family. When Aidan had thought Lucian was going to take Moses to Caelius, he'd killed Moses.

It was only recently that Lucian had forgiven Aidan. Lucian had made it his mission to torture him with every Vessel after Moses. He'd wanted him to suffer as he had suffered after losing them. Boys and their grudges. Aidan definitely hadn't deserved what Lucian had done to him over the centuries, but I wasn't about to get in the middle of that can of worms.

I guessed I was the one who'd brought the two of them together again after all those years. I could tell there was still some tension between them, but the love was there too. I didn't want to interfere, so I'd decided to stand back and let them figure it out on their own.

"Aidan is fine. He's just outside of Los Angeles," I said.

"Los Angeles? Why there?" Lucian asked.

"He thinks Caelius is tracking someone. He has an idea who, but won't tell me," I confessed.

"Ur-Nammu?"

I shook my head. "I thought the same thing, but Ur-Nammu's in Miami."

Lucian nodded in understanding. "That was always a cesspool of vampire filth." He reached out his arms and pulled me into him. My head rested comfortably on his chest as I aimlessly traced my finger in slow circles over his necklace. "Los Angeles? I don't know anyone there, so how could Caelius?"

"Maybe someone is hiding there?" I suggested.

Lucian's body tensed.

I kissed his neck, trying to distract him. "We'll have to wait for Aidan to tell us."

The phone rang.

We froze. I didn't even know we had a phone. I wanted to say it was probably a wrong number, but I knew it was Aidan.

If he was calling, then he couldn't wait for me to fall asleep.

My eyes met Lucian's.

"It's Aidan," he said.

I nodded. "I'll get it."

"No." Lucian gracefully stepped out of bed. He walked over to the phone that was apparently on the desk in our room. "Aidan—"

His voice caught.

That scared me more than anything.

I couldn't hear Aidan, but whatever he was saying made Lucian's skin pale.

He hung up the phone, and his eyes filled with anguish as he whispered one word.

"Gracuri."

CHAPTER 2
LUCIAN

Shea kept asking me questions, her tone panicked, but I couldn't hear her. I couldn't hear anything but a slight ringing.

These past months with her had been a dream—a dream I didn't want to wake from. It was as if Caelius had killed us all in that cave, and I'd died and ended up with Shea in this bliss. Granted I was no fool and needed to prepare her, but I didn't care. I didn't want to care.

Caelius and *his* world, with all his wants and needs and commands, had been my burden for over three thousand years. The weight of his power breaking and twisting me in new ways every century, the torment of torturing Aidan and killing the Vessel . . . I'd become more monster than man.

But with Shea I felt like I had in Gutium before the wars. I was finally free from the burdens of my past.

I'd hoped Caelius would just destroy the world, that it'd be swift, and that I'd be making love to Shea when it happened.

I knew that was idealistic. If Aidan or Shea were to discover my intent, they'd be furious: furious in a way one child is with another, not in the way Caelius was. They didn't understand him. They hadn't been exposed to his unfathomable rage for as long as I had. Even Aidan was blind to Caelius's *true* power.

I'd been inside him. I'd touched the center of his madness, the black hole that consumed all reason. I had become *nothing*. Everything I'd identified with—my memories, my homeland, everything that made me, that gave me reason, even my very soul—had all disappeared.

I'd never imagined a place like that existed. The lure of hell was something I scoffed at; being tormented by Caelius was hell. But that cold, dark, empty place at the center of his being . . . the nothingness . . . I'd rather be strapped to a stalagmite and have him ravage me over and over than to feel that way again.

I closed my eyes, breathing in deep. Now I felt it, the shame of what I'd been doing. In truth, I was afraid.

Shea's soft arms wrapped around my body, her concern flowing over her small frame. She pressed her head into my chest, whispering, "Whatever it is, we'll get through it together."

I sighed with regret. Who was I kidding? I hadn't been training Shea, I'd been hiding her, hoping death or bliss would take us, hoping she would never have to feel Caelius's emptiness. What if he consumed her soul and I lost her forever?

I opened my eyes and pulled back to look at her face, running my hand along the soft line of her cheekbone. "I don't want him to hurt you. This is my fault. I wasn't thinking. I should have separated myself from you and let you train with Aidan. It's my responsibility to keep my children safe. It's my responsibility to handle Caelius. I can't—"

"Are you freaking kidding me right now?" Her tone was sharp. I hadn't heard Shea use that edge since we'd first met.

I tilted my head. "Why don't you just add 'dorm monitor' to the end of that?"

Shea's eyes softened. "What I meant was that's enough of you blaming yourself. And I'm here with you because I want to be. I don't want to think about you dropping me off with Aidan and disappearing. I mean, how could you even say that?"

I reached down, kissing the small of her neck. "It's not that, Shea. Caelius is drawing me out. There's very little I care about in this world, only a handful of people: you, Aidan, and my Second-Borns—Ur-Nammu, Gracuri, Duncan, Bohe, and David—if they're still alive. I trust that Gracuri hid them well. He was probably leading Caelius away from them. He'd do anything for the one he loves, and so would I."

I stared into her, seeing the core of all I'd longed to protect, and it was killing me.

She stroked my arm, looking deep into my eyes. "Where are you right now?"

I grabbed Shea's wrist. "It's too dangerous. He knows we're together, and all of this could be a trap to get to you. He could use me to hurt you, Shea!"

She tried to pry her wrist away. "You're the only one hurting me right now."

I let go, looking at my own hand in shock. My teeth were bared. I turned away. "I'm sorry, I just . . . he can't have you."

Shea ran her fingertips over my chest. It sent chills through my mind, softening the razor-edged nerves that Caelius always brought out inside me.

"I know. I'm *yours*." Shea smiled. "But we can face whatever that a-hole has for us together."

I combed my hands through her hair, resting my forehead on hers. I could stay like this. If there was a heaven, it was in Shea Harper's arms.

I sighed heavily. She didn't understand. It was too risky, and she wasn't ready . . . because of me.

The smart thing would be to wait it out. I should let Caelius kill Gracuri and use that time to train Shea. Odds were Caelius had already bled him dry.

My stomach churned, thinking about Gracuri's severed head on a spike the way Caelius had ordered it all those years ago. I couldn't take it. He was *my* child. *Mine* to protect. And he was loyal. He was . . . irreplaceable.

Sentiment was clouding my vision. Shea couldn't risk her life for one of my children. She'd gladly do it—she and Aidan both—and that was what Caelius would be expecting. He'd want an audience.

It was a trap, any fool could see that, but I couldn't leave Gracuri to die. No doubt the agonies he'd already endured would scar him forever. I'd promised him. When I'd fed on Gracuri to charge up to face Caelius, I'd given him my word.

I kissed her lips. Shea pulled back for a moment, unsure of what my affection meant. I half smiled, cupping her face in my hands. "You're right. We'll rest tonight. Dream-Walk with Aidan and tell him we'll all meet together outside of LA tomorrow." Then I winked, adding a playful undertone to my voice. "But from here on out, I want you to take your training seriously."

Shea put a hand on her hip, eyeing me suspiciously. "I have been taking this seriously! You'll see, tomorrow I'll obliterate Caelius, and then we'll have the rest of our lives to just enjoy ourselves!"

Finally my enlarged incisors retracted. I smiled a human smile with flat, white teeth. "That sounds like a plan." I kissed her hard. It ached in me, the desire for her to fill my bones, to heal the emptiness with which Caelius had infused my soul.

I ran my fingertips down the small of her back, letting my mouth linger on the curve of her neck. She smelled like warm sunlight, like a rose just before it bloomed.

I dragged my lips up to the soft spot behind her ear. Pulling my hand to the nape of her neck, I grabbed a handful of her hair and pulled, her back arching in response. Shea gasped. It thrilled me, and so did the vibration of her heartbeat against my chest.

I kissed her, and she moaned.

Her sounds could penetrate all reason.

I laid her softly onto the bed, hovering for a moment over her frame. Her eyes were alight with passion, her chest heaving forward.

I needed her.

I knew then that I'd *always* need her. Poets for centuries had mused about touching the surface of the sun; they'd tried in muddied words to express the bliss, pain, and fulfillment of finding your soulmate. Now they seemed just words, hollow things that would never equate to the truth and beauty held in her eyes.

I leaned my hips heavily onto hers. "I love you, Shea. No matter what happens." Before she could respond, I swept inside her. Our bodies fused like blood in water.

I held her wrists, thrusting as she bit my lip and wrapped her thighs around my back. I growled instinctually and pushed harder. Her nails ran down my sides, and the marks healed as she moved. Tears welled in her eyes, and she whispered into my ear, "I'll love you forever, Lucian."

It broke me. I didn't know that I could ache for someone while being this close. It was like when she'd burned out a piece of my rib cage. Shea's words would always leave a mark that time could not erase, a hole that could only be filled by more of her, her love, her touch.

Hours passed until she fell asleep from exhaustion.

Good.

I needed her to sleep through the night.

It might give me enough time.

She slept with a slight smile on her face. Shea was transparent that way. It was so rare. I wavered. What was I doing? This could be the last time I saw her. And for whom? Gracuri?

My insides twisted again. Gracuri had been there for me. It was because of him that I hadn't killed myself looking for Shea. That pile of bodies. I shivered, the guilt gnawing at me. That had been *his* solution, but it had saved me. It was his blood that had given me the strength to stand against Caelius. Caelius had no doubt smelled it on me. I was sure he'd tortured Gracuri to madness for that alone.

I may have been a monster who didn't deserve Shea, but I wasn't a coward. I was still Gutian, and Gutians didn't leave the ones they loved to die.

I had fought against my own maker—against Caelius—for

Shea, for my very soul. I'd earned the heavy weight of the code of my people standing beside her, and now I couldn't go back to being calloused.

I couldn't abandon Gracuri and what he meant to me. I may have been a poet and craftsman as a young boy, but today I was more the warrior my father deserved than ever before.

I gently left Shea's side and walked to the balcony, surveying the outside. I'd done perimeter checks nightly while she slept. There was no sign of vampires near the villa—I'd made sure of that. She was safe here.

I leapt into the cold sky. I flew over countries and crossed the ocean. When I came to California, it was barely morning, the sun just rising over the mountains. It was breathtaking. I'd never seen Los Angeles lit up like this in daylight. I almost felt human, seeing all the people below, driving their cars, heading to work, loading children into minivans while staring at a strange floating man in the sky.

I was used to traveling at night: no eyes, no onlookers. I meshed with darkness. In daylight I'd have to be more careful. I shook my head, running my hands through my thick black hair. I was never this careless. Already Caelius had an advantage. I flew quickly to the Angeles Forest.

When I landed, I walked among the trees, picking up the scent of Gracuri's blood. Words rattled through my head from the last time we had spoken. *I can't thank you enough, Gracuri. You saved my other children from slaughter, you saved my life, and because you exposed us again, Caelius will no doubt demand your head.* I clenched my hands into fists.

My hope was that Caelius had kept him mostly intact,

wanting to wait so that I would have to watch his torture.

The tip of my boot tapped something soft—a severed hand. My shoulders sagged, and I sighed heavily. I eyed the trail of dismembered body parts. The woods were drenched with blood. It was thrown everywhere. Wasted. For sport.

I stepped back, shaking with emotion as my mind tried to steady itself. I extended my senses, feeling for Caelius. I rose from the ground slowly, hovering over the grass. The vow I had given Gracuri with such confidence screamed through my mind. *I promise, I will defend you with my last breath.*

I heard a cry, a ghastly and twisted scream that shook my bones. I'd never heard Gracuri make that sound before. Not in Athens, nor in Thebes when he'd gouged out his own eyes. Even then, his agonizing wail had been nothing like this.

I vomited, or at least I tried to. My whole body heaved, but nothing came out. I didn't have a stomach with acid in it anymore. When I drank blood, it absorbed into every cell of my body. There was nothing to pump, but the reflex kept me gagging.

I closed my eyes. *Gracuri, what has he done to you?* My fears were accompanied by the realization that I hadn't fed. I was coming to this battle weak. My concern had driven me relentlessly here, ignoring everything I'd learned battling with Adnachiel over the centuries.

"Please!" Gracuri cried. His anguish pierced me like a piece of glass through my stomach. I flew desperately to the sound of his cries. It didn't matter if I wasn't ready; he needed me *now*.

My own words played over and over in my mind. The look in those baby-blue eyes after he'd fed from me. The need. The unconditional belief when I'd said, *I promise . . . he will never have you.*

I panted for breath, covering miles in moments. Branches and pine needles tore away strips of flesh as I hurtled forward.

Gracuri.

My stomach heaved again. The thought of his dismemberment, of what I was about to see, was agonizing. The Gutian code of my people and my promise to him rang like white noise when I reached the sound of his wails, taking in Caelius's masterpiece at last.

Gracuri deserved better than this.

He was propped up on display. His wrists and ankles were chained between two giant oak trees with chains that stretched out and wrapped like a web through the woods.

I trembled.

Around Gracuri lay bloodied spikes and a whip encrusted with nails and barbs, torture devices from the Middle Ages that Caelius must have stolen from museums.

From the flayed way Gracuri looked, this ordeal had been going on for some time, long before Aidan had told Shea about his suspicions. My own words hit me again. *He'll never have you.*

I moved to stand in front of Gracuri, inches from his face. My smell awoke his blood. He looked up quickly. Tears streamed down his cheeks while he shook his head no.

I reached up to the shackle on his left arm and crushed it. As I did, fury filled the emptiness in that part of my mind still belonging to Caelius. That monster had done this just to prove that he could.

I crushed the other shackle, and Gracuri collapsed into my

arms. His knees buckled. He was double my size, but I picked him up easily, holding him like a child.

His lips trembled. "No, please. Father, you can't be here! Go, now!"

"I won't leave you." I rested his head against my chest, tears welling in my eyes at seeing him so torn to pieces. It was grotesque what Caelius had done to his once powerful frame. Grotesque and my fault.

I leapt into the air and flew, keeping his body pressed tenderly against my own, his name repeating in my mind like the beat of a soft drum: Gracuri. Gracuri. Gracuri.

I'd make it up to him somehow. I'd never let any of my children drink from me after I'd turned them, but maybe just this once, for Gracuri.

Once we were safe and I could hide him away, I'd offer him the blood he'd begged for in his youth. I owed him that much and more.

I moved my hand through his matted wisps of curly hair, comforting his jagged breath. We'd slept like this when he'd first turned and was unsure of the new world around him. "You're safe now. I have you."

I flew toward the desert as fast and as hard as I could.

"Why didn't you call out for me? All you had to do was say my name, and I would have known where you were. I could have saved you from this."

He wept into my arms. "Please, just leave me and go. He can't have you, not for me. Please—"

A spike of pain seared into my body like fire. It was worse than the burning lava of Pompeii. I plummeted like a rock to the desert below.

I wrapped my arms around Gracuri, trying to break our fall with my body. It was no use. When I landed, he broke loose from me, his body flying out of sight.

I coughed, writhing on the ground. Reaching my hand to the back of my neck, I pulled out a long wooden stake, which had plunged all the way through, crushing my spine.

Blood poured out of the wound. I couldn't get up. I couldn't feel my body.

Gracuri screamed.

Within moments, white shoes were inches from me—a pile of long spikes held together by barbed wire dragging behind them. They were Gracuri's shoes. I followed the legs up to Caelius's face.

He smiled. "Lucian. It's so good to see you, my son."

Leaning down, Caelius ran a long finger through my hair. "You fly quicker than I would have expected. I was hoping we could play this little game out in the forest, but you are a fan of *deserts*, aren't you?" He stood up, surveying the empty plain. "Isn't this near where you met your blessed Shea Harper? Arizona? Shall we infuse it with some new memories . . . *better* ones?"

Wind moved through the gaping hole in my throat. Just hearing him say Shea's name was infuriating. I couldn't think, I had to move. I struggled to rise.

Caelius shook his head, leaning down over my wincing frame. "I can't have you go slithering off, Son. I've got a show for you, and I've been waiting patiently for this moment." He rammed the long, pole-like stakes from the pile behind him through my hands, arms, and chest.

I screamed in agony, but nothing came out but a wheezing

sound: air forcing its way out through the gaping hole in my throat.

I gritted my teeth. Why was he wearing Gracuri's shoes? I couldn't turn my head but darted my eyes. Where was he?

Caelius touched my neck wound tenderly. "That was a close one. A bit over and I would have lopped off your head. It's a good thing I'm an excellent shot." The fingernail on his hand grew long and sharp, then he cut a thin line down my cheek, drawing blood. With pleasure, he slowly licked the bloody fingernail. "How *dare* you bring me to this, Lucian. You know I would be lost without you, my precious son. Your taste alone . . . there is no other I long for."

I spat, but it barely made it past my own mouth. My cervical vertebra was severely damaged, partially severed: a critical hit to any vampire. The wood had also splintered off into my bones. I struggled, but it was no use. I couldn't move.

My blood was currently being lapped up by the dry desert underneath me. Its thirst and mine grew with every drop.

But it didn't matter.

Nothing mattered but finding Gracuri and getting him away from here.

If he was smart, he'd run the instant he broke free of my arms. And if he was a fool, I hoped that any one of the Greek gods he prayed to would have mercy and save him.

I glanced briefly at Gracuri's white shoes. When I'd found him he'd been barefoot, naked, bloodied, and ravaged. But the shoes Caelius wore were clean and stark white. He'd prepared for this, unlike I had.

I tried to move and panted from the exertion, my body

struggling to respond. I was pinned apart like a mounted taxidermic butterfly.

Caelius gazed down at me with pleasure. "Now for the show." In a flash he was gone. When he returned, he had Gracuri on his knees. Caelius held him up by his curly hair, his long nails sinking into Gracuri's neck as he taunted me. "I asked my son to bring me your head, Gracuri, and he didn't. If he'd beheaded you *then*, you would've been saved from all this torture. You have your father to thank for this prolonged death."

Gracuri's lips moved, but the sound was soft, weak.

My lips mouthed the words I wanted to shout at him. "Fool! You should have run!"

My mind reeled. I wasn't sure if I thought he was a fool or that I was for believing there was any holy mercy set aside for anyone who had come to care for me.

Caelius laughed. "Come, now, we can't hear you, Gracuri. Project. From the diaphragm."

I couldn't stand it. I screamed in anger, ripping the bone of my arm through one of the spikes. Gracuri's eyes swelled with tears as his torn voice pushed out the words, "I'm so sorry, Lucian. I didn't want you to save me. No matter what Caelius says, I don't blame you. You're my world."

Caelius pulled Gracuri up to his feet, then wrapped his arms around his waist as he licked his neck victoriously. "You could learn something from this sack of meat, Lucian. *He* is loyal to his father. I devoured his children in front of him, one by one. I tortured and dismembered his favorites. And he remained *loyal* to you, even when it hurt. *Loyal.* Still, I loved watching him cry. It's rare, isn't it, tears for our kind?"

I gurgled as blood filled my mouth and my body convulsed. Caelius pulled Gracuri's eyelids open and shoved him forward. "Watch now, you pathetic excuse for a vampire. Watch as Lucian's body turns against him. He should die and revive, like you did a hundred times, but he won't. Look at his wounds. Aren't they greater and more severe than what you've suffered? Every bone in his body is broken, lanced."

Gracuri tried to jerk free, to reach for me, but Caelius held him tight. I gasped, fighting death. I always resisted it when Caelius was having his "fun." I closed my eyes and gritted my teeth until the moment passed.

When my eyes opened, Caelius laughed, dropping Gracuri to the earth like a rag doll. He crawled over to me on his hands and knees. He tried to pull out one of the spikes but was too debilitated. I looked into his eyes, sending my thoughts through him. *Gracuri, leave! I owe so much to you, let me give you this chance. I'll distract Caelius. Just run. Run, now! Save yourself and let me make good on my promise.*

He shook his head no, and Caelius laughed further.

"You see, Gracuri, the moment of death came for Lucian, but did he give into it? No. He fought the agony and held on. It's a wonder, isn't it? It would be easier to simply allow his weak body to die, then let his vampire blood, *my* blood, revive him. But he won't do it! You can imagine the things I've done to him, but he just hates, no, *despises* going to that dark, empty place of death. Which is our *home!*"

Caelius scowled as he leaned down and sat between us. He played with Gracuri's hair, lacing it between his fingertips, boredom overtaking his features.

Gracuri winced, pulling his head back in shame. When his eyes met mine, they were again filled with tears, but Caelius continued on. "That's why he's different, my Lucian. Better. Although I can't condone some of his choices. He seems attracted to mice, to rodents lower than him. Maybe it makes him feel more like a god to have pathetic servants like you and Shea around to grovel at his feet."

I moved my bloodied fingertip to Gracuri's. My pointer barely touched his thumb.

I pushed past the rips in my throat, forcing sound. It was barely a whisper, but something our kind could hear. "Why won't you just leave?" I pleaded. If he wouldn't listen to my mind, then maybe my words could reach him. I needed him to live. I needed him.

"Because he loves you, you fool! That's why he won't just leave you here!" Caelius shouted, his eyes black as night as his incisors grew to the shape of thick talons.

I struggled, pulling against the stakes as Caelius stood up. He grabbed Gracuri by the neck and held him in the air. "I tortured him for months, yet he wouldn't cry out for you! He wouldn't draw you to me! I finally had to leave a fuming trail for that dog, Adnachiel, to follow. Do you know how frustrating that was, waiting for you, my son? I had to tolerate his filth to draw you out. And how predictable. I'm sure you rushed over as soon as you caught wind of Gracuri's capture."

"Let him go, Caelius." A fourth voice joined us. I couldn't see his face, but I recognized the tone.

Aidan.

He stepped beside my mutilated frame.

I coughed, ripping another spike through my leg, freeing it in shreds. "Aidan, get out of here!" I screamed, but my voice came out as a whisper. I couldn't lose them both.

He knelt beside me, his eyes full of compassion. "Shea told me what you said. I thought I would scout ahead before we met up. When I saw Gracuri was gone, I knew you were involved."

"Did you tell her?" I choked.

Shea.

This was exactly what I'd been trying to avoid: lining up everyone I loved, all to be slaughtered, all so Caelius could revel in my agonies.

He stood up without answering.

The air was still as Caelius eyed his tall frame. I ripped another spike from the side of my torso as Gracuri's voice broke the silence. "I'm sorry, Father. I didn't want Caelius to use me against you. I would have rather died! I tried to . . . I tried to experience true death so many times. But he revived me." His voice came out in sobs, and I ached to comfort him.

"Always remember what I said to you when we first met in Thebes. I will always feel that way about you, Lucian. You've kept the deal we made then. Please don't blame your—"

Before Aidan had a chance to move, Caelius had sunk his teeth into Gracuri.

I cried out.

Aidan lunged at Caelius with his bare hands, but it was too late. Caelius flew into the air, toward the sun.

Aidan scrambled at the empty space where they'd been. His large invisible wing was useless, the other just a flapping nub from where Caelius had ripped it out the last time we'd faced him.

"Get these spikes out!" I screamed savagely, my fangs growing as they cut my lips.

Aidan rushed to me, pulling out the stakes as gently as possible. "Just tear them apart, there's no time!" I shouted.

He complied, cracking my bones as he threw the spikes miles into the air, toward where Caelius had disappeared.

I ripped my foot free of the last one, separating my arch into what looked like two giant toes.

I forced myself to stand.

Before I could leap into the air, Gracuri's voice reached my ears, a faint whisper carried on the wind. "We'll walk by the river together again. Hand in hand, like we used to. I'll see you again one day. I will always love—"

Gracuri's headless body landed by my feet.

My eyes widened in horror.

It was emaciated and drained.

"No . . ." I staggered. Aidan reached out to help me. I jerked from his grasp, hurtling my body into the sky.

The last thing I heard was the distant sound of his voice screaming out for me to wait.

It didn't matter.

I was blind with fury.

Gracuri.

Gracuri.

Gracuri.

His name had been a comfort just a few minutes ago. It had rolled like a drum in my head as I'd caressed his Greek curls. This couldn't be happening. I'd promised him. I'd had him in my arms. That wasn't his body. Caelius was just toying with me. He wasn't dead!

I broke free of the cloud cover, piercing it in a torrent of wind that howled in waves behind me.

Caelius was hovering in the air, nonchalantly licking his red mouth as he held Gracuri's head on a spike.

I screamed a sound so savage and animallike that Caelius jerked back, caught off guard. I lunged toward him, baring my fangs. I pushed him toward the earth with the force of a meteor.

When our bodies hit the ground, the desert cracked open and dirt mounded like a tidal wave around us. I ripped at Caelius's face, his chest, splattering his blood across the sand. But it wasn't his blood. It was Gracuri's blood *in* him.

I had to get it out.

Every drop of it.

Gracuri wasn't his.

Wasn't his to kill.

Wasn't his to *own*.

He tossed my body into a patch of cactus. The thorns stuck out in every direction, impaling me, but I didn't care. What was pain now that I'd lost him? I called the snakes. Rattlers moved out of their holes and slithered by my feet as I walked toward Caelius.

He smiled, pleased. The gashes on his body from my attack healed before my eyes. Having drunk a Second-Born, he was radiating power. "I love this, don't you? You're like a cub trying out his bite and growl on his father. Don't worry, Lucian. My hide is thick. I can take it."

I bared my fangs and hissed. Under my command, the ocean

of snakes slithered forward to cover his body. Some he struck away, but most of them bit hard and sank in their venom. It would have been enough to cause paralysis in a powerful vampire, but Caelius brushed them off lightly and wiggled his body as if they were feathers tickling his back.

I sneered. "I'm not *practicing* on you. My rage is not *yours*. It's *mine*! Just like Gracuri was *mine*! And his death—"

"Was *yours*!" Caelius shouted, stepping toward me. He crushed a dozen rattlers' heads with his feet as he closed the distance between us. "Gracuri's death was because of *you*. Why do you think I sought him out first?"

He was close to me now; I didn't shrink back. Caelius ran his hand down the side of my cheek as hot tears covered his fingertips.

I wasn't standing; I could only hover above the earth. My bones were all broken—they couldn't bear my weight. Ferocity had given me power, momentary strength.

Caelius smiled, eyeing my weakness. "When will you learn that nothing you have is yours? *My* blood running through you makes everyone you touch *mine*! Even that whore, Shea."

Before I could rip out his throat, he pinned me down against the hot dirt. Sitting on my torso, he gleefully swatted my face. I spat blood in every direction. When Caelius stopped, I could barely see him through the red streams flowing from my bleeding forehead.

He ground his hips into mine as he licked the side of my neck, furthering my humiliation. "My sweet boy. Still so headstrong." He sank his teeth into my neck, drinking my blood. I pushed against his chest, but I felt my strength becoming his. He'd never been able to drink me in shadow form. Other than the day Caelius had turned me, I'd never felt him suck me down.

Everything slowed.

"Stop. That's enough." A blurry figure stood behind us.

Caelius pulled back, growling. "Of course that's enough! He has *one* drop of my blood left in him, keeping his body animated. Close to comatose, but alive. He *is* alive."

I coughed, the light blinding me. As Caelius let me go, my head thudded to the earth.

He stood up, walking toward the hazy figure. My body was shutting down. This was the closest I'd come to *true* death. It felt like the night Caelius had taken me in Egypt, when I'd died in my mortal flesh. Now I would die a vampire. Without Caelius's blood in my veins, I wouldn't revive.

"Will he survive?" The figure seemed concerned.

"Of course, he has one drop. What do you think of me?" Caelius spat out in reply.

That voice. It was female and familiar. My mind filled with terror. Shea?

I rolled to my side and reached for her. "Shea, get out of here, you're not ready!"

Arms instantly wrapped around my frame and held me tenderly. She kissed my forehead and moved her hand down the side of my face. She smelled of frankincense and myrrh.

I squinted, the light behind her shadowing her face. I couldn't be certain. "Shea?"

She didn't answer.

"Shea, you have to leave me."

She placed her finger over my mouth and addressed Caelius.

"He's delirious. He thinks I'm the Vessel."

Caelius scoffed. "To be expected. His mind will recover. We need him weak so that he can remember who his *real* family is. I can giveth, and I can taketh away, Child."

"I've never left you, Lucian." Her voice rumbled like the sound of thunder in my ears. It was powerful and certain. "Ours is a proud people. I could never let you die. I will be by your side always, my love."

My jaw fell slack as my eyes adjusted. I reached my hand up, touching her face in disbelief. What was I seeing? Had I really died? Had Caelius ended me, and was this who would take me down the river of death?

There was a sweetness in her smile like there had been in childhood. "It's been a long time since you've seen me, Lucian. But I've watched over you for centuries."

I gasped, pulling her head closer to mine. "Nefertiti . . . I killed you. It's impossible. I mourned you for thousands of years."

Sadness glossed over her face.

"Um, get your hands off him." *Another* voice?

Nefertiti hissed and pulled back.

I looked up in confusion . . . at Shea and Aidan. My mind fogged. I'd lost too much blood. I couldn't will myself to move. I wasn't sure what was real. If Nefertiti was here, then I was dead. If I was dead, where was Gracuri? Had he not just promised to walk with me by the river when the time came? And what was Shea doing here?

I watched as her eyes surveyed all of my gashes. Her lips trembled in anger. "We should've come together."

I tried to whisper that I was sorry, but my mouth was too dry.

My arm just reached and thudded toward her like empty meat.

She gasped. Aidan grabbed her hand. She looked at him.

Aidan only nodded.

Caelius stood there happily. "Look what you made me do to my son, whore."

I struggled to move. This was the audience he'd been hoping for. With my last bit of strength I shouted, "You've fallen right into his hands! She's not ready yet—get her out of here!" I made eye contact, and Aidan flinched, staring into the fury of my vacant pools.

That was the last of what I had in me. My eyes couldn't stay open. I felt my body lift, and then I felt the force of the wind as everything went black.

CHAPTER 3
SHEA

"Where did she take him?" I screamed at smug-faced Caelius. At the moment, I didn't comprehend that he could probably crush me with his mind. I was too surprised that Lucian—who had been lying on the ground, emaciated and half-dead—had been in the arms of some *woman*, and then they'd suddenly been in the air and were gone.

Gone!

With some chick!

Then it hit me.

"Wait. Was that *Nefertiti*?" I yelled at Caelius.

He stared at me, auburn eyes alight with resentment. "You *dare* talk to me in such a tone, you worm? You're not worthy of—"

"Seriously, was that Nefertiti?" I interrupted Vampire Daddy's monologue. I needed to know, and I needed to know *now*. I turned to Aidan.

Aidan looked horrified, as if I'd walked in on him naked. "I . . . never really met her. Yes?" He cringed.

I was frozen in shock.

Not only was Nefertiti alive, but she was a badass vampire who had just *flown* away with Lucian.

My Lucian.

I bet she thought the same thing, that Lucian was *hers*, that he'd been hers for three thousand years. What claim did I have on him? A few lousy months? There was no way he'd pick me over her.

The thought of that struck me in a way that made me want to fall to my knees and cry.

How could Lucian want me when he could have freaking *Nefertiti*?

"You will *not* disrespect me again!" Caelius's voice boomed through the air.

I was so wrapped up in my own agony that it startled me back into my current situation.

The "Master of Darkness" was pretty upset with me.

But what Caelius didn't realize was that I was even more upset with him. He was responsible for Lucian being torn to shreds and drained of a crap-ton of blood. He was practically a living skeleton. Not even during the epic smackdown in Caelius's prison had I seen Lucian like that.

And Jerk Daddy was at fault.

He needed to be taught a lesson.

And it seemed he felt the same way about me.

Caelius threw his hands out to exert some sort of power, and I flinched, expecting *something* to happen.

Nothing.

I wanted to laugh. So I did.

This made Caelius even more furious, but before he could speak, I said, perhaps a little smugly, "You can't compel me, so I guess you're kind of screwed." I couldn't help but gloat. Probably a stupid move, but it felt so damn good.

My words were a lot more confident than I actually felt because I was pretty sure that if Caelius got his hands on me, he could tear me apart in less than a second.

As if hearing my thoughts, Caelius flew at me.

Instincts kicked in, and I connected with the earth. We were in Arizona now: my home. It gave me the strength I needed.

Even as Caelius launched himself toward me, sand rose from the ground like a giant funnel, swallowing him whole. I felt like I was in *Dune* controlling the sand worms. I could see Caelius through the maelstrom of swirling dirt as the tiny rocks shredded his skin, and he was smiling.

Caelius ripped out of the sand prison and charged at me again. I wasn't ready for it. I stepped backward, and Aidan tackled him to the ground before he could reach me, his brute strength forcing Caelius down.

But not for long.

Caelius may have been in a weakened state after escaping his prison, but he was still evil incarnate and more than a match for either of us. I knew this, but I needed Caelius to doubt himself. I needed him to believe I could best him.

I needed to make him run away.

As Aidan struggled in his losing battle to keep Caelius down, I searched the area for any signs of life. Being in Arizona, I was hoping for some Joshua trees, but there was nothing in sight except a few scraggly cactuses.

I shrugged. They'd have to do.

But first . . .

I'd figured out pretty quickly back when we fought Caelius down in his pit that he hadn't been around humans in a long time. During that fight, Caelius had put his manipulation skills to the test on Aidan's brothers, trying to convince them the Light was in danger and that they needed to leave. It was plain as day to *me*, but the angels had almost believed him. I knew then that manipulating Caelius would be child's play for a modern-day human.

I was about to try out that theory.

Aidan and Caelius were in a full-on fistfight, which I was grateful no one was around to see, as they had already created a few crater-sized holes in the ground from their impact.

I interrupted the supernatural wrestling match by shouting at Caelius, "You can't hurt me, you know that, right?"

Caelius turned from Aidan to face me. "Is that so?"

But Aidan yanked him back and started pounding on him.

"You're weak, Caelius," I said, taunting him. "You didn't complete the ritual when you escaped. No matter how many people and vamps you drain, you'll never gain your strength." I laughed sarcastically to rub in the lie more deeply. "Even when you were at full power, trapped inside your prison, you still couldn't hurt me. The worst you could do was strip me naked and pretend to rape me while I was unconscious. You know you looked like an idiot, right? When I woke up, I literally gagged. Lucian told me later how he could barely look at you; he was just as disgusted as I was." I cringed. "You're supposed to be someone he looks up to, but you're just a pervy child molester."

Caelius stared at me in rage, his eyes turning pitch-black.

I loved every second of it.

"I'm older than the sands of time, whore. I've seen the birth and death of millions of galaxies. My power is only limited by this weak, pathetic human form. It is the weakness of *your* species that keeps me tethered. And *my* son would never be disgusted by me! Any disgust is only the *human* part of his existence. You can't even comprehend the bond we have."

"I'm just telling you what Lucian told me," I countered, oozing confidence that I didn't have. "He said he wished he'd died when you made him, then he wouldn't have had to live with the embarrassment that you're his father." Oh, I sold it.

Caelius tossed Aidan aside as if he were an annoying bug.

I had just risked everything on this moment.

Connecting to the cactuses, I made them tear through the earth and smash against Caelius full force. And I kept going. I commanded every needle and branch to tear into Caelius's body, ravaging him, shredding him to a pulp.

It wouldn't kill him.

But it rattled him.

His bloody eyes grew round with disbelief.

I was pretty sure I was the only person on record who'd witnessed that phenomenon. Come to think of it, I was pretty sure I was the only one who'd *caused* that phenomenon.

But if I could make Caelius retreat, then Aidan could track him to Lucian.

Every time he tried to break free from the attacking desert

plants, I would add a windstorm of sand and earth to surround him. He choked as his body became a battered mess.

Finally, when he stopped struggling, I released him.

He dropped to the ground.

He was torn up, his skeleton more visible than skin.

I walked over to his writhing body, still terrified but trying my best to look and sound confident. "I could do this all day. You may be able to torture Lucian and your children with your little blood bond, but I'm made from the Light."

Caelius's eyes protruded out of their boney sockets. It was a nightmare staring at his mauled form, but I leaned down until we were face-to-face. "I will end you someday, Caelius, and I'm perfectly happy to make it today."

His voice was ravaged. "You can't kill me."

In a flash, Caelius was gone.

He was so fast, I didn't see him move. One moment Caelius was there, the next only a pile of cactus mush and dirt remained in his place.

I jumped when Aidan put his hand gently on my shoulder.

"Whoa, it's just me. He's gone," he said soothingly. "That was"—he looked around at the debris, his face full of awe—"pretty amazing."

I turned to Aidan, and my knees suddenly gave. He caught me as everything went black.

***

When I woke up, I was lying in a hotel bed with Aidan placing a cold washcloth over my forehead. I sat up, panicked. "Did you track Caelius? I did all of that so you could track him to Lucian!"

Aidan's arms were around me in seconds, trying to calm me down. "Shea, it doesn't work that way. If Caelius doesn't want to be found, I can't find him. My brothers and I thought that once he escaped he'd be trackable, but we were wrong. Caelius *let* me find him with Gracuri. It was all a trap."

A trap.

I knew Aidan was right, but I didn't want to accept it yet. "Why didn't Lucian let me go with him? You saw how I mangled Caelius! I could have saved Gracuri. I could have saved Lucian from . . . her." I couldn't say her name. It hurt too much, especially since Lucian probably didn't want to be saved from Nefertiti. Most likely, he was happy to see her again.

Aidan was having none of it. "If Caelius had stayed one second longer, you would have passed out in front of him, and he could've taken your soul, Shea. Your *soul*. I'd be easy to kill after that. He may be weakened, but he's not weak." Aidan was in full-on scolding mode.

"Okay, *Dad*. I still kicked his butt though," I grumbled.

"You could have died!"

"You wouldn't have let that happen." My voice grew quieter. It was a lame argument. I knew he was right, and there was no way I could justifiably defend myself. I'd acted rashly, and I could have hurt Aidan in the process.

"I might not have had a choice. I'm one angel, and I'm in *human* form. I'm no match for Caelius," he fumed.

Time to grovel.

I hugged him fiercely. "I know, and I'm sorry. I wasn't thinking. But you saw Lucian—he was so ravaged." I shuddered at the memory. "And he was in *her* arms."

I felt Aidan physically relax as he hugged me back. "It was hard for me to see him like that too."

I noticed he didn't mention Nefertiti's name. He was sparing me the agony of having someone else talk about her. It was just like Aidan to be so thoughtful.

He pulled out of the hug to look at me, his face plastered with a huge grin. "Those were some pretty crazy mind games you played on Caelius. I didn't know you had it in you."

I smiled back. "I think I tapped into the fantasy fights part of my brain. You know, where you imagine what you'd say to someone who's bullied you or something. I've had a lot of imaginary conversations with myself. This was the first time I had the balls to say it out loud though."

"Well, it worked. Caelius looked furious. Lucian would be thrilled." Aidan beamed with pride.

But at the mention of Lucian, my heart squeezed.

Aidan saw my face. "Sorry. I'll start trying to find them. Maybe I can find Lucian somehow. I know his presence better than anyone. Who knows, I may get lucky. You stay here."

"First off, no way. Second off, where is *here*?"

"Some generic motel off the highway. We're in Phoenix." I noticed how Aidan deflected my argument for him not to leave without me.

Phoenix. We were close to home, and I missed my parents terribly. Part of me really wanted to pop in and say hello since I could only imagine how worried they were. No word from me for months. Gone from campus. Gone from Arizona. Gone from their lives.

These thoughts must have been written all over my face because Aidan said softly, "You don't have to worry about your parents. We moved them to another city, and my brothers wiped their memories of us completely."

I stood up in shock. "They did *what*?" They had no memory, as if I'd never existed: all the love, my childhood, my life. All of that was gone. It hurt worse than anything.

My parents were the only ones who knew me, who remembered me as the Shea Harper I wanted to be again someday. I wanted to go back to my old life after Caelius was destroyed. I wanted to marry Lucian and have my dad walk me down the aisle. I wanted all those things. Now they were gone forever because beast-boys decided to play God?

Aidan took my hands in his and forced eye contact. "Shea, it's for their own safety and yours too, and it's not forever. If we somehow make it through all this, we can give them their memories back. Just think of the memories as repressed and replaced with new ones. They would have reported you missing, then it would have been even easier for Caelius and his lackeys to find you. We had to protect you."

I shrugged his hands away. "I can protect myself, and I'm going with you to find Lucian. I'm the best weapon you have against Caelius, and you know it." I had to admit, it did make me feel a little better knowing that my parents hadn't lost me forever. It just made me more determined to defeat Caelius so I could get them back.

Aidan couldn't argue against that, but I knew he'd try. "It's too dangerous. You're too valuable."

"Too valuable for what? Caelius has already broken out of his supernatural jail!"

"You know he still needs your soul to gain his full power," Aidan argued. "You're not going, and that's final." Aidan crossed his arms defiantly.

"And who's going to stop me?" I crossed mine as well.

Aidan sighed knowingly. "Why don't you try walking across this motel room?"

I had no idea what he was trying to prove, so I started to walk toward the door.

I almost fell to the floor, but he caught me with his strong arms.

Whoa.

The fight with Caelius had sucked more juice out of me than I'd thought.

Aidan led me to the bed and forced me to sit down.

"Just give me an hour or two," I pleaded. "I'll be back to normal."

Tucking my hair behind my ears, Aidan smiled gently. "Rest, please? I'll stay in contact, and if I find him, I won't attack without you. But I'm going to try and find him alone, okay? Just like when you were in Paris."

I stood up abruptly, ignoring my dizziness. "I'm not letting you go alone. I'll heal as we travel."

Aidan slumped, defeated. "Shea, seriously? You're going to fight me on this?"

Seeing Aidan so scared for my well-being, I couldn't force him to take me along, but I had no intention of staying put. As soon as he left, I'd leave on my own.

I sighed, trying to act defeated. "Fine. But you have to

Dream-Walk with me every night."

I must have sold it, or Aidan just heard what he wanted to hear. He pulled me in for another hug and kissed the top of my head. Gotta admit, it felt good. Aidan had always been my safe place.

"Thank you," he said. "I promise I'll keep you posted, as long as you promise not to come running at the first sign of danger."

"I'm not a *super-being*. I don't move at lightning speed like all of you guys . . . do I?" I'd never tried it, but that didn't mean I couldn't do it.

Aidan shrugged. "Truthfully, I have no clue. Just please don't try it. You'll end up running into a brick wall or something."

"Thanks." I smacked him on the chest.

"Anytime." He smiled, glowing with an expression of implicit trust in me.

Well, *that* hurt to watch, knowing I was blatantly lying to him, but I smiled back all the same. "You'd better get a move on, mister."

I felt like such a horrible person.

Aidan nodded and hugged me one more time before he left.

It was good he left quickly because I was a terrible liar, and if Aidan had stayed any longer, he would have seen through me.

I waited a good hour before I figured he was long gone and I could start my own journey.

If I could just Dream-Walk with Lucian, he would be able to tell me where he was. Not that he *would*. I had no doubt that Lucian would try and hide the location, afraid I'd risk myself by coming to rescue him. But Lucian didn't have to *say* anything, because while Dream-Walking I could attempt to see his surroundings. Then I could maybe figure out where he was. A lot of ifs and maybes, but I had to try.

I closed my eyes and meditated until I fell asleep.

***

Dream-Walking was a strange thing. It was getting easier, but I'd grown so used to doing it with Aidan that I almost jumped inside his head automatically.

Luckily, I had enough control to stop myself and concentrate on Lucian.

Nothing.

As in, a big old block.

That was odd, because I'd Dream-Walked with Lucian enough that I could jump right in anytime I wanted. Either Caelius or Nefertiti was shutting me out.

Or, worse, Lucian was.

After hours of trying, I gave up.

In my desperation to find where Lucian was, I had a crazy idea. I tried brainstorming to think of anything else, but after a while, I sighed inwardly. It looked like crazy won out.

Ur-Nammu, here I come.

We had some serious Dream-Walking together in the past, so it wasn't hard to find him. He was awake, so I had more control over what we were going to see in our shared vision.

I picked somewhere familiar: the house with a porch swing that rested in the middle of a wheat field. It was where he'd taken me the first time we'd Dream-Walked. Somehow it seemed appropriate.

Ur-Nammu looked amused. "Shea Harper. I never expected to see you again, at least not in my subconscious."

"I'm stupid like that, I guess," I replied honestly. Then curiosity got the best of me. "How can you Dream-Walk and be awake?"

"I'm a fantastic multitasker," he answered with some bemusement. "And, as you should already know, vampires rarely sleep."

"You're in a good mood," I said. "I hear you're in Miami."

He closed his eyes in a moment of contentment. "To feel the sun on my face for the first time in thousands of years is truly breathtaking. I owe that to you, and I'm genuinely sorry for my part in how it happened."

"You did it for your daughter." I threw that out there to see his expression.

Ur-Nammu raised an eyebrow as if he knew where our conversation was heading. "Let me guess, Nefertiti has taken your Lucian."

I hated it when people could see right through me. "Well . . . yeah. Can you tell me where they are?"

"Why would I do that?"

Well, at least he didn't say no, which was better than I'd expected. I knew this was a long shot, but I couldn't think of any other way to find Lucian. "Because you want me to kill Caelius?" I hoped he'd go for it.

Ur-Nammu paused, eyeing me up and down. "You think you're capable?"

"Ask your daughter," I answered cryptically.

Wrong answer.

Ur-Nammu's hand wrapped around my throat. Even though I was sleeping, I still felt like I was being choked. "What did you do to my daughter?" he said, steel in his voice.

"Nothing!" I sputtered. "I hurt Caelius though. I'm assuming they're together!" I managed to say through garbled grunts.

"Oh." He let me go. "I apologize."

I rubbed my neck and felt oxygen rush back into my lungs. Dream-Walking was crazy. I wondered if I could really die in here. I didn't want to find out. I needed to tread more carefully. This guy was a master at the craft. I was just a noob.

"Jeez, I would never hurt your precious Nefertiti." I tried to hide the sarcasm in my tone, but I really felt like being a brat. "I can tell you hate Caelius as much as I do, and the only reason you helped him escape was because you wanted to live in the sunlight with your daughter. I get it. But wouldn't it be nice to not have to worry about Caelius ever again?"

Ur-Nammu paused for a moment, then gave a reflective sigh.

"I don't know where they are," he admitted.

"But you could—"

"I can do nothing. I'm still being disciplined for helping Lucian. Destroying the overzealous in Miami is my punishment. Contrary to popular belief, not all vampires like to torture and kill. Caelius will summon me when he feels I've learned my lesson. For him, that could be centuries." Ur-Nammu was definitely annoyed.

I felt bad for momentarily obliterating his good mood, but I couldn't leave without learning something useful. "All I want is Caelius dead and Lucian back with me. Can you help me or not?"

Ur-Nammu took a deep breath. "What if Lucian doesn't want to come back? Will you still help take down Caelius?"

So, Ur-Nammu didn't think Lucian would pick me over his daughter. It crushed my soul because I didn't think Lucian would either.

But I nodded. "Yes, of course. I'm made of Light or whatever. I think that means I was born to destroy Caelius."

He smiled sadly, and the sadness was meant for me, which made it worse. "I'm sorry, Shea Harper, I truly am, but Nefertiti will always be Lucian's true love. Yours was but a shadow of what they had."

I didn't argue. My defensive button wanted to snipe back at him, but what would I say? "Nuh-uh" or "You don't know!" Both sounded desperate and lame, even though desperate and lame was exactly how I felt. "Can you help me or what?"

Ur-Nammu nodded slowly. "I will send someone who can help. They will know where Caelius holds Nefertiti and Lucian."

Something about what he said struck me as odd. "What do you mean *holds* Nefertiti? Lucian's *their* prisoner."

His eyes were distant, even sadder than before. "Why do you think Lucian didn't know that female vampires exist?"

I hadn't thought about it. I was too wrapped up in Nefertiti cradling Lucian to care. "She hid from him? I don't know."

Ur-Nammu clenched his hands into fists as he said, "My beautiful daughter went from one master to another. Caelius kept her hidden. She's been his slave for over three thousand years. I knew that when Caelius was freed from his prison, he'd allow her to show herself. She'd still *belong* to Caelius, but at least she wouldn't have to hide anymore." Ur-Nammu stared me down, his expression determined. "Once Caelius is dead, Nefertiti will be free. I will make this happen with or without your help."

"I'm helping," I replied immediately. I hated that I felt a pang of sympathy for Nefertiti, my competition. To be a slave for thousands of years, to be *Caelius's* slave . . . I shuddered. No one deserved that. No one.

Ur-Nammu nodded once. "Then we have a pact."

A pact? I didn't like the sound of that, but I'd do anything to find Lucian. "Agreed."

"I'll send her now," he said formally.

I woke up.

Her?

CHAPTER 4
LUCIAN

My eyes twitched. They were frozen open like a living corpse. Now I knew what it was like to be dead. All these years I'd felt hollow, empty, a reanimated shell. Shea had brought me back to the boy in Gutium. The boy, not the monster.

Now as my vacant eyes stared out, unable to blink, I knew that I'd never deserve her. Shea was my Eden, and I was nothing more than Adam tasting the apple's sweet nectar. It would have been better if Caelius had finished me off alongside Gracuri. I'd rather die than be used as bait.

My chest convulsed slightly. Drained as I was, the pain of his loss was unbearable. Now that I was in the same situation, I understood his foolishness completely, and his love. I would do anything to prevent Shea from coming to me. I would endure any torture if it meant her safety, just like he had.

I used all the power I had left in my weak senses to sever our dream connection. She wouldn't find me here.

Caelius moved from the corner of the room. How long had he been standing there? He laughed, casually walking over to my chains, where I was mounted to the wall like a prize elk.

He sat down by my feet. I jerked, but the chains were too tight. He ran his hands up my leg, then rested his head on my calf. "So you would still defy me, Lucian, even to your last drop of blood. How cliché and unreasonable. I find it enthralling nonetheless."

I forced myself to look down. Moving my eyes felt like dragging sand over glass. I tried to speak, to voice my hate. Nothing came out but a strange wheezing sound.

Caelius smiled, rubbing the side of his face on my jeans like a cat marking its territory. "What's that, my boy? I can barely hear you." Quicker than any movement I could register, he was standing and squeezing my mouth in fury, his lips inches from mine. It took a moment for my eyes to meet his. He waited.

I saw his distorted face. He'd been visibly thrashed; I could see the pink flesh covering his cheeks. If I'd had the energy, I would have smiled at him. I knew it was Shea who had given him that new face-lift.

He squeezed my cheeks harder. Different emotions clouded his eyes: obsession, lust, calculation. It was the last one that always frightened me. When his mind was contemplating his next step, the only real thing, the only promise, was of a future filled with agony. And Caelius *always* planned in advance. If he was planning now, then something had changed: a new calculation was being added.

Shea had changed the game.

He released my face and patted me on the cheek. My

emaciated skin hung from my bones. It twitched as he playfully tapped my jaw. I ignored the pain and watched through half-closed eyes as Caelius turned away and walked to the edge of the cell. He exited through a wooden door and left me alone.

I slowly took in my surroundings. I was in an underground cavern, and everything was wet.

Then I smelled it.

Blood.

Fresh and pumping.

Instinctually, my body jerked toward the smell, rattling the chains. I was on autopilot. My body was reacting without thought, without reason.

I tried to clear my head and regain control as Caelius returned, shoving a man and a woman into the cell. My fangs enlarged, and I snapped at the air like a rabid dog, saliva dripping from my mouth. Wherever Shea was, I was glad she couldn't see this.

Caelius stepped toward me. "Now there, Son. Don't hurt yourself any further. Let me bring them to you."

They were begging. The man was pleading for Caelius to spare his wife, to only take his life and let her live. The woman was doing the same, countering his plea with a heartfelt cry of her own for self-sacrifice. It amused Caelius at first, but then his expression shifted. His face soured from glee to disgust, then boredom. It was always that way when he thought he'd won.

"Come," he commanded, "step in front of my Lucian and offer up your necks." The man's eyes glazed over, and he marched toward my feral body, completely compelled. The woman hesitated.

Caelius stepped next to her and whispered into her ear. As

he was speaking, her face softened, then she stepped beside her husband, exposing her neck.

I yelled for them to run, but nothing came out, only puffs of air followed by maddened snapping. I tried to remember the mound of bodies and Gracuri, how I was more than my body, more than . . . this.

When they were inches from me, I smelled it. Not just blood, but a familiar scent. Did I know these people? My eyes met Caelius's in horror. Were these the lingering remainders of Gracuri's children? No. One was female, and they were still human.

Still, there was a familiar scent in the air that I couldn't place. Even as my body strained toward them, pulling savagely against the chains, within I surged against myself. I shifted that one small drop of blood floating in my bones to my vocal chords, reanimating them.

"Caelius, I'll do what you want. Just let these innocent people go."

He stepped casually beside them, straightening his all-white suit: Gracuri's suit. Not the one Gracuri had worn often, but my *favorite* suit, the one I loved seeing him in.

Gracuri had always looked like the morning, all covered in white, as if he were Helios himself riding his fiery chariot across the sky. It crushed my soul seeing Caelius flaunt it now, wearing it like a newly skinned mink coat.

The jacket should have been too big, but he'd already had it tailored. It still *smelled* like Gracuri though. Of course he wouldn't have it washed—that would take away its usefulness in reminding me of what he'd done, of what my disobedience had cost. I couldn't growl or fight. I just stared as the gleeful expression on Caelius's face returned.

My mouth pulled open, forced wide as my fangs grew longer, reaching for the woman's supple neck. I couldn't stop this. If this was even *real*. Everything was slow, indistinct, covered in a thick fog of conflicting impulses. My thoughts were everywhere, dissolving like mud across the water. But if this was happening, if I was going to eat two innocent humans while being ruled by uncontrollable instinct and not willpower, how could I look at Shea again? I was trying so hard to change. I had to be more than Caelius's pet. She deserved that much.

Caelius leaned closer, thrusting himself between the woman and me, whispering smugly, "Oh, are you still waiting for my answer? Of course I'll spare them . . . if they mean that much to you. I just thought you might be hungry. I'll tell you what, I'll let them stay the night with you and have a little Lucian sleepover. If they're alive in the morning, I'll honor my word and take them home. It's a simple deal, and I'm in the mood to make deals, seeing as I'm wearing apparel by Gracuri. Didn't you make a deal with him once as well? Wasn't that your cute little code when you turned him?"

He ran his thumb along the man's neck, his nail sinking in. The hairline cut bled instantly. Then he reached over and did the same to the woman. The smell of it was intoxicating. I shook my head, begging myself. *You're better than this, Lucian. Think of the cost. These people are important. You can feel it. They're innocent.*

Caelius slammed the rusted metal door. My eyes blackened just as my teeth savagely sunk into the woman's neck. Fear and terror etched into her blue eyes as I ripped through the meat of her throat.

***

Everything blurred. When my senses returned, I was inches away from Nefertiti. She held a rag and basin. She softly dragged the wet cotton over my face as I stared into her purple eyes. They'd been a strange color when she was alive: dark, almost black, but when the sun hit them you could see the violet.

"I always thought you were meant to be the ruler of our people, Nefertiti. Even your eyes were unique and beautiful. You were unlike anyone in our tribe." It was a strange thing to say. But my mind was lost: the starvation, the feeding. Besides, what would she care? This was just a hallucination.

I'd seen it happen before. I'd even caused it in Frank after he'd tried to drink Shea. Drain a vampire enough, and before their true death they'd see the faces of those they loved the most . . . those they'd killed.

She smiled. My insides warmed and melted the way they always had. Nefertiti wasn't a bad ambassador of death. She touched the cool rag to my forehead, wiping off blood and bits of meat. "In some cultures, purple is the color of royalty. It certainly was enough for the Pharaoh to single me out from the other Gutian women, to claim me as his own. And Caelius, well, that had more to do with you, Lucian, and less about *my* worth."

I looked deeper into her eyes. Now they seemed alight somehow, bright even in the darkness. "I would have killed the Pharaoh a million times over, had I been an immortal then. But I was just a boy when I died. And you were my everything."

She stopped cleaning my face and leaned in, bringing her lips close to mine. I closed my eyes, sensing only her fragrant smell.

She touched the engraved emerald necklace at my chest. It had been a gift to her when I was a boy. My memories were flooded with our shared moments. Our first kiss by the riverbanks: I'd been ten, and she'd been twelve. I'd thought about that kiss every night after. She'd had me then. My thoughts, my will, they were hers to do with as she wished.

She whispered, "I mourned for you in silence when you were being whipped outside my window. I never told you, but I was there when the Pharaoh was having you tortured . . . and I couldn't let you die, not my La-Narru. But that doesn't matter. I'm here with you now." Her voice was soft like gossamer. "Lucian . . ." It was rich like the aroma of rosemary. "Do you love her?"

I opened my eyes. Nefertiti's face was vulnerable. I'd never seen her look so troubled. She had always worn a mask of complete confidence, even in youth. I reached for her, but the shackles quickly reminded me where I was.

La-Narru.

That was a name I hadn't heard since we'd been children. It was the name my mother had called me. It was Caelius who'd given me a new name—Lucian—and with it, a new life.

My mouth fell open. How could I have forgotten? I hadn't been "Lucian" until his teeth had sunk into my young neck. My birthright, my very name had changed. *La-Narru*. It had meant something in my native tongue. It meant—

"Do you love her?" She leaned closer.

"Whom are you speaking of?" I pulled back. "Whom do I love?"

Nefertiti dipped the rag into the basin, then let the water pour down my face as she squeezed it over my tangled hair. "Shea Harper."

I looked at her, puzzled. "Shea is alive. And we are both dead, my sweet Nefari. You are no doubt preparing me to pass through the Nile with Anubis. Or is it to mount the Steed of Oknah in Gutium so it can carry my soul to the stars?"

I paused, holding Nefertiti's steady gaze with my own. "We both know I don't deserve either. I deserve Caelius. I deserve the black endlessness of his oblivion. But somehow you being the apparition of my harrowing tells me that my death may be a sweet one."

Her eyes softened further. "He really broke you this time. He forced me to watch, always in his shadow. The things I've seen him do to you, my only love. It pains my heart to see you so weak. I never should have—" She brought her thick, full lips close to mine. They smelled like honey, like they used to, and the taste . . . she hovered there, just out of reach.

Her violet eyes didn't blink. She was frozen like the sculptures I'd made of her likeness in Egypt. I'd molded them out of mud and straw, unworthy things that failed to mimic her perfection.

She moved closer. "My sweet La-Narru, I haven't heard you say Nefari since before I was a slave, before the Pharaoh made me Nefertiti. Do you still see me like that, like the girl by the riverbank in Gutium?"

I smiled, wanting to touch the soft curve of her back. "You have and always will be Nefari, a jewel among stones, my morning star."

She wet her lips and touched my cheek. "You are stronger

than your father ever imagined . . . stronger than I knew as a mortal woman. You are fearless now. The warrior you've become could have easily led us into battle centuries ago. And I would have stayed by your side. I would have ruled by your side. I would have been *yours*."

I pulled away—to see her incisors grow.

My head hit the wall I was chained to. Nefertiti leaned in closer. Before her lips could touch mine, one thought escaped into a single word. "Shea," I uttered.

Nefertiti jerked back, scowling.

"Why did you ask if I love her?" I demanded. "Why in death does that matter?"

She closed her eyes.

I waited in silence. I didn't know why I'd asked that. At the moment I couldn't remember what "Shea" meant. I just felt . . . felt that . . . that something wasn't right.

I was grasping, reaching, but every thought was scattered. Caelius had never brought me to the point of near extinction before. It was different when I'd been inside him, disappearing into nothingness. At that time, the ache and emptiness had burned a hole in me that no amount of sunlight could fill. But this? It was like when I was a child and had caught fever. I'd been close to death then, my mother mourning at my side.

"My mother . . . Anna-Steen." Her name caught in my throat.

I hadn't thought of her in so long. Now my thoughts drifted from beast, to man, to boyhood. I remembered the wildness of my mother's brown hair and the soil underneath her nails. She was a kind woman—too kind—and my father loved her with all the might of a raging lion.

They'd fallen in love when he and his people had raided her village. My mother had faced him, Onack the Great, with nothing more than a spinning needle in her hands. He'd often touch the scar down his left eye when he looked at her. If she caught him staring, they'd both smile, then he'd attack. They would roll to the floor, feigning brutalities like children, all the while laughing. It was how I'd known love existed in the world, that it was real, ageless, and infinite. They came from cultures that hated each other: it was in their blood. But love saw past that.

The shadow of the man that'd been left when she'd died next to me, both of us caught in the same fever, was how I'd learned what it was like to lose that love.

Then the wars had come. When my father stayed to fight, he'd begged me to leave, to live the life of a craftsman and a poet like my mother had wanted, but I'd refused. I would have rather died than leave Onack's side. But he pleaded that he wasn't strong enough to bear witness to the death of *all* that he loved, all that he had left worth fighting for.

I shook my head, remembering the tears in Onack's brown eyes. He'd been a large man, larger than the men they spit out like emaciated models now: like me. I never had the warrior's build of my father or Ur-Nammu. I had Anna-Steen's tall, slender frame, her gentle spirit, her teal eyes.

After her death, it'd been the color alone that'd prevented him from looking directly at me. Still, I shouldn't have let his tears affect my judgment—but he *never* cried. When they'd burned my mother's body, he hadn't shed a tear. He'd kept his grief trapped under layers of muscle and rage.

But on the night before battle, when I'd prepared to stand

beside him, Onack the Great's tears had tumbled out like an avalanche.

My lips parted. "How could I refuse my own father?" I gasped out the words, lost in my own conclusions. "To break his heart twice over by standing against the might of Egypt with hands that had held a paintbrush longer than a spear?"

Nefertiti's voice pulled me from the painful memory. She whispered quietly, "No one blames you, Lucian. You were being obedient, doing what your father asked, what we all asked. No one thought you a coward." Nefari's face was soft again, her eyes penetrating. My gaze followed the long black lines of makeup angled to a point on the corner of her eyelids. She looked like she had in Egypt, not Gutium.

She smiled. "Your expression, La-Narru. Your thoughts are drifting again. It's difficult to follow. I've rarely heard you reminisce about your parents."

I reached out and caught a piece of her black hair. I pulled the strands closer. They were soft and slipped through my fingertips like silk. "That's because it's too painful. Some things are better kept out of the mind . . . like you. I grieved over your loss for so long. Then I just filled that longing with sand—as I'd done with my mother's burned ashes after her funeral."

Her lips opened, and Nefertiti gazed at me like I was a helpless child. "When your father whipped you after your mother's death, that black soot covering your mouth . . . was her ashes?" She closed her eyes, and so did I. I could still hear the fury in his voice.

No one but Onack knew why my face had been covered in ash. My father had tied me to a post. The whip he'd wielded had torn the flesh from my back. I'd wept then. I'd screamed out into the sun, crying, not for him to stop, but from the pain of losing my mother.

The whole village had gathered. Ur-Nammu had tried to pull him back, but he was no match for Onack, a wild ox of a grieving man. He hadn't heard their pleas. It was only when Nefari had thrown her small body in front of my own—bracing for the whip, trying to protect me—that he'd paused.

I opened my eyes, pulling away from the memory and the pain of loss.

Nefertiti's eyes were full of compassion, her lips trembling as she spoke. "You know your father didn't mean to hurt you, La-Narru. Catching you choking on your mother's ashes must have blinded him, but he loved you." She grabbed the wet rag and let the cold water drip down my back, over the deep scars.

My gaze hardened. I felt the memory's sting as if the childhood wounds were still gaping open. "I know he loved me. But his lashings hurt more than any I received on your behalf in Egypt, Nefari. Because Onack was *right*. My mother died, and I lived. She was stronger than I was. *She* should have overcome the fever, not me."

She wrapped her arm around my neck and rested her head on my chest. "You have to know that it wasn't your fault."

I shook my head. Why lie, especially now that I was dead?

"You're wrong, Nefari; it *was* my fault. I was the one who wanted to see the marketplace. I didn't want to follow in my father's footsteps—I wanted to leave Gutium, to see the world past our village. If she'd never taken me, we wouldn't have gotten poisoned from the tea she purchased there. The tea *I* wanted. The tea I *begged* her to buy. It was the last time, before Shea, that I begged for anything. The last time I said '*please*.' My desires, my hunger, poisoned my own mother. She died because of me."

She fell silent, only shaking her head, concern flooding her features.

"I'm glad my father caught me. When Anna-Steen died and I ate her ashes, I'm glad he saw. I'm glad it infuriated him enough to beat me. I'm glad—"

She kissed my lips. Without a thought, without a word, I felt the rich, soft nectar of her touch. She pulled away slowly, her eyes burning into mine.

"Quiet now, La-Narru. Thinking of these things will keep you weak, and you have to regain your strength. Caelius has a plan for using you, but he could easily change his mind and decide to kill you, whether or not he's promised me your safety. You have to come back to me . . . you have to come back to your power, Lucian. You have to regain your senses."

I looked at her. She'd been the only one I'd loved after my mother's death, the only reminder that love could still exist in the world. I hadn't been able to stuff her ashes down my throat when I'd killed her; her father had taken her body. But I drank the sands of Egypt for years, hoping to dull the pain.

"I loved you, Nefari."

Her mouth opened, and for a moment she leaned closer, closing her eyes. Then she stopped. "You loved me, like you loved your father . . . your mother . . ."

I nodded, pulling against the chains, trying to touch her.

"Like you loved . . . Shea Harper."

"Yes."

Nefertiti stepped back, sighing. She let the rag in her hand fall into the basin. "So, it's true. You love her. It's not just boredom or infatuation."

I blinked, confused. "I'm simply reliving my life. This is the pathway before death. Mine is long because I've lived thousands of years. Some that I've killed relive their existence in a matter of moments. Are you the part of my mind that is fighting death? Why would I ask myself a question I already know the answer to?

"Of course I love Shea. I love her body and soul. With her I feel . . . alive. But it's so much more. I feel like I did when I used to watch my parents sneak kisses in the garden, that sense of wonder when I look into her eyes. Like I've known her in other lifetimes, in the depths of forever. If there is an eternity, or was, I will *always* know her. These forms we find each other in now are meaningless and will pass away, but our love will always pull us back together across time, across any distance. Like the ships of Gorthos, and Andromeda and her fated lover—"

"Enough!" Nefertiti cried. "You have said enough." Now her eyes were hard and bone-dry. "You are clearly delusional. I will continue to care for you until you regain your mind. But you should know that you're not dying, Lucian. I would never let Caelius or *anyone* take you from me. Not in Egypt. Not now."

Nefertiti's face looked like it had before battle—fierce and angry. "I'm the one who heard of the powerful man by the Nile. I'm the one who sent Caelius to find you after the Pharaoh decided to kill you. The bargain was for my life, my loyalty, and my secrecy.

"Caelius turned you because of *me*, La-Narru. After you were a vampire, he turned me in secret later that night. That was the price *I* paid to save you: eternal enslavement. When you tried to turn me, you thought I'd died, but I only feigned death. I was already a vampire. Caelius made me live in hiding afterward."

I reeled in horror. What was she saying? What torment was this? That I was still alive, and she'd been *turned* by Caelius before he'd been imprisoned? Impossible! This was the madness before death.

Caelius sauntered through the door. "I'm sorry, dear, but that's all the time I will allow you today."

Nefertiti nodded and, without so much as a second look, left the room.

Caelius moved toward me, eyeing my beaten frame. Cupping my face in his palm, he tilted his head. "See how obedient she is? I trained her well. You just have to know someone's weakness . . . and squeeze." He grabbed a tuft of my hair and pulled my head back.

He raked his lips over my exposed neck. "You and her family are *her* weaknesses. My promise to keep you all safe, to keep you together, well, that's been enough for my girl to stay obediently at my side. Nefertiti's a good pet, unlike you."

I jerked at the chains, growling. I couldn't piece together their words. It didn't make sense.

Caelius let my head drop and then sighed. "What fun is teasing you when your brain is fevered like mush? If you continue down this spiral you'll have another true death, Lucian, one I can't bring you back from. Then what would I do? I'd be inconsolable.

"It *is* curious, though. I've often wondered what would happen if I drank you down to one drop, as I did today. I'm somewhat disappointed that it's left you in what smells like some kind of human illness. Well then, let's get you mended so we can have our fun, my darling."

He snapped his fingers. As if they were mice following a flute, mindless humans scuttled in a line behind him until the entire cell was packed like canned meat.

"Dinnertime."

CHAPTER 5
SHEA

Whoever this *helper* was that Ur-Nammu was sending me, she was certainly taking her time getting here.

Her.

Another female vampire.

I was still reeling at the fact that Nefertiti was an old-as-dirt-vampire as well. It made me feel better to think of her as crone-ish. Catty of me, yet satisfying.

Maybe it was Nefertiti herself who was coming? I hoped not. I wasn't ready to face that particular demon just yet. Besides, Ur-Nammu had said Nefertiti was a prisoner and had been a slave for thousands of years.

I shuddered. Being in the room with Caelius for five minutes had been torturous, but century after century? I was surprised the girl wasn't batshit insane by now.

I needed to stay focused on rescuing Lucian. Even if he picked Nefertiti over me, I loved him regardless. I would never leave him to Caelius. Whether or not his feelings had changed, it didn't matter.

Ugh.

Of course it mattered.

I had to push those kinds of thoughts away. It hurt too much to think about him not loving me. Or worse: loving her more.

I stood up and stretched. My strength was coming back slowly but surely. I couldn't believe how much kicking Caelius's butt had drained me.

He was so powerful that every time I hurt him it took a chunk out of my energy. I hoped I'd given him reason to pause when thinking about confronting me again, but the guy was so full of himself he was probably just licking his wounds and planning his next attack.

I was going to need a lot more power if I wanted to seriously injure the guy, let alone kill him.

I sat in a dumpy hotel room that I'd paid for in cash. I was sure Aidan could find me by scent or some other angel detective skill, but I wasn't going to leave a paper trail for him or anyone else to follow. I'd watched my fair share of police procedural shows.

Speaking of, with nothing to do but wait, I decided to flip on the TV and catch an episode or two. There was always some kind of marathon running on cable. Nothing like a good detective drama to put perspective on my life. I used to think the stories were unimaginably horrifying, filled with serial killers and murderers, but now they looked like kittens and puppies playing compared to a second with Caelius.

If only people knew how much of these fictionalized movies

and shows were actually real. It was better that they didn't. No one would leave their house. But then again, maybe they shouldn't. Not if Lucian's father gained his full strength back. The world would be changed forever. It would become a nightmare.

Shaking the dark thoughts from my mind, I switched stations until I found a nice '80s movie I could use to pleasantly escape from reality. Nothing like fluorescent fashion and big bangs to make me feel warm and fuzzy inside. I wanted to find Lucian, but I knew whomever Ur-Nammu was sending would be my only hope.

My mind drifted with curiosity. Who was this girl coming to help me? A vampire to be sure, but Aidan and Lucian had told me that only *men* could be vampires. Now suddenly Nefertiti was one and, possibly, whoever was coming?

How many females were there, and how had they hidden from Lucian for thousands of years? You'd think with the amount of time he'd been on the planet, Lucian might have had some inkling that girl vampires existed. It didn't make much sense. Then again, not much in my life did these days.

I jumped when I heard a knock on the door. It wasn't loud, but I'd been so wrapped up in my thoughts that the sound jolted my psyche. My palms were sweating. I mentally prepared myself to make my blood liquid sunshine if things went south.

Taking a deep breath, I walked to the shabby motel door and cracked it open, peering through cautiously.

"Are you *her*?" I greeted her, sounding like an idiot, something I realized as soon as I'd said it.

"If you're asking if I'm the one Ur-Nammu sent, then yes. I'm *her*," the woman replied brusquely.

She looked my age, but dang—she was drop-dead gorgeous. Her skin was golden brown, and her large, almond-shaped eyes were a stunning gold to match. High, sculpted cheekbones made her face appear as if it had been carved in clay, and even her nose was perfect and straight.

I'd assumed all vampires were pale from lack of sun, but she had a permanent sun-kissed glow that took my breath away.

"Are you going to let me in?" she asked impatiently.

Oops. I'd been staring. A lot.

I opened the door all the way and waved her inside. "I'm Shea." I figured she knew that, but it was my clever way of trying to find out her name.

"I know that," she responded as she entered the room.

The more direct approach would have to do. "And you are?"

"Mekytaten." She gracefully sat on the wooden armchair in the corner.

A chill ran down my spine. I'd always been a little obsessed with the history of Nefertiti (now I knew why: stupid intuition!) so I knew all of her daughters' names. Mekytaten was her second oldest.

Man.

Nefertiti's daughter was as beautiful as she was.

I felt sick to my stomach. How could I compete with utter perfection? I was like the ugly kid-sister compared to this family tree. Why on earth would Lucian pick me when he could have Nefertiti? And it was a pretty good bet he knew all her daughters. He'd probably planned on rescuing them along with Nefertiti. When she'd died—or, more accurately, when he *thought* she'd died—Lucian's hopes and dreams had died with her.

The weird part of this was that history stated the Pharaoh Akhenaten had died *before* Nefertiti, but Lucian had said she'd still been Akhenaten's slave when she'd died. Of course, history also made it sound like the Pharaoh had loved Nefertiti with all his heart, and Lucian had claimed that wasn't true either.

It made me wonder how much of the past that I'd learned from history books was wrong. It reminded me of the telephone game, where you whisper a sentence in someone's ear and so on, until it gets back to you, and the original statement is unrecognizable. Too many half-truths and lies. People in power wanted to write their own story. What would a true recounting sound like? Probably nastier and a lot more dramatic.

"From the look on your face, I can see you know who I am." Mekytaten seemed impressed.

It was hard to imagine this girl was only a little younger than Lucian. She dressed like someone my age: striped crop, tight jeans, Chuck Taylors. I'd imagined she'd show up in robes and gold jewelry like the hieroglyphs depicted ancient Egyptians wearing. It was jarring to see her dressed as a normal teenager.

I decided I should stop gaping and actually speak. "I know a little bit of history. I admired your mother in school." I went with polite. No sense in pissing off She-Vamp.

"Admired. Past tense." She eyed me with judgment.

"It's not as if I knew she was alive . . . until today," I uttered defensively. "Where have you guys been hiding, anyway?" Might as well start with the obvious questions.

Mekytaten watched me carefully for a few moments, then smiled reluctantly. "Sorry, I'm being rude. I've been listening to my mother rage about you for the last few months. I guess it rubbed off on me."

She sounded like a teenager. It struck me as bizarre. Mekytaten was ancient. She should've been talking like Lucian, all formal and eloquent.

Mekytaten gave a short laugh. "I'm a good adapter. I have to fit in, and no offense to Lucian and his children, but their language habits don't exactly *blend*."

"Did you just read my mind?" I was mortified.

"Don't worry. I can only hear you when you direct your thoughts at me. A Vessel's brain naturally shuts out vampires, but I'm particularly good at diving into the subconscious," she explained. "As far as I know, I'm the only vampire who can do it."

Then what Mekytaten had originally said hit me. "Nefertiti was *raging* about *me*?" I didn't like the sound of that.

She sighed. "Look, my mother's been in love with Lucian her entire existence. He's never loved anyone before or after her. Let's just say, you were unexpected."

"Oh."

"My grandfather sent me here for a reason. I know where Lucian and my mother are being kept. But we can't go there . . . yet."

"Yet?" I could see she had something in mind.

"You're still weak from your fight with Caelius, right?"

I hated to admit it, but I felt like I was recovering from being hit by a car. "A little. But I could face him."

Mekytaten shook her head. "No. You couldn't. You were acting on instinct and anger before. I'm shocked you hurt him as badly as you did, but Caelius recovers fast, and you don't."

Bluntness.

I really hated that trait at the moment.

"I don't know how long it will take me to recover, and we need to rescue Lucian." I knew it sounded pathetic, but I didn't care. I couldn't stand the thought of Lucian being starved and tortured by Caelius. What kind of hell was he enduring right now? I didn't want him with his father for a second longer.

"You know almost nothing about your abilities," she stated boldly. When my face radiated defensiveness, she put a hand up to placate me. "Don't get me wrong, Adnachiel and Lucian have taught you how to use your powers, but that's just the tip of the iceberg."

Hearing her use colloquialisms was just wrong. I realized in that moment that I was a historical bigot. Aidan had an excuse because he'd been born at the same time I was, but she was so old. Ur-Nammu was all official sounding when he talked, and I was betting on the fact that Nefertiti was too. It bothered me that Mekytaten sounded like she belonged in my time. It almost felt unfair, like she didn't have the right to be a teenager, to be like me.

"Tip of the iceberg, huh?" I crossed my arms and mocked her. Man, I was being a brat, but I couldn't control myself. "You're a couple decades off in your colloquialisms." Not really. I had used that sucker quite a few times myself, but I wanted to take Mekytaten down a notch. She was just too damn pretty.

Her face fell slightly. "I didn't mean anything by it." She was embarrassed.

I made her embarrassed.

I was a jerk.

An a-hole.

A mean girl.

I sat on the bed across from Mekytaten and sighed deeply. "I'm sorry. I'm totally jealous of your mom," I confessed. "And you. And . . . that's it. I'm defensive and taking it out on you. I'm a dick." No sense in beating around the bush. I'd never been a rude or inconsiderate person.

Well, now that I thought about it, I had been just as mean to Lucian when I'd first met him. What was it about vampires that brought out the worst in me? Maybe it was our inherent Light versus Dark. I had to control my attitude, or I would alienate the only person who could help me find Lucian.

Mekytaten's face softened, and she appeared relieved. "Looking like a teenager, I try very hard to adjust myself as the years go by, but when you've been alive as long as I have, it's difficult to keep up with all the advances, especially the language. I didn't even have to learn English for a long time. My grandfather and Lucian don't have to do this as much. Lucian is older than me; though he looks like he's in his twenties, he was actually in his thirties when he was turned. My mother is a couple years older than him," Mekytaten shared.

She was giving me insight into Lucian and her mother. This only made it harder, though, because now Nefertiti was becoming a real person with a real life to me.

Mekytaten was the daughter of a Pharaoh. That was huge. That was *her* reality. She and her sisters had obviously been allowed to grow into teenagers before Nefertiti had turned them. I wanted to know all the details, all the secrets and lies, and how they had managed to stay hidden for this long.

But that wasn't what Mekytaten was here for.

And before I had rudely berated her, I was pretty sure she had been trying to help me with my powers. "You were saying before about tips of icebergs?"

Mekytaten smiled. "I'll get right to it this time. I can teach you how to heal yourself, to regenerate. I want you to be at full power when we rescue my mother and Lucian."

My eyes widened. "I can do that?"

"Oh yes. But I have to take you somewhere. Will you let me?" Mekytaten asked delicately. "It's very far from here."

I was a little leery of giving Nefertiti's daughter my full trust, but the idea of learning how to heal quickly was too tempting to be cautious. "Are we going to fly?"

"Only my mother and Lucian can do that, but if you let me carry you, I can run faster than a human eye can see." She stood up and waited for my answer.

I rose to my feet and smiled nervously. "Let's do it."

Having what looked like a seventeen-year-old girl pick me up baby-style felt a little on the odd side. But she was one of the strongest vampires on Earth, so I was pretty sure I weighed nothing to her. When Aidan carried me like this, it somehow felt all protective and sexy. With Mekytaten it was just awkward.

I shyly wrapped my arms around her neck. As fast as we were about to go, I didn't want to fly off her. She appeared oblivious to my discomfort, clearly focused on where she was about to take me.

"Mekytaten?" I asked.

"You can call me Meky. It's less formal."

This seemed to be a big deal to her, so I assumed it was an offer of friendship. I nodded and corrected myself. "Meky. Where are we going?"

"Home," she answered, and then the world became a blur of motion and colors.

I'd already experienced this with Aidan and in a drugged-out stupor with Ur-Nammu, but this was different. She was faster. I could barely contain my glee as I felt the wind hit my face with enough g-force to make my skin pull back. It was exhilarating as the scenery streaked past us. I couldn't differentiate shapes, so I had no idea where we were. It wasn't until the ground beneath turned a deep blue in contrast to the bright sky that I knew we were running over the ocean. The ocean!

Home.

The word rang in my ears.

Egypt.

I knew it with certainty. Hadn't we just left there? Caelius's prison was just outside of Cairo, and I never wanted to go back. Lucian and I had enjoyed a particularly good time in that cave, but still, too many nightmares had been born from that prison. I didn't feel like drudging them up.

When Lucian and I had finally left the catacombs behind, he'd flown me to Paris. It had been a thrilling experience, soaring through the air in his arms. I'd been like Lois Lane with Superman, except my Clark Kent ate people. I decided I didn't want to think about it anymore.

As we ran faster, the blur around us turned to gold, and I knew we were in the desert. The pyramids were so large and shapely that they were the only blobs I could actually recognize.

Then we stopped.

It took me a second to gain my bearings. I didn't want to

puke all over Meky's Converse, so I took a few deep breaths and calmed my stomach.

When I finally felt well enough to be coherent, I surveyed my surroundings. We were in an abandoned Egyptian city. A few tourists were roaming through the ruins, so it wasn't a hidden place, but it wasn't exactly crowded either.

All that was left of the city were small two-foot walls twisting over the ground like a labyrinth. They must have been part of the foundation of buildings that no longer existed. There were a few platforms and smaller staircases and only one pillar in the distance. Its circumference was large, well over six feet in diameter. The top was broken off, but it was still over twenty feet tall.

"That pillar is the entrance to the temple. Come." Meky led the way.

To anyone watching, we looked like two college students visiting the ruins. If these people knew that this was Meky's home, where she had grown up, where she had lived, they'd probably want to pick her brain for details (after being completely terrified). Where had everything gone? What had been here back then? What had it been like?

When we reached the crumbling pillar, Meky traced her finger over a faded hieroglyph of the sun god, Aten. It glowed a deep yellow in response. I looked around, making sure no one saw us. Meky took my hand when the coast was clear, and everything went dark.

It took me a few seconds to realize we were underground. Meky lit four braziers placed around the chamber, then I could see more clearly.

The room was huge, larger than Caelius's prison. It was much nicer though. The walls, ceiling, and floor all had shiny gold inlay. Engravings covered almost every inch of space, all depicting the sun and what I could only assume was Aten.

It was stunning, an archeologist's dream. There were several doorways leading to more rooms. I felt like I'd stepped into a time machine and we were back in ancient Egypt. No movie or recreation had done it justice. This was the real deal, and I was honored to be experiencing it.

"My father built this place to hide us from Lucian, although Lucian thought Akhenaten had done it to hide from him after my mother had feigned death when he'd tried to turn her.

"As Pharaoh, Akhenaten made his people change their god to Aten, the sun god. It was the only way he could justify building the sun shields. He used ancient hieroglyphs from the Book of the Dead to hold the sunlight in the shields through the night. We couldn't leave, but Lucian couldn't get in either. My mother raised us here in these chambers, and in our seventeenth year she turned us," Meky explained.

"I thought your mother hated the Pharaoh, that he enslaved her." Lucian had made it very clear that Nefertiti was not in a happy marriage.

"She hated my father for a very long time. He'd kept her like a possession. He'd enslaved her and forced her to marry him. But after a time, and after all he did to keep her safe, to keep his daughters safe, she grew to love him.

"It cut her deeply when he died. Caelius forced us into his cave after that. He didn't want Lucian finding out about us." Meky's face turned cold and hard at the mention of Caelius. I knew how she felt. Then her eyes softened. "But my memories here are some of my favorites. We felt free here, my sisters and I, even if we weren't. I sometimes long for it more than I care to admit."

I felt so sorry for her, having been caged next to Caelius just so they wouldn't ruin some crazy surprise he had in store for Lucian.

"Eventually, Caelius let us up into the world in shifts, but in exchange we were sworn never to turn anyone. We were only to feed off the leftovers of Lucian's offspring so that he'd never suspect we existed." Meky shuddered at the memory.

"You had to eat vampire scraps your whole life?" My mind put her confession into perspective.

Meky shrugged. "At least we never had to do the killing ourselves. Now we drink from blood bags."

I nodded. Innocent vampires. It made me admire her in a way I hadn't expected.

Meky reached over and held both my hands so that we were facing each other. "Your power comes from the planet, from the elements. The sun is the strongest force of energy on Earth. Because of the ancient glyphs my father inscribed here, it is a wellspring of power. Because you are made of Light itself, you are the only one who can *feed* from it."

"Did any of the other Vessels know about this place?" I asked.

"No. Lucian would force Adnachiel to kill the Vessels before there was a chance to bring them here. We wanted to, you know. We wanted to make the Vessel strong and possibly destroy Caelius for good, but Lucian was too hell-bent on revenge against Adnachiel for us to try. And we had to hide our presence from Lucian, acting in the shadows." She smiled. "We were lucky this time. The Vessel ended up being too beautiful for Lucian to resist."

That was sweet, but I hated compliments. I had no idea how to respond, especially since I felt like a troll next to her. My face burned with embarrassment and I didn't speak, Meky let out a small laugh. "And humble too. Who would have thought?" She took my hands and placed them on a small altar made entirely of gold.

It was three feet high and about a foot wide, etched with symbols and words I couldn't understand, but I heard it humming. It was singing to me. It was a part of *me*. My soul was perfectly in tune with whatever power this altar held.

Meky pulled away in sharp pain, but her smile broadened. "Vampires may be able to walk in the sun now, but true Light is still poison to us." She nodded to the altar. "Feed, Shea Harper, and become the death of Caelius."

CHAPTER 6
LUCIAN

I stared at the cold, hard stone beneath my feet. Weak. That was my problem. No matter how much power I accumulated, no matter what I'd done or survived, I was still weak.

I didn't want to look up. I kept my gaze on a crooked stone. There was moss growing in its crack. I made my irises retract. I could see the moss like I was looking at it through a microscope. All of its pores, the way it swayed from a pencil-thin breeze that whispered through the cavern.

It was alive.

Alive, and more worthy to stay that way than I was.

I tried not to breathe. Breathing to a vampire was like drinking herbal tea. The air itself was constantly filled with an ambrosia, and when it circulated through my lungs it felt . . .

I sighed.

I couldn't.

I couldn't justify the pleasures of my species. Not after this.

I didn't have to look up. I could still hear their screams bouncing around in my memory as I'd fed. Now that the fog had lifted and my mind was fully conscious, I was powerful. Externally. My body surged with pleasure. And I hated it.

Caelius had won. He'd always win. If I was damaged enough, my instincts took over. The instincts of a starved *beast* with no loyalty.

How could Shea look at me again with those soft hazel eyes? She deserved better. She deserved Adnachiel.

"Bravo." Caelius started clapping as he leaned against the corner of the room.

When the fever in my brain had cleared three days ago, I'd known he was there . . . watching. He'd sent Nefertiti in to clean out the mess, but I hadn't let my gaze fall on Nefari or Caelius. Just this stone and tiny speck of moss.

I heard his ominous steps as he moved toward me. "Are you still moping? I've been reminding you, like a good father, of who you really *are*, haven't I? And now your own thoughts repeat my sentiments, don't they? Surely now you realize how much better you are than all of them! The Vessel is unworthy of the magnificent animal that you are! She's nothing more than a light bulb trapped in cow hide."

Caelius moved his hand through my hair. He squeezed the blood from one of my locks into his mouth. I cringed as he smiled. Then, with his thumb, he dragged a long line of red down the side of my cheek and over my bottom lip. As he pulled me in, he kissed me hard.

I didn't blink. I didn't move. I just focused on that stone. Caelius, angered by my impassivity, shoved my back against the wall. It cracked from impact. The chains binding me rattled as he kissed me again, pressing his white Gracuri suit against my hardened frame. He laughed as he licked the side of my neck. I prepared myself.

He'd been doing this for three days.

He'd fatten me up, then drain me. Over and over he'd plump me, then suck me down. In the caves he'd ravaged my body. The shadow had been able to leak from his cage and do what it wanted. But it hadn't been able to do this. It hadn't been able to *feed*.

Caelius sank his teeth in deep, moaning in ecstasy as he ran his hand down my lower back. He pulled up for a moment, turning my head to meet his gaze. My face moved, but my eyes were on the moss. "Of all the galaxies I've devoured, all of the worlds I've destroyed, I must say, my son"—he ignored my expressionless eyes—"you are the most delicious creation I have ever tasted. I wonder if it's the *me* in you that makes your blood so irresistible? No. I've tasted others who carry my blood. Even Nefertiti doesn't taste this sweet."

A low rumble left my chest, and finally I looked at him. My eyes burned into the auburn of his. He smiled wider. "Oh, there you are, *boy*. I wondered how long it would take for you to come out and play. This will be so much more enthralling if you're battling me throughout. The first ten times I fed and bled this weakened body of yours you were still recovering. You were so unsure of yourself, like a puppy.

"But now, now I see that old twinkle in your eyes, that rare spark that defines you, my favorite pet." He wrapped his arms around my waist and hugged me tight, then sank his teeth in and tore, ripping a gash with his incisors from my neck to my chin. With a sigh of satisfaction, Caelius pulled back as the red gushed over and drenched my torso.

"Now that you're with me, Lucian, we can finally have some *real* moments together." He reached down and grabbed my thigh, sinking his teeth into the thick muscle.

"You see, darling," he said between slurping gulps, "these humans I've been feeding you were just a test, a theory I developed after your little harlot Shea bounced me on her lap in the desert." Satiated for a moment, Caelius stood and nibbled on my ear.

He crudely wiped his mouth on his lapel and smiled. "You have her to thank, really. If I drink you down to one drop, you live . . . but your willpower is *gone*. Granted, your survival skills are already adapting." He traced my eyebrow with his thumb, his eyes filling with twisted fatherly pride.

Then he leaned in closer, speaking with intimate passion. "But it will take you a few hundred years to master *not* feeding when *I'm* the one who has drained you." Caelius pressed his hips against mine. When he drew back, bitterness masked his features. "While you were practicing with that *whore* in France, teaching her how to use her powers against me, you should have been preparing *yourself*!"

I bit my tongue. I knew this game; he was provoking me. The more I fought, the more thrilling it was for him, and the more he'd want to raise the stakes. I shouldn't have made eye contact. But imagining him drinking Nefertiti and knowing about me and Shea in Paris . . . I had to do something.

Caelius licked my bottom lip and laughed. "Are you surprised? Of course I knew about Paris! I only used that mule Gracuri to draw you out so we could have some alone time. I missed you, darling. Speaking of that unworthy meat sack, that's our next little step in this process: your undeserving children."

I winced. Of course. Watching me feed off of my sons—my direct descendants, the three Gracuri had saved—would give Caelius the most power *and* the most pleasure.

Caelius grabbed my throat, letting his thumbnail push into my open gash. Eyes shifting, lighting like red flames, he brought his face close to mine and examined my expression. Then he breathed in deeply, enjoying the scent of my torment.

He kissed my eyes, whispering in a warm tone that was not without its own warped sincerity, "You see, beloved, I am so much stronger when feeding off of *your* blood. More so than from sucking on your sloppy Second-Borns. You are—because you are directly from me, of course—like a fine distillery."

My stomach lurched. I needed to take away anything he could use. I tried to empty myself of all emotion.

Caelius draped his arm around my shoulder and picked at my back, cutting a scar open as his temperament darkened. "I'll feed you the best cuts of meat, Lucian. The cuts *you've* chosen all these years, hand selected. And despite your *deep* affection for them, once I drink you down, you'll devour them willingly."

Then he buried his face in my chest and drank. My blood splattered across the walls as he sank his hands into my torso and fed with abandon.

He laughed, drunk on the sensation, then stopped suddenly, looking at his suit. "I'll need this cleaned again. What do you think, my love? I'll suck the delicious fermented power of your sons from your own delectable hide. Your father *needs* you, and now you can finally be of service." He grabbed the back of my neck and pulled my hair taut as he sank his teeth into my mouth. He lingered, tasting my lips before vanishing into the darkness.

I felt it; his power was radiating. If there was a God, I prayed Shea was out there somewhere practicing with Aidan, growing stronger. And I prayed that she'd never find me.

Because I needed to die, to let my body give in to death. Once I did what Caelius wanted, then, armed with the power of my Second-Borns, there would be no stopping him. It was too dangerous. I couldn't risk continuing and have him hurt Shea. But when I was maddened, I couldn't think. If I could just be conscious for a moment, one moment, I could push that last drop of blood that he would leave in me out of my bones and finally die a true death. But instincts always took over and kept it trapped inside.

A hand moved through my hair. I refocused my gaze on the mossy stone, preparing for the withdrawal. Waiting for him.

Soft fingers touched my neck, but I refused to make eye contact. I needed to focus, to be better than this. When I'd fed from Gracuri, his mind and soul had been *mine*. Now I would always carry that guilt. Even before he'd died, Gracuri hadn't fully shaken free from the influence of my feedings. It was all I could do, after every time Caelius fed, to keep myself sane and detached from his influence, to keep alive that free "wild spark" that he loved so much. But my body, everything inside, wanted to serve Caelius wholly and completely.

While at his mercy in the cave, I'd always found a way to master his torments and pull myself back together. This time was different. My mind was staying in a fog for so long . . . too long. Now I was conscious enough to see what I'd done during my blood-starved crazes that Caelius had engineered. I *knew* the countless lives I had taken.

"Lucian . . . La-Narru . . ."

I shifted my eyes from the stone and looked down into Nefertiti's purple gaze. And finally I breathed. I could be human for a moment. "Nefari . . ." I shook my head, at a loss for words. What could I say to her? The last time we'd spoken I'd thought she was an apparition. Now I'd had time to think about everything she'd said and done.

"Nefari . . ."

She placed a hand over my lips. "Don't speak. Let me mend you." She turned to the side, offering her neck.

I jerked back in disgust. "I will *never* feed off of you, Nefertiti! I'm not like Caelius!"

She paused, staring into my hardened gaze. "I know." Then she turned her neck to me again, adding softly, "But you need your strength, and this is the way of our kind."

"Caelius is not our *kind*. We are and will always be Gutian. And I will not feed on your blood like some animal. Our people deserve more respect than that. Other than your father, Nefari, we are the last of our race—"

"Enough," she commanded with the authority of the Great Royal Wife she once had been. Nefertiti waved her hand in front of my face, then sank her teeth into her wrist.

I pushed away, but she held my throat in place and poured her blood into my neck and chest. I healed in those places instantly. Dipping her fingers into her blood, she touched all the bite marks and gouges covering my back and thighs. And, when she was finished, she licked her wrist, closing the wound.

I didn't know what to say.

"I'm sorry," I mumbled. It wasn't enough, but seeing Nefari like this was destroying me. "You gave your life to Caelius . . . you let him turn you . . . in order to save me?"

She nodded.

I leaned closer. "When I was threatened by the Pharaoh, you sought Caelius out. In exchange, he gave me life. If only I hadn't been so careless. It was my fault the Pharaoh found out about us. I should never have come to Egypt. You would have lived a long, normal, *human* life by his side. A slave to the Pharaoh, maybe. Imprisoned in the comfort of a glorious palace, surely. But not *this* hell with Caelius, and for so long . . ."

Nefertiti rested her hand on my chest, her touch gentle as always, but her eyes were somewhat calloused. "I'm glad you are no longer feverish, Lucian. Caelius did not empty you this time for a reason. He wants you *conscious* when he brings one of your Second-Borns here."

She ignored the expression of horror that crossed my face to explain in very clear detail what was in store. "Caelius wants you to look at your son's terrified face—to have that as the *last* image of your child—just before Caelius empties you, just before your will breaks and *you* devour your child."

And then, because she'd been a queen used to the burden of decision, Nefertiti said in clipped, stark sentences, "We have a short amount of time. He's hunting one of your sons now. You only have three children left besides my father, but they're all well hidden. I'm sorry about Gracuri."

Sorry?

I didn't understand. She had nothing to be sorry for. Gracuri had been found by Caelius. That was not her fault. None of *this* was her fault. I could only imagine what manipulations Caelius had used to keep Nefertiti hidden from me, to keep her by his side.

She looked away. "Caelius was close to finding all of them. I met with Gracuri and told him where to hide the others. He hid them well. He should have stayed hidden himself, but *I* drew him out."

I leaned back, letting her hand slip off of my chest. "Why?"

Her gaze fixed on mine. "I couldn't reach you. I tried, but you being with the Light blocked your mind from me. I asked Gracuri to find you. Because he is your blood, he only needed to call out. He would have told you that I was alive and of my plan to stop Caelius. It would have been so much simpler that way. But . . ."

Nefertiti looked through me, no doubt rethinking her plan, and seeing its flaws. She was a more brilliant strategist than her father, Ur-Nammu, ever could be, but she was still no match for Caelius. "He found us. I'm not sure how. I was careful. I'm always cautious."

I nodded. I knew all too well of how careful she could be. It had been *my* mistake in Egypt, not hers, that had led to my death.

She furrowed her brow. "I had no choice but to act as if I had hunted Gracuri myself, to present him as a gift. Caelius was easily convinced, clouded by his lust for that particular vampire. I know Gracuri meant something to you, Lucian. For that, I am sorry Gracuri's life was lost."

She paused, and in that pause I waited, looking over her features. They looked the same, frozen like the day I thought my kiss had killed her. But inside she had changed.

"I'm sure you've done a great deal of things to survive under his embrace," I said, understanding all too well. "I don't blame you for anything you've done or will do."

I knew it was my fault Gracuri had died. If I hadn't cared about him so deeply, Caelius wouldn't have singled him out. If it hadn't been his blood in my veins when I'd fought Caelius in the cavern . . .

My mind ached with remorse. "Don't carry that burden, Nefari. It's mine alone."

Her mouth fell open, but she closed it quickly. "Are you still that Gutian poet, that boy, all these years later, La-Narru? Can you find no reason to *hate* me?"

I pulled against the chains and reached for her, the edges cutting my wrists deeper. Placing her hands over her heart, she fell into my chest like she used to when we would meet in secret by the Nile. I'd be covered in mud and straw from working with the other slaves. The Great Royal Wife Nefertiti had worn white and been adorned in jewels.

She'd let the grit of my body fall on her dress. She never cared. Nefari would bathe afterward to hide the mess from the Pharaoh, but when she was with me, she'd been more than happy to be covered in filth. As long as we were together.

I breathed in the scent at the nape of her neck. I'd done that a million times when we were alive. I wasn't smelling her as a vampire, I was smelling her like a young man, remembering a time when I'd fallen so deeply in love that I'd been blinded to the world around me.

I sighed. "I could never hate you, Nefari."

She pulled back, her hands still cupped to her breast. "I hated *you*."

I shook my head knowingly. She was as ancient as I was. She'd had time enough to think about all she had done and to grow in bitterness, to become something unrecognizable.

"I hated that I'd made that deal with Caelius because of my love for you. That one decision sentenced me to unimaginable torment. I was young, and I couldn't let you die."

She closed her eyes, probably reliving the moment of her turning like it was a fresh wound still open. "I'd just had my last child, Setepenre. She was so beautiful. A mother isn't supposed to pick favorites, but I know now as I did then: she is special.

"When I stared into her eyes, so full of life, as you were being whipped mercilessly outside my window, the thought that she would never see you—you had met all the other girls in secret, but she would never know your face—was more than I could bear at the time."

Nefertiti grabbed her waist, touching a long scar she'd received from giving birth, a scar that would never heal no matter how much blood she covered it with.

She pushed on the lesion and winced, rage covering her pristine features as it had on the eve before battle. "After Setepenre, I knew Akhenaten would kill you. You should have never made those clay sculptures of my image. And so many . . ."

I closed my eyes, trying and failing to drive out the pain of that time, the carelessness of my mistake. I hadn't been a warrior then. I had been a fool, and my love dangerous.

Nefertiti rested her soft frame against my wounded, chained body. Her lips pressed on my chest as she spoke, her voice low. "I heard whispers of a power greater than Akhenaten. 'Caelius,' they whispered, and I listened.

"When I found him, I made a deal for your salvation. I still had to watch as the Pharaoh had you tortured to the point of death. But Caelius turned you in time, changing your death into our everlasting perversion of life. Then he came for me later that night; that was our agreement. I did not resist him as he feasted on my blood.

"He said then that if I revealed myself to you before his plan came to fruition—revealed what I'd done, what I'd become— that he would kill us both. That had not been part of the agreement we had made, but, as you well know, once Caelius has you, he dictates his own terms. And then, later, he found many better ways to keep me in my place, to keep me shackled in the shadows away from your arms. But by then I had long realized my mistake. I knew it the first night I awoke as a vampire. I doomed our existence."

I leaned toward her. I used my chin to cup her neck, pulling her closer to my chest. "Nefari, you couldn't have known what he was. We came from a land of gods, a land that was ravaged without any word from those gods. And in Egypt there were new gods, and you were kept like a trophy of our failed beliefs by the Pharaoh."

An ache filled my chest. Now with the knowledge of Light and Darkness, of angels and vampires, I realized our naivety. We'd been so human then, so blind. "We'd learned through the slaughter of our kind to stop believing in anything but the love for our people, for one another. You couldn't have guessed, Nefari. You wouldn't have believed what Caelius was, what power and degradation he was capable of, even if he had told you."

I felt her lips curve as she whispered, "He did." They were soft as they moved upward on my neck. She exhaled for the first time since I'd seen her. One breath. And that was all, as if she'd been holding it for thousands of years. "I didn't believe him."

"I understand."

"Of course"—her voice turned flat—"you *would* understand." I knew her. Nefari's masked tone couldn't hide the storm raging inside. She'd always been more Gutian than I was, more passionate than the deep wells that boiled inside of me. Having become the Great Royal Wife in Egypt, she was better at concealing that passion, but it was there.

As Nefertiti pulled back, I opened my eyes. We looked at each other carefully for a moment before she spoke again, still holding tight the reins on her emotions.

"Eventually I stopped blaming you. Watching you devour the sands of Egypt in grief after you thought I was dead, it was all I could do to stay sane." Nefertiti paused, stepping farther back before she continued. "It was me, Lucian. I was the one who sealed us all to this fate. Who knows the people Caelius would have chosen as his Adam and Eve had I not turned his gaze on you. It was *my* doing. I alone am to blame for all you've suffered."

Her tone darkened, and so did her eyes, but I wasn't afraid. I knew she was hardening herself, deadening, preparing for the fury of my response. Nefertiti had waited thousands of years to have this conversation. She must have imagined a million ways that it could play out, all of which ended in my hate.

I looked at her powerful features, and all I saw was the little girl I'd grown up with. "We may have lost some of our beliefs in the war, Nefari, but the code our fathers created, that still burns. It's still alive in our Gutian bones. Those were our first words, the first thing taught to both of us. After all this time, I know you, and I know that you still believe it. I'll say this once, Nefertiti. I will *never* blame you. You thought you were fighting like our people had for the ones they loved. You thought the deal with Caelius would save my life. You risked everything—"

"For the one I love. And now he loves the Light. He loves Shea Harper."

I paused, stunned by her response.

"Nefari, I . . . I do love her."

She jerked back, out of the reach of my extended fingertips. I closed my eyes in frustration. I couldn't make it right. I didn't know how. To me, Nefari had been dead for three millennia. All I'd kept was her memory and the necklace I'd made for her as a child. I had searched for that necklace for *years* in the ashes of Pompeii. Before that I had always worn it. It was a constant reminder of her loss, of the only woman I'd ever loved. I felt it weigh heavily on my neck now.

But I had fallen for Shea, body and soul.

I needed time to process all that had happened. But it was impossible. With Caelius feeding off of me over and over like some fattened pig, I didn't know how I felt. I was lucky that I was strong enough to put my mind back together at all.

When I opened my eyes, she was staring. I looked closer. "What is it you're not telling me?"

She tilted her head curiously.

I shifted. She had a tell. I doubted even Caelius knew what it was. It was subtle. But I had watched her grow up. I'd watched the tell go from conscious to subconscious. When we'd been children, the gesture was large. But now her cheek barely moved when she bit the inside of it.

"What is it, Nefari?"

She scanned my body, looking for more gashes.

My voice hardened, and I stood tall. "I'm strong enough. Whatever you're going to say, do it now."

She nodded. "You're right. Who knows how long Caelius will be gone. Time is important. I'll only ask you this one last time. Think about your answer, La-Narru. Do you really love her?"

I would have nodded, but she deserved to hear it. "I loved you, Nefertiti. I will always love you. But you *died*. I mourned. You were buried with my heart in the sands of Egypt. I never thought I would find love again. And it's been thousands of years."

I paused. I didn't expect her to understand. To her I'd been alive all this time, just out of reach.

I breathed in deeply, letting her scent rest in my lungs, fully aware that after she heard my answer, I might never see her again. "Yes, Nefari. I love her. Shea found me when I was covered in darkness. She brought me back to who I'd been before Caelius, back to myself, to that Gutian boy who wanted life to be beautiful. She's a part of me now. I'm sorry. I'm sorry—"

"Of course." Nefertiti nodded, an impenetrable mask slowly covering her soft features. "I had to be sure. You said this before, but you were taken with fever then. I've had days to think about your response as I've watched Caelius toy with you. I watched him devour your flesh and strip you of your dignity. Even though what he's doing now is new, it reminds me of what he did to you in the caves."

"You . . . ?"

"Yes. I was there." Nefertiti's mask was almost in place, which made her pained words all the harder to bear. "No, Caelius never subjected me or my family to your unfathomable tortures. My punishment was *watching*. And I will *always* love you, La-Narru. But I understand. What you've suffered . . ."

Her hand reached up to cover her mouth in a sort of twisted horror, her eyes moving rapidly, no doubt analyzing the severity of my torment. When her hand fell away, she hardened again, certain of her response.

"You deserve better. You deserve to be loved, but also to be *protected*. Whether it's by me or Shea. And I have been working on a way to protect you. To protect us all.

"When you were fighting Caelius in the cave, I knew you couldn't kill him. If I hadn't stepped in, he would have killed all that I loved and made me watch. You don't know how hard it is to pretend to love Caelius when I truly despise that creature. I pulled him from the cell. It was a risk, but I knew the method I'd been working on could kill him. But I'll let her explain."

Decision made, she walked quickly across the room and opened a small side door. The sound raked my ears as the bottom edge of the wood dragged along the stone. My senses were heightened by Nefertiti's blood. It would make Caelius draining me that much more painful. It was agony, being juiced up on humans. I could feel every cell. Every twisted torment he concocted was done on newborn skin. And now with the power of my Second-Borns, it would be much worse. I'd go mad.

"Come in, Helena."

A slender woman entered. She eyed me in the darkness, then spoke assertively. "Why is he still chained? Is it as I've suspected? Are they angel bones?"

Nefertiti shuffled Helena closer, her voice a whisper. "If Caelius comes back before we have a chance, it will look like we're tending to his wounds. If his chains are removed, it will look like we're freeing him. We remove them at the last possible moment . . . if we even can."

Helena nodded as Nefertiti pushed her in front of me.

I stared in awe at her features. My brain still couldn't fathom the possibility, but she was here. Helena, the woman I'd befriended instead of fed on, the woman I would have turned into a vampire if my bite wouldn't have killed her. The child from Lorreto Chapel, the botanist from . . . a hundred years ago?

I stood dumbstruck. I spoke aloud, though it was more to myself. "How is this possible? You were killed in a train crash. You were pronounced dead. They never found the body."

Helena smirked and set her hand on her hip. It was an awkward gesture, but I remembered it. It was awkward because of her boyish physicality. She didn't look boyish—she was cute in a sweet sort of way—but her mannerisms had all the markings of a tomboy. She'd been raised with men. Six older brothers, if I remembered correctly.

Then Helena patted my shoulder, and her smirk widened until I saw . . . fangs.

And she saw my reaction.

"Nefertiti turned me," she explained, the scientist still strong in her personality. "Vampire genealogy is interesting. Males can turn males, and females can turn females, but you can't cross the wires."

Nefertiti stepped beside her. She wore a slight smile, as if I would be pleased. "I've watched you all these years, Lucian. When you took an interest in Helena, I did as well. I understood your fascination. She was brilliant for a human. I imagined what she could do with more time and a higher-functioning body."

I scowled. "I thought you said you'd learned over the years, Nefertiti? What was it you learned? Oh, yes, that this gift of life you gave me is a curse. I turned seven others, but I was twisted and wrong. Now I feel the regret of those decisions—"

Nefertiti waved dismissively, stopping my rambling. It was an authoritative gesture she'd picked up in Egypt. I hadn't liked it when she'd done it then, and I didn't like it now.

"It's not what you think, Lucian. Caelius forbade me from turning anyone because he didn't want you to know I was alive. He knew that you could trace any vampire that I'd turned back to me. It was too great a risk. And he so enjoyed your agony over my death and the idea of our perfect reunion."

Helena kept patting my shoulder as she sucked her bottom lip. She'd never been very comfortable talking about emotions. Science was the realm of comfort to which she belonged.

Nefertiti ignored Helena's awkwardness and continued. "When you befriended Helena, I studied her. I planned. I knew that she could help me find a cure for our condition or a way to fight Caelius, and your interest was the angle I needed. I talked about your infatuation with her, embellishing to Caelius. He sent scouts, and they watched you dance and laugh by her side, but you never fed. She wasn't like the dead humans you'd left in your wake at that time. You actually liked her as a person. That was rare for you."

I broke eye contact. At the time I'd met Helena, I'd been feeding just for the sake of bathing my hands in blood, anything to numb the boredom and pain of being what I was. And then . . . Helena. There'd been no immediate chemistry, and of course I'd tried to kill her, but she'd outsmarted me. *That* hadn't happened before. After, I'd realized who she was: the orphan from Lorreto, the one I had cared for when she'd been just a child.

Helena shifted nervously, then jabbed me on the shoulder. "How about that, Lucian? A botanist vampire. The only one of my kind. Caelius was fascinated by me for a while because of his obsession with you. But he grew bored. Nefertiti was able to convince him to let her keep me as a pet. His words, not mine."

I nodded. I was happy to see Helena, but not as a vampire. By now I was sure she knew that it would have been better had she died on that train.

Helena slipped her finger over my wrist, touching the bone exposed from pushing against the chains. She rubbed my blood between her fingertips like examining a lab sample. "It's just as I thought, Nefertiti. We won't be able to get him out easily. A smart move on Caelius's part. Lucian can't escape when he's all hopped-up on the blood of his own children."

She wrinkled her brow, looking closely at my bloodied wrists, then at my ankles, her irises widening. "Your wounds aren't healing at these places because Caelius made these chains from Adnachiel's brother's bones, the one he tortured and devoured in the caves. Caelius has stored them somehow. Maybe . . . inside of himself?" Helena's face sparkled. "Like an undigested femur in his stomach? Amazing creature, that Caelius."

Nefertiti's and my gaze fell on her with disdain for what sounded like adoration.

Helena rested her hand on her hip again, slightly embarrassed. "Not like that, I mean, not 'amazing' himself, but from an objective point of view, Caelius would be worth dissecting in a lab."

Even through my own pain, I had to grin. "That, Helena, I'd love to see."

Her eyes met mine in eager agreement. We had a similar sense of humor.

But it wasn't that much of a joke to Helena, who rattled on. "Of course it can be done; I've been working on something along those lines for a couple decades now. But first there's the matter of the parents. I've kept their bodies, but what do *you* want to do?"

My puzzled expression must've confused her. She looked at Nefertiti. "You haven't told him yet? What have you been doing in here this whole time? Caelius just left, and we need to set this plan in motion immediately, but Lucian deserves to know. And I deserve to get that stink out of my lab."

Nefertiti waved her hand, and Helena stopped talking. I assumed that over the course of a hundred years she'd learned that motion meant not to cross her. Maybe Helena really had become her pet, as Caelius believed.

"No, I haven't told him," Nefertiti explained slowly. "I wasn't sure if it was necessary. But seeing that Lucian actually *loves* this Shea, then yes, he deserves to know and to decide for himself."

Nefari paused, then faced me. "You killed Shea Harper's parents. The first night you were here, Caelius left them in your cell. You drained them. I was able to drag away the bodies. Helena has been keeping them preserved. The choice is yours."

My body collapsed. The chains holding the shredded meat at my wrists were the only things keeping me from hitting the floor. I could feel bone grate against the steel. It was painful, and I was glad for it. I closed my eyes. There was no going back from this. Shea would *never* forgive me.

That first night of Caelius's torture, caught in the blood fever he'd overwhelmed me with, I'd thought the people he brought in were familiar. I'd thought it was Gracuri's suit, but Shea's smell must have been on them, *in* them. How could I not have known?

Nefertiti's voice was low, soft. "Caelius chose them specifically your first night here. It wasn't your fault."

"Don't placate me, Nefari," I snapped.

She fell silent.

I hung there on my chains, unwilling to rise. Her words didn't matter; there was no point to anything I did now. When I'd seen Nefari again, there'd been hope. A small part of me, a part that was more Aidan than Lucian, had thought that I might survive Caelius's tortures, that I could still help Shea fight him. I'd hoped she would understand all that I'd done, that I'd not yet adapted to being leached by Caelius.

That I wasn't a monster.

But this . . .

How could she even look at me again? She couldn't. They were her *parents*.

Helena chimed in nervously, trying to distract me from

my despair. "Nefertiti is right: it's not your fault. Scientifically, a vampire becomes more like an animal when it's near death. However, even over the past hundred years, you've been able to adapt to the things Caelius has done to you. You've still remained conscious and able to resist his control. This is different. He's your . . . I'm not going to say 'father' because that, to me, is an inappropriate terminology."

She teetered back and forth on her heels, analyzing, groping to find the right words. "If you think about vampirism, or that his blood is like a *virus*, then Caelius is the original host. So him drinking you until you have one drop of his blood left is like being uninfected while reinfected by the initial virus.

"If I, or any other vampire, drained you to the last drop, you'd be injured, but for the most part conscious. You would recover quickly and be able to have some semblance of control because you are his First-Born and that strong. But this is Caelius, the 'father' of all, taking away your birthright and then returning it on his whim. It's different, Lucian. It's like a massive, multi-organ infection. I'm surprised you're not fully subservient to Caelius by now."

I could feel her cold hand patting me on the back again. When Helena was alive, her touch had been warm and firm. I knew the point she was trying to make, though. When Gracuri had fed me a small town, I hadn't been conscious then, either, but that had been because the Light was purging my blood of Caelius, the only thing keeping my decayed body alive. Now . . .

This was worse. The ownership that pulsed in the venom of Caelius's bite made me want to please him. Gracuri was the only child I'd drunk from, and it had been awful, the way it fevered his mind. How long would it take for the same thing to happen to me? How many feedings before I became Caelius's slave? What would it take, the blood of my children? Or would he force-feed me his own blood until I knelt willingly in submission?

"Kill me," I whispered under my breath.

Nefertiti and Helena were both silent in response, and Helena's patting hand froze in place.

I straightened up and looked directly at Nefari.

"Kill me."

Pain shrouded her features as she shook her head. "I would never . . ."

I shifted my gaze to Helena. "There's no reason for me to make it out of this alive. If I die, Shea never has to know that I killed her parents, and Caelius can't use that to hurt her. She won't believe him. But if I *live*, Caelius is going to use my body to harvest his full power, killing all my children in the process. He might even make me his . . . *his*! Body and soul this time! Then he'll kill Shea. Or I will."

Helena's eyes widened with the new possibilities. Nefertiti just looked away in denial of my logic.

"Helena, take Nefertiti and leave this place. Nefari—"

She continued staring at the cold stone floor.

"Nefari!" I pleaded. "Listen to me! If Caelius is using me and your father to keep you enslaved here, let me die and you can be free! Ur-Nammu is in Miami. Take him, join Shea, and stop—"

"*You* stop!" Nefertiti commanded, then stepped forward and struck me across the face. "Don't . . . don't! You can never ask me to kill you again . . . and for *her*? And it's not just you and my father, there's also—"

"I don't understand!" Helena cried, stepping between us. "I know you're against turning anyone, Lucian, but you can at least turn Shea's parents and give them back to her. You're not heartless; why wouldn't you save them?"

"What?" I reached out to grab her, momentarily forgetting about the chains. "Save them? Because they're *dead*! You have to turn someone right after you drink them! It's been three days!"

Silence

And then . . .

Helena laughed. It was dry and startling. "Oh, *that*. I've been studying our kind for some time. Of course you don't know. Here's an interesting scientific fact: a body can be dead for *ten* days before it's turned. Not eleven though. That was an unfortunate experiment."

I jerked desperately against my chains. "*Yes*! I'll turn them! Anything! What do I have to do?"

Helena leaned back and Nefertiti's mouth opened, but nothing came out. They were both shocked by the urgency of my response. But if Caelius could return at any moment, I had to save Shea's parents before he arrived. I could still find a way to kill myself after.

They were dismayed, but not immobilized. Within an instant Nefertiti and Helena had dragged in two bodies. The stench was beyond comparison. There was a word in Gutium for something that was worse than the smell of death. As Nefertiti scowled, I saw her utter it under her breath, masking the sound of her retching.

I looked at Helena. "What do I do?"

She recoiled slightly. "It's not pretty."

I looked at the purple, bloated bodies of Shea's parents. No, it wasn't pretty.

"I'll do anything," I said, trying not to vomit.

"Then pucker up."

"Pucker . . . ?"

Helena sighed, exasperated. People of intellect always hated explaining things to the lesser-minded, even if she did adore me. "It's simple: you already drained Shea's father, so you just have to give him some of your blood. For Nefertiti . . . it's going to be a bit more difficult. And it might not work. You didn't drain the mother completely; we salvaged some of her in time. Nefertiti drank what was left after your little talk the first night. Now she'll need to dip her fangs into your blood before she pours her blood into Shea's mother's mouth. It's like a claiming. A transference? No. What's the word I'm thinking of . . . ?"

"Crazy?" I stated plainly.

Helena looked at me and smiled. I didn't return her gleeful expression. This was something she must have worked out on paper, and the botanist in her was excited to see the experiment come to life. But this wasn't testing a theory. These were Shea's *parents*. It couldn't fail.

Nefertiti avoided eye contact. I leaned toward her. "Thank you for doing this, Nefari."

Her eyes stayed down. "We need you strong, Lucian. You can kill Caelius with our help. But you can't be distracted and full of self-loathing. This was another tactic by Caelius to keep you small, under his power, and hating yourself, just where he likes you. And . . ." She paused, straining. "We-we need Shea as an ally. If turning her dead mother will help that cause, I have no choice."

Helena placed Shea's father into my arms. I cringed, staring at his blue mouth. "Why is it always the lips?"

"It's interesting," Helena chirped in her isn't-science-wonderful voice. "Why can we only turn someone by the blood of our lips in an embrace? The data is fascinating. See, the tissue around that region—"

Nefertiti waved. Helena shut up.

I closed my eyes and bit my lower lip. I'd never kissed a corpse before. Not a cold one, not one that had been dead for three days, and certainly not one that belonged to Shea. Her father.

I pressed my lips against his and let my blood fall into his open mouth. Within an instant, Shea's father jerked up, gasping for air even though he didn't need it.

Nefertiti moved toward me and sank her teeth into my neck. She pulled away quickly, her mouth covered in my blood. The pleasure my body surged with when her teeth sank into my flesh was *unimaginable*. I thought I had mastered that technique, but she put my kiss to shame. I tried to shake off the sensation as Shea's father stumbled around in front of me, confused.

Then he started clawing at his skin. The first stage. Your skin feels like it's covered in ants, ants that are all biting down and chewing as the body restores itself.

Shea's father grabbed his stomach, instinctively growling. I looked at Helena. It was too soon. Usually the pangs of unbearable hunger didn't set in until the next morning, or the morning after.

Helena shrugged. "We'll have to make do, Lucian. We couldn't sneak above and procure bags of blood under the watch of Caelius. And the longer they're dead, the hungrier they are when they wake. He needs to feed now, or . . ." She paused, letting me fill in the rest.

Usually, in my dark past, I'd give my children fresh humans to feast on. I'd never given my other children a second taste of their father; I hadn't been sure of the effects. But if Shea's father didn't get more blood soon, he would die again, and no vampire kiss would revive him.

I called him to my side and presented my neck. He dug in like a thirsty teenager drinking a gallon of water after football practice. I told him to stop, that he'd had enough; my blood was too rich for a new, inexperienced vampire. He kept drinking. I warned him again. I moved to catch him as his eyes rolled back in ecstasy and he collapsed, but I couldn't latch on past the chain's reach.

I looked at Helena, and she half smiled. "He'll recover," she said softly. It was uncommon for a vampire to black out from overfeeding, but my blood was infectious like Caelius's.

Nefertiti eyed me, then reluctantly dipped her teeth into the purple of Shea's mother's mouth. Nefertiti held her teeth there. Helena nodded. "Just hold it there for a few more seconds. I'll count you down. Ten, nine, eight . . ."

Chapter 7
Shea

What.

Was.

Happening?

My mind was still buzzing from the liquid sunshine I'd just inhaled in Egypt. Then Meky had carried me at her lightning speed to where Lucian was held captive. But now I couldn't think straight. I couldn't see straight. The amount of power surging through every cell of my body was overpowering all of my senses. I had to be hallucinating. I had to be.

Because what I saw was my dad lying on the ground, dead, and Nefertiti eating my mother. And some strange female vampire was watching the whole thing with fascination while Lucian was chained to the wall.

No.

This couldn't be right.

I was seeing my worst nightmare, not reality. The sun power

was messing with my mind.

"Stop!" Meky yelled across the room.

She sounded shocked and upset.

That was when I knew it was real.

Nefertiti had killed my father, and now she was finishing the job by killing my mother.

Not going to happen.

I called forth as much of the sunshine-juju as I could muster and directed it all on Nefertiti. The force knocked her off my mother's body, and then I levitated her into the air.

It was too late.

My mother was already dead.

I froze for a second, keeping Nefertiti struggling a few feet off the ground. I stared at the two bodies of the people who'd given me life, who'd given me everything. Who were the kindest, most supportive parents anyone could ask for.

Molly and Jeff Harper.

They were gone.

Forever.

The pain was too much to bear.

I screamed.

I wished I hadn't gone with Meky to the sundial. Its power intensified my emotions beyond reasoning. All I could think of was to destroy the one who had killed the two people who meant the most to me in this world: Nefertiti.

I stared at her with all the hatred I felt pounding in my heart. Her screams only fed my anger. Good. She deserved to feel pain, like the pain she had caused them.

I would make her suffer worse than Caelius ever could.

I squeezed my hand tightly and watched as her blood poured out of her nose and mouth in a grotesque waterfall of flowing red.

Watching her suffer made me feel intoxicated. It lessened the anguish at seeing their lifeless bodies. I barely heard Meky screaming at me to stop, her hands clawing at my arm. The strange vampire woman with Nefertiti tried to attack me too, but they were no match for me.

Not even a First-Born could hurt me now.

With a wave of my hand, I trapped Meky and the other vampire with invisible bonds.

Nefertiti needed to die.

The once beautiful Egyptian princess was now thin flesh on bones. It was justice. She'd drained them, and I'd drained her.

Her screams stopped.

It was then that I realized Lucian had been shouting this entire time, the same thing over and over. "Nefertiti didn't kill them, Shea! I did! Caelius starved me, and in a frenzy I killed your parents! I killed them!"

It jolted me out of my power-induced frenzy. "What?"

The female vampire joined in. "Nefertiti is trying to save your mother! Your father is alive; he was turned by Lucian. It was *my* idea. I think it will work if you just let Nefertiti try. We can turn your mother!"

The words washed over me. I felt relief but no joy. My parents had been killed by Lucian, and he thought turning them would make up for it?

I stopped my attack on Nefertiti, and her body fell to the floor.

The choice was now mine.

Heal Lucian's ex and let her give my mother eternal life, or let my mother stay dead.

The searing ache in my chest decided for me.

I needed my parents, both of them. I longed for one hug, one look, one kiss on the cheek to tell me that everything was going to be okay. They may have forgotten me thanks to the angel brothers, but Aidan had said they could give them their memories back. I didn't even care. I just needed to see them alive, not corpses.

I ran over to Nefertiti's still form. She looked mummified from the amount of blood she'd lost. I placed my wrist over her mouth. "Drink."

I kept my blood free of the liquid sunshine I usually used when dealing with vampires. It didn't take much to revive Nefertiti. She drank deeply, and within seconds her face was flushed.

"I'm sorry," I said quietly.

To my surprise, she placed a hand on my cheek. "If I thought someone had killed my parents, I would have done the same."

"Can you still turn her?" My eyes filled with tears.

She simply nodded and went to my mother.

Her words haunted me.

I couldn't look at Lucian.

Not yet.

He'd killed them.

And yet, I didn't try to torture him. I didn't try to kill him. I didn't even yell at him. What did that say about me?

Slowly, I turned to face him.

His eyes were wracked with pure agony. I turned away. I

couldn't look at him when I felt so much pain. I wasn't ready to forgive him. I wasn't ready for anything. One thing I knew, though: the person I should be angry at was Caelius.

He probably thought it would be fun giving my parents to a starving animal, thought it would tear us apart irrevocably. Maybe he had succeeded. Could I ever really trust Lucian? What if Caelius starved him again and he started killing more innocent people?

Lucian was a vampire, and when faced with death, he'd chosen to kill human beings rather than die. Would I have done differently? I'd have liked to think so, but I wasn't sure. One thing I knew: Aidan never would. The scar on my stomach told me as much.

Aidan had been willing to kill his best friend to save billions of lives. Both Lucian's and Aidan's decisions hurt me to my core. The one who'd murdered my parents, and the one who'd tried to murder me. Both decisions had been made out of desperation, and both felt wrong, but I had forgiven Aidan . . .

At least Lucian had done the only thing he could think of to make it up to me: he'd turned my father and somehow convinced Nefertiti to turn my mother.

In a completely messed up world, it showed how much he didn't want to hurt me, that it would somehow soften the blow that he'd devoured them in the first place.

"Shea," Lucian began. "I—"

I put my hand up to stop him from talking. "I can't. Not yet." I couldn't stomach hearing explanations. I was pretty sure I'd come to the correct conclusions, and I needed to process.

Meky's voice came out of the silence. "Um, Shea? Could you

release me and Helena?"

Oops.

Helena. It was good to know the other woman vampire in the room had a name. I waved my hand, freeing them. They hurried over to Nefertiti and my mother to monitor the progress.

"Shea," Lucian began again.

I whirled on him. "I said I'm not ready—"

Dad.

He was awake now and walking toward me.

It was the worst feeling in the world. My dad stared at me with . . . hunger. Being the only human in the room—and according to every vampire ever, being the Vessel made me smell extra sweet—I looked like dinner to him. What made it even more devastating was the fact that there was zero recognition in his expression. Aidan's brothers had done their job well; my dad had no idea who I was.

Lucian's voice turned deep and commanding as he said to my father, "Shea is not food. She's your daughter." Not knowing my dad didn't have any of his memories, Lucian looked baffled as he tried to rationalize. "I'm sorry, Shea. He fed directly from me; it must be confusing him."

I could barely look at Lucian, but I had to explain. "It's not your blood. Aidan's brothers repressed my parents' memories of me." I laughed sarcastically. "To protect me." The irony was astounding as my father looked at me like I was a Big Mac.

"But she smells good." Dad sniffed the air.

Ew.

I stepped in. "Listen, Da . . . *Jeff*, you don't want to attack me. It would go badly for you." I could keep my father at bay, but I really didn't want to have to resort to that.

"How do you know my name?" he asked me suspiciously.

It stung.

A lot.

Stupid Aidan and his brothers.

Lucian answered for me, staring deep into Dad's eyes. "Shea is very important to us."

"Just don't." I stopped Lucian from continuing. Everything felt like such a mess—a horrible, sticky, hopeless mess. I couldn't imagine feeling normal again. I had thought my parents were safe. All memories of me forgotten, yes, but safe. Now they'd been killed by my boyfriend and brought back to life by him and his ex.

Ugh.

"She's waking up," Meky announced, pointing at Mom. She smiled at me as if the news that my mother was officially a vampire was supposed to bring me happiness.

Dad raced to Mom's side, touching her face lovingly.

Okay, yes, I was happy she was still alive too, but I didn't want this for her. I didn't want this for my dad. Why couldn't they be home in Phoenix complaining about how hot it was?

"What is your mother's name?" Nefertiti asked.

"Molly," I answered.

The surrealness of the situation only grew more intense as my heart seized with emotion. I couldn't do this anymore, standing by and letting events unfold. I was too angry. I was too sad. I was too . . .

Lost.

I needed Lucian, but I didn't want him. I needed to feel his arms around me and have him comfort me, but if he touched me now I'd feel nothing but revulsion. My mind couldn't keep itself together. It was still swimming with power from the sundial, and combined with everything that was happening in front of me, the power surging through me only made my confusion worse.

"Mother? Father?" My mom's voice ripped me from my thoughts. She was holding her stomach in hunger.

Lucian and Nefertiti exchanged surprised, then knowing looks, as if they could hear each other's thoughts.

Puke.

"Why is she calling you that?" I asked them with a little too much venom in my tone.

Lucian was about to explain, but Nefertiti stopped him with a glance. She was smart. I didn't want to hear from him right now. The only reason I tolerated her was because I felt horrible about how I'd reacted when all she was trying to do was fix my boyfriend's murderous mistake.

Nefertiti tried to sound as soothing as possible as she explained. "The only way to make a vampire is to drink all of the human's blood. Since I wasn't the one who drained your mother, I had to take some of Lucian's blood and mix it with mine because males cannot turn females."

"So my *mother* is now your vampire baby?" I realized in disgust.

Mom cringed at my words. "I am not your mother. I have no child. Jeff and I never had nor wanted any children," she practically spat.

Great. So by wiping their memories, Aidan's brothers had turned my parents into baby-hating pricks. Awesome.

"You may not remember because some angel a-holes erased your brain, but I'm your kid, so get over it," I snapped at my mom.

"Lucian, the girl lies. Please let me eat her." My father stared at him with wide, hopeful eyes. Gross. My dad was totally in love with my boyfriend!

"I seriously can't take much more of this," I almost shouted. With every new wrinkle in these crazy events, the sun power pulsed through my veins, wanting to release itself from my body. The more drama, the more unclear my mind became.

It was as if the sun was literally frying my brain.

I stumbled slightly.

Lucian tugged on his chains, wanting to catch me.

"Shea, are you all right?" His voice was so wracked with concern and love it physically hurt.

I was glad he was chained. I didn't think I could handle him touching me. "I'm fine. Why can't you break free, anyway?"

"Caelius created these chains out of Ashliel's bones. Only an angel can free me," Lucian answered.

"So we'll have to get Aidan here and get you out before Caelius comes back. Where is dick-face anyway?"

Caelius's small chuckle sent chills down my spine. "I'm right behind you, little sunshine."

I turned around slowly to face Lucian's father. Caelius was smiling as if watching our drama gave him immense pleasure. Next to him was a handsome man in his midthirties with short brown hair, bright blue eyes, and a slightly crooked nose that made him even more attractive. He wore a T-shirt and jeans, and I could tell he was as buff as Aidan beneath his clothing.

"Duncan!" Lucian cried out.

At hearing the terror in Lucian's voice, my mom lunged at Caelius, biting into his arm. Caelius instantly threw her off. She landed near his feet as Dad leapt to attack Caelius as well, protecting both Lucian and Mom.

Even more furious, Caelius tossed my father a lot harder. Dad hit the wall, sinking down onto the ground, unconscious.

He stared at the already healing bite marks on his forearm. "How dare you feed from *me*!" he shouted at Molly. "I choose who drinks my sacred lifeblood!"

Caelius's fury quickly turned to amusement as my mother's face went from anger to complete and total devotion from tasting his blood.

Normally, seeing my mom stare at Caelius with loving eyes would be the worst of my problems, but when Caelius turned his attention back to Duncan, I knew we were in for some serious trouble.

From the desperation in Lucian's expression, Duncan must have been one of Lucian's Second-Borns. It appeared that Caelius was finding new and horrific ways to torture Lucian. My heart broke for him. Even after what he'd done, I still loved him. I just hadn't *accepted* what he was yet. I thought I had, but having seen both my parents dead, and now vampires, I obviously hadn't. Acceptance would take time.

Time was something we didn't have at the moment.

Duncan stood stock-still next to Caelius. He seemed to be trapped under the older vampire's compulsion, unable to move or speak.

Lucian tried to lunge toward his father, but because he was

chained he couldn't move far. "Caelius, you don't need him. I'm enough! Kill me instead!" he growled. Lucian knew he couldn't defeat Caelius, he couldn't even reach him, yet he would try anyway to save his son.

Seeing my dad on the ground, knocked out cold, I was just grateful Caelius hadn't killed him on the spot. My dad was one of Lucian's Second-Borns now. Would he die for him as well?

A rush of emotion flooded through me, and I knew Lucian would protect my dad with his life. Not just because he was a Second-Born, but because he was *my* dad.

Lucian loves me.

I held on to that thought. It helped keep the surging power within me under control.

Lucian loves me.

His feral mind hadn't been able to stop him from feeding off my parents when he'd been starved, but when he'd come to his senses, he'd tried to fix the situation—for me.

Caelius loved seeing his son upset. He looked like he couldn't wait for a fight. "It took me a while to find dear old Duncan. Gracuri hid him well, but I am, after all . . . me." Caelius pinched one of Duncan's cheeks. "Hiding in plain sight on the Scottish Highlands from whence he came. Brilliant."

"You can release Duncan now," I said with way more attitude than I'd expected. After kicking Caelius's butt *before* my recent sunshine mojo, I figured this guy was toast. I might as well save one of Lucian's children in the process.

Caelius turned and smiled. "You're cute." Then he motioned wide toward the rest of the gang. "Turning the Vessel's parents. How very dramatic."

My mother stared at Caelius with big, adoring eyes.

"Mom, I mean, Molly. You hate him." I tried to give her a heads-up, but she didn't give me the time of day.

Caelius walked over to my mother and took her hand, kissing it gently. "What a lovely creature you are, Molly. The mother of a Vessel and made into one of my grandchildren by my very own Adam and Eve. Such a rare thing."

That was it.

I used the wind and threw my hand out. Caelius went flying across the room, slamming against the wall, creating a small crater with his back.

"Get away from my mother!" I roared.

Mom turned to me with a hateful gaze. "I am *not* your mother!"

Before I could think to defend myself, she was pinning me to the ground and biting my neck.

I instantly turned my blood into liquid fire, and Mom reeled back in pain.

"Devil child!" she accused.

"Me? You're the one who just tried to eat her own daughter!" I knew she didn't remember me, but I hoped there would be some kind of recognition. A flicker? Something!

"I don't have a daughter!" she shouted furiously.

Making my mother forget having a child was one thing, but *hating* the idea of having one was extreme.

Caelius brushed himself off and seemed even more pleased than before. "Just wonderful!"

My face must have said it all, and he laughed. "The beasts never seem to think things through, do they?"

In this case, I had to agree with him. "No, apparently not."

Caelius raised his eyebrow in surprise that I'd agreed with his berating, but I was so mad at Aidan's brothers, I didn't care. He looked over at Lucian. "See, my son? Even this bitch can learn."

My temper began to boil again. Using my powers on Nefertiti and then in small bursts on my mother and Caelius had only caused the sun-juice in me to surge. I needed to release the power. It felt as if I was bottling fire, and I had to pull the stopper out.

I knew that I needed to bring my parents to Aidan. He could give them their memories back, and this would all be over. Yes, they'd be vampires, but at least they'd be alive. And they'd know who I was and not be jerks.

The only thing standing in my way was Caelius.

My eyes met his.

In a panic, he grabbed the still form of Duncan, and before anyone could lift a finger, Caelius drained the Highlander.

Lucian screamed.

Caelius pounced on me.

The Light was raging inside, filling me with energy.

I concentrated all my thoughts on Caelius.

On his bones.

On the oxygen in his blood.

On the air around his body.

And I squeezed my fingers into a tight fist.

The sound of cracking filled the room as I broke every single bone in his tall frame.

Caelius's body crumpled to the floor. His skin looked like it was made of rubber with no skeleton to give him shape.

No one in the room moved.

Except Caelius, who reached his blubbery hand out for help. The vampires stared at him as if Caelius was calling out to them in their heads.

Nefertiti was the first to snap out of it. "Don't listen to him! This is our chance!"

Lucian's eyes cleared, and the intense hatred for his father showed through. He looked at me. "Shea, I can't break these chains! Can you bring his body to me? We can try to kill him!"

Helena shook out of the spell as well and yelled, "We can't! It's not time! The device isn't ready yet!"

Nefertiti looked like a fierce warrior. "We have to try, Helena. Look at him, he's begging all of us to help him! He's never done that before!"

Helena hesitated, then nodded in agreement. Meky stood at her side, ready to fight as well. That left only my mom in Caelius's thrall. I'd never been so grateful that my dad had been knocked out.

"I'm in," I said, trying to sound stronger than I felt. Crushing Caelius had depleted most of my mojo. It felt like he was stronger this time than he'd been the last time we'd fought. Drinking Duncan must have given him some extra juice. I just needed to get his body to Lucian so all four vampires could fight him. We could do this. We could finally kill this monster.

I used my power over the air and wind, lifting Caelius's body, then slamming him down onto the floor. My boyfriend had never looked happier. Lucian tore his bare feet into his father's neck, ripping flesh off with his raw strength. I was amazed at how well Lucian could fight with only his feet, his arms still chained to the wall.

But he was not alone in his efforts.

Nefertiti buried her hand in Caelius's chest and ripped out his heart, squeezing it until it burst.

Meky and Helena tried to tear Caelius's limbs from his body, but they weren't strong enough. Only the First-Borns, Lucian and Nefertiti, appeared to have enough power to shred his flesh.

My dad unfortunately woke up from the commotion, but instead of helping Caelius, he stood next to Lucian, acting as his bodyguard. Definitely weird, but better that than helping Caelius. I tried not to notice that my dad kept his eyes on my boyfriend like he was a unicorn. Seriously, that was grosser than the gore.

There was so much ripping flesh and blood, I felt like I was watching the X-rated version of Animal Planet.

Joining the killing frenzy, I connected to the wind again, since it was all I could manage at the moment. I sent an arm-size tornado burrowing into Caelius's skin. I could feel myself growing weaker, though. I wasn't going to stay conscious long.

Only my mother was transfixed from having tasted Caelius's blood. She watched the mayhem and torture of her vampire granddaddy in horror.

Still, as long as she stayed out of it, we could do this.

I started feeling the stirrings of hope.

I drilled the small tornado into Caelius's body over and over until he was unrecognizable.

He couldn't survive.

It would be impossible.

My mind grew fuzzy. I couldn't keep the tornado up much longer.

Faster than the blink of an eye, my mother moved.

I was caught off guard and too weakened to react in time.

She grabbed Caelius's broken form and flew into the air.

Flew!

Only Lucian and Nefertiti could fly!

My mom really was special.

That couldn't be good.

Covered in blood, all the other vampires huddled around the now-empty space where Caelius had been a moment earlier.

It was so sudden that we all paused for a second.

Then I realized that if we were going to get out of here, our first priority needed to be freeing Lucian. It was time to call Aidan.

Besides, I really needed to see my best friend.

I called for him in my head. It was taking the last of my strength. The room started to grow dark; I was collapsing from exhaustion.

Before I hit the ground, I felt Aidan's arms catch me. I looked up into his beautiful, concerned blue eyes and smiled. Seeing him filled me with a joy I couldn't contain. Even though he was an angel, Aidan was the only *normal* person in my life. He didn't feed off humans. He was pure. And I loved him. He must have seen all this in my expression because he shook his head, smiling. "Good to see you too, Shea."

I felt my strength slowly come back. I wasn't going to pass out. I nodded toward Lucian. "He said the chains are angel-lock only."

Aidan made sure I was able to stand and started to walk toward Lucian and the others.

Midway there, he stopped in his tracks. "Mailid?"

Meky stood up and self-consciously tried to wipe the blood from her hands. "Hello, Adnachiel."

"Mailid?" Lucian sounded just as shocked. "The Mailid I killed centuries ago?"

"To torture Adnachiel, yes, I remember. I play dead very well, don't you think?" she asked Lucian. Then she looked at Aidan and . . .

Holy crap! The girl was in love!

And what shocked me even more—so was he.

"I'm sorry, Adnachiel. I had to pretend to die. Caelius made it clear that if Lucian found out about any of us, he would take the punishment out on the rest of our family. My true name is Mekytaten." Then she added shyly, "Or Meky for short."

Lucian's eyes went to Nefertiti. She simply nodded. "All my daughters have been turned."

"But I followed them after the Pharaoh died to make sure they lived long and healthy lives!" He didn't want to believe her.

"You were following decoys, my love," Nefertiti explained.

I didn't like that "my love" comment, and I didn't like Meky and Aidan hooking up either. I was seriously a jealous freak right now. It didn't help matters to see my dad drooling over every word that came out of Lucian's mouth.

"Well, I'm glad we all know each other," I said a little too loudly, trying not to sound too sarcastic, then I focused on Aidan. "Can you unchain Lucian so we can get the hell out of here?"

So. Annoyed.

Chapter 8
Lucian

Aidan fiddled with the chains, but my gaze was fixed on Shea. The way she looked at me with stolen glances before finding something more worthy to rest her eyes on . . . it was killing me.

I hadn't thought turning her parents would make up for what I'd done to her. I couldn't remember their faces as my sharp incisors had torn through their flesh, only the bliss and the agony of Caelius's consumption of me afterward, only his thoughts rattling around in my brain.

I was glad. I was glad that her eyes saw me like I'd once seen Gracuri in Thebes: not as a boy, but a monster.

Gracuri. Now my eyes averted their gaze. I'd failed him like I'd failed her. He would never learn, but I needed Shea to. She needed to remember what I *really* was. It would help her if Caelius gained power over my mind. If the time came, I hoped she would be able to kill me easily enough if she needed to.

I sighed, looking once again at that rough, moss-covered

stone, now soaked in blood.

"Are you okay?" Aidan asked.

The words were there, but I didn't understand how he could *bear* to ask me. I looked up at Aidan. His brow was furrowed. He stared at Shea's dad, then back at me, shaking his head.

"I didn't . . . I didn't mean to kill him." My voice was barely a whisper. "What Caelius is doing to me now . . . I have no control over it yet. It's not safe for any of you."

Aidan's large, firm hand rested on my shoulder. "I know. You had no choice."

I winced. More than Caelius's tortures, those words crushed me. After all I'd done to him, how could he say that? I'd killed the only woman he'd loved other than Shea. Yes, she was alive now, but I had killed her, my only excuse being that I'd thought she was just a human in love with a beast. I'd been cruel. Hard. And now Aidan was by my side, unlocking my chains. He should've been burying his hands into the blood on my chest. He should've ended me himself.

The chains cracked, and I fell hard to the stone floor before catching myself. I recovered quickly, standing tall in the aftermath of my shame. I averted my eyes from everyone, their concerned gazes landing on the gruesome bones protruding from my wrists and ankles.

Nefertiti stepped toward me, but I waved, the same motion she was fond of using. In my mind I simply said to her, *Don't.*

Leaving me behind, Aidan walked over to Meky. He moved his hand through her hair, resting his thumb on her neck like he'd done in bed the night before I'd killed her. I'd stalked them for some time before ending her life.

Lamenting my mistakes was interrupted by my newest one as Shea's father rushed to my side, offering up his neck. I jerked away, knowing the display alone was enough to make Shea sick. I'd had no choice. Her father had needed to feed. Now, for a long while, he'd be obsessed with me like Gracuri had been, except this would be worse. I'd only fed from Gracuri. Jeff Harper had fed from *me*. He'd drunk my blood. I was his father now.

Even thinking that I was his *father* now was horrific. He was Shea's father, and now he was a part of me. I pushed him back as I stepped toward Duncan.

Jeff reached, grabbing the exposed bone of my wrist. He pleaded with me to take his blood, all of it if need be, to heal myself. He touched the shredded meat on my chest. I hadn't noticed while trying to kill him, but Caelius had gotten in a few devastating gouges himself, weak as he was.

I closed my eyes and focused on Jeff, speaking to him with my mind. *You will never again ask for my blood or offer yours to me. It does not matter how injured I am. Your only duty now is to obey Shea Harper. You are to stay by her side and keep her safe. This is the only thing that will bring me pleasure.*

When my eyes opened, Jeff had rushed to Shea's side. She jerked back from him, startled. But Jeff's gaze stayed captivated on mine as he nodded, half smiling, happy to do anything to please me.

I knelt down and pulled Duncan into my chest, holding him like a child against my torn-open rib cage. I rested my head against his, the blood from my chest oozing onto his mouth. He'd been my youngest, the last I'd turned. I had two other children left besides Ur-Nammu, but if Caelius had found Duncan in the matter of an hour, the other two didn't have much hope. But hope was not the point; they were still my *responsibility.*

Duncan. He'd been the part of me that was once carefree. When I'd arrived in Scotland, his had been the first face that greeted me off the boat. He'd been my storyteller. Everything to him was one epic tale that he wove together beautifully, sometimes in a drunken song. He'd been alive and fiery before I'd made him mine. And now . . . now he was nothing more than a juice packet for Caelius's thirst.

I breathed in his scent one last time. I wondered what story he'd have told if he could've described his death. It would have been different than *this.* In no version would Duncan MacCord have died so easily. In his storytelling, Duncan would have gone out to battle the Leguna of Aten or some fabled beast from Morocco while riding a white horse. Or in a snowstorm, he'd have been frozen like an iceberg waiting to sink the next Titanic. But this? No. Duncan wasn't dead. This was just another story for him. Another adventure. I'd just have to wait to hear his tale. And if Caelius continued to grow in power, I wouldn't have to wait long.

I let his body slip from my grasp as I stood and walked away. His empty carcass thudded to the floor like used meat. He'd deserved better, in life and in death. He'd deserved better than what *my* embrace had given him.

I looked back at the others. Helena had already gone to her lab and returned with supplies. I nodded, seeing terror crack the surface of Nefertiti's painted face as she stared at Duncan. My voice was low, resolute. "Your daughters will not have this same fate, Nefari. I promise. I'll help you find them. Caelius will never drink them like he has my Second-Borns. I would die first." It looked like a wave of relief moved through her as she reached for Mekytaten.

Shea's mouth was slightly open, as if she wanted to protest but still had nothing to say to me.

I addressed the group coldly, as I had done to hordes of warriors in the past, standing before blood-soaked fields of battle. "Shea, Aidan, Jeff, and Mekytaten will stay together. I'll stay with Nefertiti and Helena. We three will meet with Ur-Nammu and work together to find Nefertiti's daughters. Shea, I mean, *Aidan*, work on getting Jeff's memories back. Ur-Nammu can Dream-Walk, so we'll all use him to stay in contact and reconnect once her daughters are safe."

Nefertiti interjected. "What about *your* two remaining children, Bohe and David? We should find them as well."

I nodded slowly. "We'll find your daughters first, then my Second-Borns. Hopefully Caelius will be focused on us, not them."

Nefertiti pivoted on her heels and walked over to Shea, snatching her daughter from Aidan's side. "Mekytaten will stay with you, Shea Harper, as Lucian has said"—her voice was sharp, threatening—"but you are to protect my daughter with your life."

Shea didn't seem happy with Nefertiti's forceful tone but nodded her head in agreement.

Meky gently pried her wrist from her mother's grasp. "Mom, if anything, *I'll* help protect Shea. She can help us kill Caelius for good, and then we'll all be free."

Nefertiti was silent, but I knew that look. There was a low

rumble vibrating just under her stare. She was trusting Shea with her second-oldest daughter, but she was also trusting Meky. I'd only seen Nefertiti as a mother when she'd been human. It was strange seeing her now.

Aidan moved to stand beside Meky, his eyes still full of emotion. This was the love of one of his lives, now living and breathing, but a vampire. Who knew he'd be so fond of my kind?

I stepped toward them, and Shea looked at me for a moment. All I saw in her eyes was pain before she looked away.

Aidan's voice was loud and boisterous. "I'll get them as far from here as I can. Shea needs to rest. I'll stay with them until we can all meet again, so we can kill Caelius together and get Shea's mom back."

I met his gaze. At least one of us could be there for Shea. And she needed Aidan, his kind heart, his optimistic nature. My eyes shifted briefly to Mekytaten, wondering if she'd be a distraction and if Aidan, in his concern for Meky, would be able to give Shea the support she needed right now. Either way, Shea was safer with an angel and two Second-Borns by her side.

I thought about the dorm and how she'd punched a hole in my chest when I'd tried to take her. Only now did I wish she had succeeded and obliterated my existence. The pain in her heart was my doing.

Before I could say anything to Shea, Aidan swept her up and they all ran north. Just like that, she was gone. It didn't matter; I couldn't have said anything else to her anyway. All I could do now was offer my life in service of her Light.

Nefertiti stepped toward me. Cutting a line down her hand with a fingernail, she pressed her blood into my chest. I didn't protest as she moved her hand over my body. Nefertiti had drunk from Shea, so it was Shea's blood moving over my gashes, along the bones of my wrists. I breathed in deep, wanting to smell the crimson gushing from her hand. I'd held Shea in my arms. We'd made love. And now she couldn't even look at me. Having Shea's blood pour over me now was as close as I would come to her again.

After my wounds closed together and healed, Nefertiti wrapped her arm around Helena and leapt into the air. I followed quickly behind, letting the speed and distance from the stone chamber separate my emotions from the reality of what I'd done there, from what I was.

***

Flying next to Nefertiti distracted me from my torment. It was unlike anything I'd felt before. None of my children had been able to fly. The sky had been mine for centuries. It had been like a lonely island that I alone could reach.

I couldn't help but feel our connection as our eyes met. I had grieved her for centuries, and now she was *flying* by my side. It reminded me of our shared moments in Gutium.

My voice was low, treading lightly. "Remember when we were children, Nefari? We used to imagine we were birds and there was no cage that could hold us. Look at us now."

Her full lips curved as she smiled. It was a good memory. Vampires could dig up those old things in the brain, days that humans buried in the mess of living. We could choose a detail, and in an instant it was like walking through a vivid dream.

"One day we will fly, La-Narru," Nefertiti whispered softly, repeating what she'd said then. "And I'll be the sun, and you'll be the moon, and we'll soar through all the galaxies. Nothing will hold us down. We'll always be free."

That last sentiment changed her features. They shifted from fondness to agony. Freedom. The meaning of the word had been like a curse to her life, a lie she'd always longed for.

"The young woman I followed looked so much like the real Meky. It gave me a start when I saw her in Aidan's arms during the Viking era. But since I had followed her double, I brushed it off.

"I hadn't seen your children since before the Pharaoh died and they were released, so I didn't know what she looked like as a grown-up. I *never* would have hurt Meky if I'd known it was her. I always considered your children . . . my family. Why then, Nefari? Why did you hide your daughters from me?"

Her eyes widened as she increased her speed. "You know Caelius would have killed all of us if you'd found out. Once the Pharaoh died, we had to return to him. Our access to the world above was restricted."

Nefertiti let the memory come to life, her gaze filling with pain as she continued.

"The decoys of my children, that was all Caelius's idea, not mine. I watched as you cared for them from the shadows. You acted like a father in every sense, but they never knew your name. My real daughters watched as their decoys lived the loving lives that they could have had.

"Most of them know you and carry the fondness for you that they had as children. And I was filled with regret. I shouldn't have turned them, but I couldn't lose them like I'd lost you. Now it's all I can do to keep them alive and safe from Caelius's twisted mind."

Nefertiti had not slowed down while speaking, and I matched her speed. Helena held on tightly, eyes closed, shutting out the streaks of cities passing below.

We landed in Paris next to the Eiffel Tower. Helena staggered a step or two, then sat down on a bench close by, trying to give us our privacy, visibly uncomfortable with the emotional outpouring.

I grabbed Nefari's chin and turned her face toward me. "You should have told me. I would have helped free you from Caelius. Instead I wept over every child who died. I thought it was one more piece of you that I was losing, that would be gone into the abyss forever."

She brushed the back of her hand against my cheekbone. "Oh, La-Narru, still so much a boy. I know that's what you would have done. You would have fought for what you loved most. You are just as Gutian as I am, and you would have gotten us all killed."

Nefertiti was right. It was my oversight in Egypt that had brought about my death. She was a strategist, and I was more impulsive and passionate.

She closed her eyes. Her lips moved quickly. A sudden gust of wind tossed my hair as Ur-Nammu arrived and ran to our side. My mouth fell open in surprise. Nefertiti answered my unspoken question. "Of course I can Dream-Walk; I don't know why you can't. I cryptically told my father to meet us here."

Ur-Nammu looked up toward the tip of the Eiffel Tower. "Is

Setepenre all right? Is she here?"

Nefertiti shook her head. "You can see for yourself. You know she's not."

Ur-Nammu let his hand fall heavily on Nefertiti's as he pulled her to his chest, stroking her hair as he spoke. "You knew Setepenre wouldn't be here, yet you came for her first."

I was shocked to see her eyes water, her face looking lined with age for the first time. "She's the youngest, and she's always been confused, fragile, easily misled by her emotions."

They stared at each other for a moment. "It's not because she's the youngest that you worry, my love." Ur-Nammu's voice was raw, tired. "It's because Setepenre is *his*."

Ur-Nammu's gaze turned to me. They both stared, their eyes alight with expectation. I waited, and so did they.

There was a long silence.

Then it sank in.

I grabbed Nefertiti. My hands were clenched so hard around her arms that they were bone white. I shook her hard but could say nothing, my voice trapped in my throat.

Ur-Nammu's hand reached between us. He rested it against my chest. It calmed my mind as I met his gaze. This wasn't the cold stare I'd come to know over the centuries. It also wasn't the look of compassion he'd given me in the cave when he'd pulled me from the darkness of being devoured by Caelius. This was *pity*.

I growled, and Ur-Nammu slowly withdrew his hand, understanding that it wasn't his place to come between Nefertiti and me. But he didn't move away, either. She was his world, his everything to protect.

I looked down at her chest, unable to make eye contact as I hesitantly asked, "We have a child, Nefari? A child I've never met?"

"Given the circumstances, I see no harm in you finally knowing. Yes, La-Narru, before I was turned, before you were killed . . . my youngest, Setepenre, she is yours."

I let her go and stepped back. Thousands of years. Thousands of years alone, grieving for Nefari's loss, the loss of *her* children, and they were all alive. And one of her children . . . one of her children was *mine*.

A fury rose inside me as I stumbled away from them. All of this came to me *now*, when I was hopelessly in love with Shea, my soul mate, who would never forgive me, who deserved better than a monster. Now that my heart was no longer in Egypt or Gutium, all that I had wanted centuries ago had fallen into my hands.

Her soft touch caressed my spine. Nefari had done that once before, after dressing the whip marks from my father when I'd eaten my mother's ashes. I closed my eyes. This time *she* was the one who had cut me open and left me raw.

"La-Narru, I couldn't risk you knowing. My father has helped me, with Helena, create something that can kill Caelius. We couldn't risk you destroying the plan. We couldn't risk the lives of my children." Nefertiti's voice was quiet, choked with remorse.

I turned, looking into her deep purple eyes. "I was careless in Egypt *once* when I made those sculptures of you out of mud and clay. Once, out of the hundreds of times we met in secret, and it cost me my life.

"I was a boy then. How much more careful do you think

I've become after my death? After yours? I've stalked and hunted angels. I've battled in and won countless mortal wars. I've changed. I've become stronger. I was strong enough to help you. You should have come to me. You should have told me about my *daughter.*"

She nodded her head. "I know, Lucian, but I was afraid."

Again I was silent, and she waited. Nefertiti feared nothing, no one. She planned and survived. Looking at her face now, there were cracks in her seemingly calm expression. The centuries had changed her as well. The tortures she'd witnessed me suffer at Caelius's hands . . . I understood why she wanted to protect her children. It was better to work in secret than to have your intestines exposed at the mercy of his madness.

Still, I felt betrayed. Yes, Nefertiti had made a wise decision. But it went against the heart, and it had left me with *nothing.* All of those years with no hope of a family, of love. I'd experienced only a glimmer of it with Aidan, and his betrayal had hardened and killed what little I had left. In that sense, Nefertiti *had* left me to die. She'd left me to wander in agony through the ages.

I looked at Ur-Nammu. He'd kept his distance these past millennia as well. He'd been my only living link to the life I'd loved. "Why did you shun me?"

His mouth fell open. He'd been silent when I'd held Nefertiti in my hands back in Egypt. I'd asked for his help as we'd taken her cold body to Caelius. When Caelius had pronounced her dead, Ur-Nammu hadn't looked me in the eye and had barely spoken to me afterward.

His rejection was another symbolic death I'd suffered, another love I thought I'd killed by being the monster that I was. But she *hadn't* died then, only faked death. They had lied to me—Nefertiti more than anyone. She'd lied while resting dead in my arms as I wept. He'd known all this time, all of these ages, these thousands of years since.

His eyes swelled. "I could not lie to you, Lucian. It would only have been a matter of time before I told you about Nefertiti and your daughter, so I kept my distance." He paused. When he spoke again, his voice was deeper, pained.

"It was my fault. It was because I reached out to you in Egypt that you ended up a slave and were killed by the Pharaoh. I shouldn't have told you the truth *then*. I should have lied and told you that Nefertiti had died next to your father in battle. You could have lived a normal life, but instead you were enslaved because of your love for her. And Caelius is far more powerful than any Pharaoh. It was better that I stayed away from you. I could not look at you knowing what I knew, nor could I bear the consequences."

Nefertiti's voice was soft. "He disagreed with my decision. He always thought that you, as the father, should know about Setepenre. That it was your right."

I placed my head in my hands, covering my face. It was a childish gesture, but I couldn't look at them—and I couldn't leave. It burned in a way unlike the physical agonies inflicted by Caelius. Then I realized *this* was what Caelius wanted—not a tearful reunion with Nefertiti, but for me to feel the sting of all their silence, the centuries of deception. He wanted to sour my heart against the woman I had loved and died for.

A child, *my* child, hidden in secret. Caelius wanted to show me that all of these years he'd held in his possession all that I loved. Of course, my heart turning to Shea had ruined his final triumph over me.

If it wasn't for Shea, if Caelius had freed himself with the last Vessel five hundred years ago and revealed my lost family, I would have stayed. I would have stayed by Caelius's side and served him. I would have done whatever it took to keep my family safe, just as Nefertiti had done, just as Ur-Nammu had done. Now our Gutian blood was more like a curse to me, just like freedom. The foolishness in our loyal notions of love.

I fisted my hands by my side, stiffening my back. My fangs protruded, growing large enough to rip my gums. I spoke past them. "Where is my daughter? Why isn't she here?"

Nefertiti and Ur-Nammu shared glances, but it was Ur-Nammu who had the courage to speak. "I'm sorry. Setepenre is loyal to Caelius. She was the youngest. The others knew more of you and of the Pharaoh before they were turned, before they had to stay in the caves, but Setepenre never met you. Caelius knew she was *yours*. He's always kept her close."

"Has he . . . has Caelius done anything to her?" I had to ask, but I didn't want to hear the answer. His infatuation with me was grotesque enough. The thought that he would twist that obsession and turn it on my child was terrifying.

Ur-Nammu shook his head. "Caelius is intelligent. He never made Setepenre watch your torture like the other girls. She barely knows your name, only that you are her father."

He paused, scowling. "He treated her with kindness, acting like a grandfather." Ur-Nammu's expression hardened further. We all knew that there was no kindness in Caelius's heart, only strategies and poison. "We were forbidden to speak of her proud

Gutian lineage," he spat. "She sees *Caelius* as family!" His anger boiled to the surface. "Little by little, he shortened the time Setepenre was allowed above with her sisters. Nefertiti and I were only allowed to see her once a month at that time. In the last few years we've barely seen her face."

Nefertiti stepped toward me. "It was all I could do to beg her to stay hidden in Paris."

I wanted to kill. It was night, but the city was lit up, tantalizing like a candied apple. I wanted to lay waste to it, to destroy the place where I had found myself again with Shea. The place that should have held my daughter.

"She's the youngest . . ." I whispered her name, hardly above a thought. "Setepenre?"

Nefertiti nodded slowly. "Setepenre."

My face softened. In Egyptian it meant "Chosen of Ra." Chosen by the god of the sun. Chosen by the Light. The meaning made me think of Shea. When I was with her, I felt chosen. It only twisted the knife of irony further. "Who named her? The Pharaoh, Akhenaten?"

Like mine, Nefari's voice was barely a whisper. "It wasn't the sculptures of me that you made in the slums of Egypt that led to your death. It was *my* mistake, not yours. I shouldn't have had a child with you. But I . . . I wanted to have something that was *ours*. Even as you were whipped under the pyramids.

"I named her, but I had to be clever. Still, the minute Akhenaten saw *your* teal eyes, he knew. That's why he had you killed. Setepenre looks so much like you, La-Narru." She looked down, away from my injured face.

My mistake. The mistake I'd thought had cost my life, the

beating I'd endured . . . it had all been because of the sculptures I'd made of her. I cursed that part of myself: the craftsman. And when Caelius had turned me, I'd shunned creation. When Nefertiti had died, I'd embraced destruction. But it was a child, *our* child, that had caused the Pharaoh's rage.

I wanted to hate Nefari, but my eyes softened. She had birthed our child: a baby girl. I imagined what it must have been like to hold her. Pain seared through my memory.

"I'm getting my daughter back," I snapped.

Nefertiti reached out and grabbed my wrist. I jerked it from her hand, growling. Her eyes narrowed. "I know you're angry. You have every right. Your family was stolen, hidden, and I let it happen. But look at you now. This urge to run off and hunt Caelius down, it's a fool's passion. Help me find my daughters. We'll join Shea, and *together* we can defeat him."

She was right. Going off alone driven by love had ended with Gracuri's head skewered before me. I couldn't let anything happen to my daughter. I deserved my anger, but now was not the time for it. What use was it to save Setepenre if she'd still be enslaved to Caelius? I had to be a better father than that, a warrior who would fight for her freedom like Onack the Great. I looked over at Helena. "We should drop her off with Shea. She'll slow us down."

Nefertiti hesitated. "No, we need to take Helena to the underground city of Amarna—the one Akhenaten built for me—so she can continue to work."

She moved her hands over my chest, feeling around. When she found what she was looking for, her eyes brightened. Her fingers curled around the gold necklace hanging from my neck.

Her hand rested there as our eyes met. Behind the inlaid stone I could feel the rough etchings of Gutian hieroglyphs carved unceremoniously by the hands of an ignorant boy. The uncut but perfect emerald-green stone that held them had reminded me of the fallen green leaves that had been by her wet hair as she'd taken me for the first time by the river in Gutium.

The first time we'd made love.

She had pinned me down, mind set on what she wanted. It had been messy, wild, and free—a taste of what I wanted to be mine forever.

The cold stone felt heavy in her hands now. Gazing at it had anchored me on so many nights to that feeling, to that hope. As time passed, however, the weight had chained me to that anchor, pulling my heart away from hers and drowning me in the depths of loss, dragging me to the bottom of an endless night that only Shea had awoken me from.

I looked deep into her eyes. "I made you this necklace when we were children, Nefari. I carved it out of emerald from the caves in Gutium. It was the first thing I crafted. And I gave it to my first love."

She sighed with the weight of the memory, masking her tone. "I gave it back to you, Lucian, the night before battle. When you left and I stood and battled for our people."

I nodded. That had been my real mistake. "You gave it back, but the first time I saw you in Egypt, as the Pharaoh's concubine, I ripped it from my neck and placed it in your hands. I swore myself to your side and never left Egypt . . . not until my death."

She laced her hand through my black hair, the hardness in her tone crumbling into careworn love. "When you thought you'd killed me, La-Narru, you gently pulled it from my neck. Like keeping a lock of my hair. It was always close to you after that. Except when you lost it, buried in Pompeii."

My teeth clenched as I hardened. She'd let me sit in lava all those years. "I eventually stole it back from a museum. But I didn't wear it. I kept it close. It was my only touchstone to my history. To you. *You* were my history. A history of silence. I almost threw it off the balcony of a chateau in Paris when I was with Shea. *She* made me keep it . . ."

I looked at the city, turning from Nefertiti's gaze. Shea and I had been making love in a villa far away from the masses of Paris, but the whole country of France had made an impression on me. I'd thought it would always be the place where I'd finally known happiness, peace.

Now it would also be the world where Nefari had told me that I had a daughter, and that my daughter was loyal to the creature Caelius. It was a nightmare, that Setepenre considered that bestial Darkness her *family*, and that I was little to nothing to her but a name.

Nefertiti reached around my neck and unlatched the chain. I grabbed her fist as she held the emerald in her hands. "It's not yours anymore," I said, the injury of her actions adding venom to my tone.

And I succeeded. The words hurt her, and she winced. But I didn't care. The necklace, along with my heart, was not so easily handed over. They were both mine now. Mine to give as I chose.

Nefertiti called to Helena, who walked over boyishly. "Great. I guess you two are finally finished talking. I would have preferred it if you'd dropped me off first." She eyed Nefertiti critically. "You know Paris is out of our way."

Nefari scowled. "I had to see if Sete was here. The others are loyal to me alone."

Helena nodded. "I understand. It's just, without this necklace we can't defeat him."

"My necklace can't kill Caelius," I said.

Now Helena lit up. "It's what we've been working on this whole time. Because Caelius turned you first, even before Nefertiti, you are the *strongest*. But I needed to imbue something of yours, something you've had in both lives, mortal and immortal. That's when Nefertiti brought up the necklace.

"I was worried about the time it was apart from you in Pompeii. I thought maybe the connection to the object would be broken, but it wasn't. Nefertiti and her daughters helped dig you out, by the way. It wasn't just *your* digging. You may have been buried for a hundred years, but alone it would have been a thousand."

"Thank you," I stated dryly. She was missing the point that I'd still been buried in ash and lava, choking and fighting death to the point of madness, all for a lie.

Nefertiti was silent as she released her fist, letting the necklace fall into my hand.

"I'm sure you're very welcome." By now Helena was so interested in her tale that she was practically laughing with delight, nudging me like the friends we'd been when she was alive, as if this was just another one of our many adventures. "I've borrowed the necklace from time to time over the past hundred years, always returning it to that glass box inside your little sanctuary.

"I'm kind of sad you destroyed that place. The artifacts alone would have been worth testing." Her eyes grew wistful at the thought of her lost research opportunities. "I kept a few of your relics. I'm sorry, Lucian, but you didn't seem to notice, and they were fascinating."

She fumbled in one of her pockets, looking for something. When she couldn't find it, she huffed, then continued, "Well, you'll see. I need to take the necklace with me. The concoction I've been putting together, a scientific wonder really, should work."

"How?" I asked. Helena had drawn me out of my immediate anger, and I was intrigued.

"How?" she repeated. "I'm glad you asked, because Nefertiti's only interested in the results."

Nefertiti gave a faint smile. "Why don't you tell him *how*, then?"

Helena spoke proudly. "Science will make the necklace harness your power *and* the power of the sun. Together it will shoot out a blast that can destroy Caelius! In theory at least."

Nefertiti's faint smile grew serious. "You're the only one who could survive this, Lucian. It will have to drain you, and the sun's power, to work. Caelius should die before it kills you. And then we'll all be free of him forever. And we can be together . . . you with Shea, me with my daughters."

My gaze softened. "Setepenre, you, Ur-Nammu, and all of your daughters will always be my family, whether or not Shea forgives me and we are together. I lost all of you thousands of years ago. I'm not losing you *or* Shea. If this plan kills me but takes down Caelius, it will be worth it to finally set you all free.

And Shea can go back to living a normal life . . . without me."

Nefertiti nodded, but her fangs grew despite her calm demeanor. "It *won't* kill you, Lucian. I haven't survived all of this just to sacrifice you. You're mine." She stopped herself and looked away. "You're . . . hers. I know that. But you were always mine to protect. As a child. In Egypt. And now. I am a Gutian warrior. And you, my father, and my daughters are my tribe. I will fight for what I love."

I touched her cheek, letting my hand warm her hardened features. "No, Nefari. It was I who should have protected *you*. I know that. If you can forgive my weakness, I can forgive your silence. And we can move on."

She nodded quietly. "Take Helena to Egypt then. She can show you how to get into Amarna. My father and I will find the rest of my daughters and your remaining children, Bohe and David. We'll meet you there."

Ur-Nammu stepped toward us. "I just Dream-Walked with the girls. They are all safe and exactly where we left them. Let us go find the Second-Borns together, Nefertiti."

He grabbed her hand. We stared at each other for a moment, then Ur-Nammu spoke one last time. "For what it's worth, Lucian, I know you would have been a better father than I was, but I did my best to raise all her daughters with Gutian honor. Setepenre was always more *sensitive*, like you were as a boy. I'm sorry, but I need you to be the Gutian man that you are. I need you to harden and prepare for this battle. All that I care about— the lives of my girls—is at stake. And I know you love them, as you love me. Will you fight? Will your risk your life to save them?"

I clenched my jaw. "I will wear the necklace, and even if it shreds me, body and soul, I will free all of you from Caelius. I ran away *once* as a boy because my father cried and begged, because *you* and Nefertiti and the whole village asked me to leave Gutium. I wasn't a warrior then, but that was no excuse. I came back and fought in Egypt for Nefertiti, for you, but it was too late. *I* should have died on the battlefield of Gutium beside my father, Onack. But know this—I will never run again."

Nefertiti's face was moved to sorrow. Before she could speak, her father wrapped his arms around her waist and they were gone.

I grabbed Helena just as quickly and leapt into the cold night air.

CHAPTER 9
SHEA

I held onto Aidan's chest as he ran with lightning speed to wherever our new hideout was going to be. Meky and Dad followed close behind. I was the only one without that superpower, so I contented myself with resting in my best friend's arms, my safe place.

Oh, Aidan, what had our simple lives become? Only months ago we'd moved into our dorm and had been going to college. My biggest dilemma had been worrying about whether or not people thought we were a couple. Part of me never wanted to leave his embrace, even though moving this fast was making me a bit queasy.

Yup. Going to puke.

"Aidan, we have to stop. I'm getting sick," I mumbled into his chest.

He heard me, like he always heard me, and stopped. Meky and Dad quickly followed suit without argument.

"This should do fine anyway." Aidan smiled, trying to comfort me.

"Where are we?" I asked, surveying our surroundings.

We were standing in open fields of grass and weeds spreading out for miles with no sign of civilization. The only man-made structure was a dilapidated farmhouse a few hundred feet away. It had holes in the roof and looked like it would fall down if I breathed on it. Seeing as it was the only place to hide within walking distance, though, it would have to suffice.

"Can we just walk normally, please?" I could hear the attitude in my voice. I was cranky, and no matter how hard I tried, I didn't want to be nice. I wanted to be angry, to kick and scream and throw a full-on two-year-old temper tantrum. Everything was just wrong.

Dad was quickly on the other side of me, acting as my escort. I knew it was because Lucian must have ordered him to. There was still no recollection or concern in his eyes in regard to me. He was protecting me because he wanted to suck up to my boyfriend.

I looked up at Aidan. "I seriously can't take this anymore. Will you give Dad his memories back now, please?"

Aidan nodded, understanding. I moved out of the way so he could do his thing. He touched Dad's forehead, and a light flared around my father's face, causing him to stumble forward slightly. It took a few minutes for him to gain his bearings, but when he finally did, his eyes met mine.

A flood of relief filled my bones. My dad was finally looking at me like a father who loved his only girl.

"Shea?" His voice cracked.

Before I could reach out to him, he moved with super speed

and had me wrapped in his arms. With his new vampire-driven strength, he was so powerful I gasped for breath, but I didn't care. It was the best hug I'd ever had. Probably because I needed it more than anything else on the planet.

He pulled back slightly, still holding me in his arms. "We were so worried about you," he said, his voice choked with emotion. "You were missing for months." He looked over at Aidan. "Your parents were beside themselves with worry too." Then he paused, processing, focusing back on me. "Then that man, or god, or angel—I don't know what he was—came down, and suddenly my entire life had been rewritten. The fake memories are fading now, thank God. Shea, our lives were meaningless without you. We became Republicans," he uttered in horror.

We both laughed. "Heaven forbid."

But it was just like my dad to make a joke in a serious situation. It made me feel like things might turn out okay. Sure, he was a Second-Born vampire, but ultimately, he was my pops. I felt a sudden surge of love for Lucian for turning Jeff Harper.

I had been so angry because even though my dad was alive, he wasn't my *dad*. I had still felt like he was dead. But now, having him joke with me, having him look at me like I was his whole world, his baby, his little girl . . . it filled me with such an intense joy that tears began to stream down my cheeks.

Dad brushed them away. "I'm here now, Shea. We're going to make things right and get your mother back. Okay?" He tilted my chin so our eyes met, as he always did when he needed me to really hear him.

I nodded slowly.

"Come on." He smiled. "Let's get to that *Texas Chain Saw*

Massacre barn over there."

And I truly smiled back.

Even Aidan and Meky were amused.

If we could all have one millisecond of happiness, we'd take it.

As we made our way to the abandoned barn, Dad glanced over at Aidan. "I'm assuming Nancy and Alan still have their memories wiped?"

He was referring to Aidan's birth parents. Sure, the guy was an angel, but he'd had to get to this earth somehow, and that meant parents and a family. In this life he was an only child like me, but—as I'd seen the night he stabbed me—Aidan had also had two brothers in one of his past lives: a Vessel like me, and a vampire. Gunnhild had been the vampire, one of Lucian's Second-Borns. Hard to forget a guy who'd wanted to kill me. I thought I would have liked the Vessel brother, Halfdan, better.

Aidan nodded to Dad. "My parents don't remember Shea or me."

Dad sighed heavily. "I know you thought you were doing the right thing, but Aidan, the memories may have been wiped, but the empty hole was still there. Molly and I were miserable people without the memory of Shea. So are your parents.

"When you have a child, a piece of your soul is transferred into them. Then, to suddenly live as if they never existed? We *knew* something was missing. We knew. We may not have known what, but our hearts knew. It wasn't a mercy taking away our memories—it was a tortured existence."

His words hit me hard.

And yet my father continued. "Molly was worse than I was.

She started drinking and leaving for days at a time. And all I can think of now is that the person *you* created is out there with Caelius. She has no anchor to bring her back to the light. You stripped Molly of her hope and love when you stole the memories of our daughter. What kind of vampire will Molly be if she has nothing to live for?"

I whirled on Aidan. "I told you taking away their memories was a bad idea," I ranted, "but did you listen?"

I stopped when I saw the pain in Aidan's expression.

He hadn't known this would happen. Aidan had thought he was making their lives better, free of the pain and agony of losing their children. He'd never realized that the people you love are more than just memories. My dad was right: a piece of your soul was always with the ones you cared about, and that had nothing to do with your brain.

"I can't give my parents their memories back. They'd search for me forever." Aidan argued desperately, as if my father's words were convincing him to undo his brother's actions.

"Then give them a child! I don't know. Steal one from an orphanage and give the three of them new memories. Anything to fill that void," Dad suggested wildly.

Aidan shook his head. "It's too dangerous."

"It's too dangerous not to! Molly was on the verge of suicide!" Dad shouted, shocking us all. "And I wasn't too far behind."

Aidan simply nodded. He was going to do it, I could tell. I was about to reach out to him and hold his hand for support, but Meky beat me to it.

Aidan looked down at her, and his eyes were filled with relief.

I took my hand back before he could see it and wrapped my

arm around Dad's.

I should have felt happy that Aidan loved someone who loved him back the way he deserved. I knew that someone would never be me. I loved him with all my heart, but not in the way he wanted me to.

But did it have to be Nefertiti's kid? Really? A vampire who had done who knows what over the years?

I was about to voice my concerns in a not-so-nice manner when my father tugged my arm gently. "Maybe we should give them some privacy. It looks like they have a lot to catch up on."

What? I wanted to know Meky's version of their past as much as Aidan did. Okay, probably not *as* much. But seeing those two all cozy upset me. I was being horribly selfish, but I didn't want to share my best friend. I had just been through the most harrowing experience of my life. I could barely talk or even look at Lucian because he'd *eaten* my parents! I needed Aidan now more than ever. I wanted to sit down with Aidan in that crappy, gross farmhouse and just have him hold me.

But I could see in the way he looked at Meky that he wanted to be alone with *her*.

Not me.

It twisted my insides until I had to hold back tears again.

Before Aidan could see me, I pulled my dad ahead and called back to Aidan and Meky, "You guys catch up. We'll be in the barn." I hoped Aidan hadn't heard the emotion in my voice. I'd tried to sound as casual as possible.

Yeah. That didn't work.

Aidan lightly touched my arm and pulled me around to face him.

Don't cry. Don't cry. Don't cry.

I totally cried.

I felt my father let me go as Aidan wrapped me in his arms. "Meky and I can catch up later," he said, trying to soothe me.

No.

I couldn't do this to the most selfless being on the planet.

I took a deep breath and regained as much composure as I could, pulling away. "I'm fine, Aidan. You need to be with Meky right now, and I need to be with my dad."

Aidan cupped my chin in his hand, concern written all over his face. "You've just gone through the worst nightmare of your life. I don't want you to be alone."

Right? He knew me so well. My thoughts, my pain.

"I won't be alone. I've got Pops." I hugged him tightly. "I love you, you big lug." I forced a smile. "Now go. I know you want to, and I'll be fine. Just give me the scoop later, okay?" Then I looked over at Meky. "He tells me everything, so you're going to have to deal," I announced territorially.

She actually smiled, holding her hands up in surrender. "I wouldn't expect anything else."

Her acceptance of our friendship made me want to cry again. All my emotions felt too extreme. I felt like I was having the worst period of my life. Maybe this was what pregnant women felt like. I wasn't about to say that aloud. I knew my father and Aidan would cringe with embarrassment.

I felt Aidan's lips kiss the top of my head, then we both left the embrace at the same time. He gave me a smile that told me everything was going to be okay, and I turned away before I could see the two of them hold hands again.

"Come on, Dad, let's go." My father hurried to catch up with me.

Once he knew we couldn't be overheard, he put his arm around me. "I always thought the two of you would get together someday."

"Dad," I groaned.

"Not anymore, though. Shea . . ." His tone was serious.

I turned to him, knowing he was about to say something important.

"When I drank Lucian's blood"—his eyes were tinged with what I could only describe as ecstasy—"I could feel his love for you. I didn't understand it because I didn't know who you were at the time, but I was fiercely jealous of it because the feeling was so intense. No one, and I mean *no one*, will love you more than Lucian. As a father, I couldn't want anything more for my daughter." Then he smiled his old smile. "Besides, who else can claim to be a father to their father-in-law? Huh?" Seeing what must have been a disgusted kind of horror on my face, he grinned. "Too weird?"

"Yes. Definitely."

Then his words really sunk in. *No one will love you more than Lucian.*

"Oh, Daddy. I don't know what to do."

His arms were around me before another tear could fall down my face. I was tired of crying, but my emotions were overwhelming. It was probably the sunshine juice I'd sucked up earlier, or maybe I was just turning into a sap. Both options were entirely feasible.

After another moment or two of daddy-daughter bonding,

we finished our trek to the broken-down barn. It was even worse on the inside, with muddy hay and rotted walls, kind of what my insides felt like. Dad didn't seem to notice. He found a dry corner and motioned for me to sit with him.

"Tell me everything," he said. There it was. He wanted to know what had happened to me since I'd left for college. Certain things he already knew, but I needed to fill in the gaps. I did so with great pleasure since it kept my mind off of Aidan and Meky alone . . . rekindling.

I brushed that thought from my overactive brain and sat down, spilling my guts to my father. I glossed over the romantic end of things. No one wanted to talk to their dad about losing their virginity.

Dad was a captive audience, asking me to repeat certain events. I tried to ignore the fact that they were all Lucian scenes. My dad was seriously crushing. It was disturbing, but I knew he couldn't help it. Their blood bond probably matched our own father-daughter bond. Maybe it was even stronger.

We talked for over an hour, and when I had run out of story, Aidan and Meky still weren't back. I leaned against the wall in exasperation.

"Ouch!"

I pulled away and saw a disgusting rusted nail that I'd just stabbed myself with. Great. Tetanus and lockjaw, here I come.

Before I could properly moan about my injury, my father had sunk his teeth into my neck.

I was so shocked that I couldn't respond.

My dad was eating me! Sure, my mom had tried the same thing, but she hadn't known she was my mother. Dad knew, and he was doing it anyway. He could kill me.

Well, not really. I could use my Vessel powers. But still. *He* didn't know that!

I pulled myself together and made my blood into fire.

He yanked his head back and screamed in anguish.

I would have felt bad, but my neck seriously hurt, and so did the hole in my back from that freaking nail. My feelings hurt more than anything.

My eyes met Dad's.

I'd never seen him look so destroyed.

What he had done sunk in, and he couldn't seem to process it. "Shea, I-I smelled your blood. I couldn't stop."

I sighed and then scooted slightly away from him, not wanting to tempt him anymore. Closing my eyes, I concentrated on both my wounds, and just like when I'd fixed my broken leg when Ur-Nammu had kidnapped me, I healed the injuries.

I saw my father's face visibly relax a bit, but he couldn't meet my gaze. He was too ashamed. The scent of human blood, let alone Vessel blood, was too much for him to resist.

It made me realize the self-control Lucian had. He had been emaciated when Nefertiti had taken him away from me in the desert. I could only assume that Caelius had starved him further. He probably hadn't even had coherent thoughts by then, like all the stories over the years of starved hikers who'd resorted to cannibalism. When you're that hungry, you can't think rationally.

I was Jeff Harper's *daughter*, his own flesh and blood, and he had just tried to eat me. And Dad wasn't even that hungry!

Oh, Lucian.

I wished I could tell him that I understood. I wanted him

to know that, even though I was confused and angry at what he had done, I got it. The part of me that was struggling was the part that wasn't sure if I wanted to be with a vampire. Yes, I understood, I could even forgive, but could I be *okay* with it?

I didn't know.

"Aidan, Meky!" I yelled loudly. They needed to come back. I didn't care if they were buck naked in the wheat fields getting their groove on. My dad had just drunk from me, and he needed blood stat.

Within seconds, Aidan and Meky were by my side.

I filled them in. "I cut myself, and he bit me."

Dad's shoulders drooped and he lowered his head.

Meky took a good look at him. "We have to get you sustenance. I'll go to a hospital and pick up some blood bags. I can compel the nurses. They'll never know I was there."

She reached down and waved a hand over my father's face. He fell asleep instantly. "That should dull his bloodlust until I get back." She looked at me knowingly. "And his guilt. You're going to have to help him through this transition."

I nodded, knowing she was right. And blood bags? I liked the sound of that. I really didn't want my father drinking innocent people. I knew Aidan and Lucian would never let him kill anyone, but watching my dad feed off a human wasn't something I wanted to see.

I shuddered then, thinking of how Caelius was probably encouraging my mother to kill. By the time we rescued her and restored her memories, she'd have to live with what she had done. My dad could barely look at me, and he had only taken a small amount of my blood.

I stood and brushed myself off. I tried not to examine Aidan and Meky, but the obsessive part of me couldn't help it. I checked for messed up clothing, dirt and straw in their hair, anything that would indicate a make out session. I wished I didn't feel like a jealous girlfriend, but I did. Lame.

They were both clean and pressed, like I had left them. What was I thinking? I should've wanted them to have a love-tousled reunion. I'd never see Aidan in that way, so I needed to let him be happy. He'd always be my best friend, but I had to let my possessiveness go.

"So, did you guys make out?"

I'd really just asked that. I was mortified.

Meky gave me a look that suggested I was truly insane in light of the my-dad-just-ate-me circumstance.

Aidan shook his head, smiling at my idiocy.

He nodded to Meky, thankfully neither one responding to my embarrassing question. "Go get the blood." She was gone in a flash.

Then Aidan's eyes turned on me. "Were you serious with that? You are such a dork."

With all the blood rushing to my face from humiliation, I was surprised my dad didn't wake up and try to take another bite. "Shut up," was my eloquent answer.

Aidan smiled and rolled his eyes. "No, we did not *make out*."

"Well, you should have. She's very nice and pretty, and . . . you guys seem to have a past?" I was prying, and he knew it, but come on! I didn't want to be in the dark.

"Yes, we have a past. I promise I will tell you everything, but right now I need you to Dream-Walk, Shea. Meky can't seem to reach Ur-Nammu or Nefertiti. They must be keeping a block up in case Caelius is listening in." Aidan was all business.

"If Meky can't, then how am I supposed to?" At her age, the girl had to be better at Dream-Walking than I was.

"You're a lot stronger than you give yourself credit for. Meky said that Ur-Nammu has never met anyone as talented at Dream-Walking as you are. Even more than Nefertiti." He was proud of me. I could tell.

I didn't know if he'd thrown in that last part about being better than Nefertiti because Ur-Nammu had actually said it, or to make me feel superior. Either way, I appreciated it.

"All right," I agreed. "I need to lie down and concentrate."

Aidan took off his jacket and laid it down on the ground like a blanket. Always the gentleman. "Thanks," I said as I lowered myself to the floor and closed my eyes.

I was instantly standing under the Eiffel Tower.

Ur-Nammu was there alone. I knew we weren't really at the Eiffel Tower—it was just the dreamscape he had created—but it was comforting. Paris would always be special to me because of the time I'd spent there with Lucian. Although, at this particular moment, it felt like salt in the wound.

Ur-Nammu smiled at me, impressed. "I knew you'd find me. I feel I may have met my equal in Dream-Walking."

I couldn't help it—I really liked the guy. Sure, he'd kidnapped me, broken my leg, and brought me to Caelius, but he'd done it for his family. I could get behind that.

"So what's the plan?" I asked. "Are you guys in Paris?"

"No, and we can't tell you where we are in case Caelius finds a way into our dreamscapes. But tell Meky that we're safe. We're gathering her sisters and going forward with the plan," Ur-Nammu announced, determined.

"Let me guess, you can't tell me the plan either because of Caelius," I grumbled, already knowing the answer.

Ur-Nammu placed his hand on my shoulder. It was something my dad would do, and it was comforting. Looking up into his eyes, I realized that he was growing fond of me too. It actually made me feel happy that Ur-Nammu cared whether I lived or died. "I'm sorry, Shea, but no, we can't discuss our plans, not this way. Only in person."

"And will I be seeing you soon?" I wanted it to be sooner rather than later.

"We'll see. We can't find Lucian's children; they must have changed locations. Our only hope is that they are well hidden somewhere far out of Caelius's reach." He took his hand away. "I trust everything else is going well?"

"You mean did my dad try to eat me and did Meky and Aidan hook up? Then yes, everything is peachy." I may have overdone the sarcasm in that sentence.

But it only amused Ur-Nammu. "Things will settle down after Caelius is dead, you'll see. I was wrong about you and Lucian. It appears that he has indeed chosen you over my daughter. I underestimated his love for you, and for that I apologize."

It was formal sounding, but I could tell he was trying to be familial. It was kind of cute. Unfortunately, his words cut me worse than that rusted nail. "Is Lucian okay?" My voice was small.

Ur-Nammu nodded solemnly. "He's had a lot more to deal with than his situation with you. There are factors at play. I can't discuss it here, but after all he's been through, he deserves some measure of happiness."

I was suddenly frustrated. "Then why am I here?"

He sighed deeply and tilted his head, trying to figure me out. "We must keep in steady contact with each other so that when we meet, we can end Caelius for good."

"Fine. I'll make regular checkups." It sounded a bit like I was meeting with the dentist, but that was how it felt.

If only Ur-Nammu hadn't brought up Lucian. I didn't want to think about him. I didn't want to know he was dealing with more drama. As conflicted as I was, the last thing I wanted was for him to be in pain.

"Do you want me to tell Lucian anything for you?" Ur-Nammu offered politely.

Tell him I love him. That I forgive him. That I miss him, and I never want us to be apart again.

"No. Just be safe."

I opened my eyes to see Aidan watching over me. In the corner, Meky was feeding my dad blood bags from the hospital.

"Everything okay?" Aidan inquired curiously.

"Yeah. Everything is fine," I lied.

CHAPTER 10
LUCIAN

Helena and I were in the underground city of Amarna, shrouded in robes spun of gold with strange symbols woven into them. Even with the robe and not being cursed by darkness anymore, Amarna still burned when I was inside it. Helena explained that she had created these protective robes, but Nefertiti and her children didn't need them. Akhenaten had built this place so that *only* Nefari and her daughters could survive in it. Every symbol on its walls was a barrier to my kind.

How had they tolerated hiding all of those years? And the Pharaoh had done all of this to keep her safe . . . or to keep them from me.

I'd always thought Akhenaten had hidden himself like a coward after Nefertiti's death. And, worse, he'd kept the children from my gaze. It had ripped me open, her death and the way he'd blocked me from her babies. I'd been lovelorn then, newly turned and desperate to be with any part of her.

I hadn't known that she had been *with* the Pharaoh, that Nefertiti hadn't been with Caelius at that time because I hadn't been able to enter the kingdom of light, this Amarna he'd created. All of those idols, barriers, and sun shields barring my passage . . .

I'd tried so many times to break through with the hope of ripping Akhenaten to shreds and freeing Nefertiti's daughters from his slavery. I'd burned pounds of flesh trying to find a weakness, but Akhenaten had used ancient tools of magic passed down through the Pharaohs of Egypt, knowledge he'd learned from the Book of the Dead. And, even though I'd been a new vampire, my history was of Gutium, not Egypt. I'd had no idea how to combat the Pharaoh's shields of light, nor the Egyptian engravings with their protective symbols.

By the time I'd learned—by the time I'd ransacked crypts of ancient books—he'd already been long dead, along with the *doppelgangers* I had followed, the children I had cared for, thinking they were Nefari's.

I still remembered the day Akhenaten died. The people had rebelled against him and his beliefs, abandoning the city and his worship of Aten, the sun god. I'd actually cried when I saw Nefertiti's daughters again, but I hadn't revealed myself to them. Instead, I spent the rest of their mortal lives providing for them from the shadows. And when each child had died, a part of me died with her. When they were all gone, I'd mourned for all I'd lost, drinking the sands of Egypt over and over.

My skin itched, just under the surface. It felt like thousands of beetles were crawling over my flesh. I didn't care—discomfort mattered little. I'd always wanted to see Amarna, now more than ever—now that I knew Nefertiti's children had *good* memories here, that they had been safe from Caelius in this place. I walked around, touching the inlaid precious stones coloring the walls. Everything was ornate. It was a small golden city.

I eyed Helena as she mixed powders on an altar to Aten. She was using an old contraption I hadn't seen in a hundred years. It whistled as it boiled. She smiled at my interest. "Yes, I know that in today's age you have your computers and electricity, but my heart will always be with steam. I think humanity gave up on that idea too early. Think of the pollution now—that could have been avoided if I'd had a chance to perfect some of my inventions."

I stepped closer, touching Helena's hand. "If you hadn't died."

She sighed. "I didn't die."

I flicked her ear. It was something I'd done when we had traveled together and I'd needed her attention. "Yes, Helena, you did. And then you had to spend all of your time working on a way to kill the devil, not on your inventions."

She paused at my unsubtle reminder of her living death, her hand frozen, clenching a beaker.

I placed my hand on her shoulder. "It's okay. I know how you are when there's work to be done. But you can stop for a moment. There's no one around. It's just us."

Her teeth clenched. "Not now. I need to focus."

I stepped closer. Caught in all the madness of Caelius and Nefertiti, caught by grief and loss, I hadn't taken the time to really *see* her, to process what her being by my side again meant to both of us. I set my selfish desires aside and stared. Her lips pursed, and her brow furrowed in concentration.

"I missed you." I paused. "We had so many adventures. You were the only human who ever outwitted me." I looked at her distant eyes. "I'd like to think that I still know you. I said once that I would protect you, that I would fight the burdens of the world so that you could invent and create without restriction. I made promises . . ."

I brushed my hand against the side of her face.

Her whole body stiffened. "Lucian, don't."

I grabbed Helena's long braid, pulling it to the front. I took out the elastic and pushed my fingers through, letting the waves loose. "How long has it been since you've let your hair down? You only wear it like this when you're working."

She averted her eyes.

I continued. "Growing up, you always wore it back, didn't you? It was never safe to have it down around your brothers. When we met, it stayed back for a long time. But remember Tuscany? After you killed Robert and we stole that last piece of machinery you needed for your device? Remember how we rode horseback, and you finally let your hair down, the wind uncurling all of that perfection?" I laced my fingers deeper into her hair, toward the base of her neck, unknotting the braid.

Her body tensed further. Still, I knew she needed this. "You said then that you were *free*. Free from all the men in your life. Free from all the scientists who judged you unworthy because you were a woman. And your invention, the one that would make you free from death, you swore that you'd never pull your hair back again, that you'd never be something for someone else. Not for your father. Not for anyone. Not even for me.

"And I was glad, glad that I was there. To be a part of that moment with you . . . I'd seen so much of what I'd loved enslaved. Seeing you free, helping you break those chains, it was one of my fondest memories in a cold, long life. And when I was in Thebes and heard that Cumbar had killed you on a train heading home and had stolen your inventions . . . I crumbled."

Her hand tightened until she broke the glass, shattering the beaker. Her fingers were frozen in its shape. I pulled a large piece of glass from her palm. I bit my thumb, drew blood, and rubbed it into the wound, healing it as Nefertiti had done for me.

Helena's eyes shot up as she spoke. "And you killed Cumbar and everyone in the city he lived in. You buried all of my inventions in the place where you thought I'd died. You made a monument in the blood-soaked spot where my coat had been found, and you went back to hating. Hating everything that was human. Not that you fully stopped hating humans when you were with me. The spark was always there when you talked about the Pharaoh and slavery, the wealthy and powerful."

I held the back of her head and pulled Helena a little closer. We were silent.

I didn't want to see her this way—walled up, hardened—like I had been for so long.

I swallowed. It had to be said. "All you wanted was your freedom. Freedom to create, invent, and travel. I never wanted this for you. All these years, you've been Caelius's slave, only allowed to work on this weapon under Nefertiti's gaze, and that wild spirit in you died."

She fell into my chest.

There was a long silence as she balled her hands into fists with the fabric at my waist. I rested my chin on top of her head, smelling her hair. It didn't smell like the fields she would ride her horse in. It didn't smell like oil from tinkering in her lab. It was off, just like she was now.

"Helena. What you have on the inside, those are the things that time cannot erode, that Caelius can't touch. Don't hide from who you really are. Don't hide from me now. This work, this forced stand against the darkness, it will kill you if you let it. But I know you. Inside, you're still free, aren't you?"

Her breathing hitched as I felt a soft wetness bleed through my robe onto my collarbone.

I wrapped my arms around her, cradling her like I'd done when the scientific community had shunned her ideas as lunacy. She'd been lost in that moment, calloused. And she'd needed to cry then just as much as she needed to now—to mourn over the thought of what was going to be her life and to find the clarity that comes after acceptance of what is.

Still, crying was not easy for Helena; I knew that. She'd always been the type to keep it buried inside. It linked my heart to hers. I had learned that lesson recently—how to let go, how to escape the burial of emotions—but growing up, she'd been taught by her abusive father that crying and emotions were a sign of weakness, that love was weakness.

After dumping her off at an orphanage and then picking her up on a whim, her father had still overlooked the beautiful blossom that was his magnificent daughter and had married her off to some preeminent, cruel-tempered biologist. But Helena had read her husband's books while he was sleeping. She'd grown brilliant in his shadow.

I rested my head on hers.

I sighed, releasing my own fears at what she had now become. She really hadn't changed. It was good to have a friend, a friend

I hadn't injured firsthand, as I had Aidan. But even *knowing* me had brought that temporary freedom she had fought so valiantly for to ruin.

Our time together had been brief for a vampire, but it had been meaningful. With Helena, I'd seen moments in myself, moments of La-Narru.

She pushed back from me and looked away, gathering herself. When she was ready, she met my gaze, offering me a small smile while wiping her tears. She didn't have to say anything. The relief that covered her soft features said it for her. We understood each other in that way.

I pushed one of the buttons on Helena's contraption as it whistled, the liquid inside changing from clear to green. She swatted my hand away. "Don't touch that, you simpleton!"

She looked at me in shock as I withdrew my hand. I laughed, then so did she. It was such a natural reaction. It was as if she'd just woken up on the train and caught me tinkering with her inventions, as she had many times in the past.

Now the smile on her face matched the relief in her eyes. She was the first human to find new and unique ways to call me an imbecile. And I relished it. She was *never* afraid of me or of what I was.

"I'll always be here for you, Helena."

Her smile wavered, and she averted her fond gaze. "You said that when I was human too. You know I'll live a lot longer now, so you can't be so careless with your 'always.' "

I looped the ends of her hair through my fingers. She finally released her fists, the fabric falling lower to her hips, its pattern now more like crushed velvet than silk.

"I will *always* be here for you."

She stepped back. "How can you say such things after all you've lost? How can you promise anyone anything and still believe it with certainty? You just lost Gracuri and Duncan. You talked about them all the time when I was alive. They were among your favorites, weren't they?"

I winced at her words. I still needed to grieve my children properly. I still needed to find my remaining two. But I was stumbling, one step at a time, doing my best to keep up with each situation.

"I know I'm failing. But . . . but I still believe—"

"I know." She sighed, then placed her hand on her hip, leaning into it. "I'd like to think I still know you too. You loved them. You love all those you turn, and you love me. The problem isn't that you fail, or that you don't try—it's that you blame yourself for all of it. I've had to watch it for so long. You hide just as I do. I want you to believe me when I say this, Lucian. I will always be here for you too. You don't have to save me or take the blame. I'm going to save *you* this time."

Her smile returned. "Now go. Give me that necklace and leave me alone to work." Her smile widened. "Go walk the halls like some ghost. I know you're dying to see where they kept Setepenre. From what Nefertiti's told me, it was through there." She pointed toward a long, ruby-inlaid hallway. "But be quick. My work is almost complete. I'm going to charge your necklace with the sundial and add a few more gears."

I nodded, carefully handing her the emerald necklace. Curiosity was eating at me. The place my *child* had been taken, the place that had held my family for so long . . .

As I stepped inside the archway, I glanced back. For a moment Helena held the hair tie. Pulling her hair back, she paused, then let it fall. Letting her tresses remain wild as she fiddled with her concoctions, a lightness covered her face as if remembering her one, brief moment of complete freedom.

I sighed with relief, then turned away. Moving through the hallway, I saw that it intersected with a multitude of rooms. I ran through them quickly, taking it all in, lingering only momentarily in places where my family must have bathed, eaten, slept . . . dreamed.

I swept through like a tornado because Helena was right: there wasn't much time. I wanted to absorb as much information as I could. The glyphs. The tapestry. A finger painting on the wall.

I stopped.

I felt something deep inside. I knew it had to be my daughter's. I tore a chip of paint off the wall: a small blob of green. I wrapped it in a scrap of muslin. My little girl, my Setepenre.

I would keep it with me forever.

I continued to explore all of the rooms. Everything was so well-preserved: the jars of honey, the statues. In some rooms it even smelled like Nefari, especially on the bed where she must have lain countless nights while I'd mourned her death.

Everything was lavish. Had I been a mortal man, and not a vampire, I never would have been able to provide for the children like this. Yes, I would have tried, and even as a vampire I'd ensured that their doppelgangers were comfortable. But this?

I may not have been able to give them everything, but I would have *loved* them. I grabbed my chest, the pain aching. Of course, seeing this now, I realized that the Pharaoh had done just what I would have done: he had raised them here. In my absence.

I growled, darkness building inside of me. Again the word "mine" filled every thought. Akhenaten had taken all that was *mine*. If he hadn't sentenced me to death, Nefertiti never would have made her deal with Caelius, the pact that had sentenced us all to lives much worse. It was his fault. *His*. And now I was standing in the little kingdom he'd built to protect . . . to protect . . . all that he'd *loved*.

Tears rolled down my cheeks.

I folded.

I fell to my knees, clutching the small chip of Setepenre's painting. My whole life I'd been given scraps, moments to treasure. But someone more powerful always came and stole them away. Something always ripped it from my hands. And now, even as a vampire, I wasn't strong enough to protect Shea. There would always be another Caelius, another Pharaoh in my life. Perhaps that was my curse.

Helena was wrong. All of this was *my* fault. I couldn't protect them, any of them. I was weak. Worthless. She was right, however, about making promises that I couldn't keep. Why did I think the overpowering feelings in my heart would be enough to make the words true?

The weak would always be prey to the strong. No matter how I tempered my body, or my mind, I couldn't break free. My voice trembled as I spoke, a cold shiver quaking my bones. "I'll always lose the ones I love."

A soft hand wrapped around my neck as Nefari knelt beside me. Then four other young, beautiful Egyptian faces knelt around me, their hands outstretched, touching my arms, my shoulders.

Nefari spoke softly. "We are still your family, La-Narru. You haven't lost us. My daughters were raised in Amarna, but they remember the words you taught them on countless days by the river. Those times were meaningful to *all* of us. And I taught them about Gutium and our ways. Gutian blood will *always* live inside them. And ours is a proud people."

The tallest moved in closer, the oldest, the one I had spent the most time with in Egypt: Merytaten. She looked so much like Nefari. Even her voice was rich as gossamer, like her mother's. "We are many, but united we beat with one heart."

A small hand touched my shoulder and squeezed down. I turned my head slightly and recognized at once her large brown eyes: Ankhesenpaaten. With a voice as gentle as her hand, she said, "Though we fall, we will never fail because we have given ourselves over to glory."

Neferneferuaten Tasherit grabbed my little finger, like she used to by the river. I'd called her Sherit then, her sweetness revealed in her warm grin. Sherit's smile was more like her grandmother's than her mother's. Nefari's mother had come from the Zagros Mountains, and her face had reflected the beauty from that region. I could see that same beauty now in Sherit. The lineage of Nefari's mother, Shanidar.

Her words were soft. "To fight for those we *love*."

Tears welled in her eyes and fangs grew in her mouth as the last daughter, Neferneferure, spoke. "Though our bones may brittle with time, life may wear and kill the tenderness of affection, but the burning heart, the flame that is *our* people and what we stand for, cannot be stamped out of time."

There was a long pause.

They all moved in closer, embracing me, their heads resting on my back and chest like they had done as children. My family. There were two lines left. One for Mekytaten, followed by words meant to be spoken by my daughter, Setepenre.

Instead a deep, husky voice rang from behind as Ur-Nammu stepped forward, covered in a cloak. "We are etched into the very existence of all things. We are, and forever will be, a people who fight for what we love, La-Narru."

Now I understood. My people, this broken family. I understood why they'd left me suffering in the desert, why they couldn't have risked me knowing, risked Caelius killing the girls. They were *Gutian*, and they were all that was left of our people. Ur-Nammu and Nefari, along with my father, had been the leaders of that tribe. It was their duty to protect its legacy.

And it was mine.

It was my duty as the only living line of my father, Onack, and of my mother, Anna-Steen. I was Gutian, and these were *my* people. They were mine to protect. Even at the cost of my life.

Touching the girls' soft faces, I kissed each of their foreheads. I may have been weak, I may not have deserved even the scraps of love that I'd received over the centuries, but I had to try. I had to redeem myself because deep inside, even as I'd fought against Caelius's control countless times in the cave, deep within the core of my being I had always believed that Caelius was right.

Even as I'd thrown myself mercilessly into innumerable battles, I'd known that I couldn't win.

That fighting was, eventually, useless.

I'd believed that I would always lose. As I'd lost my mother, as

Gutium had lost the war. I'd lost Nefari in Egypt, her daughters, and Ur-Nammu. Then Moses and Aidan. The children I had turned I'd kept at a distance out of fear. And now I'd lost them too. One by one. Some, regrettably, terribly, by my own hand. And Shea. Anyone I cared for. I couldn't hold on to them. Like desert sand, they slipped through my fingertips.

I was weak.

At the core of myself I believed it.

So, all of these years . . . Caelius had already won.

I wasn't sure at what point it had happened, when I'd stopped believing that I deserved love, when I'd started to believe that I would always lose. But now?

Now, wrapped in these embraces, staring at all of their loving gazes, I *had* to believe again. In the Light. In myself. In *something*. I had to be Gutian again, to believe in love and its power. A power greater than any darkness. A power greater than the sum of my weaknesses. A power living and breathing in every creation. A power my father had known and Ur-Nammu had understood long before I was born.

Love wasn't our *weakness* as a people. I needed to believe that it was our strength. That we could win. That, united, we were more powerful than Caelius.

I stood up, and they rose beside me. My voice was clearer than it had been in centuries as I finished the words I had taught them by the river. "And love. Love is the soul of all that is worth fighting for."

Ur-Nammu nodded. "I'm glad you are back, La-Narru. It has been a long time since I've seen you this way."

I knew what he meant. The belief that I would always lose

had changed me. It had twisted me into something I wasn't.

Now that I was going to face Caelius again, it would have to be for everything. If I lost, I wouldn't just be devastated; it would mean that the lie had been true all this time, that I'd been born to lose what I loved. But it was a *lie*. I refused to die believing Caelius's twisted version of the truth.

I heard footsteps running down the long hall as Helena rushed toward me. She ran past the girls, but then stopped, seeing the emotional display unfolding. Nefertiti waved her forward before she retreated.

"It's finished," Helena said, holding the necklace out to me. "Are you ready, Lucian?"

I touched it, feeling its new power. "Yes. I'm ready to kill Caelius."

CHAPTER 11
SHEA

"**H**ow long are we going to stay here? It's pretty gross," I complained to no one in particular.

But it was Aidan who answered. "Until they get here."

"They" meaning the rest of the gang: Lucian, Ur-Nammu, and apparently a bunch of girls. They couldn't find Lucian's children.

Meky had just received a dream message from Ur-Nammu saying there was something wrong. He hadn't exactly elaborated. Shocker. The man liked his vagueness.

That had been two hours ago. I figured it would take them less than two seconds to get here, but I guessed they must've been trying to hide their trail from Caelius or something.

Dad was much better now that he'd filled up on blood bags. We even tried to play a game of I Spy, but since everything in this place was a muddy, rotted mess, it was sort of difficult to have any variety.

Honestly, I was mainly trying to figure out what I would do or say when I saw Lucian again. It was going to be difficult not to run over and tackle him to the ground. But I wasn't ready for that. At least I didn't think I was. The more time that passed, though, the less angry I became, and all that was left was pain.

Aidan had been a nice distraction for a little while. He'd told me a bit about his past life with Meky. It had been during the Viking days with his jerk of a brother, Gunnhild. Meky had been trying to spy on the Vessel of that time to see if his powers could be strong enough to finish Caelius off. Since Aidan had pretty much been joined at the hip to all his Vessels, Meky and Aidan had ended up falling in love. Hearing how Lucian had killed Meky (or she'd pretended to die) just to hurt Aidan only made me feel worse.

I was trying to get over what Lucian had done to my parents. Now, hearing Aidan recall old memories of him finding pleasure in torturing my best friend made things murky, to say the least. I'd told Aidan to stop telling me any more. I really didn't want to hear how evil my boyfriend was.

"Hey." Aidan sat next to me, pulling his knees to his chest.

"Hey," I answered, nudging his shoulder with mine in affection.

"I know you don't want to hear this—"

"Please don't tell me I should break up with Lucian. I kind of know that already, but it just hurts too much to even fathom not being with him—"

"I'm not going to tell you to break up with Lucian. In fact, just the opposite." He paused, probably because my face had frozen in shock.

"Everything Lucian did came from either love or hate, and the only way you can truly hate someone is to love them first. Otherwise, you'd simply feel indifference." He sighed deeply. "Lucian loved me like a brother, so when I betrayed him by killing Moses, the only other person he'd loved as a vampire, torturing me was his way of coping with the pain."

"You know, this isn't really making a great case for the guy." I knew Aidan was trying to help, but no girl wanted to hear about her boyfriend torturing the ones he used to love. "So you're saying I shouldn't break up with him or else he'll torment me for the rest of my life?"

I wasn't serious, though, and Aidan knew it, smiling and rolling his eyes. "Shea, you are so hardheaded sometimes. My point is, *I* forgave Lucian because, despite all of his cruelty, he was still my brother." Aidan's words were quiet. He loved Lucian as much as I did.

"I have to think about it," was all I could say.

"Whatever you choose, I'm behind you." He leaned down and kissed my cheek.

I peered back at Meky, not wanting another vampire attack at the moment. She stood next to my father, making sure he was doing okay, so she wasn't paying attention to us. "She's a good one."

Aidan's eyes glazed over with affection. "I know."

I felt truly happy for him. Okay, happy with just a tiny smidgen of jealousy.

I started tapping my feet. "When are they going to get here?"

As if on cue, one minute the dilapidated barn was empty, and the next it was a vampire jamboree.

Meky was instantly surrounded by what I could only assume were her sisters since they all looked so much alike. Talk about intimidating. They were all as stunning as their mother, Nefertiti. Lucian's ex. Ugh.

Ur-Nammu, Nefertiti, and Helena went straight to Aidan with worried expressions.

I knew Lucian was here too, but I couldn't bring myself to look. I was afraid my heart would stop beating if we made eye contact. He was a few feet away, but I could *feel* Lucian's presence as if he were standing next to me. It was the worst kind of torture. I wanted to run into his arms, to feel his mouth on mine, to see his beautiful eyes and how he looked at me.

But I kept my head down.

Helena was the spokesman for the new arrivals. "We have this necklace that we think will destroy Caelius, but it won't activate," she explained to Aidan. "It's fully charged, and it should be tied to Lucian's power as the First-Born of Caelius, but it's not moving. We thought maybe your angel powers might work as a catalyst."

Aidan nodded and took the necklace. He closed his eyes, concentrating.

Nothing.

After several minutes of trying, it was obvious angel mojo wasn't going to do the job.

"So this big bad plan of yours was turning Lucian's necklace into a weapon against Caelius? And it doesn't work?" That came out a lot harsher than I'd meant it to.

Nefertiti hissed at me. Hissed! It was more than a little terrifying.

I took a step back and put my hands up. "Don't get mad at

me. We can still take him down, can't we? I mean, please tell me you didn't put all your hopes into a necklace?" I couldn't seem to stop myself from being a bitch. It just irked me for some reason that Lucian's stupid necklace (the one *I'd* stopped him from throwing away) was their key to taking down the most powerful evil alive.

Nefertiti looked like she was about to rip my head off and suck out my bone marrow.

Lucian was suddenly between us, blocking me from the Egyptian queen. "Nefari, enough."

"Nefari? Is that a pet name?" *Stop it!* What was wrong with me? Evidently, I was possessed by a raging lunatic because I shoved Lucian away. "And I don't need you to protect me from *her*." I stalked out of the barn.

Now that I was in the middle of a field of weeds, leaving a building full of supernatural beings behind, I immediately felt better. It was like a vampire convention in there, and I was the only dish on the menu. Not that any of them would intentionally drink from me, but since self-control seemed to be an issue with their species, I just wanted to get away from *all* of them.

Besides, it was too difficult to be near Lucian, especially since I wanted him to grab me and take me somewhere far away from there, leave all this chaos behind. I wanted Paris back: carefree days of making love and just being together. Caelius was the biggest cock-block I'd ever met.

Thinking of the absurdity of that statement made me smile.

"You all right?" Aidan walked up next to me.

"You know I'm not." I decided not to pretend anymore. He knew me too well anyway. "Where's the necklace?" I noticed he wasn't holding it anymore.

"Lucian has it. They're trying to make it do whatever it was they thought it would do." He wrapped his arms around me from behind and rested his chin on the top of my head. It felt so normal, like we were in my backyard at home dreaming of our futures.

"We're a pair, aren't we?" I shook my head.

Aidan turned me around in his arms so he could look at me.

I cringed. "I know that face. You're about to do something I won't like, and you're afraid I'm going to try and stop you."

He smiled. "At least I always tell you first."

"That doesn't make it any better." When he was silent for a moment, as if trying to figure out how to word his next sentence, my impatience broke. "Just spill!"

He slowly nodded his head. "Shea, I don't think Caelius *can* be killed." He motioned to the barn. "They need to have hope because they've been enslaved for thousands of years, but if it were possible to destroy Caelius, my brothers and I would have done it back when we had the chance. We were only able to trap him in that prison."

Aidan wasn't saying anything I didn't already know. This whole "kill Caelius" thing felt like a fool's errand from the start. But I had wanted it just as much as Lucian. That need to be free of his father was so overwhelming it blinded us.

I could only imagine how much worse it was for Nefertiti and her girls. They had been trapped in the prison with the monster himself, unable to live real lives, watching the world carry on without them. It must have been like being buried alive, but conscious. Planning Caelius's death had probably been the only thing that gave them a reason to live.

"So what are you saying?" I asked Aidan, staying within the circumference of his arms.

"I'm saying that my brothers and I need to trap Caelius again. It's the only way to keep him from destroying everything good in this world."

"Can you even do that?" I had thought that when his brothers went back to protect the Light there was no shot at making a new prison.

Aidan nodded solemnly. "We could always re-imprison him, but we thought since he hadn't completed the ritual by killing you that he would be weak enough to destroy. Then I saw what you did to him in the desert, and Meky told me how you drank from the sundial and attacked him again . . ." He paused as if what he was about to say would offend me somehow. "And he didn't die. He should have. If Caelius had been truly weak like we thought, your powers should have destroyed him. But they didn't. Even as I'm talking to you now, he's still alive and kicking and probably killing hundreds of innocent people trying to gain his strength back."

"And making my mom do the same." I knew I should be focused on killing Caelius, but my brain kept creeping back to the horror of my *mother* being a vampire.

"Which is why I need to do this." He cupped my face in his hands. "I don't want you to tell the others. If they find a way to get rid of Caelius, great, my brothers and I are on board. But he needs to be trapped first."

I clasped his hands, keeping them on my cheeks. "Okay. But if Caelius tries to pull you into his chamber to torture you for a thousand years, I'll suck that sundial juice and get you out. You're not going to die like that."

His eyes were suddenly distant, and he was most likely remembering his lost brother. "Ashliel wasn't supposed to die," was all he said. It was cryptic for Aidan, but I didn't want to push him since the memory seemed to hurt so much.

Then he was himself again, and he kissed my forehead. "You promise you won't tell them?"

"They're going to know you're gone. What should I say?" I was a terrible liar. I'd tried to shoplift candy once. When a lady had asked me what time it was, I'd thrown the candy bar in the air and run out of the store. Yeah, real smooth.

"Tell them I went to find Caelius's location. It's simple. It's true. You technically won't be lying. You should be able to handle it even if they ask you the time." He grinned.

It only reminded me that Aidan had been with me my whole life. He knew all my stories—he was a part of most of them. No one would know me better. I hugged him as fiercely as I could, not wanting to let him go. He returned the embrace, then pulled away. "I love you, Shea."

"I love you too, Aidan. Be safe. Don't do anything heroic, okay?" I didn't want him to leave, but I knew that trapping Caelius was our best option at the moment. If he and his brothers had done it once, they could do it again.

His eyes were distant again, then he squeezed my arm one last time and shrugged. "You know me." His smile was almost sad. Before I could say anything more, Aidan was gone.

Gone.

And it hurt.

I didn't like that last look he'd given me. It made my paranoia start to grow. Anything to do with Caelius was dangerous, but Aidan and his brothers had this. They knew what they were doing, didn't they?

I groaned as I glanced over at the small light emanating from the barn full of vampires.

At least my dad was here. I'd have to ignore the adoring looks he threw at Lucian, but he was still my father, and he made me feel safe.

Kicking a stray rock here and there, I began to walk toward the shack of doom.

"Shea?" Lucian's gentle voice sent shivers through my body.

I turned. He was standing inches from me. His eyes were so unsure that it ripped my insides to shreds. I loved him so much it physically hurt to keep him at arm's length.

"Where's Aidan?" he asked.

"He went to find Caelius for you guys." Aidan was right: it was close enough to the truth that the lie had come easily. "Did you find your Second-Borns yet?"

There was a flash of pain on his face as he shook his head. "Either they're hidden well or Caelius has them. Until we stop him, there's nothing I can do." Then his eyes turned gentle as he asked, "How are you?"

His tone was so soft and concerned it wrecked me. And, like an idiot, I practically leapt into his arms. Feeling him pull me in tighter only made me want him more. We were too connected to stay apart. If that made me a moron, I didn't care. Lucian would die for me, and I for him. That had to count for something.

I stayed there with him, neither one of us speaking, just

holding on to each other as if breaking apart would be the death of us.

Finally, I spoke first. "Oh, Lucian, I missed you so much." I tried to rein in the tears I'd been holding back, but feeling his body pressed against mine . . . it felt so perfect, like I belonged there.

His hands ran through my hair as he looked down. It was as if he hadn't seen me for centuries and was trying to soak in every second. "I thought you'd never"—his voice cracked with emotion—"I thought you'd given up on me."

"I tried." I wiped away my tears. Seeing him there, with his bright turquoise eyes looking at me with such love and hope, it filled me with so much happiness. For once, in a very long time, I felt like things might just turn out okay. "I love you too much, you stupid jerk."

He smiled, relief flooding over every one of his beautiful features. "I love you more than my own life."

"You have pretty low self-esteem, so that's not really a compliment," I joked.

Lucian laughed. A real, honest laugh. I hadn't heard him do that since Paris.

Then he kissed me.

A kiss that made my whole body go numb with the sensation. It was blinding and freeing all rolled into one. No one could make me feel the way Lucian did. Everything melted away into that kiss. Nothing had any meaning except the two of us embracing in the darkness.

Then suddenly it wasn't dark anymore.

Like a giant beacon of light, Lucian's necklace glowed. It

brought the whole gang outside of the barn.

Our lips parted as we realized what had happened.

Helena broke the silence. "The necklace works!" Then she hit her hand on her head as if figuring it all out. "Of course. It takes the First-Born male and the first female Vessel." She was grinning from ear to ear. "This is it. We can finally kill Caelius!"

Everyone was beyond thrilled at the revelation, except Nefertiti. She could barely look at us. She had seen us kiss, and it must have cut her deep. I felt horrible. I knew that Lucian and I belonged together, but they had too, at one time. They loved each other. I'd always be envious of their history, but seeing the way Lucian looked at me, I knew there was no choice for him. I was it. And Nefertiti saw it too.

"Aidan went to find where Caelius is hiding. He'll Dream-Walk with Shea when he finds him," Lucian informed the others.

"Great. Let's make sure we can activate this baby on the spot when we take him down." Helena was beaming with excitement.

"Um," I muttered. I didn't think I should keep Aidan's secret anymore, especially if this necklace would actually work. What if he and his brothers actually got hurt trying to imprison Caelius again? If we could kill him, then Aidan's brothers wouldn't have to leave the Light. They could keep guarding it and let us do our thing.

Lucian's hand intertwined with mine for support. "What is it, my love?"

The way he said "my love" made me want to pass out right there. Damn him and his ridiculously sexy voice.

I broke the news. "I wasn't supposed to say anything, but now that this thing actually works, Aidan didn't only go to track

Caelius for us. He went to go trap him again." Before anyone could get mad, I continued. "He thought it would be better if Caelius was in one place, to make it easier for when we found a way to kill him."

Lucian's face went still.

I felt a lump forming in my throat.

Something was wrong.

Very wrong.

"I knew he was going to do something stupid!" Meky yelled. "He kissed me like he was saying goodbye forever, but I talked myself out of worrying!"

The sinking sensation only grew in the pit of my stomach. I had thought the same thing when Aidan left, but I'd rationalized it away as well.

"What aren't you telling me?" I choked out.

Lucian's hands slightly shook as he explained, "Shea, Aidan had six brothers before Caelius, not five. That sixth brother, Herostel, was earthbound, like Aidan is now: an angel in human form to watch over the humans. In order to trap Caelius, the earthbound brother had to sacrifice himself to *create* the prison. The prison itself is made from his *soul*."

Oh, God.

No.

Lucian only confirmed my worst nightmare when he finished, "Aidan is now the earthbound angel. Shea, he would have to give up his *soul* to imprison Caelius. It would be worse than death. He'd be stamped out of existence."

Everything went black as I lost consciousness.

CHAPTER 12
LUCIAN

"Shea.. Shea..." I ran my hands through her pale blond hair. "You're okay. I've got you."

"Aidan," she mumbled in her sleep.

I winced. Shea's first thought, her first concern, was for *him*. That idiot. Of course he'd tell her and not the rest of us. He knew the kind of monster I was. I'd never let him sacrifice his life, even if it meant saving the world. Hot and cold, it was how I ran. Even when I'd hated him, I hadn't let anyone touch him. Aidan had been *mine* to kill then. But I never had. I'd watched him choose that fate himself, over and over, killing the Vessels.

It was infuriating, his loyalty to the greater good. Thinking back on it now, I realized that I'd been waiting: waiting for Aidan to finally understand why I would never have killed Moses, why I *couldn't* have killed him, that some people were worth letting the world burn for.

When Aidan had stabbed Shea, I'd caught a glimpse of it:

his regret. Then when we'd battled over the ocean, when he'd apologized, I'd seen it again. After we'd knelt side by side and begged for Shea's life at the feet of Caelius, I knew he finally understood.

And now look what he'd done with that knowledge. I knew it wasn't for "the good of mankind." When the necklace hadn't worked, when things had looked bleak, he must have decided then. This time Aidan, that stupid beast, was going to sacrifice himself, not for the world, but for *us*: the fools he'd grown to love.

Shea shot up, shoving me back. "Where are we? This is our room in Paris, Lucian. What the hell? We don't have time for this! We have to save Aidan!"

"It's not Paris—" Again she pushed me back as I tried to comfort her. "Shea, listen to me. We're Dream-Walking."

She paused for a moment, then took a deep breath. "We are?" She looked around. "Oh, yeah, I guess we are."

I half smiled. "I'm not as good as you are. I'm sure if it was *your* dream it would be seamless. You've pulled me into your Dream-Walks but I've never actually Dream-Walked myself; that's not a power I have. I'm not even sure this counts. I think I just pulled you into a fuzzy memory."

Shea looked around at some of the blurred objects. The only pieces in focus were the bed and the view from the window, the things I remembered most. Other than her. Every feature on her face was crystal clear and beautiful.

"Why are you doing this?" she asked, looking puzzled, uncertain of my intentions.

"You passed out. No one could get through the thick wall of

darkness in your mind, not even Ur-Nammu. It's like a fail-safe, an empty barrier that protects the Light inside of you while your body is . . . comatose."

She nodded slowly, understanding, then asked, "How did *you* get through?"

I stepped closer, breathing her in. Her scent was soft and warm, like this dream. "Because I've been in this kind of empty place before, this vacuum. It will always be a part of me.

"When I was dissolving into Caelius in the cave, before Ur-Nammu saved me, everything was fragmented like this space inside your mind, tearing apart all reason and form. The scraps that I held on to the tightest were my moments with you. If Caelius had taken those pieces, what was left of my hope, I would have been lost forever in *his* void.

"And now I can only imagine what your mother must feel, having given birth to and raised the Light, and now you are simply . . . gone."

Shea crumbled into my arms, crying out. "We have to save them! We'll get Aidan and then he can give my mom back her memories!"

"Of course." My heart ached for her. I felt so helpless. It was taking all of my strength to fight the blackness seeping in and destroying this memory. I knew that if she didn't wake up soon, if we didn't get out, I'd die here and Shea would sleep forever.

She looked up at me, sniffling. "Well? Let's go."

I shook my head. "Shea, I never wanted to touch that emptiness again. But when the others couldn't get through to you, I threw myself inside your mind. Where we are now, this is *your* void. *I* can't get us out."

Panic crossed her features. I stroked her hair, uncertain if I should tell her the full truth. "When I first entered, I started dissolving, like I had with Caelius. I reached for this memory in the darkness, and I appeared here when you did. But you were asleep. I've been waiting. Time isn't real in this place, but it feels like I've waited for hundreds of years, just holding you while you slept, keeping the darkness from swallowing us whole."

Shea's mouth fell open. "What? Seriously? That's awful." Guilt rushed over her features. "I meant the time thing, not the holding me part."

I shrugged lightly. "I had a beautiful view."

Her eyes quickly turned away from me, to the window, but mine stayed on her. It had healed me in a way, all of that time sitting in silence with Shea in my arms. But we had to leave. I'd been trying to wake her for some time. My strength was waning, and I needed to save Aidan as well. I owed him that much. I loved him that much.

And Nefertiti, her children. And Setepenre. As happy as I could be just holding Shea for eternity, we had friends and families worth fighting for. Worth dying for.

Shea was rallying quickly. "Well, now that I'm awake, I mean, strong enough to Dream-Walk with you, let's get back."

She closed her eyes.

Nothing happened.

She squeezed her hands into fists, clamming up. "Why isn't this working?"

I shrugged. "I've been focusing all my energy on this place to keep it from dissolving. You're still weak from when you used the sundial. Its power came with a high price." I rested my hand on her cheek, a sharp pain twisting in my chest. "I think it almost killed you, Shea. When's the last time you really slept?"

"I don't remember. I mean, time is all jumbled up, it's . . . been a while."

"Your body is exhausted. I was worried—you had no heartbeat. That's why I leapt inside to follow your consciousness as deep as I could, to find you and bring you back."

Shea closed her eyes and felt her chest for a moment. Then, opening her eyes again, she shook her head. "Don't worry, Lucian. I'm very much alive. I can feel my juices rattling around. I just need to wake up so we can get back into the real world."

She began walking around the vague, dreamlike room. Every place she stepped filled in with detail, became crisp, clear. Shea smiled. "I think I have a better memory of this place than you do."

She touched a table, and the swirls of wood filled in. The lamp she brushed by turned canary yellow. Shea's power was filling in the void. It was strange, though, because the clearer everything was, the less real it started to feel.

When everything was just like the night I had left to save Gracuri, she stopped. "This is what it all looked like, but we're not leaving the dream. This is how it's done, you gain control, I . . ." She looked at me with confusion. "I don't understand, this should have worked. Why am I not waking up?"

I touched the small of her back, half smiling. "There's one more memory to fill in."

Her cheeks flushed. "We don't have time for that. Even if there is no 'time' here."

I nodded. "I know." And her fear wasn't because of Aidan or

Caelius. Shea was afraid of *us*, was terrified of reconnecting with me and having her heart ripped open again.

I understood her trepidation. I still couldn't face what I'd done to her parents. And I still couldn't fully believe that we would win, that I could stand against Caelius and actually succeed. I needed to believe that it wasn't my fate to lose her. But I was afraid.

Afraid that if I failed, Caelius would use me to destroy Shea. Poised against that possibility, I knew it would be better if she stayed away from me, better, even, if she hated me.

Her lips landed softly on mine.

I wrapped my arms around her.

How could she still love me? How could Aidan? By now they'd both seen the monster inside.

"Lucian," she whispered. "I *need* you."

My mind stopped. Nothing else mattered. I pinned her to the floor. Her back arched under the weight of my hips. I let my lips seep into the small of her neck. I *needed* her. More than she knew. "Shea Harper, you saved my soul from darkness."

That was enough. She moaned, and my spine stiffened. I felt every muscle in my body come back to life as she ran her hands over them. She bit my bottom lip as she tore off my shirt. I raked my hands over the small blue dress she was wearing, tearing it open at the sides.

Her hips lifted to mine as her mouth moved to my ear, her hands slipping off my buckle. I eased into her. Gently at first, but then the torrent of our passion broke the wooden floorboards under her back.

Shea rolled me over, and we laughed at the absurdity of

anything breaking in a dream. Still, by the time we were finished, the room looked like it had been hit by a tornado.

She lay against me, naked, panting for breath. Her eyes met mine as her soft face filled my view. She was everything I had always wanted: a love that was more powerful than death.

"I think I needed that," she said with a laugh.

I nodded. With all the madness, it was a moment of bliss. A reconnection.

"Shea, I love—"

We were back, out of the dream. I was blinking, holding her body outside of the barn, surrounded by my Gutian horde and Helena.

Jeff Harper reached for us. "Are you all right?"

Shea and I exchanged looks. I wasn't sure if Jeff was asking me or her, but I bit my tongue. Yes, we were back. Back to what our lives had become after Paris.

Shea sighed. "I'm fine, Dad. And *Lucian's* okay too."

I grinned. I was more than okay. We shared another look, and her smile matched mine.

Nefertiti stepped toward us and placed a hand on my shoulder. "How did you get through the barrier? How did you get her to wake up?"

I paused for a moment, unable to answer.

Shea stood up, her face flushing.

Nefertiti backed off. She probably figured out the "how" in an instant after seeing our shared glances and masked her concern with apathy.

Shea fumbled her words. "How long was I out?"

Meky stepped forward, her face wracked with worry. "You've

been unconscious for two hours. You were out for an hour before Lucian went in. Once your heart slowed, then stopped, we weren't sure what was happening."

We'd been making love for a while in the void, enough time for Shea to recharge mentally. Luckily, it had only been a few short hours.

Shea nodded. "We have to get to Aidan." She looked at me, and I nodded in agreement. If I knew Aidan, he'd already talked to his brothers by now and had convinced them of what needed to be done—at the cost of his life.

Shea started to walk but stumbled slightly. "I need to juice up," she said quickly. "Meky, can you take me?" Her voice was resolute.

I spun on my heels, grabbing her arms. "Are you out of your mind, Shea?" Despite myself, I was shaking her, my fangs growing. "This little blackout was the aftermath of the sundial! I'm not going to let you risk your life like that again! You woke up this time, but—"

Nefertiti stepped in. "She's right, Lucian. If it takes the two of you to power the necklace, the more power she has, the better chance of it working."

Helena chimed in. "It's the *only* way the necklace will work."

"Thank you for your *scientific* analysis," I growled, "but no, we're not saving Aidan at the cost of Shea." It was *my* life that I was willing to risk, not hers.

Shea stroked my back like she'd done moments ago in our dream room in Paris. "This is Aidan we're talking about, Lucian. Nothing you can say will change my mind."

I stopped. This was wrong. I turned back to Helena. "What's

the theory? We distract Caelius, then Shea shoots her power into the necklace while I'm wearing it, then the necklace uses that power and leaches all of my own to kill Caelius? And it won't hurt Shea?"

Helena began to answer, but Shea interrupted. "Wait. What do you mean leaches all of your power? Are you saying the necklace could kill you?"

Helena shook her head. "No. Because Lucian is the First-Born of Caelius, it shouldn't *kill* him, technically speaking. And it shouldn't kill you, either, Shea. There. Two questions answered. Now can we please start planning our attack? I have other experiments and a life to get back to once this is all over."

Shea listened to Helena, and in her eyes I could see the resolution. Then she stepped toward Meky. "Let's go. Carry me."

I moved between them. "You're coming with me, Shea, not with Mekytaten."

Shea's mouth fell open, ready to protest, but nothing came out. I turned to the others.

"Get ready for battle." I paused, looking at Nefertiti's children, then at Helena and Jeff. "Nefari . . . your father, you, me: we're Gutian leaders. This is in our blood. But everyone else should stay here. They need to be safe. We can't risk their lives. I *won't* risk their lives."

Nefertiti nodded, agreeing. Warmth returned to her features, and relief.

"We are Gutian too!" Meky said, ready to protest, her sisters grumbling in support.

Nefertiti waved. They were all silent as she said, "My children, you are the last of the Gutians. We need you to carry on our legacy. No matter what happens. If we succeed, you are finally free, a gift I've always wanted to give you. If we fail, Caelius will think that you are all still loyal to him. And you can survive. You can plan."

They nodded in reluctant obedience, but I could feel Nefari's rebellious warrior blood pumping in their veins. Every one of them wanted to fight.

Helena leaned into her left hip, resolute in her defiance. "Sorry, Lucian, but this is one adventure I wouldn't miss for the world. And I'm keeping my promise. My invention *will* save you." Her jaw hardened, but in her eyes there was a softness. "I haven't forgotten, you know, the way you stood by my side when I presented my inventions to the scientific council. I was human and afraid—they might as well have been Caelius in my ignorance then. But you stood in full daylight, steaming in the gray shadow of a pillar, just to be there.

"This time, when you're by my side, I won't fail. My invention will work. I'll make sure that it does." Her eyes weren't on Nefertiti, but locked on mine.

I smiled. "I don't doubt your intentions or your invention, Helena, but I need you to—"

"Don't."

"I *need* you to stay behind."

"Need? You *need* me there. I invented the damn thing powering that necklace!"

"And you don't know for certain if it will kill Caelius."

Helena had no answer; the scientist in her believed in the theory of her invention but knew it was only a theory. Untested. I could see the hurt in her eyes at the implication.

Her face sagged, so I softened the blow with my next words. "If we fail, I need you safe. You're the only one I trust to work with the girls."

It was too much to ask, and I knew it. If we died, I was asking her to dedicate her existence into looking after Nefertiti's children.

She looked down, refusing eye contact.

I left Shea's side and flicked Helena's ear. She looked at me with fury, that wild spark igniting in her. "Lucian, I will make it work if I'm there!"

"No, Helena. Shea and I will power the necklace—that part of your invention has already been proven. We don't need you there."

"Lucian, I can—"

"Not just for their sake, Helena, but for yours. I believe in you. I always have, even in Lorreto. If this necklace doesn't work, your brilliant mind will. Eventually you'll find a way to kill him and free yourself."

Her fists balled at her sides. She gritted her teeth, her anger willfully kept under the surface. "Lorreto? I don't know what you're talking about. This argument is cyclical and taking up time." She didn't call me an idiot, but her furrowed brow and the sneer of her lips did it for her. "If you don't want me there, that's fine. I'll start working on another way, just in case the necklace fails."

That last word hung in the air, and I could see it deflate the belief previously burning in her gaze. "I'll start working now. Just in case." She pulled a piece of elastic out of her pocket and tied her hair back. "Good luck." She turned and left us without a second glance.

Now I felt her pain. I needed to believe that our plan would work. And I did. I just didn't believe that, if we all went, everyone would live. But seeing Helena so defeated, as if it might fail, seeing her pull back her wild tresses in slavery . . . I was again filled with doubt.

Jeff spoke up, his voice small, his eyes pleading. "If my wife is there, I have to be too. Don't make me stay behind, Lucian. Please."

But it was Shea who answered him. "Dad, Caelius will use your love for Mom against you. You're too young as a vampire; he could give you some of his blood and make you his mind puppet in a heartbeat. He could make you kill her, or me, or *Lucian*." Shea apparently threw that last part in because she still wasn't sure if his vampire bond was more powerful than his fatherly one.

Jeff was on the verge of arguing, but then nodded slowly. Shea reached out and hugged him. "We'll be back for you, Dad. I promise."

"I can't lose you again. I just got you back." Jeff's face was pained.

"I can't lose you either," Shea said with determination.

It was enough for Jeff. He kissed the top of her head. "Come back to me."

My shoulders sagged, doubt of our success still plaguing my mind as Shea reached for my hand. "Let's go then," she said.

I nodded.

Ur-Nammu looked at Shea. "Nefertiti and I will search for Aidan. We'll send you his location as soon as we find him. When we've regrouped, we'll kill Caelius."

That was all I needed. I held Shea in my arms and flew into the air. I'd never flown so fast before. I kept her head carefully pressed to my chest, my hand covering her eyes so that she wouldn't get the urge to look. If she did, she might get sick.

We landed in Amarna, and I walked to the pillar and traced my fingers over the symbol of Aten just as Nefertiti had told me. It glowed bright, and the door opened.

I threw on the cloak Helena had made and led Shea underground. I brought her to stand at the apex of the Pharaoh's secret chamber. We stood in front of the sundial where a single thin shaft of light from a precise hole drilled painstakingly through layers of rock illuminated it. I gritted my teeth, imagining the poor slaves the Pharaoh had forced that job upon.

"Let's do this," she said, gripping my hand tighter and walking toward the bright circle.

Before she could touch the sundial and activate its power, I grabbed her. "I'm still not sure of this, Shea. I always lose. I can't keep the people I love. The fact that you can look at me, that you still love me, is beyond my comprehension. But I *want* to believe . . . I *need* to believe—"

She kissed me. I closed my eyes. I *couldn't* lose her. I had to stop this.

Instantly my lips started burning. I jerked back, releasing Shea. She'd set her hand on the sundial mid-kiss. She must have known that I was changing my mind, that I wasn't going to let her do it.

I tried to grab her, but my fingers blistered.

Her eyes widened as light shot into them. The light moved into her mouth, into every pore. Ignoring the pain of touching her, I tried to pull her back, but the power pushed me aside, burning my skin. It filled me with fury. The same Light-born fire had defeated me when the Pharaoh had moved Nefertiti's children down here and I'd tried to follow.

"Lucian!" she screamed. Something was going terribly wrong. The Light was out of control. "It's too much! I can't stop!"

I lunged in. Now I screamed.

It was worse than when I'd filleted myself with the Enochian blade to track her. The light burned me from the inside.

Still, I didn't stop.

I could smell the meat, the singed flesh as my skin charred.

I held on.

"Lucian!" she cried out.

"Shea! I have you!" I answered through fire-seared lips.

I pulled through the maddening pain. I was burning alive, dying. I saw her desperate eyes, Shea's desperate belief in *me*.

I *pulled*.

As she came away from the sundial, we both collapsed on the floor.

I couldn't hold her any longer. I couldn't move. I was a black piece of coal.

But now I had hope. If being in that pure blast for one moment had injured me this much, I hoped the necklace might be enough, combined with the sundial's power, to kill Caelius. I couldn't die. Not yet.

Shea jerked up, recovering, taking in a deep breath. Then, seeing my charred remains, she screamed, "Lucian!"

She grabbed my arms, but the muscles fell off in chunks. She screamed again.

I couldn't speak. My vocal chords were fried. I was in agony but no longer without hope. And I knew now that as long as one drop of Caelius's blood remained, I would recover. I wanted to tell her that I could heal, that it was possible.

Shea placed her neck to my blackened lips. "Take what you need!"

My fangs instinctively grew, but I retracted them quickly. This wasn't the same as with Caelius. Even half-alive, as I was now, I could control myself. With Caelius it had been different—his draining had been like a fevered infection that pushed me to devour mindlessly. But I wasn't his chained puppet now. And I would *never* drink Shea.

"Lucian!" Shea shouted. "You have to! I let Nefertiti drink me for God's sake! Just do it!"

She pushed her neck closer, but I refused. I had never taken blood from Shea. I couldn't lose that. It was one of the scraps I had clung to in the darkness. I'd never been a vampire with her, just a man: the real me, alongside the monster.

She closed her eyes, frustrated. When she opened them again, they were focused. Shea began to move her hands over my body, obviously having to fight back the repulsion as strips of my flesh peeled off. "If I can heal myself, I can heal you," she said, as much to convince herself as to reassure me.

Her certainty grew stronger as all of that radiant Light inside of her bounced around like pulses of power, filling the room with brightness. Had I not known her, had I been just another vampire, it would have been terrifying.

Then it burned. As her hands moved over my skin, it burned worse than Pompeii. I screamed in agony. Tears dripped from

Shea's cheeks as she continued. I was finally able to move my neck, and I watched as new flesh formed, as the marrow in my bones filled in.

I could heal quickly, but wounds like this would usually take months, or oceans of blood. Now, being healed by Shea's power, within moments I was fully restored. She smiled triumphantly.

I pulled her into my arms. "Shea, are you all right?"

She was silent. Then she pushed me back. "Am *I* all right, asks Mr. Charbroiled?"

I smiled. "You said it was too much, that you couldn't stop."

She jabbed my side. "Maybe you were right about the sundial. It's dangerous. But we need to get Aidan and my mom. And we need to kill that a-hole Caelius."

She looked at me, but her eyes were again filled with horror. "Lucian!"

I couldn't respond. Her features faded away.

Everything was black.

Then I was by a small river in Gutium, next to the house where I'd grown up.

I reached down, letting the river's water move through my fingertips. It wasn't wet or cold. This was a dream. A *forced* Dream-Walk. This river had dried up and died, like I had, ages ago.

But no one was here. I looked around. "Shea?"

Silence.

Someone had pulled me into this dream, someone powerful.

I walked around the riverbanks, not daring to go inside the small house. I didn't want to see it. It was a memory I didn't like to think of: the house where my mother had died.

"Lucian!" someone called, but it was distant.

I ran toward the voice.

I ran *slowly*.

Whoever's dream I'd been pulled into, my vampire powers were useless; I was mortal.

I ran harder, but my legs ached. My *small* legs.

I looked at my hands, at my little fingers. I was a boy. This was a very old memory. "Nefari!" I shouted. "Where are you?"

Something was wrong. These were her memories. She should have been right by my side when she summoned the dream.

"La-Narru!" She wasn't calling me.

She was screaming.

I ran. There were splotches of emptiness, spots of memory that weren't filled in. They were vacant or out of place. Memories were mixed, shifting, out of control.

Now I was grown, the age I had been when I'd left my homeland.

I must have crossed our entire forest before I came upon the empty field by Gutium. And there they were, all of my people, the Gutian tribes . . . slaughtered.

This memory was vivid. Every detail. The smell of death. The ache of defeat. I took in the massacre. I'd never seen it; I hadn't been there. I'd wept for the loss of my people but had never returned to Gutium. It had been isolating, bearing the weight that I was the only Gutian left in the world. I'd been a young man, but it had been devastatingly lonely. The hum of the code of my people, decaying my heart with guilt. When I'd found Nefertiti and her father *alive* in Egypt I'd been overtaken with relief and vengeance.

Now, seeing this, I finally faced my shame. I should have been here, with my people, with my father, Onack. On the field of slaughter I recognized the rich blue fabric of his cape. His frame, a large mound surrounded by hundreds of dead Egyptians. Nefertiti had *seen* all of this. Lived it.

I walked over to him: Onack the Great. Twenty spears had been shoved through his body like a stuck pig. His sword was still clenched in his fist, even after death. I fell to my knees by his side, tears forcing their way down my cheeks.

"I'm sorry, Father." I rested my head on his chest. I should have been here. I should have fought and died by his side.

After he'd whipped me for eating my mother's ashes, I'd never forgiven him—because I'd never forgiven myself. When he'd begged me to leave, I'd hated him for it. These were childish things I'd unknowingly held on to all of these years. But seeing him now, dead . . .

He'd died *alone,* without his family by his side.

My father. My *real* father.

"La-Narru!"

I jerked up. Nefertiti was on the battlefield, covered in blood. I rushed to her side. "Why are you dreaming this? What's happening?"

Her voice was soft, weak. "We found Aidan. He was trying to summon his brothers. We were telling him about the necklace, how it works now, when Caelius showed up and ambushed us.

"We're mid-battle. I pulled you in here because this is my most powerful memory, and this is where we are. You may not recognize it now, but it's the field by our village where you used to pick wildflowers for me in the spring. It's all I can do to get this message to you before—"

I was staring at Shea. The dream had disappeared as quickly as it had come. She was shaking me, repeatedly calling my name.

"I'm here, Shea. I'm here."

"What the hell happened, Lucian? Your eyes went black and then you were just gone!"

"Caelius has them: Aidan, Nefertiti, and Ur-Nammu. We need to go, *now*." I pulled her into my arms.

Shea nodded. "Okay. I'm ready."

I flew toward my home. I didn't doubt that this place had been handpicked by Caelius. The battle I never got to fight was here, now. Except this time I wouldn't run.

When I landed in what used to be Gutium, the scene was similar to the massacre from Nefertiti's dream. Aidan's blood was everywhere, and Nefertiti and Ur-Nammu were pinned down like grasshoppers in a field, trapped under the weight of a giant shadow. Setepenre was lancing Aidan open while Caelius sat back against a large stone, laughing, commanding her to continue.

Just seeing Setepenre's face threw my mind out of the battle. It was no wonder the Pharaoh had known Nefari had slept with me. Her teal eyes, lightly tanned skin, thick black hair, even the structure of her cheekbones . . . she was mine.

The awe quickly faded as she opened Aidan's gut, adding her laughter to Caelius's as she eyed him for approval.

Fury boiled to the surface. I had to kill him, to crush Caelius so Setepenre would never look at him like that again, like he was her *family*.

I called to Aidan. "The necklace works! Grab Setepenre so she doesn't try and take the hit!"

He nodded, spitting out blood as he wrapped his arms around her, his strength revealed. He'd been holding back, trying to get to Caelius without hurting her. Aidan and I shared a look; he knew she was my daughter.

She tore her teeth into his neck as he squeezed her tighter and ran toward the Zagros Mountains behind Gutium.

I quickly clasped the emerald stone around my neck. As Shea blasted her Light into the necklace, it shot fanged metal teeth into my sternum, clutching on to bone.

I staggered forward. It hadn't done that before. When Shea had kissed me outside the barn, that small spark from her Light had activated something, but this was different. With the metal from the stone's encasement growing deeper into my chest, I knew that this was going to work, or kill me in the process.

Caelius's eyes met mine, and his face twisted with pleasure. "I'm glad you're finally here, my son. I was getting bored having my Sete play with that puppy." He eyed Shea. "And you brought your bitch. Good. Now the real fun can begin."

I didn't respond. I used all the power I could summon, all that I had learned in Egypt with Moses. I called the essence of everything I had deep inside of me, shoving it into the emerald stone, feeding it power.

The necklace shot out an infused gray light—straight into Caelius's chest.

His flesh burned.

He howled in agony.

But I had no time to enjoy his pain. The necklace's power was sucking away my energy. As the blast bored into Caelius, its fiery power consuming his flesh, my body weakened further.

I fell to my knees. But it was not only me whose strength was being taken away as the blast continued. Shea joined me on the ground. Helena had been wrong; the necklace was *killing* us.

I tried to stop it, to rip off the necklace, but I couldn't. The metal—infused with whatever concoction Helena had devised, and combined with the powers of Shea and me—would finish what it started.

I choked.

The necklace was absorbing not just my body, but my will.

I looked at Shea. She looked weaker than I was. I reached for her. Our hands intertwined.

Was this how we were going to die? Side by side, giving our power over to kill the living incarnation of Darkness?

I prayed. If there was anything out there, if the Light cared about its small piece in Shea, I prayed that it would spare her. *Please*, I prayed, *let her break free*.

Caelius screamed one last time, then there was silence.

The necklace made a humming sound.

Then it fell from my chest, smoking. The bright green emerald had turned black.

I fell forward. Nefertiti, now free from Caelius's shadow form, ran and clutched me in her arms.

Ur-Nammu stepped over to hold Shea.

My voice was weak. "Is she okay?"

Nefari's eyes were firm. "Of course she is."

"I'm fine," Shea croaked out next to me. "I just feel like someone dropped a thousand-ton brick on my face."

"Is Caelius dead?" Nefertiti looked at Ur-Nammu, and he nodded. "There's nothing but a pile of ash."

His voice was filled with relief—as mine would have been too. After all of these years, after everything we'd been through, we'd *done* it.

I sat up and reached for Shea, pulling her into my arms. She rested her face on my chest. I leaned my head on hers.

We'd won.

Ur-Nammu stepped over to Nefertiti and held her. I caught a glimpse of her face as one small tear left the hardened mask. Then she broke, falling into her father's arms. They wept together. Thousands of years of slavery . . . finally at an end.

Tears welled in my eyes as well. Were we finally free? "Is it over?" I said aloud.

Now we could live. Paris could be every day. There was nothing to imprison our souls, nothing to chain us. And Shea was a Vessel. A Vessel could live as long as a vampire. We would have the ages to love each other.

I pulled back. "Where's Setepenre?"

Shea jerked up. "Where's Aidan?"

CHAPTER 13
SHEA

As if hearing me, Aidan was instantly by my side. The three of us held one another for a long time. Lucian and Aidan had an extensive and complicated past, but now there was nothing to keep them from being brothers again. My boys. It was nice to feel completely content, even just for a moment.

We pulled away when we heard Setepenre's scream as she raced to Caelius's ashes.

I felt heartless because I didn't care.

All I cared about was the fact that we were finally rid of Daddy Evil.

Setepenre was obviously one of Nefertiti's daughters from the looks of her, and apparently she was on Team Caelius. Then I saw her eyes . . .

Those perfect teal eyes.

I turned to Lucian, and his expression confirmed it: Setepenre was *his* and Nefertiti's daughter.

"I just found out today," Lucian confessed.

Okay, my perfect moment of contentment was now a little skewed. Still, honestly, even love child revelations couldn't shake my mood completely. I knew I should've been freaking out, but it made a weird kind of sense. Lucian and Nefertiti had a history. A long-ass history. And it didn't really surprise me that they had a child together.

Besides, I knew I could deal with my feelings later because right *now*, in *this* instant . . .

We were free.

Free!

If I felt this good, I could only imagine how Nefertiti felt. Sure, she'd have to deal with her psycho daughter, Setepenre, who was currently wailing like a banshee. And I was pretty sure she'd be looking for revenge. But Lucian and Nefertiti could probably pin her down long enough to wipe away the brainwashing that the master of evil had created. At least I hoped so for Lucian's sake.

I slowly stood up with Lucian. "We have to find where Caelius stashed my mother."

Aidan nodded and jumped to his feet. "I'll try to track her."

Setepenre finally came to her senses and whirled on Nefertiti. "How could you allow this? He was your father!"

Nefertiti's face was wracked with desperate concern. "My little Sete, Caelius was no one's father. He was a plague that needed to be stopped. Ur-Nammu is *my* only father, and *your* only grandfather. You will see, in time."

But Setepenre wasn't buying it. "Time cannot erase your betrayal! Grandfather was the only one who understood me, who loved me, who told me the truth and not your filthy lies! And now look what you've done! He's ashes. As if he never existed. Not even his true form survived!" she cried hysterically.

Not even his true form survived.

Chills raced down my spine. From everything I'd learned since this whole thing had started, Caelius was Darkness incarnate. Yes, we could destroy his flesh-made body because he had chosen to give up his shadow form to be human, but wouldn't that mean he would go back to being only Darkness again? Shouldn't we have seen some kind of crazy smoke monster or shadow creature or something, like we had when he'd been caged in his prison?

Maybe I was being paranoid, but that tiny seed of doubt was beginning to grow into an entire forest. I grabbed Lucian's arm. "Let's get out of here."

He reacted to the urgency in my voice. "What is it?"

"I just . . . I don't know . . . I don't want to jinx anything." I couldn't say what I was thinking. Maybe it was just an irrational fear.

Then we heard laughing.

A familiar, nails-on-chalkboard chuckle that made my whole being sink with dread.

I hated being right.

Nefertiti's gasp of disbelief and anguish made my heart squeeze for her—and for us.

This wasn't over.

Not by a long shot.

And we had nothing left to fight Caelius with.

Before us all, Caelius's body grew out of the ashes until he stood perfectly formed without a scratch on him.

Setepenre, still on her knees, grasped and held on to his leg in total adoration. Her tears were now tears of joy at seeing her "grandfather" in full health.

Caelius acknowledged her by placing his hand on her long black tresses and petting her like a dog. "My sweet Sete. You are the only child who stood by me, who is grateful for the life I've given you, the only one who is loyal to me and me alone."

Lucian placed his body in front of mine and was slowly backing us away from our worst nightmare. I could only imagine what was going on in his head, seeing his newly found daughter for the first time and watching as she lovingly stared at the creature he hated most in the world.

My brain could hardly take in what was happening. The sundial's power still surged through me, and it was making my mind fuzzy again.

I almost wanted to laugh out loud. This couldn't be happening. We'd defeated him. We'd killed him. Our powers united had finally destroyed the evil monster. And yet, the only thing that kept repeating in my head was the quote from Dark Helmet in the movie *Spaceballs*.

Evil will always triumph because good is dumb.

And then I *did* laugh. I couldn't control myself. Everything was so wrong that this whole situation struck me as absurdly funny.

Caelius appeared amused by my mirth. "I think your bitch has finally cracked, Lucian."

Lucian didn't respond. His body was rigid, battle ready, waiting for what his father was going to do next.

I stopped laughing. Things were starting to come into focus

again. If we were going to survive, we'd need to escape and go back to our life on the run. I needed to create a distraction.

Caelius milked the moment for all he could, knowing he had everyone's rapt attention. "My children"—he glanced at me and Aidan—"and *others*." He offered his hand to Setepenre, helping her to her feet. "I want to thank you from the bottom of my heart—"

I threw my hands forward, and a large beam of light engulfed his entire body. Setepenre was thrown back from the force, her skin burned from being so close.

Instead of screaming in pain, Caelius simply chuckled again, and with the snap of his fingers, my sundial-super-attack turned into a yellow, harmless mist, leaving only dust behind. Caelius brushed it away and looked at me with amused contempt. "Your Light doesn't work on me anymore, little Vessel." He pointed at Lucian and me. "You two made certain of that."

Nefertiti and Lucian exchanged puzzled glances, but I had the sinking feeling that I knew what was coming next. As in, refer back to the *Spaceballs* quote.

"We need to get out of here," I repeated. If super-juice couldn't affect Caelius, what could three vampires and an angel do?

"You're not going anywhere until I've crushed every cell in your body," Caelius said to me. I thought I would melt from his glare.

His threat sent Lucian into protective mode. He growled at his father and bared his teeth.

Caelius wasn't even remotely threatened, he simply looked more amused. "Did you think that I wouldn't know what your little gang was planning?" He looked at Nefertiti as her nails dug into Ur-Nammu's arms, her eyes wide with horror.

"Your pet, Helena, is a fascinating woman—and very inventive. You didn't think I would notice her little experiments? Well," he drawled, "I did. And, once I realized what she had in store for me, it wasn't difficult to tamper with her fragile mind and make her reverse that little device of hers."

Before we could absorb the truth of what he had just said, Caelius focused on me. "I needed to know what I was up against, of course, to know exactly how much power I'd be feeding on. I wanted to find out if it would be enough to bring me back to my full strength. I *let* you attack me before, with Gracuri. I lured you in with Lucian. I waited for you in that wet, dark cave, feeding him your parents. I didn't expect Lucian and Nefertiti to turn them, but that was icing. I pleaded for their help as you crushed my bones." He laughed again, making my skin crawl. "You never hurt me, Vessel. I was just gauging your power."

Caelius reached out to Lucian. Though he was yards away, the shadow of his hand brushed Lucian's cheek. "When you two used your joint powers with that necklace, you weren't killing me." He smiled viciously. "You were *restoring* me." He motioned with glee to the remnants that used to be his body. "Like a phoenix rising from the ashes. Tell me, Vessel, how does it feel to fail so completely to the Dark that you've even lost your *soul?* Do you all see how foolish you were to stand against me?" His shadow hand pulled back from Lucian and wrapped lovingly around Setepenre. "It matters not. I know who my true family is."

No soul?

He had taken my soul?

I still felt like I had a soul, but what would that really feel like anyway?

I had to push the thought aside so that I could survive this moment.

I couldn't believe we all just stood there, listening to his monologue. It was as if we were too shocked to believe that this was actually happening.

Setepenre bared her fangs at Lucian and Nefertiti in response.

It must have killed Lucian, seeing Setepenre's hatred of him, but he didn't show it. I knew he would spare her, but from the way he blocked me from Caelius, I also knew that he'd die protecting me.

This was it.

If we didn't run now, it would end with Caelius killing us all.

He was at full power.

Unstoppable.

Indestructible.

"Run!" Aidan screamed and launched himself at Caelius. He knocked Setepenre aside as if she were made of air, then began to speak a language I didn't recognize.

"No!" I shrieked.

Aidan was going to sacrifice himself to save us. He wasn't waiting for his brothers. He was going to die and transform himself, his soul, into Caelius's prison.

I didn't know if I had a soul or not, but I had to try and stop Aidan from killing himself. I threw my hands out to use all the power I had left in me. I connected to the ground, making the earth shudder and roll, trying to interrupt Aidan's chanting, but he continued.

His body started to glow.

I couldn't lose Aidan.

Not to Caelius.

I wouldn't let him die for me.

I brought out the wind, creating a hurricane of dirt and leaves, but it was as if Caelius and Aidan were in the eye of the storm, untouchable.

I had been so focused on my own terror, I hadn't noticed that Lucian had tried to rescue Aidan as well, but Setepenre stopped him. Her teeth sunk into his neck, and he was trying to pull her off without hurting her.

Then Aidan stopped his incantation and stood there looking as confused as I was.

Knowing that Aidan hadn't turned into super-prison-incarnate made me feel relieved. I immediately felt the drain of all the power I had been using. I dropped my connection to the elements; the air and ground went still.

Only Caelius seemed to know what was going on. He looked pleased with himself.

Again.

"You stupid beast. It's been over three thousand years! Aren't you wondering why your brothers haven't come to join you? It's because it was a onetime deal. Your prison won't work on me anymore! You failed your mission. I can't be killed or trapped. Your brothers will never leave the Light now, not even to save you." Caelius barely touched Aidan's chest, and his body went flying until it smashed into a boulder. I knew a fall like that wouldn't kill him, but seeing my best friend lying unconscious on the ground made me worried all the same.

Lucian managed to throw Setepenre off. She landed at Caelius's feet with a loud thud. I saw Lucian cringe at the impact.

I was growing weaker by the second. I wasn't sure how long I could stand.

This was it.

I was going to die.

All that time we'd spent on the run, planning, training, learning my powers . . . we were exactly where we'd started the first time we'd faced Caelius. Except now we didn't have Aidan's brothers to help.

I looked over at Nefertiti and Ur-Nammu.

They were with me.

All differences aside, we were together. If we were going to die, we'd die trying to hurt Caelius enough so some of us could escape.

I nodded to Nefertiti.

In this moment, we were soldiers bonded by our desire to take down our common enemy. She nodded back, respect gleaming in her eyes for the first time.

Here we go.

But before we could charge, six bodies raced onto the battlefield: Nefertiti's five daughters and my dad.

Normally, the last person I'd be afraid of was Jeff Harper. He was an architect for goodness sake! But seeing him with his fangs out gave me chills. I thought Dad grounding me for taking the car out when I was fifteen had been bad, but the way he looked now was terrifying.

I knew it wouldn't be enough to hurt Caelius, but maybe we could damage him so we could *all* run and survive.

We had to try.

Meky grabbed Aidan's still form and looked at her mother. "I have to save him."

Nefertiti gave Meky a nod of approval. "Go. And if none of us make it out, remember our Gutian oath. Let it live in you. Have the love that I cannot."

Tears streamed down Meky's face as she wrapped her arms around Aidan. They were gone in less than a second.

I felt immediate relief. Aidan would be safe. At least for now, anyway. Then it sunk in what Nefertiti had said. *Have the love that I cannot.* If I felt horrible, Lucian must have been feeling even worse.

"Oh, wonderful!" Caelius grinned. "The nonessentials have arrived. I was getting hungry."

My heart crushed from terror.

Daddy.

Chapter 14
Lucian

"**W**ait! Stop!" Why were they here? "You all have to run!" They had to leave!

"We are not leaving our family!" Jeff shouted as they all rushed Caelius, ignoring my pleas. He plowed through them effortlessly. My Sete was helping him, cutting her sisters open as they flooded in.

The ancient fear instilled by Caelius stirred in me, the belief that nothing I could do would be enough to keep those I loved alive. Caelius would win.

There was proof in his power now, in the destroyed amulet and our mass failure. But I was Gutian before I was *his*. I thought of my father on the battlefield, alone. And now, seeing this horde, my tribe—the people I loved—fighting the darkness that was Caelius, I would rather have died by their side than escape with Shea and live in the aftermath of their butchered bodies.

I closed my eyes.

The earth below my feet rumbled.

I called on the blood of every creature I could reach. Thousands of insects crawled from the ground and completely covered Caelius's new skin. He screamed. I made them form a shell around his limbs, entombing his body.

Setepenre howled, but I trapped her in the swarming insects at her feet, pinning her to the earth. I couldn't hurt her, not my daughter. I didn't care if she was loyal to Caelius. Even her screams as she tore at the insects scraped down the sides of my skull. *My Setepenre.*

"I will stay and fight, the rest of you leave!" I yelled.

They all shouted their protests as Shea stepped beside me and grabbed my hand. "We'll hurt him enough so that we can *all* escape together! We are weak, but we can do this; we can buy ourselves time!"

I couldn't give up hope yet. I still had to believe that love could win against Darkness. And if it couldn't, then I'd gladly bury my body here with my people and my heart in my homeland.

Caelius's cries turned to laughter as he reached out of the mass of insects.

Shea summoned the earth and lifted the ground, making it swallow Caelius, breaking every bone in his body.

He recovered quickly, bursting through the surface, his skin already fully healed despite being crushed. He reset his bones, his spine cracking with every vertebra as he stretched. He turned to me as he snapped his neck into place, his long form resembling a snake as he restored his concaved skull with the power he had derived from us.

Shea summoned the air, and I used it to carry my locusts.

The wind thrashed at his skin, tearing apart his reassembled bones while my insects crawled into every orifice, eating his insides.

Still Caelius laughed.

I knew it wasn't enough.

Was he growing stronger from our efforts?

I refused to accept my fears and dug deep. Yes, I was exhausted—the amulet had sapped all the reserves I'd had—but this was my *family* at stake. And if I was going to die here, I was going to make sure that Caelius remembered this place: Gutium, my home. I hoped this land would burn in his mind forever.

I closed my eyes. I drew strength from the surroundings, my true heritage. I pushed upon powers I had only suspected to exist. There was no time to doubt now, no time to question. What I suspected, what I hoped for, *had* to exist . . . or we were doomed.

The ground started shaking, but this time it wasn't Shea's power over the earth. Caelius looked at me with a new regard, like a proud father. I gazed at him in hate.

I called every mammal, every creature whose mind was easy to control. I had mastered insects, snakes, and a few other sea creatures, but this was different. I felt every heartbeat, every animal that had blood pumping in its veins, and I summoned it to our cause. I expanded my control, calling beasts from Gutium to Saudi Arabia. Their hooves and claws shook the dirt around us, the sky turning black with birds as they rushed toward our battle.

Shea pinned Caelius to the ground as the beasts attacked and devoured his flesh. She used the trees, shredding their limbs into stakes, shooting thousands of sharpened spears through his torn body, crushing his brain into the mud as large crows tore and dug out the pieces.

Setepenre began weeping again as her sisters and Jeff tore and ripped at what mush was left of Caelius. I joined them, using my bare hands as my power over the mammals faded along with the last bit of my strength.

"Everyone run, this should be enough!" I screamed.

Shea stood back, staggering. I reached, but she hit the ground before I could catch her.

"Shea!" I rushed over, knelt down, and held her still form to my chest. She had a heartbeat, but it was slow.

Something splattered on my neck. I held Shea close, one last time, and then set her gently on the grass. I touched the back of my hair: blood.

I didn't want to turn.

A gnarled claw dragged me to Caelius's feet. He laughed, lifting me from the ground into the air. He turned me around savagely. My mouth fell open, my eyes fixed on his visage. I'd seen this face on him before.

He flung Jeff toward Shea. Jeff's mangled body fell next to his daughter's.

Then Caelius held the rest of us suspended in the air with black claws that protruded from his stomach. His mouth oozing blood, his face twisted, he looked like the shadow creature from the caves. But it wasn't smoke this time, it was real—the monster that was inside Caelius piercing through his human flesh.

Spikes protruded out of his back like long, sharp hairs. His fangs were as large as his face. There were no whites in his eyes. They were red. Red and gushing blood.

I looked at all of the others' horrified faces. Even Setepenre was aghast at what her false "grandfather" had become, at what he *really* was.

I wasn't shocked or afraid. The only feeling burning in me now was anger. They hadn't escaped in time. I had to keep fighting for my family, for Shea.

I wanted to conjure the smoke, the shadow within myself, like I'd done in the cave. But, having devoured me, Caelius owned that part of me now, and conjuring it would make me his puppet. I cursed myself and my weakness. I was failing, and they all needed me now more than ever.

Caelius dragged Merytaten to his mouth, then ripped her open. Victorious, he snapped her in half and poured the blood of Nefertiti's oldest daughter over his face and mouth, lapping it up like the mutant beast he was.

"No! Stop!" I screamed, struggling to free myself from his grasp.

Everyone cried out, fighting against Caelius's claws. Nefertiti's voice was the loudest. He dropped Merytaten's body onto Setepenre. She screamed, reeling in disbelief. "Grandfather, no! You said you'd *punish* my sisters, but you wouldn't *kill* them! We're a family! We are *your* family!"

Something happened. His eyes cleared, the auburn color returning. Caelius scowled, lowering us to the ground. And then he spoke, his voice dark.

"Don't worry, Sete. You won't remember any of this. It was Shea who killed your sisters. You'll still be my little pet."

She hesitated, unable to fathom his betrayal.

Nefertiti called to her. "Leave, Setepenre! Save yourself!"

It took all of my strength, but I moved the insects that still had her pinned to the earth. Before Sete could run, Caelius flung her through the air. I lunged, but the barbs on his claws that were piercing through my torso grew deeper, cracking my rib cage in half. His grip was too tight, and I was weak.

He growled, pinning us all to the ground.

"Don't worry, Lucian. I just sent her to the place I'm keeping Molly. When my lovely Sete wakes up, she'll have new memories of this moment."

He reached for Ankhesenpaaten, her sweet brown eyes filled with terror. The Gutium words she'd spoken to me in Amarna sank to the pit of my stomach. *Though we fall, we will never fail because we have given ourselves over to glory.* Before I could plea, before I could move, he unhinged his jaws and swallowed her whole.

I cried out. "Stop! Stop, Caelius! *Please!* Setepenre was right! We are your *family*!"

Nefertiti begged. "Please, Caelius, I made a mistake! I'll never stand against you again! Just let them live! I'll serve you!"

Caelius only laughed in response, pulling Nefertiti's second youngest, Neferneferure, close. He brushed her hair, drinking her as he spoke to Nefari through the holes in her daughter's body. "It's not you that I want, dear Nefertiti. It never was. Besides, you had your chance. Our original deal was that if I saved Lucian, you and yours would be loyal to me.

"This is *your* doing, Nefertiti. I always keep my promises. If you had behaved, you wouldn't have to watch me eat your children." Neferneferure's eyes stayed on her mother, courageous until the last drop, when she shriveled into ash, drained to nothing under the power of Caelius's gaping, life-sucking mouth.

This was what I'd been afraid of. This was why I hadn't wanted them to come. Tears rolled down my face. I kept pounding my fists against his barbed claw around my waist. My knuckles were bloody, the bones crushed to mush, and still I couldn't loosen his grip. I tried to summon the beasts again, to do *something*. But the harder I struggled, the closer I came to blacking out like Shea.

"Spare them!" Ur-Nammu begged. "It was me! It was *my* idea to betray you, Caelius! I filled their minds with poison! I controlled them! Let them live! You can . . . you can *convince* them to stay. They'll be loyal! Kill me in their place!"

Seeing Ur-Nammu offer up his life, as if that was the only strategy left, broke me. And I knew it meant nothing to him; there was no quarter given by Caelius. No mercy.

I tried summoning anything alive that would listen, and still there was no response.

The power of Caelius was emanating in destructive circles, killing the grass, scorching the earth under our backs, and rendering me useless.

Caelius covered Ur-Nammu's mouth. "I tolerated you and the scratchy sound of your voice for all these years. Now, thanks to your disloyalty, I'll finally be rid of it. But there's an order to things. We can't just have chaos."

He stood us all up.

"The parents should always be the ones who watch their children die. I'll drink them first. Then your daughter, Nefertiti. You will be honored last, Ur-Nammu. I'll give you the pleasure of watching your child and all of your grandchildren cease to exist."

I closed my eyes. No, Caelius wasn't mentioning his ultimate triumph of torture; *I* would be last. All of this pageantry of death was to service his pleasure—and my pain.

Caelius had won.

He would always win.

I gritted my teeth as he laughed. He forced my eyes open with another one of his jagged claws. "Stay alert, Lucian. I need you to *see* what your life has cost. After Ur-Nammu, I'll drink your precious Shea, since her existence ruined my perfect Adam and Eve. Still, Nefertiti proved her unworthiness. But you, my boy, for you I still have *great* plans."

He shoved his claw deeper into my abdomen, crushing my spine, clenching down harder, holding me in a fist.

Blood poured from my mouth as I choked out, "Caelius, *please* spare them!"

"Your pleas means nothing to me now, boy." He wrapped his mouth around the fourth-born daughter, Sherit, whispering into her throat. "Your *whore* mother served her purpose, didn't she?" He shook her like a doll. She winced in pain but disappointed him with her silent acceptance of death.

His agitation shifted as he then stared at Nefertiti. The tears hadn't stopped falling from her eyes since Merytaten's death. The woman who rarely cried was now weeping uncontrollably. Caelius had destroyed her.

Feeding off of the fear and pain in Nefari's trembling limbs, Caelius's mood elevated as he continued. "Nefertiti did, after all, birth Lucian's baby, my beautiful Setepenre. She made a vampire with him as well: the Vessel's own mother. Two wonderful spawns of my favorite plaything. I think Nefertiti was Eve enough. And you, Sherit, like your sisters, were just a child of that meat sack

Akhenaten. You were always disposable. I never cared for you." Tears streamed from Sherit's eyes as they closed. She mouthed to Nefari, her voice a whisper, "Be strong, Mother. The flame that is *our* people and what we stand for cannot be stamped out of time . . ."

He licked the side of Sherit's face, a face I'd never see smile again. Her features reflected the beauty of her grandmother, the people from the Zagros Mountains—a people that no longer existed.

Her words boiled inside me. Our Gutian code was dying, along with its only living descendants, on the very soil of our homeland. I thought about my mother, about Nefari, about Aidan and Shea. Caelius was right—I would always lose what I loved at the hands of those who were more powerful. I would lose because I always fought for what I loved. Now I needed to give up, to stand against the code of my people and let love go.

"You're right, Caelius," I growled. "You never cared for them."

He paused.

"You never cared for anyone . . . but me."

His grip on Sherit loosened. "Are you finally ready to play, my boy?"

I nodded. "All this time, I never saw it. But now I do."

Caelius stepped toward me. He released his claw, retracting it back toward his long frame. I stumbled forward, coughing as the gaping holes from the barbs spilled blood down my chest, soaking my pants. It didn't matter. Nothing mattered now but this last sacrifice, this surrender.

I stepped toward him. He looked shocked and pleased as he eyed Shea. "Her body must have given out now that it's soulless.

What will you do, boy?"

He wanted me to grab her and run, to leave the rest of them to die. I stood tall, imagining Onack's last moments on the battlefield, all of those spears stuck through his torso, the empty place by his side where I should have been. "Even this battle, you picked Gutium for *me*, didn't you?"

I felt his power lessen as his focus shifted to me alone.

I staggered closer, holding my open wounds. "I'm what you want."

He half smiled. "Is that so?"

"I'm all you've *ever* wanted, since you became flesh."

The smile left his face, and he was still. A sort of relief moved through his shoulders as his claws sagged. Finally, I was acknowledging his true desires.

I was also aware.

Aware that Aidan had returned, unnoticed by Caelius. He must have convinced Meky that he was going to fight. That or he'd lied to her, his love for Shea stronger than any bond.

I let a piece of my mind connect with his.

Aidan. I called to him beyond Caelius's focus. *I know why you came back. Get Shea and the others out of here.*

Aidan's voice was like the wind—soft, barely audible in my mind—as he protested. *I won't leave you, my brother. I will stay by your side and fight.*

But it was too late.

Caelius ran his fingertips through my hair, his large teeth receding, his face reforming into that of a flawless youth. Caelius's eyes filled with longing as his voice curved with a twisted sort of fondness. "Of course I handpicked this place. You may not remember, but this was the first time we met, not in Egypt. I have watched you your whole life. I never drank a human until I took you."

I swallowed hard. I couldn't fathom what his words meant, or how long he'd played a role in my life, how long he'd been watching me from afar.

I pleaded in my mind with Aidan one last time. *Please, brother, look around you! You'll have one chance. When I distract Caelius, get them all out of here.*

Seeing the mutilated bodies of most of Nefertiti's children, with Jeff and Shea passed out and Nefari and Ur-Nammu weeping, Aidan finally agreed.

Caelius chuckled. "I'm at full power now that I've drained the Vessel of her soul. If it pains you so much, out of kindness, I'll kill her first."

I prayed Caelius was wrong and Shea still had her soul. Either way, I knew what I had to do.

I placed my hand against Caelius's chest. He looked at it curiously, pleasure filling his gaze. It was the same look I'd seen in the caves when he'd bent me to his will, playing with his favorite toy.

"You are right, *Father*."

Now he smiled. A full grin. His grip on everyone was loose. He was barely holding on, his mouth salivating. "And so, boy, *this* is what it takes for you to finally call me Father."

"I was wrong, Father. All this time. I know now that I can't win. Not against you. I'll stop fighting. Now . . . now that I know it has been *you* all along." I knew what I had to say, what his ego and empty heart wanted to hear. I pushed further. "I didn't realize, but I see it now. It is you whom I've wanted, you whom I *need*. You're the only one who really cares about me. Look at all you've done to prove it. After all of this time, you're my *God*, aren't you, Caelius?"

Caelius lunged forward and kissed me, claws and spikes disappearing into his chest as he dropped the others like useless sandbags. I kissed him back, hard, pulling him deeper into the embrace. He wrapped his body effortlessly around mine and lifted us into the air.

The others were gone in an instant. They'd escaped. Aidan had saved them.

Caelius didn't care. He was busy with me, tearing my clothes off, sinking his teeth into my neck. For once, I didn't resist. I needed to give them time. He moaned with ecstasy.

"You're all I've ever wanted," Caelius whispered into my ear as his hips shoved against mine.

"I know." I practically gasped the words. Caelius mistook it for passion, believing that the fire I felt was for him. Yes, there was fire, a gasping from the effort. It was all I could do to stop the spark within me from fighting him off.

The others needed to hide themselves. And to buy that time, here in Gutium I was offering up my life and my pride, as I should have done all those centuries ago on the battlefield next to my family.

I peeled off his clothes.

Our bodies pressed against each other, naked under the light of a full moon.

"I surrender everything. I will serve only you."

When he learns how I've betrayed him, I hope that my death is at least enough to buy them the chance to live.

I whispered into his ear, "I am yours now, Caelius, body and soul."

EPILOGUE
MOLLY

I waited patiently for Grandfather. He'd said he had to punish his misbehaving children (my parents) and then he would be back. That statement alone was the reason I'd never had kids. It made my skin crawl just thinking about how that Vessel had called me "mother." How dare she? As a human I had never even considered having a child, and for her to speak such a lie in front of my new parents and Grandfather? It was humiliating.

Still.

There was something so familiar about her.

I pushed the thought from my head like Caelius had shown me. It was quite easy now. Anytime a stressful thought crept into my mind, I would visually swat it away like a fly. It was empowering.

I wished I had possessed that skill as a human. My depression had been so strong, I'd been ready to die. When Grandfather had tried to compel me to feed Lucian with my blood, I'd hesitated at first, but then he'd whispered in my ear that I'd find peace. It was as if the Universe had finally given me my wish and was letting me end it all.

When I'd awoken as a vampire, I'd been crushed. All I'd wanted was the peacefulness of death that Grandfather had promised.

But I loved my life now. Draining mortals made me feel powerful, as if I could do anything. I'd never felt that way as a human. Back then I'd been weak, tired, and miserable. Jeff had been my only light, but I'd kept him in the dark for so long that I didn't know if he still wanted me. I missed him terribly, but Grandfather had said I might not see Jeff again and that killing him may have to be one of the punishments for my parents.

I didn't see how killing my husband would mean anything to Mother and Father, but Grandfather seemed to think Father would be hurt the most by this because of his feelings for the Vessel. Why did she care about me or Jeff anyway? She must really believe we were her parents. She had been so convinced. So sure.

I pushed the thought away. I couldn't even remember her name. Grandfather had said it wasn't important, since he was going to kill her anyway, and that I should just refer to her as the Vessel.

My heart surged when thinking of Grandfather. He was so good to me, and I wanted to show him how much I loved him. He'd given me a mission to find Father's last two Second-Borns, and I wasn't going to fail him. So as soon as Grandfather left, I used my amazing new sense of smell and found them almost instantly. Soaring across the skies was the most exhilarating sensation—I was so fast!

I had captured and brought both of Father's Second-Borns to my hiding place in less than an hour. I couldn't wait for Grandfather to return and see that I'd succeeded.

The only problem was that they smelled so good. I wanted to pop their heads off and drink them myself. I pushed the thought from my brain and sat, comfortably waiting for Grandfather to arrive. I just wished he'd hurry.

I was *really* hungry.

GUTIAN CODE

"**A**re you afraid of me?" I asked Bohe, who sat quietly in the corner.

"I stopped fearing death long ago," he replied calmly.

I wouldn't have blamed him if he *had* been scared of me. *I* was scared of me. And currently, I was scared *for* me.

Grandfather wasn't going to like this.

Father's last two children, Bohe and David, were *my* responsibility. I was supposed to keep them safe for whatever Grandfather needed them for. I was relatively sure it was to make Father happy, which only made what I had done worse.

I'd drained David.

There was no way to tell if just a drop of Grandfather's blood was in his system, because that would be enough to revive him.

And I got scared Grandfather would be angry if he told on me . . .

So I'd decapitated him.

Afterward, I felt horrible. He actually seemed like a good person, if vampires could be considered good. And now my fear of David telling on me for draining him was replaced by my fear that Grandfather would torture me for *killing* him.

And a very small part of me hated to admit it, but I'd never tasted anything so delicious.

Bohe smelled divine as well, but my fear of Grandfather stopped me from taking a bite of Lucian's last living child—well, not quite the last. Jeff, Ur-Nammu, and I were his children as well.

Jeff.

My heart squeezed with longing at the thought of my husband. Why wasn't he with me? Why was he with *her*?

Shea.

The Vessel. Claiming she was my daughter! As if I'd have kids.

But I did.

I had Shea.

I loved her.

What was I thinking? Was this a trick from the Vessel? Was she that powerful?

No.

These thoughts were coming from me. They grew stronger the longer Grandfather was away. I used to tell him every time I had that kind of thought, but I stopped because he'd always feed me his blood after. And I didn't like it. The taste was mind-blowing, the power indescribable, but . . .

I didn't like it.

I didn't like forgetting *her*.

My little girl.

No.

She was the Vessel. She was evil. She was the enemy of Grandfather and of me. She'd destroy us all, she was so powerful.

Confusion overwhelmed me.

What was happening?

"Is the Vessel trying to brainwash you again?" Grandfather's voice sounded from behind.

I knew he was going to give me more of his blood. I almost longed for it at the moment. I didn't want to remember anything. I didn't want to feel this pain. I nodded.

He was alone, but I could hear Father in the next room, struggling against the chains. Grandfather had made me secure him to his bed. He'd said that Lucian would be honored to be tied with the bones of Ashliel. I didn't know Father all that well, so I'd done what I'd been told, but from the sound of Father's angry screams, I didn't think Grandfather was correct in his assessment.

"I need to be with Lucian. I don't have time for your weakness," Grandfather scolded.

I glanced briefly at David's dead body, feeling guilty.

Grandfather nodded. "His blood made you vulnerable. It's how the Vessel reached in and probed your thoughts, filling them with lies."

But I thought David's blood had made me stronger.

I didn't know what was real anymore.

"Make me understand," I begged.

Sighing, Caelius pricked his finger with one of his fangs and drew a single drop of blood. He never gave me more than that. It wasn't enough, but I'd take it, even if it only allowed me to think clearly for a short while.

I drank, and before I could utter a response, Grandfather left to be with Lucian.

I waited for the blood to take hold.

Where was I?

I looked around and saw Bohe in the corner, sitting next to the headless corpse of David.

I tried to remember what I had just been thinking, but nothing came to mind.

I felt a twist in my gut, but it had no meaning.

Maybe it was the fact that I had killed one of Father's children.

I looked at Bohe and asked, "Are you afraid of me?"

He only answered me with silence.

CHAPTER 1
SHEA

Was I Dream-Walking? Had I died? Where was I?

Looking around, all I could see were miles of white. There were no walls or floors. My feet felt like they were on the ground, but no matter how hard I searched, there was no surface beneath me. It was as if I was floating.

My instant reaction was one of panic, but every time I thought I would go into full-on anxiety mode, a sense of calm would wash over me and I'd relax again. It was a strange cycle that kept repeating until I thought I'd go mad.

Seriously. Where was I?

I did a complete body check. I could feel my legs, arms, head . . . Yup, everything was real and *here*. Wherever *here* was.

Before this place, I could remember pieces of what had happened. I had used my elemental powers to take Caelius down. I'd shredded trees into spikes, pinning Caelius to the ground so Lucian and the others could hurt him enough so we could all escape.

But it had been too much.

I had expended every ounce of power I had, and my body had finally given up. I must have passed out.

Helena.

She had betrayed us. That, I remembered.

Caelius had said he'd jumbled up her brain. We'd thought Lucian's necklace was our superweapon, that it would destroy him. Unknowingly, she had turned it into a device that had given him immense power and he'd gloated that it had also taken my soul.

Yeah.

Feeling a little stupid.

And looking around at all the white surrounding me, it was a good bet that I'd croaked.

Maybe with no soul I was in some kind of afterlife waiting room, as if the universe wasn't quite sure what to do with me. And since I was completely alone, it looked like I was the only one.

I didn't *feel* soulless though.

But what would not having a soul feel like? I needed to take some kind of morality test.

Did I still love Lucian? Yes.

Did I still want to save the world from Caelius? Yes.

Did I still want to rip Caelius apart until all that was left was a gooey mess of skin and guts? Yes.

Wait. That sounded pretty soulless.

"You have your soul," Aidan's voice said from the ether.

"Aidan?" I called out, feeling a surge of hope.

A shape transformed in front of me, but it definitely wasn't Aidan's.

I should have been terrified by what I saw, but the figure

was stunning to look at. His lion's head, with hundreds of eyes, stared at me with kindness. His torso was that of a man, perfectly muscled like a Michelangelo statue, but his bottom half was ox, thick and powerful. On his right side was one giant wing in the shape of an eagle's, and on the left side, where another wing was supposed to be, was only a nub.

Gazing into the hundreds of blue eyes before me, I saw . . .

My Aidan.

It *was* him.

I'd know those baby blues anywhere.

His lion head and expression looked unsure, as if he didn't know how I'd feel about seeing his true form.

He could have been in the shape of a razor blade for all I cared. "Can I hug you?" I asked, not sure what the protocol was for embracing angels.

And that was what he was: an angel. It was easy to forget that when Aidan was in human form—the only way I had ever known him. Since he was an earthbound angel tied to the Vessel, it meant we'd been born on the same day, minute, and second. Having been raised together in Phoenix, Arizona, I didn't know anyone as well as I knew Aidan, but I felt like I was seeing who my best friend truly was for the first time.

And it was glorious.

"Of course you can hug me." Aidan smiled.

It was a little strange to have a lion's head with hundreds of eyes smile at me, but I fell into the embrace like he was my savior. Because in that moment, he was. These arms would feel the same on any plane of existence—strong, powerful, and cozy like a teddy bear. I never wanted to let him go.

But after a long moment, Aidan pulled away. "I had to bring you here. We need to talk to my brothers."

Okay, I knew it was Aidan, but lion's head . . . lots of eyes talking. Very surreal.

Aidan seemed to sense what I was feeling and laughed. "Is it weird, talking to me this way?"

"More so when you laugh. It's like talking to your Animoji on the phone. Is that why you always choose a lion?" I asked, and we both cracked up.

With a wave of his hand, Aidan's angel body shimmered in front of me until he was back in human form. Though Aidan's angel form was beautiful in its own way, his human form rivaled it. Wearing a simple white T-shirt and jeans, Aidan looked like he had just worked out for fifty hours in a gym somewhere. His swoopy brown hair was perfectly messy, and his giant blue eyes sparkled at me like they always had. My best friend. Nothing would break our bond.

"Better?" He smiled.

"You don't have to do that. You're making me feel like an angel racist." I felt like a jerk for teasing him before.

Aidan's easy smile was about the best thing I'd seen in a long time, then he said, "Yup. Shea Harper: angel bigot."

I smacked his chest, laughing. I suddenly wished we could stay like this forever. It was easier to forget everything that was happening with our loved ones when we were isolated up here in this land of glowing white.

Speaking of which . . .

"Aidan, what happened in that last battle?" I looked around with doubt. "I'm assuming since we're here that Caelius is still on the loose, but . . . who made it?"

His face showed what I feared the most. He didn't want to tell me. That was bad.

"Lucian?" I could barely speak his name, I was so terrified of what Aidan would say.

"He's alive, Shea." His voice cracked as he continued. "Lucian sacrificed himself to save the rest of us: you, Meky, Nefertiti, Ur-Nammu, your dad, and Sherit."

"What do you mean *sacrificed*? You said he was alive!" I stood in front of him as if I was a wall trying to break a storm.

"He gave himself to Caelius . . . willingly." Aidan's voice was quiet.

Oh, God.

My entire being froze in agony. Lucian *gave* himself to Caelius. All Caelius had ever wanted was Lucian, and now he had him. What was Lucian enduring while we stood here in this place? We needed to save him! We needed to get him back.

I hadn't thought it was possible to hurt this much. I was crushed by the excruciating weight of helplessness and guilt. Lucian was probably being tortured and ravaged by Darkness itself.

And my mom . . .

"Aidan! My mom is there too, isn't she?" I felt another surge of panic.

Aidan nodded and took my hands to calm me. "She drank Caelius's blood. She worships him now, so she's probably safe for the time being."

I wanted to believe that, but how could I? This was Caelius we were talking about. Two people I loved with all my heart were in his grasp. It was excruciating. I looked up at Aidan. "We have to help them. We can't leave them there."

Pulling me in for another tight embrace, Aidan's words rang in my ears. "We will. That's why we're here—for help, and to get some answers. We have to do everything we can to stop Caelius so that we can get them back."

It didn't feel like enough, but I knew it had to be. Lucian had given himself to Caelius so we could escape, and I didn't want that to be in vain. We needed the inside scoop on Caelius and the Light, and the only way to get it was through Aidan's brothers.

Pulling away from the hug, Aidan kept his grip on my hand like he used to when we were kids. "It's time to talk to my siblings."

I nodded and motioned for him to lead the way.

Closing his eyes, Aidan concentrated.

The whiteness around us grew brighter and brighter until I shut my eyes, afraid I'd go blind from the intensity.

"You can open your eyes now, Shea." Aidan's voice was soothing.

I looked at Aidan, and his three brothers stood before us. I'd seen them before in our first epic battle against Caelius. They were in their man-shaped bodies, which was probably Aidan's idea. All joking aside, Aidan really was making me feel like I was too fragile to see angels in their true form. We had bigger problems to worry about though, so I didn't say anything.

Sabrael, Harahel, and Gavreel were well over ten feet tall. They looked like they were sculpted out of marble, skin smooth but perfectly muscled. They were wearing simple white robes. If I saw them on the street, I'd think they were three very tall supermodels going to a toga party. I kind of wanted to see their true forms, since I couldn't seem to get the image of them making fashion poses in a photo booth out of my head. I had only caught glimpses of their true form when we had fought Caelius: wings the size of a dragon's and even more of a mishmash of the animal kingdom than Aidan.

Maybe it was better to see the beautiful toga boys in front of me after all. I'd probably stare too long if they were in their real bodies.

Which, of course, Aidan had likely guessed because he knew me so well.

It was Gavreel who spoke first. "Welcome, Vessel."

Sabrael and Harahel echoed Gavreel's words. "Welcome."

Awkward.

It felt so formal, like I was in some kind of movie where I was at the pearly gates and everyone suddenly spoke like they were in a Shakespearean play.

Harahel interrupted my thoughts by saying, "We have much to discuss, Vessel."

"Can you call me Shea, not Vessel?" I looked at Aidan for support, and he gave a slight nod to his brothers.

Sabrael replied, "To us, all Vessels are the same, made from the drippings of Light. But if you wish for us to call you by your *human* name, we will do so."

"Uh, thanks." Smooth. I was definitely representing *all* Vessels with my eloquent speaking skills.

Gavreel continued. "Your soul is made from the Light, and Caelius still needs this to regain his full strength. If he is to succeed, he will destroy everything in his wake, *everything.*

The three of us cannot leave the Light to help you. If it's left vulnerable, Caelius could abandon his mortal form and consume the Light completely."

Harahel finished his brother's words. "If this were to happen, all of creation would be lost."

I almost couldn't comprehend what they were saying. Caelius had the potential to destroy the world, but now they were declaring that if given the chance, he would consume *all of creation*.

Yeah. I didn't want these guys to leave the Light either.

I was by no means a martyr, but I suddenly understood why Aidan had been willing to kill all the Vessels before me and then die himself. It was the Vessel or all life on Earth. Kind of a no-brainer.

What he had done still hurt like hell, both physically and emotionally. But I understood it now more than I ever had before. And that was just stopping Caelius in *human* form. If Caelius were to return to his "natural state" and the Light wasn't being protected by the angel squad? That was it. Game over. No more life in the universe.

"So, we should make sure he stays mortal?" I asked. Darkness incarnate on the loose seemed a lot more dangerous than mortal Darkness. Maybe Aidan's brothers could tell us how to capture him again or how to defeat Caelius once and for all.

Gavreel shook his head. "No. Caelius needs to go back to his true form. The Light gave him a chance to live the life of a mortal, to experience what it was like to be human. He was to observe but not to interfere with human life. When he gave his blood to the first human, Lucian, he broke his promise to the Light and had to be imprisoned. Caelius's blood will turn a human into what you call a vampire; it's like a sickness made of Darkness. If a human has even a drop of Caelius's blood inside them, they will remain a vampire, feeding on life itself."

"Blood," I said, clarifying what "life itself" meant. Blood was what made people live, so it made sense that the only way for a vampire to stay alive was to drink it from a living, breathing person. But my brain still wasn't comprehending why the angels didn't want Caelius to stay in a mortal body. "Isn't Caelius more dangerous in his true form, as Darkness?"

"As long as we protect the Light, Darkness cannot win," Sabrael answered. "It's a balance between the two. Clearly, Caelius doesn't like this. It's his nature to destroy. The Light thought that putting him in a human body might give him more empathy, maybe even allow him to understand what it means to create. But even in Caelius's desire to create something of his own, he made beings that want to ravage all living things, like he does."

"Not all of them do," I blurted out. Lucian wasn't like that, and neither were Nefertiti or Meky or my dad. The angels stayed silent, neither agreeing nor disagreeing with me, which in angel-speak meant they thought I was mistaken.

I wanted to argue more, but I knew it was pointless. I knew the things Lucian had done in his past, and they weren't exactly peachy. And Nefertiti had been a warrior *before* she'd become a vampire. And how well did I really know Meky? She'd claimed that Caelius had never let them drink from a living human, that he'd only let them have leftovers from all the male vampires, but what if that wasn't true? What if all vampires were killers just like Caelius was? It meant that Caelius's blood turned anyone who had it in their system to the "dark side," whether they wanted to or not.

"Is there any way to remove Caelius's blood from someone who's turned?" I wanted to rip him out of every vampire I knew and cared about.

"We do not know," Harahel replied. "But if the blood *is* removed, the vampire would become mortal again. Most creatures with immortality would not give this up easily."

Aidan finally spoke. "Lucian would give up immortality in a heartbeat if it meant being with Shea."

My chest squeezed. Lucian and I would both be human then. We could have a family. We could just be . . . us. I needed to get him back from Caelius's clutches. I needed to get my mom back. I felt so useless at the moment. What could I really do? Caelius needed my soul in order for him to be at full power. Was I really thinking of walking into his *lair* like a meal on a platter?

Yes, I was.

Sabrael's voice cut through my thoughts with anger. "The Light does not care for Caelius's creatures, and as the guardians of the Light, neither do we." Turning to Aidan with scolding eyes, he said, "We will give you all the powers of the Light we can so you may fight Caelius in battle. But Adnachiel, Caelius *must* return to his true form. If he drains the *Vessel's* soul, he will destroy *all* life on Earth."

Why aren't they killing me then?

I couldn't help it. My brain heard their words, and that was the first thing that popped up.

If the world would end by draining me, why wouldn't they end me right now?

I decided to keep that little revelation to myself.

They obviously had their reasons, and if I was being honest, that was what worried me the most.

And we were back to *Vessel* again. I knew Aidan had chosen to protect me, but his brother's words about not being able to kill Caelius still hit me hard. He was going to take down the world if we didn't somehow force him to give up his human body.

Damned if we do, damned if we don't.

"How can we get Caelius to give up his corporeal form?" I asked. "There's no way."

"You must find a way," Harahel said with authority.

Then without warning, Sabrael, Harahel, and Gavreel reached out and each placed a hand on Aidan's chest and mine.

Our bodies glowed white, and I could see both Aidan's human and true form all at once, as if I were seeing double. Before my eyes, Aidan grew back his missing wing until both of his wings were over twenty feet in length.

I could feel the Light coursing through me, strengthening me, making me feel invincible.

Then their hands left our chests, and so did the glow.

Gavreel spoke for all three brothers. "Aidan, your wing has been restored. You can fly again—you always could. It was your shame over Moses that kept you grounded all these years. You must toss such petty things aside and use flight in this battle. We have filled your blood with Light so that you can heal, so that you can burn and pull energy from the sun."

Then he turned to me. "And to you, Vessel, we have given our power. We hope it is enough to return Caelius to his true form when the time comes. But you must not run to confront

Caelius. If he takes your soul, all is lost. Only attack him when the timing is in your favor and you're sure you can turn him back to Darkness. You'll have one chance. Use it well."

Thanks. Could they have been any more vague? Attack, but don't attack? Which one was it? I decided I'd leave strategy up to those of us who were left fighting.

After a moment, the light died down, and I turned to Aidan. He was fully in human form, but he looked like he'd just drank ten energy drinks in a row. I imagined I must have looked the same because he gave me one of his goofy grins.

"It's time to leave now," Aidan said, and everything went dark.

***

I slowly opened my eyes to see my dad, Jeff Harper, sitting in a chair next to me. I was lying in a somewhat comfortable bed in an empty room I didn't recognize.

Dad's eyes lit up when he saw that I was awake.

"Shea, oh thank goodness." He took my hand and squeezed it. "We were so worried."

I looked around at the empty room. "*We?*"

Dad shrugged. "Well, you know, Nefertiti and her family show worry in their own way."

I supposed that was true to a certain extent, but my guess was that Nefertiti wanted me alive not for any feelings of friendship, but because I might be able to help her rescue her daughter Setepenre. And probably Lucian, but I didn't want to think about Nefertiti's feelings for my boyfriend.

Dad let go of my hand and stood up. "I'll go get everyone." He left the small room, and I got a better look at where I was. There were no windows and just one door leading out to a hallway. It made me think we were somewhere underground.

I didn't want to wait for the others to come to me, so I stood up from bed and tried to follow my dad. As soon as I was in a standing position, a wave of dizziness hit me. Luckily it passed after a few seconds, but I was still unsteady.

How long had I been out?

Carefully watching my steps, I walked out of the room and into the hallway beyond. I had no idea which way my dad had gone, seeing as the floor was the same linoleum tile as my pseudo-bedroom, and it wasn't like he'd left any footprints. From the stucco on the ceilings and the army-green paint covering the walls, I was pretty sure this building had been built in the '70s. Or if it hadn't been, the interior designer needed to join this decade. Left seemed like a good idea, so I headed down that way, hoping I'd catch up with my dad.

Nope.

It must have been forty-five minutes of me walking down endless hallways of green tiles and white walls before I finally heard Aidan's voice. "Shea? Where are you?"

And so began our game of Marco Polo, where eventually I found Aidan in the middle of one of the numerous hallways. I sighed in relief. "This place is insane. I've never seen so many freaking hallways in my life."

Aidan's smile instantly warmed me as he hugged me tight. "Crazy, right? I guess it's some kind of underground bunker. Nefertiti says it was built by some rich guy in the '60s in case there was a nuclear war. Helena found it abandoned in the '80s and kept it on her list of hideouts. Nefertiti wants us to be in a place that Helena can find. Hopefully when we see Helena again we'll know if she's . . . you know, not on our side anymore."

It was sad to not be able to trust Helena. We all knew she had been brainwashed by Caelius, but was she still?

Looking at me, Aidan shook his head. "And Vessel or not, your body has been in another astral plane. You should be resting."

"*You* should be resting." I really had nowhere to go with that. I just didn't want to lie down again, not when Lucian and my mother were with Caelius.

Chuckling, Aidan pulled away and nodded in the opposite direction of where I'd come from. "Come on. This way."

We eventually passed the room I'd woken up in, and by taking a right instead of a left, we entered a large study with several couches and chairs. I wanted to smack myself in the head; I had been so close. Leave it to me to go the opposite direction.

Ur-Nammu and Sherit sat on a couch together talking while Nefertiti and Meky stood by a giant fireplace that looked like it hadn't seen fire in decades.

Dad leapt up from an armchair and walked toward me. "There you are. I told you I was going to bring everyone to you. Why did you leave?"

"I thought it'd be faster if I came to you."

Dad, Aidan, and I all laughed.

Then Dad said, "Yes, you got here *much* faster."

Nefertiti walked over with Meky by her side. Meky gave me a slight wave while Nefertiti eyed me like I was a disappointing boxer she'd have to train for the championship.

"We were discussing strategies on how to get Lucian and Setepenre back, but Aidan says you have to sit this one out." Nefertiti watched me carefully, gauging my reaction.

I whirled on Aidan. "What are you talking about? I'm the best chance we have of getting Lucian, Sete, and"—I turned to Nefertiti with slight annoyance—"my *mom* back." Only mentioning Lucian and her daughter had been expected, but a part of me wondered if the reason she hadn't mentioned my mom was because she didn't think Molly Harper was saveable.

"Yes, of course, your mother," Nefertiti added as if she were placating a child. "So you *do* plan on helping us?"

Aidan stepped in. "Shea, you heard my brothers. You can't be anywhere near Caelius yet. We're not ready for the big takedown. If he drains your soul, he'll be at full power, and we'll have no chance of getting him to give up his mortal form. He'd destroy the world first."

"Can't he do more crap when he's Darkness again?" I asked what I thought was an obvious statement. I hadn't been satisfied with Aidan's brothers' answers. Being all Darkness sounded way more sinister and dangerous.

Shaking his head, Aidan sighed. "No, Shea. With my brothers protecting the Light, he will be put back into the cosmic balance of the universe when he becomes Darkness. Here on Earth, as a human, he can physically destroy anything he wants. It's one of the perks of being human, remember? Free will. Ever heard of it?" His sarcasm was not lost on me.

"Don't give me attitude." I looked at him with pleading eyes. "Don't bench me when my mother is brainwashed. She has no memory of her own daughter because of your brothers. And

Lucian is probably being tortured as we speak!" Tears welled in my eyes. "I just can't. I have to do *something*. I have to."

Nefertiti nodded. "It's settled then. When we attack, Shea will come with us. Sherit, Meky, and Ur-Nammu will stay behind, of course."

Aidan laughed, annoyed. "So everyone who matters to you stays behind, but all the rest of us are expendable?"

With an edge of fury, Nefertiti said, "I lost *three* of my daughters in that battle, and Caelius made it very clear that he plans on taking the rest of my family if given the chance, so yes, *Beast*, my girls and father will stay behind."

I joined in at that point. "Okay, no more of this *beast* talk. We're all friends here . . . kinda. Can we at least come up with a plan? Because if your strategy is to just 'storm the castle,' we're screwed."

Nefertiti had no response, which meant that was exactly her plan.

"We need someone on the inside to get to Caelius so we have eyes and ears on everything he's doing," a woman's voice said from the doorway.

All heads turned.

Helena walked in.

With everything that had happened, no one knew how to react. Caelius had confessed that he had controlled Helena. Lucian's necklace had been our greatest weapon, but Caelius had compelled Helena to turn it into a full-blown battery to juice him up instead.

No one could blame her for having been mind-controlled.

But no one could trust her either.

Helena continued. "I have someone with me who may be able to help us."

Motioning to the doorway, Helena signaled.

Everyone stood dumbstruck as a man we all thought dead walked into the room.

Duncan, Lucian's Second-Born who had been murdered by Caelius and had died in Lucian's arms, stood before us with a half smile.

"Hullo. Lang time nae see," Duncan said in a thick Scottish accent.

What did he just say?

Chapter 2
Lucian

I stared vacantly at the endless white above me. If I wasn't a vampire, I would have thought it flawless. But there were specks, dirt from age, and a hairline crack that ran from one corner of the ceiling to the other.

I tried to move but couldn't. Aidan's devoured brother's remains had been reshaped and now formed bone chains at my wrists and ankles. Even in death, Caelius would make use of Ashliel. Even in death, there was no escape from Darkness.

I looked around the room. It was an elaborate hotel . . . in Paris. The subtleties in the air gave it away. Paris had a scent I had relished long before I'd met Shea, a scent that now made every part of my body ache and long for those nights we'd spent here.

Of course Caelius would pick Paris. His jealousy knew no bounds, and I'd been as imprudent as ever, thinking I could fool him for long. I ran through Caelius's relentless lovemaking in my mind. I had fought back every urge to resist, every grimace and ounce of Gutian pride, all to give them a chance, not to hide, but to *live*. I'd thought I could distract him with my body, at least for a few thousand years or more, at least for Shea.

I wanted her to love someone else, to experience the world, to see beauty and to find happiness, to laugh, to feel *anything* before she felt Caelius's cold desire carve out the soul from her flesh. I wished he'd never found out that the necklace hadn't worked. I would die to spare her that fate now. In fact, what I valued most inside of myself already had. Even still, Caelius was Darkness, and he was right to call me a *boy*. Of course he would see through me. I had been foolish to think otherwise.

I hated his icy hands running over every inch of my body. I hated the idea of making love to anyone who wasn't Shea. And it wasn't making *love* with Caelius. That was the problem. I had tried to convince my mind that it was just sex, that it didn't matter, but in all my years with Nefertiti, I had never once cheated on her. Then, out of all the centuries that had passed in the shadow of remorse after Nefari's presumed death, it was only Shea who had pulled me toward love again. And because of that, my severe loyalty to her had instinctively outwitted my reactions. I didn't love Caelius, and I couldn't fake it.

I sighed. "How long are you going to sit there, watching me?"

"Grandfather can't look at your face right now." Molly sneered in disgust. "And stop talking!" she spat, her words full of malice and desire. Bloodlust was pulsing in her tone like the shadow in Caelius's black heart that had covered her own.

She had finally answered audibly. I had been trying to convince her for days on end that Caelius was a monster, that he had manipulated her. It was no use now. She was restless and angry. Mostly she mumbled and argued with herself, as if I wasn't chained three feet from her.

I'd thought I could exploit her obvious conflict to my advantage. Yesterday, she'd paused as if my words had broken through, and for that instant, I thought I saw compassion fill her gaze. Then he'd beckoned, and she'd run from the room. When she'd returned, she was in ecstasy. That's when I knew: Caelius was giving her *his* blood. Not the blood of Second-Borns, but his own. No amount of convincing was going to break the brainwashing that liquid Darkness could have on a vampire.

Looking at her now, it was hard to believe she was related to Shea at all.

That sweetness, honesty, and sense of humor, if only I could see a glimmer of it, a piece of Shea in this new hell. Instead I was reminded of my mistakes. Killing her parents and turning them had been *my* doing. It was only fitting that the vampire version of Molly torment me now.

"At least you smell like Shea." It slipped out.

I closed my eyes.

In an instant she flew to my bedside, her hand extending like talons as her nails hovered over my neck.

"If Grandfather hadn't commanded me not to *touch* you—" Small specks of saliva landed on my face, her mouth open, baring teeth as she spoke. "I am nothing like the Vessel! I won't believe your lies!"

"Now, now, La-Narru. Don't provoke her." Caelius stepped into the room, and everything went cold. His voice usually carried a childlike whimsy with an undertone of vindictive contempt. But now? There was no humor to it. It was a mixture of rage and tenderness. If I didn't know him so well, it would almost sound like he was heartbroken.

"Leave," he commanded.

"Of course!" Her hands moved away from my throat as she obediently made her way out the door. "But, Grandfather . . ." She hesitated. "I know it's not time yet, but since I've held back and behaved so well, can't I have another drop of your blood? I can't stand it, the time in between feedings! I need it, Grandfather, please!"

He growled, and the walls shook around us.

"Obey." One word, and he didn't make eye contact. Instead, his gaze burned into mine.

She deflated, slinking out the door like a child who'd lost their security blanket.

Obey? Usually he had more style than that.

"You're losing your edge, Caelius. If you're not careful, I'll turn Molly to my side. I've always been good with women." I let a half smile slip.

"No, you won't," he mocked. "One drop of my blood will keep her subservient for weeks, and I won't give useless human cowhide more than that."

He wasn't taking the bait.

I swallowed.

He stood at the edge of the bed. His determined gaze was worse than Molly's hand hovering over my throat, threatening to choke the life from my body.

"Are you just going to stand there?" He didn't move. There was no banter, no snide Caelius-like remarks. "I don't know why you're keeping me here. As soon as I convince Molly to get me out, I'll be back with Shea. And we'll *kill* you this time. And I'll laugh! I'll laugh over your pathetic ashes, you perverted piece of sh—" He covered my mouth with his hand.

"You want to provoke me so that I will end your life." He paused, and I held my breath. "I would ask *why*, but the answer you gave me days ago was enough. I'm sure it's still the same. Because you love *her*."

My eyes bulged, and I screamed obscenities into his palm. Despite my outburst, his vision seemed so clear. I realized now how cloudy it had always been when he'd looked at me. Still, if I could just exploit that lingering tenderness he was feeling toward me, I could protect Shea. And if I couldn't, he was right, I would spit curses at him until he cut off my tongue and ended my life.

"I'm going to keep my promise, boy. It seems I'm the only one who will." He took his other hand and pulled it through my hair. Over and over he repeated the motion, staring at me with those burning auburn eyes. "You fear I will use you against Shea, so you prefer death. But you already *died* in Egypt under Nefertiti's window."

He moved the pad of his thumb over my bottom lip. "And with this same mouth you promised me your afterlife. As a boy by the river in your homeland where we first met, you promised to be mine, calling me God. *Your* god. Just like you unconsciously did again when you surrendered to me. Pity, I thought being in Gutium had made you remember . . . but it was all a lie!"

He pulled my lip down, running his index finger along my bottom teeth. "I was omnipotent, wasn't I? I watched over you. I didn't interfere with your life until it came to its natural end in Egypt. I let you have your free will." He pulled his hand away from my mouth, staring at the fingers now coated with my saliva. "Unlike the pathetic mortals in your life, I will *make* you keep that pure promise you enticed me with." He moved his fingers to his mouth and licked the wet slowly, his eyes never leaving mine. "As you have ensnared me throughout time—again and again, tempting me with your words and body—you will ensnare Shea Harper, destroying her with your own hands . . . as you have destroyed me. As you destroy *all* who care for you."

He half smiled to himself, but it wasn't the Caelius smirk I had known over time. It was a grimace, a painful thing. He placed his hand back over my mouth. "Even though you do it so fluidly, turning love into hate is no small feat. So first, let's start with something easy, shall we? I'll have you hold something tender against you, something tender that you will come to despise."

I knew before he walked in, his scent reaching me as soon as the door opened: *Camellia sinensis*. My mind thought of the Latin first, but I had memorized it in every language because he had taught it to me. He had drawn out the words like painting long strokes with ink as he spoke its praises.

He had told me its origin once, holding the hot cup and serving it as tenderly as one would present a newborn to its mother. He'd explained that in 2737 BC, Shen Nung had been sitting beneath a tree while his servant boiled drinking water for their journey. Some of the careless leaves fell inside. Shen was known for herbalism, and instead of punishing his servant for the chaos of nature's whim, as most nobles were inclined, he'd decided to try the concoction.

Now everyone just called it *tea*. It was prepackaged in tiny contained bags, all that was wild, mysterious, and raw now bleached and dried for the world to consume at its thoughtless leisure. But back then—the passion for it and the aliveness when he'd told me the stories, beaming with pride of his rich heritage—it had seemed so much more to me than just a tea leaf. It was an art. *His* art.

"Liu Xie." I spoke the words into Caelius's palm.

He nodded at the muffled sound. "Yes. Emperor Xian of Han. The last in the Han Dynasty. The failure you adored so perversely that you even gave him a pet name. It was Bohe, if I'm not mistaken."

I swallowed, unable to speak. Even though Shen Nung was eventually despised by the people, Bohe had idolized him in his youth, so much so that he always smelled of tea. Drinking it, bathing in it—it was one of his greatest mortal pleasures. I remembered long nights in China smelling the hair at the nape of his neck, the herbal infusions there having a calming effect on my tormented mind. And here it was again, that calming scent, this time filling me with agony.

"Finally silent, darling? Are you surprised?" Caelius stroked my hair one last time before sitting in the corner of the room, where Molly had been.

I took my eyes off of Bohe, looking back up at the ceiling. In that glance, he'd looked as innocent and frightened as he had been when the warlord Dong Zhou had killed his older brother. He'd forced Bohe to become emperor at eight years old. In the years that followed, he became an ornamental finger puppet, a lapdog for that vicious war-hungry murderer.

How many centuries had passed since he'd had to play the part of a lonely marionette? How long had I protected him from re-experiencing anything from his childhood? And yet, here it was, having come full circle. Because of me, his strings were once again pulled, and he would be forced to play the puppet.

"You turned this doll after Pompeii, no?" Caelius clicked his fingernails on the wooden chair, leaning his head casually on the heel of his palm. "After you dug yourself out, of course." He smiled, but the tenderness in his gaze was giving way to fury with every word he spoke. "Does your pet know that you *watched* him, and how long you watched him for? You and I are not so different, are we, Son?"

My mouth felt dry, and I swallowed as shame cast itself over my senses. I met Bohe when he was a boy. He'd been kind to me, this *thing* walking the night. The fresh ache of Adnachiel and the madness of being trapped in cooling lava and clawing my way out inch by inch over a hundred years had made me more animal than man. And there he was.

I closed my eyes, remembering that moment as if living it again for the first time.

He had been small, and his cheeks were round and soft—a chubby boy in silk robes hemmed with gold. I had never eaten a child before, even at my lowest. But I was still burning with the scars of Pompeii, and I despised royalty because of Akhenaten. The idea that any man thought he was above another because of birth or station disgusted me.

I had thought that the little ruler would grow up to be a monster like all the rest I had known and seen throughout the ages. I was close to devouring him whole, to losing the only boundary I had left. But then he had asked if I was hurt, concern filling his blameless face. He had taken me into his private chambers. His small hands had trembled as he'd tried to mend the blood spilling from my gut. It was an open wound I hadn't noticed. I had been numb for so long then.

He'd bandaged me tenderly. Then he gave me food, the garnet ring adorning his finger, and some of his favorite tea that he had kept hidden under his bedding. I thought it strange then, for the son of an emperor to hide something so meaningless. But when he spoke of the herbs and smells, I could see how precious it was to him, more so than the bejeweled ring he willingly stripped from his pinky.

But most surprising of all was when he'd bowed and spoke into the innate carpet at our feet. He had asked that I sell the ring and live a safe, honorable life free of violence. Then he pleaded with me to leave in haste and to never return, that it was a dangerous time and if anyone found a vagrant on his grounds, it would mean their death or worse.

I watched him silently, bent in submission. And for the first time in a long time, I felt something beyond the pain of Pompeii. I willingly obeyed the little ruler. It was only as I staggered through the open doorway, back into the gardens that I had clawed my way into, that a violent wind shifted the loose silk robes from his shoulders. I paused. There, half naked before me, was the reason he had shown kindness to the rabid dog that wandered into his palace. How else could an emperor's son know how to properly mend an open wound?

He had been beaten.

Wrapped in white, pressed with herbs, I saw that his back was bleeding from fresh shallow cuts. His wounds were something I had known all too well as a young slave in Egypt. Even as a boy after my mother's death, as the honored son of Onack the Great, I had publicly endured the lash from my own father's hands.

I stared at the would-be emperor. I didn't have to know *who* had given him those wounds; I knew what they meant, and in that moment, I saw myself—the part of me that I hated the most. He was unwanted, and he would suffer greatly for it. I had to know just how helpless he would be to fate's twisted plans for him, if his life would mirror my own, if he would become the monster he now set free back into the world.

It was only then that I'd started observing him.

At that time, I *needed* to turn someone; even in my stupor I'd been aware of that much. There was a pattern: around the time the new Vessel would arrive, or not long after, I would get this deep, unquenchable ache for company. I called it many things, but in truth, it was loneliness and despair.

Turning a new Second-Born temporarily kept me from acknowledging those erupting feelings. When they were first turned, they'd worship me. The adoration, the bond, it was unbreakable . . . for a while, at least. Even if the soothing was a placebo effect, their comfort would usually see me through for a decade or more. But with Bohe, because he was just a child, I had waited. And I had wanted to. A sick part of me needed to see what kind of man he would become.

It was the first time I had stalked someone I knew would one day be mine.

"Look at him, La-Narru." Caelius's voice grew impatient. "I've dolled him up for you; the least you can do is appreciate a pig wrapped in fine garments."

I bit my bottom lip and looked again at Bohe. His long black hair was looped delicately like the inside of a nautilus. Decorative sticks protruded in every direction, breaking the perfect Fibonacci sequence that had become his dark tresses. His face was powdered white, save for the red paint drawn on his lips and the pink blush painting the apples of his cheeks moving upward to dust black-lined eyes—eyes that implored me to do *something*, anything but lie there helplessly.

I pulled against the angelic chains. It was more of a gesture for Bohe, by now I knew it was useless. I'd thrashed while Caelius had ravaged my body in every position for months.

There was no escape from this for either of us.

My eyes traced over his petite frame. When he was alive, he had been more delicate than the men of his region, and the vampirism cast him even more profoundly in a feminine light. I focused on his minute hands, hands that were now trembling under Caelius's watchful gaze. It wasn't the first time I had utterly failed Bohe, but it might have been the last.

I strained further, trying to lean my torso up from the mattress. "He's dressed in a Hanfu? And he's wearing stage makeup." I feigned a sarcastic laugh. "What are you playing at?"

"Quiet!"

I could feel the energy surging off of Caelius like black waves flowing over my body.

"He looks like a doll like this, so I prefer it for my fantasy." He licked his lips and stood up. He walked slowly until his large towering frame stood behind Bohe. "You're going to do just as I asked, aren't you, little Liu Xie?" Bohe's face flushed, and he nodded in obedience.

"Don't!" I gritted my teeth. "Don't touch him!"

Caelius growled. The room trembled, and it vibrated the white sheet that had been carelessly covering my naked torso. Bohe eyed the bruises and bite marks littering my frame in horror.

"And what would you have me do instead, lover?" The room grew still as Caelius relished his handiwork.

"Let him go; feed off of me instead."

Bohe's eyes warmed. If he had been one of my Second-Borns who could cry, I might have seen it then.

Caelius's eyes, in contrast, were cold as stone. "I've already *tortured* you. Now I need something *more*." He paused. "What do you expect your little emperor to do? Should he fight me? Run? Beg?"

What would I ask from him? To resist Caelius like I always did? And for what, for my benefit?

I stared into his dark brown eyes. Bohe had suffered so much in his mortal life; his own mother had tried to abort him before she was poisoned. He'd been hated, tormented, and used. The more I had observed him, the more I had come to want him. But still I had waited.

Caelius eyed me as he looked down at Bohe. "You know, *Emperor*, he watched you. He let you be that warlord's puppy. He watched as you fled your captors only to be captured again and again. He watched until the end of the Han Dynasty was official, until you were forcibly made to give up your title. It was the only thing you had left at that time, if I recall. How many times did he stand by while someone more powerful made you *theirs*, to use as they needed? Now I'm giving you the chance to make him *yours*. To use him as *you* desire, little emperor. Aren't I kind?"

Bohe's eyes were pained as they looked down on me.

"It wasn't like that, Liu Xie!" I called in desperation.

"Oh, but it was," he whispered into Bohe's ear. Caelius's eyes met mine, but he left his lips where they were. "He thought he was being patient, letting you have your sad little mortal life before he gave you a new one, before he gave you bliss and eternity. All so that you would adore him. I understand—I made the same mistake. We are alike after all, aren't we, La-Narru?"

"I'm nothing like you!" I lunged forward. My wrists were already raw, but I pulled harder at the restraints. "I know what you're doing! You're trying to convince me, to show me how you feel through some twisted game of comparison!"

"Oh. Is that what I'm doing?" His hands fell idle at his sides.

My chest twisted. It was true. In the beginning I was watching, waiting to turn him when he was old enough. I was desperate and cruel at that time, but I had grown to care for Bohe. I had never been conflicted about turning someone until then.

"I didn't *want* to turn you!" I shouted.

He winced. With my words the hurt in Bohe's brown eyes seemed to cut even deeper.

"It's not that I didn't want you!" I reached out to him, but the shackles held me back, the white sheet finally falling to the floor as the chains clanged against the stone tiles. He had been unwanted his *whole* life.

I sneered, looking at Caelius. I was playing right into his hands, giving him the drama he longed for. "Bohe . . . before you, I turned Gracuri."

Caelius's head jerked back, the fury in him returning. "Even now you bring up *Gracuri*!" He spat out the name like a curse.

I ignored him, looking only to console Bohe. "I enjoyed

Gracuri's company, and our lazy walks by the river. We were friends before I turned him. And because of that affection and mutual respect, after he became a vampire, I left Gracuri to live out his life as if he hadn't been turned. As a mortal with power, he was a Greek god among men. The tales of his heroism mark history books, even today. We would meet, and I would bring him treasures from my travels, and he would tell me stories of his latest triumphs. But when I returned to Thebes . . . when he . . ."

"Yes, yes." Caelius laughed. "Though they don't call him *Gracuri* in the books, do they? Sophocles was too much of a coward to use his *real* name. But you can read about that little swine everywhere, can't you, La-Narru?" Caelius looked around the room, placing an exaggerated hand on his hip. "Where did I put that suit of his? I lost track of it after I stuck his head on a spike."

I pulled uselessly against the chains. Gracuri—*my* Gracuri—tortured and impaled by this *thing's* hands.

"Oedipus." Caelius turned and whispered into Bohe's ear. "What a tragic tale. A tale that should have ended there. You see, I commanded La-Narru to kill him for overexposing our kind, but he didn't *obey* me, and Gracuri suffered just as you will suffer, Bohe. All because he won't keep his promises."

"Why—" Bohe's voice was soft, and it carried with it the musical tone it had always had in youth.

"Go on, Duke of Shanyang," Caelius said. "Talk to your daddy."

Bohe swallowed, looking down at my chest, his eyes not meeting mine. That was the title he'd been given *after* he was finally dethroned. It was a polite title that carried with it all the weight of his defeat. "Lucian, what does Gracuri—"

"Oedipus. Let's call him by his historical name. Since La-Narru is so offended by such things, we should really stick to the history books from here on out, as fallible as they are. The history and titles of piglets are so important to La-Narru, aren't they, *Duke*?" he mocked, his gaze darkening further.

Bohe cleared his throat. "Yes. Of course, Grandfather. As you speak it."

I winced at hearing him say that word. Caelius was no grandfather, nor was I a father. All of this twisted dialogue around vampirism, all of this corruption, because Caelius was Darkness in human form but no better than a spoiled, ignorant child.

"Because of Oedipus . . . you didn't want me?" Bohe's voice was smaller than before. The way his tone shifted at the end—half question, half acceptance—was agony.

"No." I leaned back onto the bed, sighing. "Yes." I swallowed. "Because of Gracuri."

I hesitated. This was a memory I'd never wanted to return to. "He'd been pure and noble, even after he was turned. He refused to eat humans and survived on animals alone. And he laughed, laughed with the coming of dawn, laughed at the stars blinking in the night sky. He was an abandoned, starving orphan, and still, I thought there was nothing that could take the smile from his lips." How many years had I spent hiding from that smile, the memory of it, a ghost that I couldn't bear the sight of?

"He turned every misfortune and dark idea into a philosophical question that ended in the hope for a better future, not just for himself, but for all of mankind. He *believed* in the good in everything and everyone. He reminded me of Adnachiel in so many ways, but he would never betray me. He would never kill . . ." I paused. "The innocent." This was a painful conversation that wasn't meant to be had with Bohe, but with Gracuri himself. It was a conversation I had wanted to have a thousand times over, but I'd never had the courage to face myself, to face him.

And now it was too late.

"You didn't want me because you wanted someone like that angel who betrayed you? The one you loved so much, who was like a brother to you and Moses?" Bohe clenched his jaw, his small hands forming fists at his sides. It was a rare sight. Bohe had never been a fighter.

I blinked. He didn't understand what I was confessing to. "No, I . . ." Taking in another long breath, I damned my own lips. If it wasn't so painful, I could tell him quickly, but every word was like unearthing splinters hidden deep inside bone. The burden of my guilt was a heavy, ancient wooden box that I had packed away a long time ago, never intending to open.

Caelius had to be enjoying this. If he'd had his fill of causing me physical pain, then emotional pain was the next item on the menu, and using my own words to hurt Bohe only amplified my misery and added to his delight.

"I let Gracuri go. I traveled and put distance between us. We would meet every summer, once a year, by the river. We would talk and walk until nightfall, then I would leave again, even if he begged me not to. I thought I was protecting that smile I'd come to rely on. But he was still newly turned, and I was careless because he was dear to me, giving him the freedom I had once craved in Egypt, to live as he wanted to in Athens."

My jaw clenched. If only it had stayed that way. If his

honorable heart had been left intact, I could have visited him over the centuries and *never* turned another. His laugh would have given me the strength to hold on after every Vessel died and Aidan disappeared from existence. How ignorant and dangerous thoughts like that had been.

"It was my fault." My chest seized, and I could see the corners of Caelius's mouth start to rise in amusement. "Because Gracuri was a *vampire,* when he discovered that his wife was his biological *mother* and that he had killed his real *father* . . . had he been just a mortal, all those people wouldn't have died." I remembered the smell of it. How long had he been there by himself in that infected filth and decay before I'd arrived?

"He laid waste to the whole kingdom—children as well. You know it's something I forbid, the only rule I have for our kind, and he broke it a hundred times over. Their small bodies, twisted and broken." I cringed, wishing I could burn the image out of my mind.

"When I found him, he had gouged out his own eyes. His body was in a pool of dried blood surrounded by rotting corpses. He didn't feed on them, just butchered them, wasted in a fit of madness and rage. He cried and screamed and wailed for days without ceasing, refusing to be comforted. Every time his eyes grew back and he saw what he'd done, he would rip them out again." I'd never seen anyone mutilate themselves like that, over and over . . .

My body shook with the memory. I had loved him, and seeing him in a pool of red, his body growing thin from blood loss, starving and mad, his beautiful smile twisted in inconsolable grief . . .

"His agony and the sound of his wailing stay with me, even to this day. When the wind shrieks through empty streets, I can still hear it."

Nightmares.

I'd had my share of them after my mother died when I was mortal and actually slept. As a vampire, I was thankful we didn't sleep or dream, at first. But over time I realized that vampires dreamt in a different way. Our minds could act out memories in the dark–haunting echoes, regrets that followed us because our shadows did not.

"His screams . . ."

Bohe's soft hand reached for me, but Caelius grabbed it at the wrist. "Let's not interrupt such a fine memory, *Duke*."

I swallowed. Gracuri's eyes, crushed in his own hands . . . He'd been one of the rare children I'd made who could still cry. Even as an immortal whose tear ducts should have dried with the change, what twisted irony to make a boy that could only laugh, weep. "I consoled him for a long time."

"Just to be clear, I had sent La-Narru to kill him. But instead, he *consoled him for a long time*." Caelius's tone was like ice, the hand around Bohe's wrist tightening painfully.

"I finally persuaded him to live on and let his eyes grow back." I remembered his surrender to my coercion, his limp body falling into my arms, the light in his newly forming eyes, dull.

"He changed after that. He never again cared for human life, for anyone, other than me. And I . . ." This was that splintered box I hadn't wanted to open.

"Continue. Don't keep us in suspense," Caelius jeered.

My words creaked as Caelius forced open the lid. "I

abandoned him. I couldn't look at him the same, and he was so observant. He kept remarking on how my glances weren't like they used to be." I thought of my cutting words to him, how I hadn't known how to mend what I had broken. "Eventually, even I blamed him outright, calling him a monster. He moved around after that. It was a lonely life, I'm sure. I'd always meant to tell him that it wasn't his fault . . . to apologize. Instead I separated myself and made it seem like a punishment, but in reality, it was only I who had failed. The true reason I couldn't look at him the same wasn't because of what he'd done, but because I missed his smile. I missed who he'd been, and I couldn't rectify what I had turned him into. He was *never* to blame, *I* was. And now he's gone. He'll never laugh again, like he did by the river. I'd always hoped to hear it one more—"

"Boring." Caelius pushed Bohe's wrist behind him, into the small of his back, resting his chin on top of his head. "Who cares about that incestuous cow? We want to know how that relates to *us,* don't we, Bohe? We're jealous and tired of hearing about your love for that dead Greek tragedy. Does he even love you at all, Liu Xie?" Caelius twisted Bohe's wrist further. "It's always someone *else* he talks about, isn't it? The Vessel, the angel, Gracuri, Nefertiti, blah, blah, blah. When is it *our* turn?" he growled, and for a moment Bohe did too before he caught himself.

His face reddened with embarrassment, and Caelius smiled. "Did I hit the nail on the head, Duke of Shanyang?"

"Caelius, stop!" I smacked the chains just for the sound, to draw Bohe's attention to *my* words and not his. "I was afraid to turn *anyone* after that, even though I still craved it for my own selfish reasons. I thought, 'What will become of him if I turn him now?' I didn't want to *ruin* you like I had ruined him. Gracuri was a *good* man with a lion's heart, and he was *never* the same. Without all of that blind power, he could have remained an orphan and happy, smiling by the river, a mortal who would have lived and died with the laugh of life still inside of him!"

My lungs squeezed. Every time I remembered his laugh, it felt like a knot in the center of my chest was pounding against that buried box of guilt, and I couldn't breathe. "After he gouged out his own eyes, I felt responsible for him in a way I wasn't responsible for any other child prior. I still feel responsible, even now. His death hasn't changed that."

"Us! We don't care about your regrets! You should have listened to me and killed that fake-smiling swine!" Caelius's nails grew, and the tips left indents in Bohe's skin that pooled with blood.

"Gracuri's the real reason I watched you, Bohe! That's what I'm saying!"

Caelius relaxed. "Finally. Out with it, boy."

"I was afraid to do anything that would change the course of your life, afraid to turn you and ruin your light. But after you gave up your role as emperor, after your final submission, you fell ill. The doctors in that region were barbaric and ignorant. I killed them after they covered you in leeches. I tried to mend you with the herbalism of my own people and what I'd learned through my travels. Nothing worked, and your body grew still and cold, your breath rattling in a cage of ribs, like your soul was trying to claw its way out of your body forever."

I looked at his full lips. They were now painted red, but then they had been blue and dry. "In the end, I couldn't lose you. I gave into my selfishness, hoping it would be different." I reached for him but couldn't touch the cheeks I had stroked then. "And it was. You were not Gracuri. Bohe, you are beautiful and unique. Because of you, I turned others. I was able to move forward for another century. The regret I now feel for turning all of you is because of Caelius's blood and torment, not because of who you *are*. I have always been proud of the man you became, Liu Xie. I have *always* wanted you."

"I have always wanted you." Caelius chuckled miserably to himself. "You so easily say the words I long for to this worthless dynasty boy." A chill ran through the room as he laughed. "Unbelievable." He ran a hand through his hair. "That whole story, just so you could prove he was worthwhile. You care for him that much."

I swallowed hard. Caelius's tone was not bemused. It was angry. My eyes left him and jerked to Bohe. I was surprised to see Liu Xie's face looking elated. His body sagged in relief, even as Caelius's hands held him firmly in place.

"I'm glad, Father," Bohe said quickly.

His words were lost under the growl of Caelius's heavy voice. "Don't flatter yourself, *Duke*. He's good with words, but he's terrible at following through."

My mouth fell open, but I was silent.

This was not the time to provoke him.

Caelius relished my silence, and for a moment I could see his old spark return, the pleasure in my agony. "*In the end, I couldn't lose you*. How poetic, La-Narru, almost like you were in childhood. Perhaps if I had spouted those same words you would have forgiven me like you are expecting this doll to forgive you now. As if forgiveness means anything."

He laughed, looking toward the ceiling. "He watched you suffer all those years, *Duke*. Just like I watched him become a slave in Egypt. He thinks me cruel, but we are the same. And I do not need his forgiveness, and you won't pardon him so easily, will you?" he jeered. "The Light speaks often of forgiveness. I still think it's meaningless, but your fragile kind clings to it so desperately. I wonder why. Is it mortals who forgive? Is it because you're weak? Or is it because you're desperate?"

Caelius grew the nail on his index finger and traced the sharp tip of it down the red paint on Bohe's lips, cutting a deeper red into it. "Say it then, doll. Say it for Gracuri and *all* his children who never had the chance. If my lover needs to hear it so badly, let's have you appease him this one time, for me." Caelius tightened his grip around Bohe's arm, and he flinched from the pain.

"Don't say a word, Bohe. You don't have to do anything to appease me. I've never been your master. I've never done to you what those throne-stealing bastards did, and I won't now. You're not my puppet. Hate me if you like. Just . . ."

Escape. Just get away from here, and I'll handle Caelius.

I pulled on the chains again.

I had said a million things in an attempt to provoke Caelius after he had discovered my betrayal, useless words that had fallen flat on the ears of Darkness. There was nothing I could say or do now that I hadn't already. What did I have left to give?

I took a deep breath. "I'm sorry, Bohe. I'm sorry that I turned you and now you're in the hands of a warlord worse than any you experienced in China." I couldn't meet his gaze. All of this failure was stacking on top of me and crushing my will to fight.

"Good boy, La-Narru. Knowing when you're beaten is the first part of the process when you're breaking a pet." Caelius yanked the Hanfu down so that Bohe's shoulder was exposed. I looked at the deep teeth marks. Caelius had already fed on him, which meant most of his mind wasn't his own anymore.

I let out an exasperated sigh. "Nothing I said matters now."

"Nope!" Caelius laughed jovially to himself. "He's already mine. I have been beating and feeding on the emperor, and trust me, what little willpower there was in this doll is no more."

He pulled the large sash in front of Liu Xie, untying the knot. "Isn't that right, puppet?" Bohe's lips tightened, and he nodded. The yellow sash slipped to the floor. "I don't know why you would use these *things* to console yourself, La-Narru. My grief was inconsolable after I found out you'd lied to me, and breaking him brought me no pleasure whatsoever."

"I'm going to destroy Paris this weekend. Shea ruined my lovemaking, so I'm going to ruin the memory of yours. But I don't want my precious La-Narru to get bored in my absence. Today I will watch, but tomorrow and the next I will leave you alone with him, and he may do as he pleases." He grabbed the back of Bohe's neck. "You are going to spend the next three days with my precious La-Narru. But you're not to take a drop of his blood, do you understand?"

"Caelius!" My mouth dropped open. "Don't! Isn't it better to have a powerful, willing vampire at your side? You could accomplish so much more with a brilliant strategist like Bohe. Don't abuse him, and he'll be loyal. You'll have an invaluable asset, just don't make him do what those generals used to—"

"What is this concern for *my* safety? As if I need a strategist when I myself am a master at the craft." Caelius smiled. "What, you'd prefer your son sacrifice his pride rather than have him take yours?" He shoved Bohe by the neck so that his face was inches from mine. "No such luck. Enjoy how done up he is for you. Enjoy his little chubby cheeks because in a moment his actions will erase every sweet memory held between you. And I'm going to watch. I think I will quite enjoy watching this doll play with you."

Remorse filled Bohe's gaze as much as it echoed in my own. There was nothing I could say, and I knew how this would end. Still he waited, as if I could give him the words he needed to hear. I should have said, "Caelius will hurt you anyway; you don't have to do anything he says. Run, fight, but don't obey." It was true, and we both knew it. But I couldn't give up on Bohe now, just like I couldn't all those years ago when he'd fallen ill in China. I still wanted him alive, and if obeying Caelius meant that he could live, then I didn't care what he did to me. Even if he became loyal to Caelius, even if I never saw him again, it would be enough if I knew he was *alive*. All these years, just knowing he was out there in the mountains—studying, drinking tea, living in peace—had brought me some comfort during long nights when I feared insanity would take me.

Even now, I still couldn't lose him.

"See how selfish your maker is, even after his flowery words of confession? He has nothing to say to you now that you're the one in a position of power," Caelius said. "Remember that in the days of my absence."

I looked at the tension running through Bohe's body, the

terror every time Caelius spoke. I hated seeing it: his obedience to the now-reigning warlord. It was an old wound, and Caelius was exploiting Liu Xie's traumatic childhood, using him like he had been used his entire life as a mortal. After I turned him, he'd made me promise that I'd never let anyone make him a puppet again, that even I would resist the temptation.

And I had kept that promise, until today.

I looked at the fear in his dry eyes. "I never wanted this for you, Bohe."

Caelius pulled the chair from the corner of the room closer so that it was right next to the bed and sat down. "How sweet." He wet his mouth as his eyes took in my helpless exposed frame. "Now, now, *little emperor*, dance for me like the marionette you are."

CHAPTER 3
SHEA

I sighed a breath of relief as everyone's attention turned to Duncan and Helena. Nefertiti had been pretty set on putting together some kind of kamikaze rescue mission that would have most certainly ended in our deaths and me getting my soul sucked. What would that even feel like, anyway? I really didn't want to find out.

Duncan nodded to me, and suddenly I was the center of attention again. "Gracuri told me to stay away from ye since ye were Lucian's. Ye have to be pretty special to make him kill an entire line of vampires just to prove a point. I'm sorry, the last time we met, I was being killed myself." Duncan laughed.

And I found that I instantly liked him.

He reminded me of Aidan, with his warm smile and pleasant demeanor. Thinking about it, Lucian had probably turned Duncan for that very reason. I'd realized pretty quickly that Aidan and Lucian's bromance might even rival the love Lucian and I had for each other. It made a kind of odd sense that he'd turn a guy who reminded him of Aidan. And now that Duncan was talking a bit more, I found it much easier to understand his accent.

"I didn't realize Caelius had been controlling me until *after* the necklace had been used." Helena broke my train of thought with her remorseful tone. "I got all my memories back at once. Somehow I was able to rig the necklace to power him up without stripping Shea of her soul, though I have no idea how I managed that."

Nefertiti answered for her. "Because you have the strongest mind of anyone I've ever known." She walked up to Helena and placed a hand on her arm in support. It was very unlike her; she wasn't exactly the touchy type. Or was she? The more I thought about it, the more I realized that I didn't really know Nefertiti or any of her children. I knew Aidan, but I was still in the dark about his past lives. So really, all I had was *Dad*. But now that he was a vampire and had almost eaten me when I'd had accidentally cut myself on a rusty nail, I felt like I couldn't really trust anyone.

I didn't even know if I could trust Lucian. That thought scared me more than anything.

Helena looked relieved at Nefertiti's touch and continued. "I appreciate it, but I wish I could have done more. Caelius knew what we were doing, and I wasn't aware of it, even though I was *living it* side by side with the devil himself muddling my brain." Her eyes were haunted, then she focused on Duncan. "I went back to Lucian's prison, trying to find anything that might help us, and that's when I saw him. His body should have been desiccated, but he still looked alive. When I went over to him,

I realized that Caelius's blood had touched his lip. It must have fallen in when Lucian was crying, some of the splatter washing off into his open mouth. I had no idea his blood was powerful enough to do that."

Duncan chimed in. "It brought me back te life, but I had a wee crush on ma grandfather because of the stuff."

Helena nodded. "Thinking about it rationally, I now realize that it's possible. Caelius's blood is what gives vampires life, whether it's a drop or a hundredth of a drop. Duncan had just enough to bring him back and to be loyal to Caelius."

"And now?" I asked, suddenly worried about these two.

"Duncan was still weak, so I was able to chain him down," Helena replied. "It took a few days, and luckily it was just a tiny drop of Caelius's blood. I gave him an entire hospital's shipment of blood bags to clear his head. Now he no longer feels an obsession for *evil incarnate*."

Shrugging, Helena added, "I didn't know I was being controlled. Now that Lucian has been taken by Caelius because of my failure, I just . . ."

I felt the need to intercede. "You saved my *soul*. I'll always be grateful for that."

Nefertiti's eyes were distant as she said, "We all know how strong Caelius's blood compulsion is. He's made us do things we never thought possible, and he's erased memories we never thought he could."

Whoa.

That sounded like drama I wasn't sure I wanted to hear or not. I didn't need to be reminded how evil Caelius was, but I still needed to know what I was up against.

Before I could form a question, Duncan said, "Whatever we decide we should do, we need to do it quickly. Have ye seen what Caelius and his little army have done to Paris?"

Gulp.

Paris?

Aidan walked over to a small boxy television resting on an end table and switched it on. The TV was black-and-white and should have been in a museum. When there was nothing but fuzz, Dad joined Aidan's side and pulled up two metal antennas to get a local signal. I thought they were called rabbit ears, but I couldn't remember. I'd only seen old TVs like this on . . . TV. After some serious finagling and turning a knob a few times to go through the stations, a news channel finally came in clear.

My heart thudded in my chest.

The footage we all stared at was terrifying. It looked as though Paris had been hit by a nuclear bomb. Destroyed cobblestone, bricks, and broken glass littered the ground. Not even the Eiffel Tower stood; it was just a twisted heap of metal that had been bent into a million different shapes. The strength it must have taken to literally destroy every building in Paris astounded me. If this was Caelius at half power, then I didn't want to imagine what he'd be like at full power.

I could barely hear the anchorman as he listed the number of fatalities, which currently was over . . .

A million.

People.

Dead.

I couldn't breathe.

I was having a panic attack.

I'd had them before, but recognizing what it was didn't help me break out of it.

I felt like I was dying.

Strong arms held me up as I crumbled to my knees. Aidan's voice was soothing and strong as he said, "Shea, are you okay?"

No, I was not okay. None of us were okay with Caelius out there. He was going to destroy the world, and I wasn't sure if we could stop him. I wanted to say all of these things, but my voice wasn't working.

Through my panicked haze, my eyes focused on the television, and suddenly Caelius's evil grin was there, laughing as he stood on a pile of dead bodies while thousands of bullets bounced off his skin. A tank, a bazooka, a grenade—all attacked him, but he stood unmoved, only laughing harder, calling the humans ants.

The anchorman was scared out of his mind. "We don't know what he—what *it* is. But it can't be stopped!"

My dad switched off the TV, and no one argued.

Without the horrors of what had happened in Paris playing, I was able to breathe again. Aidan's arms never left me. He was my set of human crutches.

"I didn't see Lucian or Sete in that newsreel," Nefertiti said with a tinge of hope.

My dad lashed out at her. "But Molly was right there with him! We just saw her kill thousands with her bare hands!"

I hadn't seen that. I wanted to vomit. I still couldn't speak. This wasn't happening. This wasn't my life. It was a nightmare I needed to wake up from.

I pushed away from Aidan and finally found my voice. "Caelius picked Paris because of me, because that's where Lucian and I were, together, after Caelius escaped. We were happy there."

Meky crossed her arms. "Caelius is nothing if not predictable."

Nefertiti directed her words toward me. "He must know by now that the necklace didn't drain your soul, and Lucian can't truly hide how he feels for long. Caelius will see through him, and when he does . . ."

"Caelius won't compete with you, Shea," Ur-Nammu said. "He'll simply erase you from Lucian's memories."

My mind came into focus at that.

"What?"

Then Nefertiti stood before me, her expression oddly soft. "Caelius's blood compulsion was powerful before he was released from his prison, but now? He's probably shoving his blood down Lucian's throat. Caelius will be able to create any memory he wants, and Lucian isn't strong enough to fight it."

"Lucian is stronger than any of us!" I was immediately defensive. "He can fight it! He won't fall for Caelius's lies!"

Nefertiti, Ur-Nammu, and Meky all shared a look of . . . what? It was as if they were remembering something.

It only made me angrier. "What?"

"Shea, Caelius has done this to Lucian before, and he never remembered what Caelius compelled him to forget." Meky's tone was kind, but it didn't help soften the blow.

"It's true," Nefertiti said with absolution.

"Don't even try it." My defensiveness knew no bounds. "I know you're about to say something like he compelled Lucian to forget his love for Nefertiti or something stupid like that, which is bull-crap. He completely confided in me that he loved you. It's obvious the way you two look at each other . . ." What was I saying? I was so scared of Caelius erasing me from Lucian's brain that I was arguing a case for Nefertiti to be with him again? All of this was making my head spin.

Nefertiti held my arms until our eyes met. "Shea, listen to me." When she was sure I was paying attention, she continued. "Lucian never forgot our past, that is true, but Caelius never wanted him to. Caelius did make him forget that we *reunited* once, a thousand years ago."

"Maybe Lucian did remember," I said weakly, but I knew it wasn't true. If Lucian had thought for an instant that Nefertiti and her children were still alive, he'd have searched for them until the end of time. He never would have given me a second thought. Finally, I asked, "Why did Caelius make Lucian forget? I thought he wanted you two to be his Adam and Eve or something." My chest and heart ached. I didn't even know why I was asking the question.

Meky stepped in. "It was my fault, really."

Aidan shook his head. "No, it was mine."

Nefertiti rolled her eyes with annoyance and pulled her hands away from my arms. "It was Lucian's fault, and his alone." She eyed Meky. "He beat you to a pulp! If he had decapitated you, you really would have died!"

The realization hit me: the Gunnhild Viking era, when Aidan and Meky had fallen in love. Lucian had "killed" Aidan's lover to hurt him, not knowing that it was Meky and that she couldn't be killed by normal means.

Nefertiti almost growled at the memory. "I was furious. The deal I made with Caelius was that my family would keep to the shadows in exchange for his protection, but when Meky almost died? Even he couldn't stop me from confronting Lucian. In Egypt Lucian had made a Gutian vow that he would protect my daughters' lives even if it meant losing his own. And he put hands on Meky? His favorite! Beating her for the sake of hurting"—she nodded disdainfully at Aidan—"*him*?"

Yeah. That would piss me off too. I was about to ask Nefertiti how the confrontation went, but I was pretty sure I knew already. Lucian would have been devastated. "He never would have forgiven himself, so Caelius wiped the memory of you confronting him," I guessed aloud.

Nefertiti nodded. "Caelius only wanted our reunion to happen when he was *freed* from his cage, so he sent Ur-Nammu with his blood and compelled Lucian to forget. Caelius still let Lucian hold on to the memory of killing Meky because he was happy that the act of hurting an angel brought Lucian so much joy." She barely glanced at Aidan. "He really felt betrayed by you."

Aidan didn't argue.

No one did.

"So not once did he remember seeing you?" I just couldn't believe that Lucian's brain wouldn't remember *Nefertiti*. He had loved her so much. I was still jealous of their history, of what they had. I was feeling so insecure.

When Nefertiti shook her head, confirming that Caelius had succeeded at wiping out that memory of her, I knew with certainty that if Caelius used his blood to compel Lucian to forget me, it would succeed. We had only been together about a year—what was that when Lucian had been pining over Nefertiti for thousands? I was a blip. She was eternal. If he forgot her, he'd most definitely forget me.

The pain was too much to bear.

Leaving the small group of vampires and an angel, I walked over to one of the couches and sat. Millions of people were dead because Caelius was jealous of my relationship with Lucian. Of course he'd compel me from his brain! Why wouldn't he?

If he could erase me, then Lucian would be *all his*.

Surprisingly, it was Duncan who sat next to me. "I know I should be leavin' ye to your thoughts, but I have to tell ye, Lucian's heart is strong, stronger than I've ever seen. Try to have some faith even if it's none ye see."

It didn't help a lot, but it did help. "Thanks, Duncan."

"We're going to be good friends. I can see it already." Duncan's crooked smile was small, but it was genuine.

And weirdly, I felt the same way.

"Besides," he said, "let's figure out a way to get him back so ye won't be worryin' about the possibilities that may or may not happen."

Feeling a surge of hope, I slowly nodded my head. He was right. The fact that Lucian wasn't in any of the footage indicated that he wasn't Caelius's lapdog yet, which meant he was still Lucian and we could save him.

Nefertiti's plan of blindly breaking in suddenly seemed a lot more appealing.

"Now what is this plan of yours?" Ur-Nammu asked Helena. "You want Duncan to go in as a spy?"

Duncan whispered in my ear, "They're talkin' about me when I'm sittin' right here. Something yeer used to, I suspect?"

"Considering I'm the Vessel, yeah. It's my soul on the line, and everyone wants to make decisions for me, but all I want to do is get Lucian and my mom back." I didn't know why it was so easy to open up to Duncan. Maybe it was because I didn't know him. He couldn't judge or tell me what to do. Or maybe it was because he was just a nice guy that genuinely wanted to listen. Either way, I appreciated his company.

"For it's a man, he spoke. I told him not to," Helena suddenly said, a surprised expression on her face.

Duncan and I exchanged confused glances as Helena continued to spout gibberish.

Goose bumps instinctively rose on my arms.

Duncan noticed and stood. "Trouble," he said.

I nodded and stood up with him.

We both walked over to the group. As we approached, I could see Helena's eyes darting back and forth as if she were caged inside her own body. Then she said, "He will to for a name. I found the her for you."

Nefertiti placed her hand on Helena's arm. "Helena. Breathe deep. What's happening?"

Ur-Nammu said, "I'll Dream-Walk inside her mind. Maybe I can see what's going on."

Helena pulled away from Nefertiti with a jerk, her eyes still wild. "For to me a child."

Ur-Nammu's eyes closed, and I knew he was astral projecting inside Helena's head.

Helena's eyes stopped moving when they suddenly focused on me, but it was almost as if it wasn't her. She went from terrified to . . . furious. Helena stared at me with a hatred that radiated off her body.

Quicker than I could follow, Helena ran the distance between us and pinned me to the ground. Sharp fangs pierced my neck as she drank deep and fast. Aidan and six powerful vampires tried to rip her off of me, but she was like a pit bull, jaws clamped down and not budging.

I was losing consciousness, but I had to make my blood liquid sunshine as I had in the past. It required a lot of concentration, which I didn't have.

I grew weaker by the second.

Was this how I was going to die? I couldn't seem to summon the Light inside of me. I kept reaching for it, but it was just out of my grasp. I called out to Lucian in my head, knowing full well he couldn't hear me, but I wanted my last thoughts to be of him. Then maybe he'd know I was with him, that I loved him and that our souls would always be connected.

For just a second, I thought I heard him call back.

Even if it was just my imagination, it somehow gave me strength. I connected to the Light inside me as if it were the easiest thing in the world. I filled every blood cell in my body with the pure Light of a Vessel.

Helena screamed as she pulled her teeth out of my neck. It was enough for the others to drag her free of me completely. I sat up, gasping for air, suddenly realizing that Helena's body had been pressing so hard on my chest that I hadn't been breathing.

Nefertiti took charge of the attack, being the warrior queen that she was. The others circled Helena like backup bodyguards, giving Nefertiti the space to attack Helena fully. But I could see by the way Nefertiti held Helena's arms down that she wasn't trying to hurt her; she was trying to snap her out of whatever had caused her to attack in the first place.

"When I Dream-Walked, I saw nothing but black!" Ur-Nammu shouted over the commotion.

We had underestimated Caelius's mind control.

He'd left some kind of brain-bomb in Helena, making her attack me. The gibberish had probably been Helena trying to fight it. It made me realize just how strong-minded Helena truly was. I wished that I could fix her, that I could take away any kind of control Caelius still had on her. If I could fix her, then I could fix Lucian if I needed to.

Helena tried desperately to gain her freedom, her eyes still focused on me. But Nefertiti was Helena's maker, and the longer she held Helena down, the weaker she seemed to become.

"Helena, listen to my voice," Nefertiti commanded. "You are safe. You are free from Caelius."

At the mention of his name, Helena thrashed, but Nefertiti's hands might as well have been iron.

"Helena!" Nefertiti boomed.

The sound of her name jolted Helena to tear her head away from staring me down, and she looked up at Nefertiti.

In a voice just above a whisper, Helena pleaded, "Nefertiti, please . . ."

It hurt my soul in a way I couldn't describe. I could see the terror in Helena's eyes; she had no control over her body or mind.

I had to try *something*.

Knowing I might aggravate Helena more, I crawled toward her anyway. Her eyes glossed over with rage again, and she renewed her struggle to break free. Aidan and the wall of vampires blocked me from her.

"Shea, get out of here!" Aidan cried out.

At this point, Helena was a rabid dog that no one wanted to put down, but the situation was growing dire enough that I suspected everyone was considering it.

"I can help!" I yelled back, not knowing if it was true or not. The Light had healed Lucian's wounds when he'd been burned to a crisp by the sundial in Egypt. I had to see if I could heal Helena's brain. It was worth a try.

Aidan moved aside, and I felt a wave of love for my best friend. He trusted me, even if he shouldn't. I crawled past him and touched Helena's leg to form a connection with her. Helena shrieked in a kind of crazed glee at being so close to me, and Nefertiti looked downright pissed at me for being there.

"Do what you're going to do!" Nefertiti screamed. "Just do it fast! She gets stronger when she's near you!"

No pressure.

Closing my eyes and Dream-Walking inside Helena's mind, I could instantly feel that Nefertiti was right. Caelius had made it so Helena would grow in strength when near me, which explained why no one had been able to pull her off of me before. How he could do that, I had no idea. I just needed to find Caelius inside her. It wasn't his blood though, like Nefertiti had suggested. I could feel that right away. It was something *else*.

A shadow with . . . instructions?

There were words and thoughts burned into a black mass floating through Helena's entire body, constantly moving so it would stay active and impossible to eradicate.

But I was made from the Light.

And Light casts out shadow.

I mentally chased it while hearing Helena scream viciously

on the outside. That was when I knew: she wasn't screaming—it was the shadow, knowing I was coming for it. It was crazy racing through her body. It felt like a movie I'd watched in middle school where a scientist had found a way to shrink and travel through blood vessels. I was able to go everywhere, through her heart, lungs, arms, and legs. It was like a crash course on the internal workings of the human body, except I was chasing something dark, something evil . . . and it was terrifying. The banshee shrieks alone made me want to run away, but I knew the only way to help Helena was to track Caelius's shadow and annihilate it.

Using all the strength I could muster, I mentally leapt toward the shadow and grabbed it, infusing it with Light. I could feel my hand on Helena's leg heat up to the point where I thought it was on fire. It burned badly, but I kept holding on, pushing my Light into Helena and surrounding the cloud of darkness that was Caelius's mind control.

My ears rang from Helena's intense cries, but it was working. I could feel it.

Whoosh!

And just like that, it was gone.

I searched her body one last time, but there was nothing, no darkness.

Opening my eyes, I noticed that Helena had stopped screaming. Nefertiti held her in her arms, and Helena desperately clung to her. I pulled my hand off Helena's leg, and we both let out a grunt of exhaustion. A perfect gooey handprint was on her calf, and it looked *nasty*. She dug her head in and cried in Nefertiti's arms.

Aidan waved his hand over mine, and my pain was instantly gone. Shaking his head at Helena, he said, "The Light inside me will only burn you more. You'll have to heal with blood."

Helena didn't seem upset by this at all. She just looked relieved to be herself again.

Nefertiti let Helena use her body for support as she stood up. Meky stayed a step behind in case she fell. Helena hobbled weakly toward me. "Is it gone? Can Caelius take me over again?" Her expression was terrified.

I shook my head. "No. I saw what he used to control you, and I chased it away. I didn't see anything else."

Relief flooded every feature on Helena's beautiful face. "Thank you, Shea. I owe you."

Then I threw it out there. "Maybe I could do the same with Lucian if Caelius mind-controls him?"

The look in Nefertiti's eyes made my heart squeeze with disappointment. Shaking her head sadly, Nefertiti said, "Caelius will control him with his *blood*." Then she said with slight hope, "But if Caelius uses both blood *and* his shadow, then yes, you may be able to break one at least. It could mean the difference between life and death for him."

"It's too late for Lucian," a familiar voice said, making my heart stop.

Mom.

I turned around to see Molly Harper, my mother, holding a small box in her hands.

She stood about twenty feet away. There was something different about her. She looked . . . sad? I couldn't tell. She was so unlike the mother I knew and loved. When her eyes met mine, there was no recognition. They were just empty and horrifying to look at.

Then her attention turned to Dad. "Hello, Jeff." Her voice was thick and pained. "Are you ready to come with me yet?" It was almost a plea, and my heart ached for her. Even if she couldn't remember me, she remembered Dad and loved him deeply.

Dad stood next to me, placing his hand on my shoulder, and said, "I'll never leave *our* daughter."

"She's *not* our daughter!" she screamed, shaking her head as if warding away some kind of evil.

Aidan stepped toward her. "Molly, let me give you back your memories—"

"Take one step toward me and I'll be gone before your next breath!" Mom's eyes darted toward me. I wished Aidan could leap across the room and fix this, but she could fly like Lucian and Nefertiti, so it was useless to even try.

It took a moment for Mom to compose herself, but once she did, her face turned sad again. "Lucian felt the Vessel's presence moments ago, and that's how we found you. Grandfather likes the chase, so you'd better run far and fast because he's going to come here next." Then she tossed the box at Nefertiti's feet, her tone colored with even more sadness. "You're to come with me, Nefertiti. Grandfather sent that as an incentive."

Nefertiti tried to hide the terror from her features, but I could tell she was scared to open that box. Ur-Nammu, Sherit, and Meky stood rooted as well, knowing that whatever was in there would most likely devastate them too.

Kneeling down, Nefertiti slowly pulled back the lid.

Her daughter Merytaten's severed head lay inside. Caelius had killed her in their last battle, and her flesh had already decayed to the point of seeing the skull beneath.

"You're a mother!" Nefertiti hissed at Molly. "How could you do something like this?"

Molly stood silent. It almost seemed like Nefertiti's words had broken her. She wasn't yelling that she wasn't a mother. If she was struggling like this, maybe she could fight Caelius's compulsion. Maybe she could remember . . . me.

After what seemed like an eternity of silence, Mom finally spoke in a monotone voice. "I'm sorry for your loss, but Grandfather says it's time to make a new deal if you want to protect the daughters you have left."

"Why did Caelius send *you*?" I asked before Nefertiti could respond.

Molly paused, unsure, then said, "Caelius wants to torture you. He despises the Vessel."

The fact that she paused gave me hope. I took a step forward. "If you truly believe you're not my mother, then how would seeing you be torture for me?" I tried to reach her with logic, then a thought suddenly occurred to me. "And if Caelius really wanted to torture me, why wouldn't he torture me through Dream-Walking? I have no defenses when I'm asleep."

I had a theory that had been rolling around in my head for a while now, and I hoped my mother would be able to confirm it. It was a conversation I'd had with Nefertiti, when she told me that she had Dream-Walked with Gracuri to keep him and the last of Lucian's Second-Borns hidden. She had been cryptic and careful during her Dream-Walks, but she expressed her doubts about Caelius having the ability. I knew she, as a warrior, could never fully trust that it might be true. It would leave her too vulnerable. But the more I thought about it, the more I felt that Caelius would have gone straight for Gracuri and probably tortured Nefertiti for trying to hide him in the first place. But Caelius never brought it up.

I reiterated what I had said before, trying to reach that part of her that remembered she was my mother. "With Dream-Walking, Caelius could torture me as long as he wanted, never allowing me to wake. I'd be in torment forever."

Molly stood there for a long while, staring at me.

"He won't hurt you. Grandfather is kind," Molly said, unsure.

"Of course he will. He wants to take my soul. He wants to kill me." Then I pushed further. "All he'd have to do is Dream-Walk with me, and he'd be able to control me to do anything he wanted."

Molly shook her head. "No, Caelius can't compel you because of your Light, and he can't Dream-Walk. Darkness can't *create*, and walking through dreams is building a true connection with someone and the scenery and . . . it's not just about control, it's . . ." She trailed off, talking as if in a daze.

I was in shock that not only was I right, but that I had gotten my mother to admit it.

If Caelius couldn't Dream-Walk, then we had an open line of communication with no fear of Caelius listening in.

This was huge.

I exchanged looks with Nefertiti and Ur-Nammu. They were trying to hide their surprise from Molly.

Then her eyes cleared. "I don't know why I told you that."

"You told her because you trust her." Dad stepped forward.

"Because she's *ours*."

A flash of emotion illuminated Mom's eyes. There was definitely something there.

My heart squeezed.

But the moment erased itself as soon as it had come, as if she'd been fighting some inner battle and had lost. She nodded toward Merytaten's head with true sympathy and said, "We should leave before he kills any more of your family."

There was a moment where nobody moved.

Then finally Nefertiti set the small box down and walked toward Molly.

Ur-Nammu held her back. "Please, you can't go. Caelius will kill you."

Nefertiti shrugged him off. "Then he'll kill me. As long as my daughters are safe, I don't care. It is our code, after all."

Ur-Nammu had no argument. He knew that, to her, only her daughters mattered.

As she reached my mom's side, she said, "Let's go."

Before they left, Nefertiti stared at me. She was giving me a message. Helena's original plan had been to have Duncan act as a double agent, but Nefertiti was going instead.

She was going in.

And she was coming back with information, or she would die trying.

CHAPTER 4
LUCIAN

Bohe took the blade Caelius gave him and hovered over my torso, biting his bottom lip.

It was painful to watch, but I couldn't take my eyes off him. Sweat covered his supple skin, and every muscle was taut. He was trying to resist, as if a force, and not his own compulsion, was pressing his hand down.

His arms trembled as he finally stopped. "I'm sorry, Lucian. I defied him for days, but I–I'm not myself. I'm not strong like you are."

My eyes squinted as I felt the knife on my throat. "Liu Xie, you are one of the strongest people I know. This doesn't change that."

"You'll hate me after. What he wants me to do to you—"

"It's all right." I tried to make my tone comforting. "He's already done the worst to me himself." From the corner of the room, I could see a faint smile cover Caelius's lips from the sentiment. "Whatever you do, Bohe, it's already forgiven."

"It's so important to your creations, isn't it, Light? This *forgiveness*. How childish," Caelius taunted.

Bohe clenched his teeth as his breath hitched, and he finally met my gaze. "Even with your forgiveness, it's painful to hurt the one I love. I won't forgive myself as readily. I know I have no right to ask, but please, remember me like I was before." He closed his eyes, and so did I.

Like he was before . . .

I thought of the days that passed in China, of our long conversations over tea. The smell of his skin had always brought me comfort. Now the delicate fragrance of *Camellia sinensis*, however, was overwritten with the strong scent of fear. It was like a lotus pulled back down into the muddy pond that had birthed it. I sighed. Bohe—who had kept his delicate light, even when subjugated by warlords—was drowning in the mirth of Caelius's darkness.

And I was helpless to save him.

All I could do now was honor his request and remember him like he was before.

I felt rough skin on my lips.

Rough and cold.

It was strange. He had always been so soft to touch.

He didn't move, as if frozen in place, embracing me one last time as he had done the night I turned him.

Then the texture on my lips struck a disgusting chord of familiarity.

They weren't lips pressed to mine.

My eyes flew open.

Caelius's hand was between our mouths, his irises ablaze like fire. My eyes darted back and forth from Caelius to Bohe. He pulled his lips from Caelius's palm in shock. I jerked my head away from his hand and yelled, "Bohe, run!"

"Grandfather, what's going on? I thought before I cut him, I could say goodbye in my fashion—"

Caelius pulled him back by his hair.

I knew that look. "Caelius, don't! It was nothing! He'll only do what *you* ask from now on! He's loyal, you can keep him alive, he'll tortue me, he'll serve you and I—"

He elongated his nail and slit Bohe's throat.

Blood rained down over our bodies.

My mind froze in horror.

Liu Xie gagged for breath, his hands desperately grabbing his throat, trying to close the gash. Caelius wrenched them away, pulling the yellow sash from the floor. He ripped it into four pieces and tied Bohe's arms and legs to my own. "Now, now— stay in place, or I'll tear off your arms next."

His slick red chest convulsed as he writhed on top of me. "Bohe! Hang on! It's okay, it's just pain, your body will heal! It will pass!" I looked up at Caelius brimming with hate. "You monster!"

Caelius's hands balled into fists as he looked at the two of us. "He'll heal, the pain will pass? That's a problem, isn't it, darling?" He pulled a bone from his pocket and shoved it in the open wound at Bohe's neck. "Problem solved."

I lashed out, the chains shaking both of our bodies, trying to loosen his knots so that he could move his hands. "You crazy bastard, let him go! He was doing what *you* wanted!"

Caelius reached down, running a hand through my hair. "That's *angel* bone, boy. He won't heal. Your body will be his immortal grave. How romantic."

Bohe's frame jerked, his head thrashing as more blood spilled over us. I could feel the hard pounding of his heart, its erratic rhythm in time with mine. "Please, Caelius! What do you want? I'll give you—"

"You."

My mouth fell open. Bohe wheezed, his torso trying to push away from my blood-soaked chest, but the knots were too tight, and he was weak.

"Fine! Have me! Have whatever you want! Just let him go," I begged.

Now the hand in my hair gripped into a fist as he tilted my chin up. With his other hand he ran the pad of his thumb over my bottom lip. "No, I don't. I don't *have* you." He looked down at Bohe in disgust. "But that doesn't mean I'm going to let anyone kiss you, either."

His hand relaxed, and he stepped away, looking at the bloodied mess.

"This isn't the view I was hoping for." He moved the back of his hand over his lips, kissing the spot where mine had been. "I thought seeing someone else torture you would help diminish you in my eyes. I hoped it would lessen my desire for you. But the idea of this swine kissing without my permission what I know is *mine*—" A low rumble quaked the room as he scratched his nails down Liu Xie's back. He cried out, thrashing again, his blood now splattering the walls as Caelius flung it whimsically about the room.

Bohe's heart started to slow, his motions less exaggerated but all the more desperate. I stared at his wrists wrapped in the yellow sash. They were burning where they touched my angelic shackles, burning and keeping him weak. Because he was a Second-Born, anything made of Light was like poison. My lips trembled as I heard the scream of flesh around the bone in his throat, sizzling with every moment that passed.

"Caelius . . . don't do this," I pleaded.

Emperor Xian, the last of the Han Dynasty, my lifelong friend Bohe, degraded to this monster's plaything . . . because of me. "I get that you're jealous, but it's *my* fault for turning him in the first place. Punish *me* for wanting anyone other than you!"

The auburn of Caelius's eyes burned even brighter. "You care for him that much." He tore a new line down Bohe's back.

I paused.

My pleas were making it worse.

My mind turned and turned, but I didn't know what to say. How could I negotiate with Darkness? What card did I have left to play?

Bohe's heart slowed further, no longer in time with my own. His body twitched, the strain of his muscles giving in to exhaustion.

Caelius turned and walked toward the door.

"Wait! Don't leave him like this! Caelius, please! Father!"

His back hunched. "Father? Please? Words that mean nothing to me now."

I remembered what he'd said when he was deep inside me, the longing in his eyes as he spoke. He didn't want to be called Father—that was always meant to be a stepping-stone. He told me that as a child in Gutium, when I had thought him more than mortal, I had moved him with my words then. I could move him now.

"God, spare him. Aren't you more than human? Aren't you *better*? Only a human would do something this cruel to someone he desired, but not a god. Be merciful. Caelius, be *my god*."

I could hear his breath hitch as he turned slowly. There it was again, that tenderness I had seen emerge in the time he had thought I was his. I had given my body over to him, lying with words of praise, all to buy Shea and the others time to heal and hide.

His gaze softened.

I'd found it, his weak spot.

He stepped back toward me. Bringing his hand down, he stroked the back of it against my cheek. "Even though I know you are saying this for *him* and not me, I will be merciful. I will be *better* than human. After all, everything I do is for you, La-Narru. Remember that."

He reached down to Liu Xie's neck.

I held my breath as he grabbed the bone and pulled it out.

Instantly, I could see the wound start to heal itself. I could also see the deep black burn its presence had left.

My blood was all that I had left to give him, and if I could convince Caelius to leave, I would gladly give Bohe all of it. Killing me would help Shea, and the strength in my blood would make Bohe strong enough to get out of this place. His large brown eyes rose to mine. Relief flooded his features and reverberated through my bones as well. "It's okay, Liu Xie," I whispered, kissing his forehead. "My precious *Camellia sinensis*."

I looked up. "Caelius, thank you. I—"

He sank his teeth into the still-pink flesh at Liu Xie's neck and, with one violent inhale, drank him dry.

Bohe's emaciated body fell back to my own, limp like a wooden doll whose strings had been cut. The tears that had been at the corners of my eyes fell down and into my open mouth. I stared at Caelius in horror.

He grimaced seeing my expression. "I don't understand. Are you not pleased?" He tilted his head to the side in confusion. "You were asking for mercy, were you not? A quick death? Surely you weren't expecting me to let him *live*? Not after you all but confessed to loving him."

My mind reeled at his words.

"You disgust me." I spat into his face. It landed just below his eye. "You're sick . . . you . . . you're—"

"Careful." His expression hardened, the tenderness shifting from confusion to rage. "If I'm not mistaken, you still have one Second-Born left, besides the Vessel's parents. Ur-Nammu is one of your favorites as well, is he not? If I were you, I wouldn't put my *maker* into such a foul mood. For *his* sake, of course. Because that's all you do things for, right? For someone else? How selfish of you."

I clenched my jaw. Hate radiated from my every pore—every pore that could feel Bohe's cold dead skin resting against it.

Caelius moved his thumb over my spit, wiping it off his cheek. He stared at it a moment. "A parting gift for the Duke of Shanyang." He smeared it into the long black tresses of Bohe's now-uncoiled hair. His eyes matched the fury in my own. "I'll remember this, and next time I won't show mercy, no matter how hard you *beg*." He turned and moved toward the door, lifting a hand and waving it as he passed through. "See you in a few days, handsome. Like I promised, Bohe will keep you company in my stead while I continue to destroy Paris. Enjoy the fruits of your pleading."

He slammed the door behind him.

I screamed.

I screamed as loud as my lungs could stand, and then I screamed more. I could feel him, could feel Bohe's delicate wrists and ankles tied to mine. His chest, molded to my shape, his head resting under my chin as if in sleep. We had done this before. I'd held him like this, his body slack in my arms, when I had drained him of his mortal life. The fever that had wrecked his body had left him, along with the last warmth of human blood. I'd hesitated then, remembering Gracuri, worried that I'd destroy the beauty of Bohe more than any mortal had in his lifetime.

I struggled against the chains, wanting to touch him.

I needed to hold his head in my hands, to stare at his lips, his soft cheeks, like I had then. In doing so, I had convinced myself that I couldn't live without him, that the world was better for having Liu Xie in it, even as a vampire. But I was not Lucian the Merciful. The longer I had stared then, the more I had felt my own selfish desperation. The loss of Adnachiel had been renewed by Pompeii. The loss of Gracuri was fresh. In that moment I had felt all the losses over my lifetime: from Moses to childhood, the death of all of Gutium, the loss of my own mortal life.

Now here, with his body against mine, I felt it all again. It was like a wave that had been held back by a low tide, filling in all the crevices of my grief.

Why was it always like this? One domino and my mind relentlessly connected all the times I'd felt this way before. But it was so much worse now. Now that Shea had revived my heart and I couldn't bury the pain under thousands of years of well-developed callousness, I was raw and open to my feelings. Tears streamed from my eyes, and I screamed again. I couldn't fill my mouth with the sands of Egypt. I couldn't stuff my self-hatred with dirt. I couldn't bury the pain with my own hands in the blood or life of another, and I couldn't bear it.

"*Wǒ ài nǐ,*" I cried out.

He and I should've been dressed in white. The dirt I despised should've been under my feet as I walked a traditional funeral march by his casket. There should've been a ceremony and an offering. Had he still been a ruler in his own time, the complex funeral rights of China had tombs that rivaled ancient Egypt. There would've been provisions left for the deceased, provisions to carry them into the afterlife like Qin Shi Huang and his nine thousand statues, his terra-cotta army meant to protect the first emperor of China.

In his burial, respect would've been paid to his ancestors as a sort of filial piety. He had decided to become Buddhist in his later years, and Buddhist ethics dictated, to some extent, that it was a virtue to respect one's elders, parents, and descendants. It was a sort of last respect given, even upon death. The family was also expected to take vigil, watching over the casket of the beloved deceased for days, ensuring that the soul had support as it journeyed into eternity. Unless . . . unless you were an unmarried bachelor. Unless, of course, you weren't human anymore.

Moreover, Bohe had already had a funeral.

Though it wasn't as elaborate or as honor bound as it should have been. At that time, his title of Emperor had been stripped, and he'd been reduced to the Duke of Shanyang. No one visited his grave to offer incense or flowers or to tidy it up when time destroyed it. Not that any of that mattered to him. But it mattered to me, just as it did now.

When he'd opened his eyes then and looked at me, the dark brown almost black, it had been the happiest I'd seen him. Instead of instantly craving blood, he had kissed me. It had been quick and soft. When he'd pulled away, all he'd said was, "I'm home." As if that was what my arms were to him.

I gritted my teeth. Was I now a fitting casket to hold him? If he could awaken now, would he look at me like he had then? Would he be relieved to know that he died in his home?

I gasped for breath.

This was agony.

"I won't leave you, Bohe," I whimpered, choking in air to steady my breath. "It's tradition to stay by your side until you pass over. If your spirit *is* here, I'll pray for you—I'll chant so that my words may light a path to your *true* home. I was never really home for you. In the end, I used you like I used everyone else. I'm sorry."

I closed my eyes, feeling the weight of his body on mine. I whispered into his hair, cupping his head under my chin. It was the only way I could hold him now. I uttered a small blessing in his native tongue. Not traditional, not any chant I had heard him spout over tea, but it was the closest translation I knew for the blessing in Gutium for fallen warriors on the battlefield. It was something that was mine, that I could still give him.

I didn't know what or whom to pray to. Would I need to bargain with Anubis for his safe passage down the Nile, or the Steed of Oknah to carry his spirit to the stars? I didn't deserve either. I deserved Caelius and his endless black oblivion. But Bohe had deserved so much more in life . . . and in death.

I whispered into his dulling hair for the last time. "From my home to yours, Liu Xie, Emperor Xian of Han, the last of the Han Dynasty, my *Camellia sinensis*, my beloved Bohe." Tears rolled down my chin, leaving splotches on the drying blood at my chest. "If you find no home for you in the afterlife with the emperors of China, I am the son of Onack the Great, leader of Gutium. I consider you one of my own. If your people will not have you, mine will. You are welcome there. I cannot hold you anymore, but surely the arms of my mother, Anna-Steen, will." I choked on my own words. "You may have my home, my place, if you still need somewhere to belong."

I wept.

This was useless.

I had given up on believing in gods and the afterlife a million times over when I'd been mortal, and then more so when I'd become this. And yet when I could not escape my pain or desperation, it was to some invisible force that I prayed. Did that make me a fool? I tried to breathe in deep, but it came out in jagged gasps. I would give anything to run from this place, to bury him properly. I would give anything to hide from these feelings.

Alone.

Why do I always end up alone?

The weight of it, and Bohe's body, crushed me deeper than

when I'd been buried in the fiery mountains of Pompeii.

I was alone then.

I would always end up alone.

It ached.

I couldn't breathe.

"If there's no afterlife," I gasped, "if my mother is not there to hold you . . . if you are truly gone, I will burn your memory into the existence of all things. You will be everywhere I look, as with my other children. I will never forget you. As long as I exist, I will be a living tomb for the memories of your life. But please, *Mother*, if you are there . . . hold him." I panted for breath. The pain was incredible. I couldn't bear this, having his dead body tied to mine for days. I would go mad. I felt the chaos in my mind seeping in like thick black smoke. Better to go mad than to remember this gruesome end, than to have it forever carved into my soul as some pawn in Caelius's useless game.

"La-Narru, don't."

I blinked and searched the room.

Am I really losing my mind?

"It's just a body."

I smelled a rich herbal blend of earth and leaves all around me.

"I'm not there."

A light kiss brushed against my lips.

My eyes widened, and I jerked up. "Bohe!"

I looked down as his body half slid from mine. "Bohe, you're still alive!"

I moved again. "Bohe!" His face shifted up.

Dead eyes frozen in anguish stared back at me.

They were empty.

I looked around the room. Was this an illusion, a trick, a hallucination? I stared at his petrified body. "Bohe, *please*. Kiss me again, like you did the day I turned you. *Live* again. Don't leave me."

A silence as cold and as dead as he was filled the room.

I stared at his sunken cheeks.

He was gone. There was no reviving him now.

Just as the realization broke me, I felt a strange lightness there. Words echoed off the bloodstained walls. "I'll see you when you come home. That's where I'll be waiting."

My mind fought the peace attempting to overcome my mourning with facts about Darkness always winning and nothing being sacred. Still, the room *felt* different than it had before. Was this the peace I had heard mortals speak of? Humans said they had felt their loved ones say goodbye, but I had known only grief. I bit my bottom lip. It felt warmed by the lingering sensation of touch. Was this really the taste of Liu Xie? Was it possible, or was this a waking dream because I didn't sleep and my mind couldn't cope with reality?

Bohe.

He had become spiritual as the centuries passed: secluding himself in the mountains, in temples, studying enlightenment and trying to forget his time as a young puppet emperor. It was why I'd seen him less and less. He had changed, and I had remained much the same: scared, alone, and savage. That peace he'd found, that evolution . . . was that why I could hear *something*? I swore it was his voice that'd spoken, that it was his smell, his taste.

An overwhelming feeling of light covered me for a moment,

and I felt another presence.

"Shea?"

Was Shea reaching out to me?

Was it her heavenly Light that had touched me and Bohe because his body was tied to mine?

Was that why I could hear him?

"Shea!" I reached my hand forward as it was caught by the chains. "Shea, where are—"

I stopped myself.

I growled, hardening my emotions.

No.

I'd sacrificed my dignity and pride so that she could escape, so that she would be safe. Reaching back to her now would only guarantee her death. Even though I wanted her comfort—even though the Light that touched me and Bohe now was nothing but divine, and underneath it was Shea Harper, real and flesh and blood—I had to protect her. She was a piece of Light that I could never touch or hold again. My soul mate. My world.

I fixed my gaze back on the ceiling.

I had to reconnect with who I'd been before I'd met her. This vulnerability would only cause her death, and I would lose her like I'd lost everyone else.

She had to stay away from me.

I had to be the one lost in battle this time.

Though there would be no words spoken over my corpse. I prayed only that she could let me go or kill me if she had to.

I guess I have one more card to play after all.

I didn't know if she could hear me through the wall of Caelius's Darkness, but if she could, I sent my thoughts to her one last time. *End me, Shea Harper. End me before Caelius does to you what he's done to Bohe, what he'll do to everyone and everything I love.*

***

Five days passed. The horrid stench of Bohe's rotting body was only matched by the smoke and ash pouring through the crack in the door. I had no need to scream—all that I felt was being voiced for me in the slaughtered sounds of what had once been Paris. Would there be anything left of it by the time Caelius finished? Would the Eiffel Tower at least stand?

This was what Shea had tried to stop. This was why, even before Shea, I had kept Caelius locked in his cage, only feigning to take the Vessel to hurt Adnachiel. I winced. If only I had talked with Aidan sooner about Moses, if only we had spent decades working on a way to kill Caelius rather than my childish obsession with revenge, this might have all been avoided.

But he'd pierced my heart when he'd taken Moses.

The pride of the Gutian people was that we lived by a code that was governed by the ideals of loyalty and love. My father used to say that you couldn't really kill a Gutian; our souls would fight beyond the grave. Our code was etched in the existence of all things. Only when my mother died, alone in the dark holding her cold body, had he commanded that I look.

"This is the only way to truly kill a Gutian," he'd whispered, "to pierce them directly through the heart, to take away what they are fighting for, leaving nothing in their hands but remorse. She will live on, mounting the Steed of Oknah to rest with our kind in the stars, because her soul was made to *fly*. But look closer now, La-Narru, for today you have not lost a mother, but a father."

It was hard to breathe, remembering his words. It was no wonder I'd eaten her ashes after that.

Now, at the end of the world, when I had done all I could to save the ones I loved, I understood his words more than ever. I'd lost so many; they'd died in my arms as my mother had died in his. If I lost Shea too, I would truly be dead.

The door flung open.

"Look who's feeling more himself!"

Caelius sauntered over, soaked in fresh blood. "Did you miss me?" The tips of his hair dripped crimson onto my cheek. "Oh?" He stared a moment longer. "And here I was referring to myself, but look at you." He smiled. "You have that cold callous look in your eyes." He traced his bloodied hand down the length of my side. "What's wrong, La-Narru? Did Emperor Xian not entertain you enough while I was gone? Did you get bored like I used to in my cage, longing for you and you alone?" He leaned forward and grabbed the back of my neck, forcing my lips open as he kissed me hard.

I jerked my head away. He laughed, wiping his mouth. I spat, trying to get the blood out of my throat.

"What's wrong, darling? Not hungry?" he jeered.

"I don't know where it's been," I shot back, hardening further.

He placed his hands at my wrists and pulled the yellow sashes free. "You don't want the blood of the innocent to taint you?" He smiled. "Oh *please*, don't act so virginal." He walked to my feet, untying the knots there as well. He pulled him off. The loss of his weight was replaced with an inescapable emptiness. I almost asked him to leave the body with me. I wasn't ready, even after he had started to smell, to let Bohe go. In truth, that was why I'd turned him. I would never be ready to lose him.

He threw Bohe over his shoulder like a doll. The look of it cemented the reality aching in my chest: he was gone.

Caelius moved his thumb over my mouth. "If their swine blood has touched the lips of a god, then trust me, it is purified enough for *you*." He adjusted Bohe on his shoulder. "Isn't that what gods do, La-Narru? Purify. In history, Paris will be an example like Sodom and Gomorrah. The desecration of those cities was seen as the Light's holy glory, just as taking Paris will be my glory. I brought them brimstone and fire, after all." He touched the creases by my eyes. "And it looks like you've done enough crying to be my symbolic pillar of salt."

My muscles coiled as I clenched my jaw. My tears were not for him to relish; they were for Bohe. "All that I have and am is not yours and never will be. And you are no *god*. You're just Darkness that needs to know its place—"

"You're the one who needs to know his place, boy." His playful grin subsided, and he paused, taking in a long drawn out breath. "It took a whole city to get the bounce back in my step, and one minute with you to remove it. Why is that?" He scrutinized the hard lines on my face, as if looking would procure some sort of answer. He sighed again, uncertainty moving over his features.

"Well, onward and upward, or so they say." He tossed Bohe's body through the open door. It hit the wall with a thud and crumpled into a pile like trash.

"Don't treat him like that! Have you no respect for the dead?

No honor?" I stared in abhorrence at Liu Xie's now-concave face.

"How cute that you still care after days with that *filth*." He laughed, low and long. "That puppet won't dance for you anymore. Its strings are cut. Best to throw it out."

Caelius ran his hand over my face. "If nothing else, you are my favorite plaything, but more than an empty puppet, I'll make you *mine* without the strings. I'll make you keep your promise, La-Narru. It's all I've ever wanted since I became flesh. And the point of life is to get what we want, isn't it?"

I bit the inside of my lip, hatred boiling over. "Don't call me that. My childhood name isn't yours to use so candidly."

"I will use you and it as I please!" He slammed his fist next to my face. It punctured a hole straight through the mattress. "I gave you the name Lucian! It was *mine*!" He ripped his fist out, cotton spilling in tufts, the fibers floating through the air like snowflakes. "And until *you're* mine, I'll call you by the name of the boy who begged for me to be his god by that river in Gutium! I'll taste the sweetness from your lips as you call me it over and over! And *this* time you'll mean it, like you did then! This time when I create your name anew, you will treasure the name Lucian like the gift that it was!"

"I'll die before that happens."

"Maybe." His irises blazed like rubies. "But not until I've tried *everything* to keep you." A sort of sadness filled his gaze as he wiped the mattress stuffing from his hand onto my chest.

"You're wasting your time—we both know that." I leaned forward, as close as I could before the chains pulled me back. "Just kill me now and save yourself the trouble."

He drew his face closer to mine, then licked the side of my

cheek. "Oh, it's no trouble." He straightened up, humming to himself, savoring the taste of my sweat.

I gawked in disgust as he motioned toward Bohe. "I want some privacy. Close the door, but do pick that puppet up and dispose of it, dear. The sight of it seems to be troubling my lover."

I scowled, looking toward the doorway. "It's sick how you've made Molly your errand boy."

"Molly?" He laughed. "Does it exhaust you, being wrong all the time?" He squeezed my cheek and patted it. "Not the brightest, but at least you have your looks."

A shadow moved from the dark hallway. She stepped forward. I didn't need light to illuminate her face. I knew who it was. I had made clay sculptures of that shape for years.

"Nefertiti."

She refused to meet my gaze, gently picking up Bohe and slamming the door closed.

"What have you done to her? Why is she *here*?" I pulled furiously against the chains.

He covered my mouth with his hand. "Look at you squirming like a fish on a hook every time there's new information." He moved his other hand down Bohe's dried blood, caressing my torso. "It's enough to make a god want to take you all over again." He slid his long fingers down between my thighs, pulling on the meat of them. "But there's time for that later, time when you'll give it up to me without resistance. You'll be supple and willing."

I hardened, trying to close any lingering vulnerability inside.

"Nefertiti was part of the original game. It's frustrating to plan something for so long and not have it work out, don't you think? You must have felt that a million times by now." He laughed, squeezing my inner thigh harder. "I want to see how it would have worked, you and Nefertiti reunited at long last. You have a child together, after all."

He placed a hand over his forehead in feigned despair. "And that whore, Shea, killed some of Nefertiti's children and almost all of yours, attacking us without provocation. It's really Shea who's ruining your life, she and that Adnachiel you hate so much, the one who betrayed you and killed Moses.

"I'll rewrite everything for you so that you can finally forget your strange obsession with her and be happy, like I'd planned for centuries. I'll take care of you, darling, and you'll appreciate me for it. With a little work and time, you'll be mine eventually."

My eyes widened. It wasn't possible, was it? He'd driven me mad before, I had killed Shea's parents unknowingly because of it, but I was stronger now, and I had eventually come back to myself. There was no way I would think that Shea had killed anyone. He couldn't take her from me. She was all that was left in my heart, all that was keeping me alive. She was burned into a part of my soul that even he couldn't remove.

I swallowed. Darkness had limits. Everything did. He couldn't remove love. He could hide it for a while, but he could never remove it. I was about to tell him just that when I thought of Molly Harper—Shea's own *mother*, someone who loved Shea more than her own life, who'd birthed her . . . and now she hated Shea with every fiber of her being.

Caelius slowly removed his hand from my mouth. "Do you understand what I'm going to do to you?"

"It won't work," I choked out.

"Well, well, you've given more convincing speeches from the

other side of my cage." He licked his lips. "What's this doubt I smell past your perspiration? Come now, if even Nefertiti was willing to allow me to do this to you, Gutium's strongest warrior, surely you know that this truly is the end."

"I'll die, Caelius. Without Shea—"

He laughed. "We'll see."

"You're using Nefertiti's children against her. I know she wouldn't—"

"*Your* child in particular, La-Narru, let's not forget. The one she cared so much for that she found me in Egypt, begged me to turn you, and promised me her life and her children if only to save you, so that her precious Setepenre would know your face." He smiled. "Nostalgia. Of course, she never knew that I was going to turn you anyway, that even then I desired you more fiercely than she."

I shivered. Guilt, shame, fear—this helpless feeling I had spent lifetimes trying to run from—swelled all around me. Ever since I'd watched my mother's fevered body grow still, I'd known it was my fault; all of this was because of me. She was my first loss, and every loss after was mine to bear alone. My father was right. I was no one's son now, except this monster's. I brought nothing but pain and death to all who knew me.

Caelius leaned forward, kissing my cheek. "Don't despair, dear one," he whispered into my ear, cupping my face. "I'll rewrite your mind, and you'll be happy once again, as you were in Gutium before the wars. And you'll worship me in return, and we will have our Eden. You and I. Forever."

"You're going to make me be with Nefertiti?" My voice quivered. "In front of Shea. To hurt her."

He kissed my cheek again tenderly, moving down my jaw, kissing in small breaths as he spoke. "Yes." His voice was soft. "You'll finally be freed from the guilt of Nefertiti's death. The reunion will be a happy one. She's not to sleep with you, but I can tolerate a few kisses here and there. Maybe. We'll see.

"Then she's to convince you that she is *not* your salvation, *I* am. Not that you'll need much convincing after I give you everything your heart truly desires." He ran his teeth along the side of my neck. I braced for the pain, but it didn't come. He closed his mouth, pressing soft lips to my throat instead.

He leaned back. "I give Molly a single drop of my blood and it lasts for weeks. It's enough to keep her *hating* her own daughter. Her mind and her loyalty are mine completely." He scowled. "I hate it. My blood is too precious to give to any human pig. But for you, darling La-Narru—"

He cut a long line down his wrist. With his other hand, he forced open my jaw, holding it in place, pressing his elbow into my solar plexus, opening my throat in a gasp.

I thrashed as he poured his blood into my mouth like emptying a jug of water down the sink.

I choked trying to resist, trying not to swallow, but it was still getting in, seeping into my very being.

My body instantly felt like it was on fire.

I writhed in agony, but he didn't stop.

It was too much.

My mind jumbled.

I could smell everything, see everything in the room on a microscopic scale like it was being torn apart, broken down into atoms. Time slowed. Stronger than any drug, stronger than my will, his blood moved with an unholy power inside of me.

No.

This was what he meant.

My mind, my memories, my heart.

Shea, please, no.

I couldn't lose her too, not like this.

I tried to hold on to that one word as everything went black.

Shea.

I felt myself, my true self, sinking into an endless pit of mud, blinded by all-consuming Darkness.

Shea.

Further and further down I sank.

My soul was being ripped, torn from every vein, every muscle. Torn from skin and bone and pushed deeper into blackness.

Sh—

What was that word I was holding on to?

What was that feeling?

It was all for something.

Or for someone.

What was it?

"Come now, boy. Say my name."

"Caelius, I can't breathe!"

Was that the name I was looking for, alone in the dark?

"Call me God."

"God, I'm dying, save me!"

"Of course, darling. Always."

Caelius, my god.

Caelius, my savior.

That was the name.

The only name I needed to reach out for in the darkness, to never be alone.

CHAPTER 5
SHEA

I stared in shock, and a little bit of awe, as Ur-Nammu decapitated one of Caelius's vampires with his hand.

His freaking *hand!*

It was like Ur-Nammu had transformed it into a butcher knife, the head came off so clean. I was in the middle of trying to connect to the wind, to create some kind of hurricane or something, but watching Ur-Nammu fight was mesmerizing.

Here on this strange battlefield, an abandoned playground outside of Toledo, I could truly see the warrior he'd once been. He no longer looked like the grandfather figure I had grown used to. He was in his element and had been born to fight.

And he was terrifying.

He was currently protecting Meky and Sherit, not that they needed it. Nothing registered on his radar except his grandchildren, not even protecting me, who was supposed to be a superweapon against Caelius. Though at the moment, Ur-

Nammu did *sort of* inch his way toward me when another vamp got closer.

Luckily, there were no witnesses to see this epic battle. The playground was next to a condemned elementary school in a neighborhood that had been demolished in favor of a slew of McMansions. Construction hadn't begun yet; there was only dirt and debris for a half mile in every direction. Whenever Aidan's angel-sense picked up that vampires were close, we'd book it to the nearest unpopulated place. The last thing I wanted was for any innocent bystanders to be killed.

This was the tenth attack so far.

Mom hadn't been kidding when she said Caelius would come after us. Luckily, he'd sent what Ur-Nammu called "lesser vampires," which were no match for a group of Second-Borns, an angel, and a Vessel. As if to prove my point, Duncan easily ripped one of the vampires *in half* before decapitating them.

We had killed thirty already. My dad had taken out the first two quickly, and Helena had used some kind of device to take out the next three. The rest were a joint effort with Ur-Nammu and Duncan doing the heavy lifting.

Now there were only five left.

Suddenly, a particularly vicious vampire made a mad dash for me, her red hair flying behind her like some kind of comet with teeth. Without thinking, I connected to the air around me and, in a flash, there was a ten-foot tornado wrapping itself around my attacker. I couldn't tell who looked more shocked, me or her.

Another vampire took his chance and leapt toward me, completely clearing the eight-foot parallel bars between us, but Ur-Nammu was on it. He grabbed him by his head in midair and squeezed with his hands and—

Pop!

Gross.

I think I just swallowed a piece of brain. Nope, scratch that—it was skull.

I could feel the tiny piece move down my esophagus like a half-eaten tortilla chip.

What was Ur-Nammu's obsession with heads? He was either decapitating them or popping them like grapes. I wasn't complaining, but it was pretty disgusting. Thinking about it a little more though, taking out the head was most likely the quickest way to kill a vampire.

Three left.

Meky jumped on the back of a large vampire who must have been a linebacker before he was turned. Her petite frame looked like she'd be no match for him. But Meky was a Second-Born, not to mention the daughter of a badass warrior queen, which kind of made her a princess warrior in her own right. With no effort, Meky ripped off both the large vampire's arms at the same time, held them like trophies, then tossed them to the ground. Before the vampire could react, she easily ripped off his head and tossed it next to his arms. What was left of the vampire's torso slumped over, hitting the end of a slide.

Two more.

Duncan snapped another vampire's spine, breaking her in half before ripping off her head. Everyone had their signature move.

The last one was all Aidan. Placing his hand on the vamp's chest, he poured Light into the woman until there was nothing left but a black husk of charcoal.

"Is that tornado girl coming back?" Sherit asked.

"I really don't know," I answered honestly.

"I don't sense her. I think she ran." Aidan walked over to me. "You okay?"

I wasn't. But I nodded. "Yeah, we should get going though."

Dad leapt over a broken seesaw, landing at my side. "I killed those first two *vamps*. Did you see?" He looked at me for approval.

I still wasn't used to my parents being immortal, but I was glad he could take care of himself now. And he wasn't killing people, he was killing vampires, which was good . . . even though *he* was one, and so were all these other people, and my mother, and ugh.

"Yes, good job, Dad," I answered. "You killed some *vamps*." I couldn't help but tease him. He was my dad—it was my job. And shortening vampires to vamps was very *dad-like*.

He laughed. "Would you prefer bloodsuckers? Leeches? The Vampeer?"

Aidan and Duncan nudged each other, both appreciating the humor. They had become fast friends. Their personalities were so much alike that it had proved my theory correct: Lucian had turned Duncan because he reminded him of Aidan. Duncan didn't seem to mind though. He actually seemed honored by the fact, calling Aidan his brother-from-another-mother.

Walking toward the minivan we'd rented, we all smooshed in and drove away. To where? I had no idea.

Twelve hours later, we pulled up to a small motel outside of Duluth, right on the water of Lake Superior. Driving for that long had made me more than a little stir-crazy. At least if we got into a fight here, I could use the water to our advantage.

It had been a while since Nefertiti had left with Mom, and we were exhausted from the constant cycle of running and fighting. Looking over at the motel, I noticed that the building itself was run-down and appeared to only have ten rooms. There were two cars parked in the lot, so at least it was empty-ish.

"Please tell me we're going to book a minimum of three rooms this time," I complained from the back of the eight-seater van that squished Dad, Aidan, Ur-Nammu, Meky, Duncan, Sherit, Helena and me together. With the speed all vampires seemed to possess, I'd thought we'd travel by supernatural means, but I guessed that method was the easiest for Caelius to track. Since the guy had been trapped underground for the last three thousand years, he didn't know much about technology, hence the deluxe minivan we were all currently crammed into.

Everyone, including me, felt better with Dad at the wheel. He had the most experience driving, and with the amount of road trips he'd done over the years, he knew his way around the States.

"One room," Aidan called back from the front passenger seat, his tone leaving no room for argument. Since I was the only one who needed sleep, we'd been renting a single room and paying cash, for safety's sake. We didn't want any detective-vampires to track us the old-fashioned way like the diner vamp had with me and Aidan when all of this had just started.

"I'll order an extra cot so it won't look suspicious," Aidan announced, as if that would somehow make me feel better.

"Yeah, because four grown men and women renting a single room isn't suspicious at all. That extra cot will totally make us seem legit." I didn't bother to hide the sarcasm in my voice.

Duncan laughed and gave me an approving nod from the first row.

Aidan ignored me, but I could see the remnants of a smile as he left the van and headed to the lobby.

"Can we get out now?" Meky was losing patience as well. I couldn't blame her. Since we were the smallest, we had both been designated to the middle seats in the van. With Duncan on her right and Ur-Nammu on her left, the girl was pancaked. At least I had Helena and Sherit next to me, which gave me a lot more elbow room.

Duncan jumped out and slid open the side door so everyone could leave. Only Dad stayed inside, ready to park the car in front of our new temporary abode. I practically shoved Helena out to get some air, but she didn't mind. She was just as relieved to be free of our minivan prison.

Aidan came back, dangling a key.

Off to our motel room prison now.

I wished Caelius would die already.

"We're over there, number 4." Aidan turned to lead the way.

After hearing the number, Dad drove ahead and parked in front of our room.

Exiting the van, he walked over to me. "You got your things?"

Such a dad.

I walked over and pulled a small bag out of the back of the van with all my toiletries. "Got it." Being the only human, I was a little jealous that no one had to brush their teeth like I did. Luckily, my dad had packed everything I needed before we'd even started our cross-country-runaway-from-Caelius-a-thon.

Aidan unlocked the door, then ran off to get the cot.

Walking into the motel room, I tried not to cringe at the carpet. It looked like it hadn't been vacuumed in a century. There were two queen beds, a small desk, a dresser with a television on top, a chair, and a door to the bathroom. Same room, different city.

I'd wanted to get an Airbnb, except I didn't trust my newbie vampire dad to not eat the homeowners. And besides, with everything that had happened in Paris, Airbnb hosts weren't exactly in a trusting mood either.

America still acted like it was immune to a massive attack, despite Paris. But keeping to the smaller towns and cities definitely helped in terms of visibility, although it did feel like we were on the verge of a zombie apocalypse.

Plopping down on the bed, I secretly hoped Caelius's goons would find us soon because this place was a real crap-hole. Carrying a cot over his head, Aidan entered the room and set it down in front of the dresser, making it even more cramped.

"Glad you got that cot." I couldn't help myself.

Aidan shook his head and chuckled. "You're such a dork."

Duncan laughed too. "Lose the cot, lad. I'll compel anyone who looks at us funny."

"I can't return it now. That'll be even weirder." Aidan looked appalled at the thought.

"Oh, for crying out loud." Dad took it and left the motel room, grumbling.

I savored the moment.

Not because it proved my point that we were overcrowded, but because it reminded me so much of how things used to be.

In that moment, Aidan was my best friend growing up, and Dad was . . . Dad, rolling his eyes at Aidan being too embarrassed to return anything. He was the adult, and Aidan was the child—a child he'd helped raise, since Aidan had been glued to my side our entire lives. It made me miss those days terribly.

Seeing my expression, Duncan placed a hand on my shoulder. "I can get the cot back for ye, lass, if ye want it that badly."

I shook my head. "No. I was just remembering simpler times."

Duncan seemed to understand completely, his expression turning solemn. "We'll have them again."

A moment later, Dad walked back in with another set of keys. "I got the room next door." Before Aidan could object, Dad nodded toward a closed door I hadn't noticed next to the dresser. "They open up to each other. We can guard two rooms. It'll be fine, Aidan."

He reluctantly nodded, and I leapt into my dad's open arms. "Thanks." I grabbed the key and walked outside, letting myself into the nearly identical room. After opening both adjoining doors, we officially had two whole rooms to hang out in. It was luxury living as far as I was concerned.

I lay down on one of the queen beds and enjoyed being alone, even if it was just for a moment. I knew it wouldn't last long, but it made me feel so much better.

And it lasted for all of three seconds.

"Shea Harper, may I speak with you?" Ur-Nammu walked into the room cautiously. His expression said that he didn't want to bother me, so I knew it must be important.

I sat up on the edge of the bed. "Of course. What do you

need?" I motioned for him to sit on the bed across from me.

He complied and took in a deep breath. "I'm not sure what to do."

That was intense language for Ur-Nammu.

"We're in this together. I'll help any way I can." I tried to put the ancient vampire at ease.

Taking a moment to gather his thoughts, Ur-Nammu finally spoke. "I've been trying to Dream-Walk with Nefertiti since she left. Now that we know Caelius can't hear us, there's no reason why she wouldn't communicate with me." He paused, unsure of how to continue. "I fear the worst."

"You think Caelius *killed* Nefertiti? No way. Wouldn't you *feel* that? And Caelius would want to rub it in our faces. He'd make that public. She's not dead. I'm certain." I wasn't certain, but I couldn't just watch Ur-Nammu suffer like this. We had a complicated relationship at best, but I was certain of one thing: family meant *everything* to him.

"Then maybe she's under his blood control," Ur-Nammu said with a kind of helplessness I completely related to. "It's unlike her. We've always been close. Human or immortal, there was never a time she didn't confide in me. Not in Gutium, not in Egypt."

"Maybe she's gathering intel that will help us defeat Caelius, and she doesn't want him thinking she's Dream-Walking? And if she's being blood-controlled, then we have to assume Lucian is *definitely* being controlled. I just hope I can do something about it," I vented. This whole blood-compelling crap had me more worried than I let on. I knew from what I had accomplished with Helena that I could remove Caelius's shadow, but blood?

Ur-Nammu sat forward, anxious. "I know it's not proper to ask, but will you try to reach Nefertiti? Maybe she's too ashamed to talk to me, or afraid that if I learn that she's in danger, I will try and find out where she is and get myself killed rescuing her."

Ding. Ding. Ding. "Yeah, it's that last one. She would totally think that because it's true, right?" With sudden clarity, I was positive that Nefertiti was keeping her distance from Ur-Nammu on purpose.

His face told me that I was right.

"I can't just leave her there with *him*," he grumbled under his breath.

Shaking my head and commiserating wholeheartedly, I reached over and lightly touched Ur-Nammu's hand to comfort him. "I can't promise anything. Nefertiti and I don't exactly have the greatest of friendships, but I'll try."

Ur-Nammu squeezed my hand. "I appreciate the effort. Thank you, Shea Harper."

"It's just Shea. You don't have to say my last name like I'm some kind of celebrity or something. It's weird." I smiled, teasing him. Although I really shouldn't have complained. Aidan's brothers only called me Vessel. My whole name was a huge improvement.

But Ur-Nammu smiled back. "Thank you again, *Shea*."

Aww. We were having a moment.

I didn't want to spoil it by saying something stupid, so I pulled my hand away and lay back on the bed. "No time like the present."

Ur-Nammu stood up and, with a slight pep to his walk, left my side and began to close the door that joined the rooms. "I'll give you some privacy."

Nodding, I closed my eyes, knowing full well that Aidan and my dad would have that door opened seconds after Ur-Nammu closed it. But I tuned all the background noise out and concentrated on falling asleep anyway. I took deep calming breaths. I'd learned to switch into Dream-Walk mode much quicker than I used to.

Concentrating on Nefertiti, I breathed in and held . . . breathed out and held . . .

Breathed in . . . and . . .

Opening my eyes, I was in the middle of . . . Miami Beach?

I could tell because I could see the famous hotel from the movie *Goldfinger.* What was it called? The Fontainebleau? I'd always wanted to go there, but being a college student, it was way out of my price range. Plus, finding out I was a Vessel and being hunted by what equated to *the devil* kind of put a damper on traveling for pleasure. Besides, Miami was supposedly a cesspool for rebellious vampires. Caelius had sent Ur-Nammu there once to keep the extra murderous ones in line. But still, even being in this dreamscape made me worried that I might get bitten.

I stood on the white sand beach and waited nervously.

This was definitely not a regular dream. I was definitely Dream-Walking.

But with whom?

I sighed in relief when I heard Nefertiti's voice. "It's about time you came."

Turning around, I faced the annoyingly beautiful vampire. "I hadn't realized you were ignoring your own father."

Why did she always bring out my angry side? Oh, right. She was Lucian's ex, and I was extremely jealous of her.

"My father would only get himself killed," Nefertiti said with a sigh.

"He's really worried about you. He thought you might be blood-controlled." I chose to lose my attitude.

"Thankfully, Caelius doesn't deem me worthy enough to drink his blood. He's reserving that for your mother and Lucian." Nefertiti's expression turned hard. "He's giving Lucian gallons of it. It's the only thing that will erase you from his memory."

I didn't know if I should be flattered or puke. Luckily, I was in a dreamscape, so if I threw up it would just disappear, but I wanted to curl up and cry for Lucian. What would that much of Caelius's blood do to him?

"My mother too? The tons of blood, I mean?" I didn't want to ask, but I had to know.

Nefertiti shook her head. "No. He only gives her a drop a day. It used to be a drop a week, but the memories of you are powerful." She paused as if what she was about to say next was difficult. "It seems you are well loved."

My feelings were so conflicted I could barely think straight. Lucian and my mother were being force-fed Caelius's blood, but they were so strong that they were fighting it. I hoped I could help somehow. I just needed to be in the same room with them, to touch them, to hug them, to *be* with them.

"I brought you here for a reason." Nefertiti cut my thoughts short.

"You brought *me* here? I'm the one who contacted you." There was my weird defensiveness again.

"Like I said before, I've been waiting for you to Dream-Walk with me for a couple of weeks now. Some of those vampires

Caelius sent were messengers, not assassins. They were the worst of our kind though, so I can't say I'm not happy they were killed. Caelius wants to make a new deal with me and my family, and I have to agree to keep them safe.

"I'll still work as a double agent, but I'm only communicating with *you,* not my father. Caelius knows this. He can't overhear us, but if he really wanted to, he could feed me his blood and make me tell him everything we talk about." Nefertiti paused thoughtfully, then continued. "I doubt Caelius would do this. He abhors giving your mother even a drop. He only wants Lucian to have it. The thought of giving me his blood makes Caelius physically wretch. He hates me because Lucian loved me unconditionally."

She stared at me intensely as she said, "But Caelius hates you more than the Light itself because every fiber of Lucian's soul is entwined with yours."

And from the look on her face, I got the feeling Nefertiti hated me just as much for the same reason.

It didn't give me comfort hearing those words though.

I loved Lucian just as much, if not more, but the reason Caelius was torturing him was *because* of our love. Our love would destroy him. Caelius would rather see him dead than to see him love another. Caelius wanted Lucian all to himself, and that would never happen because of how he and I felt about each other.

Nefertiti didn't wait for my response as she said, "The plan is simple. Caelius wants his Adam and Eve again, but he wants an Eve he can control: me. He's rewritten Lucian's memories so that *you* are responsible for the death of my daughters and his Second-

Borns, including the torture and murder of Gracuri." She let that sink in. Her eyes actually showed sympathy, but her speech did not.

She was all soldier as she continued. "Caelius wants Meky and Sherit returned to me and Lucian so that Caelius can convince Lucian his memories of what you did are real. Ur-Nammu will be exiled but not killed. Caelius *will* kill my father if he sees him again. Are we understood?"

I stood paralyzed.

My heart and brain squeezed in pain.

Lucian's memories of me were *gone*. They'd been replaced with fake ones where I was the enemy who'd killed the people he loved.

He'd never forgive me.

He wouldn't even want to.

Lucian would look at me with hate, and I didn't know if I could survive that.

Nefertiti waved her hand in front of my face to get my attention. "Shea? I need to know that you understand the situation."

I tried to gather my wits, but it was difficult, so I focused on the part of the plan that caused me the least amount of pain. "Meky will never agree to go to Caelius, and why would you want her to? Caelius could kill her or Sherit on a whim. You're willing to risk that?"

"Meky will do as she's told to save her family," Nefertiti said plainly. "And trust me, Caelius keeps his promises. He kept his promise to me for three thousand years."

"Was that before or after he decapitated Merytaten?" I knew

it was harsh, but I couldn't believe she was considering putting Meky and Sherit in danger like that.

"I betrayed Caelius, and the deal was off. It was fair rules of battle. I would have done the same to an enemy who'd broken an agreement," she said.

"Are you being serious right now? Nothing that Caelius does is *fair*. Caelius would have no issues whatsoever killing your daughters and then claiming he was justified. If you think any different, you're delusional." I was angry for Meky and Sherit, but mainly angry at the fact that I was helpless to do anything for anyone.

Nefertiti paused, then eyed me carefully. "I have no choice. If Meky and Sherit don't come, Caelius promises he will kill *all* my daughters. At least this way they have a chance."

"Don't do this! We're going to find a way to kill Caelius, you just have to be patient!" I was taking all my frustration and anger out on Nefertiti, but I couldn't stop myself.

"Patient?" She stayed calm but stern. "I waited and planned for decades before you were even born. We failed. We will always fail. And my children paid the price. I will *not* risk that again. If you have a plan, you will execute it with my daughters safely by my side."

She stepped forward, her stature commanding. "Tell Meky and Sherit to meet here, where we are standing at Miami Beach, in the real world. Miami is Caelius's next conquest. He's preparing to destroy the entire city as he did Paris." Then her expression softened as she said, "Please, Shea, convince my daughters if needed. I can't lose another child to this madness."

I was out of steam. I couldn't argue anymore, so I simply

nodded in agreement.

"And one more thing," Nefertiti said flatly. "I used this connection to figure out where you are, and I'm going to tell Caelius as soon as we end this Dream-Walk, so I suggest you leave quickly."

With a loud clap, I was thrown out of the dreamscape, and my eyes flew open.

Sitting up in bed, I noticed I was alone, but like I had assumed, the door was open.

Hurrying into the other room, I yelled, "We have to get out of here! Nefertiti is telling Caelius where we are!"

"So she *is* being blood-controlled," Ur-Nammu said.

"No. She's her stubborn self, but she's still playing the double agent, so she gave me a heads-up that she planned to tell Caelius where we were." I made sure my eyes met Meky's then Sherit's as I said, "You have to meet her in Miami Beach near the Fontainebleau."

I quickly explained all the details of the conversation I'd had with Nefertiti.

Meky was livid. "She wants us to lie to Lucian and pretend we're one big happy family? No way. This is ridiculous!"

Sherit, on the other hand, didn't seem as upset. "Meky, Mother knows what's best to keep us alive. She's been doing it for over three thousand years now. We need to trust her."

Whirling on her sister, Meky argued, "And you're okay with throwing Shea under the bus? Telling Lucian that Shea killed our sisters and his Second-Borns?" Meky turned to me, shaking her head. "I won't do it, Shea. Don't worry. I have your back."

Aidan looked at his girlfriend with pride and clasped Meky's hand. "I'll keep you safe this time."

"I can keep myself safe, but I love you for being so protective." Meky smiled.

I wanted to keep our group together, but the more I thought about Nefertiti's words, the more I knew she was right.

"Meky, you have to go," I found myself saying.

"Shea, no. I won't," Meky said stubbornly.

"Caelius told your mom he'd kill *all* her children. Sete is already there. I won't be responsible for her death. Lucian would never recover. Plus, I need you there. You're the only one I trust." I hurriedly looked at Sherit. "No offense."

"None taken," Sherit replied back. "My mother and I respect you and everything you've done to try and destroy Caelius, but we have no affection for you. Not like Meky does, apparently." Then Sherit added, "No offense."

"I don't know how anyone could be offended by that," I said sarcastically, but Sherit had proven my point. Meky and I had grown closer since the final battle, and I considered her a true friend. Heck, she was most likely going to marry Aidan, so that practically made us sisters anyway. I turned to Meky one last time. "Please, Meky."

After a long pause, she finally nodded. "All right, I'll go. But if Caelius tries to hurt you, I'm out."

"Deal. Thank you." It wasn't much comfort, but it was a little.

Aidan looked like I'd ripped his heart out, but he didn't argue. He leaned down and gently kissed Meky. It made my heart squeeze in guilt.

Ur-Nammu stepped in. "I'm going with you girls all the same. I know Miami well. I can keep to the shadows as not to be found out by Caelius, but there is nothing you can say or do that will stop me. I'd gladly die if it means your safety. I'll be near if you need me."

Not surprisingly, no one argued because everyone, including Nefertiti (though she'd be reluctant to admit it), knew that no one could stop Ur-Nammu. Nefertiti would be livid, but there was nothing I could do.

Helena glanced at the window. "Caelius's goons will be here soon. We should leave."

"On to the next hotel?" Dad asked, a little too excited to get back into the van for my taste.

"I'd rather use the water in that lake out there and transport us all in a giant wave than go back into that van," I grumbled. "Or maybe air? I could tornado us to the next state? Or if I could master earth I could earthquake us to California? Anything but that horrible van!"

Helena froze.

I was instantly on guard.

From the look on her face, the goons must have arrived.

Duncan noticed too. "Helena? What's wrong? Are they here?"

Helena shook her head. "No. I think I just had an idea of how to destroy Caelius, but it involves Shea mastering all four elements, which means we need a place for her to practice."

Meky raised an eyebrow. "Are you going to use that other contraption you used to talk about, the one you said was too risky and would never work?"

Helena nodded, then explained it to the rest of us. "It's a device I abandoned, but I was mind-controlled at the time. Now that I'm myself again, I think Shea's powers just might do the trick. I have a lab that I'm certain Caelius knows nothing about. In all my years as a vampire, I never visited it once. I must have subconsciously protected it. I would have taken us there earlier, but I didn't want to be forced to destroy it if Caelius found us. It's worth the risk for this now though." Her face brightened at the thought. "This could work!"

I tried to match her enthusiasm with a smile, but my stomach turned at the realization that whatever this device was, it relied on me mastering *all* the elements.

No pressure.

Can I vomit now?

CHAPTER 6
LUCIAN

The Light.

I'd done it.

I'd brought the Vessel to Caelius, and he was free.

But why?

Why would I want him *free*? I'd always used the Vessels to torture Adnachiel. It was strange. I must have gotten bored to the point of madness, because now, looking at his auburn eyes, I questioned my judgment. They were searing into me, alight as if they were on fire like my blood was.

I was radiating power. I could feel it move in waves off of me, vibrating between his body and mine. But his blood fogged my brain like a thick tar pumping through my synapses. I was desperately trying to piece together why I would *willingly* free him, knowing this would be the outcome. He caressed my cheek as a memory pushed through the fog: our bodies intertwined, him lifting us into the air over the fields of Gutium.

I pulled away from his touch. "Why would I do that . . . ?"

He pulled me back toward him, holding me tighter in his arms. He licked his lips and pressed his mouth to the soft spot behind my ear as he spoke. "What is it, darling?"

My body tensed instinctively as he moved his hands up and down my back, finally resting them on my hips and squeezing hard.

"We . . . I *willingly* gave myself to you, in my homeland?"

He licked a long line down my neck, nipping at my collar bone, then sucking it gently, leaving a bruise that healed quickly as he pulled away. With agitation, he glared at the place the mark had been. "Permanence. I want all the things I give and do for you to last, Lucian." He leaned his torso back and locked eyes with me. "Because you're *mine*, after all."

Mine.

It was a powerful word for our kind, and I felt it in every inch of my body as it yielded to him. It yearned to be held a while longer. I ached for Caelius. "It's your blood. That's why I'm like this."

He bit the side of his lip, scrutinizing my features. "We've gone over this, my sweet. After you freed me in the last battle with the Vessel, she almost killed you. I had no choice but to feed you my blood. It was to save your life, just as I did in Egypt when you were killed by the Pharaoh, just as I promised when you were a boy in Gutium. I was and will always be your salvation. I've wanted you for so long. Can't you *feel* it now, the knowledge that we will *always* belong together?"

I did.

There was no way I *couldn't* feel him, his desire, his obsession, his body. Right now he was my world, but he had broken me enough times in the cave before he'd been free for me to understand what his blood was doing. I knew this wasn't real; this was a fevered intoxication created and controlled by him alone. However, understanding my situation and being able to resist him were two different things.

"I don't . . ." I couldn't look away from his eyes. It sickened me, but I *wanted* him to be the one who gave me the answers. I *wanted* him to be my salvation, my lover, my everything. I tried to choke down the yearning, but it was impossible. "What's happening to me?"

He smirked, looking over my body. "It's been a few days, and you haven't let me leave this bed. Even now the look of desire, the longing for me to fill your loins, it's enough to drive even a being like me into heat."

I swallowed hard, realizing that we were indeed in bed. His body was just as naked as my own; we were meshed, flesh against flesh with our legs intertwined.

"How did I get here?" I meant that in more ways than one. I didn't even know what city we were in. By the look of the bedding and room, I was wrapped in his arms in some high-priced hotel.

This had to be the effect of his blood, blood he had happily given to save my life. In the cave, he'd spoken of it for centuries like it was holy. It was something he would never give to any human swine, yet he was feeding so much of it to me that I *yearned* for it.

It didn't make sense. I was long since healed from the damage of the Vessel. I didn't *need* it. I had to wean myself off of him or risk losing myself to his control completely. As it was, I had no memory, only his words that elicited images that *must* be memories. But they were foggy and incomplete.

Scattered.

Like I was.

The only thing that felt familiar was this feeling of dissolving like paper in water. It was like a black emptiness was hollowing out something important inside of me. What was it that I was clinging to besides him? Wasn't there anyone else? Where were my children, my Second-Borns?

Gracuri would answer me honestly. He was a part of the world, enough to know what was going on outside of Caelius's control. I could trust him. I could contact David, Duncan, or Bohe . . . no. Bohe I could trust, but he was secluded, and it was better for him that he stayed that way. He was safe from all of this. My chest ached with a strange sensation at thinking of my children. Where were they now? Why couldn't I *feel* them? It was as if our strings had been cut. Was Caelius's blood strong enough to break the maker-bond between me and my children?

The ache persisted. Was this loss? Guilt? Sorrow? How many days had it *really* been since I last knew what was real and what was Caelius?

He pulled my chin up, steadying my darting eyes. "Rest assured, I will repeat what happened as many times as you need me to. But first, let's get you dressed. Like a good god, I have a present for my obedient son."

I instinctively leaned forward and kissed his lips, a moan escaping my mouth.

He laughed, flicking his tongue against mine before pulling back. "Not that kind of *present,* darling." He was enthralled, his body limp and relaxed. He looked almost as drunk as I felt. But there was something else behind his affectionate gaze, something under the surface I couldn't scratch no matter how many times I clawed his back as he sank his hips into mine. His restlessness to reveal what was buried matched my desire to find it. What was I looking for? What was he hiding?

He looked over my body as a painter would his masterpiece, touching the fading bruises and teeth indentations. "I was gentle this time, wasn't I? I stayed flesh for you. I didn't do anything you didn't like."

I laughed outright, then caught myself, choking back my outburst. It was true that he hadn't taken me in shadow form, but that didn't mean an immortal body had been any more forgiving.

He smiled nonetheless. "It was gentle for *me*, I suppose. I am a god, you know."

He scanned my face, that same strange look overtaking his features. "Where are you really, La-Narru? Will you ever come to me again by choice?"

I looked at the tossed sheets and dented bed frame. "I'm here with you now, aren't I?"

He touched my face, letting his hand rest at my cheek. "Do you remember meeting me for the first time yet?"

"Uh . . . yes. I—"

"Don't placate me, boy." His hand dropped, and he averted his eyes. Those eyes, the same ones that had looked up at me with such hope a moment ago, were now tinted with bitterness. "We went over this last time I was deep inside you, and yet you've forgotten. This is a *real* memory, it happened, so why can't you pull it from the recesses of your mind? It's so important. Why can't you remember me?"

I fumbled, unable to follow yet yearning to please him all the same. "I'm sorry, tell me again—"

"Before Nefertiti laid her *tainted* lips on you, before you lost your mother to sickness, you loved me. *I* was your first." His voice grew distant as he looked out our bedroom window.

"I don't know the age in human years, but you were young." He turned his face to meet mine. There it was again; the longing I thought would be satiated after days in bed still burned when I saw the deep auburn of his eyes.

"I had been in human form for some time. And it bored me. It was a little wager, an experiment between me and the Light. This planet had its time, just like every world, but the Light protected it, extended it past reason and balance, and I couldn't fathom why. The Light offered a deal: I could experience what it was like to be alive, just this once. And I was . . . disappointed."

I winced, and my jaw hardened under his tender touch. "Of course you were disappointed." That felt true on every level. No matter what state I was in now, it would never be enough to quench his eternal needs.

He pulled my head up and placed a small kiss on my mouth, nibbling on my lower lip before he pulled back. "Until I met you." He licked the side of my face, the salty sweetness that must have been my skin, enthralling him further.

"Darkness in human form is still not human, after all. And you could sense it right away." He stroked his hand gently down my frame. "You were awestruck. The things that you said to me, I often replay the moment in my mind. The words that you *can't remember*, I will never forget."

"Is . . . is that when I called you God?" His eyes searched everywhere but my own. Then he leaned his face closer so that he was all that filled my gaze.

"Yes. You asked if I was a god. And I said that I could be *your* god." He pulled away as I grimaced. "Are you embarrassed?"

"N-no." I couldn't fathom the child part of me that would be so foolish. But before the wars we had been raised to believe in gods, and in that ignorance I had enticed a being of Darkness.

He looked away again. The uneasiness that had settled earlier sank further into my skin. All of this stuttering and placating. It was similar to the behavior I'd exhibited when I'd been *forced*, when he had broken me in the past. But this was different. This time he wanted more—

"La-Narru."

My eyes shot up. I still hated hearing him call me by my Gutian name.

"The meaning of your birth name in your native tongue couldn't be more true. However, it's the custom of *your* people to be given a new name after you've proven yourself as a warrior to the gods, though your father never gave you the honor after your Harrowing. When you asked me to take you, to save your life under Nefertiti's window so that you could see her again, did I not honor you in your own tradition by naming you Lucian? By claiming you as my own? I let you live a mortal life, unhindered by my touch, until it came to its natural end. Then your life was *mine*. It's what you asked for as a child: that in death we would join, that you could be with me again, your *god*. You promised. Have I not . . . have I not given you everything you've asked for?"

My mouth fell open. Incensed, I tried to grasp his words.

"Everything I've asked for? I would have never asked for this—"

"Careful." He hardened his jaw as if holding his rage in place.

I softened my tone. "I don't remember. I only remember the night of the Harrowing. I'm sure I was too young to understand what my words meant."

He rolled his neck, stretching his shoulders and straightening his back. "Why is the feeling of vulnerability now growing alongside disgust?" He stood tall. I struggled to rise next to him but fell to the floor, my legs weak from his passions.

"I want to help you up, to hold you again. At the same time, my mouth is filled with bile." He coughed, reaching for me and lifting me to my feet all the same.

"I wasted my one chance, my one time being human, on you, *boy*. Look at us now, all because of some stupid promise I made to you by that river." He laughed, the sound full and rich and bitter. "The Light's little dogs never would have imprisoned me if I hadn't broken that single arbitrary rule to save you. I was never supposed to take a life. And now there is no escaping it; what's done is done. Because of *you* I suffered all of this time in mortal form, caged for *thousands* of years. Now I will set this world on fire as my revenge. I will destroy everything you've loved . . . just to have what you promised me in Gutium."

His fingernails grew instinctually and pierced my arms.

"I don't understand. I'm yours! How else can I prove it to you?" I fumbled, fearing what his threat meant. I had nothing left to lose, but Caelius was inventive, and I had my Second-Borns to think of. "I only want to please you." It sickened me, but it was true enough. His blood pulsed inside me with every word he spoke.

He let me go and sighed. "Of course you do . . . *now*. But this isn't the way I wanted it. When you willingly offered yourself to me, I thought you were finally keeping your word, that you at last returned my feelings, but it was a lie spoken for *their* sake."

"What lie? For whom? What do you mean?" I couldn't remember what he was talking about.

"Never mind that, little one. Power. Control. Forcing you to my will. That is something I know well. And now, out of the cage, I can do it completely and make you *mine* for good. None of this 'willing acceptance of love.' If you're not going to *give* it to me freely, then I'm going to take it, darling."

He kissed me long and deep, then pulled back. "Don't worry your mind with these things. I'm just talking to myself, working things out, as it were. You just relax into my presence, and enjoy my fevered touches like you have been. You are clay now. Trust the hands of your sculptor; I have your best interest at heart. That is why I prepared this gift for you."

He dressed me slowly, fitting me in a silk Hanfu with a bright yellow sash. It was beautiful.

He watched me closely as I studied the fabric. "Is this the gift? It feels familiar somehow."

"This isn't the gift. This is just a Hanfu I've cleaned for you, sweetheart." His gaze was resolute. "You liked it, so we took it off the dead body of a boy. He never would have looked as handsome as you wearing it. No harm done, right?" There it was again, that look in his eyes, like he was masking something important. "And the yellow sash I picked up anew. It sounds like a wedding rhyme, doesn't it? Something borrowed, something new, something yellow . . ." He brushed his thumb by my eyes.

"Something blue." He smiled, but his teeth were clenched in anticipation. "Do you like it? Is it not agreeable?"

I couldn't explain the warm affection I felt for this Hanfu. "It feels . . . like it's *mine*." It felt like it had been pressed up against me, held in my arms, like it was something precious I couldn't put words to. "It's like it belonged to me before, but I have no memory of it. I lost it."

I lost it.

My own words struck the growing ache in my heart.

The feeling of loss.

That was familiar too.

Caelius took in a long breath. "No memory, huh? Think hard, dear one." He waited. His eyes were now cold and calculating. The quick shift from affection to distaste was jarring. As the moments passed, my mouth felt dry. Was this some kind of test? Was I *supposed* to remember something?

I searched, but it came up empty, like a gaping hole had been dug out of my mind with a rusted spade. The only thing remaining was a nameless ache.

Still, he leaned closer, like a cobra gazing down at a cornered mouse, the black in his irises opening like slits, threatening to overcome the vermilion.

"Like the memory from childhood. *Should* I remember something?" I whined. "I'm sorry, Father, I don't . . " I looked up at him in desperation. I felt like that lost mouse, wanting nothing more than to be comforted by his hands, even if he was the hunter who had brought me here.

I felt so alone.

Without my memories to anchor me, the pain of the past

felt more present. The death of my tribe, the loss of Nefertiti and Moses . . . the loss of Adnachiel.

He sighed, elated. "Of course you don't remember. It was just some material you liked off of a dead boy, nothing important."

He seemed pleased, but I hated it. I had my past, a past where I hadn't been subservient to Caelius. A past full of betrayal and torment. A past that I had always wanted to forget but now clung to like it was precious milk, feeding my life's purpose. And I could remember all of it, every detail. Everything except this last *year*. The question kept repeating: How had I gone from hating Caelius and keeping him in his cage to lying in his lap like some schoolboy in the arms of his first love?

"My present awaits." Caelius fiddled with the yellow sash, tying the bow at my back a little tighter. "You can come in now. This will be the *fourth* time, but hopefully I'll get the reaction I'm looking for." His tone was cold as his gaze shifted to the door, but it warmed considerably when he wrapped his arms around my waist and whispered into my ear. "I think you're ready this time, darling."

"Fourth time for what?" I squirmed in his grip.

He released me and sat on the bed candidly, his eyes again intent on the doorway.

A figure stepped through.

I blinked, then fell to my knees.

"Impossible," I muttered. "You're *dead*! I killed you myself!"

Her gaze flickered to Caelius in a flash of contempt before returning to me and softening. There were lines on the sides of her eyes, grooves that the black eyeliner couldn't hide. There was a weariness there I had never seen in Nefertiti in all of our days in

Gutium, nor in all of the long nights in Egypt.

She walked toward me, then knelt at my feet.

"It is I, my love."

Caelius sneered at her words, but I couldn't take my eyes off of her. I pressed my head into her shoulder. My body ached to weep into her, to believe that this wasn't some blood-induced dream. Tears tumbled down her back, the wet falling on her skin like it had in the endless dunes of the Libyan desert. Every tear that had evaporated in the sand had screamed her name. And now in her arms, I found myself doing the same. "Nefari! You're alive," I wept.

Through the weeping she spoke, but I couldn't hear her. I clung to her as I had when Onack had whipped my back as a boy, when I'd lost my mother, when I had eaten ash and she had saved me from my father . . . and myself.

Finally, there was another name besides Caelius in the dark. "You're really here, aren't you, Nefari? *Please* be real. I don't want to be alone anymore."

"Of course I'm here beside you, La-Narru. For ours is a proud people," she said. In her voice I heard a hesitancy that was also unknown to me. "We are etched into the existence of all things. Are we not then bound by love and fate? Do you think that anything could truly smite the Gutian tribe?" Her grip tightened around my back, almost painfully. To hear our Gutian code referenced so easily through Nefari's lips—as if it had always been there, as if time had not eroded it away—was a dream, a dream I didn't want to wake from.

"How? Besides your father, I thought I was the last Gutian left," I whispered, my chest convulsing. The girl I had kissed by the river in our childhood, the girl I had made love to by the Nile, the daughter of Ur-Nammu, future leader of Gutium, the wife of the Pharaoh, my everything, she was *alive*.

This must be it.

Even as my blood pulsed for Caelius, a part of me resisted with everything I had left. A part of me was reaching for *something*. It was as if I were clawing like an animal trying to dig itself out of a stone cave, buried deep in the black. This must've been the name, the memory I'd been looking for in the nothingness: Nefari.

"It's you. It has to be you." I clung to her arms. "It's always been you."

I held on to that resolution.

And it brought me peace.

This must have been what I'd been missing in the year gap.

I realized now why I had been so desperate to remember.

"Nefari. My love. Jewel among stones, my morning star. How could I have forgotten your resurrection?"

I held her for so long, I lost track of time.

The longer I clung to her, however, the more that strange hollowness crept in. Was this just the effect from Caelius's blood? It was small at first, but eventually it groaned like an expansive crack with wind whistling through.

I held her tighter, trying to fill in the gap, ignoring the emerging sensation. This *must've* been what I'd been searching for. All I'd ever wanted was Nefertiti alive and in my arms again.

Now I had it.

Caelius had given me my dream.

Caelius was my savior.

I felt a surge of affection for him that quickly shifted to anger.

"Wait." I pulled back from her embrace. "I don't remember what happened this past year. Explain to me how this is possible." I glared at Caelius. "When I brought her to you, you said she was *dead*, that my kiss had killed her because male vampires cannot turn females. You said there was nothing to be done!" As anger rolled off my lips, his blood pulsed inside of me, aching for any explanation that wasn't betrayal.

"I was able to save her, true enough, but she was weak and in a deathlike sleep. I wasn't able to turn her fully until I was more powerful and free from the cage." Caelius knelt down behind me, wrapping his arms around my stomach. "We've been over this, dear one. Last year I restored her and revealed her to you the instant I was free."

He stroked my hair with one hand, his other tightening around my waist. "Why do you think I so fervently asked you to bring me a Vessel? I wanted to revive her, to bring you two together. As I've always said, you mean everything to me. It's all for you."

I blinked.

His words seemed habitual, as if repeated. I *had* heard this before. He had in fact told me. But wasn't this the first time? "I drank the sands of Egypt in grief. Why didn't you at least tell me she was *alive*? I suffered for so long!" I looked at Nefertiti's flawless skin, the deep purple of her eyes—a color that had pained me every time I'd seen it after her death. *That* was familiar. It was more familiar and trustworthy than Caelius's words in my ear.

His lips pressed against my hair as he whispered, "It's all for you. At least remember *that*."

Her hands cupped my cheeks, pulling my head away from

Caelius. The feel of her—that I knew more than any thought in my own brain. "Nefari." My lips trembled. "Love of my life." I leaned forward and kissed her. It was nothing like the aching need of Caelius's blood, the possession that forced me to crave him. My heart yearned in a way that only Nefertiti had ever made it yearn. In the way a boy loves a girl. *She* was and would always be my first true love.

My only love.

The name I had been looking for in the dark.

Nefari.

I closed my eyes.

I could feel her resistance under my mouth—a slight pause before giving herself over completely—and I did the same. I was swimming in the deep sea of our lifelong bond, letting it lift the dregs of Caelius's blood from my mind. *This* I knew.

This was home.

Gutium.

Our code.

Our family.

An image pulsed through my mind: her children crying out, being ripped apart.

Mutilated.

My eyes flashed open.

Caelius pulled me back from the embrace, his voice agitated. "Why did I wait, you asked?" He turned my chin to face him, relieved to have my full attention. He shifted my shoulders, pulling me out of her arms. "You would have been helpless, watching her sleep. Better to think her dead, to grieve and go on living, in case you never procured a Vessel. But that's in the past.

Now she's here, a gift for you, a gift from the *god* who cares for you more than any man or woman ever could." He bit his thumb and ran the red over my teeth.

My blood churned. I swallowed, licking my incisors, a fever overtaking my internal rhythm.

"Yes," I said involuntarily.

Yes.

His words made a kind of sense, a sense that might have infuriated me if I wasn't so enamored with every sound his mouth made. His blood was inside of me, calling to go back to its home. It was unlike any home I'd had in childhood. The home inside his body, the creation drawing back to its maker, was all-consuming.

I felt my will crumble.

I nodded in compliance, as if my words weren't enough, and he smiled. It was a dull smile, but he pulled me farther away from Nefertiti's arms and deeper into his.

"Her children. A memory . . ." I spoke slowly, not sure of what answer I wanted. "They were . . . killed in front of us?"

His smile shifted quickly, a hard line overtaking his lips.

"And?"

"A gruesome death. But they died in Egypt a long time ago, didn't they? I watched over them."

"You are so close to . . . remembering, my sweet." He took a deep breath. "Let me go over everything a few more times; we'll perfect it. By the time I'm done, you'll remember everything fully." He pressed a sigh into my neck as he kissed my nape. "Leave, *hag*. I'll call you in, and we'll do this again tomorrow."

She rose silently. Her mouth opened as if to speak, but it hung there, unable. Finally she closed it, speaking through her teeth. "As you wish, Father." She left as quickly as she had entered.

"What's going on? Why can't she stay?" I panicked. I tried to reach for her, but his grip constricted. I was nothing more than a mouse coiled in his arms. "What have you done to us, Caelius?"

He played with his nail, pressing it against my wrist in an idle threat "*Caelius*, you say. How quickly we revert to old bad habits, La-Narru. I believe the word you were looking for was Father or *God*." He pressed the nail into my skin until blood covered the tip. "Because the sight of her kissing you is so revolting, I nearly ripped her apart, just like I did her children and yours. That's why we'll do it over until it's *perfect*. But next time, she's not to kiss you—not unless she wants me to go against our new deal. With her affections removed, this time I'll be able to keep my composure and answer you properly."

"What? You ripped apart her children and mine?" I thrashed in his arms.

Brainwashing.

That's what he was doing.

And somehow he'd brought Nefertiti back from the dead to do it.

What kind of hell was I really trapped in?

"It's okay, my sweet."

I clawed at his skin but still couldn't move.

He licked the blood moving down my wrist and moaned. "I haven't drunk from you this whole time. I've been gentle, and you're being so stubborn." He bit his lip and smeared it along my filleted wrist. The wound closed instantly, but his blood mixing with mine filled me with desire. My tense body relaxed instantly.

He nuzzled his head into mine. "We'll do this until you get

it right. I'll change some things, make a few tweaks here and there to make sure the blame falls on the proper channels. You are *so* close. Although, I won't regret spending more time in bed with you, rewriting your mind. The sex is amazing, and you're so defenseless like this." He cupped my face in his hands, affection overtaking his venomous features.

Tears rolled down my face, as if my body knew something my mind couldn't grasp. "Stop this. Stop this madness, Caelius. No matter how many times you brainwash me, I'll never be yours!"

There it was.

As my lips trembled, a name escaped the blackness.

Shea.

"What a fun word." Caelius smiled to himself. "Brainwashing. A washing of the brain. Yes. As your *god*, I am cleansing it of all the clutter and trash. I'm cleansing it of the *lesser* beings you've clung to like a child clings to his filthy worn-out blanket. All that would make you miserable and keep you from being mine, I will expunge from your existence. Be thankful I am leaving Nefertiti . . . for now."

He cut his wrist and shoved blood into my mouth. My arms instantly fell limp at my sides. I was already at the place where I could not physically resist his control. My mouth lapped up the red as if it was natural, as if I had been starved and aching for it. How long had it taken to become like this?

The name that had risen to the surface vanished, and with its absence, the hollowness returned.

No.

I just had it.

Who was it?

They were important.

I closed my eyes as he poured and poured, an ocean of Caelius swimming in my veins as he whispered into my ear.

What was I looking for?

Blackness.

Nefertiti . . .

A woman.

No.

The Light.

Yes.

I did it.

I brought the Vessel to Caelius, and now he's free.

He saved me from her; she tried to kill me.

I'm in his arms.

Caelius.

My god, my everything.

Caelius.

The name that will save me from the dark.

Caelius.

*****

Light filtered in through the window.

I sat with Meky and Setepenre by my side, staring into the beautiful eyes of my world: Nefertiti.

I sighed in both contentment and pain. The Vessel had murdered her innocent children. She and Adnachiel had killed *all* of my Second-Borns except Ur-Nammu, who was nowhere to be found. They'd even killed Gracuri, who'd been so adept at hiding.

I understood Ashgar and Gunnhild, but they'd slaughtered Bohe, David, and Duncan, the kindest and most evolved of our kind. They wouldn't have hurt anyone. They'd been living off of animals for decades. How could that dog, Adnachiel, kill beings who were so . . . so much more human than the mortals alive today?

That *beast*.

I scowled.

What was I thinking? If he could kill Moses, he could kill anyone without remorse.

So why now? Why had he finally chosen to spare a Vessel? He had failed his mission and let her live, which had unlocked Caelius, and now he was traveling with her, trying to kill all of us off. It was definitely a new move. Instead of sacrificing his queen, he was keeping her close and going after my king. Maybe he was tired of playing the pawn. But to be desperate enough to kill the innocent . . .

To think, at one time I'd considered him my brother. I hadn't known then what a merciless liar he was. I should have known by the knife in the back of his sibling Halfdan. Still, him helping the Vessel murder Nefertiti's children was a new low I had not thought him capable of. They were vampires, but they were blameless and had never spilled human blood.

How the righteous had fallen.

I looked at Meky and Sherit as I played with Setepenre's hair. She leaned against my shoulder with a contented sigh. They were the last of the Gutian tribe now, and I would give my life to protect them. I squeezed her tight. She was *mine*. My child. She'd been hidden by Ur-Nammu, and when she'd come of age, she'd been half-changed and left asleep with her sisters and the body of their mother. Caelius had turned them all fully when he'd escaped the prison.

I had barely gotten to spend any time with the other girls before the Vessel and that dog had slaughtered them. What was worse was that it was time I couldn't remember spending. That truth ached in me. As a mortal, I had helped raise them by the Nile. But I had missed so much of their lives, and now I would never have the chance to be the father I had always wanted to be to them.

It was Ur-Nammu who had insisted upon hiding Nefertiti and the children from me. How could he have been so selfish? Even though Nefertiti hadn't been fully restored, just knowing she was alive would have eased much of my suffering. He was to blame for this ache I was feeling now.

Caelius had tried to convince him otherwise, but as their grandfather, Ur-Nammu had said it was his right to decide. I'd been betrayed and lied to. I couldn't believe it, but it *felt* real and burned down into my gut. Ur-Nammu had *lied* to me for so long. And now that it was all out in the open, now that we had lost so much to the Vessel, he was hiding like a coward, unable to face his own shame.

I clutched onto my daughter, eyeing the other two girls.

Caelius had plans for us to rule the world, but for now he wanted me to spend time with him and my family, to fully heal from the Vessel's attack. I didn't know where we were exactly: a forest overlooking a lake in a beautiful cabin somewhere. Surrounded by family and nature, I felt more Gutian these past few days than the vampire I had become over the centuries. It was peaceful and empty, simple, almost like I was human again.

I sighed, but it hitched in my throat. It was peaceful, wasn't it? Was that the right word? Why did I have to repeat that to myself every day? Why did I feel such unrest?

It must've been the *Vessel*. I couldn't stop thinking about her. She was out there somewhere, even now, looking for us.

Hunting us.

I almost laughed. I had hunted every Vessel since the dawn of Vessels. And now this one, a woman, had almost defeated me? Was this karma? At the time Caelius had been freed, he'd been weak and unable to consume her soul and restore himself completely. To face off against even a half-powered Caelius with only the *beast* at her side . . .

She must be the strongest Vessel ever made.

The frustrating part was that I didn't remember how she'd done it. Caelius had said the shock of it—the physical damage and loss of the children and my Second-Borns—must have been too much for me to process fully, that even his blood couldn't restore my memory completely.

Still, he had saved me.

Caelius.

As if the thought of him had summoned his ghost, he stepped behind me, squeezing my shoulders.

Setepenre looked up at him affectionately, and I cast my eyes to Nefertiti. She stared out at the lake. She, Sherit, and Meky barely met my gaze these days. I understood. I had failed to protect our family from the Vessel. Shame flooded my body. I wouldn't fail them again. I would rid the world of the Beast and the Vessel, then Nefertiti would fall back into my arms, and I could raise the remainder of our family properly, like I had in

Egypt.

I stared at Nefari with longing, my cheeks flushing like they had when I'd been a boy in Gutium.

Caelius leaned down, nibbling my ear. "Don't blush on account of me." His voice was whimsical, pleased.

I jerked my head from him.

He had used his blood to save me, but Caelius's blood was nothing to play with. He had given me a large amount, and I knew all too well from my own children that even one drop was enough to bring on infatuation, an affection that lasted an age. That one drop gave them immortality and slavery all at once.

Now that some time had passed and my memories were somewhat restored, I was out of the fog his blood had induced. I felt more myself. I straightened my back, shrugging his hands from my shoulders.

"What is it you want, Father?"

He pulled the chair next to me closer and plopped down. He rested his head against the back side of his hand. "You, of course."

"Stop it," I growled.

He licked his lips. "I miss the Lucian that was like a puppy, suckling on my blood," he bemoaned to himself.

I swallowed, feeling a tremble shake through me.

Setepenre leaned up, looking at Caelius. "But he's healed now, Grandfather. He doesn't need your blood." Her voice was sweet and innocent, a smile lifting her sculpted cheeks.

Now Nefertiti and Meky turned to me, but their eyes fell on Caelius alone.

He licked his lips again. "True enough." He reached over and patted Sete's head, eyeing me like dinner. "Besides, you became quite boring, darling. I like it when you come to me of your own volition, tasting of that old rebellious fire we used to share."

"You'll taste nothing." I scowled.

I was fully aware that I'd repeatedly slept with Caelius in my blood-drunken haze. He had taken advantage of the situation and relished in it. Those memories were etched in my soul like a brand I couldn't carve out: his hips against mine, his tongue in my mouth.

I shuddered.

It would never happen again. As it was, I couldn't call him by his name. Everything in me wanted to call him *God*. I knew that he must have repeated that word over and over. "Father" was all I could muster, and even that sickened me. "I'll serve you, I'll burn this worthless world to a husk if that's what you want, but make no mistake, I do it for the sake of my family, not you."

"But your family is *my* family, dear one." Caelius laughed. It was a cold dead thing, lacking whimsy and the airy nature of most of his jaunts. "Children are so difficult, aren't they, Molly?"

"I don't know what you mean." She fidgeted with her hands, stepping from the doorway.

I had hardly noticed her. Apparently Nefertiti and I had turned her in hopes of dissuading the Vessel. But the Vessel didn't care, so Caelius had wiped Molly's memories in order to protect her from the pain of having to battle her own daughter. It was a secret we were supposed to keep for Molly's sake.

Just who was this Vessel really? What kind of woman would willingly kill her own mother just because she was a vampire? It was as if being a vampire was a crime in and of itself. She was probably dogmatic, the religious sort. Good and evil, black and white, drawing rigid lines like I'd seen humans draw across centuries, lines that always ended in massacres. Every generation claimed that some other faction of human was *evil*. What would the world do now that they knew there were vampires?

I thought of Bohe and Gracuri, of Duncan, David, and all the good men who'd *still* been good men even after the change. They hadn't been perfect, they'd killed on occasion, but people didn't go around obliterating all things with sharp teeth that killed in nature. What would the world be like without sharks, lions, bears, alligators? What right did she have to decide what was *divine* and what was unholy? What right did she have to kill my kind without question?

I looked down at the Hanfu I was wearing.

She had killed them all in one swoop, more or less. All their deaths felt fresh, but none so raw as Bohe's. He'd practically been a monk.

I bet he didn't even fight back. I bet Duncan and David didn't either.

I shifted nervously. And what of Gracuri? The smile I had hoped would one day return to his lips was something I would never see again. What kind of monster was she to rob the world of such men?

In truth, I'd thought Gracuri's end would come from Caelius. He hated him, that much I knew. Caelius would have killed him *slowly*. Although . . .

I looked back at him. There was something in his eyes lately, something I had never seen in the cage: a sort of affection. It was like the seeds of love that could grow in any other person, but in someone as corrupt as him, they just remained seeds. They were scattered throughout his irises, visible if I looked long enough.

Scattered.

That was familiar.

Still, his eyes had changed.

He had changed.

A timeless being of Darkness was evolving.

He looked deep into my eyes, stroking my cheek with the back of his hand.

"I'm bored, darling. Let's destroy Miami together."

I swallowed.

Vacation was over.

CHAPTER 7
SHEA

Duncan was floating above me in a gust of wind I had taken control of, and Aidan was buried knee-deep in the ground.

Neither one of them could move.

It was epic.

I was pretty impressed with myself.

We were right outside Helena's secret fortress. It looked like a simple one-room cabin on top of a cliff, but really it was a maze of rooms built deep into the mountains.

"Shea!" Helena shouted from the front doorway. "What did you do to my floors?"

Oops. Earlier I had experimented with using my earth powers indoors and ripped up the wood flooring of the cabin, creating a hole looking down into the room below, hence why we were outside at the present moment.

"But hey, look, she's mastered earth." Aidan came to my defense.

"I can fix it. Don't worry." I hoped I wasn't lying. "I just wanted to come out here since I was on a roll. Hang on."

With a simple thought, I maneuvered the dirt surrounding Aidan and raised him out of the ground, then controlled the earth to seal it back up.

I was about to walk back into the cabin with Aidan when I heard a friendly voice behind me.

"As much as I love flyin', I'm wonderin' if you'd let me down now, lass," Duncan said with a laugh.

Embarrassed, I turned around and lowered the Scotsman safely to the ground. I found it so cute that Duncan called me lass. Of course, he called every woman that, but still. And equally adorable was when he called my dad lad. Jeff Harper was hundreds of years younger than Duncan, even though he *looked* twenty years older, so it was extra amusing to see Dad treated like a youngster. And if I was being honest, I was pretty sure Dad liked being one of the youngest in our group too.

Walking inside the small cabin, I saw the giant hole I had created and cringed. I could see the room beneath it through the opening, but the hole itself was a mess of cement, wood, and dirt.

Now to try and fix it.

I could do this.

Concentrating on the wood itself—the grains, the knots, the inkling of life left inside what used to be a giant oak tree—I envisioned the floor repairing itself. Then I added the rocks and the dried water from the broken cement, weaving in and out until . . .

Well.

At least it wasn't a hole anymore.

It was a mangled mess of wood with a little bit of gray cement mixed in, but it was solid.

I turned to face Helena's wrath, but she was actually leaning on her hip and smiling. "Good job. Not pretty, but impressive work."

"Oh, cool, thanks," I said in relief.

It had been just the five of us for a couple of weeks now: me, Dad, Aidan, Duncan, and Helena. The more time passed, the more I worried about Lucian and my mom, not to mention Ur-Nammu, who had gone off the radar completely. But if Caelius was feeding Lucian his blood and wiping all memory of me, what could I really do? I just hoped there'd be a sliver of recognition. I had seen it in my mom when she'd confessed Caelius's inability to Dream-Walk. But I kept my longing to myself, afraid that if I expressed any emotion about mom remembering me, I would jinx it.

I asked Helena, "How's it going on that device, or invention, or whatever it is that might stop Caelius?"

Helena's expression was distracted, which was pretty normal for her, but she forced a smile. "Slower than I'd like, but I feel like we'll be able to do some testing in a couple of days. You're doing a wonderful job training."

I couldn't tell if she actually meant that or if she was trying to be encouraging. Either way, I'd take it.

Looking awkwardly at the mangled mess of concrete and wood, I said, "I should probably practice a bit more."

Nodding, Helena walked toward her lab table. "Good idea. Just try and keep this place in one piece." Without another word, she pulled her hair back and began working on what appeared to be gears and electronics. I couldn't really tell.

One thing I knew: Helena was a mad genius. It was a shame that she hadn't been recognized in her own time. It made me wonder how many other brilliant women in history had never received the accolades they deserved.

I looked out the window and took a moment to appreciate my surroundings. Helena's "lair" was a cabin in the middle of the Colorado mountains. Seeing glimpses of the range through the bay window in the distance was breathtaking. Crooks and large peaks let in the perfect purple glow of magic hour. It never failed to amaze me.

It had taken quite a hike to get here, though I'd been able to practice my wind moves to help myself up a few tricky cliff walls. Vampires and angels didn't have that problem. Dad, Duncan, and Helena had kind of zoomed up the walls, while Aidan had tried out the new wings his brothers had given him. It was strange seeing Aidan fly, though I couldn't actually *see* his wings. For some reason they were invisible to me since I was part human. As a Vessel, I'd hoped seeing angel wings would be a perk, but nope. Aidan had just looked like me, kind of hovering in midair until we reached the top of the cliff face. So anticlimactic.

The cabin itself was simple in build—four walls, a couple windows and doors—but it was what was inside that made it special. It was like stepping onto a movie set about Nikola Tesla with the amount of what I referred to as Helena's "invention stuff." There were giant electricity conductors, moving gears from the size of a nickel to the size of a small car, beakers, Bunsen burners, wooden tables, and bookshelves full of both ancient books with no authors and newer books by modern scientists like Neil deGrasse Tyson (I may have thumbed through a couple of those), Stephen Hawking, and Carl Sagan.

And that was just the top floor! A staircase led down to more rooms and more staircases with gears and inventions that Helena probably hadn't touched in years. I only explored four or five levels down, but Helena said she had built rooms going at least a mile deep.

Honestly, I didn't want to leave.

It was cozy.

Sometimes isolation was perfect for avoiding reality.

I had my dad. I had my Aidan.

Even Duncan and Helena were becoming fast friends.

And staying here, in a kind of reality-denial, helped ease the aching guilt of the thousands of innocents who had been killed by Caelius. I couldn't erase that entirely. What if Lucian and my mother were murdering people against their will? Could I forgive them? Could they forgive themselves? I had no answers, so I stayed in my protective bubble here at Helena's lair.

Aidan nudged me affectionately. "You and Duncan got this? I'm going to try and contact my brothers and see if they have any new information."

I nodded, turning to Duncan. "If you're okay with it?"

Duncan's smile was contagious. "Of course I'll help ye. Fire's next, right? We should probably head outside again so we don't burn the building down."

"Good plan."

I walked outside with Duncan, and the cold breeze hit my face. It was stuffy inside the cabin. Some of the rooms deeper down in the lair were cooler, but there was nothing like fresh mountain air. Even though it was still fall, being this high up in the mountains, it might as well have been the arctic.

As much as I liked the breeze, I'd get chilled fast. It didn't help that I'd been born and raised in Arizona. My body definitely couldn't handle the cold very well. The vampires couldn't care less, and Aidan said he was cold, but I didn't believe him for a second. He was just looking out for me, which was why he kept the fireplace going in the upstairs room twenty-four seven.

"What do ye have in mind for me, lass? Burn a hole in my chest?" Duncan winked.

"Are you seriously making a joke of when I seared a hole in Lucian? It was by accident, by the way." I shook my head.

Laughing, Duncan replied, "Aye, Gracuri told me of that one. Scared me at first telling, but now that I know ye, I'd be honored if ye laser beamed me through ma ribs."

"I'm pretty sure it hurt. Like *really* hurt. Let's try sticks, in a very safe fire pit, that won't burn down the forest."

"Your decision, lass, but I'm volunteering if ye need it," Duncan said, almost too cheerfully.

Walking over to the fire pit at the side of the house, I sat down on the bench facing it. Duncan sat next to me, concerned. "What is it? Ye thinking of Lucian and your mum again? We'll get 'em back. I swear it to ye."

I didn't want to talk about it.

It only reminded me of how little control I had in my life right now.

"You haven't had any blood since we got here. Are you going to be okay?" I knew I was evading the subject of Lucian and my mom, but I really was curious. Duncan hadn't eaten anything since this trip had started.

"Ah." Duncan leaned back on the bench. "I don't drink from anyone alive. I don't drink animal blood either. I've got no stomach fer it."

"Wait, what?" I was shocked at his admission. "You can't digest it?"

Duncan threw his head back and laughed. "Nae, I can drink it just fine, I just choose not to." He paused, then added, "It's what drove Lucian and me apart. He never understood."

"So you don't drink humans or animals?" I couldn't process what he was telling me. Finally, I replied, "That's so noble. I kind of want to hug you right now. But how do you survive?"

"Much like Nefertiti and her children must've. Hearin' their stories about Caelius not wantin' them to kill anyone and only eating leftovers, I only drank from the dead. At least back then anyway. But now I drink from blood bags. Fer the last hundred years or so." He smiled. "I'm a Second-Born. I'm powerful enough to live off of air for four to five weeks at least."

"Wow." I had no words. A vampire who didn't want to feed off of humans or animals. It made me wonder if there were more vampires like Duncan. Did that make him a vegan vampire? It made me feel an intense affection for him that I couldn't explain. Then something he'd said finally registered in my brain. "What did you mean when you said it's what drove you and Lucian apart?" I didn't really want to ask, but I had to. "Is it because he wanted you to kill?"

Sighing heavily, Duncan nodded. "When I first met Lucian, he had come straight off the docks in Edinburgh, and I admit, there was somethin' about him that caught ma eye. He had an aura 'bout him. I could tell he had some great stories to tell. And since ma favorite thing is tellin' stories, I steered straight to him and started tellin' him how I had just defeated a savage twenty-foot brown bear that had torn apart ma village." Duncan nudged me with a smile. "It was a complete lie, o' course, but Lucian actually smiled, and it was the most magnificent sight I'd ever seen." He paused, as if remembering that single moment.

I completely related. Lucian's smile was epic, probably because it was such a rarity. But I liked thinking of Duncan amusing Lucian. It somehow made me feel better about everything that was happening.

Continuing, Duncan said, "Tha two of us were inseparable after that. He'd always be askin' for more tall tales, and since it was my favorite pastime, I'd oblige. We went on like that for a good three months, all through summer. But the fall was on us, and King James IV called on all Scotsmen to battle the British. I decided to fight like all men of my time did." Duncan's eyes looked to the mountaintops, his usual jovial demeanor turned somber. "Lucian wanted to fight too, and tha two of us joined the thirty thousand strong and marched to the Battle of Flodden. It was horrific. I can see it as clearly in my mind's eye as if it happened yesterday.

"Lucian destroyed twenty men right before ma eyes in less than a second. Scots or Brits, he just tore open their flesh and moved on to the next. He was a vampire. I dinnae even know such monsters existed." Duncan looked as if he were reliving every second of his past.

"I froze. I dinnae know what to do. I saw Lucian rip ma own countrymen to pieces. They were as terrified as I was, but since they'd seen me in Lucian's company the last few months, they thought I was with him. Before I knew it, I had been stabbed straight through with a broadsword." Duncan stopped. I could see that as difficult as it had been to tell his story thus far, what was coming next was far worse. I almost didn't want to hear it. I had heard enough of Lucian's monstrous behavior in his past to last five lifetimes. But I *needed* to hear it. I needed to hear about the kind of vampire Lucian used to be because Caelius had probably turned him back into that very monster.

Duncan continued. "Lucian screamed to high heaven when he saw me drop to the ground. I'm admitting to ya now, lass, I wanted to die. I wanted to pretend that what I'd just seen was battlefield hallucinations and that I could be reunited with ma mum in Heaven." He nudged me to break the mood a bit. "Ma mum was famous for her feasts, and I expected a right good one when I arrived at the pearly gates." Then he took a deep breath and said, "Lucian turned me instead."

I looked at him, and his expression of true regret and grief gave me a sudden chill.

Turning his face toward the mountains again, Duncan shook his head. "I had so much of Lucian's blood in ma system I couldn't think clearly. With the thousands of men surrounding me, I only saw one. It was as if Lucian were an angel come down to Earth to make me his undying servant. And I wanted to please him with every fiber of what soul I had left." He shrugged and looked at me. "It was the blood, of course. Lucian's blood is as potent as it gets, next to Caelius's, and if he would have told me to slit my own throat, I would have done it happily. That's how much control a maker's blood has on their children."

"You didn't want to be a vampire," I said, already knowing the answer from the look on Duncan's face.

He shook his head. "I truly wish I had died that day." Duncan managed a melancholy smile. "I really did want to see ma mum. I still want to."

"I'm sorry." I didn't know what else to say. My heart ached for him. So far, all I'd seen was the happy-go-lucky Duncan who was so much like Aidan it had been comical. To see this side of him gave me a reality check into how unreal my life had become since I'd found out I was the Vessel.

After a moment, Duncan continued. "Lucian's bloodlust was still high, and once he had turned me, or what he'd thought was 'saving' me, he told me to 'drink until I was full.' " There was a catch in Duncan's voice, the memory was so painful.

I instinctively grabbed his hand and held it. "Oh my God, Duncan. I . . ." I had no words. I knew what was coming. I just wished it was another one of Duncan's tall tales.

Squeezing my hand for support, Duncan plowed forward. "Like you know from your da, new vampires dinnae have much control. I killed my entire clan before I knew what was happening. The guilt of what I'd done overpowered Lucian's blood, and I fell to my knees, sobbing. Lucian was enjoying the slaughter too much to notice. When he had killed almost ten thousand men, he finally saw me, alone in the battlefield, surrounded by ma family and friends who I had murdered with my own hands and who I had . . . fed off of." That last admission hurt him the most. "Lucian ran up to me, and the look I must have given him stopped him dead in his tracks. I'd never seen a man look so . . . broken.

"He knew then what he had done, and he knew I'd never forgive myself. He tried to take the entire blame, saying he had 'forced' me to kill those men, but blood control or not, *I* killed them. *Me.*"

The silence between us was deafening.

I knew that even monster-Lucian wouldn't have been able to stomach Duncan's devastation at killing his friends and family.

"I haven't killed a living soul since, unless you count other vampires. I've killed a lot of those, especially the ones who kill for sport." Duncan pulled his hand away.

"And you and Lucian? What happened after that?" I asked.

"I pushed him away until he finally left. I hated what I was. I refused to drink blood. I thought I could starve myself to death, but it only made me motionless and caused excruciating pain. I deserved it though. I was lying in a cave, mummified, a hundred and fifty years after the battle, writhing in pain that was only fitting for what I'd done, when Lucian appeared.

"Lucian carried a large stag on his shoulders and told me he hadn't killed it, that I could smell the gunpowder from the bullet that had killed the animal. The hunters had abandoned the corpse, and it would go to waste." Duncan turned to me with a sad smile. "He was trying to make it okay for me to drink. Lucian understood that I'd never take another life again, and he wanted me to stop torturing myself. I nodded as much as my head could move, and he gently placed the enormous stag next to me." Duncan finally laughed. "I'll spare ye the details of how messy that eating session was, but it brought me back to myself. I was able to feed from people and animals who were already dead after that, and that allowed me to live with myself."

Becoming contemplative again, Duncan added, "Lucian and I didn't see much of each other after that. He wanted to stay the monster he pretended to be, though I could tell he longed to live like me." Patting my shoulder affectionately, Duncan said, "Your love is what brought him back. He's not a devil anymore, and that's all because of ye."

I didn't want to say that Lucian probably *was* that old monster again—not after everything Duncan had just told me.

"I go to those Highlands every year and say ma prayers to the souls I took that day. That's where Caelius snagged me. Everything else you're up to date on." Duncan gave me a supportive smile. "I just thought ye should know ma history with Lucian. I'm the last son he made besides yeer father, and I think there's a reason fer it. We only knew each other fer a short while when I was human, but I'd do anythin' fer him, and him fer me. That's still true enough."

I knew it too. I may have been the catalyst that'd brought Lucian back from being a monster, but Duncan had been one of the seeds.

"It's cold out here." I concentrated on the sticks in the fire pit, and they instantly lit into a roaring fire. I turned to Duncan, surprised, and we both smiled.

"Look at you, lass. Caelius should fear ye."

My smile faded slightly. "Even if I master everything, I'm still no match for Caelius."

"Don't ye worry about that. Helena is makin' some kind of Caelius-death-contraption, and she needs *ye* to power it." He waved at the fire. "And in less than a couple weeks, yeer already making bonfires with yeer thoughts. I'd say our team is doing pretty well fer itself."

As if he were the sound of doom, Aidan poked his head out of the cabin door. "You guys better get in here."

"Uh-oh." Duncan said what I was thinking.

I stood up and walked toward the door.

Aidan noticed the fire and said with an appreciative grin, "Nice one." Then he added, "Better put it out though."

I focused on the fire, and just to playfully show off in front of Aidan, I snapped my fingers, and the fire snuffed out.

As I reached the door, he smiled. "Really? You going to snap every time you put out a fire now? Because you know the fire went out like three seconds *after* you snapped."

Laughing, I smacked him in the chest. "Shut it."

Inside, Helena and Dad were hovering over a small television that rested on one of the worktables. Like with Paris, a demolished city was showing on every piece of news footage, the captions reading: *Miami destroyed. Demons or aliens? Countless death toll. The whole world is under attack.*

The world was ending.

And I was snapping fire on and off with my fingers.

The footage put everything back in perspective.

I may have been training, and Helena may have been perfecting this device no one knew anything about, but it felt like we were hiding. It felt like we were allowing millions of innocent people to die.

I needed to do something.

"This is horrible," I finally uttered.

No one responded. What could they say?

I needed to Dream-Walk. I needed to connect with *someone*

in the loop. I needed to know what I could do because sitting around in a cabin wasn't working for me.

"I'm really tired. I'm going to lie down for a bit," I lied. But no one suspected anything. They all gave me looks of approval and words of encouragement.

Walking over to the small cot that was my bed, I lay down and closed my eyes.

***

"Good, you're here." Nefertiti's voice came out of the dark.

Sights and sounds swirled around me until we were standing on the same beach in Miami as before. But instead of the beautiful Fontainebleau behind her, it was only burnt ruins.

Before I could speak or ask questions, Nefertiti said, "How long has it been since you've slept? I've been waiting here for you for two days." She seemed angry.

Thinking about it, I realized I hadn't slept much in the last week.

Nefertiti stood there, not speaking. I could tell she was having a full-on inner battle with herself. About what, I had no idea, and frankly, it kind of worried me.

Thinking the worst, I asked, "Is Ur-Nammu . . . okay?"

Nefertiti looked even more upset that I'd brought up her father, which made my stomach sink. But she answered, "I told you to stop him from coming, but that aside, he's fine. He's been watching from a distance. We Dream-Walk when we can."

"Then what's wrong?" I swallowed hard.

Finally, she said, "I need to meet with you in person. Just

you though. No one else. You can't tell anyone. I know it sounds bad, but it's the only way." Nefertiti walked up to me, her eyes pleading. "Lucian needs you, Shea. If you don't come, it may be too late for him."

The pain I felt was desperate. "Where?"

Relief glimmered in her eyes. "Here. I can sneak out during the day. Can you be here by tomorrow?"

"I can't exactly fly like you." The frustration was real. I'd barely been able to lift myself up the small cliff faces using wind. What did she expect me to do, tornado myself to Miami?

"Where can you get to by tomorrow?"

Thinking it through, I could "wind" myself down most of the mountains, grab our van, and drive at least a few hundred miles from where we were. I hoped it was enough to not give away the others' location.

"Santa Fe?" I offered.

"I'll be there. Tomorrow at 4:00 p.m." Nefertiti popped out of the dreamscape, and I was yanked awake.

Staring at the others watching the television, I knew I had to meet Nefertiti to save Lucian. I had to keep it secret. And I had to do it alone.

Aidan would be pissed.

CHAPTER 8
LUCIAN

New Mexico.

Santa Fe was beautiful when it was spoken of in songs and poetry, idealizing the Spanish colonists that settled there in 1610. It was then glorified, like a husk for dead cowboys, in cinema with every new generation's exploratory epiphanies on the exaggerated life of the old West. In reality though, despite the commercialism of most "historical" sites, there was still something mysterious, adventurous even, in the look of the place.

I remembered the city appearing old, even when it was first made—old and worn out like I was. The lingering scent of dried spices used to remind me of the early settlers. They'd been full of hope, and so many of them had ended up as rotting corpses whose bones had been bleached white buried under the sands of the desert sun.

The Pueblo-style architecture and crooked streets often led to adobe cathedrals and old churches; one specific chapel in Loretto had become invaluable to me because of Helena. Santa Fe was not my favorite place, not since I'd thought she'd died.

Its history was laced with slavery, oppression, war, and heat. Deserts.

Why was it *always* the desert?

Did fate have a sense of humor? Did it enjoy bringing me to these places again and again? I was never myself under its sweltering unyielding rays. It was as if the eye of Light itself was mocking my pain, watching me toil and suffer as I had in Egypt. In truth, if I were to describe the life I'd lived after leaving the fertile mountains of Gutium as a young man, I would say I'd left on a sea of gods and had washed up on the shore of a desolate, burning world, hungry and alone. It was much like the story of Eden. That was what had become of my life: starving in the desert. I'd been landlocked from an oasis that had once carried a people, now erased from history and out of reach forever. My homeland.

Until now.

Now I had been reunited with Nefari and our children.

They were what was left of my people.

They were my everything.

Then why?

Why was this happening again, and in the desert, no less?

I held on to the piece of my rib cage threatening to fall off. I pressed it, bone to bone, and gritted my teeth. Gluing the broken fragments together with marrow and muscle, rather than having to grow the chunk back completely, was one of the first lessons I'd learned as an immortal. My body was mangled from shielding Nefertiti and the children, but I didn't care about the pain. I was glad I'd taken the blows for them. I slowed my breathing, letting my blood heal what it could. I straightened up, cracking my shoulder back into its socket, surveying the damage.

Santa Fe, and the staircase I had once sculpted here with my own hands, was . . . gone.

I looked at the Vessel as Caelius pinned it down. A being so puny had held its own against all of us. It gave my foggy memories more validation. This *thing* must have killed them all.

I stared at her.

There was something familiar about the heat and the way the sun reflected off of her wavy blond hair.

Shea Harper.

It was not a name that should invoke fear, but in our previous battle, it had no doubt been on the lips of Nefertiti's children and my own as they breathed their last.

I moved closer.

She was small framed but curvy in all the right places, and her hazel eyes bored into mine with an ache I couldn't comprehend. A thirst bellowed in me like it always had since I'd left the mountains of Gutium. Even though Nefari was by my side, staring at the Vessel made me feel landlocked and far from home.

I finally bridged the gap between us.

"Don't do this! Lucian, you have to fight him! I love you!" She spoke the words as if they had been said before, but they were foreign to me.

I cringed as Caelius laughed. It was a laugh that filled the empty spaces where the rubble of adobe homes lay in waste at our feet. "She thinks because she is a female that she can seduce you, boy." His eyes lingered on my frame, the wound over my ribs already mending.

I let my laugh follow his; it was a small sound chasing an echo. "As if I could be charmed by someone who *murdered* my family."

Caelius's smile faded. "Yes. That's right," he whispered in a tone that was more befitting a church. Maybe it was the ruins of them surrounding us that made his words seem like a silent prayer of remorse. "How could you ever forgive someone who had done that?" He trailed off as if the sentiment wasn't for me, but a reflection for himself.

"I couldn't. My will is not so weak." I puffed my chest, hole and all. It was a childish habit I had picked up from my father. Although, when Onack had broadened his chest and spoken, it was affronting like a lion, a roar that called for submission. It worked with humans, but as a statement against Caelius, it was laughable.

He motioned toward the Vessel, and the strange feeling that had crept up as I stared into her pleading eyes faded with one recollection: she had killed them, mutilating Nefari's children and my Second-Borns.

"You're a monster." I spat, and it landed on her stomach.

I watched it move up and down with her jagged breaths.

There was a small scar there.

Had I kissed that stomach?

I wet my mouth as if the nectar of her skin had been there before. Maybe I had, in battle somehow? That didn't make sense, yet in this desert I thirsted for the Vessel like she was water on dry land.

I averted my eyes, looking around at the battle we had just

survived. We were all panting like mad and more exhausted than we'd ever been in human form, but since I'd taken most of the blows, everyone else was relatively intact. Sadly, Santa Fe wasn't.

Caelius kept our battle in the middle of this city. "Two birds with one Vessel," he'd mocked. Destroying her and the human ants of New Mexico was a joint bliss for him.

I didn't mind the people that couldn't evacuate being fodder, but the buildings themselves, that was a real shame. All of that history I had seen grown around itself like an unkempt garden was a sort of living thing in its own right. That mud and clay, the rustic beauty of it, was now sticking up in jutted broken columns, much like the bleached bones it had once covered. Soon even that would be eaten away by the sun until there was nothing left, like the decimated steps I'd made for Helena.

Our battle, the force of our bodies and the Vessel's elements, had laid waste to what was now the ghost of Santa Fe. In this modern age, would settlers even bother rebuilding it? It would never look the same if they did. And given that Caelius was going to rule the world, I doubted that humans would be allowed to build cities again, let alone churches. Most likely the larger cities would be ravaged, and the smaller would be reduced to farms for human blood. I cringed, thinking of what was going to become of this "new world" Caelius envisioned for us.

I glanced over his body; he didn't have a single mark on him. He healed much faster than the rest of us. Even at half power, he was stronger than I could have imagined while I'd mocked him from the other side of his cage.

He held the Vessel down patiently as she chatted away. Her mouth grew dry from shouting. Each plea was more ridiculous than the last. It was an obvious string of lies meant to confuse me. Finally she stopped, almost hoarse, and shifted her gaze to Nefertiti. Again her pleading went on for some time, words like, "How could you betray me? We could have saved them all *together*," and so on. It fell flat on Nefari's ears, as it had my own.

What was she thinking, that her Vessel mind-control would work on us as it had my Second-Borns? She was powerful but not stronger than all of us together. If memory served, she had separated us and attacked by using the element of surprise. She had even, once, with Adnachiel, tried to broker some kind of treaty—another trap, of course. This Vessel was as clever as she was deceptive.

We had the upper hand now. We had caught her *alone* and off guard. Even so, she must have thought she could take us and was now shocked at her predicament. Caelius remarked how she was stronger than the last time. Her vain belief in her growing power had been her final mistake. If she was a religious zealot then she should have known the words best: pride comes before a fall. What arrogance, to think we would be unprepared this time.

Nefertiti shifted her gaze away from us and turned her back to the Vessel. Surprisingly, Meky did the same, glaring daggers at her mother. It was unusual. The Nefertiti I remembered, the warrior, would have been the first to sink her hands into Shea Harper's chest and rip out her heart. It would have been payment for the lives of her daughters. And Meky? She hadn't fought the Vessel at all. She'd stayed on the sidelines, frozen as Nefari had fought harder, almost *for her*. Had Nefertiti been trying to protect her from injury? Then why the strange unspoken fury between them? Were they fighting again?

Everything had been off since we'd left the cabin. Sherit was obviously obedient to Nefari, without the fury between them that Meky displayed, but even she seemed distant now. Destroying Miami hadn't brought us any closer together, as Caelius had promised. Although, he had thoroughly enjoyed himself in the slaughter. It was visible by the bounce in his step that had remained until Santa Fe.

The only child who had let her guard down had been Setepenre. She'd fought by my side and relished in conquest as I had in the days of old, before I'd lost the taste for it. I was thankful for her attachment to me, but not her viciousness. In my absence, what had she grown into under Caelius's influence? Had I been there for her, had I known, I would have made different choices. I'd missed so much of her life, and slaughtering the world and the Vessel was not how I wanted to reconnect. Still, once all of this was done, Caelius would let us rule the humans like masters over sheep. If I wanted to give her the world, I had to accept that this was one way of doing it.

Once the Vessel was dead, we'd have peaceful days again like we'd had in the cabin. I'd make sure of it. Then the rest of the girls would come back to me. Maybe they would call me Father again, like they had by the Nile when we'd all still been human.

I breathed in deep.

I remembered all of Nefari's children embracing me in some underground lair preparing for battle. Each of them had spoken the Gutian code, their hands reaching for me across the darkness, clinging to my back. It was a moment I held on to, a clear image in the fog of my scattered memories. It must have been just before the Vessel had murdered them. Their love and oaths still burned like hot coals in the pit of my stomach.

I will etch them into the existence of all things. Their memory, I will not lose again, and I will take care of the loved ones who remain. I will be the Gutian father they deserve.

I looked at Sherit and Sete. They were resting at a distance from where we were, keeping Molly restrained, on Caelius's orders. I wasn't surprised. Caelius had said she'd tried to *kill* the Vessel while we were battling. I hadn't seen it myself, but by the way she was thrashing, I believed it. Killing her was not the plan. Maybe that was why Nefari had turned away; she was fighting back the urge herself.

We needed to *subdue* the Vessel, and just as Caelius had predicted, once she used all of her powers, she was spent and quite helpless. It was a relief and something to catalog, that even a being like her had limits, although the knowledge was useless now. Once Caelius was done, she was going to be the *last* Vessel. What use was it to record the weaknesses of a dying species? I looked down on her like she was the last dodo.

"I thought you were stronger than this. I'm disappointed." I pressed the toe of my white shoe into her rib, feeling the dissatisfaction in her failure as if it were my own. "Do you recognize these? They were Gracuri's shoes. Caelius saved them for me after you *slaughtered* him." I looked deep into her eyes, the ache of his loss trembling down my spine. "He wasn't perfect, but he was precious like *all* of my sacred children. And you decapitated them like *trash*."

"I didn't kill them, Caelius did! Lucian, you have to believe me—"

Caelius covered her mouth. "Oh, this one likes to tell stories as much as your Duncan."

I flinched when he said his name, but I didn't know why. In the short time Caelius was free and my Second-Borns were alive, he had met him. He'd told me as much. That must have been enough time to know what Duncan was like.

Still, for him to speak of my son like we shared the knowledge of who he was disgusted me even now. Duncan *hated* Caelius. There were only a few of my children, the warmongers, who would have given anything to see Caelius off his leash, to kill and participate in the end of the world. But Ashgar and Gunnhild were dead, along with those who would have wanted to save it, like Bohe and David, Gracuri and Duncan. In her ignorance, she had killed her best defense against us.

Caelius nudged his foot next to my own as Shea struggled weakly in his arms. "Have a good long look at your enemy, darling. Thoughts? Hatred? What are you *feeling* in those deep turquoise eyes, my sweet? Share with Papa."

I scowled. His tone was gleeful, but there was hardly any red in his eyes; they were consumed in black. Maybe it was being so close to the Vessel, and his long-held dream of being restored to full power, that made him like this. It was all he'd wanted for so long. That must've been why the darkness was emanating off of him in powerful waves. But those waves were directed at me, not Shea Harper, the Vessel crippled in his arms.

What was he doubting?

My loyalty.

I leaned down to her face, sneering up at him. "Because it took me so long to bring you one of these *things*—is that why you're not doing it yourself? Is that why you want *me* to drain her? Do you doubt my devotion?"

Without a moment's breath, he said, "Yes." It was plain and colorless. But what followed was loaded and heavy. "You made me wait," he shot back, the black around him expanding. "I've been waiting for *you* all this time. You failed your tasks and broke your promises. Now prove that you are *mine* and mine alone. That you serve me, if nothing else."

My tongue flicked at the roof of my mouth. It was dry. Everything was so arid and surreal. Staring at her fear-driven eyes, in that moment she looked not like a Vessel but like a young woman. More than that, she looked *innocent*.

I hesitated.

I had seen innocence taken enough to know the feeling of it. I had choked it down myself when I'd turned my Second-Borns. It had been taken from me that night outside Nefari's window by the very Darkness asking me to do it again now.

"I didn't fail you, Caelius." I refocused, ignoring her seemingly pure gaze. "I brought her and freed you from your cage, didn't I?" I moved closer. "Late, I'll give you that, but still I succeeded."

Caelius leaned his head back in shock, the red finally returning to his eyes. "Of course." He gathered his thoughts before speaking again. The blackness emanating off of him calmed and dissipated into the clay and dust at our feet.

"But you failed with every Vessel before that, and you allowed her to kill so many of our kind. They were invaluable to you, and because of that they were invaluable to me. Am I really asking too much of you, sweetheart?" His voice attempted to warm, but there was still a growing agitation behind it. "I know, as a rebellious boy, you hate these kinds of tests, but I'm being more than fair here."

He paused again, looking at the pink skin covering my rib cage, and there it was, that peculiar look he wore recently, as if a demon like him could feel real concern. "I don't want to endanger you unnecessarily." His voice warmed further. "I can–" He paused. It was strange to see Darkness unsure of itself, even for a moment. "I can let her go. We don't have to do this right now."

I blinked in shock. "What?"

"I used to think she was important. Being trapped in that cage for so long led me to false delusions. But she's not important. The Vessel never was. *You* are." He placed both her wrists into one of his hands and held them above her head. "We'll let her go until you're ready to obey my simple request." Reaching out his other hand, he stroked my face. "What do you think, precious? Should we try this again at a later date? When you're ready?"

I chewed my bottom lip, sinking deeper into his auburn gaze. Something about his words bothered me, particularly the words, "try this again." I didn't know why, but they filled me with an inescapable terror. "What game is this? You *need* her so that you can be restored!" I tried to mask my feelings with words that seared out of me like hot pokers ready to gouge those red eyes out. "I know it's all that matters to you. Don't pretend you'll let her go just to mock me—"

"Ask me now, and I will." His eyes locked on mine, steady and unwavering. All the doubt dissipated like the black that had been around him. I bit the inside of my mouth, hard. There was a threat beneath that gaze–a control, a passionate obsession to have and consume. If I was thirsty and lost in the desert, Caelius was the desert itself. How much more did *he* ache for the things he thought he needed than I?

He leaned forward, his black shadow falling over Shea's body, blocking her from my sight. "If you are too fragile from your last defeat, we will wait and try again. If you recall, I am very good at waiting, my sweet. And for you, I will wait for all of time, until you're ready."

There was another long moment between us. Was this Caelius's twisted form of devotion? Did he really care about my rehab? As if I was so crippled by her that I needed the patience of a snake cloaked in black. And his *waiting* would strike me, not her. I would again be filled with the venom of his blood. I knew there was no true absolution for those who failed him.

I ripped myself from his mesmerizing gaze as he moved his hand from my cheek and leaned back, revealing the Vessel. She had stopped thrashing and was now staring at me, as if she hoped I would ask him to release her.

No.

I looked longer at her face.

It wasn't as if she *hoped*; there wasn't a shred of doubt in her eyes that I would do just that, that I would tell him I wasn't ready. Was my shattered state so apparent, even to our enemy?

Nefertiti and Meky turned back toward us, their eyes burning into the back of my skull.

Indignation boiled inside me. If Gunnhild were alive today, he'd kill me himself. Weakness could not be tolerated. I had made that one truth palatable for him over the cruel years we'd spent together eradicating the Vikings. And still, he had fallen for Ashgar. And still, he'd had that one exploitable weakness.

It was strange that they'd been killed separately. At least that was what I'd been told, but there was no way Gunnhild would have let that happen. He was too intelligent to be fooled so easily by the Vessel, and he hadn't been more than three feet from Ashgar in over a century. Ever since I'd told him to keep his enemies close but his weaknesses even closer, he'd never left Ashgar's side. He had taken my words as a threat, even though I'd made it clear that I would allow him this *one* love. After all, I had turned Ashgar for *him*. Besides, what benefit was there in killing my own children?

I took a deep breath. Killing my chosen, there was nothing that could push me to such madness, even if Gunnhild wanted my head. I couldn't even kill Gracuri in Thebes when I'd been commanded to by Caelius himself. Then why was I hesitating to kill this Vessel? She was nothing to me. She was not *mine*.

I looked deeper into her eyes. It wasn't the desert flowers filling the air with sweetness that was making me so uneasy–it was her skin, the scent of her sweat. It was throwing me off. I knew I was strong enough to obey Caelius. The problem was my body, not my mind. My mind raged at what she'd done, screamed for justice, for penance, for her head on a spike.

Head on a spike . . . now that *felt* familiar.

There it was again, that cognitive dissonance between what I knew and what I felt. The problem was, I *felt* no hate for the Vessel, even after all she'd done. Maybe Caelius was right: I was too broken. Was I mournfully numb from the loss of the children, and was that preventing me from accessing the full range of my emotions? My mind gave me that answer, and it made sense, it fit with the small flashes of images that I could recall in the black hole my memory had become. But my *body* wasn't listening.

I sighed, heavy and low. This circular battle within was getting me nowhere. I had to trust my mind. My instincts and my body, they could be controlled by the Vessel. Maybe this was part of her allure—this helplessness, her intoxicating aroma, the way her body moved, the way my fingertips desired to slide along her pale skin, even with Nefertiti standing so close by, watching. This familiar feeling between us could be *fabricated*, and Nefertiti wouldn't lie to me, not the warrior queen of Gutium, not the power behind the Pharaoh of Egypt, not my childhood friend and love, Nefari. *She* was true. She was real. I had to depend on that.

I looked up, pleading into her purple eyes. Instead of a fearless affirmation, a death sentence, her gaze looked as dejected and uncertain as I felt. I swallowed. My saliva was thick with a thirst only the desert could produce. Nefertiti had lied to the Pharaoh all those years in Egypt, but that was only so that *we* could be together. She would never lie to *me*, right? I had known her since birth. We were more than lovers. I looked at Setepenre in the distance. It had been Ur-Nammu who had kept everything a secret; *he* had kept them hidden. Ur-Nammu was the liar. The Vessel was the murderer. I needed to remember these simple truths.

But there it was again, that inescapable hollow feeling, as if my words and thoughts weren't connecting to my core self. I clenched my hands into fists. It didn't matter. I'd be damned if I let the Vessel, or Caelius, see me broken. I'd be damned if Nefertiti looked on me again with pity, as she had when I'd been a slave at her feet. I was the first and only son of Onack the Great.

I was just as much a leader of the Gutian people as she was. I wouldn't abandon my heritage again, and I wouldn't fail her like I'd failed to protect her daughters in our last battle. My thrashed body and splintered bones should've been proof enough of that.

Now that felt real, the ache caused by my failure to protect them.

"What exactly do you want from me, Caelius?"

"Caelius." His eyes grew dark again. "Try on Father. Or my favorite, which you have yet to master: God."

I stared at him blankly. "Enjoying yourself?"

He licked his lips, tracing the outline of my frame with his eyes. "When you were cradled in my arms, you called me both."

"Stop it," I said with disdain.

He smiled, pressing a hand over the Vessel's mouth as she again rallied to speak. "What do I want? I want you to *feed* on this little light bulb whore. I want you to make her weak enough that my hand can easily pop in and take out her tiny, insignificant soul." He pressed his body closer to hers as her limbs fell limp, the fight leaving them.

I felt that too, the hate at seeing his skin against hers.

Was this possessiveness because I had hunted her and vampires were notoriously proprietorial of their prey? I wouldn't put it past myself. I at least had some memory of the hunt: locusts, a dorm in Arizona, a hall monitor, and then . . . then . . . only blackness and words remained. The words in my mind said that I had destroyed the dorm and taken her to Caelius right away. It was strange that the journey to Caelius was just *gone*. How badly had I been injured in our last battle to have forgotten a *year*?

I did remember a moment of her in his cage though, his skin

pressing against hers.

"Disgusting," I uttered.

Caelius smiled. "I agree. The blood of a Vessel will taste like swine compared to mine."

I blinked. *He* was disgusting. The word had slipped out, and it'd been meant for him alone, though I wasn't sure why. He wasn't altogether wrong; her blood would be sour after ingesting the blood of my maker for . . . weeks? Months? He still never gave me a clear estimate when I asked. Who knew how long I had been coddled, helpless in his arms.

Disgusting.

"I've got ahold of her, and she's weak enough so she can't turn her blood into light. It should be *easy* for you, darling, unless you are still unwell." He paused again. "Lucian, if this is making you feel . . . uncertain, I can take us back to the cabin and mend you more thoroughly. My arms do miss your weight, my pet."

I instantly pressed my lips against her neck.

Like hell I would let him drown me in his blood and exploit the fever it induced.

Like hell I would make Nefertiti and her children watch what a subservient worm I became after every feeding.

No.

I needed to prove to him, to all of them, that I was fine, that I would never need his blood again. I had to break the cycle of control he had over me. Even if every cell in my body was fighting to stop, to not hurt the Vessel, I had to resist it. I couldn't be broken like this, not when they needed me the most. I looked again at Nefertiti and her daughters. If Caelius wanted me to prove myself, if that was what it would take for him to stop force-feeding me, then I'd gladly accept the challenge. I had to be there for my family now, what was left of it.

My teeth grazed her supple neck, and she flinched.

I've only been a man with Shea. Never a vampire. I will never feed from her. The words floated to the surface of my mind but were drowned out just as quickly as they'd come.

What was that?

Was the Vessel trying to manipulate me in a desperate attempt at salvation? Did she think such cheap parlor tricks would win against *the* First-Born of Caelius?

I sunk my teeth in deep.

It was sweeter than honey.

I felt both the tensed shock of her body and the relaxed palm of Caelius's hand against my back.

"I'm so glad," he said calmly, resting his chin on my head as I fed feverishly, lapping up her blood like nectar. "I am the only one, Lucian. She is *nothing* to you. You doing this for me means everything." He paused, relishing the moment. "Forgiveness is important to your kind, isn't it? I forgive you then. I forgive you for all of it. Let's never be apart again." He nuzzled his head against mine.

I drank as fast as I could. I just wanted this to be over. I wasn't doing this for *him*.

What?

I choked, swallowing down more of her sweet blood.

What was this?

Tears were streaming down my face.

I heard Nefertiti gasp at the sight. The pain in my chest felt raw, like the Vessel had singed a hole through my rib cage, but I was intact. I drank faster, trying to bury the feelings spinning like a hurricane at the center of my heart. I felt out of control.

Loss.

So much loss.

The grief was inescapable.

Why was drinking her making me feel like I had lost the most precious thing in this world? It didn't make sense. *Nefari* was my world. This Vessel was nothing.

"Okay, Lucian. That's enough, dear one." Caelius stroked my back, tugging on my Hanfu.

I clung to her with my teeth, wrapping my arms tight around her waist.

"I said that's enough, boy." He pulled the fabric harder, his tone threatening.

I couldn't stop; I wouldn't stop.

She was *mine.*

The word growled in me, deep, like a hunger that would never be satiated, like an ocean breeze moving over the desert, calling the sailor *home.*

"Mine!" I shouted through my clenched blood-soaked teeth.

I pushed him back, yanking her free from his grip.

Then I felt it.

I'd had the same feeling in Pompeii when I'd drunk the Vessel then. It was as if I were starting to pull at her soul, drawing it out like Caelius had planned to do for himself.

Did I even have that power?

"Enough!" Caelius threw me back with such force I heard the sound barrier snap in my wake.

My body smashed into the earth like a meteor, the crater

surrounding it filling up with a mushroom cloud of dirt. Through the haze I heard Meky's voice. "You should be ashamed to call yourself Gutian!"

"Meky!" I stood up quickly, coughing out the grit choking my lungs dry. "Where are you? I'm sorry! I'll fix it!" I tried to see her through the cloud, but it was too thick. She was right—what was I doing? The Vessel was *mine*? Was I intentionally trying to piss Caelius off and get us all killed? I should've been ashamed; I'd humiliated myself in front of them, no more Gutian than some rabid newly turned vampire.

"Wait, don't!" Nefertiti called through the storm cloud of silt, and I ran toward the sound.

"Nefari!" When I arrived, Caelius had a hole burning in the side of his skull like a fist made of fire had punched through it.

"What happened?" I shouted, looking around desperately.

Meky and the Vessel were *gone*.

Nefari fell to her knees, pleading at Caelius's feet. Caelius glared at Nefertiti before kicking her off and shifting his one remaining bloodred eye to me. His teeth grew, splitting his gums, drool pooling at the tips. "You failed. That's what happened."

CHAPTER 9
SHEA

"**P**lease wake up. Please, please wake up." Meky's voice was filled with worry. "I'm so sorry. I'm such an idiot for putting up with that charade for so long. I didn't even know what was happening until we arrived. If I'd have known, I would have warned you, I swear . . ." Meky trailed off, obviously not knowing if she was talking to an unconscious person or not.

I tried to open my eyes or move any part of my body, but I couldn't.

After blasting one last firebomb at Caelius's face, which had felt really good, I'd found myself whisked away by Meky, then I'd blacked out. But like a giant boulder to the brain, all the memories of what had just happened hit me with terrible impact.

I moaned. It was all I could do.

But it was enough to hear a huge sigh of relief from Meky. "Oh, thank the gods! Shea. Shea, can you hear me?"

Moan number two. It was meant to be a yes, but nope,

couldn't quite form words yet.

"I've got to get us to Aidan and the others. They'll be able to help you. I just don't know how." The desperation in her voice was heartbreaking.

I didn't blame Meky at all. I didn't even blame Nefertiti, though she was the one who'd lured me into the trap. I blamed Caelius.

I'd had to fight them all, though thankfully, Meky had steered clear. She'd even body-slammed her mother and sister a time or two when they had come close to attacking. Lucian had been too busy focusing on me to even notice, or if he had, it hadn't seemed to register as odd.

What was scary about the whole thing was the fact that even his view of the fight was distorted. Every time I'd tried to hit Caelius, he would shadow-yank one of the girls in front of him as a shield. Then Lucian would jump in front of said girl, and I'd end up blowing a hole in *him*.

Lucian had thought he was saving Nefertiti and the others from *me*! As much as I was furious at Nefertiti, I hadn't wanted to hurt her. I knew she was only doing this to save her daughters. And poor Sherit. I'd blasted her four or five times when Lucian wasn't there in time. Only Sete had been into the fight. She'd kept coming after me like she was a cat and I was the laser. I'd had to use some serious wind power to keep her away, but I hadn't tried to hurt her either.

The only shining light from that horrible confrontation was my mom. When Sete had pinned me down at one point, Mom had yanked her off me like the poor girl was a rag doll. Then my mother had looked me in the eye and said, "Shea? *My* Shea."

Sete and Sherit had pulled her off of me and kept her restrained for the rest of the fight.

But I'd seen it in my mother's eyes: love.

She'd remembered me.

I knew it wouldn't last long. No doubt Caelius was giving her blood even as I had these thoughts, but it gave me hope.

Lucian, on the other hand . . .

I thought I'd prepared myself to see him brainwashed, but nothing could have prepared me for what I'd seen.

When he wasn't attacking, he'd looked at me with a blankness that had made my knees weak with pain. I'd tried so hard to get to him, to remind him of our connection, of our love for each other, but . . . there was nothing.

Not even when I first met him in Arizona and he'd only seen me as a Vessel had he looked at me like that. His expression had been so full of emptiness, it made me wish I had the power of a thousand suns to destroy Caelius.

And when Lucian drained me . . .

He'd just kept drinking and drinking.

It was Caelius who had stopped him.

He would have killed me.

The Lucian I knew was gone.

I felt so helpless.

Oh! A finger. I could move my finger.

I hated that I was completely incapacitated because of Lucian drinking from me. He had promised he never would, even when I had given him permission at the sundial. He had been so burned, I'd wanted to help heal him, but he had refused.

If he ever did remember the truth again, he'd never forgive

himself.

"Meky." My voice was back, but it was gravelly from screaming.

My eyes opened. I was leaning up against a tree in a dense forest of pines. Meky stood in front of me, her expression full of concern and shame. Kneeling down, she touched my arm gently. "I told my mother what I thought of her and her little scheme to trap you. I swear I didn't know, Shea. She disgraces the Gutian name."

I found the strength to clutch Meky's hand. "Please, don't blame her. She just lost your sisters; she can't bear to lose any more of you. She'd do anything for you. You know that." I didn't know where my sudden defense of Nefertiti had come from, but I knew I spoke the truth. If sacrificing me saved her daughters, she would do it without question. *I* could never trust her again, but Meky could.

"You're seriously too nice. It's probably all that Light flowing through your veins. She was over the line, and she knew it. But at least Lucian seems to be fighting his blood control, so that's a positive, right?" Meky had a glimmer of optimism in her tone.

"How was drinking my blood and almost killing me 'fighting his blood control'?" I asked incredulously.

"You didn't see him?"

"Kind of hard when his teeth were in my neck." I tried not to sound too wounded. It still hurt to think about Lucian wanting to drain me like that.

Meky squeezed my hand and smiled at me. "Shea, he was crying the whole time, as in, waterfalls. His soul is fighting to remember, even if his brain can't because Caelius is shoving his blood down his throat."

"But Caelius was the one who stopped him. Lucian kept going." I wanted to hold on to the shred of hope Meky was giving me. If he had cried while drinking me, then he remembered on some level who I was and what I meant to him.

"I don't think Caelius liked it when Lucian claimed you. His own ego made him pull Lucian off. Let's just say screaming 'mine' probably means another brainwashing session for Lucian." Meky tilted her head to the side and sighed. "Plus, I'm pretty sure Lucian tapped into your soul like he did in Pompeii with the third Vessel. It brought Aidan's brothers in to protect the poor guy, and then Aidan had to . . . you know . . ."

"Kill the Vessel? Don't remind me. I still get aches from where *I* was stabbed." I thought about what Meky was telling me for a moment, then said, "My soul, huh? So Caelius threw him off of me because he was jealous and afraid Lucian would eat his power-up pack?"

"Yeah," Meky confirmed. "I wouldn't have let Lucian kill you, Shea. I was already running toward you when Caelius threw Lucian off. I'm just grateful you had one last fireball in you, or I'm pretty sure Caelius would have popped my head off when I got there."

I knew she was right. Caelius wouldn't have hesitated if I hadn't distracted him with a face-bomb, and I would have been blamed, yet again, for killing one of Nefertiti's children.

Meky continued. "When you blew his head half off, I took you and ran. Ur-Nammu came after me to make sure I was okay, but now he's back to spying on Mom and my sisters. He's being a coward too, letting doubt make the decisions for him. I'm seriously the only one who's even acting like a Gutian."

Standing up once more in frustration, Meky shook her head, then put her hands out as if displaying the trees like a prize. "Welcome to the Black Hills National Forest in South Dakota. I ran until I was sure we weren't being followed. That could change very quickly though, so we need to get to Aidan and the others."

"Agreed. I need to Dream-Walk and tell them where we are. I've done it with Aidan before, so hopefully he'll be ready for me." Taking a deep breath, I paused. My strength wasn't getting much better. "I don't know if I have the mojo to do this."

Meky sat down across from me. "Your Vessel powers are tapped, so it's going to take a while. Just try and see what happens. If you can't do it, I'll keep us moving toward the cabin. I'm not going to let anything happen to you."

I felt a burst of affection for Meky. Nodding, I closed my eyes. "Here goes nothing."

It wasn't difficult to fall asleep, as exhausted as I was. It was nice that my brain was so used to Dream-Walking that I ended up standing next to the swing set in the backyard of the house I'd grown up in. I remembered Dream-Walking with Lucian here, back when we barely knew each other. It was somehow comforting and devastating rolled into one. Still, being back home, I felt relieved. Aidan and I had hung out on this swing set every summer, all the way through high school.

"Aidan? Are you here?" I called out.

"Shea! Is that you, or am I having a weird dream about our backyard?" My *dad's* voice came from behind me.

Surprised, I turned around and saw Jeff Harper, the best dad anyone could ask for. He pulled me into a hug. Whether it was a dream to him or not, he was obviously terrified, not knowing where I'd gone and what had happened to me.

Gently pulling away, I kept our hands clasped together as if I were a little girl that still needed her daddy.

And I was.

I *really* needed him now more than ever.

"It's really me. I'm Dream-Walking with you," I said. "I thought for sure it would be Aidan that would show up because I've done this with him before, but obviously my brain decided I needed to see you instead. I could really use some 'Dad' time right about now."

My father framed my face with his free hand and looked at me as if I were the most beautiful creature in the world. Such a dad. "Thank *God* you're okay." His expression quickly turned worried as he pulled his hand away from my face. "You *are* okay, aren't you?"

"Yes. I'm all right. Meky saved me. Nefertiti lured me into a trap, and I fell for it like the naive sap I am," I grumbled.

"Don't apologize for being a trusting person; it's what makes you better than everyone."

"Everyone? Really, Dad?" I smiled at his unwavering devotion to me. It made me feel safe. And a little bit better about what I had just been through with Lucian.

"Yes, *everyone* in the entire universe. You're the best there is." He smiled at me as he squeezed my hand with affection. Then he sighed. "So Nefertiti is definitely bad news, huh?"

I shook my head. "No. She was just protecting her daughters, but that fact alone now makes her untrustworthy." I tried to stop the catch in my voice, but I couldn't when I said, "Lucian thinks

I killed his family. He hates me, Dad. As in really, really *hates* me."

Dad pulled me in for another hug, and I took it as my cue to cry my Dream-Walking eyes out. I knew I wasn't really there in physical form, but it felt good to let it out anyway. After I regained my composure, I took a step back, realizing I hadn't told him about Mom.

"Dad, Mom recognized me. She said, '*My* Shea' and tried to protect me from being attacked by Setepenre."

His face brightened at the possibility. "We have to get her away from Caelius. She'll remember everything on her own if we can just get her alone. I know it."

"Or if we can restrain her in the vicinity of Aidan like we did with you, he can fix her." I really hoped it was possible, but I didn't think Caelius would let me near my mother after witnessing her momentary lapse in judgement.

My father placed his hands on my upper arms to steady me. "First things first. Where are you two? We need to come get you."

Duh, that was the whole purpose of this Dream-Walking session. I had been so happy to see my dad, I had almost forgotten. "Black Hills National Forest, South Dakota. I can't be any more specific than that."

"Don't need to." He took his hands away and tapped his nose. "Super smeller now. Just need to be within thirty miles or so, and I'll find you."

"Super smeller?" I groaned. "Dad, you're such a dork."

"The first vampire-dork in existence. I'll take it. Maybe I should start thinking of some good 'dad' jokes for the ride back to the cabin." He laughed.

"Nothing would make me happier," I teased. But I actually meant it. My dad may have been a Second-Born vampire, but he was still my dad. "Just hurry. Caelius has probably sent a goon squad to attack us, and I'm weak. I'm going to need some time to regain my strength."

His expression turned serious at that. "We'll leave as soon as I open my eyes." Reaching down, he kissed my forehead. "I love you to the moon and back, Shea."

"I love you too, Dad."

I opened my eyes, and Meky was staring at me expectantly.

I allayed her tension immediately. "They're coming."

With a sigh of relief, her posture relaxed a bit. "I'm trying not to be mad at my mother, but I can't help it. She's never been weak, and she's always stood up for what was right. She never let fear rule her."

"Maybe she'll come around. You rescuing me might have woken her up a bit." I tried to comfort her.

"I doubt it. She's too stubborn." Meky made a face of disgust. "Let her have Sherit and Sete. Sherit was always a follower, and Sete . . . she's always belonged to Caelius." She shrugged. "Which basically has made her a mean girl her whole life."

"She's probably never had the chance to really be herself or even know who she is, not if Caelius influenced her." Was I defending the brat who'd almost killed me? I just didn't want Meky to hate her family. "I mean, look at my mom. She's pretty horrible because of Caelius, but back when she had her memories, she was just my mom. She was the kindest person you'd ever meet. We just need to destroy Caelius, then you can decide if you hate your sisters or not."

"I guess. It's just easier for me to be angry," Meky confessed.

"I get that. I'm angry too." I really was. I simply didn't know what to do with it.

My eyes grew heavy again. I wasn't healing fast enough, and Dream-Walking had drained me even more. "I think I need to rest for a bit."

"Of course. They should be here soon. I'll carry you if you're still asleep."

"Thanks," I said as I closed my eyes. My exhaustion was too deep to stay conscious.

Just as I was drifting off, I swore I heard the flapping of giant wings . . .

***

"Shea?"

Was that . . . ?

"Mom?" I opened my eyes. I was standing in a swirl of colors, as if I had jumped into a child's painting.

I was Dream-Walking, I knew that right away, but where was I?

And had I imagined hearing my mother's voice?

I tried to give the environment shape, turn it into a forest or my old backyard, but the spinning blobs of color continued to swirl instead.

I knew then that I wasn't controlling this Dream-Walk. Someone else was. Someone who didn't know much about it, or at least couldn't seem to figure out how to make a real-life setting.

"Shea?"

Definitely my mom. But where was she?

"Mom, I'm here. Can you hear my voice?" I called out to the whirlwind of blues and pinks flying in front of me.

"Yes." Her voice sounded relieved. "Yes, I can hear you. I can't see you though."

"Just concentrate on me as hard as you can. Think about our house. Our life. Our—" My voice caught in my throat. It was painful to even think about how perfect life had been growing up. I really took it for granted. I had two amazing parents that, frankly, I didn't know if I deserved.

The colors began to take shape and form into furniture until I stood in my childhood bedroom. Everything was decorated as it was when I was eight. *Harry Potter* posters adorned almost every wall. There was even a small poster of *Twilight* I didn't remember having. Ironic much? A four-poster canopy bed was in the corner, and a small rolltop desk sat across from it.

"Mom?" I tried again.

Molly Harper materialized in front of me, sitting on the edge of the mattress with her hands in her lap. Looking up at me, I could see the confusion in her eyes. "Is this real? Is this your room?"

I nodded, not wanting to spook her. "I was in love with Ron Weasley." I motioned to the posters and the fact that most of them were of Rupert Grint.

Mom actually smiled at that, then looked as if she were trying very hard to remember something. "We named our cat Weasley because she was orange."

I sat down next to her, and she flinched slightly. I scooted away so there was at least a foot between us. "Yeah, you'd call her your little gingerbread because you thought she was so sweet when she'd sleep on your chest."

Tears rolled down her face. "I remember that."

I was too scared to say anything that would cause her to leave.

A long silence passed.

Finally, she said, "It comes to me in flashes. I used to tell Grandfather whenever I had one, then he'd give me a drop of his blood, and it would go away. I craved that at first. I didn't want to remember. It was too painful."

"But now?" I asked tentatively.

"Now I don't tell him because . . ." She turned to me, unsure. "Because I *want* to remember. I can feel it, this overwhelming sensation, and it fills me up like nothing ever could. At first I thought it was love for Grandfather, but it isn't." Mom paused, a frown deepening her brow. "I don't think I like him very much at all." Shaking her head, she continued. "When I saw Sete attack you, I realized all that love is . . . is for you. Isn't it?"

I felt like her words would burst my heart on impact. It was almost too much to hope for. I was terrified that this was a trick, a horrible joke that Caelius had put my mother up to, but her eyes . . . they looked sincere.

"I love you, Mom." I decided I'd go with honesty. If she was faking it, these words would make her break character and attack.

But she simply said, "I love you too, my little girl."

I swallowed down the intensity of emotions that threatened to drown me. "If Caelius finds out . . . he'll erase this from your mind. You won't remember any of it. Or me."

Mom's eyes brightened when she said, "Shea, I'm evolving somehow. He already gave me a drop of his blood after the fight. It did nothing. I remembered everything, and I didn't feel bonded to him or the false sense of love that his blood normally gives me."

"You're saying his blood control isn't working on you anymore?" I asked, doubtful.

"I think so. I don't know. Maybe if he was giving me the amount he gave Lucian it would work, but the one drop? It doesn't affect me at all anymore." She was actually smiling, proud of this new power.

"It must have something to do with you being a child of both Lucian and Nefertiti, or maybe it's because you're my mother." I began to work through it out loud.

"Mother of the Vessel, daughter of the First-Borns." Mom repeated my sentiment with a nod of agreement. "I don't know what I am, but I know above all, I'm your mother, and I never want to forget that again. My soul and mind are filled with you, Shea. The most important thing I've ever done in my life is being your mom. I will kill Grandfather myself if I have to. Blood or not."

"Oh, Mom." I couldn't control myself. I leaned over and hugged her desperately. She embraced me back with even more intensity. "I don't ever want to leave here."

I could hear her crying openly. "I don't either."

I pulled out of our embrace, desperate. "Can you escape? Can you get to us? We can protect you! Mom, I need you. I need you to be safe from Caelius and his blood."

Mom's face became pained. "Shea, I can't. I can't be with you yet. Grandfather is so much stronger than you suspect. He could squash all of you with the snap of his fingers. He's choosing not to because of his obsession with Lucian. Lucian is all Grandfather cares about. He's trying to reshape Lucian's thoughts and memories over and over until he gets it perfect."

Pausing a moment, Mom made sure our eyes were locked when she said, "Lucian fights for the memories of you like nothing I've ever seen. His will is so strong, it's what made me determined to start remembering. If he loved you that much . . . and you kept begging me to remember that I was your mother . . . I just had to know for sure." She shook her head with sadness. "Shea, Lucian has remembered you so many times despite the amount of blood Grandfather feeds him. Still, I'm afraid he may never recover from this."

Not what I wanted to hear, but I knew I needed to. It only made me more motivated to save Lucian, and the only way to do that was to kill Caelius.

"But why do you have to stay? Why can't you find us and fight with us?" I asked. I could hear the panic in my voice.

Mom took one of my hands and held it in hers. "My fight is being by Grandfather's side. He has to believe I'm his alone. I don't know what his plans are, but I have to find out for *you*. If you want the chance to destroy him, you need as much information as you can get, and I'm the one who can get it for you."

"It's too dangerous. He'll know you're lying. He'll kill you." Now that I had a shred of my mother back, I couldn't let her go. It hurt too much to even contemplate.

Mom smiled. "Oh, Shea. Grandfather is completely clueless. He's probably the original narcissist, and you know how I handled Ms. Thompkins from the school board."

Comparing Ms. Thompkins to Caelius actually brought a

smile to my face as well. She was the worst. She was a classic narcissist, didn't care one iota for the kids, and only wanted to push her agenda with the school. That had basically equated to making everyone else do her job while she sat back and collected a paycheck for doing nothing. The stories of how my mom had manipulated Ms. Thompkins into actually working and doing great things for the schools was legendary. If Mom could do the same with Caelius, we might actually learn something useful.

It just scared me to think of her putting herself in danger like that.

"What if he—"

"Trust me, Shea. He's been holed up for thousands of years; he's completely vulnerable to modern-day manipulation."

I remembered that after Caelius killed Gracuri, I had made some things up about what Lucian had said about him. Caelius had gone nuts. It had been pretty easy too. I'd been trying to enrage Caelius, and he had fallen for it hook, line, and sinker.

If Mom thought she could handle Caelius, I had to trust her.

I nodded slowly. "But if you think for a second he's figured you out, you have to promise me you'll run."

"I will." Sighing, she said, "If I see you again in person, I might not be able to stop myself from going with you anyway, or die trying."

"Don't say that. We will all come out of this *alive*." As I said it, I wondered if it was true. A deep dark knot in my stomach threatened to overwhelm me, but I pushed it down.

Squeezing my hand with affection, she looked at me as if it were the last time. "You're healing now, I can feel it. I can feel you, my beautiful daughter. It's time to wake up."

***

A surge of warmth filled every cell in my body as I jolted awake. Bright lights and rainbow reflections blinded me as I blinked. I felt like I was back with Lucian in his small house; he had used crystals to heal me after Aidan had stabbed me. But as my eyes adjusted, I saw that I was in Helena's cabin again.

Someone turned off the lights, and I saw Dad, Aidan, Meky, Helena, and Duncan enter the room with hopeful looks.

"There she is. Welcome back, lass." Duncan smiled.

My mom had been right—I was healing. The refracted light had restored me just like it had at Lucian's home.

"I'm okay." I sat up.

Helena looked me over like I was a patient. "Back when I was human, Lucian asked me to find a way to heal with light. I didn't know then that he wanted this knowledge to heal creatures of Light."

Aidan nodded. "Lucian wanted to torture the Vessel, then heal them, then torture them again, knowing how much it would hurt me."

Duncan placed a hand on Aidan's shoulder. "I would've given him a right kick in the arse if I had known you then, brother."

Brother was new. And my heart really loved it.

"I Dream-Walked with my mom. She remembers me now," I said in a small voice, as if I couldn't quite believe it myself.

Dad clasped my hand and squeezed it. "Is she coming to find us? Will she come home?"

I shook my head. "No. She thinks she can find out more for

us if she stays." I hated saying it out loud.

Dad nodded, though I could tell he was heartbroken. But he tried to stay positive as he told me, "Helena is so close to finding a way to destroy Caelius, Shea."

I turned to Helena, hope surging through me.

Helena nodded. "There's just one missing ingredient, but I know I'll figure it out. I just need a little more time."

"I'm not sure we have it. Caelius will find this place soon."

"I've gotten everything I need from the cabin. The rest needs to happen here." Helena pointed to her head. "The missing link is right in front of me, I know it. I just need to percolate for a bit."

"It's not me?" I asked. The whole assumption was if I learned enough of my powers, I'd be able to juice up one of her contraptions to kill Caelius.

"That's the thing. It *is* you and it *isn't*. I can't explain it. I need to think about it more." Helena looked as if her mind was racing.

Aidan took my hand from my dad and helped me to my feet. "In the meantime, you need a bath."

I looked down and was finally able to see what he meant. My clothes were practically in shreds. There was dirt caked on my skin, and I was pretty sure there were leaves and blood in my hair from the big fight with Caelius.

Gross.

"A bath sounds nice," I said.

"Good, because you really do stink." He smiled.

Aidan's joking made me suddenly feel normal, and I was grateful for it. I grabbed him before he could pull his hand away and hugged him tightly, making sure I rubbed as much dirt on him as possible.

Laughing, he tried to push me away, but I just held tighter. "What's the matter? You don't want to hug me? But I missed you so much."

After a moment of struggle, he finally gave in to the hug, despite my odor. He looked down at me with his gentle eyes and said, "Don't run away like that again, okay?"

I let go of him and nodded solemnly. "I never will."

And I meant it.

I'd never make that mistake again.

Chapter 10
Lucian

You should be ashamed to call yourself Gutian!

Those words echoed through me as Caelius pulled his body off of mine. He stood up next to the bed. The sun shone on his skin, and it glistened from our mixed sweat, making him shine like the god he was. I worshiped him more than Nefertiti, more than anyone. It sickened me how he had pounded that truth into every muscle of my body, every cell in my veins, until I'd screamed for him alone.

I wiped the red from my lips. Despite swallowing a gallon of blood, I was still thirsty. Caelius's feedings *always* left me hungry for more. He obliged the tremors of my aching need by giving me all I desired . . . at first. It was my body, not my will, that had responded so readily. Now that he had both at his disposal, he gave me just enough blood to keep me begging shamelessly for more. Still, it was just enough that I wouldn't go through total withdrawal and recover. Addicted. That was how he wanted me, and although part of me knew his game, knew what this was . . . every other part worshiped him.

My legs trembled, unable to stand from the long hours of being bent into submission. He hadn't let me leave this bed for over a month, or had it been longer? Time ran together like the pulsing of his blood in my veins. I hadn't seen my family for so long, only *our* bedroom. No matter how hard I screamed, no one else dared enter. My world consisted solely of Caelius now–his words, his next "fun" idea for us to try out.

He looked down at me and smiled, reaching his hand around my neck.

"My adorable pet," he mused, squeezing my throat.

I was bound by angelic chains, but I was drunk enough with his blood that he could tie and keep me in any fashion he liked. I wondered how much of this was really punishing me for disobedience. He seemed more like a convict that had just escaped prison and the first and only thing that drove him was lust.

I blamed the Vessel for this. I'd been off of his blood, and my mind had just started to clear, but my failure to obey Caelius had forced me right back into his arms. Meky's words as she left were never truer than in this moment; I wasn't Gutian—I was Caelius's plaything.

I felt the restraints cutting into the bruises on my wrists as he pulled my hair, my spine arching painfully. I winced but said nothing. Despite my addiction, if I could keep his focus on punishing me and not the others, I would gladly take the brunt of Caelius's twisted sense of justice. The thought dwindled as I mocked my current state—as if I had any pride left, as if I could resist him now, even if I wanted to.

I squirmed as he twisted my body against the chains. "Uncomfortable, pet?" He released my hair and pulled me by the neck, lifting my lips to his.

"Please," I gasped.

I shifted my weight restlessly. The boy who had sworn never to beg for anything after his mother's death was pleading–as if I was the *pet* he so called me. "More blood," I panted.

He leaned forward and cut his thumb, shoving the red tip into my mouth.

My head jerked up in anticipation as my lips curled around my thumb, licking the crimson in a blissful agony that was the definition of being with Caelius.

He jerked his finger out suddenly. "Please, what?"

"Please, *God*, it's not enough! I need more!"

His eyes flashed to mine, and as mixed as I felt, he looked the same.

"I like it when you call me God." There was a spark of pleasure as he thrusted his thumb farther into my mouth, cutting it on my elongated fangs. "As insincere as it is." And there was the stab of pain.

"No," I moaned instinctively. "Your wrist, like before." I suckled, but the few drops escaping his thumb weren't enough.

He didn't yield.

He toyed with me for another hour after that.

He released my chains when he was finished, and we panted in each other's arms. He cradled my head to his chest, weaving my dark hair through his pale fingertips. I looked up at him with an adoration my body *felt*, but the longer this went on, the more

I realized that I was just under his control. And the more aware I was of his influence, the longer these sessions became. In the end, all I was aware of now was that I'd lost myself.

I'd had questions in the beginning. Why was I crying when I drank the Vessel? Why did her name sound like salvation, and Caelius never used it, like it was a curse? Why couldn't I remember that *name* in the darkness? What really happened in the year I lost?

All those questions were like stories erased from a chalkboard; they were abstract numbers and letters, scribbled mathematical theories that were half-formed and impractical in real life. All that was real, was now, and right now I had to be obedient to Caelius to protect my family.

Questions about the Vessel were meaningless while stuck in purgatory with only penance and no release. Even my lips couldn't form the words to ask him to stop. They only begged for *more*. This wasn't purgatory at all, but hell itself. I should have known that by the *thirst*.

He kissed my forehead, and I practically purred.

"Good boy." He patted my hair, nuzzling his face against mine.

I looked briefly at the door.

Salvation wasn't coming.

I could hear her voice just beyond it, but Nefertiti didn't interfere. I was glad she kept her distance; Caelius was too powerful. It did make me see her in a different light, however. Nefari was not the woman I had fallen in love with back in Gutium. She was broken and compromised like I was. I couldn't trust her after all, no more than I could trust myself and my fractured memories. My one constant, my morning star, my jewel among stones . . . had fallen.

Caelius could've been lying about everything, and most likely he was.

But that didn't matter.

What mattered was survival, *their* survival: the remnants of the Gutian tribe. However, Meky was right; I didn't deserve to be called a part of that tribe anymore. Our code—a code that had been engraved across our tapestries, woven into our minds, spoken like a nursery hymn over every child in Gutium—was more meaningless text erased on the chalkboard that had become my mind. And it left me . . . empty.

In all my years hating Adnachiel and the Vessel, hating myself and what I'd become, I'd never felt so despicable as I did now. This baseless devotion to a master that made me call him God, the humiliation of it–if it weren't for my family, I would kill myself while there was still a self left to kill. Even that desire, over time, would be consumed by Caelius and his ravenous hunger to devour all that I was and could be.

The sad thing was, his shallow ache for complete devotion actually robbed him of what he truly wanted: the real me he had renamed in earnest. The more I dissolved into him, the more I realized he'd made that mistake too. Calling me Lucian, making me "new," changing me, it all only added to the pain so evident in his eyes. He was bleeding out his own pleasure with every ounce of blood poured down my throat.

The more I became his, the less he wanted what I was becoming.

Pleasure and pain.

He was stuck in the same hell I was, only he didn't know it.

Could the devil even know he was in hell? Maybe that was what kept him there. He would never want to admit that, in defeating me completely, he had defeated himself and torn what was precious out of his own hands.

Now, looking up at him with such devotion, I was really *Lucian*, the one he had made. I was no longer looking at him as I always had, as La-Narru.

Meky was right.

Everything Gutian about me was dead.

***

"What kind of *god* would I be if I didn't believe in second chances?" Caelius laughed to himself. "Or, in your case, a thousand chances." He laughed again, but this time it was full of resentment. "I've never tried so hard for anything in all my existence. I've swallowed galaxies more willing than you." He frowned, looking up toward the ceiling. "Kids. Am I right, Light? They're the *worst*."

When his gaze met mine, I felt nothing but subservience.

He did that often now, talking to the Light as if they were old familiar rivals.

I crossed my hands in front of my chest, touching the silk that covered it. It was nice, wearing clothes again.

"Come now, pet, it's time." He paraded me out into the living room like some sort of finished masterpiece.

Having spent the sole of my time in the bedroom, I hadn't realized we were back at the cabin. All the girls were silent; not even Setepenre met my gaze. They were no doubt devastated because Meky was missing. She'd been taken by the Vessel I had failed to give over to Caelius.

"Now we will all *try again*." He moved his fingers through my hair, eyeing the bruise around my neck. I flinched as his hands moved to his side. I could still feel them at my throat, and in that, choking me during sex had served its purpose well. I would always feel them now, like a collar reminding me whom I belonged to. He wanted permanence on a body that could heal from wounds, and he'd found a way to do it. Even as the purple began turning cream, the others could tell just as readily that he had indelibly marked me as *his*, whether the bruising was still visible or not. Nefertiti made no motion to bring me comfort, as she had upon our first reunion. She stood by the window, as cold and distant as the mud sculptures I'd made of her in Egypt.

Caelius leaned forward. "I believe in second chances, so I'm going to—"

"Grandfather . . ." Finally Sete's gaze lifted as she scanned my body, eyeing the visible cuts outside the Hanfu. It was the same garment he had dressed me in before. There was something comforting about it being close to my skin, as if it were alive somehow, as if I weren't so achingly alone, standing at the center of what should've been my family. I had become alien to them in my absence, consumed by long nights pinned under the weight of my new god.

Setepenre swallowed, looking over my wounds one last time before shifting her eyes to Caelius. "I understand wanting to punish *us* for the Vessel escaping, but . . . you took all of your punishment out on my father, and for so long. In the beginning he was screaming for days, begging you to stop. After that, he was moaning and . . . and we could all smell how much blood you were giving him, but he's not even injured. I mean, he's injured now, but that's from *you*, not the Vessel. It just seems unnecessary, cruel even."

Her face twisted, as if Caelius's behavior was shocking. "I don't understand. Aren't we a *family*?" She turned her chair, facing him. "You used to read me bedtime stories from the human world. You said we'd be like *that*. You said it would be perfect, like a dream. This doesn't match what you promised when you were imprisoned, saying that my real father and I would finally be reunited at last."

I had thought it impossible for the room to become quieter, but after she spoke it was like we'd flown to the moon. Fear pulsed through Nefertiti so fervently that I could taste it on my own lips. Sete had confidence in her voice, as if she believed she could talk to Caelius so casually, as if she didn't completely fear him like the rest of us. "What you're doing now is nothing like those fairy tales. If anything, you're acting like the villain—"

Stop! I reached into her mind and shouted that one word over and over.

She stuttered as she met my sharp gaze, ending her deadly progression of syntax.

"But—"

I shook my head at her as Caelius stepped forward, palatable rage emanating off of his limbs. He raised his hand to strike, but I quickly laced my arms around his waist, pulling him against my chest. I rested my head on the nape of his neck, as if I weren't terrified. "You're wrong, Setepenre. It is *my* job and my responsibility to handle the Vessel. I failed. None of you would have even been there had I done my job centuries ago. The blame is mine alone to bear. The consequences are mine alone to reap."

Caelius leaned back into my arms. "As if I, a god, would break a promise to you Sete. Only a human would think something so idiotic. All of you, you're the promise breakers. The whole lot of you. Maybe it's a Gutian thing," he taunted.

Nefertiti's subtle tell of biting the inside of her cheek when she was upset wasn't subtle anymore. The left side was sunken in, as if she'd had it for breakfast. I couldn't blame her; they all looked gutted from the remark. Caelius, in short, was calling our homeland a tribe of liars.

Reaching up, he patted my head, our devastation cooling his rage. "What a good pet *you* are though, finally taking responsibility for your failures."

"Have mercy. She doesn't understand the complexity of the situation." I held him tighter.

"Agreed. A momentary lapse on her part . . . and mine." He stroked my arm and winked at Sete, as if that were an apology for almost smacking her head off.

Nefertiti's eyes were still down, but she scowled deeper. Her shoulders sagged with relief at Sete's safety and what I could only guess was shame. I had to guess because I'd never seen her look the way she did now. It wasn't in my catalog of Nefari emotions. This wasn't a "tell" she had developed over time that only I knew. This was something I hadn't seen, not even as a slave in Egypt.

This was *defeat*.

"But Grandfather, don't you think—"

"Enough." I spoke before Caelius had the chance. Openly

defying him, doubting his choices, talking back: those were all things of the past that could have been done and survived, if barely, from the other side of his cage. This was different. He was free now, and she didn't need to learn what that shift meant. My body should have been proof enough for the both of us. "Caelius knows exactly what he's doing. He's not a villain; he's our savior. Anything on the contrary is blasphemy. Let it rest, Setepenre. Not. Another. Word."

She looked surprised, as if I, above everyone else, should have joined her in protesting my treatment.

As if I would be that selfish.

She was still mine to protect. Even if she felt undermined, even if in the end she hated me for it, it didn't matter. It was a father's greatest desire to shield his children from all the ugliness of the world, and right now that ugly was leaning against me, fiddling with the sash around my waist. For a brief moment, I was glad that Onack had died in battle. To see his son like this . . . would have killed him.

"Good, *very* good, pet. Better than expected even. But be careful throwing my name around. You know what to call me." He pulled the sash tighter and then grinned, taking a long moment to stare at each of their disgusted faces before continuing. "Now as I was saying before I was so rudely interrupted, I believe in second chances." He moved out of my arms and stepped behind me. Pulling my waist against his hips, he wrapped his hands around my shoulders as he spoke into my ear. "I'm going to let Lucian try again, if he thinks he's ready."

"I'm ready!" I yelled instinctually.

"Oh, such eagerness," Caelius growled, his breath hot against my neck.

"Are you *really* ready, puppy?" he whispered. "Or do you need more *training?*" A vampire could hear a whisper a mile away. He wanted everyone in the room to see the intimacy of his lips pressed into my skin, his ownership clear.

"Yes, I'm ready!" It almost sounded like a bark, the way it exploded from my lips.

"Yes, *what?*" His grip tightened.

"Yes, *God.*"

They cringed together, as if one breath had moved around the room and touched all of their skin. And technically it had. Caelius's breath was moving, activating his blood that now lived in all of us, blood that lived in *every* vampire in the world thanks to me because I'd turned humans who then turned more humans. I had the arrogance and ignorance to call them children, but in reality, *I* was the child. Broken, lost, and suddenly immortal, even then Caelius had me by the throat, when all along I had thought myself a man and not a dog. I was playing Caelius's game the instant I turned Ur-Nammu.

No.

It was when I lay in his arms dying in Egypt and he asked if I wanted salvation for *her*: Nefari. The moment I agreed, I had unknowingly forfeited my eternal freedom.

He squeezed my shoulders, pinning me up against him like the master he was.

That same Nefari wouldn't even look at me now. I scanned the room. Setepenre, Sherit, and Molly were all staring at the floor. I was glad Meky wasn't here, so she too wouldn't see me like this.

In all my years as a slave, I had never been so broken down by a master. A whip could crack the flesh and spill blood, but it could not infect it with intention; that alone was left up to willpower. I had seen many slaves turn on their own kind, giving up information and sinking rebellions before they started, just to be spared the rod themselves. They would claim they had *no choice*, but in the end, as slaves, that was all we ever had. At that time, I had never compromised my Gutian integrity. Not once had I begged. Not once had I revealed anything. Even as the Pharaoh beat me to death, I'd protected what I loved. I'd protected *her*.

In Gutium, I'd left, but only after my father cried that he would surely fail in battle if I were by his side, dooming our entire village. I was all he'd had left to fight for, so he'd sent me away. That mistake had created in me the desire to never run from battle again. In fact, after I was turned, I ran *toward* war.

I vowed to never abandon my principles and pride, not for all the tears in the world, not even for the ones I loved, which was why I'd kept my Second-Borns at such a distance. Yet here I stood, giving up myself and my dignity for family. A family that, by the looks on their faces, would've rather seen me dead than Caelius's sock puppet. Was this worse than betraying them, like the slaves of old? Was this equal to my fleeing of Gutium the first time? Wasn't I doing the right thing? Wasn't this brave in its own right?

"I will not fail you this time, God. I give you my word as a—" I couldn't bring myself to say Gutian. I couldn't envision Onack the Great looking at me as if I were his son. This *thing* I'd become was more dog than man. I wasn't La-Narru anymore—

this last feeding of Caelius's blood had made sure of that.

I was Lucian.

Now and forever.

"I swear on my life."

Caelius clicked his tongue. "It's something precious to me, however, that life is not *yours* to swear on and lose. Remember, it's *mine*. And that life is the only reason I have for staying flesh." He nibbled the side of my neck, nuzzling his nose in the back of my ear. "Your vows excite me all the same," he whispered.

He pulled his head back and looked at the others. "But we will all formulate a plan and try again together, as a *family*. I'll supervise, of course, and this time you *will* drain her without those pathetic tears, stop when I command, and hand that meat-sack over to me so I can take her whore of a soul. *Understood?*"

"Yes." I didn't hesitate. "You know best. I'll do whatever you want."

He released me, then sat at the table, looking casually at the rest of them. "Well, family!" Their eyes were on him in an instant. "I *said* we'll make a plan together, didn't I?" He patted Setepenre's head, as if this approach would somehow appease her.

He slid his hand to the chair next to him, tapping his index finger on it. I rushed over and sat, quickly obeying the small command. He stared at Nefari and Sherit. "Sit." Only Nefertiti paused. And when she did, Caelius ran his hand through Setepenre's hair. "I keep them safe, don't I? The least you can do is obey without hesitation." She instantly sat in the chair across from me. It was strange, seeing the pride of Egypt afraid. Not in battle or beside the Pharaoh had she ever shown such fear.

No.

That didn't feel right. When her daughters died, she must have been afraid then, but I couldn't place it. I could still hear her screams though, the sounds her body made as they were torn apart in front of her. The Vessel had made her less Gutian in that moment, just as Caelius had done to me.

She was hollowed out, and it showed.

"Now." Caelius casually carved a light bulb onto the table with his pinky. He then ripped it apart with his long nails, cutting the table savagely as they grew thick, splitting his fingertips until they oozed dark blood. When he stopped, his eyes were black and filled with wrath. "Let's all be good little children and kill that slut once and for all, shall we?"

***

This was the first night Caelius let me sleep in the living room with my family. For the past few weeks he'd been giving me less blood. I was "dieting," as he liked to call it. The sex that followed lasted for a few hours; it wasn't an all-day affair like it had been. His hope was that, in time, I would be ready to drink the Vessel and give her over to him with nothing of the strange possessiveness that had overtaken me before. He explained that his blood "healing" wasn't supposed to be a punishment, but to undo the mind control and power the Vessel had over me.

Even though the pain and hunger was unlike anything I had experienced, I was thankful that some of my senses were finally returning. I could question and think, at least somewhat, for myself again. I thought about the task ahead. I found it odd that, simply because she was a woman, she was able to possess such control over a First-Born like me. Not in all my years hunting the Vessels had I ever encountered something so devastating.

Was she really *just* a Vessel? Was there nothing more to it? I shook my head, drawing a hand through my dark hair. I was always thinking about her. If Caelius knew that, he'd never let me leave his side. Just how strong was her mind control? I balled my hands into fists. All that mattered now was that I captured her for Caelius.

I couldn't wait.

He was going to fatten me up and then starve me like he was now until he thought I was ready. He had only given me a few drops today, but the lust in his eyes was insatiable. He was going to drown me in red soon, then pull out again. Each time he would give me less and less blood than the previous time. Each time the hunger for his return would grow, and that was exactly what he wanted: for me to spend the rest of my life *craving* him.

The way Caelius had looked at me this morning, like I was the oasis trapped inside his desert, didn't give me any confidence in an immediate time frame for this "plan" to be executed. When I asked *when*, he'd responded, "You're so close. We have a plan, but we are immortal, so we have time, darling. I need you to be foolproof. I want you to get this *right*. It will mean a lot to me, and to you too, in the end."

Was making me "foolproof" more important than him becoming whole? I had known of his obsession with me in the cage, but this was to a new extreme. How many times would he break my legs so I couldn't run away, mend them, and then break them again? I wasn't myself anymore. My personality and rebellious nature felt like a distant dream, much to Caelius's displeasure. He remarked how he wanted the *old* Lucian back, but perfected: the old Lucian, but subservient and infatuated with him. That was like taking the ingredients out of a soup, then complaining there was no flavor. It wasn't broth anymore, just boiled water, and that was what I'd become under his "care": empty.

Empty, but smart enough to know that I needed to redeem myself, not in his eyes, but in the eyes of my girls. Even though I was allowed to socialize with them again, they wouldn't look at me. Even Setepenre had distanced herself after I'd reprimanded her in front of Caelius. It was for her own safety, but she took it as a personal attack.

I sighed.

It was quiet at the cabin as the days passed, but not like it had been before. Before I could have stayed there forever, but now their distant eyes made my body sweat with the overwhelming feeling of failure and shame. If I brought Caelius the Vessel and did as he asked, he would have no need to feed me *period*. Without his blood, if I was still in there somewhere, maybe I could regain myself like I had done in the past. At least enough of myself to protect what I had left . . . which was dwindling before my eyes.

I thought of Meky.

The Vessel had taken her right in front of us, but not even Nefertiti was making a move to rescue her. Was the fight so gone from Nefari that she'd given up on her own daughter? We couldn't wait for me to be "ready" in Caelius's eyes; he didn't care about Meky. While he was force-feeding me, I had all but forgotten about her myself. Only her words that I wasn't Gutian had remained. Once his dosage had lessened, her image, her laugh, all of it came rushing back. What in Caelius's name were we doing just sitting here?

What?

I caught my own thoughts.

In *Caelius's* name?

My shoulders sagged in defeat. He had really become my god. I had so much of him still inside of me, I could feel his body against mine, his hands forever around my throat. I coughed. I was so *thirsty* . . .

I had to get out of here.

If sucking down that Vessel and bringing her to him would end this hell, if it would save Meky, then what was I waiting for? I had already taken the worst of Caelius's punishment. I knew what was coming if I failed him again: his words, his touch, hollowing me out, sculpting my flesh into something made for him alone. If that was what I was *now*, what did I really have to lose? And if I died trying, it might be a relief to the girls, no longer having to look at how pathetic I'd become. In truth, I couldn't feel any worse than I felt now, but if the Vessel hurt Meky while we were all just sitting here, I'd never forgive myself.

I went to the terrace overlooking the lake. The moon was hidden out of sight. It was the blackest night I'd seen since we'd been here, but it still had stars, unlike the blackness inside Caelius, the vacuum of nothingness.

I looked back at Nefari. Those Egyptian lines on her eyes faded in the soft light as she clung to Sherit, rocking her in her arms. Sherit didn't resist her mother. She stayed silent as Nefari spoke to her in both Egyptian and Gutian. It was a mangled mesh of words and phrases, and among them was, "You're all I have left now." Even though I was hollow, I was alive enough to feel her loss. To see the great Nefertiti broken like this, it must truly have been the end of the world.

I sighed, looking back at Caelius's bedroom. The door was shut. I knew he was giving Molly a drop of blood. "One drop to console her," he had said earnestly. But ever since she'd stood up to him, Sete had been asked to join them inside, and afterward she would reek of Caelius too. Was he drugging her as well? A fury rose in me, then sank like a rat drowning in water.

With every breath I felt subservient to him. I had to finish this and get my mind back, no matter the cost. When I returned I vowed I would find a way to protect her. I would convince him that Sete didn't need *any* of his blood . . . that I would take her share, if that's what he wanted, as long as she was free from him.

I licked my lips.

That's what *I* wanted.

More.

More of his blood.

I should take all *of it.*

I shook my head again. Even my love of Sete was getting clouded by hunger. And to think, I had spent all those years calling Adnachiel a dog. I ran my tongue along the growing tips of my incisors. Only Caelius could satiate this hunger now.

The Vessel.

An image emerged of her long locks streaming like liquid gold, bouncing down her shoulders in the sunlight. It was wet and wild, and her soft cheeks were flushed like she had just gotten out of the bath.

The image was so clear, but I couldn't place the memory.

All of that gold flickered deep in my mind, and for a brief moment I forgot my ravenous emptiness and called out to her.

Shea . . . where are you?

It felt like a strange light was weaving through my mind, like an unconscious part of me was pulling something through.

It burned.

It burned until the only words left on my lips were "Help me."

CHAPTER 11
SHEA

As I stepped out of the claw-foot tub, which had probably been made in the late 1800s, I almost slipped on the wood floor. It wasn't my normal clumsiness; it felt like something had tugged me forward. Grabbing the towel from the hook hanging on the wall of Helena's never-ending fortress of rooms, I felt it again.

Okay, it was full-out *yanking* now.

I looked around and hugged my body. I wasn't actually moving, so what was I *feeling*? Quickly throwing on my jeans and T-shirt, I reached for the door to find the rest of the clan to tell them about the weird sensation, though I had no idea how I'd explain it. *Hey guys, I know I'm not moving, but I swear I'm being pulled somewhere. Weird? Crazy? Insane?*

All of the above. Ugh.

I hesitated as I turned the knob, not sure if it was a good idea to get them riled up about something that may be nothing.

Maybe I should see if it goes away?

It could've been magnetic something or other because I was made of Light and we were all locked in a multilevel laboratory created by a real-life mad scientist.

Yeah, that had to be it.

I opened the door.

My Dream-Walking form was fully yanked out, and I watched in horror as my physical body dropped to the floor, unconscious. Suddenly I was grateful I had gotten dressed. Nothing like having someone walk in with me splayed out naked on the floor. Why was my mind even going there? Probably because I was terrified that I couldn't break free from whoever was pulling me out of my body.

It had to be Caelius.

If I could breathe, I would have tried to take deep breaths to calm myself. I needed to figure out a game plan, but what could I do? Caelius was Darkness. Maybe this was how he would devour my soul and come into full power. If he could separate my spirit from my physical form, then I'd no longer be a threat. I couldn't connect to the Light without my body. Maybe he just had to suck my soul out and drink it, as if the air itself was his straw.

I instinctually ducked my head as I passed each floor, helplessly flying through the levels of Helena's lair. I didn't see anyone as I finally pushed through the top of the cabin and into the sky. I tried to fight, but there was nothing to fight. It was just me being yanked to my inevitable oblivion. My mind squeezed with a powerlessness that sent surges of terror through me.

Until the pull began to feel *familiar*.

Warm almost.

Like home.

I knew with a sudden certainty that Caelius wasn't the one pulling me toward him.

It was *Lucian*.

My heart soared in anticipation as I flew past rivers, valleys, and mountains. Maybe he had broken free and was scared and alone. Maybe he needed the *essence* of me in this form to be strong, to fight Caelius's control.

I pushed myself into the stream and flew faster. I was even more sure now. I could feel him. I knew his spirit as if it were my own. I was so close. I leapt forward blindly, my surroundings a blur from the speed I was soaring.

Without warning, everything was suddenly black.

Um.

"Lucian?" I cried out.

Could he hear me? Was this really him? Had my desire for him clouded my reason, and had I just walked into Caelius's trap? I desperately wanted Lucian to call my name, to let me know he wasn't gone forever. The scenery around me shifted and moved until I was standing in the middle of a desolate wasteland.

Paris.

I recognized the twisted, mangled form of the broken Eiffel Tower in the distance. There was no sign of life anywhere, only abandoned cars and destroyed buildings lying in piles of rubble. Even the cobblestone streets had been ripped and torn to pieces, scattered across the broken soil like extracted teeth in a bowl. It was horrifying. What once had been a beautiful city, bright in its long history, was utterly destroyed. There was no recovering from this; there was nothing to rebuild. There was only dirt and crushed stones.

Suddenly Lucian was standing next to me.

Even though I was Dream-Walking and my physical form wasn't really here, it felt as if my heart had leapt into my throat. I turned to him, desperate. "Lucian! Are you fighting Caelius? Are you in Paris?" I rambled at his still form. He didn't respond to my voice. He stared straight ahead, as if soaking in every detail of the demolished city.

I had to reach him. He obviously brought me here for a reason, but why couldn't he see me? I stood, waving my hand in front of his saddened eyes. "Lucian! It's me, Shea. I love you. I love you." My voice broke. What else could I say?

"I love you," I whispered, no longer able to speak without falling apart.

His expression was anguished, as if seeing what he and Caelius had done to the people and this beautiful city was too much to bear. Then he reached down and picked up a small pink barrette made for a young child, and a tear fell down his cheek.

"Lucian," I said helplessly.

A shuffling from behind caused me to whirl around, and my brain froze in shock. Another Lucian stood there, *watching* the one that had just picked up the barrette. But the new Lucian's eyes were empty, blank, as if he couldn't comprehend his own existence.

I turned to this Lucian and tried again. "Can you hear me? What is this?"

No response.

Terror raced through me as Caelius walked toward the Lucian with the barrette. I turned to run but then noticed he wasn't paying me any attention.

I was in a memory.

Lucian's memory.

Caelius grabbed the pink barrette out of Lucian's hand and tossed it aside. "Why aren't you celebrating our victory? Instead you come here and wallow over a child's hair thing."

"A child *you* killed," Lucian choked out.

Caelius shrugged. "I killed lots of children. And *you* killed lots of men. And lots of women. That's why I want to celebrate." Caelius scowled. "You're ruining my excellent mood with this nonsense." Then he sighed heavily. "I thought I could take you out of our bedroom, to test you, but it seems you're still as headstrong as ever. No mind. I'll erase all this from your memories anyway." Taking Lucian's hand, he nodded. "Come on, back to the angel bones for you."

The Lucian behind me stepped forward and now stood next to me. I looked up expectantly. If this was a memory, then the Lucian watching was the *real* one, the one who needed to see this for some reason. And whether he knew it or not, his subconscious had yanked me into his mind too, and we were visiting the memory of the aftermath of Paris falling. Since he didn't have the power to Dream-Walk, that may have been why everything was so strange and he wasn't able to interact with me.

Cautiously, I took the real Lucian's limp hand. "Why are we seeing this? What does it mean?"

Nothing.

I might as well have been talking to one of the bricks on the ground.

Then hope filled me. His eyes and expression were blank, but Lucian's grip tightened, his fingers lacing through mine. I had to break through, and this was a good start.

The scenery swirled and shifted again. We were going somewhere different: a new memory. I kept my hand firmly in place. There was no way I was letting Lucian go, not when I was so close to reaching him.

As the scenery took shape, I recognized it immediately.

We were in our villa just outside of Paris.

If my dream self could've blushed, I would have. The memory we had stepped into was of Lucian and me making love. This memory was burned into my brain. It was our first day in the villa, and we hadn't been able to get enough of each other.

Feeling Lucian's hand gripped in mine as we watched ourselves getting busy was . . . intense? Weird? Uncomfortable? But pushing aside my own embarrassment, I realized Lucian was remembering this moment for a reason. Insecurities ruled my life, so to see that Lucian had held on to this memory at all made my heart soar.

It was actually beautiful in a non-porny kind of way. We almost looked like we had been fused together, blending into each other. The intensity was probably making my actual body, lying on the floor of Helena's bathroom, sweat.

That would be embarrassing.

I looked away from our past selves and stared up at the Lucian next to me. He gave no indication of knowing I was there or that *he* was there. If he hadn't been squeezing the life out of my astral fingers, I wouldn't have known if this was really happening.

With a loud boom, we were no longer standing in the bedroom of our villa.

We were standing on what was left of it: smoldering, burning heaps of ash for as far as the eye could see, mixed in with blackened lumps of what used to be walls and furniture. The only reason I knew we were still at the villa was because a charred corner of the bed frame was burning on the ground in front of us.

Past Lucian returned and flew to the ground, alone, viewing the charred ruins with devastation. This was the first place Caelius must have destroyed. Past Lucian looked more like himself than the one squeezing my hand, who showed no emotion at all.

I was broken.

Seriously broken.

I tried to get through to him again. "It doesn't matter if Caelius destroyed our villa. It was us being *together* that made that time magical. We can do that anywhere."

Again, no reaction.

But he didn't let go of me.

The ash began to swirl, and I knew we were headed to a new location. When the memory came into focus, we were standing on a floor covered in dried reeds of grass. It was some kind of one-room hut. House? Definitely a living abode with mud for walls and a thatched roof. There was a bench that looked like it was also used as a bed against the wall. It framed a stone trough that could hold a fire, but it was burnt out, an empty cauldron hanging useless above it. A few rabbits hung from the walls, abandoned and already rotting.

Two identical twins caught my eye. They were dead, lying next to each other on the ground. One had a large knife wound on his back that was covered in dried blood; the other had red streaking down his hand.

It was Aidan.

He had just stabbed the Vessel: his brother, Halfdan, I thought his name was. Sadly, I couldn't remember Aidan's name during this lifetime, mainly because he'd always been Aidan to me. Now, seeing the real person he had been, I felt like I was dishonoring his memory.

The door opened, and Meky walked inside. I wanted to run up to her and hug her, but I knew she wasn't really there, just a memory. Past Lucian was in this house somewhere, watching, or we wouldn't have been able to see this.

Meky didn't seem to notice as she raced to Aidan's corpse. Her beauty was just as perfect back then as it was today, her long locks of hair falling over Aidan's body as she cried. My heart ached for her. I knew how she felt about Aidan, but seeing her like this was devastating to watch.

"You Moors are tougher to kill than I thought." Lucian walked out from the corner of the room that had been cast in shadow. "I won't make that mistake a second time."

Meky's head flipped up to face him, furious. At this point I knew Meky well enough to know that anyone with an ounce of sanity should run away as fast as they could, but the Lucian of the past didn't know who she really was. Or *what* she was. So instead, he leapt at Meky, teeth bared.

He didn't reach her.

He was thrown back so hard his body crashed through the mud walls and landed violently on the ground. But it wasn't Meky who had tossed him as if he were a twig . . . it was Nefertiti.

And she was a seething storm of beauty and rage.

Lucian raced back inside the house, then stopped dead in his tracks at seeing the woman he used to love standing before him filled with hatred. Shock drove him to his knees, eyes wide with disbelief. "It can't be. What trick is this? Did Adnachiel's dogs conjure you to torture me?"

Nefertiti walked like a huntress as she approached him, her voice furious. "It is no conjuring! You broke your promise to me! To the Gutian code! You beat Meky to a pulp; you could have killed her!"

Lucian couldn't comprehend the sudden accusations. His eyes immediately turned to Meky, who sat next to Aidan's body, holding his hand.

"No." His voice was a horrified whisper.

"Yes." Nefertiti's was like ice, her expression set in unwavering anger.

"My love? Is it really you?" His voice cracked with emotion.

My love? Awkward. Of course I knew they had a love story for the ages, but it was so long ago, my mind could almost look past it. But seeing it in front of me as if it were happening now made me feel out of place, like I'd never really had a chance with Lucian, like I was a distraction for when he and Nefertiti reunited, just like Caelius had wanted.

Leave it to me to turn this into a personal attack on my self-esteem. I needed to stop my introspection and watch, to remember everything. Lucian's subconscious was stuck in these memories, while his conscious mind was controlled by Caelius's blood when he was awake. Where we stood now was the part of his brain that was repressed but untouched by Caelius, so he had to be trying to remember these moments for a reason.

"Don't speak to me of love when you almost killed my daughter!" Nefertiti was having none of it. When it came to her girls, not even Lucian was exempt. "And besides, I see what you do to the ones you love!" She eyed Aidan's corpse.

Lucian's face went blank as he really heard her words. He looked over at Aidan with Meky leaning over him. Instead of the anger and betrayal he always seemed to show toward Aidan, it was replaced by . . . shame?

Meky stood up and said softly to her mother, "You know I'd never let anyone destroy me." Then she seemed on the verge of tears as she said to Lucian, "*Physically.*"

Ouch.

Talk about guilt.

I knew him enough to know how much that hurt. Past Lucian lost all pretenses of the monster I'd just witnessed. He was *my* Lucian, brokenhearted at what he had done. Lost. Wracked with emotion.

He stayed on his knees, placing his hands over his face from the pain. It seemed to be all hitting him at once, as if he didn't know how to react to what was happening around him. That was when Nefertiti's expression finally softened. In that moment, I think she saw the boy and the man she'd fallen in love with. Going to her knees to face him, Nefertiti gently took his hands away from his face.

Their eyes met, and if I wasn't completely and totally in love with Lucian, I'd almost have been rooting for them to kiss.

But no. Not that mature.

Please don't kiss. Please don't kiss. Please don't kiss.

I hoped the Lucian holding my hand couldn't hear my thoughts. I looked up, but he stared at the memory as if he didn't even know he was there.

Past Lucian spoke. "I can't believe it's really you." He glanced at Meky, though his eyes were so full of guilt he could barely stay focused on her. "Your daughters, are they all . . . ?"

"Vampires? Yes. Caelius made me, and I was able to make them." Nefertiti brushed her hand over his cheek. Lucian took her hand and kissed it.

"My Nefari. My love. My morning star. I thought you were dead, and now you've returned?" He grew stronger in his conviction. "Whatever the reason, I'll never leave your side again."

Nefertiti looked as if she was going to kiss him, but another man entered the house.

Ur-Nammu.

"Daughter, stop," he commanded. He looked scared. I knew that fear—I'd seen it many times. He was afraid for the lives of his family, and he'd do anything to save them. *Anything.*

Nefertiti stood and turned to her father. "We could run. Caelius is stuck in his prison. He can't hurt us."

"You know that's not true. His shadow form has more reach than his physical form. We live by his will alone. Don't think it otherwise, or we'll all be killed, and your daughters will be first; that much he assured me of before he sent me here."

Nefertiti seemed on the verge of protest, but after a moment, she slowly nodded.

Ur-Nammu stepped up to Lucian and lifted a metal flask. "A drop of Caelius's blood is in here. It's enough to make you forget that you saw us."

"No! I will not go back now that I have seen that they're alive. I held her dead in my arms. I drank the sands of Egypt and still couldn't escape the pain. I won't go back to ignorance! The ache of her loss is unbearable. I can't." Lucian looked desperate.

And he was.

He needed to hold on to the piece of him that was good. He'd been living in loss and vengeance for so long, I could see that just a tiny shred of hope had changed him instantly.

Ur-Nammu grabbed his arm with his free hand. "Lucian, if you ever cared for Nefertiti and her daughters, then you must do this. If you don't, it means their *true death*. You know Caelius. He will punish them to great lengths before he kills them. He'll forgive this one misstep, because you tried to kill Meky, but their existence *must* remain a secret, as per his and Nefari's original agreement."

"I can't," Lucian begged. "I need her. I need Aidan. I need all of them. I'm so alone, Ur-Nammu. Ever since . . ever since I left Gutium as a boy . . . ever since my mother died . . . I can't lose them again."

"Yet lose them you must, or they will *suffer*. I won't make you. You must choose to; it's what Caelius asked. A willing choice guarantees that you won't remember, because at the core of it, you know it's to protect the ones you love," Ur-Nammu said with authority.

He was invoking that damn Gutian code again. My heart ached, but I was selfishly relieved to see Lucian nod in agreement. Caelius's threat was real, and I'd seen firsthand what breaking Nefertiti's agreement had cost her.

"It's her children. If Nefari agrees . . . who am I to protest?"

"I'm sorry, La-Narru. I will find a way to free us—I promise. But the risk right now is too great." Nefertiti's eyes were pained.

"I love you."

He choked down tears. "And I you. I trust you with my life. If this is the only way to protect all of you . . . give me the blood." He stared at Nefertiti and Meky, as if their eyes would soften the blow of what he had to do next. "Know that even though I will think you dead, you will always be *alive* in my heart. I will cherish you through the ages, even if it's in grief alone."

Ur-Nammu opened the flask and handed it to him. He drank the drop quickly, like pulling off a Band-Aid. Then his eyes went blank, much like the current Lucian who stood next to me.

Ur-Nammu spoke the words that would make Lucian forget everything he had just seen. He then prompted him to bring the next Vessel in, as per Caelius's command. Well, I knew *that* hadn't happened. Past Lucian had obviously fought that part of the compulsion five hundred years later with a Vessel named Brummel, I thought it was.

The scenery shifted again, and we were headed into another memory. I wondered how many of these he was going to take me to. I needed to keep track, to remember as many details as I could.

Everything turned yellow and brown until we stood on the cliff face of a jagged canyon overlooking a dry, cracked desert. Even though I didn't recognize the people, I knew exactly what we were witnessing.

And holy crap, I was seeing Moses. *The* Moses! Even though this moment was intense, I couldn't help but be awed. The Bible had always felt like fiction to me, but learning what I had from Lucian, I knew that it was actually a variation of the truth, but it *was* the truth. Moses was real, and he'd been a Vessel—the first

Vessel.

And I was the last.

It was a circle that immediately made my brain freeze. I was a part of something so huge that if I had been in my corporeal form I would have barfed.

Moses.

A Vessel like *me*.

Could Lucian be remembering this for that very symmetry?

I needed to know why we were here.

Events unfolded in front of us almost too quickly to follow. An old man ran up the craggy rocks that made up the cliff face to reach Moses's side. I didn't need any introduction. He had a different face, but I'd know those eyes anywhere: Aidan.

"I can't let Lucian take you to Caelius. He'll free him, and it'll be the end of everything." Aidan's face was wracked with guilt. I knew that guilt. It was the same expression he'd had right before he stabbed me.

Past Lucian landed in front of them, hearing every word Aidan had just said. "Adnachiel? What is this? After all these years together, why would I betray you and take Moses to Caelius? Brother, I don't understand." His eyes showed his shock. "Have I not proven what you mean to me? I love you both. This is madness. Come, let us sit. We'll sort this out *together*. Isn't that what we always do? You taught us that, Moses." He extended his hand out to them, a slight tremble in his fingertips. "Let us make good on his teachings now, brother."

"Don't lie, Lucian! Caelius is your father and Darkness incarnate! And Moses and I are the Light," Aidan said, panicked. "I know what you've planned, and I can't let you free him! All of this was a lie! You used us for your own gain!"

With frightening speed, Ur-Nammu ran up to the trio. "It's time to bring in the Vessel, Lucian."

Moses was hurt and betrayed as he looked at Lucian. "My brother, what is this?"

Lucian growled at Ur-Nammu. "Go back to Caelius! I will not betray them!"

Aidan froze in doubt. Even though I knew what had happened, I almost thought he'd change his mind.

Ur-Nammu said, "We've waited too long! The Vessel must be taken to Caelius. We already discussed this, and you agreed!"

"That's not true!" Seeing Aidan's expression turn to one of resolve, Lucian panicked. I could see that he was scared that Aidan would make the wrong decision. He raced forward and grabbed Moses, flying into the air.

I knew it was to save him.

But man, did he look guilty now.

I could see Aidan lifting his chest, his face sad but determined. He leapt after them.

The Lucian who held my hand squeezed tighter as we flew with the memory. I searched his face for a sign of anything, but there was still nothing, just a vacant stare as we both watched the most horrifying thing I'd ever seen.

Aidan caught up to them and grabbed Moses's arm, trying to wrestle him back from Lucian. Moses cried out to Aidan, "Brother, you must do it! He has betrayed us! We can't release Caelius; he will destroy the world!"

Past Lucian was devastated. That this was what they thought of him broke him apart. He released Moses to Aidan. "Listen to me . . . I'm not a monster. I want only to live by your side in *peace*, like we have done. We freed a people together. Do you not believe in the truth of who I am?" he cried.

Then Moses's expression changed, the realization hitting him as he saw the sincerity in Lucian's eyes. "Brother?"

Lucian nodded, desperate for them to believe him. "I would *never* hurt you."

Moses's face filled with shame. "Forgive my weakness. Fear overcame the wisdom of my heart." He turned to Aidan, eyes once again alight with faith. "Adnachiel, he won't betray us. I was wrong to doubt our oath!" Moses yelled over the wind.

Tears streamed down Aidan's face. He wanted so badly to believe, just like he had wanted to with me. But he'd been created to protect the Light and the Earth itself. "I can't take that risk."

"Aidan—"

With a quick thrust, Aidan stabbed Moses straight through the heart.

Both their bodies fell from the sky, crashing to the hard ground below with a loud crunch of bones.

Past Lucian screamed in agony, and it tore my insides apart. The pain was so intense I almost let go of the Lucian next to me, but I held on tighter instead. I hoped that on some level he could feel me, that I was there with him, sharing this heart-crushing moment.

He'd lost both his brothers that day.

For no reason.

The scenery changed again, and I was grateful. I didn't want to see him cry over their bodies like I knew he had.

But when everything came into focus, I was shocked at what

memory we were in.

We were back in the ruins of my dorm building. I had pushed my hand into Lucian's chest, searing a hole in its center. Past Lucian said with sadness, "I couldn't save them." Now, knowing what Lucian had felt, I knew he'd been talking about Moses and Aidan.

When we were in Paris, he'd confessed that he'd been so relieved I was alive he didn't care that I'd punched a hole in his chest. It had been the moment he knew he loved me, though he hadn't been able to admit that yet.

I watched as I destroyed the rubble holding Aidan down.

Past Lucian tried to warn me. "Wait, Shea, you don't understand. He's not who you think he is. He'll kill you . . . I won't let anyone touch you. Just come with me. I know I'm a monster. I know what I've done . . ."

Lucian had terrified me, but now I knew he had been telling the truth. It was so sad that with Moses he hadn't been the monster he so easily confessed to being with me. Then he'd uttered his biblical threats toward Aidan, followed by the words I would never forget. "Shea Harper is *mine*!"

The Lucian holding my hand let go. I tried to grab for it again but froze when his eyes were suddenly alive and awake.

"Help me," he whispered.

***

I woke up on the bathroom floor, as if I had been rubber-banded back into my body. I coughed, choking on unbidden tears. I couldn't control anything—my body, my emotions, my brain. It overwhelmed me to the point of deep sobs.

And suddenly I felt Aidan's arms wrap around me. "Shea, what is it? Are you okay? What happened?"

I managed to pull myself together for only a moment as I sputtered, "Aidan . . . he . . . needs us."

Shock and sadness covered every feature on Aidan's face. He nodded slowly, then held me against his chest. "We will save him, Shea. I promise you."

CHAPTER 12
LUCIAN

I awoke from a strange mental fog and was back in the living room of the cabin. What had just happened? One minute I was here, the next everything had gone black. I looked at the clock in the corner of the room; I'd lost an hour. I'd never experienced a blackout like that before. The light and burning I'd felt before it started when I was thinking about the Vessel dissipated once I'd regained consciousness. And what was left in its wake was emptiness accompanied by an unshakable ache.

I wanted to drown that ache in Caelius's blood.

I clenched my fists, steadying myself, shaking the experience from my mind and replacing it with an urgency I felt boil up inside: I needed to escape. I leaned away from the visibility of the doorway. Aside from my strange lapse in time, I had been waiting for this moment. They were all finally preoccupied at the same time. It was now or never. I had to make my move.

Without a moment's hesitation, I leapt into the night. It

didn't matter where I flew first; I just had to create some distance between Caelius's presence and my physical body.

It was agony.

It felt like my skin was being pulled apart by a million hooks linking me to him. Every part of me screamed to go back, to fall into his arms like a puppy suckling milk.

I *needed* Caelius.

I needed my *savior*.

I cringed at my state and flew faster.

I tried to think only of Adnachiel, and it felt good. This was something familiar. *This* I remembered: hunting that beast and the searing feelings of betrayal his memory induced. To feel anything so deeply again, even pain, was bliss to me now. I longed for the recollection of Moses to pull me from apathy. I was reaching into the nothing for a hand, even a hand that I despised.

"Come back to me, Aidan," I whispered.

His scent was easy enough to find. Now that I was hopped-up on Caelius's blood, I could visibly *see* his Light trail. It was no wonder Caelius had said he could find them whenever he wanted, that it really was just about me being "ready." I tried not to think of him, the taste of my maker calling me to his feet.

I was so *thirsty*.

Just a few drops would be enough, wouldn't it?

I gritted my teeth, trying to shift my focus. That angel-beast, where was he going? Following a trail of heavenly light felt familiar somehow, even though this was a power I'd not possessed before. The image of Gracuri and a pile of dead bodies at our feet flashed like a quick bolt of lightning through my mind. Then, just as quickly, that image was replaced with Caelius.

My pace quickened.

Every time my mind went back to Caelius, I tried to refocus on Adnachiel's scent, his boyish nature, the way he had gutted our brother, Moses. It was strange—the more I thought of him, the more bizarre images would blink into my mind. Just as strange, however, was their immediate deletion, as if they'd never existed. Was I so fractured that my thoughts were like a shaken jigsaw puzzle? So it wasn't just the girls that made me feel out of place; even alone I felt disjointed.

It was all right though.

Caelius's blood would sort me out.

I sighed again, flying hard enough to break the sound barrier.

"We are not looking for *Caelius's blood,* we are looking for *Adnachiel*," I reminded myself over and over until I caught the mistake. I trembled, feeling a grip tighten around my throat. Caelius had so infected my subconscious that I now called myself "we." I shivered again, racing harder toward Aidan.

When I landed, I gasped for breath and leaned against a tall cedar tree. His trail had finally met the Vessel's and Meky's in South Dakota, and I'd followed it to this end here in Colorado. I winced, noticing that most of my skin was stripped off. Even an immortal's body wasn't meant to move that fast; after all, my original form was still flesh and bone. As it was, I felt like my body was barely containing the new strength Caelius's blood allowed. If *I* felt like this, how was Caelius's power not ripping his mortal body to shreds? Was he in pain like I was?

I stopped myself again.

We don't need to think about Caelius. Remember why we're here.

I took a quick breath. The cool air helped fight the pain as skin slowly grew back, but nothing helped the *hunger*. I crushed a large rock under my foot as a bird began to sing in the trees behind me.

Music.

I'd forgotten that it even existed outside of Caelius's bedroom.

I tried to think of my favorite songs across the ages. Words of men made from strings of beats. Harps and pianos, drums and electric guitars. Even remembering lyrics felt religious and holy. I was so relieved—relieved and terrified at how far gone I was.

I looked up at the snowcapped mountains. They were beautiful and untouched by man. It made me feel clean in a way I hadn't been. Even washed, bathed, and wrapped in the white sheets and walls of our bedroom, I'd still been filthy. Caelius's touch and the eyes of my disapproving family had assured me of that. I stared at the gently falling snowflakes in the distance. It was comforting to see that it wasn't only Caelius's blood that made the world anew.

I looked around at the adjacent mountains. Nestled in the center valley, Aidan's trail had led me to this peak. In contrast, the mountains surrounding it were giants. This was the smallest point, hidden in the center, dwarfed by the others like David had been, surrounded by Goliath and his armies.

I smiled with the recollection. Goliath had been quite the man in his day, but he was powerless once he had fallen in love with David. I rested my hand against the sharp edge of a rock at the mountain's base. In my experience and observations throughout history, it was not faith that could move mountains, but love. Of course, love could also take magnificent giants and bring them to their knees. I cringed as the rock I was leaning into cut my hand.

Blood.

Was such a thing more powerful than love itself? I looked past the red and stared up at the tiny mountain being overshadowed by the others. How had my friend David been so brave, and Goliath so foolish?

My friend.

It was something David had always called me, even at the end. He hadn't been as charming as Moses, but he'd had that way about him, inviting in even the worst among us and calling them companions, forging allies instead of enemies. He'd used that same language with Goliath, who'd only been called a giant, a *beast*.

If ever there were soul mates, they were proof enough. But in the end, Goliath chose David over immortality, and David chose his people over Goliath. The betrayal and regret that followed had hollowed out the warmth in David's eyes as the years passed. He never loved again: not his children, not his wives, not the kingdom he had won after the war. He never forgot that, as Goliath breathed his last, the only words left on his lips had been "I love you."

My friend.

Had I been a true friend, I would have killed him to end his suffering. At one point he'd begged me to, but even then I'd ensured that no harm came to him, that he fully lived his immortality, crushed by the weight of the choices he'd made in his youth. It was part promise, part punishment for what he'd done: choosing political victory over love. It was only in the last hundred years that I regretted keeping my promise to Goliath:

to protect David until the end. Who was I, Lucian the Merciful? I should have killed him the day Goliath died. In the wake of all I'd lost, I should have known that even a coward deserved that mercy.

I turned my gaze to the soft white above me. At least my past was still mine. It didn't belong to Caelius, no matter how painful it was. The reality that David, along with all my other sons, was now gone pained me further. That pain made me crave the comfort of Caelius's blood like a fever.

Wash away Goliath and his David. Wash away the promise of love and its inevitable betrayal. Wash away all my sins and mistakes. If I am yours, I do not have to be my own. I do not have to be responsible for my failures.

I groaned as the thirst grew.

Caelius.

My salvation.

I closed my hand over my mouth, trying to push back my jutting fangs. Their eyes . . .

I tried to remember the icy look of Nefari and our girls. I held on to it. Even with all I'd lost, I still had something to protect: a family worth fighting for. I couldn't give in to oblivion like Goliath, who'd only had his David.

I needed to end this.

I squinted. The Light trails led to a large house at the peak. It was visible and open once you passed the outer mountains. The way through the ice caps would be treacherous if you couldn't fly. I, however, could just jet up and grab her. It was an exciting thought, the Vessel snatched so quickly in my arms, but they would see me clear as day through those endless glass windows adorning the cabin.

I clenched my teeth, letting my eagerness be replaced by rationality; with a Vessel this powerful, I couldn't let her know I was coming. I had to sneak in through the center and take her before anyone could respond. I needed every advantage, and surprise was a good one. Surprise had taken down kings, even the great Caesar. He was another interesting man, another giant that fell because of his love of Brutus.

I paused. Why was I even thinking about the past by pondering love's betrayals? What was it about the Vessel that brought on such worthless recollections?

I need *her.*

That sentiment alone struck me in a strange way.

Let's rephrase.

We need her dead.

I stared at the large stones around me, collecting myself.

There had to be another way in.

The treetops waving in the breeze cast fragmented light across the rocks, and an unnatural glint caught my eye. The boulders had been moved and put back in place. I ran my hand along the hairline cracks. The seams were flawless; not even my kind would have noticed. But I wasn't just some vampire, not anymore, thanks to Caelius. These misplaced stones were a hidden door, most likely an emergency exit if things at the top went south. I smiled. Only one scientist I knew of would be this clever: Helena.

Caelius had said the Vessel might have brainwashed her and kept her alive to use against us, but to not hold out hope. With her aiding them, however, Adnachiel had procured himself a rather ingenious advantage. I sighed with relief. "Helena, you're alive," I whispered. Touching the grainy surface, I searched for a small hole. Shadowed by a large bulging rock, I slipped my finger into the crack underneath it.

Just as I had thought, there were small gears hidden inside. A key could be lost or forged, but this was a code, a pattern. Having to turn the cogs with the tip of your finger until they locked into the correct sequence was ingenious.

It was just like the prototype she had been working on when we first met. She hadn't yet known of my full capabilities as a vampire, that my sight was enhanced enough to see through the spaces in her metal "do not touch" boxes. Trying to hide any of her work from me had been fruitless, but it was just like someone so brilliant to miss a calculation; she hadn't taken into consideration how long I had known her before we became friends. I knew more about Helena than I'd ever confessed, though I'd come close to telling her such in Loretto.

I smiled as gears moved and the boulders parted. She had an affinity for lemniscates—all the shapes in her machinery reflected it in their designs. In that way, she was an easy code to crack. I stepped inside, and immediately the rock door sealed behind me, not that I would be going out that way. Past this point, there was no going back for me.

My eyes adjusted to the dark until I saw perfectly. I was inside a small tunnel with equations scribbled along the sides. No doubt she'd had ideas flash in her mind as she was coming and going. Wood pulp was nonessential to geniuses: their world was made of paper.

I looked closer. The writing was old, forgotten. Something must have happened to make her abandon this lab. My smile faded. The Vessel was using her, making her reveal her sacred places like they were hideouts and not something to be cherished.

My hands balled into fists. I'd had a place where I had kept all of my keepsakes: trinkets accrued over centuries. It was a long lonely life being immortal, but that refuge had been like an anchor to my sanity against the storms. I had even stored Nefertiti's necklace there. I'd searched all of Pompeii for that tribute, and where was it now? If I could offer that necklace to Nefari again—like I had as a boy, then as a man in Egypt— perhaps she would look at me like she used to.

The Vessel had done all of this. I didn't know how that light bulb had found my hiding place, but she had destroyed it completely, as she would do to Helena and her lab once she was done with her. I couldn't let that happen.

I moved forward.

The narrow hallway let out into a large circular room. It was hollowed out, like a cyclone had dipped down into the center of the mountain. The walls were covered in moss. I looked closer. Under the carpet of wet green were cyclical lacerations in the stone, each an inch thick and perfectly equidistant from the other.

I was wrong; this was nothing as unpredictable as the wind. This was symmetry carved out by a machine with large claws. Of course Helena would invent something to hollow out the base of a mountain. Even as a human, I had thought her mind unstoppable. People that judged scientists as technical and not creative had never met a *real* scientist like her. She was the embodiment of both.

Distinct patterned dots of light filled the entire cavern and made it look like a classic pointillism painting. It reflected her tastes. She admired Georges Seurat's work. When I stole the original *A Sunday Afternoon on the Island of La Grande Jatte* as a gift for her birthday, she'd been livid. At the same time, she'd made no demands for me to return it. In fact, it was the first thing she would unpack every time she moved to a new lab.

When she was stuck on a particularly hard equation, she would get close enough to the painting that her nose almost touched it. She'd remark that anything without objectivity became impossible for the observer to see clearly. Then she would lean back and look at the painting again, watching as all of the dots started to form a larger image. When she would do this, I always took it as an invitation, and sure enough, I would provide the wanted distraction, and sure enough, when she returned, physically worn out and wild, she'd solve the problem within minutes. We worked well together in that way.

She could have changed the world if she had been given the chance. In her generation, they'd been too sexist to see her infinite possibility, and now, as the world was, science didn't matter—not in this transformed planet Caelius was envisioning.

Blood, teeth, and servitude were the new reality.

I moved toward the center where there was a singular helix-shaped staircase that led upward. I could see now that the light at the top moved its way down by refracting off of polished stones. I stopped and marveled. More than a pointillist painting, the bottom chamber was colored like the stained glass reflections of an old Catholic church. I never thought I'd see it again, not after Caelius had destroyed it, but sure enough, the staircase itself mirrored the one at Loretto Chapel in Santa Fe. The nuns there had called it the "miracle stair," saying it had been built by St. Joseph himself. It had become a legend to the faithful.

I smiled, waving my hand through the specks of color as I touched the staircase. Had the nuns known Joseph, they wouldn't have called him a saint. Now *that* was a man who could drink. Still, he was always honest, which was why I'd brought Helena to New Mexico, just before I *thought* she'd died.

I was going to confess who the saint had been, but I fell short, seeing her come alive. She'd marveled at the arithmetic and artistry of the carpenter, who had used crude tools and no electricity to complete such a masterpiece. The nuns had filled her head with stories of a saint coming in the night hours, and for once she'd listened and hadn't argued science over faith. And for once, I'd listened and hadn't argued either.

Even as a drunk, Joseph had been a better man than me; at least his legend could inspire belief. She'd confessed to me then that her father had abandoned her once in that very monastery as a child, that she herself had witnessed the miracle and had some faint memory of the man.

In truth, there'd been no miracle. In that era, they took in too many orphans who needed food and schooling. The nuns had been desperate for space and needed a second floor. Children were forced to stay outside in shifts, suffering the blistering heat or the unrelenting cold depending on the season. I had no love for Catholicism, but after wandering the streets, a child covered in mud had asked fervently for my help. She either hadn't noticed the bloodstains on my shirt or didn't care.

When I shrugged her off, she pleaded on bended knees, gripping my shins, refusing to let go.

I asked for her age and name and was surprised that she was younger than I had been when I'd lost my mother. She was just a little thing, and still she was so determined. She spat her name like it had only ever been spoken as a curse. She said it was Helena, but it should have been *Henry*. I knew what she meant. At that time there were plenty of households that only wanted boys, so much so that they abandoned their own children in merciless places like Loretto.

The Gutian Harrowing had allowed young ones to prove themselves, despite their gender, but these children were thought worthless by *birth*. As I stared at her muddied hands and fierce eyes, I was sure that she would have passed the terrifying nights alone. She would have made it home and been honored and renamed, given a place in my tribe as a warrior.

Yet there she stood, proving herself worthy to no one, with blistered hands and raw cheeks.

It pulled on my old rumblings as a Gutian, and I agreed to help her, despite what I was.

Even the nuns didn't acknowledge Helena; instead they said I was sent by God. It made me laugh, the idea that God would send a devil to do his work. All the same, it was a welcome challenge at first. As a boy I had enjoyed crafting things with my hands. I had been so caught up in destruction as a vampire that I hadn't tested my new capabilities as an immortal. Sure enough, without needing sleep, I had designed and constructed the staircase in a matter of days. It had been easy. Too easy.

I hadn't felt the old satisfaction I had as a child, laboring to create beauty. The only pleasure I took from it was the look on Helena's face once it was completed. Despite the nuns' appreciation, it was her gratitude alone that I cherished. She polished the stairs daily like they were precious to her, and eventually, that made them precious to me.

Then her father came.

Without so much as a thanks to the nuns who had raised her for *three years*, he dragged her screaming back to the wealthy mansion he'd ejected her from. Some stranger with a birth certificate, that's all he was, yet that paper gave him power over her life.

I could have stopped him. I wanted to, but I was what I was.

A vampire couldn't raise a child.

I watched as her rags were exchanged for dresses hemmed in gold. I listened as she sang the songs from the church, like a sad canary, out her open window at night. Once she even called for me, the Carpenter Saint of the Loretto Chapel. I had thought my presence hidden then, but she spoke my name all the same, believing that I was always out there somewhere, creating miracles for her little church in the shadows.

I couldn't bring myself to answer her call.

I was no saint.

Eventually she stopped singing, and I couldn't bear to watch her grow into the shape of her father's delusions. I left her side, as I had left so many others in a long line of abandoned heartstrings. I scoffed at my recollection. Lucian the Merciful, indeed. I had been a coward, afraid to raise and lose a child like I'd lost Nefertiti's. At the chapel, rumors that Joseph had built the stairs took hold, and I didn't care. Without her, those steps were just empty planks of wood. Time passed, and I put her out of my mind along with the whole of New Mexico.

Then by accident, over a decade later, I tried to kill her.

I was roaming the sleek cobblestone streets in London and got hungry. I let myself into an estate that was lit up like a candy shop. I decided that a fluffy little debutante in a dress was just the right amount of fatty blood that I needed to tide me over until I reached the next continent.

When I stepped in, I knew immediately that it was just the kind of party I hated: an upper-class young woman was making her first appearance in *fashionable* society. It was a fancy butcher's shop, and she was the piece of meat for sale. The wealthy suitors were already surrounding her, making their assessments. They might as well have opened her mouth to check her teeth. One of them leaned in close when she was laughing, and I had no doubt he was doing just that.

I decided then to save the pretty young thing from a life of servitude by wetting my appetite and cutting the pearls at her neck off with my teeth. But she outwitted me; with wild eyes and muddy hands, she'd fought me back. I was dumbstruck by the memory of a child in Loretto with eyes just as fierce: Helena. She had grown in the shadow of her father into something magnificent.

She had taken my pause as an opportunity to strike the final blow. Had I been a murderer like Jack the Ripper, she would have won. But my skull healed, and I came back for her the next night, this time offering companionship.

As the years passed, she accepted what I was and our friendship deepened. Secretly, I'd vowed never to leave her side again, but I still longed for her to know me, to remember, so I took her to the chapel. To my disappointment, as awed as she was by the sight, her memory was blurry, and she barely remembered the nuns' names, let alone the saint.

Or so I'd thought at the time.

I cast my eyes upward. Was I again looking for some kind of redemption for not telling her when I had the chance, in this handmade church of Helena's? Had my influence left such an impact that she'd subconsciously built this staircase, a replica of Loretto's? I had never confessed to being the saint from her childhood, and now that staircase was dust, along with what had been Santa Fe.

I looked at the thin steps spiraling above me with no central support beam. It was a beautiful stretched-out nautilus, like the perfect sequences found in nature. Many had remarked that my design defied physics, but really, the only thing keeping it afloat was math.

My smile returned. She'd done well. I gazed at its perfection and simplicity. Beautiful things were like that: infinitely intellectually complex but simple in a fundamentally endearing way.

That was Helena.

All this time I'd thought she was dead, but she had been asleep next to Nefertiti and her children. She was another "loving" surprise kept secret until they could be turned fully and released from the prisons of their dreams. But the prince that awakened them had been a monster of Darkness, and the kiss had been a vicious life-sucking crunch to the neck. Their transformation was more in line with *Grimms' Fairy Tales* than the popularized version of *Sleeping Beauty*. Even Duncan with his silver tongue wouldn't have created such a hopeless story.

She deserved better. Perhaps if she did remember meeting me as a child, she would have cursed the day she asked for that staircase. It had been free, but the cost had been her eternal servitude to Caelius.

Muffled voices pulled me from my thoughts.

The sounds were moving down the stairs, losing dialect and tone as they absorbed into the moss and scattered along the stones. However, one word did manage to filter through: friend.

There that word was again. As with David, it had been important to Helena. I sighed, feeling the heavy weight of it. I had failed many friends in my lifetime, but I had to save Helena, even if she belonged to the Vessel now.

I fought back a growl.

My Second-Borns had been brainwashed before being butchered, David among them. But once the Vessel was *dead*, her control would leave Helena, and I could convince Caelius to spare her. It would no doubt take time to undo the damage to her mind, but it would be a welcome relief to have her by my side again. I had lost all of my chosen Second-Borns, and my family was small now, thanks to the Vessel. Helena was precious. I had to do this for her as much as I had to do it for Nefari.

I moved noiselessly up the stairs, hovering over the steps. To my surprise, the staircase branched off like the base of a tree trunk. Small bridges extended to more doors. Some were open, revealing bedrooms or labs. Some were closed with massive locks and sheets of metal drilled into them. Experiments gone wrong, maybe? If I had time, curiosity would have prompted me to open those doors. As it was, I had to be ready. I needed to harden myself and prepare for battle. I had to think of the beast.

My smile grew.

The thought of seeing Adnachiel filled me with relief.

I caught the sensation and crushed it.

Relief?

How far gone was I that the sight of that beast should bring me *relief?* Maybe it was the familiarity of torturing him that calmed my mind. If thinking of Helena had softened me, that angel, in contrast, should've filled me with the desire to fight. I shook my head, trying to refocus. The Vessel was too powerful, and I couldn't fail. Caelius would continue to do the unspeakable to my body and mind if I came back empty-handed.

He would give me blood.

I licked my lips.

So much blood . . .

Thinking of Helena had distracted me from feeling just how *thirsty* I was.

I moved closer to the top, where the light was coming in.

The final door.

I shattered it with one quick punch and ran into the room that held them. The wood splintered and fell down on everyone in the room like rain. Power surged through me in waves, radiating down my spine. I hadn't used my juiced-up body for anything other than Caelius's pleasures, but now that I was moving on my own accord, I could *feel* the difference in strength. I was more powerful than I had ever been.

My body moved in a flash like lightning. I snatched the Vessel and Meky in an instant and smashed through the walls, flying high into the endless blue outside. I made my way quickly to the thing my blood longed for: Caelius. I *needed* to get back to him, even if our flesh peeled off in the process.

I flew faster.

With this kind of speed, I was confident that Adnachiel would never catch up. Not even with his ability to hover midair could he compete with flight like this. Nothing could.

They both struggled in my arms, shouting, but it was Meky's words that slowed my pace. "What the hell are you doing, Lucian? Let me go! Put us both down this instant!"

I looked at her face; her eyes were furious. "I-I'm sorry I failed you before, Meky. But I'll take the Vessel and make it right. Let me at least have the honor of your rescue." She was so disgusted with me that she didn't even want me to save her.

"Are you insane? *I* saved Shea! I wasn't kidnapped! Caelius is lying to you, Lucian. Wake up!" Meky screamed, squeezing my arms with all her might.

"What are you talking about—" I heard a crack in the sound barrier as huge white wings surrounded me, then something yanked the girls from my arms. Before I could move, I was flung to the earth. I landed on my face. It caved in with the force. For a moment I was blind, rolling on the ground like a worm as my bones and eyeballs hung out.

What was that?

I scratched at my bright red skin. It burned like my body was being eaten by fire ants. Healing was always a painful process, but it seemed more intense now that I was fattened up with Caelius's venom. I clawed and clawed until my face finally returned along with my vision. I panted, weary from the effort.

"Beast?" I stared at his soft features. "What . . . what's happened to you? How did you get your wing back?" I blinked as my eyelids grew into place. Adnachiel's wings were extended. They were vast and magnificent, shining like glory itself. His whole body looked blessed and more kissed by the sun than ever. I was awestruck until I saw that he was cradling both Meky and the Vessel in his arms, as if they belonged to *him*, as if a creature like that deserved to even *touch* them.

I brushed the dirt off my Hanfu. "Impossible. You haven't been able to fly since you killed Moses. You're earthbound, you dog." I cracked my neck, preparing for the fight. "Did that Vessel restore your wings somehow? Does she know that your true form is *ugly*, covered in eyes and animals? Does she know that you're as ugly inside as out, that you gutted all the other Vessels along with Moses and—"

"I know." She moved out of his arms and took a step toward me.

"Shea." He spoke desperately, his hand wrapping around her wrist.

"I know, Aidan, it's okay." She pushed his hand away, and he growled like the dog he was.

"*Aidan*?" I laughed out loud. "So you have the same name that you wore back when you killed Moses. It was the last word on his lips as he died in disbelief at your betrayal."

Adnachiel scowled. "Caelius let you keep the painful memories of your past, just not anything recent. I mean, you really don't remember having us swallowed by a whale? That was pretty epic. It was a first for me at least." He shifted his gaze to the ground and moved his hand down his muscled arm in the insecure way he used to when we first met. "We're over all of that now. I apologized, and you forgave . . . well, you said . . . that we were *brothers* again." When his eyes found mine, they were sad, dimming some of the glory his body was emanating.

What was that, guilt?

Pity?

I blinked, again dumbfounded. Aidan was a lot of things, but he wasn't nonsensical; a *whale*? What kind of lunacy was he referring to? "We'll *never* be brothers again. You saw to that with Moses and every Vessel thereafter," I hissed. None of this mattered. "I don't have time for this. Whatever game you're playing, it's not going to work."

"Okay, just stop," the Vessel said. She stared at me with a strange look of longing. "How can you not remember? You let me into your mind! You sucked me into your memories and asked me to help you! Isn't that why you're really here? Some part of you ran to me, I know it!"

"Are you talking about Dream-Walking? With *you?* That's not even a power I possess!" I didn't know what kind of mind game she was playing, but she was obviously misinformed. "Even the dog knows that, Vessel. How moronic can you be? In a game of wits, it's obvious you'd lose. I won't fall for your childish deceptions."

"It wasn't Dream-Walking; you took me into some of your memories! Maybe your subconscious is more powerful because you're hopped-up on Caelius juice—it literally grabbed me! I still don't know why you picked those specific moments, but maybe we could figure it out . . . together." She reached her hand out for me to take.

I stepped toward the Vessel, then stepped back, shocked at my body's obedience. What kind of power was she using?

Adnachiel pulled her back, placing himself between us. "I should be the one to offer peace. I'm sorry, but we really are here for you—"

"I don't mind going *through* you to get to them, Beast. Don't forget, I know who you really are, and she is no safer behind you than in front."

Adnachiel clenched his jaw. "Listen to Shea. Some part of your brain reached out to her and asked for her help. Brother, listen like I should have before Moses—"

"Don't you dare call me brother!" I lunged forward but stopped before contact.

My nails were so close to the skin at Aidan's throat, a slip of paper couldn't pass through. Meky stood between us, her face inches from mine, her arms pushing me back. "It's not him you'll have to go through, Lucian! It's me!" She struggled with all her might to hold me in place, but it barely felt like butterfly wings touching my skin. "I won't let you hurt him! I love him!"

My eyes widened in surprise. "You don't mean that!" Meky in love with the beast? It wasn't possible. "You have to trust me; the Vessel has *brainwashed* you. She's created stories as elaborate as the old fables I used to read to you and your sisters in Egypt. It's all fabrication. You have to trust me, trust what your heart *knows* to be true—"

"Look who's talking." She smacked my outstretched hands away and laughed, but it wasn't with any of the joy she used to have when I would braid her hair by the Nile, back when we'd *both* been human. "Caelius has turned you into his pet and rewritten your memories. Lucian, you are on *our* side! We're working together to kill Caelius. Doesn't that *feel* familiar?"

It felt like a bomb had gone off in my mind.

My ears buzzed. She was still talking, but her words were drowned out. All that remained was a pulse—a dark, devouring pulse repeating words into my brain, pounding it into my body. The pulse spoke the truth. The Vessel was brainwashing *them*. It had killed her sisters. Meky was deceived. Her words were lies created by the Vessel's power.

I had to get back to Caelius, my savior.

I needed his blood to protect me from her manipulation.

I shook my head, everything coming back into focus as my mind reeled at the sight; out of breath, traveling on land, stood Helena.

"Lucian, stop! Listen to reason," she panted, tucking in her loosened shirt. "Should I be offended that you only took Shea and Meky?"

I staggered. "Helena, I can't express in words how glad I am that you're alive. I . . . will always care about you." I stumbled forward, wanting to reach for her. "I can't." It took all my willpower to keep myself glued in place. "You have to understand. I will save you too, once the Vessel is dead, but I can't bring you back now. Caelius will *kill* you, if not out of jealousy, then because of what you've done."

That's right, the voice in my head whispered. "You created some kind of invention to harness the Light and used it against us." I shook my head, grabbing my chest. An invention to harness the Light; now that *felt* true. "Once I've proven myself to Caelius, I will plead to him and Nefertiti on your behalf. It's not your fault that her daughters died—you were being used. You are still . . . my friend. I will save you and your lab from this Vessel, I promise. I know it's too late, now that Santa Fe is destroyed, but I'll finally tell you about the staircase in the Loretto Chapel. We can save that church in our memories, if nothing else."

Her hair was pulled back, which meant she had been working. She swayed nervously from foot to foot, her eyes darting back and forth, calculating just as she had as a human. Finally, she rested her hand on one hip. The movement was so familiar that it put me at ease.

I straightened my back and hardened my resolve.

This was part of the trap.

The Vessel was trying to disarm me by shielding herself with the bodies of the people I cared for. She wanted me to hesitate. She was just waiting for the right opening to attack.

"Lucian," Helena said. She pulled the tie from her hair and slowly untangled the braid. My mouth fell open, but I didn't respond. Seeing her tresses fall free like they had decades ago when we were riding horseback across the plains felt more recent than nostalgic. "I need you to listen to the science of it."

I chuckled. "Still trying to convince a vampire in a world of chaos that there are irrefutable laws and facts? Oh, Helena, if you weren't brainwashed, I would . . ." How was I going to finish that sentence?

I would embrace you like I did before and tell you everything.

It was all I could do to not grab her in my arms.

"In the last battle, you were on the Vessel's side," she said quickly. "The device I made was meant to harness your power and hers, to kill *Caelius*, but he had warped my mind with his Darkness, his shadow. Consciously, I was a puppet, but subconsciously the true me still existed, even if it was buried, and I sabotaged his plan to absorb the Vessel's soul. I know deep inside, the true you still exists too. You brought Shea into your memories. A part of you knows exactly what happened. You just have to find it."

"Enough!" I motioned for Meky to move. "I don't want to hurt you, but I can knock you out and bring you back. Your mother is worried to death—"

"My mother is a traitor! Listen to Helena! She knows you!"

"The Meky I know would never speak ill of Nefari," I snarled.

Meky's hands balled into fists. "The Nefari *I* know would never sacrifice La-Narru. She wouldn't act from a place of fear or loss. She's given up her Gutian code; she thinks she's protecting what she loves, but you can't protect what you love by destroying it. She was letting Caelius *destroy* you, and that was destroying the rest of us. She's not worthy of being called Gutian anymore."

Her words burned down my throat as I swallowed. "So neither your mother nor I are Gutian to you." I paused, letting the callus wash over me. "So be it."

"Lucian, that's not what I meant—"

I moved to grab Meky, but Helena stepped between us, thickening the shield around the Vessel.

"I was barely able to resist Caelius!" Helena interrupted, just as brave and socially awkward as the mortal she once was. "I can't imagine, scientifically, the miracle it will take for you to resist his blood. But I know a drug addict when I see one. You're stronger, sure, but look how *thin* you are. Look at the dark circles under your eyes. You're barely hanging on. Lucian, he's *killing* you . . ." Helena's voice trailed off. It was rare to see her unable to complete a thought because of emotion.

Rare and unwarranted.

Caelius had *healed* me, and I was stronger than ever. I hadn't seen a mirror, but there was no way I looked as bad as she was implying. Most likely, I was as radiant as Adnachiel.

"The lass is right, brother. Look at ye. Ye reek as bad as a dead spawnin' fish upriver. Of course, Caelius be the body layin' eggs, and ye the body dying. Not the sort a story I got planned for ye."

"How?" I ran forward and grabbed him instinctually. "Duncan!" I pulled him into my arms. "You're alive! I thought you were dead like the others!"

"O' course! It'll take a better tale than that to kill ol' Duncan. I guess that worthless bucket o' black dinnae think to remake a memory of me livin' since he dinnae know it. There ye go! I'm alive, and he dinnae have the chance to get to that part in yeer brain! That's proof, brother!" He hugged me back, hardy and strong as he laughed. The sound of it vibrated through my chest. I relaxed a little into his warmth.

On drunken mornings on grassy hills, we'd laughed and embraced like this. There were long nights and tall tales. There was an endless summer where we looked at stars while walking down cliffs to the ocean. He spoke of magic, lore, and fairies, and I listened. His mind was as endless and as deep as those stars, and he could have created whole universes had he the power of a god and not a man.

But he'd been a man before the war.

Before I'd turned him into something he hated.

Before he hated me.

He patted my back. "There, there, brother. I'm here with ye now. Ye saved me in tha caves when I was lost, longin' fer death.

Ye brought me a dead animal, remember? I'll save ye now that yeer lost. Come with me. This Shea, she means tha world to ye, even though ye dinnae remember. She's who ye want to protect from that dobber, Caelius. Not tha other way around."

I slunk out of his tight grip and stepped back. "I see. Another shield has arrived to aid her." I looked back at those hazel eyes alight with the power of a Vessel.

Behind me, another familiar voice called out. "Hey, sorry I'm late. You guys are a little faster than me." Jeff Harper moved a hand down his shirt, straightening it with embarrassment. His eyes looked up and down my body, and he smiled. "H-hey. It's been a long time, Father. I mean, Lucian. Sorry." He laughed to himself awkwardly. "The father thing is weird, especially since you're with my daughter."

I looked at him with disdain. "I only turned you in hopes that the Vessel would join us and not doggedly despise vampires like the religious Light-worshiping zealot she is. I am not, nor have I ever been, *with* her."

Jeff threw up his hands. "Hey now, that's my daughter, and we've never been particularly religious in our household, so that's totally uncalled-for. Surprising for a couple raising the Light though, right?"

I scowled. "How candid."

"Yeah." He walked toward Shea. He moved with an ease in his own skin, even though he was newly turned. "It's good to see you though. Helena's right, you look rough, but you're still very handsome. I mean, you know, the blood you gave me really creates like an, uh, infatuation, right? So if I'm being weird, that's totally why." He blushed a little. Surprisingly, the Vessel's face looked just as mortified as I felt. "No, I'm just, what I'm saying is if you drank Caelius's blood, you probably worship the guy by now. Think about it."

"I do." I spoke without hesitation. My devotion to him wasn't something I could resist. Helena's words seemed to make some sense in that respect. *I know deep inside, the true you still exists too.* A small part of me still knew that Caelius was poison, but the rest of me wanted him like a drowning human wanted air.

"Caelius is my salvation." I spoke as if his hand was still on my throat. In truth, I could feel it there, even as far away from him as I was.

"No, Lucian, that can't be true," Adnachiel said from behind them.

My eyes momentarily locked with his, but he didn't make a move. It bothered me, this whole situation. Why hadn't he tried to kill her? He'd killed *every* Vessel throughout time. When it came down to saving them or saving the world, he always chose his *true* family: the Light. What had made him change his mind? Was she controlling him as well? And if she was this powerful, how had I succeeded in bringing her to Caelius in the first place?

I shook the thoughts from my head.

This was what she wanted, to throw me off-balance so that she could kill me or make me her puppet like the others. Was this why Caelius wanted to pump me with his blood until I was ready? Did he know how effective her manipulative tactics would be?

None of this mattered in the long run.

Caelius was free now, whether the light bulb was alive or not.

The rules had changed.

I looked at all of them like they were strangers. The relief I'd felt at Duncan being alive faded. They were the Vessel's pawns now. "There must be some part of all of you that knows you're being manipulated. The Vessel killed all the other Second-Borns, Duncan. She killed your *sisters,* Meky. You both at least feel *that,* do you not?"

Duncan shook his head. "Yeer so stubborn, in right or in wrong. Ye killed some of yeer own children to save her, and Caelius drank the other lot like ale. Drank me right in front of ye. With yeer own eyes, ye cried for me. It was ye cryin' over my body, that's why some of the devil's blood fell in ma mouth, and I'm alive now because of it."

"Your accent gets thick when you're nervous. I bet she can't control that, but it's a tell. You're good at making up stories, and she's using that to her advantage, Duncan." I sighed. "Even you must understand how ludicrous this all sounds."

"I can't help my accent–I always get excited when yeer around. Come now, lost lamb. What are we gonna do? Won't you let me save ye? Please. I'm sorry for pushin' ye away all this time and never saying it; I still love ye, Lucian. I can't forget what ye did, but I can forgive it." He reached out his hand.

Crazier than his words was the fact that I reached back to him before yanking my hand away. What was I thinking? First she'd used Helena, now Duncan. Just how powerful was this Vessel at mind control? I moved farther back.

"How dare you use him to speak of love." I glared at the Vessel before my gaze met Duncan's and softened. "Don't worry, once she's dead and your free will returns, I won't hold you to anything you're saying. I know you *hate* me, and it must be killing you, having to choke out words otherwise."

Duncan's hand remained outstretched as he shook his head and sighed.

Meky reached out her hand as well. "He ripped through his mortal flesh, the Darkness in him trying to contort into a more suitable *physical* form, with spikes and blood for eyes. He had black claws and huge teeth that ate—" Her face twisted in horror and grief. "How can you not remember the sight of it?" She shivered, haunted by the fake memory.

I had seen something similar in the caves, when he would take me and bend me to his will in shadow form. I had felt the horror she spoke of. It was nightmarish and not something I could forget. I shook my head again. All of this could be fabricated by the Vessel. No doubt she knew the various forms of Darkness.

Why was I even listening to them? By now Caelius had figured out that I was gone. I couldn't fail. No matter how much I wanted it, I couldn't be forced to drink gallons of his blood again. I needed to stay clean, for my family.

My dry tongue moved along my teeth. It didn't matter how *thirsty* I was, he could always do something worse if I failed. He could have me watch as he tortured the children, especially Setepenre because she was *mine*.

They all stepped around me and inched in.

This was the trap I had known she was setting. The Vessel called them all to her. She was controlling their minds, and because of my fondness for these familiar faces I had allowed myself to be surrounded.

She was smarter than Adnachiel, I'd give her that: using Meky as a shield, using Helena and Duncan to sway me and keep me raw. I had played chess with the beast for centuries, but this was pure exploitation, to use family and friends. It was something *I* would have done, not Aidan. How had she caused such an angel to turn against all that he valued when my torment over the centuries had not?

For that alone, she needed to die.

I lunged forward and knocked Meky down. I'd have to come back for her. I punched Adnachiel in the chest, angling it so he flew into Jeff and Duncan. Caelius's blood had allowed me to hit harder than I had expected. They soared so far out of sight, their scent trails were masked with debris from fallen trees and mountains.

Helena wrapped her arms around Meky and shot me a defiant look, as if I would go after her and risk injuring them both. "I lied to you." Helena's voice was resolute. "When you took me to Loretto Chapel, I acted like I didn't remember. But I never forgot you or what you did for me, Lucian. *Please* don't leave me again."

I paused. My heart felt crushed. I wanted nothing more than to take her then and there. "I can't." It pained me, and I saw her then as the child she once was, calling my name out her window. "I'm sorry for abandoning you then and for what your life has become because of me. But you're not safe until this is over. I *promise* I'll come back for you when she's dead and your mind is clear. We'll talk about everything. I'll make it right somehow. Trust me this one time, my friend, and I will never leave your side again. I . . . love you."

I leapt into the sky with the Vessel pressed against my hips, her head resting on my chest. I had to leave my feelings unresolved at Helena's feet. I hoped she would understand once this was all over.

I flew backward as fast and as hard as I could, shielding the Vessel's body from the ripping force of the wind. Meky had slowed my pace, and Adnachiel had used the element of surprise, but it wouldn't work twice. There was no way, even if that beast had functioning wings, that he could catch me, as strong as I was now. The only *thing* that could was probably Caelius himself. I winced at the thought. I had to get back to the cabin before he lost his temper, before he accused me of taking Shea for myself.

That was not what this was.

I grimaced.

Why did that idea feel so familiar, as if it were a real possibility? I shrugged it off. Whatever rebellious leftovers were still cooking in my brain, Caelius had baked most of that out in heated hours of blood and lust. I would make sure he questioned *nothing*. I would drink this light bulb down enough for him to get her tiny, insignificant soul.

Then we will be fed.

We are so thirsty.

The Vessel's voice wheezed, not able to reach past the frequency of the wind and muffled further still by the pounding of my frantic heartbeat. Then I felt it, wet and sticky. I stopped midair, pulling her back.

"I threw up," she moaned pitifully.

"Obviously," I retorted in disgust.

She looked dizzy and pale, as if she might do it again. I pulled her farther from my torso, holding her at arm's length, her legs dangling like wet noodles.

She looked down, and fear replaced nausea. "Oh my God,

we're so high! Lucian, I can't fly yet. I've barely mastered enough wind to hover, like, a few feet off the ground, if that!" She wiggled her legs, clutching my arms. She jostled herself enough that my grip loosened, and just as she had predicted, she fell. It was comical really.

My grip wasn't as tight as it should have been. Why had I been holding such a repulsive thing so gingerly? I'd even cradled her head against my chest to protect her from the wind. Just as troubling was the fact that she'd thrown up so easily, like she was a regular human, unaccustomed to moving at high speeds. *This* was the Vessel that had defeated Caelius, that had defeated *all* of us?

Pathetic.

I watched as she flailed helplessly. The panic must have made her forget herself, unless she was still weak from the last battle or the strain of manipulating all of those vampires below us. How could she use such powerful suggestions and not have mastered enough wind to fly?

Her voice reached me in an instant.

She was screaming my name.

As if it meant something to her.

As if I would *willingly* save her.

As it was, she was falling into an active volcano. She had chosen the perfect spot to throw up. Had she no sense of self-preservation, to vomit over something like this when she couldn't fly? Caelius was right—humans were idiots.

We should let her get burned a little, maybe lose her legs in the heat.

She didn't need to be intact for Caelius to get her soul.

The idea instantly filled me with an unexplainable fury, as if I would punish an entire volcano if it dared touch her.

What was this, jealousy?

It was the same possessive anger I'd felt before, when my teeth wouldn't let go of her neck.

That same word tried to vie for importance: *mine*.

What was she to me? The Vessels were just mindless little puppets created by the Light to—

"Lucian, help me!"

An image burned through my mind hotter than the magma that would dare singe her beautiful long hair: the same words had been on her lips as Aidan held a bloody Enochian blade, like he had with Moses. Her gut was lanced, her hand reaching toward me . . .

Something snapped.

Before my mind could stop my movements, I was clutching her in my arms, kissing her like she was some sort of homecoming to a boy lost in the desert. My mouth took hers in again and again as I lifted us higher into the air. But as high as I went, I couldn't escape the heat. I burned for *her*, and with every gasp of breath, with every moan, I felt satiated in a way that oceans of Caelius's blood could not. When I finally released her lips, I looked at her long and hard.

"Sh-Shea?"

Something flickered, so raw and bare it terrified me. "Is it your name I've been trying to find? I've been so . . . so *thirsty*. Ever since I left Gutium, all these centuries wandering in the sand . . ."

The look in her eyes as tears rolled down her cheeks was

overwhelming. "Lucian, you saved me." Love, whole and completely unfabricated, was what I saw there; that was what I felt in her arms.

And I let her go.

It was a while before she started screaming again.

I watched as that name I had called her drifted just as far out of reach as her body.

What had I done?

Why had I *kissed* the Vessel and said such delirious things?

Why did that name mean *anything* to me?

I reached for the memory again, but it was already turning black.

Her name.

The feel of her lips on mine.

I hovered midair, frozen, my blood at war with my heart.

She fell closer to the flame.

She screamed as the heat started to scorch her body.

What did she matter?

She was nothing.

Nothing like I was.

The name calling me home was . . .

Caelius.

It was Caelius who was always by my side.

With him, I was never alone.

Caelius was my savior.

My everything.

Caelius was the name I was searching for in the dark.

CHAPTER 13
SHEA

I was going to die.

The heat from the lava was already blistering my skin as I plummeted downward toward its embrace. Where the heck were we? Hawaii? Lucian had flown far and fast.

I needed to protect myself from the magma. I had to dig deep and tap into my fire element, or I was going to die or be burned beyond recognition. I didn't even think Helena's rainbow light show could heal me from being swallowed by molten lava.

I was concentrating so hard I didn't notice Lucian diving down toward me.

My heart leapt into my throat.

Did he . . . ?

Was he . . . ?

Nope.

He stopped as if a giant hand had halted him midair.

And suddenly I was filled with a rage so deep I couldn't see straight.

Before I knew what I was doing, I connected to the fire inside the liquid magma as if it were an extension of my own body. I pulled on the wind to separate me from the burning substance, and it answered my call like it was my loving savior.

And it was.

Floating above the lava, I stared at Lucian, anger filling my veins, fire itself reaching into my blood.

Caelius did this.

Caelius turned *my* Lucian into his broken plaything.

No.

I was never going to let that happen again.

Lucian would detox from Caelius's blood whether he wanted to or not.

Our eyes met as I moved closer to his body. He hovered midair, trapped in indecision. I could see the conflict brewing behind his beautiful teal eyes. He had kissed me. I knew *my* Lucian was still in there somewhere. He had reached out to me through his memories, though his conscious mind was still clueless. His lips had parted mine like they had the first time in Arizona. It had been instinct, but it had come from his *soul*, from the Lucian who had clasped my hand desperately in his memory.

I had to believe that.

Otherwise . . .

Lucian would be lost to me forever, and there was no way I would let that happen.

The problem was, I needed to trap him before his super-vampire reflexes kicked in, which meant I needed to distract him.

I kept my mental hold on the lava, ready to strike, while I

used the wind to float face-to-face. Lucian was still frozen in a mixture of shock and anguish. I didn't even think he knew the anguish was there, it was so deeply shoved down by Caelius's blood control.

"Oh, Lucian," I said out aloud, staring at his cold eyes.

"Are we going to fight?" he asked. Though his tone was fierce, his body looked worn and tired.

"What has Caelius done to you?" I couldn't hide the catch in my voice. It was excruciating to see him like this, like a feral animal that desperately wanted to be loved but snapped at anyone who tried to come near it.

"He's made me stronger. He's made me whole. He is my salvation. He is my god, Shea." He stopped himself when he said my name, as if he was surprised that he had uttered the word. "Wait, that name . . . it's gone again."

I knew for certain Lucian was still in there. I just needed to connect to him. "Caelius has taken *everything* from you, not just me, Lucian, but your whole family—"

"I have my family!" he interrupted with rage.

"Not really though," I answered calmly. "Nefertiti isn't the same, right? And Sherit? She's such a sweet and loving girl; when was the last time you saw her laugh? Or smile even?"

I could see my words were reaching him. Lucian was struggling internally. He was so exhausted, he couldn't even hide it anymore. "They're just angry . . . at you . . . *you* took their sisters away . . ." Lucian said this like a mantra, something he'd practiced over and over.

More mind control.

"And what about Paris? Why do you think Caelius destroyed

that villa just outside the city *first*?" I used the memory Lucian had shown me to try and reach him.

"Because . . ." Lucian began.

He didn't have an answer, so I gave him the truth. "Because it was where we stayed after our first battle with Caelius. We made love every day, and our lives were perfect, just like you showed me in your memories. Caelius needed to destroy it *first* because he needed you to forget me, to forget that we love each other more than we could have dreamed. And I do love you, Lucian. Even when you look at me with hate, I love you even more because I know how hard you're fighting to hold on to . . . us."

He didn't speak.

He didn't move.

He just hovered like a statue.

For a moment, I was afraid I'd broken him completely.

Finally he said, in a dull lifeless voice, "Caelius is my everything now. I'm bringing you back to him. Then this will all be over."

I controlled the wind to move closer to Lucian until we were only inches from each other. I knew it was dangerous, but I had lava awaiting my command. My stomach churned, but I had to keep him away from Caelius's blood. I remembered the night in Paris when he told me the torture he'd gone through, buried in ash and lava after fighting Aidan's brothers in Pompeii. I was about to do the same thing to him.

He might never forgive me, but I can't see any other way.

Lucian was too strong to subdue otherwise, unless I could break Caelius's hold on him first. Maybe Caelius had used a combo of blood and shadow control. If I could just touch Lucian long enough to see inside his mind, I could remove at least some of Caelius's power. Maybe it would be enough for Lucian to free himself.

I had to try.

"You saved me. When two of your Second-Borns tried to take me to Caelius, *you* killed them to protect me, and when Aidan stabbed me here"—I lifted up my shirt to show him the scar— "I asked for your help, and you didn't hesitate. You smashed a boulder on Aidan's body and took me to your home where you healed me with light."

I couldn't help but notice the brief smile at the mention of smashing Aidan with a boulder. I didn't know if that was a good sign or a bad one, but I continued. "And we made love for the first time in that house. It was intense and magical and all the things that musicians write songs and poets write poetry about." I gently held his hand. "*Us.*"

"Mine," he mumbled in a daze.

Not what I was hoping for, but at least it was some kind of memory of the two of us.

I slowly tightened my grip on his hand.

And . . .

I closed my eyes and used Dream-Walking to push my Light inside Lucian's body like I had with Helena. What I saw inside of Lucian made me want to scream in anguish and horror. Black swirled everywhere I could see. Where tiny pricks of light would rise, it would be snuffed out before it had a chance to grow.

Lucian's soul was being devoured whole by Caelius's Darkness.

Even though I was inside Lucian's head through Dream-Walking, I could feel his outside body trying to pull away from me. It wasn't him that wanted to retreat—it was the Darkness knowing the Light was there to extinguish it. Helena's body had reacted in the same way.

I used my power to yank the lava up and hold Lucian in place, only covering his legs and hips. I could hear him scream from the agony, and my heart broke at the sound, knowing I was the one responsible for it. Not wanting him to suffer any more than he had to, I did something I had never done before.

I called on all four elements at the same time.

A surge of power raced through me as I pulled water from the nearby ocean, dirt and rocks from the volcano itself, air from the wind, and fire from the lava. With my mind, I knit a layer of protection between Lucian's skin and the molten magma itself. It was made with water to cool and harden the lava, and dirt to pack Lucian in tight so he could heal but not escape.

Since I was still inside his head, I could only *hear* that my barrier of protection worked because he had stopped screaming in pain.

In fact, he was absolutely still.

I nearly cried when I realized . . .

Lucian *wanted* me to destroy the Darkness inside him. That tiny bit of him that had reached out to me through his memories was letting me do this.

He may have been consciously fighting with his brain because of Caelius's control, but his body was reacting on instinct, like it had when he cried while drinking my blood. His *body* knew me and would always know me, even if his thoughts battled it out with Darkness.

Quickly, I used my Dream-Walking form to chase every

shadow I could find. Just as Helena's shadows had been etched with words and instructions of how she was supposed to act and react, so were Lucian's. The difference was, Helena had one set of instructions, whereas Lucian had *thousands*.

It was terrifying and overwhelming, but I had to fight for him.

I couldn't destroy Caelius's blood control, but I could destroy his shadow. How much of that would bring back Lucian's memories, I had no idea. These instructions could be behavioral and have nothing to do with memories and feelings, but I knew I still had to clean house. Lucian's mind would never heal if he was constantly contending with both blood *and* shadow control.

Encasing him in lava would dry him out of his blood addiction, but destroying the shadow control?

Well, to put it like Lucian would: destroying the shadow control was *mine*.

Pushing my Light through Lucian's veins must have been excruciating like it had been for Helena, but he kept quiet regardless. One after the other, I destroyed the hidden pockets of Darkness. I had no idea how long it took, but it felt like hours until I finally snuffed out the last shadow.

There was light again.

Caelius's blood was still swarming around like deadly wasps inside Lucian's body, but the shadow control was gone and some of Lucian's precious soul was returned to him.

Pulling out of Lucian's mind, I opened my eyes.

He stared at me, still holding on, though his hand was red and burned from where I had entered with my Light.

I couldn't read him; it was almost as if he was in some kind of coma.

I stared into his blank eyes.

"Lucian?" I wasn't sure what to do or say.

He didn't respond.

He just kept staring at me, expressionless.

"Lucian? Are you okay?" I was starting to feel like I may have broken him for real this time.

"You're so beautiful when you sleep." The words came out, but there was still no life in his eyes.

"Lucian?" I choked off my forming tears.

He pulled me in tight and bit into my neck viciously, drinking with savage desperation. On instinct, I turned my blood into Light. Lucian didn't let go, the pain not seeming to affect him at all. I knew then that Caelius's blood control was too strong to overcome. Even eradicating the Darkness wasn't enough to wake him up.

It was finally time to detox.

I barely felt the heat even though I was connected with fire. Something had changed inside of me when I used all four elements at the same time; I knew now that I was one with each, making them a part of who I was. I had complete control.

Pulling more lava up, but making sure the water and dirt kept him free from pain, I made it reach up and cover his back and then his head so I could yank myself free. I saw a glimpse of his tear-filled eyes before quickly encasing him in the liquid magma. When I was done, a mountain of dried lava stood in front of me, forming a peak.

"That will hold him for a while." Aidan's voice rose up beside me. "You did the right thing."

I nodded, not wanting to say anything.

I was exhausted and devastated.

Aidan drew me into his arms so that I wouldn't have to use wind to levitate anymore. "We found a safe house, but honestly, if he can follow our Light trails, I don't think any place is *safe* anymore."

I leaned my head against his shoulder and let him carry me as he flew across the ocean and toward the mainland. A deep depression rose inside of me, to the point where I couldn't even cry. Only sleep felt like a reasonable solution. I closed my eyes but was haunted by Lucian's empty expression as he'd said, *You're so beautiful when you sleep.*

***

"Shea?"

I opened my eyes.

I was standing in the doorway back in my old room from childhood.

My mother sat on the edge of the bed as she had before, but upon seeing me pop into the room, she quickly stood up and embraced me.

"Oh, Shea, I was so worried. I thought Lucian had gone to *kill* you."

"Mom, he's so broken." I could barely form words. All I felt was pain.

"Did you . . . ? It would be okay if you did. I wouldn't judge you for it." Mom said the words, but I knew the bonds between maker and vampire were strong. It only showed how much she loved me, that she would forgive me even if I had killed Lucian.

"No, Mom. I could never kill him. I'd die first." Dramatic, but it was how I felt.

We both sat down on the bed, keeping our hands clasped.

"Lucian hasn't returned yet. Caelius will only hold out for a day, maybe two, then he'll come for you, and I just . . . I don't think he can be stopped." I could tell that was difficult for her to say. The Molly Harper I knew would never tell me I wasn't capable of something. To her, anything was possible, and that went double when it came to me. So for her to say that she didn't think I had a chance of stopping Caelius shook me to my core.

"Helena said she's close to figuring something out." That sounded way lamer than I'd intended.

"And you trust this Helena?" My mom actually sounded . . . hopeful?

"I guess. I don't really know her that well, but she's super smart, and she was the one who rigged that necklace . . . where she pretty much juiced up Caelius . . ." I wasn't exactly instilling confidence about Helena's capabilities at this point. "Anyway, she moves around her lab, tinkering with things and saying 'ah-ha,' and 'maybe if I . . .' She never really finishes those sentences though. I dunno."

Mom smiled. "You make her sound like Doc Brown from *Back to the Future*."

I smiled back. "Yeah, she is kind of like that. And hey, if he can invent a time machine, maybe she can invent a way to kill Caelius. She has a device already, it's just the powering-up part she's having trouble with." I shrugged optimistically. "Originally she thought I could be the one to power it if I mastered all four elements, but then she seemed to think there was something else she was missing. But, Mom, I actually used all four elements at the exact same time. I've never done that before. When I wake up, maybe it'll help Helena somehow."

"Shea! That's huge!" My mom's eyes widened with pride as she squeezed my hand. "That could mean the difference."

"You think so?" I asked. It felt like when I was a little girl and Mom had encouraged me to try out for the gymnastics team. It had been a total failure. I fell off the balance beam with stunning impact, landing flat on the mat with an on-land belly flop. Before that, Mom and Dad had been cheering in the stands like I was Simone Biles. Until I fell. Then I had two mother hens racing to get to me. Actually, make that three; the third, Aidan, got there first. Where had my wind power been then? Huh? Stupid late-blooming superpowers.

Mom shook her head as if I amazed her. "You are truly special, Shea. I'm just so honored that I was the one chosen to be your mother. You're the Vessel; I still can't wrap my head around it. From the way Grandfather describes it, you were made of burning sunshine that was meant to destroy everything he loves. But he talks about the Light itself sometimes as if they were friends once, as if they shared some kind of bond that no one could ever fathom or understand. When he talks like that, I think . . . my daughter is made from that Light. *My* daughter." Her hands squeezed mine tighter.

"Thanks, Mom. It is weird, isn't it? We had such a normal life. Now look at us." I casually glanced around to indicate that we were Dream-Walking in my old room again. "A Vessel and a vampire mother."

Mom put her head down in what seemed like shame. "I hate that I'm a vampire. I can feel the Light inside me too, and I fight with the Darkness every day. It's so difficult sometimes."

"You can feel Light in you?" I asked, curious. Now that my mom was "normal" enough to talk to, I found that I wanted to know as much as I could about what she was going through. She really was an anomaly: the mother of a Vessel and Lucian and Nefertiti's vampire baby.

"I haven't told anyone, not even Grandfather."

"Could you not call Caelius that? It makes it . . . weird. And I hate him with every fiber of being, so there's that too." I tried to be delicate but couldn't.

Mom nodded. "Of course. I don't even know I'm doing it, to be honest. It's probably that drop of blood that keeps me in check. I want to hate Grandfa—Caelius . . . like you do, but I see such sadness and desperation in him. I-it must be the blood," she said, almost embarrassed.

"No, I'm sorry. You just don't know him like I do." I didn't really want to make her feel bad, especially since we had such little time together, but it was difficult not to when I knew she had witnessed all the horrible things Caelius had done to Lucian and to the world.

I decided to change the subject. "So, the Light, when did you notice it?"

"Right away. I just didn't know what it was. As a vampire I can feel it like a foreign substance pumping through my veins. It doesn't hurt exactly, but it doesn't feel natural either. I never told Caelius about it because, this is going to sound weird, the

Light wouldn't let me. In the beginning when I thought only of Caelius, I wanted to tell him everything, but I physically couldn't. Every time I tried, nothing would come out of my mouth."

"That's crazy," I said in wonder. "I guess it makes sense that you'd still have some of the Light in you, since you gave birth to me."

Mom suddenly sat up straight, as if hearing something. "Grandfather is having a tirade. I have to get back. Maybe Lucian has returned."

"I doubt it," I said guiltily. "I kind of encased him in lava to, you know, detox. And I destroyed all of Caelius's shadow control. Does the shadow go back to him? Do you think Caelius knows?"

Mom looked uncertain. "I don't know how it works, but that sounds likely. Don't worry, I won't tell Grandfather anything. I have to go now though. I don't want him to suspect me." She kissed my forehead and popped out of the room before I could utter a goodbye.

Taking a deep breath, I woke myself up.

***

I had the feeling of déjà vu as I opened my eyes to rainbow light.

"All right, all right, enough with the healing stuff." I sat up in bed as the lights snuffed out.

Like before, Dad, Aidan, Meky, Helena, and Duncan were all huddled around me like I was their dying patient.

"I'm okay. I swear. Helicopter parents much?" I teased, but it honestly felt good to know how much everyone cared about me.

"Dinnae expect that smash-and-grab by dear ol' Lucian, if I'm being honest," Duncan said. "I'm just glad yeer in one piece."

"Really. I'm better. I Dream-Walked with my mom again. She thinks Caelius will come after us if Lucian doesn't return in a day or two, so we have to be ready." I proceeded to tell them the entirety of the conversations I'd had with Lucian and my mom.

Helena was the first to speak. She looked like her mind was racing. "Your mother has a piece of the Light inside of her? Maybe we could use that. I don't know."

"Do you think it's important?" I asked. All eyes were now staring at Helena.

The scientist began to pace, nodding her head and, like my mom had observed, looking very much like Doc Brown.

"Maybe, but I'm thinking more about the fact that you used all four elements at once." Helena turned to us with a giant smile, which was completely out of character for her. "I think that may be the answer."

Dad said, "You mean . . . ?"

Helena nodded. "Shea mastering each element separately wasn't enough, but being able to use them all simultaneously as if they were one . . . I think we just found the way to kill Caelius for good."

No one spoke.

We didn't have to.

It felt *right*.

I just hoped Caelius didn't kill any more innocent people before then.

I really did hate that guy.

Chapter 14
Lucian

I was entombed like the Pharaohs I'd despised in Egypt.

The irony was laughable.

I wasn't adorned with gold for my passage down the Nile, however. There was nothing but dirt. Another suitable irony considering my relationship with it. It seemed I was destined for things like this.

What have I done.

I let out a long breath.

Finally, the word "we" was gone.

I could feel how empty the space outside of my tomb was.

The Vessel was gone too.

I felt filled with her and the absence of her at the same time. Her scent was in all the elements, wrapped around me like an embrace, but she herself had left with that beast, Adnachiel. His words about her doing the "right thing" seared hot like the magma that had burned my legs. She'd tricked me into lowering my defenses, then captured me like this. She and that dog deserved each other. He'd tricked me too once. I'd come to rely on that kindness in his eyes, like it meant something, but he had only been out for his own gain. He was selfish in the way he defended the world—selfish, untrustworthy, and yet . . . the Vessel hadn't let me burn, just as Aidan had saved my life from his brothers in Pompeii by burying me.

Was it that same kindness, however, that left me alone in my agony now?

That was familiar.

I knew loneliness well.

Maybe they were *holding hands* while laughing at their triumph over me.

A flash filled my mind: Shea holding my hand, walking through the ruins of Paris, standing next to Aidan as he betrayed me and Moses. I shook my head. It was like a memory, but it was something else. Maybe the Vessel's manipulation? She was powerful, after all.

"Where are you now?" I hissed. "Why didn't you finish me off?"

Maybe she and Aidan were pressed against each other in comfort, pitying themselves for knowing such a monster. I clenched my fists. I didn't want to acknowledge the spark of extreme jealousy that thought produced.

In a moment of desperation, I'd let her do it: burn Caelius's shadow out of my soul. Now that my mind was clearer, it made sense. Why wouldn't I allow her Light to chase him out? As "healing" as he claimed his blood was, and as much of this year was still a mystery, I still had my memories of the past. I had been bent by that same shadow when he was in the cage. I'd been tortured enough times by its ravishing to know what it felt like when it was still inside of me.

The pain of her chasing it had been like having my intestines slowly pulled out by rolling them on a spit over a fire; it had been pure agony. I'd endured because, as much as my blood wanted to serve him, I owed it to my family to be more than Caelius's dog.

I didn't do it for her.

I didn't do it . . .

Even as that thought arose, I felt its falsehood.

I did do it for her.

I swallowed hard.

Why?

The image of her sleeping peacefully, like a beautiful pearl wrapped in the sheets of my bed, sprung to mind again but left just as quickly. If I wasn't so tightly encased, I would have physically shook the thought from my head as I'd done before. " 'Why' doesn't matter right now, nor do these strange images."

I had failed.

Right now, Caelius was no doubt aware of my absence.

Right now, my family was in *danger.*

I growled, guttural and real.

As exhausted as I was from her burning my insides, the absence of the shadow made me feel much stronger. Even though I'd cried again, it had been wise to drink her blood to repair myself. Who knew how long it would have taken my body to recover from her bleeding the Darkness out had I not. I didn't have the luxury of time that she apparently thought *she* had, while resting in the comfort of Aidan's arms like a coddled child who had everything and everyone at her feet.

As if she were precious simply by being.

I growled again and this time acknowledged that it was indeed jealousy.

But of whom?

The Vessel or Aidan?

I thought of the beast. They really were perfect for each other. Everything came so easily to him. He was immortal and lived countless human lives without having to feed on blood. He'd been born to protect the Light, born next to the divine creator of all things. He was loved by the Vessels, his brothers, and loved by his god. The only pain in his side was me.

And I'd been born a worm, tortured and played with by Darkness itself. That precious Light of his did nothing to protect me because I was not its *angel*. I was nothing more than another human it had abandoned to some game with Caelius. I was not gifted with divine purpose, but the Darkness had carved one out of my soul. I was left to struggle, caught in his web, with potter's hands forced to bathe in blood, the poetry in me drying up in the rage of an unfair and unwanted existence.

"Only you." The words rang through me, and my tongue felt swollen against the roof of my mouth. "Only you. You are all I've wanted since I became flesh. You are my *everything*. Let me be your god, and I will give you this world and any other that you like." Caelius's whispers at night, as he pressed long kisses into my neck, were a twisted sort of comfort.

It was unlike the comfort I felt when I kissed Shea.

My eye twitched comparing the two in such sharp contrast.

With her it felt . . . even her blood was . . . truly healing, like an oasis on dry land.

With Caelius, every action was carefully planned, all so that he could increase his control over me.

His embrace, no matter how thorough, always left me *thirsty*.

If she was an oasis, he was the desert itself.

He would force my submission.

He would *make* me obedient.

I laughed, feeling my body quake in the encased magma. Wasn't this force as well, and where was she? Was she by my side, or now that she had stopped the *vampire* from bringing her to Caelius, was she done with me? All of that affection, was it just a powerful manipulation like Caelius had warned me against?

Still . . . images kept creeping up in my mind, then dissolving: we were on a bed in Paris, my hands moving across that small scar on her stomach, the taste of her sweat, haunting, like it was telling me all of her secrets. There were moments of clarity reaching through to the joy and pleasure of loving her, not through the suffering and pain of my past.

Her scent was like a balm that lingered even now, provoking such musings.

And yet, where is she?

I growled again.

If she was *mine*, why was I alone?

I hardened myself.

These memories, sorting them, feeling anything toward *my* enemy, was a mistake.

Caelius was more powerful than all of us combined. More powerful than Shea Harper.

That I *felt*, and with that came an image so savage and unholy

I gasped, sucking in the dirt around my face: Nefertiti's children were ripped apart, devoured by giant fangs. The Darkness exploded from Caelius's human form, searching for a way to extend its power out, holding us all like tiny flies clutched in his engorged claws.

Death and failure. I broke into a cold sweat. Was this the *detox* the Vessel had wanted? Were these images even real? My body shook.

There was something else . . .

An offering.

I'd offered myself at the end of the last battle, to save them.

To save *her*.

The bones of my shoulders sagged into the meat of muscle, unable to lower into the stones around me. I paused for a long breath, wetting my bottom lip with my teeth as my eyes darted back and forth in the black.

If this was true . . .

Then *united* we had already failed.

What choice did I have but to go back to him, to save Nefertiti?

I winced.

Nefari, her cries as her children were killed in front of her, and her embrace now, the hollowness of her gaze . . . the commander of Gutian armies, the great ruler of Egypt, had finally been brought to complete ruin, as had the son of Onack the Great.

"Is that what you believe? Were all of our deaths for nothing then?"

My breath hitched with the familiar voice. I searched in the darkness the Vessel had concealed me in. Was it really him?

"Do you plan on forgetting all of us? Will you desecrate our memories by becoming Caelius's puppet?"

I flexed my muscles. It couldn't be.

The excitement made my teeth grow large enough to split my gums as I shouted, "Bohe! You're alive! Thank the gods! Thank your gods! I never thought I'd see you again!"

I struggled against the elemental prison, extending my claws and tearing at the earth between me and the magma. I had to get out of here. I had to aid him. It was better that Caelius didn't know he was still alive. "I'll keep you safe! Just wait a moment! We'll go back to your lonely mountain, together! I'll hide you until I sort things out!" I clawed frantically, clumping handfuls of dirt.

Bohe was *alive*.

"I don't blame you for resigning yourself to your fate, La-Narru. When I was mortal I had done just that, knowing that I could never win against those who sought the power of my throne. I was used willingly because I thought it guaranteed my protection, that I would, at the very least, live. And I did. I led a horrible defaced life because of it."

I clawed, ripping my teeth into the earth. I swallowed it, creating space around my head. That was all I needed, a few inches to shatter this small mountain whole. "It's all right, just wait a moment longer!"

"I fell prey to that same weakness again under Caelius's torture." Bohe's tone was low, saddened. "Even after all that time as a monk, he made me lose myself."

I was used to swallowing dirt, having drunk the sands of Egypt. I chewed and slashed, his words pulsing both ferocity and urgency through my veins. "I don't know what Caelius has done to you, but I will protect you from him as soon as I break free! He won't lay another hand on you; it's me he wants!" I snapped at the earth and shifted my weight, feeling power surge in my muscles. His face, his voice—I felt like I could see them through the darkness, as if they weren't form but light, pulling me toward him.

"But you were never like that, were you, my friend?"

I froze.

No.

Stop.

A memory was trying to push through.

Something so agonizing that I wanted to rip my skin and scream.

Bohe's dead body was tied to mine with a yellow sash. He'd been wearing the same Hanfu I was now, before Caelius removed it. He was pressed against me, as cold and hollow as Caelius's gaze that watched my every reaction.

My mouth fell open, breathless, as I squeezed my claws into fists full of dirt. The garments around me now, I had been wearing them like a blanket of familiar comfort, and the familiarity was because they had adorned Bohe before he died in my arms.

The images couldn't be real.

Bohe was alive.

I thought the Vessel had killed him, but if he was here . . .

"Bohe, I'll save you! I saved you from death once before; I can do it again! Just wait for me!"

"For all the things that you are, Lucian . . . *you* don't give up. You think yourself a coward for abandoning your people in

Gutium, a weight I always saw you carry, a deeper scar than the lashes of slavery that cover your body. But you were obeying your father. *That* was not *this*."

Emotion welled up inside of me. I had to cover the pain his words were unearthing. I struggled, hearing the cracks of magma as well as my bones as I started throwing my body against it.

Still, the image kept returning.

His lifeless form had been tied to me for *days* as I'd wept and prayed for his safe passage into the afterlife.

"It's not true! If I'm speaking to you now, the memory is *wrong*. You're alive, aren't you? Please be alive." I winced at the sound of desperation in my own voice. The memory was *wrong*. "You're alive."

"You have fought lifetimes over. You are a fighter, but it doesn't have to be in the way of Nefertiti or your father, Onack. Fight like La-Narru fights. Lucian was *his* name for you, wasn't it? Have you forgotten what your name means in Gutian? Have you forgotten who you really are? Son of Anna-Steen. Poet. Friend. We have *all* loved you. Will you forget the way we died as you have forgotten yourself?"

I stopped moving and leaned against the dirt and magma for support.

My eyes flooded wet and hot.

"No. You're *not* dead. Please, Bohe. You're here with me now, aren't you?" It was a desperate question, and it quivered as it left my lips.

"Just as your mother never left your after she died, even as you spent years in the desert wandering, thinking yourself lost and alone, I will never leave you. None of us will. Do you not see, even here, covered in Darkness, that the Light is with you, that our love is *here*, La-Narru?

"Even Gracuri waits for you in the form of a boy, laughing by the river where you first met."

I clutched my chest. Gracuri's words echoed in my ears: *I'm sorry, Father. I didn't want Caelius to use me against you . . . Always remember what I said to you when we first met in Thebes. I will always feel that way about you, Lucian. Please don't blame your—*

Caelius.

He was wearing Gracuri's shoes and holding his head on a spike.

"Rest assured, La-Narru. He smiles like he used to, and he still believes that you were his salvation. He will wait with his hand outstretched for yours; that was the deal you made when you returned to him every year before Thebes, and he is still honoring it. He will *always* wait for you to return to him, in death as he did in life."

I couldn't breathe.

What was this?

Was I hallucinating? Dying?

"He can't still think that after how many times I failed him, after I rejected his confession of love." The pain was too much to bear. "Stop this madness, Bohe." I slumped farther. "I'll save you."

"Gunnhild and Ashgar can love without fear now, and they do just that. They don't blame you; instead they wish for you to think of them with favor. All they've ever wanted is your approval. Will you continue to hide your fondness for them, even now? Will you not give them rest?"

"No! I didn't . . . hide my fondness . . ." Was that what I'd been doing this whole time, safeguarding those closest to me by keeping them at arm's length? "I was protecting them."

"David still calls you what he whispered on his deathbed: *my friend*. Can you not hear his voice when the moon is full like it was then? Can you truly not hear him calling you? He waits beside the mountain Goliath, hand in hand, their love offered to you as well."

I turned my head away from the voice. "I . . . I don't. I don't hear anything. I don't feel *anything*. Just Darkness and loss."

"And what of me? I have been speaking to you this whole time. Will you deny my voice as well? Will you call me a waking dream like you have to other ghosts from your past?"

I opened my mouth, but nothing came out.

"You spoke to me in my own tongue, a Gutian blessing. You said you loved me. You asked that my soul find the light. You said you would carry me with you *always*. Have you easily forgotten such loyal words?"

My eyes darted.

I wouldn't.

I would never willingly forget anything between us. I cherished him. "Bohe, I—"

"I rest with your family because you gave me that gift in your blessings at death, and I *chose* yours over mine. I will always choose you, as you chose me in life. Will you reject me now, your *Bohe*?"

Another image flashed through my mind.

The dejected look on Bohe's face as Caelius toyed with his hair, the guilty feeling accompanying it as I tried to explain myself; my mind filled with the memory of his mother trying to abort him and how that was just the start in a life that would make him feel unwanted by all who touched him.

I tried to turn my face back toward the voice, reaching out to it, clawing handfuls of dirt. "No, Bohe, I'm sorry. I would never reject you. I just don't know—"

"Nefari's daughters and your parents wanted you to remember that no matter what happens in this life, you are always Gutian. You still have a home. You are not without a tribe. I like the words of your kin. They taught me something precious in my stay with them. Will you hear it?"

I felt like he had stabbed me in the chest.

I had felt orphaned when my mother died, and twice over when Nefari told me of the slaughtered fields of Gutium in Egypt. What right did I have to still belong to any of them? "Bohe . . . stop."

"The code of your people is right. United, we beat with *one* heart. Because you offered me a place with your own, what's yours is now mine, so I can say with certainty, the flame that is *our* people cannot be stamped out of time. We are etched into the existence of *all* things. And love is truly the soul of all that's worth fighting for. Have you forgotten those simple truths, La-Narru?"

"No." I closed my eyes. "Yes." I gasped for breath. "I don't know. Everything's so confusing. I'm sorry." I felt like the hollowness was filling in and flooding, like I would drown in this sarcophagus, swimming in the ache of my tears.

"Our memories of you and the love we shared have only grown in our deaths. And they live on."

I made fists. "What are you saying?"

"You aren't and never were *alone*."

My body shook. I closed my eyes, as if it would shield me from his truths. The sweat at my palms mixed with dirt. I wanted to bury my eyes in that mud, to rip them out as Gracuri had done in Thebes.

"They can live inside of you, my dearest friend. You carry your home on your back like the World Turtle. You are not lost, for you are fused with all of our histories and stories, our rich cultures and memories. Duncan would like that, wouldn't he? Even though he's still living, will you deny him as well? You think your life has been a failure surrounded by loss, but loss is an illusion, a *lie* of the Darkness, a lie the Darkness itself believes, for it is the opposite of the Light. In truth, Caelius clings to you because he is afraid of being alone."

His voice was a whisper now, but it didn't take away from the power of his words.

"You studied too much in the mountains, Bohe. You've become wise." I laughed, or at least tried to through the ache in my chest. "Is this why you can speak to me, because you were the only one of my children that became enlightened?"

"We are *all* here. You are not alone."

I clenched my teeth.

"Fight him. But fight him the way La-Narru would. Not as a singularity, but held by the love of your people. *All* your people."

The cracks in the magma began to fill with a strange sort of light, a light that grew externally as it grew inside of me.

"Can you feel it now, what has always been here? What will always be here for you?"

"Yes," I muttered.

Love.

It was all I could feel emanating from that light. It beckoned me back to who I'd been as a boy, summoning a call from a childlike self within. For the first moment in a long life, I felt clear, like the clarity after a long walk in the fog of heat from the illusions of the desert.

I grabbed my chest, feeling a tidal wave, an ocean inside of me that had been kept at bay for too long. I had been afraid of these emotions. I had thought they would destroy me after my mother died, when my small hands had turned to fists that held her burned body. This whole time I'd been eating the ash of all that I had loved and lost . . . this whole time I'd been grieving. So I'd run, from everything and everyone, only to arrive at the center of my grief again and again.

When my father said that Anna-Steen's death had killed him and not her, it was in that moment that the lie had formed; loving me had a *cost*. Love was fragile and easily burned, and my existence was nothing more than kerosene, my very breath fire, turning the ones I held close to embers in my hands.

I'd become afraid, afraid of myself and terrified in the loneliness that followed. With every century the lie had become a self-fulfilling prophecy, and it burned. My small hands, still covered in ash, had turned into the hands of a man.

But she'd been with me this whole time, my mother, Anna-Steen.

And so was Gracuri.

Gunnhild and Ashgar.

David.

Bohe.

The girls, my father, my tribe.

They were all *here*, the family I was born with, and the one I had created and loved, with those same desperate hands.

"Fight. And remember who you are. Remember we are *all* Gutium now." Bohe's voice faded, and I felt his presence lift, but it didn't fill me with hopelessness as it might have before. His love, all of their love, was with me.

I wasn't alone anymore.

I didn't need Caelius's twisted devotion to stave off my childhood fears of abandonment.

I shattered the mountain in half, erupting from the tip like a geyser. As the pieces fell to the earth, I felt the lies fall with them, and I flew with the lightness of a boy.

I gasped, sucking in air.

Ever since my mother died, I had been unconsciously holding my breath.

I smiled, finally feeling the warmth of her love as I had known, so long ago, as an innocent child of the mountains.

The lies I had believed had stolen her from me twice.

I flew like a lightning bolt, cracking the sky open.

I landed, my heart and the ground thudding together, at Caelius's feet.

"I finally understand how to save you. You don't have to do any of this. It was all a lie!" I yelled into the cloud of dirt that surrounded my landing.

We stared at each other as the dust slowly cleared. As it did, his blazing red eyes came into sharp focus. I looked around, suddenly realizing that it was pitch-black, a darker night than all I had seen on the desert plains of Egypt while wrapped in death.

Just as it had then, with the dark came uncertainty. It struck me as quickly and deeply as the truth had moments before.

I looked around again, feeling that sensation of being lost.

"Bohe?" I called out into the black, but there was no answer.

Caelius's brow furrowed with the name. "Lucian." He stepped forward, reaching for my hand. "You seem *confused*. Are you unharmed?"

I stepped back. The presence, the light that had surrounded me, was gone, and I was standing in front of the absence of, as if it couldn't follow me into this place—as if Light and Darkness canceled each other out. A fear, visceral and instinctive, moved through me. Empowered with truth, I had felt strong enough to stop him myself, but now that I felt my mortality sinking in with every heavy breath as his eyes bored into mine, I questioned my sanity. Perhaps I had lost my mind after all, trapped in that tiny mountain.

I swallowed.

The trees rustled behind him as Nefertiti and Molly stepped out.

We were in a forest halfway between the cabin and where Shea had encased me.

I swallowed again, stepping back. "You were coming for me?"

He moved closer, his hand still extended. "Of course, darling. Why wouldn't I?"

There it was.

In the way his words curved when he said "darling." Uncertainty, fear, loneliness—it was all there smothered in his breath. I had seen glimpses of it before, lingering in his gaze, but with Bohe's wisdom still ringing in my ears like the gongs at a funeral pyre, I knew the lie that those emotions held.

"More so than anyone, I know your loneliness." I convinced myself to step toward the Darkness, toward his outstretched hand.

He froze in place. "Is that so, boy?"

"It aches in you, like it's a void that can't be filled." I stepped closer.

He smiled, a cruel wry thing, a defense to cover what was momentarily exposed. "I think you can *fill* it just fine."

He snatched my hand and pulled me into his embrace. His mouth was wet, his kiss hasty and forced. I pushed back, but it was no use. My physical strength couldn't match his. I was like a wilting flower in the arms of stone, but I didn't have to fight in the ways of Onack or Nefertiti.

When he pulled back, he sighed, relief filling his gaze. "I was worried that I had lost you, but you came back to me of your own free will." He buried his head in the nape of my neck, rubbing his face against the place where his deep bruises had bored into me like a dog collar. "You came back."

I clenched my teeth, pulling my head back, trying to create some space between us. "You're not going to punish me then?"

He straightened us both up, trying to mask his elation. "Oh, what a good suggestion." He laughed.

"Caelius, I came back to tell you the truth. Listen, I know why you're doing this—"

"Caelius?" The softness in his gaze disappeared, replaced by the monster I had seen tear through cities, engorged with death and rage—the monster that had truly killed Nefertiti's children.

My eyes searched for her. She was staring at the ground. I had never known this Nefari, the one that would not meet me head-on with honesty and pride. I sighed with an inward knowing; fear could destroy even the brightest of stars.

"I believe you were calling me *God* when we last touched." He ran his hand down my side, lingering in the space between every rib.

I growled in anger. "*Don't.*"

He scoffed and seized my shoulders, breaking the bones underneath his grip with the force.

"Grandfather, stop!"

I must have looked surprised and my face matched his as we stared at Molly.

"What's this now, *child?*"

She hesitated, then shifted against her heels, steadying herself. Nefertiti's eyes met mine with relief, as if she had been holding back and finally someone was brave enough to speak in her place.

"You thought the Vessel might have killed him. You've been inconsolable this whole time. Why are you acting like this? I'm sure Father left for a good reason, and now that he's back, our family is reunited." She folded her hands in front of her in a nonthreatening gesture. "I'm just saying, shouldn't we *celebrate* that he's safe and he returned to you? You don't . . . you don't have to *hurt* him. We're all tired of it. Let's just be a family. Isn't that what you really want?"

To my surprise, he released me.

He moved as if he were going to rush Molly and snap her neck.

But he didn't.

He looked up, as if contemplating. "A *family.*" He tilted his head toward me. "Why did you leave me?"

"To prove myself, to return the Vessel to you." It was quick and moved like a flood out of my mouth, fear already hastening my tone. I was surprised at how whole I had felt minutes ago, and how that wholeness felt like it was bleeding out of me with every breath of the black air emanating around him. His fear was my fear, and it was powerful.

He looked me up and down. "You failed, I imagine. As you always do."

I thought for a moment. I wanted to keep confronting him, to tell him there was another way, but maybe that was something gradual I could do over time, maybe facing him now would only result in my torture and continued brainwashing. As it was, the few pieces of memory that I had regained were like images of stained glass, each separated by missing information like a line of black grout. At least they couldn't be disregarded as false anymore, and among them, one thing was certain: Caelius had to be stopped.

"I'm sorry," I said. "She trapped me in lava. The instant I broke free, I flew back to you. I wanted to do it myself, to prove to all of you that I deserved your . . . affections."

He smirked at the word, then thought for a moment longer. "You've always been like that, even as a boy, rushing off to do things on your own. You're so obsessed with *proving* your worth. In all honesty, I shouldn't have been surprised, but there I was, like a fool whose lover had run off in the morning." He growled, but there was no threat to it this time. "Nefertiti, I'll return your children to you, since no harm was done."

"You'll what?" I looked at her, but her eyes were fixed on

Caelius.

"I told you I hadn't betrayed you. There was no need to bind them in the first place!"

He growled again, and this time it was hungry and horrifying, the threat palpable in the air itself.

Nefari instantly bowed her head in reverence. "What I meant to say was thank you, Father. Thank you." She lowered her head inches from her ankles.

It was disgusting to see, and I hated stomaching it.

"I'll go get them for you, Grandfather!" Molly leapt into the air, and as quickly as she left, she was thrown down.

I raced to Nefertiti, protecting her instinctively in my arms.

Molly looked startled as Caelius wrapped his hands around her shoulders, lifting her back up. "Tut, tut, Molly. You're not going anywhere. That was quite an independent speech you gave earlier. I think you and I need to spend a little more time together. After I have some alone time with Lucian, that is."

Molly nodded in compliance as Nefertiti's arms tightened around my waist.

Time together meant more blood.

"I'm not strong enough to ask you to leave, to damn the consequences. But that's exactly what you should do." Nefari's voice was barely a whisper, light enough that a distracted Caelius might not hear her plea.

"I won't leave you like I did in Gutium. I won't abandon the girls either." I held on to her, hoping to hold on to myself. I had to keep this oasis I had found inside of me alive, even as Caelius wrapped us in the black pulsing from his body.

A feeling came over me as I clung to her. We had done this

once as children. By the fire on a dark night like this one, when our fathers spoke of the Great Unknown and the endlessness of existence, when they spoke of monsters and gods, she had clung to me. It was as if our arms were a tether, the only thing keeping us from being sucked into the abyss of night. And here again, staring at Caelius, we were tethered, but it wasn't her arms I longed for. This wasn't the safety and reassurance of a love that would last through all of time, the promise to stand against Darkness as our Gutian code had reassured us of; I didn't feel that from Nefari anymore.

She had broken our tethered oaths with every whip mark on my back in Egypt, even before Caelius had taken me as his own. Even now, as I held her close, I knew I couldn't trust her. She had forfeited my life to that very Darkness we had sworn to protect each other from. As he fed on me and his will became my own, she had let go, and I was sucked into that abyss.

Our chord had snapped.

I thought of Shea.

I didn't know why, but it was her I longed for now. I wanted to feel her soft breath against me as she slept in my arms. We could ignore the Darkness like it wasn't reality, but a nightmare we could awaken from just as easily as a dream. The image made me wish that I was a man and not a vampire, so that I could sleep with the same peace that covered her resting face.

Images and the sound of Shea's words called to me. They pressed, like a thumb, against the inside of my ribs in the opposite places Caelius had touched, like the other side of a coin: love versus fear. I felt a pressure build in my brain, like at any moment it would pop and I'd remember everything, if only I could get away from this Darkness.

You are not alone.

As Nefertiti clung to my back, I was more certain that the ghost of Bohe had spoken the truth; it wasn't just her arms embracing me, steadying me against the Dark.

They are all with me.

I clung to that realization, squeezing her tighter.

I wouldn't run anymore.

I was fortified by love, and I would fight the Darkness *my way*.

I just needed to find out what that way was.

I just needed a little more time.

"Egypt." Caelius turned to me, his eyes ablaze. "My darling, I will give you Egypt."

Nefertiti's grip left mine, and she stepped away from me, her gaze unable to meet Caelius's. Her body instantly obeyed his silent order to not touch what belonged to *him* and him alone.

"What is there in Egypt?" My voice was low. I was uncertain how to play this new hand.

He released Molly. "Don't make me repeat my movements. Stay put." She nodded, and he walked toward me.

He pulled his hand through my hair, his fingers tracing the outline of my face. They felt cool, but they started a burning within: his blood. His blood was still inside me, and it was calling back to itself. I was still his possession in that way, a claim he had wrought as deep as my bones, but not my soul. I could reach that at least, thanks to Shea's "detox."

Thanks to all of them.

"I hate it because it's where I was imprisoned, but you hate it too, don't you, my sweet?" He fondly kissed my neck in the same spot he had first bit me when I was turned. It was a spot he often touched tenderly after sex, pointing out that very fact. "They made you a *slave* in the desert. That place scarred your precious back and destroyed your people. The Egyptians slaughtered your father like a *stuck pig*."

I cringed thinking of the heat and long days enslaved by the same Egyptians that had burned my village and tribe to ash. On the deathbed of my people's slaughter, Akhenaten had taken Nefari as his living prize of conquest. At first she'd been his slave, then his wife. I'd had to watch as the love of my life was impregnated over and over again, then paraded around like some spoil of war. My only offering to her was my slavery, to never leave her side, and even that was stolen with my demise. The death I'd suffered at the hands of the Pharaoh was as brutal as my father's had been, my bones crushed and my back bloodied by a thousand gashes. Egypt had been my personal hell before Caelius.

"That was a long time ago." The words were soft and broken, as my heart had been then. "I'm past it." I sighed. "You should move past it too. That's what I came back to help you with. To move on."

"They still worship him, you know."

The thought started to mask the tenderness of love with dark rage, a rage that was fueled by Caelius's blood pounding in step with my heartbeat. "Akhenaten?"

"They worship *all* like him, as if being Pharaoh was some *divine right*. Kids these days even think it's *cool*. Should we show them, darling? Should we show them what a nameless boy from the mountains can really do?" He smiled, and I felt something wicked fill my face as my teeth grew. "A boy not written in their sacred texts, or even mentioned once in the glyphs of Akhenaten's tomb, could be their demise. Let us unite and destroy a place that has marred your life since you were a boy." He ran his hands down my arms, then rested them against my palms, clasping tight. "As a thanks for your return, I will help you kill your ghosts."

"Wait." I struggled. I was already losing myself; his persuasions and presence were so powerful they unmoored me.

He smirked. "Let us go as a family. Let us unite and watch the living and entombed lords of this world shake in fear. I want you as my *equal*, Lucian. Convince me that's what you are, then we'll talk all you like about this *loneliness* you speak of." He squeezed my hands. "Do this with me, and I'll even let the fact that my shadow is gone from you slide."

I swallowed as he pulled me closer, then licked the side of my neck like sampling a delicacy.

He yanked my hair back and thrust his wrist against my elongated incisors.

Blood.

It poured into me as he tightened his hand around my throat.

"Did you think I wouldn't notice what that *whore* did to you, pet?"

CHAPTER 15
SHEA

Now that we had a plan, I felt rejuvenated and ready to fight.

Whoa.

Strike that.

A sudden wave of weakness washed through my body.

I lay back down. Maybe I needed to rest a little.

No one seemed to notice as they talked fervently about the new revelation of me using all four elements.

I wanted to tell someone about my abrupt change, maybe get some more light therapy from Helena, but I couldn't seem to form words. My mind could barely focus on my surroundings. Everything sounded muffled. I couldn't even tell where I was anymore; my vision started to blur.

That was when I realized with clarity . . . I wasn't recovering.

Using all four elements was supposed to bring me to my true self, my true power. Wasn't it? So why did it feel like I was breaking apart from the inside out? I tried again to speak, to ask for help, to do *anything*, but I could no longer move.

A giant gush of light burst from my hand, rising upward like a beacon of white fire, then immediately snuffed out.

That couldn't be good.

They were all paying attention to me now.

Aidan's voice sounded in my ear, his face inches from mine. "Shea? Can you hear me? Say something!" His tone was desperate.

I knew exactly how he felt. I couldn't calm him because I couldn't freaking move anything.

"What's happening to her?" Aidan screamed.

Helena answered, but her voice was so distant I could barely hear her.

Stand closer, woman!

It sounded like she said, "I have no idea," which pretty much summed up my life right about now.

I wished I could say something, but what would I say?

I didn't know what was wrong with me.

And I was scared.

So yeah.

Help?

That was all I had.

Another burst of light flew out of my right thigh, rising like the other one before, then blinking out of existence.

What was happening to me?

Aidan's voice was next to my ear again. "We're going to try and induce sleep, see if Dream-Walking can snap you out of . . . whatever this is. Helena thinks it might have something to do with you using all four elements at once. Maybe it's some kind of consequence for using that much power?" He paused, his voice shaken. "I really hope you can hear me."

I can hear you!

No words came out.

I tried to calm my mind, to help whatever kind of "inducement" they had planned for me. Knowing Helena, it was probably some kind of device or tonic. Either way, I was glad I couldn't see all that well because whatever it was would most likely freak me out.

Then I heard my father's voice, soft and reassuring.

He began reading *The Lion, the Witch and the Wardrobe* by C.S. Lewis. It was the book he always read to me before bed when I was a little girl. We read the whole series in third grade, and it had been pure magic. After that, I would beg him to read the first book whenever I had trouble sleeping. I was embarrassed to admit it, but Dad had read me this book through high school.

I didn't need any of Helena's contraptions to help me fall asleep. It was just going to be my father being his true self, not a vampire, just a dad reading to his daughter. If I'd been capable of crying, I would have. I listened to the words he spoke. They were so familiar that I knew them by heart. They made me feel like I was . . . home.

I could move!

Overjoyed, I did a quick jumping jack, then noticed I was standing in the living room of my *parents'* house.

I was Dream-Walking.

Well, at least I could move in my head.

I'd take it.

"Shoot. I thought we'd end up in Narnia for sure," Dad said as he materialized in front of me.

I hugged him tightly, then pulled away smiling. "I don't think Dream-Walking works that way, Dad, but trust me when I say being back home is better than Narnia right now."

His face was wracked with concern. "Are you okay? What's happening to you?"

I shook my head. "I have no idea. I used my powers, got really tired, then felt fine and excited to attack Caelius, then suddenly I lay down and couldn't move or speak, with light bursting from random parts of my body! My guess is as good as yours."

"What's happening to you?" Mom suddenly appeared in the living room with us, eyes wide with worry.

Dad whirled around to face her. When their eyes met, it was like watching a romance movie. Normally, I'd make hurling noises at my parents' obvious love for each other, but at this moment, it was the best thing ever.

I quickly assuaged my mother's fears. "I'm fine. Please kiss, or hug, or something. I promise I won't be grossed out."

They both smiled at me like they used to when they thought I'd said something witty, and for just a second, everything felt completely normal. I wanted to hold on to that sensation for as long as I could. "Normal" had such a bad rap as being boring or uneventful. What was wrong with normal? Nothing. Absolutely nothing.

Embracing each other, my parents kissed passionately. This was their first reunion with both their memories restored. They weren't the wiped robots that Aidan's brothers had left behind. They were Jeff and Molly Harper: a father and mother with a lifetime of experiences we'd made as a family.

They eventually parted, and Mom reached over, grabbing me

by the hand, pulling me in for a group hug. It was wonderful.

Parting enough so that she could see my face properly, she placed her hand under my chin and forced me to make eye contact with her, just as she had done when I was a child and she wanted a truthful answer. I'd hated it then; I loved it now.

Mom said, "Spit it out. What's happening?"

"I swear I don't know. I used all four elements to bury Lucian so he'd be safe, and suddenly I was exploding light and couldn't move," I explained lamely.

Mom released her hand and turned to Dad. "Does anyone from your group know what this is? Is Shea going to be all right?"

The look on Dad's face made me feel guilty for being so candid. "We have no idea what it is. Helena's trying to figure it out," he replied.

Mom nodded. "Good. I hope you two haven't misplaced your faith in her, but I trust you." Then her expression turned grave. "Caelius is attacking Egypt as we speak. I told him I needed to rest for a moment, but I have to get back soon. He's being very possessive of all of us. I think he suspects we'd leave him if we could, which is absolutely true. Luckily, he's too obsessed with forcing Lucian to *worship* him right now that he let me have a few minutes without them."

My heart sank into my stomach. "Lucian broke free of the lava?" It hadn't been enough time to rid himself of Caelius's control. With one sentence, everything I had sacrificed to save Lucian was for nothing. My powers, my inability to move, all of it was so that Lucian would never have to go back to Caelius and be his slave again. Now they were apparently destroying one of the oldest civilizations still left on the planet. Yay, Caelius.

Realizing what her words meant, Mom's arms were around me again. "Oh, honey, I'm so sorry. If it means anything, I could feel a physical change in Lucian when he came back to us. Whatever you did helped him regain some of his old self. He's fighting so hard." She stopped herself, not sure if she should continue. I couldn't see the expression on my face, but if it was anything like how I felt, it was pretty bad.

"I just thought if he could get a few days away from Caelius's blood, maybe he would remember . . ." I didn't know what else to say. I had failed. I had probably made it worse. Lucian's torture would be maddening now that he had some of his sanity back. What had I done? I just wished he would pull me into a memory again. Maybe I could help him in that way. Maybe I could figure out what those experiences meant.

My mother kept her arms around me in support. I hadn't realized how much I had missed this kind of contact with her until it was gone. Just having her near me, fully my mom again, was everything.

"Don't regret what you did. Lucian is better for it," she said.

"But you guys are ravaging Egypt right now. How is he better if he's *hurting* people?" I didn't want to think about the fact that Lucian and my mother had most likely *murdered* for Caelius's sake. How could I forgive that? How could I forgive anything? Depression overwhelmed me. Was this how family members of serial killers felt? On one hand, you loved them—on the other, they *killed* people.

My mom allayed my fears. "Oh, honey, we're not killing anyone—none of us, not even Nefertiti. And Lucian is destroying pyramids, tombs, and any structure he can get his hands on.

He doesn't even seem to see the people around him, which is a good thing. We're making Caelius believe we're killing, but we're draining people to unconsciousness. There's lots of blood everywhere, but no one is dying from *our* hands. Caelius's victims are another issue. We can't stop him. I know it sounds awful, but now that I'm truly *awake*, I will never harm another living soul again. I promise you that." She spoke the last sentence while staring at me directly.

I believed her, mainly because I wanted to, but also because she was my mother and she had never lied to me before.

As if hearing something in the distance, Mom turned her head, listening. "I have to get back."

Dad touched her arm, and I realized he had been simply watching the two of us the entire time. He looked like he had been basking. Dad was definitely a basker.

Mom held our hands, one in each of hers. "I'll try to break free, but I don't know if it's possible. Being a spy is pointless now. It's now or never. I'll return to you or die trying."

"We'll come to you," I said.

Even Dad's eyebrows rose. "Shea, we don't even know what's wrong with you."

Shaking my head, I said with confidence, "This ends now. Helena said she was close to finding a way to turn Caelius back into his shadow form, and whatever's happening with me, shooting out powerful beams of light, can only help." I had no idea if that was true, but somewhere down deep, it felt right.

Mom didn't look pleased, but she nodded. "If Helena finds a way, let's end this and be a family again."

"It's happening." My confidence didn't waver.

Smiling at me, Mom kissed my cheek, then kissed Dad. "I love you both."

And with that, she was gone.

Turning to my father, I held both of his hands. "Let's get back."

Dad stared at me, eyes crinkled in worry. To him nothing had changed; I was still in a semicoma, but something inside of me had awoken.

Seeing my mother, knowing she and Lucian were in danger, knowing that Caelius needed to be stopped . . . I was finally ready.

And it was time.

Closing my eyes, I squeezed my dad's hands with determination.

***

My eyes opened.

I was in a hotel room sitting on a chair.

I could move.

I could see and talk.

"I'm good," I assured them. Then I turned to Helena. "It's time."

To my surprise, her expression showed that she agreed. "It's your powers *united*, Shea. All four elements, that's the key. No gadgets, no inventions, just pure Light and the energy of the Earth itself should be enough."

"Yes." I nodded. It was as if we were the only two in the room. I could feel the intensity behind her words. As much as exploding Light out of various parts of my body was terrifying, I also knew that it had the potential to free us from Caelius.

"I can control it now." That was a total lie, but I hoped to figure it out by the time we got to Caelius. I needed them all to believe me, otherwise they wouldn't agree to go. I was being reckless, but I couldn't stand a second more of Lucian and my mom being held captive.

I physically and mentally couldn't take it, and the world couldn't either.

Too many innocents had died already.

Caelius needed to be stopped before any more people were killed.

Aidan faced me, forcing me to focus on him and not Helena. "Are you sure, Shea? *How* can you control it?"

Freaking Aidan with his direct questions! I managed to muster up my confidence. "I can't explain it, but I can control it, just trust me."

He stared at me, trying to read my body language.

I remained determined.

Finally, he relented and agreed. "I will always trust you, Shea. I'm in."

Meky was the first to respond after Aidan. "I'm *definitely* in."

Duncan echoed Meky. "Ye know where I stand. 'Til tha end."

"May the Force be with us."

Dad, seriously? It was so "him" that I had to laugh. Aidan joined in, and soon we were all smiling despite the terrifying confrontation we were about to run straight toward.

"Aidan, you take Shea. The rest of us will run," Helena said.

Our smiles faded as we fully realized what we were about to do.

It was fitting that I was going to be flown in by an angel when I was about to fight the devil on Earth.

I just hoped we'd *all* survive this time.

***

Soaring over Egypt was a nightmare. I felt as if I were watching a horror movie where the bad guy had destroyed one of the seven wonders of the world. The pyramids were *gone*, flattened to the ground in crumbles of stone and sand, along with every other ancient structure that used to exist. Knowing that Lucian had been responsible for most of it made my heart hurt. Seeing living history being destroyed was both terrifying and incredibly sad, though I knew Lucian had lived at that time and he was finally getting vengeance on the symbols he had helped build while he was a slave.

Now that the large monuments were ruins, it was easy to see where the action was happening. Large clouds of dust and dirt flew in every direction, along with streaks of red. There may have been a city here before, but it was gone. Nothing but desert and blood remained.

I kept reminding myself of what Mom had said, but as many people as they spared, thousands of others were dying anyway because of Caelius.

It made me sick.

I had to end this.

Through the chaos and hovering midair, Aidan looked at me with his usual concerned expression, then said, "Are you *sure* you can do this?"

No. Not at all.

"Yes. I'm sure."

Aidan nodded, and we made our descent onto the sands of Egypt.

Caelius and the others didn't even notice; they were in full destruction mode.

I needed to make myself seen.

But I also needed to clear out all the dust and debris to get an idea of what we were truly up against.

Here went nothing.

Taking a deep breath, I called on each element: water, fire, earth, and air. Water burst in giant crashing waves from the mighty Nile. The blood in its waters erupted with it, and the force looked like some kind of biblical red sea. I focused on fire next. There were millions of tiny sparks from where the desert sun burned into the sand so deeply that they almost acted like embers. I tapped into each overheated grain of sand and lit the debris around it using fire. I shook the earth violently, forcing everyone to stop in their tracks. And then I connected to the winds and blew the sand, ash, and dirt away from where Caelius stood.

Standing in the remains of the mighty pyramids and the civilization that had grown close to them was devastating. Everything was gone. All of it.

Now that I had Caelius's full attention, I wiped the elements away so all that remained was . . .

Silence.

Only the whimpering of the injured people could be heard.

My eyes met Caelius's.

He looked at me with deep hatred.

Behind him stood Lucian, my mom, Nefertiti, Sherit, and Setepenre. They stared at me with hope mixed with fear, like they were yearning for me to free them.

I wouldn't let them down.

Mustering up the courage, I walked closer. "It's time, Caelius. It's over."

He laughed. "Time for what, little Vessel? Time for your death?" He motioned for Lucian to stand next to him, and he immediately obeyed.

"Kill this one, Lucian. I don't want her dirty little soul anymore. I'm powerful enough without it. I only *need* you. Now that I have rewarded you with Egypt, prove to me that I'm the only one and destroy this hollow skeleton of your past," Caelius ordered, though his voice was soft, almost loving.

Lucian didn't move; he simply watched me with calculating eyes.

Was he still in there?

Did taking away the shadow inside of him help?

Caelius didn't like the hesitation. He turned his head so that his eyes met Lucian's. "Do this for me, boy, and all is forgiven. I will never doubt you again."

I hated that I could see conflict on Lucian's face. Darkness itself had swallowed him whole, and yet I could see that he was fighting its grip on him. I wanted to run over and physically separate Caelius's blood from Lucian's body.

But I couldn't.

I had to end this first.

Without warning, a burst of light shot out of my shoulder, almost reaching the clouds, then snuffed out.

I tried to look as if I had done it on purpose, but I almost collapsed from the force of it.

Maybe I didn't have this whole Light thing under control after all.

My vision blurred slightly, but after blinking a few times, I was *almost* able to see clearly.

Okay, not clearly, but at least I could still tell people apart.

I needed to get it together or Caelius would win.

Again.

"Will you look at that, darling?" Caelius's laughter broke the quiet.

Aidan's hand rested on my arm, and I turned to him. "Did you do that on purpose, Shea?"

"Yes," I lied. I was really getting this lying thing down. I just didn't want Aidan to pull me away this time, and I knew that was exactly what he would do if he thought I was in any danger.

Helena, Duncan, Dad, and Meky all arrived at the same time. They looked strong, refreshed, and ready to fight. I was proud to stand with them. This was the team. We were the ones who would take Darkness down once and for all.

Then one other arrived.

Ur-Nammu.

He gave me a small nod. "I've been watching and following my daughter and granddaughters as they have been serving that *thing*. I did nothing out of fear for my family's lives, but I can tolerate Lucian's and their abuse no longer. I stand with you, Shea Harper. As the sole surviving leader of Gutium, I am honor bound to take a stand against Darkness. I am a Gutian, and I will die as one."

Caelius stopped laughing for a brief moment as he viewed Ur-Nammu with disgust. "That can be arranged." He sighed, exasperated. "Ur-Nammu, a backbone can't be grown overnight. You've lived like a weasel since the day you were turned."

I wanted to punch Caelius in the face and hug Ur-Nammu at the same time.

But I could see it in the way Ur-Nammu held himself. He was there to fight with us to the bitter end. We had our differences in the past, but we'd resolved them, and having another father figure here made me feel safer, like everything would be all right.

But everything wasn't going to be all right unless I destroyed Caelius, who was laughing again.

Again. I really wanted to know what was so funny. When evil people laughed, it was usually because they knew something the good guys didn't.

And that scared me.

I was yanked forward by an invisible force and came face-to-face with Caelius.

Aidan leapt to my defense, but as he took flight a long shadowy arm grew out of Caelius's body and pinned him to the ground.

More sinewy tendrils of black smoke flowed out of Caelius like a creature from my deepest nightmares. Arms of smoke grabbed hold of every person for as far as the eye could see, tightening and squeezing them into submission. And it wasn't just my rescue team; it was Mom, Nefertiti, Sherit, and Sete as well. Even the humans were pinned down by his shadows, dead and almost-dead alike.

Caelius's trust was gone.

He didn't want to risk any surprise attacks, even from his own army.

Okay.

Definitely up to me now.

Staring into his hot red eyes was more terrifying than it had ever been, probably because he was a bit on the blurry side, but also because there was a black shadow moving and swirling around his entire body. I was finally seeing Caelius for what he truly was: the thing that made monsters themselves.

Lucian stood close to him, arm in arm, the black smoke almost caressing him. His eyes looked me over as if he wasn't quite sure what to do with me.

And could Caelius stop laughing already?

It was *really* annoying.

Finally the manic cackling stopped.

He placed his hand gently on my chin.

I swatted him away, which only entertained him more.

"You have no idea what they've done to you, do you?" he asked, knowing full well that I had no clue what he was talking about.

I didn't answer; I didn't have a good enough lie to back me up.

When enough time passed, Caelius chuckled again in an irritatingly satisfied way. "Aidan's precious brothers decided you were *disposable*."

What now?

I spoke, but my voice was shakier than I wanted it to be. "They made me *strong*."

"Oh yes, they definitely did that. I'm guessing you were supposed to be cautious and wait to fight me. They didn't count on you using their little Light-bomb to trap Lucian in magma while you chased out my shadow. You used all four of your elements too early; now your power is waning, and you're going to disintegrate right before our very eyes. Not even your soul will be left, little light bulb." Caelius's smile was cruel, and he was the happiest I'd ever seen him. "Looks like you won't have to lift a finger after all, darling. Her fate is already sealed." He moved his hand down Lucian's side.

No.

They wouldn't do that.

Would they?

"He's a liar, Shea!" Aidan yelled behind me as the shadow pinned him to the ground.

Caelius's gaze quickly turned to Aidan. "You think so much of your brothers, but they know you better than you know yourself. You'd never let anything happen to *this* Vessel, you've proven that much. But to them, she's just a carrier of Light, a weapon to be used to force me back into shadow form. They don't care if she dies and loses her soul. They only want the balance back where *they* think it belongs. Do you deny it? As a protector of the Light, wouldn't you do the same if you were in their position, *angel*?"

I looked at Aidan; his face was full of doubt.

And I knew at that moment that Caelius was telling the truth.

Aidan's brothers had over-juiced me to rid the world of

Caelius; they didn't care if my soul survived. It was probably why they kept calling me Vessel instead of Shea and why they never told Aidan their plans because he'd never agree to it.

And I had ruined it.

I'd tapped into my powers too early when trying to stop Lucian from burning in the lava, and now I didn't have enough juice to do the job I was meant to.

Or maybe I did.

Maybe if I gave everything, even my soul, I could force all the Light inside of me to consume Caelius. Then he'd be forced to turn back into his shadow form and leave his human body behind forever. It would be the only way he could save himself. I had to try. I had to save the ones I loved. I was just a Vessel, made for the purpose of restoring balance to the universe. At least I'd die for a *reason*.

Facing Caelius, I took a deep breath. This was happening.

I saw a flicker of fear in Caelius's eyes.

Good.

I wanted him to be scared for once.

Drawing the elements to me, I . . . fell forward as a wrenching pain hit my body.

Looking down, I saw Caelius's arm sticking through my stomach.

He had stabbed me with his own hand!

I couldn't connect to any element; the pain was too overwhelming.

I was going to die like this, and I wasn't going to be able to take Caelius with me.

I had failed *again*, miserably.

I turned to Lucian. I wanted the last thing that I saw on this Earth to be him. Whether he remembered me or not, his love had changed my life, changed who I was. It had made me into someone who would sacrifice herself for the greater good.

Our eyes locked.

And there he was.

My Lucian.

Fully himself.

Looking at me with the intensity of a thousand suns.

His eyes moved toward Caelius.

And he was seriously pissed.

CHAPTER 16
LUCIAN

The wholeness I felt from the Vessel trapping me in lava and stripping the Darkness from my soul, locked into place when I realized that she might actually *die*.

Shea Harper.

Finally, I understood.

That was the name I had been searching for in the dark.

I had tried to hold on to it before Caelius's brainwashing consumed me completely.

And finally here it was again, rising to the surface like a powerful force of light, burning my blood until I felt it boil up inside of me. I was weakened by the corruption of that tainted blood, but I was stronger than Caelius knew. My mind was fortified by the love of Bohe and all of my people. Now that Shea was here, I could feel them reaching for me again, like a horde fighting to push back the lies of Caelius's sequestered void. Their love was here for me now, in the shadow of my poisoned heart.

That truth was *powerful.*

More powerful than Caelius.

Even a solitary candle could dissipate darkness.

And that was what Shea was: a light.

My light.

How dare he even *touch* something so precious.

I growled, and in a sudden fit of rage I wrenched Caelius's arm back and threw him across the desert. Had the pyramids still been standing, he would have pierced right through them on his way to Libya.

I looked into Shea's eyes as she collapsed into my arms, red making its way down her parted mouth. The others, pinned back by Caelius's shadows, had been released when his body went flying. They ran to our side. I could feel their hot, untrusting gaze against my back, but I didn't care. Their judgment and the pulsing obedience commanding my heart's loyalty to Caelius could do nothing to control the feeling that a life without her would be more of a true death than I had ever known.

I pressed her forehead into my chest. Her scent filled my senses and, like a flood, memories rushed forward, overwhelming me. With every new memory came an adjoining agony. Faces screamed through my mind like wailing banshees, furious at the insolence of how I had forgotten their importance.

I had killed Gunnhild and Ashgar to save Shea.

I clenched my teeth.

I killed my own children with my own two hands. That was something I'd never wanted; no matter how callous I'd become over the centuries, they were still mine to protect. I lifted my hand as it shook, now covered in Shea's blood. I had done it for *her,* hadn't I?

He had killed the others.

Duncan had been sucked dry, and although I never saw David's demise, I was sure it was agony because Caelius had brutally tortured Gracuri and Bohe right in front of me. How could I have forgotten their deaths? I was still wearing the Hanfu Bohe had bled out in, while Caelius wore Gracuri's shoes on the days it pleased him. When he wasn't wearing them, or making me wear them, he kept them on a *spike* outside the cabin.

This was a sick joke.

It couldn't be real.

I squeezed Shea tighter to my chest as a more terrifying impression pulled through. This wasn't the first time. The words "try again" repeated from Caelius's lips like there was still a chain around my neck. How many times had I remembered, only to have his blood make me forget everything again?

Caelius's betrayal seared in me, but my betrayal of memory to the ones I loved scorched hotter. It was against the code of Gutium; it was our duty to burn the ones passed into the existence of all things. It was a brand we carried until our own death was carved out, in turn, by those left behind. No matter the pain remembering had wrought over the centuries, it was a tradition I had never broken . . . until now.

I thought of my father on the hills of Gutium, his people slaughtered at his feet, his body pierced with spears like a "stuck pig," as Caelius had called him. Onack the Great came to such an unworthy end, and he had spared me of it. Only now, as every new pointed memory pierced through, the code of our people erased, did I feel that I was indeed my father's son.

But for Onack, the devastation was glory as he proved his right as our leader and fought for love. The things Caelius allowed, and the things he took from me, weren't in the name of love, but were in the absence of it. All of my torment over the centuries was for *his* pleasure, just to show that I was a slave in more ways than Akhenaten's whip had ever made me. There was no honor in it, and only in defeat was I like my father.

Defeat . . .

I remembered our last battle and how Caelius had torn Nefari's children apart.

Maybe it was that moment, as I committed another betrayal of our code, that had led me to this place now. I had fought for the ones I loved, but in the end I had *surrendered* to save them— something my father would have never done. Was this fate's cruel sense of irony, to lead me to the same choice again? Was it only Gutian to know such ruin?

I looked at the faces of those surrounding us.

They were here again, in no better state than before.

We would lose.

I wept into Shea's back.

My mind flashed with the memory of a different desert. It was Arizona and, despite my mission, I was falling in love with the Vessel. Her pale blond hair and light hazel eyes healed me in a way that blood never could. Memories of Paris and our nights together rose and lifted the veil that had blinded me, the compulsion finally overcome.

My body tensed as I remembered *everything*: the entire year I had lost.

Shea Harper wasn't just the name I'd been searching for in

the dark; hers was the name I would always search for, until the end of time.

She was my soul mate.

A part of me knew that in the first moment we met.

A part of me would *always* know her.

My lips moved against the nape of her neck. If she were a vampire, I would offer her every drop of my tainted blood, anything to heal her. But it was because she was not that she was able to bring me so fervently home. As with every time I met her, it was her humanness that had returned mine.

"I'm so sorry, Shea. Please . . . I will fight Caelius myself."

Leave here.

Run.

"As long as you are alive, I can keep fighting." I pushed my hands through her thick hair. "If you are by my side and anything more happens to you, I will surely die. You are all I have left. Please *hide*." It struck me, the arrows of memory twisting further. These were, in essence, the words my father spoke the night before battle, begging me to leave Gutium. All this time I had resented that he'd asked me to leave, and now that his bones were no more than ash, like my mother's, I finally understood his love.

I'm sorry, Father. Forgive me as I now forgive you.

I couldn't look at her face.

The dishonor of all of it.

I had fed off of her.

I had hurt her.

The one person I had sworn never to be a vampire with—just a man.

And now I was begging her like my father, as if I still had any right to call on the loyalty of our love.

The only other woman I had longed to be mortal with offered me support. Nefertiti reached down and placed her hand on my back. "It's all right, La-Narru. You didn't have a choice."

I recoiled from her touch. Now that all of my memories were alive again, I rejected her pale platitude of comfort. "I *remember*, Nefari. It was you, not Ur-Nammu, who lied to me."

She was silent, and in her silence grew the rage of a thousand lifetimes.

"You should have killed me when I *asked*—when I was chained, before we fought him the *first* time! I told you he would use me against her. He used me against *all* of you. You shouldn't have let me become Caelius's lapdog. You promised in Gutium; we both did. 'Death over servitude.' It is the Gutian way, and you robbed me of that birthright."

Her hand dropped. Her voice was jagged, more like stones scraping together than words. "I thought we both agreed in Egypt. That was a part of our people's code we'd have to leave behind to survive, along with our life together in the mountains."

"Don't rewrite history as if I wasn't there. *You* asked me to vow to live on; *you* wanted to survive. And when death finally did come for me outside your window, *you* gave me over to Caelius and had me turned . . . then left me in the wake of mourning your loss."

"I know," she whispered. Nefertiti had once spoken with authority in this very place. Her confident words had flooded over an entire people—her *new* people—after Gutium's demise. She'd ruled alongside Akhenaten and had even commanded his armies from behind the throne. Her natural ability to adapt and lead had not been inhibited by her new station. True to her Gutian name, Nefari had shone bright through oppression. She'd been a morning star, a jewel among stones.

Now she felt to me like a burning coal embedded in my stomach, a constant ache that I had returned to again and again, unable to move past.

"How many times have I been tortured because you couldn't let me die in peace? How many thousands of years have I hung on because your last words in Egypt asked me to deny my right of death over servitude?" My tone was steady, unlike her breath, which became more jagged with every word I spoke.

Rulers across nations had come to see the Pharaoh's prized wife, whose eloquence had given her a reputation, an adoration even amongst the slaves. After she made us vow to live, the mere whisper of her name—even as my bare feet pressed mud into hay and whips lashed my back—had persuaded me to fight on. Her speeches from high above the palace reached me, even there, in the squalors of hell.

I withstood torn flesh and broken bones because I knew with that same powerful mouth she would whisper the sweetest of lullabies to her children and kiss promises into my neck in the moonlit nights along the Nile.

Promises she never fulfilled.

I wanted to bury it, along with any love I had for her— choke it down like I had the sands of Egypt when I'd grieved for lifetimes over her loss.

Now, holding Shea in my arms, stabbed by Caelius because Nefertiti would not end me, all of the betrayals I had suffered by loving her since Gutium linked together.

"I knew this would happen; you should have let me go. I may understand *why* you've done what you have over the ages, but you broke me in the process, Nefari. And without Shea, I can't . . ." I clung to Shea's body, tormented like a man possessed by grief itself.

Nefertiti stepped back as if I had lanced her gut.

"Please," I whispered into Shea's hair. "Tell me what to do. I'll do anything." I didn't want to know a world without her light. There was no sacrifice I wouldn't give. "Death over servitude," I whispered. "If that's all I can offer you, I will. My life for yours, a million times over. I can't begin to apologize for what I've done to you."

She breathed in deep, running her face along my chest. I felt the wetness of tears. She was clinging to me—she had been this whole time, in both thought and action. She hadn't let me go.

I clung back in desperation. "I tried, Shea. I tried to hold on to you too. But I was so lost."

"Lucian, I know." She squeezed, and there was a fierceness in her grip, despite her mortal wound. "I love you." Her words were sobs, and they broke my already splintered heart. "It's okay, I'm just glad you're back."

How could she respond so easily?

No punishment.

No resentment.

She was better than I was. Her love was pure and unselfish; it was unlike anything I had experienced with Caelius. His affection came with conditions; it had to be constantly earned, proven, and above all else, it came with a *price*.

Like the very thought of him conjured the demon itself, smoke filled the air.

Caelius was furious.

I could already feel the agony he was going to burn into me as black started covering my skin.

"Lucian, let go!" Shea shouted.

I clung tighter. "I won't lose you again!"

If Caelius wanted her, he'd have to kill me, and I would die as my father had, with my people at my back.

"I said let go!" she screamed, struggling in my arms.

The smell filling the air around us was grotesque.

I waited for his hand to grab my throat, but it didn't come.

I looked up briefly.

Caelius was still far off, sauntering back at a slow pace. Even as flames rose around me, I could see that his face was downcast, looking more like a kicked child than Darkness. Defeat weighed his shoulders down in a way I had not seen, even in the thousands of years he was caged. His red eyes were staring at the sand. Instantly, I understood what I was seeing. I too had looked at that same Egyptian sand with such bitter heartbreak once.

Now we both had.

I for Nefari, and he for me.

He must have finally realized that the love I had for Shea was more powerful than his control and that I would *never* belong to him. It was a death of expectation—the agony of an unquenchable desire left unfulfilled.

It hurt.

I knew well enough.

It *burned*.

"I said let go!" Shea pushed back in my arms.

I looked down.

The smoke wasn't coming from Caelius; it was coming from me.

He wasn't the one burning me up from the inside. *She* was.

Shea's skin was starting to emanate light.

Everyone had been screaming, their hands trying to pull me back, but I hadn't noticed. I had been so lost in my returned memories—my agonizing over Nefari, Caelius, and Shea—that it'd been as if the whole world had fallen away.

I looked up in a blur at the desperate faces around us. They yanked at my limbs, trying to distance Shea from my body. Their voices were a mix of her same sentiment.

"Let go!" they shouted over and over.

I grabbed her shoulders, hard.

I wouldn't let her go again.

Not for anyone.

Everyone was forced to retreat, shielding their gazes and bodies from the fire consuming us.

Through their desperate cries, I held on tighter, wrenching her back into my arms.

Her eyes met mine as my skin burned with a holy flame I had experienced once before, when I had clung to her after she had charged her powers with Akhenaten's sundial.

Except this was worse.

Much worse.

I fought back screams of anguish.

"Shea, are you all right?" My words were almost a screech alongside the sound of my skin frying like bacon. "What's happening? What did Caelius mean about Aidan's brothers and your soul? Are you overpowered? Is this the sundial again?"

Her smile made my insides burn hotter than my skin. "You *remember*."

I missed her. I would *always* miss her. "Shea . . . *I love you*."

She nodded. "I love you too."

She took in a deep breath, then tried to jerk herself out of my arms.

"No!" I squeezed, blisters covering my hands. "Stay with me, tell me what to do to save you!"

"Just let go." She paused, looking at my burns as if they hurt her more than me. "This whole time you've been fighting a long fight. Deep inside you've been doing everything to hold on to me—I *know* that now. Even when you were lost, you still couldn't kill me. You pulled me into your memories when you were at your worst. You still felt it: *our connection*."

I kissed her; my longing and my scorching lips ached.

She lingered for a moment, then shoved me away. "It really is time. Please understand, I have to do this. You have to let me go. This world, all the people . . . *you*, Lucian, are worth dying for. You have given up your life and so much more. Don't you think I love you just as much as you love me?" She took in a quick gasp. "I'm sorry, but it's my turn to die."

My body flipped back as hers burst with light, healing the gaping hole in her stomach. I fell into the sand, skidding face-first down a dune. Choking on the dirt and brushing it off of my skinned cheeks, I coughed as I stood up, screaming out her name. "Shea!"

She was already hovering in the air, her whole body aflame

like the sun.

I squinted, unable to make out her face. "No, Shea, please, wait! Let this whole world burn, and me with it! Just live! You're all that's worth fighting for!" I clawed at the sliding dune like a worm trying to make my way back to her, but the waves of power pulsing off of her body kept forcing me back.

Then gears and the fierce beating of wings sounded behind me.

I turned and saw everyone fighting Caelius. His moment of melancholy had passed, and he was *savage*. But to my surprise, he wasn't the only one.

Aidan blasted him with light, fighting him from the air without restraint, his wings creating whirlwinds in their wake. I stumbled forward with the residual force of it, caught between his power and Shea's. He looked now as he had just before he'd stabbed Moses. His grief and confusion were evident as much on his face as in his shrieking war cries. After all these centuries, his agony finally matched my own. He loved Shea as much as I did, and his brothers' betrayal, to that end, was a shock to him alone. I knew what they were like after Ashliel was abandoned to the pit. Now so did he, as he threw heavy fists and wings at Caelius.

For all my years spent hating him, not once would I have wished to see him as he was now. Despite the weight of my torment through the decades, and even though his build was enormous like Gracuri's, Aidan had bolstered a careless lightness about him. It was like he was a caged bird with hollow bones that still remembered how to sing. I saw none of that lightness now; he had changed. He was finally flying again, but he was without the holy dignity and righteousness he'd always held.

He looked heavy as stone.

The sound of gears that followed after him belonged to Helena. She was using a device that flung bottled concoctions into the air. Some landed hard hits, exploding in glass and colored vapors that boiled Caelius's skin; others were brushed off, as if she were throwing pebbles into the ocean. Looking at her slumped stance, I realized that Helena had changed too.

She looked more bitter and unsure since our last battle, where she had been unknowingly brainwashed by the very being she stood toe to toe with now. That kind of self-doubt, even for a levelheaded scientist, was detrimental, and it showed.

Her hair was pulled back and filthy from hands that were smeared with the blackness of lubricated gears as she forced them into place. The delight of seeing her creations work was replaced with frustration and the fear of failure. The last time I had seen her this haunted was when she'd been isolated by her abusive family. Back then she believed their lies: that she would never belong in this world, that an intelligent woman had no place in it and was powerless against the force of a society ruled by men.

Nefertiti was quickly by her side. She must have caught the same gaze I had because she shouted, "Are you a man that you should give up so easily? Where is your pride as a woman of science? Have you abandoned reason for defeat?" In that brief moment, I could see that their time together as the years passed meant more than I'd initially understood.

Helena's resolve hardened along with Nefari's.

They had become friends, like Helena and I had a hundred years ago.

"Science never yields to weaker minds," Helena said through

clenched teeth. "A belief in absolutes is weakness; failure is the true path to success. A will to keep *trying* is the only real measurable outcome of greatness." She parroted the words, words I had heard her repeat to herself millions of times in the lab. That sort of ritualistic affirmation paid off; it steadied her now when she was at her lowest.

Nefertiti nodded, pleased, and kissed her hard on the lips in a quick moment of passion. When she pulled back and gazed into Helena's stunned eyes, she cupped her face as gently as she had her children's. "I believe in you, Helena."

I was shocked. Nefari only believed in the capabilities of her own hands. She had never once said those words to me, or to *anyone*, but they flew from her lips just as fluidly as the embrace had. Perhaps she had become *more* than friends with Helena, as I had with those I'd turned in the past.

Ur-Nammu stepped beside Nefari as Meky and Sherit joined them. He extended his hands, and for a moment the girls all linked together. It was painful to see what would be the last unified Gutian front in history. When they released one another, they all attacked Caelius with fists and teeth, tearing bone and hair in handfuls.

I wasn't sure if it was Helena's kiss that had awoken her, but finally the fire had returned to Nefari's gaze. The drawn black lines around her eyes were smeared and imperfect, but now they resembled war paint as the ink ran down her cheeks. She looked more the leader of Gutium than the queen of Egypt, and I was glad for it: to see her return to herself here, at what would truly be her end. She knew it, and now so did I. There was no forgiveness or plan that would make Caelius spare her this time.

I hadn't realized the resentment I had been harboring toward her until the careless words had spilled from my lips. In truth, I hated that she hadn't left with me in Gutium, on the eve before they battled Egypt. I hated that she hadn't run away with me in secret, escaping Akhenaten with the girls. I hated that she'd hidden with Caelius while I was tormented by his obsessions, all the while grieving her. I had lived a life of longing. I hated that I'd always waited for her, but she'd never come. And now that I had finally disowned our love, I would lose her again, as I always lost Nefari.

Still, at the end, despite the fear that Caelius would slaughter more of her daughters, I had finally seen her return to the image I had held of her as a child and desperately clung to as a man. It was an image that had never changed, even though she had.

She paused and looked at me.

No, not at me; she looked past me.

I turned and saw Setepenre frozen in place. She couldn't bring herself to raise a hand to Caelius, but she didn't help him fight her family's unified attacks either. Even as he called for her, her eyes stayed down, refusing to meet his gaze. She had finally seen enough in the past few months with the degradation of her family to doubt all that she had been raised to believe as his granddaughter.

She left his side, beginning a slow walk of isolation in the very desert she had grown up in. Her shadow was lit by the sun as she gazed back at me, then she silently disappeared, like a mirage leaving nothing but waves of heated sand.

It was a judicious choice, but then again, she was a part of Nefertiti and had no doubt inherited the diplomacy from her mother. For that, I was glad. There was solace in thinking that once we were all dead, Caelius might just spare her.

I looked at Nefertiti. Her eyes found mine, and for a moment we shared in that relief.

Then Duncan's cries turned our heads. He spat Scottish hymns and chants at Caelius. One was familiar. It was a dark poem he'd made up as a boy to ward off trolls. When we'd crossed the Highlands and he walked over bridges, he would speak it under his breath like placing a holy curse.

He now looked like the young man I had met coming off the boat in Scotland. He spat his troll-ward at Caelius, sinking in heavy hits reminiscent of his days as a street boxer. There was glee in the way he moved, a bounce in his step. He'd always loved a good fight, but I had robbed him of it when I made him mine and slaughtered his kinsman, expecting him to do the same. His love for battle had ended that day, along with his life.

At least his stories remained, and *this* was one he would have told with fervor. This was a death he wanted: a fight in the blaze of glory against the devil himself. It was a tale worth telling, unlike his death before: being drained and left without a grave like the nameless dead in war.

In fact, his rise from a second death and then coming here to save the world was worthy of the *Iliad*. Gracuri would have liked to hear Duncan's interpretation of his own death, as he used to listen with awe in amphitheaters playing Greek stories battling gods with men. They had become friends over the years. He would have sat, leaning off the edge of his seat, the boyishness in his demeanor apparent, while Duncan spoke in earnest, his hands waving about with the telling. There was no doubt that

Gracuri would have fought by our side without hesitation. So many of them would have. All I had to do was ask, and they would have followed me to this glorious end. Instead I'd isolated myself, and them in the process, thinking that I was alone.

It was painful realizing I was surrounded by so much love but that I hadn't seen it. I labeled it as petty things like lust and amusement. At times, I'd even been afraid to call them *friends*, but that, and so much more, was what they had been to me. This whole time they'd been sending me messages in a bottle carried on an ocean of acceptance, while I'd shut my heart away inside a solitary desert of loss. If anything, it was my fear of loss that had kept me losing the ones that I had come to love.

It had kept me thirsty and aching with insatiable hunger.

A hunger that not even Caelius, with all of his blood, could fill. He said that swine weren't worthy of a single drop and guarded it from everyone but me, like it was holy. I watched as they tore him apart, that same blood now strewn carelessly across the sands like a giant inkblot test.

Molly and Jeff moved around Duncan, bobbing in unison. They were so close to each other. I noticed they were holding hands as they attacked with fervency, as if their lives depended on it. But they didn't.

It was *her* life.

I struggled in place, still held at bay by the force of her mounting power.

Why weren't they trying to *stop* Shea like I was?

Then it finally sank in.

I knew exactly what they were doing.

"All of our lives rather than yours!" I shouted up at her.

"That's what we're all saying, Shea!" She hadn't made a move yet because they were blocking Caelius with their attacks. "If we can stop him ourselves, you don't have to do this! We won't give you up! Not to the Light, nor to the Darkness! Power down, and let's do this *together*!"

I ran away from her, toward Caelius.

My people's creed wasn't wrong; love was a powerful force.

It was stronger than his Darkness, stronger than the lies I'd been living my whole life.

Light exploded past me.

It landed on Caelius's body, blasting everyone around him back. He shrieked—a sound in all my years I'd never heard him make. A ghastly sound.

And I wanted to scream with him.

Shea was doing it anyway, despite everyone's efforts.

Instantly, a shadow with enormous limbs sprung out from his diminished frame, reaching its claws for the Light.

Shea didn't relent.

I turned and ran the other direction, back toward her. "Stop!" If I had to sacrifice myself, I would. I didn't matter. As long as she was alive, my soul could rest at peace. But there would be no peace for me left if she died and her soul disintegrated.

As I made my way to her, the light emanating from her chest began to sputter like the backfire of an old truck.

She fell.

I caught her in my arms before she touched the ground. The light pulsing on her skin faded until she was dull and weak, her breath jagged. Her skin shifted between translucent and a sickening gray. It was like she was dissolving in my arms, turning to ash like my mother had . . . like everyone I loved.

"It wasn't enough." Tears rolled down her cheeks as her body flickered in and out of existence.

"No matter the outcome, you will *always* be enough, Shea Harper." I clung to the ghost of her. "Please, stay with me . . . or take me into oblivion with you. Don't leave me here." I had said similar words to Anna-Steen on her deathbed. My hands felt just as small and helpless now as they had been then.

She ran her hand through my hair, but it felt formless, like a gust of wind. "I have *more*. There's more Light inside of me," she whimpered. "Help me, Lucian. Give me the strength to finish this for all of us."

I stared at her beautiful hazel eyes. She had awakened so much that had been dead and forgotten, filling it with light so it could finally start to heal.

"No." I pulled her fiercely into my lap. "I have given up everything and everyone I have loved, one way or another, out of arrogance or fear. I have made so many mistakes; I can see that now. Don't ask me again. I won't give you up as well—"

"But, Lucian!" She took in a long pained breath, her eyes still fixed on mine. "Ours is a proud people."

The breath I gasped in shock mirrored hers and quivered like she had reached her hand into my stomach, as Caelius had just done to her.

"Shea, don't—"

"We are many, but united we beat with *one* heart." She pressed her hand to my chest as it phased in and out. It was cold, unlike the warm desert wind at my back.

"No. I won't help you lose your soul, no matter what you say."

"Though we fall—"

I winced. How many of my people had spoken these very words before death, their slaughtered bones piled by Onack's?

"We will *never fail* because we have given ourselves over to glory."

I pressed my forehead against hers. This wasn't fair. "Stop. That damn Gutian code, it's just words made up by dead men."

"To fight for those we *love*." She breathed in deep, but it puffed out in an uneven wave. "And though our bones may brittle with time, and life may wear and kill the tenderness of affection, the burning heart, the flame that is *our* people and what we stand for, cannot be stamped out of time. They are more than words, Lucian, and they were created by your *father*."

"Shea, please—" I held on to the hand at my chest. I could feel it, the warmth in her touch slowly returning.

"We are etched into the very existence of all things, you and I."

"Please don't leave me. I don't want to be alone again," I muttered, but even as I said the word "alone," something shifted inside of me—a stirring, as if the old weight it carried, the old lie, was leaving.

"You are not alone because we are and *forever* will be a people who fight for what we love. And love"—tears steamed down her porcelain face as she choked out the last words—"love is the *soul* of all that's worth fighting for."

Her words rang out alongside the laughter of my mother, Anna-Steen. It was warm and strong like my father's arms had been when he'd carried me on his back, alive and happy. The words of our code were true and wise like Bohe under a waterfall as he meditated. They were soft and wild like the curls in Gracuri's hair as he waited by the river for my return. The voices of all of those in my past began mixing with hers in the Light as her body started to regain its color, warming the skin of my forehead and melting my heart under her touch.

She laughed to herself. It was light and kind as it had been in Paris, before all of this. "Ur-Nammu taught me."

I squeezed the hand at my chest that was now fully solid again.

"He said as an elder it was his right to allow me into the tribe of Gutium. He said he'd forgotten that it wasn't just about blood. He talked about his wife and your mother, how they *became* Gutian. Then we argued and made up." She laughed again. "He's seriously super stubborn. Still, I get to live and die by your code now, just like the rest of the Gutians." She smiled to herself, her mind resolute.

"Lucian, that's what love is; it's all the same. I see that now more than ever. All the people of the world are *my people and your people*, and we are all singing the same song, we are all shouting this same code, aren't we? We are not alone standing against the Darkness. You feel it too, don't you? I know I'm connected to the Light right now, but I know you hear them calling you, calling *us*. That's why I have to do this, because they are *all* our people. The whole world is Gutium."

My mouth opened, but nothing came out.

How had I forgotten the people Onack had taken in? Most of the elders alongside him had come from conquered tribes. People had been integrated as equals from all parts of the world for generations, long before Onack and Ur-Nammu unified and created the code of *our* people.

Had Nefertiti's children been any less Gutian by having the blood of the Pharaoh? All of my Second-Borns were from different generations and cultures. Had blood ever really mattered when it came to *love* or *family*?

I looked back at the fight still raging behind us. They were all tearing at Caelius's grotesque spider body, which had been torn open by her Light.

Blood.

I closed my eyes, sighing.

I couldn't deny the truth she had discovered. I had been close to understanding similar truths while buried in her magma. Ur-Nammu was wise like my father and must have discovered it for himself while in exile.

Being Gutian was *never* about blood.

Another lie woven in the Darkness was broken.

I had been willing to let the whole world burn for Shea.

But she was right.

Only now did I fully understand what Bohe had meant when he said, "Remember we are *all* Gutium now."

A hand grabbed my shoulder.

It might as well have been my neck.

Caelius.

My late-blooming revelations didn't matter now.

It was too late.

How could Shea's words, how could any of their words, reach me if I was consumed again in his Darkness? I still felt his blood burning, threatening to overpower my every breath.

The hand squeezed.

I closed my eyes and did the only thing I could think of to protect her. I used all the strength I had left and pulled her into my mind, like she said I'd done before unconsciously.

Everything went black.

CHAPTER 17
SHEA

I was back on the craggy cliff face with Aidan, Moses, and Lucian. It was the aftermath of Aidan's betrayal, the part I didn't want to see. Aidan and Moses were dead, stabbed and crunched by the fall.

But what I saw in front of me wasn't what Lucian had always said happened. He had hated Aidan for killing Moses, so much so he wreaked havoc on the world for three thousand years to punish him. Lucian always talked about how he had held Moses after Aidan killed them both. Though it was true that he held Moses's hand, it was actually Aidan he held in his arms.

And his cries. I knew I wasn't there physically, but I felt my heart squeeze with agony at the sound and sight. I never knew how much Lucian loved Aidan until this moment. And his betrayal was so much deeper than stabbing their fellow brother. Aidan had taken his own life. And that had almost killed Lucian.

"Shea," Lucian said.

I looked up at him. He stood beside me, holding my hand just like last time, but unlike before, Lucian was *awake* and truly present.

Turning away from the scene was a blessing; it was too difficult to watch.

"You always told me it was Moses you held." I motioned.

"That was how I remembered it." Lucian seemed surprised at witnessing the truth in front of us.

He stared at his past self crying over Aidan's body, holding him close.

"I loved them both, but it was Aidan who brought me out of the tailspin of losing Nefertiti. We were *brothers* then. You know him. You know his spirit. He helped me . . . he changed me . . . then he took it all away, and I was more alone than before."

Lucian turned to me, a deep sadness in his eyes. "What he showed me in that brief moment was that, even though I trusted him completely, he didn't trust me. He must have always been wondering, in the back of his mind, if I would betray him and take the Vessel to Caelius.

"It only took a few words of doubt from Ur-Nammu, and Aidan was willing to die and kill Moses. My hate and anger grew with each year that passed. I longed to show him that he had created the exact monster he'd believed me to be.

"So I hunted and cornered him, each time giving him the choice: to believe in me or in the monster. I never had any intention of taking those early Vessels to Caelius. Even after Moses." Lucian shook his head. "And each time, he chose to see Lucian the Monster. And each time, my agony *grew* with his." He ran his hand through his hair in anguish. "Why are we seeing this now? What purpose do I gain by remembering the pain of this moment?"

As if to answer, the scenery changed to the memory where I seared a hole in Lucian's chest in my old dorm building.

In our last excursion to memory lane, these two memories had been shown in this order as well. It had to mean something, but what did it have to do with what was happening outside of his mind? And did it *really* matter? We were in our final battle. Aidan's brothers had given me the power to send Caelius back into Darkness. We needed to get back!

"Lucian, our physical bodies are in the battle of our lives. We can't stay here and relive your worst memories," I said. "I know you think you can somehow save me this way, but you can't. You know what I have to do."

Lucian didn't respond, he just stared at his past self where a small smile of relief crossed his face when he realized that I was alive. "That was the moment I knew I loved you."

Squeezing his hand harder, I responded gently, "I know, Lucian, you've told me that before."

He looked down at me, wonder in his eyes. "You don't understand. After Aidan, I never thought I'd love again."

"But you loved Gracuri and Duncan and all your Second-Borns to some degree, right?" I was trying to make sense of what was happening and how it could be important to the battle at hand.

"Yes, I have loved. But it wasn't the same as this. I had no hope for true love, for true happiness. There were times when my strength would falter and I'd let myself slip into false hope that I could love again. That was when I'd turn someone."

As Lucian said this, the background changed to Gracuri covered in blood with dead bodies all around him, eyes gouged out. It was gruesome, and I had to look away from the sight.

Lucian's voice was steady as he said, "But look where that hope would get me. I met beings capable of the very love I desired, and I turned them into beasts. It was a cursed cycle I knew I'd never break."

I could see the scenery changing again at my feet. I looked up, and we were in a cave. A skeleton rested against the wall as Lucian walked in carrying a large deer. Then the skeleton moved, and I knew right away that it was Duncan, desiccated, as he'd said he was when he told me this story.

Lucian dropped the deer at his feet.

"Duncan reminded me of Aidan. I didn't consciously see it at the time. I pushed my emotions down, but there was no denying his spirit was pure like Aidan's had been. The carefree way he laughed, his smile, it was so close. Then I turned him, and in his bloodlust he killed all his clansmen and family. I broke him, Shea. Broke the very thing I loved most about him. When I saw him there, almost dead, refusing to give in and drink human blood, I knew: Aidan had been right. I was the evil one, the monster. And he was right to distrust me."

In a flash, we were back at the cliff face with Lucian holding Aidan's body with one hand while holding Moses's hand with the other.

Just as quickly, we were back at the dorm building, my hand burning through his body, but his small smile was real.

Back and forth, back and forth on a loop, switching every few seconds. It made me dizzy.

"I can't seem to stop this," Lucian confessed, a tinge of fear in his voice.

"It must mean something," I said, trying to see how these two moments tied together. "But Lucian, how will this help us fight Caelius, even if you do figure it out?" My mind was racing. My mother and father were fighting as we stood trapped in Lucian's mind. I couldn't see how anything we discovered here would help us.

"I think I'm beginning to understand. Even if you lost your soul, you can't just force Caelius to leave his earthbound body by torturing him with Light. He could withstand that for eternity. We have to find a way to *convince* him. It has to be his choice." Lucian's face was animated, almost desperate.

And I realized in that moment he was right.

If Lucian thought we could find the answers in his memories, then I trusted him wholeheartedly.

"Okay," I said, pulling our clasped hands to my lips and kissing him gently. "We can do this." I tried to focus on each memory as it flashed by, but they switched too quickly for me to see any details. "Is there any way you can freeze the Moses memory?"

With some effort, Lucian halted the background so we were now staring at what was essentially a 3D photo of the scene. It was much easier to analyze this way, not having to see Lucian sob in agony in real time.

So what were we missing?

"Let's look at this objectively." I put on my detective hat, as much as I could anyway. "Your mind wants you to remember something about this moment."

"My pain? My love? My betrayal?" Lucian said in anguished tones.

He was way too close to this. I'd have to be the one to help him navigate through. "All those things, but the fact that you rewrote history in your waking life has to mean something. Why would you blank out that it was Aidan you held?"

"Too painful," he said.

But I ran with the seed of an idea. "Too painful because you began to think he was right in not trusting you, and because you felt that he was able to see you as a monster before you even knew you were a monster." Oops. I hadn't meant it like that.

Lucian didn't seem to notice, which just showed we both had serious self-esteem issues. Mine were looking far less scarring than his at the moment.

"I remember losing hope that I'd ever be able to love again." He looked at me, eyes helpless. "That was the strongest feeling I had after it all happened. It was the same feeling when my mother died."

"I feel like we're close, but that's not quite it. How would losing hope for finding love again convince Caelius to go back to shadow form?" I wondered aloud.

Lucian shrugged. "I don't know."

Nodding, I asked, "Can you show me searing that hole in your chest now?"

A small smile reached his face, and he touched my cheek with his free hand, sending shivers down my spine. How was he able to do that when my body wasn't even there? Seriously!

A 3D freeze-frame of my hand inside his chest, glowing from the Light melting his skin and bone, appeared.

Ew.

We both stared at his obvious expression of relief.

"And this is when I got my hope back that I could love again," he said.

"I don't think you're wrong. I just think we're *looking* at it wrong." I tried not to get frustrated. Losing hope and then gaining hope was huge, I felt that, but Caelius wouldn't care about that. He only cared about Lucian; he meant *everything* to Caelius. He was willing to destroy all life as we knew it just for the slight chance that Lucian would be with him.

We all knew that wasn't going to happen.

I stopped looking at past Lucian's expression and started watching my own past self's face. What had I been thinking at that moment? I tried to remember.

Then it hit me.

"At that moment, when I saw what I had done, my whole body ached with regret and loss," I said.

Lucian turned to me, surprised. "But you hated me back then."

"No, I never hated you. I didn't understand you. I was angry with you, but I never hated you. And when you tried to hurt Aidan, I acted without thinking and did . . . *that*." I nodded to the frozen scene of melted-chest. "I thought I had killed you. And it almost killed *me*."

Lucian stared at me, then looked back at the memory.

"Lucian?" The ideas were forming in my head like puzzle pieces coming together. "Do you think it wasn't that you were afraid you'd never find love again, but that you felt no one would ever love *you* again?" Before he could answer, I continued. "And this moment wasn't you realizing you were capable of loving again, but it was seeing the regret and horror in my eyes, and you knew . . ." My voice caught from emotion, but I pushed forward. "You knew that *I* loved you."

Lucian's eyes found mine, and he pulled me into his chest. "I would never have presumed, not back then."

"But you can see it, here, in this memory. *I* can see it. My whole face, my eyes—I loved you, and you saw a glimpse of it, not daring to believe it, turning it into your own obsession." The words felt right. I was onto something.

Lucian pulled back. Taking both hands and cupping my face, he looked at me as if I were the only thing that existed in his world. "Yes. Even when Gracuri or my other children expressed their love, I never believed it because they had my blood in their veins. I never gave them the chance to love me when they were human, so I never knew if their love was real or not. And I never believed it was. And if Aidan was willing to die and kill Moses with only a few words from Ur-Nammu, it meant he never really loved me either." I was about to argue, but Lucian stopped me, continuing. "I know that's not true now, but back then it was my only truth and why I turned so bitterly against him."

"This is it, Lucian. This is the connection we need to convince Caelius to give up his physical form. All he wants is for you to *love* him, and he can't seem to force you to do it. You know how he feels. For thousands of years you believed you were unworthy of love because of what Aidan did to Moses, and you relived it every five hundred years until you met me." I pulled his head down to mine so we were forehead to forehead. "And I love you with every fiber of my being. I truly love you. Even knowing and seeing all the horrible things you've done, I still love you."

"I love you more than my life, but I can't love Caelius. I can never love Caelius. I'll never be able to give him what he wants." Lucian seemed panicked.

"You can't love him because he tries to force you to, but if he can see that sacrifice is the key to your heart, he might let go." I knew I was right, but I also knew what I had to do to get Caelius into a position to actually hear Lucian out.

Lucian instantly saw it in my eyes. "No. I'll try to talk to him, but we don't need you to sacrifice yourself. I can do it without you."

Tears came to my eyes. "You know that's not true. You need me to lock him down, and the only way to do that is the Lightbomb Aidan's brothers armed me with."

"But your soul will evaporate!" Lucian screamed, unable to hold back.

I was terrified but resolved. I nodded. "Yes, but it'll be worth it."

"Not for me! Not for anyone who knows you! I can't, Shea. I can't!" Lucian looked like a caged animal.

Our surroundings changed again, and we were standing in the empty bedroom of our villa in Paris. "We can stay here for a long time. No matter what happens outside, we'll be safe. Not even Caelius can fully reach us. You know this from before when you collapsed after the sundial, and I leapt into the vacuum of your mind. My memories of us in Paris are the one thing the Darkness can't dissolve completely."

"Lucian," I whispered. "We can't."

"But we can!" he insisted. "I'm keeping you here. You're *mine*, and I won't let you go. I won't lose you!"

"And now who do you sound like?" I said, knowing it would hurt, but also knowing he'd see more clearly how he'd be able to connect to Caelius.

Lucian flinched, and my heart nearly broke, then he said softly, "I'll die without you."

I reached up and brought him down to my lips, kissing him with all the love and passion I had in me. Pulling away with tears streaming down my face, I said, "Then we'll die together, saving the ones we love."

"I will love you forever." Lucian kissed me again.

"I will love you forever," I repeated.

It was time.

Chapter 18
Lucian

When my eyes jerked open, the hand released my shoulder as Molly sat down next to us, the memory over. Her clothes were splattered with the black ink of Caelius's blood. "Don't worry, we have some time. They're still going at it." She motioned behind her. "But that won't be enough to kill him; he's already getting his power back."

Shea was cradled in my arms. She reached past me and grabbed her mother's hand. "That's why I have to finish this, Mom, even if I have to die doing it. We need to give Lucian time to talk to Caelius. I can weaken him, then Lucian can convince him to turn back to his shadow form."

Molly patted me reassuringly before I could retort. "Don't worry, Lucian, it's not the job of the daughter to die before her mother." Her eyes were kind, but her words carried a loving authority I had not heard in thousands of years, not since they'd last been spoken by my own mother on her deathbed. "It's okay.

I know what's best, child."

"Mom, *please*, I have to—"

"Sh." She brushed Shea's cheek, and as she did, it became more solid.

I squeezed Shea's arms; they were fatty and flesh. Her lips regained their pinkish hue. She shook her head no, her eyes locked with Molly's. "Listen to me, Mom, this is serious! This is what I was made for!"

"Sacrifice." Molly took a deep breath. "It's one of the Light's most powerful moves: to sacrifice yourself wholly and completely. That's why it's in the Gutian code, right? It's not just about fighting for those you love." She addressed me, but her eyes stayed on her daughter. "Lucian, you were right to give up last time in order to save them. You weren't disgracing your people, you were honoring them."

She kissed Shea's forehead. "You are so *brave*, my little girl. To think at one time I had you safe in my belly." Tears rolled down her cheeks, and Shea's followed. "And now you are strong enough to sacrifice yourself for the world. My precious, beautiful baby."

Molly looked up at my desperate face. "I'm going to be the one to save her this time."

She gently pushed me aside and pulled Shea out of my arms and into hers, squeezing her tight. She whispered, "It's a mother's job to sacrifice herself for her daughter. It's always been a mother's job. That's what Light is: the mother, the creator of *all*, who loves its children more than anything."

I felt helpless watching as they wept together, and Shea continued to protest in vain.

"Light is the *mother*, you say?" Caelius's voice stopped all of ours. "Then I guess I am the *father*. And what She creates, I will happily destroy." A darkness swept from behind us, followed by the screams of everyone left on the battlefield. They were pierced and pinned down just as Nefertiti's daughters had been in the last battle, before he'd gouged their necks open and sucked out their lives. I could see by the hate spilling off of Caelius's ghastly form that this was all repeating, except this time there would be no one left to tell the tale once he was done.

He rose upward like the base of a spider, lifting above his long clawed legs, hovering in the sky like the god he thought he was. "Besides, what do *you* know of the Light, hag? The Light and I have been together since the dawn of time, and even I don't understand Her. What could you possibly know that I do not?"

I stood up, placing my body between them and Caelius. "Even as a mortal, I know more about the Light than you." That came out wrong.

He leapt into the air, landing over us in an instant. "Careful, boy!" he sneered. "Or the next *makeover* I give you won't be as gentle."

"Love." My voice quivered as I shot a quick, knowing glance to Shea. "I know more about the Light because I know *love*. Tell me, Caelius, what have you been wrestling with this whole time, trying to understand, trying to know for yourself through me?" My voice was shaky, but my determination was resolute. I wasn't sure what Molly had been talking about, how she could sacrifice herself instead of Shea, but if I could persuade him now, Shea wouldn't lose her soul. Maybe my words would be enough to pin him down. As convincing as she was, I wasn't going to lose her.

He encased us in the coils of his twisted black limbs, pulling me close to his face as he wrapped his other claw around Shea, covering her mouth. His incisors grew as he spoke in heated gasps. "You, mutt-child of *Gutium*! What do *you* know of love? What do *you* know of sacrifice? *I* was willing to give up that Vessel bitch's soul. *I* was willing to give up becoming whole, all so that I could keep you. In all of my existence, I have never chosen to give up power. I have never cared for anything as I have for *you*!"

He was right.

Like the rest of us, he had changed too.

There were so many new emotions he had been trying to hide, but they were evident, even here, as he shook us in his fists. This wasn't the same monster that had pierced his claw through my chest in our last battle. He was holding me so I couldn't move, but he wasn't *hurting* me this time. If anything, even as he squeezed the others tighter, he held me gently.

As angry as his voice sounded, there was something else there, something I'd seen evolve over our time together but hadn't named. In truth, I hadn't *wanted* to name it. I'd explained and written it off because of what he was doing to me then.

But Shea had helped me bring it to light through my memories.

And here it was again.

In this momen, I knew him as I knew myself.

Shea was right.

Caelius wanted to be *loved*.

Perhaps now was the right time, and I could fight *my way*, as Bohe had suggested. Perhaps the nightmare of Shea's death didn't have to be a reality.

Caelius shook me again for emphasis. "The moment I saw

you, La-Narru, by the river in Gutium, the moment you called me God, I *wanted* you, and I can't stop—I've tried. I can't control you or change your affections to return what I feel. It's Shea now, but it was Nefari then. And once I kill Shea, it will be someone else. If you understand the Light more than I, then tell me what I have to do to make you *love* me. Tell me now, and I might spare your precious Vessel's life!"

Fear and loneliness accompanied by an ache to be understood and loved in return—I knew these words well and had spoken them myself over the centuries. I had threatened Moses before Aidan, Gunnhild before Ashgar, Gracuri before Bohe, David before Duncan. On and on, one after another, I had threatened Vessels, angels, and Second-Borns, daring them to love me even though I couldn't love myself. I'd threatened the world, daring it to *make* me understand.

And finally, it had.

"Alone." My lips moved on their own, and his gaze followed the sound, awaiting my answer.

"Finally willing to speak up, darling, now that the offer to spare your whore is on the table!" He laughed painfully to himself. "Of course, always defending your precious *family*!"

"Such isolation and loneliness," I whispered, feeling the words sail like arrows through my own chest.

"How dare you speak as if you know anything of the isolation of *Darkness*." He jerked his head, spit landing on my face.

"I tried to talk to you before, to tell you what I've only recently come to understand. You're not alone, Caelius. Loneliness is a lie, a lie *you* created. In our despair as mortals, we believe that lie when we experience loss. But it's not true, is it? The love I've had and the love of those passed is with me now, even in all of this. They are here by my side. I was *never* alone."

He pulled me to his chest, finally squeezing me as tight as the others. "I told you to be careful. I don't want to hear about your love of swine and their continued obsession with you."

"Or what, you'll kill me?" I scoffed.

He stared at my insolence, dumbfounded; even he was blind to how much he had changed. The Caelius that might have accidentally taken my life in blind fury a year ago was too afraid to lose me, and now I knew why.

His teeth receded as he brought me closer to his face. "What are you offering then?" His eyes sent shivers over my skin as he looked over every inch of it. "Another bargain, perhaps?"

"Would you take it?"

I could see Shea struggling against his grasp, screaming into the fat of his thick spider-arm. She thought it was her turn to die, but I would die a thousand times if it meant the salvation of her soul.

He hesitated, searching my features for a tell. "It would be a lie. I would *know* that this time, boy."

"I think you knew it last time."

He winced, then scowled. "Aren't we cocky?"

I cleared my throat. "Even knowing, would you take the deal? My imprisonment for their freedom—not just Shea's, but the world's."

"I would." There was no hesitation in his voice now. "But you will be fully conscious this time as you give yourself over to me; no blood, no memory wipe, no Nefertiti or Vessel, no games. There will be no one else, just you and me traveling this land for all eternity. I've said this before—you're all I've wanted since I became flesh. *That's* the deal."

I swallowed, realizing what immortality with him would be like: my own unimaginable handcrafted hell. I had created a plan with Shea to convince him to go back to Darkness, but she wanted that plan to include her sacrifice, along with words that could reach him after. But I couldn't sacrifice her, and even though I was a poet as a boy, now my tongue knew nothing of the art. This wasn't the best way, but it was *a way* for them all to live. And that's what mattered most. "If that's what it takes to save them, it's a dea—"

"And that's what you don't understand about sacrifice." Molly's voice was soft, but her authority commanded his attention. "Devotion isn't a *bargain*. It's not something you manipulate and force. If you truly cared for Lucian, you would prioritize his happiness over your own selfish desires. You'd give up your mortal form and go back to being Darkness and let him go because that's what *he* needs."

She sighed. "You've never been a parent. I can't expect you to understand what I mean, but surrendering your power to get what you want is not the same as sacrificing your life. Lucian gave his *life* to save Shea. She tried to do the same. And I would die for my daughter."

Caelius shook his head and laughed, as if the thought was ludicrous. "You would have me *die* to prove myself, *Mother*? How convenient that would be for you and your little Vessel; me dead and all of you holding hands. Don't make me sick."

She pulled her arm out of his grip and cupped his cheek. To my surprise, he let her hold him like that as she spoke. "It's what the Light would do."

"Is it now? Is that what the *Light* and everyone else would do? Do you really believe in that stupid code his fat father Onack made? He was just a man, but I am a *god*! Why should *I* follow such human drivel?" He shook all of us in rage.

When he stopped, his limbs sagged. "This is exhausting. I'm *tired*," he choked out, his voice cracking for the first time. "I'm not *supposed* to be in mortal form, you dumb cow. It's proven . . . difficult. Even I have my limits."

He shifted his eyes back toward mine. "Last chance, boy. Take the deal, or I kill them all in seconds, and you'll be mine anyway."

I gaped. Of course I would take the deal, but Molly, without knowing what Shea and I had discovered, was circling the revelation. I looked at her hopelessly.

Molly nodded, not letting me speak. "I know you're tired, Grandfather. It's okay." Her tone was so motherly, even I felt somewhat reassured by its promise. "It's been hard for you, and there's so much you haven't understood."

"That being said"—he jerked from her embrace—"I am not the *Light*. It's always giving up pieces of itself to save its pathetic little creations. That is not *my* way. By nature it is not. By nature I am the opposite; I am different from everything that is or was. There is Light, and there is Darkness. The one remaining truth is that we are *not* the same. I am not created by the Light. Just as it exists, I am a singularity."

"And yet here you are." She leaned closer. "And yet you took this *bargain*. What were you looking so desperately for in this playground of the Light? What were you trying to understand after eons of being what you've always been? Can't even the

Darkness want to change?"

He paused, and the wind around us grew still, as if it had been sucked out into the vacuum of space. "I don't know."

"That's not true."

I was astounded; Molly Harper was talking to Darkness as if he were a rebellious teenager. She was speaking for me while I gathered my thoughts in her shadow.

"Ever since I became mortal, I've felt strange. I've been searching for . . ."

"Is strange really the word? And searching? Haven't you already found what you were looking for?"

"I thought I found it"—he tilted his head toward me—"when I found him."

"But you couldn't hold on to it?" Her voice was low as she leaned even closer to him. "You considered it worthwhile enough to come here, to suffer in this small form just to understand it."

"I was patient," he spat, "like you're supposed to be with fragile things. I waited. I didn't pluck his life until the humans snipped his string for me. I let him have the experiences he would have had, and after that he was supposed to choose *me*. He *promised* to be mine. He was supposed to be grateful, he was supposed to—"

"Love you."

He froze, blinking at her soft round face.

"Yes, of course."

There was a long pause.

I was still unsure of what to say. For all of the things that I had felt for Caelius, *true* love was never one of them. Even now, I understood him, pitied him even, but I did not *love* him, and

I never would.

I squeezed my fists. This was what I needed to convey, that *my* love didn't matter.

I wasn't what he needed.

How could I make him understand what had taken me thousands of years to realize? How could I reach him, now, when he was vulnerable and open?

This might be my only chance.

I had to follow Molly's lead, as inarticulate as my dry tongue felt. "But love is in everything the Light touches, Caelius, even you!" I shouted, breaking their silent gaze.

When his eyes met mine they were sadder than before, and I could see the tiredness he had spoken of. He looked ancient and weathered, so unlike a pompous lord strutting his arrogant wishes over humanity, over me. "The Light doesn't touch the Darkness, boy, so it is not *in* me." He half smiled, but there was no humor to it, only desire. "As I have been *in* you, I know what I speak of."

"But—" I was thrown off by the lingering lust in his gaze. "I don't know how long you were watching me for, but the morning I met you . . . was the night after my Harrowing, wasn't it?"

He eyed me up and down. "Of course I was there."

I swallowed. I thought that might've been the case; I had watched a fair share of my Second-Borns before turning them.

"So you saw it." I paused, remembering that night vividly. It wasn't uncommon for cultures, even now, to have a rite of passage for boys becoming men. In Gutium, however, it hadn't been gender specific; all children underwent the Harrowing, and that was what I'd been, a *child*. It was worse for me. My mother had just died, and instead of waiting three more years, my father decided that if I was old enough to cause her death, then I was old enough to become a man.

Others had to last a night in the mountains alone, but as the son of our leader I had to survive a week. It was his verdict, and I believed it a fitting punishment for her loss. It was brutal. I had barely learned to speak, let alone hold a bowl, and there I was . . . in the black woods, lost and alone.

He tilted his head, eyeing my scowling face. "It is the reason you called me God and reached for me the next morning, not yet understanding what I was." He looked at me for a long while, pained by his own words. "You were afraid then, as you are now." His eyes saddened further by the truth of his most treasured memory. "You've always been afraid of the dark."

"Yes." I nodded. It was not only an innate fear for all humans, it was something that had terrified me specifically as a child because of the Harrowing. Even so . . . "That last night, I discovered something in the dark before I met you."

His eyes flashed, his interest piqued. This was a conversation he'd never thought of having. "You don't speak of the days surrounding your mother's death often. And your memory of the next morning with me has been all but forgotten." He bit his bottom lip, salivating. "Isn't this a mistake, Lucian?"

He bit harder until there was blood. My teeth grew in anticipation. It was an enticing threat. I watched as it moved from his chin down his neck.

"Think clearly, lover. The more I learn about you, the easier it will be to take you apart later. You know that by now, don't you? I will hold nothing back next time."

"I know." I swallowed, *thirsty*. I had to force my gaze from the red of his blood to that of his eyes. I wouldn't let him stop me from saying what I should have said as a boy, instead of mistakenly calling him God.

"After feeling the fear of night and crying for my mother, I was lost for days. Alone, I lay on my back clutching my stomach, ready to die from the unyielding pains of starvation. It was then that I saw the full light of the moon. It had been there the whole time, but in my terror, I had only looked down, never up. Then as I walked, easily finding the path back home, I also noticed the stars. There were so many, it was overwhelming; I felt . . . that I wasn't alone anymore.

"There are daytime things we forget about in the dark— things we take for granted, things we get too afraid of or blinded by. But I saw it then. I've forgotten it a million times over, just like you have, but the light of those stars, they stood *with me* in the dark. They were *inside* of it, just as they are inside of you."

He sighed, moving his fingers through thick pitch-black hair. "Is that what you think?"

"Yes." I wrung my hands nervously. I needed to drive the point home. "I should have told you then; the Light is not *separate* from you. It's not standing in opposition fighting some ongoing war over territory. It is a part of you, just as you are a part of it. You have never been alone.

"Just as the moon carried me home when I was lost, the Light has been by your side this whole time, *loving* you." I thought of Shea and those I'd turned. I thought of Aidan and Bohe, Gracuri and Duncan, all the people who loved me, but I hadn't been able to see it, all because of a lie . . . the same lie Caelius was caught in.

"Can't you see it in the world it's created? Day and night,

summer and winter, up and down, everything coming in pairs to create and sustain more life that then gives way to death. It didn't strive to make a world *without* you; out of love, it etched you into the existence of all things, just like our Gutian code. It never stopped loving the Darkness who thinks he is alone.

"Without asking you to change, it will *always* love you. Out of all the things that do change, that has remained the same. You are worthy of love, Caelius. The Light knows it more than all of us, paying homage to your existence in everything it touches."

His claw moved from around my waist, craning my head forward to meet his. "That night, I was taken in by *your* light, boy. That's why I spoke with you that next morning. You were radiating something I couldn't touch, and I fell for you—for that something I saw in your gaze. Then you called me God, and I was never the same."

I opened my mouth but hesitated.

He sighed again. Our faces were so close that his hot breath moved over my cheek. "And now you say you were radiating with the knowledge that Light and Darkness are one." He brushed his lips over mine. The blood was dry now, but I had to use all of my strength not to lick it clean.

I jerked my head away.

He wrapped his darkened limb over my mouth as if hiding the temptation from himself as well. Shea and I now matched, our bodies and our voices muted. He leaned back, lowering his legs to the ground and us with him.

He looked up into the sky at the moon blocked by brilliant rays of sun. "Through the mouth of babes, huh, Light?" He glanced at me and chuckled to himself. "And what a *mouth* it is."

He stared back up for a long while, analyzing my words. "To think these humans could forget something you and I have known for all of time." He squeezed all of us a little tighter. "To think that even *I* could forget."

His shoulders slumped. "Do you still shine upon me, even now? Do you not despise me, Light, for all I have taken from you in my forgetting? For all I *will* take, even now that I know?" He readied himself, shifting his eyes from the sky to the sand covering the tops of his feet.

The wind finally returned in the vacuum his powerful emotions had created. It flowed past us and circled him for a fraction of a moment. It was so brief and subtle that if I hadn't been a vampire I would have missed it.

"Is that truly what you believe, Light?" He laughed to himself—the disheartened laugh of the defeated. "That's your answer then? In a small still voice, just like always. Patient. Gentle. Constant." He sighed again, returning his gaze to the sun. "How annoying." He paused. "Not that I don't like it." His chin raised higher toward the blue that veiled the blackened night and its stars. "This whole time, it was *me* then. I was the one who didn't understand *you*, not the other way around."

Slowly he released his hold on all of us, his shape returning to that of a man's. I ran to Shea's weakened body and propped her up in my arms. She clung to me, pulling my Hanfu into a ball at my chest.

"Don't you *ever* think about sacrificing yourself again!" She was trying to yell, but it came out low and hoarse. I held her close, knowing it might be the last time. If anything, Caelius was unpredictable.

He still might kill us all.

And as I thought his name, his gaze met mine.

"You really do love her." His tone was even more deflated. "Even though I offered you immortality, unlimited power, and a seat to rule the world and all we touched . . . if only you'd stay by my side."

I nodded reluctantly, not wanting to provoke him. "I would choose her every time, for all of time."

He stumbled back, as if struck. "Of course you would."

"But the Light chose *you*."

"So it said." He smiled wryly. "But I want to hear it from *your* lips. Tell me again, boy. Tell me in a persuasive way that only a poet born of a warring race could. Tell me of love and loneliness, La-Narru, and this time, and only this time . . . I will listen. So make it *convincing*."

I cleared my throat. It was always unnerving when he spoke my childhood name. I wished that I had kept writing poetry, that I had searched relics over the ages for wisdom like Bohe had, instead of power. I sighed, trying to remember that it was the inarticulate child by the river in Gutium who had won his heart the first time. It was La-Narru he had fallen for, and at the heart of me still lived that boy, no matter how much I had hidden him from the world.

"I'm sorry, Caelius." I held Shea tighter. "Looking back on it now, I can see that I was never meant to be by your side."

He stumbled again. "Gentle now."

I swallowed. "I was always meant to be the *messenger*. You weren't supposed to keep me. You saw the boy but not the message of love that the Light had written for *you* in the stars that night. I think the Light gave you the chance to become flesh so that you could watch us and learn—so that you could embrace each other again."

I took in a sharp breath, trying to steady myself. "The Light risked all of its *favorite* creations by having you come here. It even sent a piece of itself to be carried by a human Vessel so that you wouldn't be alone, trapped and imprisoned forever. It didn't stop you from devouring Aidan's brothers, its beloved angels. It hasn't tried to stop you, has it? Only the free will of its creations has ever stood in your way. And you act as if you're not loved." I scoffed.

Caelius's eyes widened.

"You are more loved than *all* of us." My body began to shake in fury. "You, who are more loved than all of creation, forgot? How absurd. How . . . human." I laughed as Caelius's look of shock grew. "You who have been jealous of *me*. You who are a part of us just as much as the Light. You are loved no matter what you do, no matter how you change or don't." As my resentment grew, I felt something else overshadow it: the same peace I'd felt as a boy staring up at the moon. In truth, there was so much love in the universe, and we were *all* a part of it.

A solitary tear ran down Caelius's face.

I gasped unintentionally at the sight.

He tilted his head, as if rolling the words around. "How very human indeed." He played with a chunk of his hair. "I suppose it is possible that the Light loves me as much as I love *you*." His gaze moved back to the sky. "I feel it reaching, trying to hold me, arms that have been outstretched since the dawn of creation. Arms I ignored, then forgot existed, even in my longing for them." He chuckled to himself. "The prodigal son returns. After all this time, after what I've done and who I am, the Light still cares for Darkness. What an idiot."

He peered into the sky. "It has a better personality than I do. Out of all our games, I suppose it won this one." He reached up and spread his fingers, letting the sunlight fall through them, casting a shadowed hand over his face. "I'll win the next one though."

He lowered his hand and touched his face, moving his thumb along the wet trail at his cheek. "Crying, that's a first for me, even though you weaklings do it all the time." He scoffed even as his voice cracked. "I don't get why it's supposed to be *healing* or why it was created as a function to a mortal body." He sniffed, wiping his nose on his arm. "It's disgusting." He patted his face dry, shaking his head. "It's a strange sort of release, different from destruction, but . . . I suppose I do feel better for having done it."

His gaze met mine. "How cringeworthy and cheesy your little poem was. You should be embarrassed. You spoke less, but it meant more when you were a child. Still . . . despite your failings, I do understand that I am loved and not alone anymore and blah, blah, blah."

This time the weariness I had seen in his gaze faded, as if the fatigue of time itself, the burden of it, was gone for a brief moment. He extended his shadow out to me. I flinched as it patted me on the head. "Don't worry. You did well enough."

He retracted it, then balled his hand into a fist at his chest.

"I know where I'm wanted. I'm ready then. I'll go." He squeezed his fist until the knuckles paled. "And I'll do it for *you*, La-Narru. *I'll* be the god you need this time. Not because of your little speech or the Light's lame confessions."

He unclenched his fist and reached it toward me. "But there's still a price. I can't pop this mortal flesh without the *key*." His nails extended. "I need the Vessel's soul to become whole, to give up this contract and return home. It's why the Light sent her, after all. I'm sorry, my love, but as we all have a purpose, this was always hers."

I followed his outstretched fingertips toward Shea.

My mind was reeling. "No, I won't—"

She kissed me hard. I blinked, staring at her face as she poured her passion into it. She pulled back with the intent of leaving the embrace and stepping forward. I clung to her, not letting her go. "I lost you once."

"We'll be together again someday," Shea said with a small smile as she eyed our entire family. "All of us."

Caelius's nails retracted as Molly stepped between him and her daughter. "I told you, Shea, that's *not* your purpose."

"Mom?" She leaned toward her as I steadied her trembling legs.

"Caelius, *I* am the mother." She walked up to him and took his outstretched hand in hers. "I felt her life in my womb. I held and kissed her tiny fingers in my arms as she cried. I have watched her and loved her all of my life. If she is the Vessel, I am the vessel that held the Vessel. I am the child of your two First-Borns. *I* am the key to bringing you home. That is why her soul broke you out of the cage but has eluded you since. It was never meant for that." She looked at Shea with affection. "I love you."

"Mom, no!" Shea lunged forward, and I followed her.

Caelius's shadow emerged around the ground at our feet and held us in place *easily*. It was only then that I realized just how much he'd been holding back. This whole time he'd been playing a long game, not to win against the Vessel, but to win my affections over time.

He could have effortlessly killed all of us, the whole world in fact, with one flood of his overwhelming power. He was Darkness itself: a force just as vastly immense as the Light.

He stepped toward Molly, then looked again at the sky. "Is this how it is, old friend? I would have *preferred* to take the whore." He talked for a while longer under his breath, as if arguing. He tilted his head toward us. "Although death would be quick for her, taking her mother will elongate her suffering. That's not a bad deal, but I still want the girl."

Molly squeezed his hand. "I know you want her, but I am the mother and it is my place."

"Mom, no! It has to be me, please!" Caelius's shadow covered Shea's mouth. I clung to her as if my insignificant arms were strong enough to save her from the power of his oblivion.

"Fine," he snapped at Molly, then met my desperate gaze with resolution. "It would feel good for a while, but I supposed watching Lucian stumble around miserably for the rest of his days without me being able to comfort him would bother me, even in abstract form." He licked his incisors. As much as he'd tried to fill his words with callousness, to harden the vulnerability he now felt, it was still visible on his face. After all this time, the truth that the Light had been trying to reach him with was already bridging the gap, and he was changing more rapidly than before.

"Come then, *Mother*, give me your little soul, and I'll leave this world . . . forever." He flinched with that last word as if struck by a heavy blow, the weight and weariness returning briefly to his eyes. This time doubt met my gaze as he looked over my body with longing.

"But you won't be going back to who you were before, Caelius." My words rushed in to displace his fears.

"What I am, not *who*, child. I am not human." He shrugged, a smile spreading from one side of his mouth to the other. "And yet a *human*, one that I have tortured to make mine, offers me this simple truth in my final hours as a mortal. Even I'm not foolish enough to turn down such a decadent deal, boy: the Light as company, the memories of our time together, and your words. It's not a bad trade. All I have to do is forfeit this sad flesh-sack." He pinched his own arm in disgust. "It wouldn't have been able to hold me in an appealing form for much longer anyhow, and I wouldn't have wanted you to see me otherwise."

He laughed, and this time it wasn't full of malicious intent or hate; it was hearty and wild—wild like dark nights in the forest with howling animals and strange eyes. Then it struck me: for all of the order and stability of Light, Darkness was the unknown that Light pulled its creations *from*. They were each other's soul mates, one the completion of the other.

I looked at Caelius somewhat anew. Was it thrilling for a being like Light to have something unknown existing beside it? I moved my hand unconsciously through Shea's hair. The unknown parts of her, I wanted to seek all of them out, all of her corners and vast spaces, to know her and lose her, only to know her again, throughout every world and every lifetime.

That was what the Light had felt for Darkness all this time. What would change for Caelius now that he remembered the

Light's affections? What would change for all of us existing inside their eternal dance?

"Think on me, won't you, boy?" Caelius's words penetrated my thoughts, his shadow moving intimately along my spine.

"You said that those who have loved you and passed are with you now. They think of you, and you remember them. You may not have cared for me, but I have always *loved* you. Will you answer this last request, as the child at the base of a mountain who looked at me in wonder and thought me a god?" As wild and untamable as his eyes had been before, they shifted with every word he spoke. They were uncertain, inexperienced, and afraid— the other aspects being in Darkness produced for mankind.

I bit my bottom lip. "I will. I can never forget you, Caelius." For better or worse.

He sighed in relief, then squeezed Molly's hand. "It would have been nice for you to call me *God* one last time, but, things being as they are . . ." He pressed his other palm against Molly's chest. A light emanated and moved like pieces of stardust into his veins. "I will rest in your love for a good long while, old friend. It's been an eternity, hasn't it, since we've embraced Light to Darkness?" Molly's light ceased, and it filled Caelius like white spots sprayed on black canvas. He began lifting into the air as her body fell limp and cold to the earth.

Finally Caelius's shadow released us.

"Mom!" Shea shouted. She ran to her side. I followed her but stopped as Caelius floated between us.

Another trick?

The thought flashed through my mind.

I was foolish to think he would change.

Now he was all-powerful.

Now there would be no stopping him.

I gazed up at him in rage.

But his face . . . his whole body became black and started to fill in with the cosmos above us. He reached down and kissed my lips. As much as it was cold and foreign, his form shifting, there was an abiding tenderness there.

"Goodbye, Lucian. I cannot create life, but you were and will always be the only living thing I loved and named as my own. And like a good puppy, you led me back home to myself and to the Light. For that, I will be forever grateful." His face was evaporating, but I could feel the Cheshire smirk lingering on his lips. His red irises danced like flames, flickering over my skin one last time before he dissolved completely.

And just like that, the being Caelius was no more.

And just like that, balance was restored to the universe: Light and Dark in their *rightful* place.

But now they were no longer separated by an idea that had turned into a lie, that had gained power over the one that had created it and caused the Darkness and the world to suffer in loneliness.

Now they were one, as Shea and I could finally be.

They were together, and all of humanity, all of life, and all of us . . . were finally free.

CHAPTER 19
SHEA

5 YEARS LATER

"**M**ommy, do I have to wear this tie? It makes me choke. Are you *trying* to choke me?"

I stared down at my little boy with his oh-so-serious expression and tried not to laugh. He looked so much like La-Narru it made my heart sing every time I saw him. Even though it had been difficult to get used to at first, I completely understood why Lucian wanted to be called by his birth name, his *true* name. Now I didn't even think about it anymore. He was just my La-Narru, a name that meant "the way home" in his native tongue.

I shook my head at Ash with a smile. "No, I'm not trying to choke you. Go ahead and take it off, but keep your jacket on."

Ash was short for Ashliel. He was named after Aidan's brother, who'd sacrificed himself to trap Caelius in his "human" prison all those years ago. It felt right. We did it for Aidan, and he was honored. Even though I'd been mad at his brothers after our final battle with Caelius for juicing me up with a Light-bomb that would have evaporated my soul, Ashliel had still made the ultimate sacrifice to save humanity. His memory deserved to live on. And it would, through our little boy.

Ash's four-year-old hands happily yanked off the clip-on bow tie at the neck of his adorable little tuxedo. He let out a huge sigh of relief as if I had intentionally tried to choke him.

Dang, he was cute.

I was still amazed that Ash even existed. He was only possible because Helena cured Lucian. A few months after my mother's sacrifice and Caelius's return to Darkness, Helena discovered that vampirism could be eradicated like a disease. One injection of the formula she made destroyed the last of Caelius's blood in a vampire's system, turning them back into a human.

A cure.

An actual cure.

Even a few years later, it still stunned me.

Helena said it wouldn't have been possible if Caelius was still in human form and his blood tied to the mortal world, but as Darkness, it had no solid connection to Earth anymore and therefore could be eliminated. Essentially, in scientific terms, Caelius's blood was a virus and her serum was the cure.

I wished my mother was alive to see it. She would have been cured and a proud grandma to Ash. My heart still hurt thinking of how she had sacrificed her life for everyone, for me. It was easier now that five years had passed, but the wound would bubble up whenever I thought of her. I missed her so much.

As I looked at myself in the mirror in my wedding gown, I wished she was here with me. I could feel her sometimes: her presence, her love. It had taken me a long time to get to this place of peace, and if I was being honest, I wasn't sure I'd ever truly be okay with what had happened, but I was happy in this moment, and I knew she would be too.

It was my wedding day, for crying out loud!

"Why are we the only two stuck in this room? I want to go see Uncle Aidan," Ash complained.

"Are you sure it's Uncle Aidan you want to see?" I teased, knowing full well Ash had a crush on Aidan and Meky's daughter, Lulu. Lulu was only two months older than Ash and pretty much the most beautiful little girl ever. It made perfect sense of course, considering she was half Egyptian princess, half celestial being. Not to mention the fact that she was the sweetest, most mild-tempered child in the history of all children, or at least compared to Ash anyway. Stubborn, willful, and intensely passionate pretty much summed him up, which made him quite a handful at times. Like father, like son.

Ash sighed, his voice sounding a lot older than his actual four years of existence. "You can tease me, Mommy, but I plan on making Lulu my girlfriend. She's the prettiest girl in the whole world, and I love her a lot."

My heart melted. "Well, I didn't know it was so serious. I won't tease you again," I said with as much sincerity as I could muster, though all I really wanted to do was scoop him up in my arms and kiss his cheeks a million times. "And we're here alone because I thought it'd be nice to spend some time with my little boy before you and Grandpa walk me down the aisle."

"I guess, but I'm not that little." Ash looked contemplative, then said, "You look really pretty, Mommy."

"Thank you, sweetie. That means the world to me." I leaned

down and kissed the top of his head, and he smiled.

I smoothed out the cream satin fabric as I stood back up and looked in the mirror. I felt like a movie star, wearing a form-fitting dress that trailed out into a long train. I loved how the strapless neckline framed my face and hair but hoped that I wouldn't get cold in the evening. Maybe the long, bouncy waves that Meky had spent hours curling for me would give me some kind of warmth.

There was a knock on the door and through it came Aidan's muffled voice. "I know you said you wanted to be alone, but we have a slight emergency out here."

I nodded to Ash to open the door, and he made a mad dash to the knob, throwing open the door as if he expected to see a fire. "What's the emergency?"

Aidan smiled at Ash's intense expression. "Hold on, little man. I said 'slight' emergency, and I was actually lying. I just wanted to see the bride before she heads down the aisle."

Ash almost looked disappointed but waved his hand out to welcome Aidan into the room.

Aidan's eyes widened when he saw me. "You look stunning."

I hugged him tightly. "Thank you. How's everyone doing out there?"

We separated from our hug, and he laughed. "Well, La-Narru is more excited than I've ever seen him. You did make him wait for five years. He actually smiled for ten minutes straight, if you can believe that."

"I can't. And I didn't make him wait; I just wanted it to be perfect, and sometimes that takes time. But continue," I said with a laugh.

"Meky is trying to organize everyone and everything. I think you picked the perfect wedding coordinator. She's found her calling in life. She says it's just like organizing a battle, but without all the blood." Aidan smiled again.

"I'm sure that's not far from the truth. Though I am a bit worried about the 'leftovers.' " And by "leftovers" I meant the vampires who had eluded Nefertiti and Helena's grasp. The two women had not taken the serum that cured vampirism because they'd made it their new mission to hunt down every vampire on the planet and force-inject them with the cure.

It wasn't surprising that a large portion of vampires didn't want to lose their immortality and super strength. Those of us who'd fought Caelius, however, knew that the vampire "disease" needed to be eradicated, whether the vampires wanted it or not. More importantly, there was a whole faction of vampires that enjoyed killing, loved that they were a predatory species, and only thought of humans as food. They needed to be taken out.

Nefertiti and Helena had volunteered to hunt the last of them down. Helena had invented a device that was able to track Caelius's blood, so they knew there were exactly 234 vampires left in the world, not counting them and Duncan. Duncan desperately wanted to be human again, but his sense of duty was a stronger pull, and he wanted to help turn every last vampire human.

Lucian had called it "self-penance" and tried to talk Duncan out of it, mainly because he felt guilty about turning Duncan in the first place. But Duncan was stubborn, and he wanted to feel as if he had righted his wrongs in this lifetime. Tracking down vampires seemed like the only thing that would satiate his guilt.

Aidan understood the meaning of "leftovers," code for vampires, so Ash wouldn't know what I was talking about. Aidan also understood why I was worried about possible vampires wanting to crash the wedding of Lucian the First-Born. Killing La-Narru would be like winning a trophy to any vampire left.

Aidan shook his head. "My brothers are hiding this church from anyone with Caelius's blood in them. I had to bring Nefertiti, Helena, and Duncan myself or they never would've been able to find it. I'm pretty sure my brothers did this as a thank-you for returning Caelius to Darkness, by the way."

I couldn't trust Aidan's brothers after they duped me into being a Light-bomb for Caelius. "I appreciate the gesture. That was nice of them," I mumbled under my breath.

Picking up on my state of awkwardness, Aidan changed the subject. "Your dad is beside himself with excitement to walk you down the aisle. I don't know if he's happier for you or *La-Narru*."

I playfully punched Aidan in the arm. "He does not still have a crush. Would you stop?" Unfortunately, even though he was human again, my father's feelings were very strong when it came to my future husband.

"Okay, but the way he looks at La-Narru, I'm just saying," Aidan teased. "And Ur-Nammu has been waiting at the front of the church to marry you two for the last hour." Aidan laughed.

"He has not!" I laughed with him, and even Ash cracked a smile.

"I kid you not, the man is prepared," Aidan said in an amused tone. "And the Gutian wedding ceremony is what, two minutes long? It's not like he has much to prepare."

"Oh my God, he's so adorable." I felt nothing but affection

for Ur-Nammu now and saw him as the grandfather I never had, since both sets of grandparents had died before I was even born.

"Yeah, and Lulu is glued to his side. The two are inseparable," Aidan said.

"Lulu? She's at the front of the church?" Ash asked with interest.

Both Aidan and I laughed again. Then I said, "Go on. You can stay up front with Ur-Nammu and Lulu and watch me come down the aisle with Grandpa."

Ash didn't wait for me to change my mind. He raced out of the room toward the main church.

Aidan and I watched him go with smiles plastered on our faces.

We could hear the grunts of Ash tangling up with someone in the hall, then Meky popped her head in the doorway. "You look like a dream."

"Thank you," Aidan said.

"Not you, dork, though you always look like a dream to me." She winked. "We're ready for you, Shea." Meky was beside herself with happiness.

Butterflies threatened to yank themselves out of my stomach and do a tap dance on my head. "I'm ready."

"Yeah you are. Get over here." Meky grabbed my hand and led me out of the room with Aidan trailing behind. She turned her head to him. "When we get up to the altar you'd better do your best man duties. La-Narru needs you. That boy is practically fidgeting out of his suit."

"I will, I promise."

Walking down the long hallway of the church, I had never

felt so happy.

Even though my mom wasn't physically here, I knew she was with me and loving me from afar. I felt it so clearly, my heart was full.

Finally we reached the closed double doors that would lead to the inside of the church. Dad stood there waiting for me, smiling from ear to ear.

He placed his hand on his heart. "You are so beautiful."

I hugged him. "Thanks, Daddy."

Holding me tight, he said, "Your mother would be so proud."

"I feel her here," I said, trying not to cry.

"Me too," Dad said with a slight catch in his voice. Then he pulled back from the embrace, holding his arm out for me. "Shall we?"

I nodded. "We shall."

Meky was in control. She and Aidan stepped in front of us as the best man and maid of honor. They opened both doors, and the music started. It was a song from La-Narru's childhood in Gutium. Nefertiti had hired musicians to record it. It was a simple tune with just flutes and drums. It was both sweet and dramatic, perfect for our wedding.

Meky and Aidan walked down the aisle first.

Then after I counted to ten, like Meky had instructed me to, my dad and I followed after them.

The pews were full on both sides of the church. There were people we'd met in the last five years who knew nothing of our past or what we'd sacrificed to save them. The destruction of the cities that Caelius had wreaked havoc on had been rationalized away as terrorist attacks with super sophisticated weapons that had made the attackers invulnerable. Only a handful of people on Earth knew what really happened, but they just looked like conspiracy theory nuts talking about vampires demolishing cities.

The front row was filled with our family: Duncan, Sete, Sherit, Nefertiti, and Helena.

Setepenre gave me a quick wave and smile. I smiled back. We'd become close over the last couple of years. It was easier for her to talk to me rather than family, and I was a willing ear. After being brainwashed by Caelius for the last three thousand years, she hadn't even known who she was after she got free. It took her a while to understand what had been done to her and to get to know her family, for real this time.

It had been difficult, but Sete was generally a happy person, though I could tell her past life still haunted her. She was still struggling with her relationships with her sisters, mother, and La-Narru, but they were getting there. Ash helped immensely. It was a new relationship for her, and she wanted to be a good role model. The fact that she was here meant the world to me.

Then I saw him.

La-Narru.

His bright turquoise eyes stared at me with the intensity only he was capable of. Being human hadn't changed that part of him at all. He was much lighter in spirit, but the boy would always be intense; that was just who he was—a true artist.

Ash and Lulu held hands while Ur-Nammu waited patiently for me to arrive.

It almost took my breath away, the sight was so beautiful.

I wanted to run up there and give them all a group hug, but I followed the beat of the song and slowly made my way toward the altar. Aidan and Meky made it there first and stood to the side. Aidan gave La-Narru a gentle nudge in the arm for what could only be described as bro-love.

But La-Narru's eyes never left mine. Once his focus was on me, it would take a mountain falling on him to tear his gaze away. I still couldn't believe how lucky I was. To defeat Darkness itself and come out of it alive was a miracle none of us were taking for granted.

I just couldn't believe it had taken us this long to walk down the aisle. After everything that had happened, we were simply happy to be together. Then we'd had Ash and life had become . . . life: finding a home to settle down in, buying furniture, decorating Ash's room (with Ur-Nammu painting ancient protective symbols on the walls, then painting over them thinking we hadn't noticed), and just being *us* for once without murder and mayhem looming over our heads.

It was amazing.

The only thing missing was Mom. That's why I'd waited so long to have the wedding. La-Narru had wanted to do it a few years back, but I just couldn't. It felt wrong somehow, to have a celebration when she couldn't be there with us. A couple of months ago I saw a hummingbird fly into a lupine flower. Hummingbirds were my mom's absolute favorite. She had told me one time that she thought they were messengers from the ones we love that had passed. I'd known then that it was time.

As soon as I gave Meky the word, she was on it, planning this wedding as if she'd been planning weddings her entire life.

It was absolutely perfect. We were in a small chapel in the countryside of France, and the amount of flowers decorating the walls and pews astounded even me. The vaulted ceiling was framed with rich brown wood that was centuries old, and the stained glass windows brought the perfect amount of light into the sanctuary.

My father and I reached the altar, and he turned to me with tears streaming down his face. "I love you, kiddo."

"I love you too, Daddy."

Dad took my hands in his and leaned down, kissing my cheek, then turned to La-Narru. "My little girl is in your hands now, and I couldn't be prouder of the both of you."

My father might not have been a vampire anymore, but his sire bond with La-Narru hadn't seemed to lessen much when he'd become a human again. I didn't mind it. My dad had been a little too overprotective of me and who I dated before I went to college, so it was nice that he wholeheartedly loved La-Narru, even if some of that love had been blood-based.

Dad held my hands up and lowered them into La-Narru's.

As we touched, a thrill surged through my entire body. I knew that would never change. Our connection went beyond anything imaginable, and I wouldn't have it any other way.

Ur-Nammu pulled out a white silk scarf and began wrapping our hands together. It was a little tight for my taste, but this was a Gutian tradition. With each tug and wrap of the scarf, I only felt more bonded to La-Narru.

Ur-Nammu began speaking in Gutian as he worked the scarf. Only a handful of us understood his words. La-Narru had spent the last three years teaching it to me and Ash, and I didn't care that all our new friends had no idea what Ur-Nammu was saying. When they realized how short a Gutian marriage ceremony was, it would make up for not understanding what was being said.

As he wrapped each layer of scarf, then tightened it with a large tug, his words called out to us. They spoke of bonding, loyalty, and love.

Ur-Nammu completed tying the scarf around our hands at the same time he finished his ceremonial words.

"It is done," Ur-Nammu said in English. "These bonds bind your heart, body, and souls together in this life and the next."

That should have been the end of the ceremony, but he sighed and added, "You may kiss the bride." I could tell it pained him to say something so Western, but he managed a smile all the same.

And so did La-Narru.

Realizing he couldn't hold my face because our hands were fastened, he leaned down and our lips met, sending an explosion up my spine. I wanted to grab him, but all we had were our lips, which was probably a good thing considering I'd forgotten we were in a room full of people. I had never felt a purer kiss in my life, and that was saying something, considering how many times I'd kissed this beautiful man. But having our hands bound together, standing in front of everyone we loved, was a snapshot of true happiness.

La-Narru's lips left mine. "Because of you I am whole again. I love you, Shea Harper."

"I love you too, La-Narru, with all my heart and soul." Words didn't do justice as to how I felt.

An eruption of cheers and applause filled the air.

I couldn't believe it.

We were married.

And we were still tied together.

Ur-Nammu began unwrapping the silk scarf from our hands, and I could feel the circulation come back to my fingers. Dang, that man could tie a mean knot.

After he was done, La-Narru kept hold of my hands and brought them to his lips, kissing them gently.

My smile was big enough to slide off my cheeks. "So I guess this means you're officially *mine* now," I teased.

"I was always yours, from the moment you slammed the door in my face at your dorm," he teased back.

Aidan laughed at that. "Best moment ever."

Meky motioned for us to move. "Get down the aisle. Everyone is staring. Besides, you guys have no idea how amazing your reception is going to be. One word: epic."

La-Narru kissed me one last time, and we both went to grab Ash's hand to walk with us as we left the church.

Ash was in the middle of tying his hand to Lulu's with the silk scarf he'd snuck out of Ur-Nammu's pocket. "You're *mine* forever now too, Lulu."

Trying not to laugh at the obvious like-father-like-son moment, La-Narru gently took the scarf away from Ash. "No one is a possession, Ash. Lulu is to be respected and adored. Did you even ask her if she wanted to be yours?"

"No," Ash said solemnly. "But I *do* respect and adore her. That's why I want her."

Lulu looked thoughtful and replied, "It's okay. I love him too."

Ash's smile was so big it made my heart squeeze with cuteness. "*See?*"

Lulu smiled back and took Ash's hand. "But I'm not *yours*,

okay? We're equals."

Ash nodded vigorously. "I will love you forever, Lulu."

Ash led Lulu down the aisle, and the two of them giggled at all the elaborate hats the guests were wearing.

La-Narru held his arm out for me to take, and I did so happily.

"You ready to celebrate?" La-Narru smiled.

"For all of time," I said, and we walked out of the church and into the next chapter of our beautiful lives.

Epilogue
Caelius

So . . . I was Darkness again.

Not that I was complaining. Honestly, the heartwarming moments between me and the Light were nice enough.

For now.

I destroyed a galaxy or two when I first returned, just to blow off steam. It had been painful being human, having my unlimited power confined to weak mortal flesh. Ah, but that flesh knew things that I had not, and the sounds Lucian made when he was mine would ring in my ears brighter than the songs of all creation.

It was a first for me, to love something other than myself, and a creation of the Light no less. It was long ago, so I had forgotten, but I had once loved Light itself in that way. Then jealousy erupted as It expanded past our union and made things out of Us. Jealousy, contradiction, confusion, rage . . . a million other feelings emerged that hadn't existed before, if you could call them *feelings* in the void. They were creations in their own right, though I wouldn't call them *mine*.

Our relationship was hard to define, as we'd both always been. It wasn't easy to know how you felt about something that was so much a part of you, other than to separate from it. But I'd gone too far. I'd gotten lost in the undoing. I'd forgotten that, in stepping away from your dance partner, the next step was to pull them back in. Luckily Light remembered. It was good about things like that.

I understood now why Light created form. To further Its understanding of Itself, and of me, It played this little game with life. And It did it for *us*.

How flattering.

Being human taught me much in a short time.

And now time was a part of everything and not measured by human standards, so I drifted as I always had, keeping balance. As Light created stars, I took the old ones and gave them rest. As things lived vivaciously, I held them quietly as they died. There was a mercy in endings, a gentleness I had forgotten, except when I'd touched Lucian's hair while he slept. It was a gentleness I had wanted for him alone when he had praised me as a god by that river in Gutium, a gentleness that had made me forget myself and remember myself all at the same time.

Now that I was formless, all of that seemed like what humans called a dream. It was a dream I replayed in my memory often, nonetheless. It was not the way of Darkness to hold on to things. If anything, it was my way to constantly let go. But for this memory, this bright spot that was no doubt a dark spot for him, I would hold on to Lucian. For all of my existence, I would remember him. I was Darkness, but I held on.

Was that love?

Before I tortured Bohe, that little mouse had spoken of Yin and Yang: a fascinating human concoction, but not altogether far off. Now that I was reconnected with Light Itself, I had a white circle inside my Yin, just as my connection with the Light added a black spot in Its Yang. I liked Lucian's interpretation better, referencing the moon and the stars, living and moving inside of each other . . . as I had moved inside him.

Cute.

And you act as if you're not loved.

What an adorable face Lucian had made when he realized how much the Light wanted me. Ah, if he was here now I would try and make him show me that face one more time.

Alone and unlovable.

What a wild lie I had created and believed for so long. It was a good one. I knew because it had been easy to believe, and just as easy for the Light to refute. Good lies were like breathing, just like good truths. We were opposite and similar in that way. How bold for the Light to finally destroy something of mine, and such a powerful long-held belief at that.

How ballsy.

I laughed.

I had done horrible things.

I still might do horrible things.

I would still do horrible things.

And the Light would love me, *always*.

I missed having lips. I supposed if I had them, I might have smiled at that.

As it was, I was looking over Earth now.

I visited often, watching them muddle around.

Watching *him.*

I was sure Molly was watching too. She was with the Light now, no doubt blissed-out like all beings on that side were.

Today I could've used some of that bliss. Because today *my* Lucian was marrying that Vessel.

He would have made a better wife to me than a husband to that light bulb. Still . . . their child was *adorable.* If I could do it again, I would keep Ash and Setepenre and raise them as *our* children.

I kept watching. They were all so happy.

I sighed, feeling the Light comfort me in the way that It did.

"I know." I leaned my presence against the moon, making a crater that looked like my human face had. "Now the next time Lucian is lost and looks up at the moon, he'll remember me and what he said about Darkness." I caressed its shape. "No one wants to be forgotten entirely, darling." I embraced the Light, as much as we could embrace without destroying each other completely. "You have churches and synagogues and all of that, you lush. I just want this *one boy.*"

"He really is something." We sighed together as the Light spoke in warm waves.

"Oh, don't flatter yourself. How cheesy to say that it was worth all of creation just to make something I liked." I warmed further but still refused to yield. "You know, he was *mine* too, wasn't he? I had my blood *in* him. I remade him a few times over; I even renamed him. Give him to me."

I growled, which was more a tremble in space rippling

through time than an earthly sound.

It made a tidal wave that sunk a populated island.

Oops, was that Japan or Hawaii?

It was the same for Atlantis last time.

Oh well, they'd make up stories and find it amusing later.

I smiled. "I know, I know. All that you have is mine, and all that I have is yours. And they are created out of both of us and so on. But you know what I mean. I'd like to keep him for myself in a less *corporeal* way, but I won't hurt you by leaving your side again."

We spoke often now and at great lengths. We planned things, worked together, fought together, reached the far corners of our beings and touched where we could. And I was changing, and so was the Light.

I wasn't sure what that meant for creation, if it meant anything at all, but integration had been harder when I was human—riddled with feelings of love alongside possessiveness and the need to destroy. Maybe as the Light and I eventually found our rhythm again, creation would as well.

Maybe that is my final gift to you, La-Narru.

The final gift to the humans you love.

That you could set aside the lie of loneliness. That you could feel in your souls the peace of creation, and finally rest like I have, in the joy of eternal balance.

COMING SOON
NOVELLAS :

VESSELS: LUCIAN & AIDAN
THE HUNT: NEFERTITI, HELENA & DUNCAN

Other Books by Hina McCord

Ivory

Love & Dark Series (with Becca C. Smith):
Vessel
First Born
Gutian Code

Other Books by Becca C. Smith

The Riser Saga:
Riser
Reaper
Ripper

The Atlas Series:
Atlas
Grigori Returned
The Underworld

Alexis Tappendorf Series:
Alexis Tappendorf and the Search for Beale's Treasure
Alexis Tappendorf and the Search for Atlantis

The Dream Diaries:
The Dream Diaries
The Dream Diaries: Blood Ties

Love & Dark Series (with Hina McCord):
Vessel
First Born
Gutian Code

SHEA Chapters Written by:
Becca C. Smith

Becca fell in love with storytelling at an early age. The first book she read was *The Lion, The Witch and The Wardrobe* and she's been looking for the door to Narnia ever since! Becca is a passionate reader, consuming anything sci-fi or fantasy. Mix it in with YA and she's a fan for life. So it's no surprise that she writes in these genres as well. When Becca isn't writing, she loves to sew. From *Mortal Instruments* rune pillows, to elaborate *Firefly/Serenity* bags, Becca loves to create!

LUCIAN Chapters Written by:
Hina McCord

Hina McCord is a novelist, aka an avid bullshitter; that's why she lives in L.A. She's been writing for as long as her ancient mind can remember, devouring tales like an anemic vampire roaming the streets in hot-pink heels, always thirsty for more. When she's not writing, she's making steampunk weapons, sewing giant plant-eater Mario plushes, making costumes for some film bloke or cosplayer, and sculpting/casting movie prop replicas while gardening in her urban apartment. Her favorite tools? A soldering iron, a blowtorch, a band saw, a sonic screwdriver, a replicator, and an active imagination.